INSTRUCTOR'S ANNOTATED EDITION

Third Edition

FUENTES

Conversación y gramática

Debbie Rusch
Boston College

Marcela Domínguez
Pepperdine University

Lucía Caycedo Garner
University of Wisconsin—Madison, Emerita

with the collaboration of

Donald N. Tuten Emory University
Carmelo Esterrich Columbia College Chicago

Houghton Mifflin Company Boston New York

Publisher: Rolando Hernández
Sponsoring Editor: Van Strength
Senior Development Editor: Sandra Guadano
Senior Project Editor: Rosemary R. Jaffe
Editorial Assistant: Rachel Zanders
Art and Design Manager: Gary Crespo
Senior Composition Buyer: Sarah Ambrose
Senior Photo Editor: Jennifer Meyer Dare
Manufacturing Manager: Karen Banks
Associate Marketing Manager: Claudia Martínez

Cover photography: Harold Burch Design, NYC.

Credits for texts, photographs, illustrations, and realia are found following the index at the back of the book.

Printed in the U.S.A.

Student Text ISBN: 0-618-46523-5

Instructor's Annotated Edition ISBN: 0-618-46524-3

Library of Congress Control Number: 2003116167

1 2 3 4 5 6 7 8 9-DOW-08 07 06 05 04

Instructor's Guide

Contents

Philosophy of the *Fuentes* Program

Fuentes: Conversación y gramática (FCG) and *Fuentes: Lectura y redacción* (FLR), Third Edition, present an integrated skills approach to intermediate Spanish that develops both receptive and productive skills simultaneously. The primary objective of the program is to offer students an opportunity to acquire communicative skills while developing their awareness and appreciation of Hispanic cultures.

The two texts are coordinated by chapter theme, grammar, functions, and vocabulary. Although FCG and FLR are designed to be used together, they can also be used independently of each other. For information on coordinating the two texts, see FLR.

The following are the leading principles that inspired the creation of the *Fuentes* program:

- **We learn by doing.** By using the language to communicate original thoughts, in oral and written form, and by interacting with written texts and recorded conversations, students will acquire a high degree of proficiency. See Activity 11 in Chapter 4 of FCG and Activity 7 in Chapter 8 of FLR.
- **Skill integration promotes language development.** Each skill reinforces the others; therefore, students learn to comprehend and produce language while practicing specific strategies for listening, reading, and writing. Many activities combine skills to better reflect real-life language use. See Activities 1–4 in Chapter 5 and Activity 11 in Chapter 4 of FCG, Activity 23 in Chapter 4 of FLR, and Activity 21 in Chapter 3 of the Workbook section in the student Activities Manual.
- **Language is culture, and culture is reflected in language.** By being exposed to real-life situations and by comparing the new cultures with their own, students acquire an awareness of and respect for other peoples. See Activity 21 in Chapter 10 of FCG and Activity 12 in Chapter 3 of FLR.

- **Spiraling of material is essential to move students from learning to acquisition.** Continuous and systematic reentry of previously studied material while learning about new topics leads students to acquisition of language needed to carry out specific functions. See the table of contents in FCG for a list of specifically recycled material.
- **Learning is enhanced when it is enjoyable.** If the material presented places students in a relaxed, pleasant atmosphere, and if students enjoy class activities, their rate of success increases. See Activity 13 in Chapter 3 of FCG and Activity 23 in Chapter 6 of FLR.

New in *Fuentes*, Third Edition

- The *Fuentes* Video features twelve video segments in a news-magazine format titled **Videofuentes**. Filmed in Mexico, Spain, Argentina, and the United States, the segments include interviews with the actor-comedian John Leguizamo and Elena Climent, a Mexican artist; a tribute to Celia Cruz; clips from a film by the Spanish director Pedro Almodóvar; a Chilean short-subject film; reactions from students who have studied abroad; overviews of Mayan culture, the cultural heritage of Spain, nightlife in Madrid, agrotourism in northern Spain, Latino Recognition Day at Fenway Park, and the "desaparecidos" and their children in Argentina. Related activities expand on and reinforce cultural and language topics presented in the chapters.
- The **Fuente hispana** quotes, comprised of comments made by Spanish speakers of all ages (those under 30 predominate), allow students a personalized view into the cultures of numerous Spanish-speaking countries. Twenty-seven Hispanics from eleven countries express their own opinions or relate actual events. They are not representatives of their respective cultures, but rather simply a window to an individual's perspective. An icon signals each **Fuente hispana** paragraph.

- Open-ended activities that present and practice rejoinders commonly used in everyday conversation (e.g. **No puede ser. ¡Caray!**) promote improved communicative skills.
- Some new listening selections, including an interview with Cuban artist Alexandre Arrechea, develop listening skills as well as cultural awareness.
- Revisions in grammar sequencing and presentations to better balance chapters include less emphasis on the present tense and more attention on past narration (imperfect and preterit), which in the third edition is the primary focus for Chapters 2, 3, and 4.
- Updated cultural information in activities and **¿Lo sabían?** readings offers insights on diverse theme-related topics.
- The Appendixes now contain review information on **ser, estar,** and **haber,** adjective formation, and use of the word **a**.
- A student CD-ROM that provides additional language practice for each chapter reinforces topics in an interactive setting.
- A revised testing program with two self-contained quizzes or a quiz and test for each chapter offer improved instructor support. The Instructor Test Cassette contains the listening portion of the quizzes and tests.
- Increased self-checking in the Workbook minimizes instructor correction, and the option of an Online Activities Manual that includes the workbook and lab activities, plus the lab recordings, offers a convenient alternative for students to self-check many activities and monitor their own progress.

Features of the *Fuentes* Program

Functionally and Thematically Organized Components

- Structures and vocabulary presented are functionally grouped so that students can more easily practice and assimilate them. For example, in Chapter 2 of FCG, the preterit, adverbs of time, and the pluperfect are presented to support the function of narrating in the past.
- Themes presented in the initial listening section of each chapter in FCG are focused on throughout the chapter.
- Themes are expanded upon in FLR and in the ancillaries to provide students with a solid base of cultural knowledge.

Clear and Concise Grammar Explanations

- Explanations recognize the knowledge gained during the first year and expand upon that knowledge, pinpointing specific problem areas.
- Examples illustrate concepts and include contrastive sentences for key topics such as the subjunctive. See pages 119–120.
- Easy-to-locate charts and diagrams provide helpful visualization of important points for study and review. See pages 65–66.
- A grammar appendix with explanations of tense formation and verb conjugations serves as a handy all-in-one reference for consultation throughout the course.
- Activities in FLR recycle and review structures and vocabulary presented in FCG.

Ample Number of Activities

- FCG provides an abundant variety of activities for each topic, allowing instructors to use all or some of them.
- FLR provides three readings per chapter. Instructors can choose to do some or all of the texts and some or all of the activities that accompany each individual selection.
- Activities in FCG are contextual and personalized and move from controlled to open in nature, encouraging students to express personal wants, needs, desires, and opinions.
- Both FCG and FLR provide opportunities for students to express themselves orally and to exchange ideas and information through pair, group, and class activities that also include opportunities to engage in connected discourse.

Integrated Listening Comprehension Program

- All chapters of FCG contain a listening section accompanied by pre-listening, ongoing listening, and post-listening activities.
- All chapters of FCG (except for the Preliminary chapter) contain a video section accompanied by pre-, ongoing, and post-viewing activities.
- The lab program provides additional practice for students to improve their listening comprehension.

Reading, Writing, and Listening Strategies

- FLR systematically presents, practices, and recycles reading and writing strategies.
- Additional writing practice is available in the Workbook section of the accompanying Activities Manual and through the journal entries in FLR.
- The lab program presents and practices listening strategies that parallel the reading strategies presented in FLR.
- The *Fuentes* Video provides additional listening practice.

Culture Integration in All Aspects of the Program

- Authentic texts from newspapers and magazines, literature, realia, and interviews with native speakers provide students with an inside view of Hispanic cultures in FLR and FCG.
- The new **Fuente hispana** quotes enhance and personalize the cultural component.
- The new *Fuentes* Video allows students to view the Hispanic world and hear people discuss various aspects of their cultures.
- The **¿Lo sabían?** sections of FCG provide additional cultural insights related to the content of each chapter.
- Activities ask students to make inferences about cultural topics and to examine their own culture and opinions.
- Both large-"C" and small-"c" culture are included.

Student Annotations in FCG and FLR

- Annotations in the margin of the student text provide information to students while studying, help focus students while doing activities, and offer additional cultural information.

Instructors and institutions that wish to incorporate elements of the National Standards in their programs will find ample opportunity to do so with the *Fuentes* program. The five Cs (communication, cultures, connections, comparisons, communities) are reflected in numerous aspects of the program. The Cs of communication and cultures permeate FCG and FLR. For example, there are paired activities where students make decisions and exchange information (FCG Ch. 6, Act. 7; Ch. 10, Act. 30), listening and reading sections where students are exposed to differing cultural perspectives and encouraged to relate and compare them to their own experiences and culture (FCG Ch. 11, **¿Coca o cocaína?**, p. 272). Comparisons are done through the **Fuente hispana** feature where students are frequently asked to make comparisons to their own culture (FCG Ch. 2, Act. 23; Ch. 5, Act. 21). Video activities ask students to compare their culture to what they have seen (Ch. 4, Act. 3). Connections to other disciplines form the backbone for some chapters with themes dealing with topics such as art, business, ecology, economics, geography, history, music, and sociology. These themes also form the base for video sections. The C of communities is addressed via web activities and cultural links where students are introduced to a vast Spanish-speaking community on the Internet. Students are also encouraged to find out about volunteer opportunities in their own university which could put them in direct contact with Spanish-speakers in the U.S. or abroad (video Ch. 11, Act. 4). In addition, the final video segment was filmed to encourage students to travel abroad so that they truly enter into a Spanish-speaking community.

Program Components

For the Student

- Student Texts: FCG and FLR
- In-Text Audio CD (contains all text conversations)
- Activities Manual: Workbook/Lab Manual
- Workbook Answer Key
- Quia Online Activities Manual
- *Fuentes* Video
- *Fuentes* Student Website
- *Fuentes* Multimedia CD-ROM 1.0

For the Instructor and/or Institution

- Instructor's Annotated Edition (IAE)
- Instructor Class Prep CD-ROM
- Quia Online Activities Manual
- In-Text Audio CD (contains all text conversations)
- Lab Audio CD Program
- Instructor Test Cassette
- *Fuentes* Video
- *Fuentes* Instructor Website

In-Text Audio CD This CD contains recordings of all listening sections in FCG. Transcripts for the audio are located at the end of this Instructor's Guide and in the Activities Manual. The CD is packaged with the FCG student text and IAE.

***Fuentes:* Activities Manual** The Activities Manual contains the following:

- A Workbook section with controlled to open-ended activities corresponding to material presented in each chapter of FCG
- A Lab Manual section that offers pronunciation practice, systematic presentation of listening strategies, and listening comprehension activities (answers to the Lab Manual are found in the Instructor Class Prep CD-ROM)
- Scripts for the listening sections presented in FCG
- A **Workbook Answer Key** is available to students at the request of the instructor.

Quia Online Activities Manual The Online Activities Manual contains the same content as the print version of the Activities Manual in an interactive environment that provides immediate feedback on many activities. The audio portions corresponding to the lab activities are also included.

The online version includes automatic grading of discrete-answer exercises and the capability for instructors to review and revise grading decisions, give feedback to students, and grade open-ended exercises individually. Instructors can customize exercises, as well as create their own.

Lab Audio CD Program The lab CDs contain recordings of pronunciation and listening activities for each chapter, coordinated with the Lab Manual. The lab CDs are available for use in the language lab and/or for purchase by students.

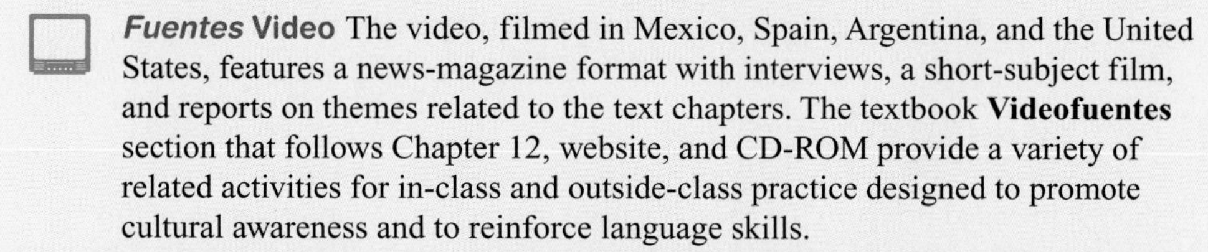

***Fuentes* Video** The video, filmed in Mexico, Spain, Argentina, and the United States, features a news-magazine format with interviews, a short-subject film, and reports on themes related to the text chapters. The textbook **Videofuentes** section that follows Chapter 12, website, and CD-ROM provide a variety of related activities for in-class and outside-class practice designed to promote cultural awareness and to reinforce language skills.

***Fuentes* Multimedia CD-ROM 1.0** The multimedia CD-ROM helps students practice each chapter's vocabulary and grammar, and provides immediate feedback so that students can check their progress in Spanish. Among the various types of exercises are art- and listening-based activities and recording activities, all of which help students develop reading, writing, and speaking skills. Access to a grammar reference and a Spanish-English glossary is available for instant help. The CD-ROM also contains complete chapter episodes from the *Fuentes* video and related activities based on clips from the video. A progress report for each chapter shows the percentage of activities completed, the number of attempts on each exercise, and the full text of answers to open-ended exercises.

***Fuentes* Website** The Student Website includes the following:

- Activities linked to Spanish-language sites to learn further about chapter topics and to practice chapter grammar and vocabulary
- ACE practice tests to provide additional practice with vocabulary and structures
- Video exercises based on clips from the *Fuentes* Video
- Exercises based on feature length films
- Cultural links for each chapter for exploration of topics presented in FCG and FLR
- Overview of FLR Reading Strategies
- MP3 files of the chapter listening passages

The password protected Instructor Website includes the material from the Instructor Class Prep CD-ROM, with the exception of the testing program and answer keys to the Workbook and Lab Manual, and a guide on use of technology components.

Instructor Class Prep CD-ROM The Class Prep CD-ROM includes the following:

- A Testing Program, with accompanying answer key and audio transcript of the listening portions of quizzes and exams. Quizzes and tests are offered in ready-to-copy PDF format and as Word files so that instructors can modify them to suit their classes.
- A transcript of the Lab Manual recordings and answer key to the Lab Manual activities
- A transcript of the video segments
- Communicative Activities, consisting of (1) selected activities from FCG (role play, interview, and information gap activities), which can be reproduced for use in class so that each student views only his/her role, and (2) an additional information gap or pair activity, often art-based, that can be used in class.
- Overheads and PowerPoint slides of illustrations for use in vocabulary and conversation activities with chapter correlation and suggestions for use.
- Overheads and PowerPoint slides of grammar charts from the text.

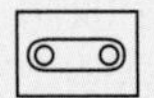

Instructor Test Cassette The Test Cassette contains the listening portions of chapter quizzes and tests for use when administering tests.

Communicative Language Teaching

Although intended primarily for inexperienced instructors, the information in this section may serve as a useful review for experienced instructors. It describes six steps or phases for ensuring an effective communicative class: overview, input, drill, activity setup, the activity, check.

Overview

When planning a communicative class, functions[1] are center stage. Ask yourself these questions: (1) What structures are being presented? (2) What is the vocabulary being

[1] *Function* indicates the purpose of the utterance (to express likes and dislikes, to ask and give information, to describe physical appearance, to ask and give directions, etc.).

presented? (3) What are the functions highlighted by the text? (4) How do these high-frequency functions coincide best with the background knowledge and interests of the students? (5) Where, when, and by whom are these functions used?

Once the function and context have been identified, they provide the basis on which to plan the lesson and give students an overview of the material to be presented. For example, in the case of an introduction to narrating in the past (the preterit tense), students could be told, **Uds. ya saben decir qué van a hacer mañana y qué hacen todos los días. Ahora van a aprender a decir qué hicieron ayer.**

Input

When presenting a new topic, comprehension should precede production. Plan some sort of "comprehensible input" at the "i + 1" level[2] so that the students will hear the functions in a somewhat realistic setting. This can be done by you as an individual or through the use of a tape, a video, or a reading. You might rely on acting ability, creativity in constructing examples, or the use of visuals. Many times it is a combination of the above. The input phase doesn't mean explaining but rather exemplifying.

During this phase, you will need to make sure that students comprehend by "negotiating meaning"—in other words, by having students demonstrate that they understand what they hear. To negotiate meaning, have students respond physically (i.e., gestures, actions), answer yes/no questions, answer either/or questions, give information, and even laugh at the right time to demonstrate that they have understood. For example, when working with the subjunctive to express the unknown, you might say **Jane** (a student in class) **busca un novio que sea inteligente. ¿Tiene Jane novio?** Students reply **no. ¿Existe esta persona?** Students respond **no.**

The input phase may be short (two minutes) or long, as the material and class dictate. *Clarity in presentation is of the utmost importance to ensure comprehension.*

Drill

The next step, after the input phase, should be devoted to drilling. The purpose of the drill is to give students the structural or lexical practice needed to carry out the function or functions highlighted in the overview and input phases. If students don't see the relationship between the input and the drill, you should point it out (e.g., **Estamos hablando de alguien que no sabemos si existe o no. Para eso necesitamos usar formas especiales de los verbos. ¿Quién sabe cómo se llaman esas formas? Sí, presente del subjuntivo.**). You can plan the drill around the individuals in your class and their interests, something a text can never do. The drill will be more meaningful to students if you talk about individuals in the class and their abilities, especially if accompanied by some humor. Personalizing the drill helps to solidify form and meaning, which is the aim of the drill phase—an ability to manipulate certain forms so that students can carry out a function. Many people call this the "skill-getting" phase, and correction is needed during this period. Drills may take as little as two minutes for a simple structure or longer, depending on the needs of the class.

Drills can take the form of a game. The **dice game** will help students master verb conjugations and also take responsibility for their own learning.

Write the following on the board:

1. yo	4. nosotros
2. tú	5. vosotros
3. él/ella/Ud.	6. ellos/ellas/Uds.

[2] *Comprehensible input at the* ***i + 1*** *level* is language that is a little above the students' current level of production.

Pair students, assigning one to do the even numbers and the other the odds, and give each pair a die and a handout containing 50-60 infinitives listed in columns:

1. cerrar 2. acostarse 3. necesitar (etc.)

The student who does the odd numbers rolls the die for verb 1; depending on the number rolled, he/she must give the proper conjugation (e.g., verb 1 is **cerrar,** the student rolls a 4, the corresponding subject pronoun is **nosotros,** so the student says **cerramos**). The other student does 2, etc. Model the activity with the students. Students depend on each other for correction and verification. When in doubt, they should ask the instructor.

Activity Setup

This part of a lesson is sometimes referred to as the "skill-using" phase. The activities in this phase should be *task* oriented, communicative,[3] and usually done in pairs or small groups. The objective is to utilize the function or functions focused on in the input and skill-getting phases. Activities will most likely include functions previously studied (in earlier chapters or lessons), since the very nature of communicative activities builds in a certain amount of recycling of previously learned material.

Clarity in direction giving is imperative. Before doing an activity, you need to "set it up." You should approach the setup phase as if the students did not have any printed instructions in front of them. Setup may include pairing the students, giving them roles, telling them where the conversation takes place, physically moving them, etc. Then focus the students' attention on the structures and/or vocabulary needed to carry out the functions by practicing a few of the key phrases that they will have to use. Show how the activity works, modeling the beginning of the activity with a student, if needed. Rather than following up instructions with the question "Do you understand?" have students *show* that they understand. Then comes the last step of the setup: giving a time limit. The time limit may be shorter than the time you expect the activity to take. A short time limit can motivate students to get down to business right away.

Forming Pairs. Forming pairs and small groups should be quick. Here are a few tips for their formation:

1. Point at individuals sitting near each other and say, **tú con él, Mary con John y Phil, Uds. dos,** etc.
2. To form pairs or small groups with students who don't sit near each other, have all students stand, point at them and say **tú con él, Mary con John y Phil, Uds. dos,** etc. As you call out names, the students make eye contact with each other and sit down. When you are finished, they all move to work with their partner.
3. As students enter the room, have two piles of paper—one with capitals of countries, one with the names of countries. Organize the papers so that the top one is Madrid and the bottom one is España, the second from the top is Caracas and the second from the bottom is Venezuela, and so forth. Hand out one from the top and one from the bottom, thus always ensuring a pair. As a warm-up, have students find their partner. Other topics could include dates and events (**711/invasión de los moros**) or famous people and what they did (**Andrés Segovia/tocaba la guitarra**).

[3]A *communicative activity* is often a paired or small-group activity in which the instructor can predict the functions that will be used and, therefore, the structures/vocabulary needed to carry out the function(s). The instructor may or may not be able to predict exactly what message the students will want to convey since the students will be creating with language.

4. Some activities require assigning a role. This can be done while forming the pairs, by pointing at the students and saying, **A y B; padre y madre; profesora y estudiante; cliente y agente de viajes; jefa y empleado;** etc.
5. If you have an uneven number of students, form one group of three. The instructor should not participate in paired activities, since his/her responsibility is to mingle and monitor.

The Activity

While an activity is in progress, the instructor and the students have very specific duties. Discuss with students their responsibilities during activities at the start of the year in order to form good habits. This is best done after a day full of paired activities. Instructor and student responsibilities are as follows:

Instructor Responsibilities	Student Responsibilities
Monitor, but don't hover. Circulate among the groups.	Work on task.
Offer suggestions if needed.	Work cooperatively.
Answer questions, but don't be overly available.	Look only at your own information if appropriate: don't peek at partner's.
Correct individual errors when communication is impeded.	Ask partner for clarification if needed.
Note grammatical and pronunciation errors for further classroom work.	Enunciate and speak clearly.
Call a time-out to correct a common error that will be repeated a number of times in the activity.	Correct each other's grammar when needed.
Abandon the activity if it isn't working. Failure could be due to poor setup or not enough linguistic preparation.	Speak only in Spanish; use gestures if needed to convey meaning.

The instructor should also decide when to stop the activity. It is not necessary for all groups to finish each activity—when two or three groups have finished, either they can reverse roles, or you can end the activity for the whole class.

Check

Depending on how you choose to end the activity, you may or may not need to do a check. For certain types of activities, it is important that the students know how they will be held accountable for what is accomplished during the pair or small-group activity. Here are a few suggestions for possible wrap-up activities:

1. Have some individuals report their findings to the class.
2. Identify a group that has done something humorous and have them share with their peers, either by reporting back or by acting out the activity for the class.
3. Have students self-check in pairs by putting their books side-by-side and comparing their pictures, lists, data, etc.
4. Collect and correct for accuracy activities that require a specific interchange of data.
5. Assign a brief composition, newspaper article, follow-up letter, etc., based on the contents of the activity.

The preceding steps may occur a number of times within a single class period. The class should be conducted in Spanish so that students' exposure to the target language is as great as possible. Remember that the input phase should be at "i + 1," but the communicative activities should not. The purpose of the skill-using phase is for students to acquire language, not to invent language. It is when students are pushed beyond their ability that they rely on their native language for assistance, and more errors occur.

Suggested Strategies And Techniques For Working With FCG

Chapter Opener

The chapter opener contains a photo or work of art that introduces the chapter theme, followed by a list of communicative goals that will be the focus of the chapter. Use the opener to ask questions or elicit comments that orient students to the theme, and encourage them to refer to goals during the course of the chapter as a check on their progress.

Listening Comprehension

An initial listening comprehension passage accompanied by pre-listening, ongoing listening, and post-listening activities is designed to give instructors a means of helping students develop their listening skills as well as introduce them to the chapter theme. Many of these conversations, ads, monologues, interviews, etc., are designed to provide natural-sounding passages, and others are completely authentic in content. In all cases, aspects of Hispanic culture are presented and discussed by the students.

The photographs, expressions, and pre-listening activity before each conversation serve to focus students' attention on what they are about to hear. They help to activate background knowledge so that students can better comprehend the content of the passage.

The next two activities provide ongoing listening practice. Instructors should go over instructions and read any items given in lists prior to listening. In this manner, students know what to listen for and can *scan* for specific information without being concerned about the meaning of each and every word. The instructor should then play the listening selection and check responses. The second of these two activities usually asks students to listen to the selection again and answer more specific questions, put items in order, take notes, etc. At this point, the instructor can vary the presentation:

- Play the selection and then ask the questions.
- Read the questions, play the selection, and then ask the questions.
- Read a question, play the selection, pause when the answer is given, and pose the question again to the class. Continue this process until finished.

The post-listening activity at the end of this section provides students with an opportunity to expand on the theme and cultural elements presented in the passage. Many times this is followed or preceded by a **¿Lo sabían?** reading that provides additional cultural knowledge.

The scripts to the chapter listening passages can be found at the end of this Instructor's Guide in FCG as well as at the end of the Activities Manual.

Functional Grammar and Thematic Vocabulary

Functions (for example, narrating in the past) and the grammar that supports them (preterit, time expressions, pluperfect in Chapter 2) are presented in building-block fashion. Each explanation is followed by a series of activities that progress from more controlled to open, allowing students ample opportunity to use their new knowledge to express their own ideas in a meaningful fashion.

Vocabulary is presented in thematic groups (such as politics, employment, the environment) and usually appears near the start of the chapter. Lexical items are also presented, when needed, in grammar explanations (e.g., time expressions to sequence past events). Each presentation of lexical items is followed by a series of activities to enable students to practice the words as well as the chapter functions in meaningful contexts.

All functional grammar explanations and thematic vocabulary lists can be assigned for study as homework. Workbook activities and some controlled activities from the text can also be assigned to reinforce students' learning as they progress through the chapter.

In class, regardless of whether the students have already studied the point in question at home, the instructor should provide *comprehensible input* when presenting a topic—that is, highlight the new construction in a functional and meaningful context (e.g., when presenting the preterit, discuss what you did yesterday). Next, try to elicit rules from the students if appropriate to the topic.

Oral and Written Activities

FCG provides a variety of activities ranging from controlled to more open, for individual, pair, group, and class work. Instructor annotations provide information for carrying out many of the pair and group activities, follow-up ideas for connected discourse, and answers to many controlled activities. The first instructor annotation in each chapter opener lists a series of activities or parts of activities that can (but need not) be prepared at home and later checked in class. These activities are more controlled or provide students with an opportunity to think about their responses prior to class. If they are assigned as homework, the following tips may help make the class run smoothly:

- Write homework assignments on the board or post them on the Internet in the order in which they are to be done to help students organize their study time.
- Collect textbook activities. If they are corrected in class, you can simply check them off as done or not done. If you collect them, students will do them.

Many activities in FCG are communicative and should be done in class. Most of these are for pairs or small groups. For information on how to implement these activities as well as how to form pairs, see the "Communicative Language Teaching" section on page IAE 8. It is also advisable to get the students out of the textbook whenever possible by putting an activity on an overhead transparency. The activity could be intact as printed in the text, or it could be slightly altered to include examples pertinent to your class or events in the news.

Circumlocution and Connected Discourse

Many activities in FCG encourage students to practice circumlocution. In the directions to these activities, students are encouraged to use specific phrases, such as **es una cosa que..., es una acción que....** An example of this type of activity is Activity 24 in Chapter 6.

Opportunities for students to engage in connected discourse are presented throughout FCG. An example of this type of activity is Activity 6 in Chapter 6. When giving directions for paired and small-group activities that require connected discourse, it is important to provide students with a model that clearly shows them what your expectations are. When checking these activities, encourage students to explain their opinions or to expand on what they are saying by asking leading questions, such as **¿Por qué?, ¿Y?,** and **¿Qué quieres decir con eso?**

Error Correction

When teaching a language with a communicative approach, instructors are confronted with a dilemma: when to correct and when to ignore errors. To help reduce the possibility of errors during communicative activities, make sure students are prepared lexically and linguistically to carry out the activities by providing a clear input and drill phase.

Correction is needed and accuracy is important; however, balance correction with encouragement so that students will be willing to take chances and to speak in class. Students must realize that errors are a part of the learning process.

- Correct frequently during the drill and set-up phases of activities.
- Correct by simply using a student's response and offering the correct form, then follow up with an opportunity for the student to self-correct.
  S: Yo **fue** al cine el sábado pasado.
  T: Yo también **fui** al cine. **Fui** al Roxy. ¿Adónde fuiste tú?
  S: **Fui** al Majestic.
- Use a faded cue to lead the student to the error and allow him/her an opportunity to self-correct.
  S: El sábado pasado yo **fue** al cine.
  T: El sábado pasado yo (*raising voice slightly*)
  S: Ohh, **fui**. Yo **fui** al cine.
- Offer an option (without actually indicating the correct response).
  S: Me **gusta** las películas.
  T: ¿Te **gusta** la película o te **gustan** las películas? (*implying, I'm sorry but I didn't catch what you said*)
  S: Me **gustan** las películas.
- Elicit help from other members of the class and, when needed, review appropriate rules.
  S: Vi John y Jim ayer en una discoteca.
  T: Vi...
  Ss: Vi **a** John y **a** Jim.
  T: ¿Por qué?
- React to what is said, showing the student that he/she has miscommunicated.
  T: ¿Qué hace tu padre?
  S: **Tu** padre es ingeniero.
  T: No, **mi** padre no es ingeniero, es médico.
  S: (*Realizing his/her error, the student self-corrects and says:*) **Mi** padre es ingeniero.
- During pair and small-group work, circulate and offer brief error correction. Certain errors heard in pair and small-group work can be noted and then used as the basis for future class warm-up activities.
- If an activity just isn't working, abandon it. Return to the activity at a later point when students are better prepared, repeat the instructions, or omit the activity altogether.

¿Lo sabían?

Throughout each chapter, pertinent cultural information is explained in the **¿Lo sabían?** sections. These appear sporadically in each chapter to expand on or provide information related to the cultural content of the listening selections and activities. Many times, the **¿Lo sabían?** readings end with a discussion question that asks students to examine aspects of their own culture or cultures to gain greater insight into Hispanic cultures.

These cultural readings can be assigned as homework or read in class. Have students compare their own culture with the target culture. Check comprehension by asking either/or, yes/no, informational, or opinion questions. Allow time in class for students to briefly discuss questions posed after reading the text. Remind students that differences in culture are usually of degree and not kind.

Fuente hispana

The **Fuente hispana** quotes appear sporadically throughout the book. These short written texts present comments by Spanish speakers from numerous countries on cultural topics related to the chapters. Students should realize that these segments reflect the opinions and stories of the speakers and may not be representative of a culture as a whole. Help students understand that, through the comments, they can begin to enter into other cultures and gain insights into other ways of thinking and living. Many times the **Fuente hispana** segments form part of an activity, a vocabulary presentation, or a **¿Lo sabían?** reading. They may be assigned to be read at home or read silently in class. To ensure that students understand the message, ask a few comprehension questions as needed before focusing on cultural comparison. Most **Fuente hispana** sections ask students to compare their own life, opinions, stories, etc. with that of the native speaker. By doing this, it is hoped that students will not only begin to see glimpses of the cultures that make up the Spanish-speaking world, but also have a better understanding of their own culture.

Fuentes Video

The *Fuentes* Video allows students to gain insight into Hispanic cultures while improving listening comprehension skills. Each segment is approximately six to eight minutes long and complements the chapter theme while recycling and reentering chapter structures and vocabulary. There is a video segment for each chapter except the Preliminary. Although the video may be shown at any point in the chapter, it is suggested that it be shown closer to the end or even after completing the chapter as a review. The textbook **Videofuentes** section, following Chapter 12 in FCG, contains pre-, ongoing, and post-viewing activities to accompany the video. These can be done in approximately twenty to twenty-five minutes of class time. In addition, FLR contains discussion questions for in-class use or homework.

When working with the **Videofuentes** activities, have students read through the items in the **Mientras ves** activities prior to watching a particular video or segment of a video. By having a task to do while watching, students are more focused and comprehension increases as does cultural awareness. Many of the post-viewing activities can be expanded or done as homework, particularly those that may include composition writing, skit writing, and research.

Skit Integration at the Intermediate Level

Students at the intermediate level can be asked to prepare a skit that can be videotaped or acted out in class. As opposed to presentations, script writing and the rehearsal of skits is a collaborative effort. They have a captive audience since they are developed by students for students. Topics for skits can be TV shows (dating games, reality games, etc.), children's stories, parts of a famous or classic movie, etc. Set up students in pairs or groups of three and then hand out a schedule with details; for example, when each group will turn in the first and possibly a second draft of their skit, and the date each group will present it or show it to the class. Skits should integrate functions and vocabulary that have been learned up to that point. For example, if the class has already been working with the subjunctive to give advice in Chapter 5, a skit on a dating game could have one of the male contestants tell another contestant who is fighting over the same woman **Te recomiendo que busques otra chica porque ésta es perfecta para mí.** To ensure a successful skit, instruct students about key factors to take into account:

- The skit should contain some sort of twist. Something should happen in the story, preferably something unexpected. When their peers finish watching the skit, they should be able to say what happened. If the skit portrays two people saying what they did over the weekend, the audience can become bored very quickly. If, on the other hand, the "actors" are discussing who had the most terrible weekend, then it becomes more appealing to the audience.
- It should contain repetition, especially when an important point is being made so that the audience has a chance to understand what is going on. This can be in the form of echoing by another speaker (A: **No quiero estar más contigo.** B: **¿Cómo que no quieres estar más conmigo?**).
- It should contain cultural aspects of the Hispanic world that students have learned in class. In retelling *Cinderella*, for example, the party she attends could be a **quinceañera** party.
- Lines should be memorized so that exchanges between characters look more natural. When grading, take into consideration the quality of the first and second draft, the originality of the project, the quality of the delivery of lines, pronunciation and intonation, and overall impression.

Planning A Syllabus

The *Fuentes* program was written keeping in mind different course configurations and teaching styles. Course goals and the total number of class meetings available vary from one institution to another, so these will be key elements to consider in planning a syllabus. During the study of Spanish at the intermediate level, some institutions have classes that meet four times a week, others three times, and some only twice. The *Fuentes* program can be used in all of these possible scenarios with slight adaptations or omissions.

Although it is best to use both FCG and FLR in conjunction, doing most activities presented, if an institution chooses to focus on listening and speaking skills as provided in FCG, allowances can be made to pick and choose from the readings in FLR. On the other hand, if the institution opts to focus more on developing reading and writing skills in FLR, it can place less emphasis on FCG. The *Fuentes* Video complements both volumes, and instructors are encouraged to consider it an integral part of the program, using a combination of in-class and outside of class time for viewing and activities.

Both FCG and FLR contain a wealth of activities and instructors should feel free to pick and choose which to use in class. Although it is best to finish all 12 chapters, the last chapter is a review chapter and can be omitted.

Sample Syllabi for the *Fuentes* Program

Semester System. First semester, three-day-per-week schedule: four quizzes, one midterm exam, and a final exam scheduled during the semester. The exam will take the complete hour and quizzes half a class period. The number of days allotted per chapter assumes use of both FCG and FLR.

Second semester, three-day-per-week schedule: four quizzes, one midterm exam, and a final exam scheduled during the semester. The exam will take the complete hour and quizzes half a class period. Chapter 12 in FCG serves as a review for the course and the final exam.

Semester 1				Semester 2			
Week	Day 1	Day 2	Day 3	Week	Day 1	Day 2	Day 3
1	Prelim.	Prelim.	1	1	Review	7	7
2	1	1	1	2	7	7	7
3	1	1	Quiz, Ch.1	3	7	Quiz, Ch.7	8
4	2	2	2	4	8	8	8
5	2	2	2	5	8	8	8
6	Quiz, Ch.2	3	3	6	Quiz, Ch.8	9	9
7	3	3	3	7	9	9	9
8	3	3/Review	Exam, Ch. P–3	8	9	9	Exam, Ch. 7–9
9	4	4	4	9	10	10	10
10	4	4	4	10	10	10	10
11	Quiz, Ch. 4	5	5	11	10	Quiz, Ch. 10	11
12	5	5	5	12	11	11	11
13	5	Quiz, Ch. 5	6	13	11	11	11
14	6	6	6	14	Quiz, Ch.11	12*	12
15	6	6	Review for final exam	15	12	12	12

*Chapter 12 FCG reviews material from the entire course.

Quarter System. First, second, and third quarters, three-day-per-week schedule: one midterm and a final exam scheduled each quarter. The number of days allotted per chapter assumes use of both FCG and FLR.

Quarter 1				Quarter 2				Quarter 3			
Week	Day 1	Day 2	Day 3	Week	Day 1	Day 2	Day 3	Week	Day 1	Day 2	Day 3
1	Prelim.	Prelim.	Prelim./1	1	Review	5	5	1	Review	9	9
2	1	1	1	2	5	5	5	2	9	9	9
3	1	1	2	3	5	5	6	3	9	9	9
4	2	2	2	4	6	6	6	4	10	10	10
5	2	2	2	5	6	6	Midterm, Ch. 5–6	5	10	10	10
6	Midterm, Ch. P–2	3	3	6	7	7	7	6	10	Midterm, Ch. 9–10	11
7	3	3	3	7	7	7	7	7	11	11	11
8	3	3/4	4	8	7	8	8	8	11	11	11
9	4	4	4	9	8	8	8	9	11	12*	12
10	4	4	Review for final exam	10	8	8	Review for final exam	10	12	12	12

*Chapter 12 FCG reviews material from the entire course.

Lesson Planning

When planning a lesson, keep in mind the following general points.

1. Clearly define your daily objectives.
2. Plan your lesson thinking of your students as individuals.
3. Write homework assignments on the board prior to starting the class or post them on the Internet for easy access.
4. Begin the class with an active warm-up.
5. Involve students actively in the learning process.
6. Anticipate possible student errors or questions.
7. Do not do anything for your students that they can do for themselves.
8. Maintain a brisk pace.
9. Allow for a variety of activities.
10. Establish a pleasant, relaxed atmosphere.

Each day, after class, ask yourself the following questions.

1. What percentage of the class time did students talk?
2. Did the students and I manage to use only Spanish?

When planning a lesson using the *Fuentes* program, keep in mind the following points.

1. Do activities from both FCG and FLR in the same lesson rather than having days dedicated specifically to one or the other.
2. Pick and choose from the various activities presented. It is not necessary to do all of them. Pick those that best match your students' needs and your teaching style.

3. When assigned, textbook activities from FLR and FCG should be collected and may simply receive a check mark indicating that the instructor glanced at them. In many cases, these will be checked in class. In other cases, the instructor may wish to provide an answer key, to check them, or to spot check them. If they are collected, students will be more apt to do them all when assigned, which will ensure that students are well prepared for each class.
4. The CD-ROM is optional as are the activities on the Web, but the activities can be a valuable tool for those who require more practice to master material or simply enjoy on-screen work versus pen and paper. If the instructor actively promotes use of these programs, students will be more apt to try them and thus benefit from them. Instructors may also choose to make these actual assignments that can be emailed to the instructor or printed out to be handed in.
5. If you have students do the **Cuaderno personal** entries in FLR, collect them in small batches during each class period, except exam and quiz days.
6. Assign Workbook activities during the course of each chapter and collect them at the end of each chapter on the day of the quiz or exam. Since answers are provided for most activities, students can be held responsible for correcting their own answers. If you are using the Quia online version of the Activities Manual, you may want to spot check to make sure students are doing the activities as assigned. In both the print and online version, only open-ended sections need to be checked, and although thorough checking is preferable, you may choose to simply spot-check.
7. Assign the Lab Manual activities the last few days of each chapter and have students hand them in on the day of the quiz or exam. Answers to the Lab Manual activities can be provided to students for self-correction, or the instructor can choose to correct these. The lab activities and audio files are also available through Quia in an online version and are automatically checked whenever possible.

Sample Lesson Plan For Chapter 3

Note: If using the print version, all Workbook/Lab Manual activities will be handed in at the end of the chapter the day of the exam (many are self-checking in nature). If using the online version, you may spot check at any time during the chapter or check it at the end.

Day 1

The following is the homework students should have completed prior to class on Day 1. Instructor will need a CD player and the In-Text Audio CD containing the legend.

Estudiar:	I. Narrating in the Past (Part Two): A. Preterit and Imperfect: Part One, p. 65–66, FCG
Hacer:	Act. 4 y 5, FCG, para entregar Cuaderno de ejercicios Act. 1-4
Leer:	¿Lo sabían?, p. 64. Using Sentence Structure and Parts of Speech to Guess Meaning, p. 39, FLR
Hacer:	Act. 2, 3A y B, 4, 5A, FLR, para entregar
Opcional:	Actividades correspondientes en Internet y CD-ROM (Note: these can be assigned as homework and printed out to turn in or they can be optional assignments for additional practice as deemed appropriate by the instructor and individual student.)

Warm-up with pre-listening activities (5 minutes)

- Have students look at the opening pages for both FLR and FCG side-by-side and ask questions about the photos. Then do Act. 1, FLR and Act. 1A, FCG.

While-listening (12 minutes)

- Read the directions for Act. 1B, FCG, and play the story. Allow a minute for students to discuss and then have a few groups report back.
- Do Act. 1C, FCG. Play the story again, pausing at appropriate points and having students add details to the story. Prod with questions if needed. Remember that yes/no and either/or formats are easier than information questions.

Post-listening (4 minutes)

- Do Act. 2, FCG.

Pre-reading (4 minutes)

- Transition from listening to the reading in FLR. Discuss possible answers to Act. 5, particularly #2. Inform students that they will be reading about the fall of a civilization for the next class.

Provide input for narration in the past (5 minutes)

- Using the story of Quetzalcóatl, provide input dealing with past actions with no clear start or end, actions in progress that were interrupted or two simultaneous actions in progress in the past.

Practice narration in the past (20 minutes)

- Do Act. 3–6, FCG. Consult instructor annotations in the margin for tips on how to best present the activities.
- When doing Act. 3–6, it is good to change pairs at least once.

Collect Act. 4 and 5, FCG (if assigned, simply check them off as done since they were corrected/used in class).

Collect Act. 2, 3A and B, 4, and 5A, FLR. Options for correction include (note: some are time-savers for instructors, yet make students work):

- Simply mark them as done.
- Correct each one individually.
- Glance at them and spot check.
- Mark them as done and hand out an answer key, email out an answer key, or post an answer key on the Internet.

Day 2

Homework to be completed prior to class on Day 2

Repasar:	I. Narrating in the Past (Part Two): A. Preterit and Imperfect: Part One, p. 65–66, FCG
Estudiar:	B. Preterit and Imperfect: Part Two, p. 68–69, FCG
Hacer:	Act. 7, 12A, FCG, para entregar Cuaderno de ejercicios Act. 5-7
Leer:	¿Lo sabían? p. 71, FCG. *Autopsia de una civilización*, p. 42, FLR
Hacer:	Act. 6, 7, 8, FLR, para entregar
Opcional:	Actividades correspondientes en Internet y CD-ROM

Warm-up (3 minutes)

- Have students retell the story of Quetzalcóatl that they heard in the previous class.

Input (Preterit and Imperfect: Part Two) (5 minutes)

- Transition from the story of Quetzalcóatl to use it as a summary of narration in the past. As you do this, you may want to make use of time lines on the board. For example: write *descripción de una escena* on the board and write a few sentences below it that the students may have given you (**Había una colina con un hormiguero.); ***acciones habituales* (**Las hormigas trabajaban mucho todos los días**.); review and include actions in progress.

Do Act. 7–14, FCG (omit Act. 13) (35 minutes)

- Note: You may pick and choose from these activities as time permits and based on the needs of your class.
- Transition to Act. 7 by discussing the Aztec civilization. Check in class and ask a few comprehension questions while doing so.
- Transition to Act. 8 by asking students to name other indigenous civilizations in Latin America and where they were. Do Act. 8.
- Transition to Act. 9 by saying the lives of the indigenous peoples of the Americas were forever altered after 1492, just as lives were altered in more modern times with technology. Do Act. 9.
- Continue with Act. 10–12.
- Transition to Act. 14 by asking students if they were told any stories as children—Jack and Jill, Jack and the Beanstalk, etc. Then ask them to create the legend of how the buffalo came to be.

Do Act. 6–9, FLR (7 minutes)

- Transition to the post-reading discussion by telling students that in many countries children are taught legends that help keep the ancient cultures alive. If time allows, correct Act. 6, 7, and 8.
- Do Act. 9. Note that the use of the imperfect subjunctive can be avoided by providing model sentences for students to use where students react by saying **No es verdad/cierto.** + *New sentence with information*.

Collect FCG homework and simply mark as done if corrected in class. If not corrected in class, provide an answer key and mark papers as done. Follow a similar procedure for FLR homework.

Day 3

Homework to be completed prior to class on Day 3

Hacer:	Cuaderno personal 3–1, p. 45, FLR
Estudiar:	II. Describing People and Things: A. Descripción física y B. Personalidad, p. 75–77, FCG
Hacer:	Cuaderno de ejercicios Act. 8–13 Act. 10–12, FLR, para entregar
Opcional:	Actividades correspondientes en Internet y CD-ROM

Warm-up (20 minutes)

- Do Act. 13, FCG, as a warm-up. Prior to doing, reenter uses of the preterit and imperfect. You may do this by discussing a pet that you own or used to own, saying what the pet used to do, did one day that was funny, and perhaps, even how the pet died. When doing Act. 13, encourage students to use their imagination.

- Transition to Act. 15, FCG, by discussing what happens when a new pet is introduced into a household (especially interesting when a dog enters a household with cats or vice versa). Discuss how territorial fights might ensue and how one may dominate the other. Elicit from students what might happen when one country invades another. State that this is what happened post 1492. Then read and discuss the statements in the **Fuente hispana** section.

Description (25 minutes)

- Provide input by showing pictures of indigenous peoples and conquistadors and have students describe them. Then show pictures of mestizos and do the same.
- Transition to physical descriptions of individuals in the class or famous people and include personality traits.
- Do Act. 16–19, FCG. Note that Act. 19 reviews past description.
- Read the **¿Lo sabían?**, p. 77. Ask students what nicknames they would give family members.

Pre-reading for Panorama cultural, FLR (5 minutes)

- Transition to pre-reading by saying that many adjectives also have related words that are verbs: **gordo–engordar; flaco–enflaquecer; delgado–adelgazar**. Check Act. 10–11, FLR.
- Briefly discuss Act. 12, FLR.

Collect all homework.

Day 4

Homework to be completed prior to class on Day 4

Estudiar:	C. Describing: **Ser** and **estar** + Adjective, p. 79–80, FCG
Hacer	Act. 21A, FCG, para entregar
	Cuaderno de ejercicios Act. 14–15
Leer:	*La presencia indígena en Hispanoamérica,* p. 47, FLR
Hacer:	Act. 13–14, FLR, para entregar
Opcional:	Actividades correspondientes en Internet y CD-ROM

Warm-up (7 minutes)

- Act. 20, FCG, reviews description and habitual actions in the past while using the vocabulary items.

Input (5 minutes)

- Provide input dealing with **ser/estar** + adjective.

Do Act. 21–24, FCG (20 minutes)

- Check Act. 21A, do Act. 21B.
- Continue with Act. 22–24.

Do Act. 13–16, FLR (18 minutes)

- Check Act. 13 and 14.
- Do Act. 15 and 16.

Collect all homework.

Day 5

Homework to be completed prior to class on Day 5

Estudiar:	D. Describing: The Past Participle as Adjective, p. 82, FCG
Hacer:	Act. 25, FCG, para entregar
Estudiar:	III. Indicating the Beneficiary of an Action, The Indirect Object, p. 84–85, FCG
Hacer:	Act. 27–28, FCG, para entregar Cuaderno de ejercicios Act. 16–18 Cuaderno personal 3–2, p. 51, FLR (debes estar preparado/a para discutir tus opiniones en clase)
Estudiar:	Using the Bilingual Dictionary, p. 51, FLR
Hacer:	Act. 17, 18, FLR, para entregar
Opcional:	Actividades correspondientes en Internet y CD-ROM

Warm-up (5 minutes)

- Have students discuss their responses to the Cuaderno personal 3–2 in pairs or small groups.

Act. 17–19, FLR (25 minutes)

- Quickly correct Act. 17 and 18 or simply collect these and supply an answer key.
- Do Act. 19A–C. Do A as a shout out, then have students as a group make guesses as to the content of the story based on the vocabulary words provided. Do C individually or in small groups. If done in small groups, this could be done orally or in written format. When finished have one or two groups relate their story to the class.

Introduce past participles as adjectives and do Act. 25–26, FCG (10 minutes)

- Transition by asking students to look at the word **perdido** in Act. 19A, FLR, and stress this is a past participle and an adjective. Stress that it will agree with the noun it modifies. Quickly provide input with other past participles as adjectives and correct Act. 25.
- Do Act. 26.

Introduce the indirect-object pronoun and check Act. 27 and 28, FCG (10 minutes)

- Transition to the use of the indirect-object pronoun by referring to the drawing in Act. 26 and asking, **¿El gato está muerto o dormido? ¿Alguien le dio algo malo para comer?** Continue by saying, **Hay regalos en la mesa. ¿Quién compró estos regalos? ¿A quién le dio o a quiénes les dio esos regalos?**
- Check Act. 27 and 28.

Collect all homework.

Day 6

Homework to be completed prior to Day 6

Repasar:	III. Indicating the Beneficiary of an Action, p. 84–85, FCG
Hacer:	Act. 31A, FCG, para entregar Cuaderno de ejercicios Act. 19–21
Leer:	Biografía de Augusto Monterroso y *El eclipse*, p. 54, FLR
Hacer:	Act. 20–21A y B, FLR, para entregar Cuaderno personal 3–3, p. 56, FLR

Escuchar: Manual de laboratorio para el día del examen parcial
Opcional: Actividades correspondientes en Internet y CD-ROM

Warm-up (5 minutes)

- To review indirect-object pronouns and past narration, have students say what gifts they received in the last year, from whom they received each gift, and why they like it or not. Then have them say what they gave others and why they liked the gifts or not.

Do Act. 29 and 30, FCG (10 minutes)

Do Act. 31, FCG (5 minutes)

Discuss the reading *El eclipse*, FLR (20 minutes)

- As a transition, discuss the fact that Cortés realized that Malinalli was a bright woman who could help him in his quest, but that many times other conquistadors underestimated the knowledge of the indigenous population.
- Check Act. 20, then 21A as a class shout-out activity.
- Do Act. 22.

Do Act. 23A and B, FLR (10 minutes)

- Instruct students that they will be writing their own myth and as practice, you will tell them one. Discuss the *Popol Vuh*. Then tell them the story (see instructor's annotation) and have them take notes. In groups or as a class, have them retell the myth.

Collect all homework.

Day 7

Homework to be completed prior to Day 7

Repasar: Todo el Capítulo 3, FCG
Leer: Using the Bilingual Dictionary, p. 51, FLR Hacer: Act. 24, FLR, para entregar
Escribir: Act. 25, FLR (Entrega tu esquema, tu lista de palabras, tu borrador y tu versión final de la composición)
Opcional: Todas las actividades en Internet y en el CD-ROM del Capítulo 3

Video FCG (25 minutes)

- Warm-up: Do Act. 1, p. 319, FCG, which provides a pre-viewing activity that has students say as much as they can about indigenous peoples.
- Do Act. 2A and B. These are while-viewing activities that help to focus the students. First make students aware of what to listen for and then show the video, stopping to check partway through.
- Do Act. 3. This is a post-viewing activity that will help students make links between what occurred and is occurring in both Latin America and their own country.

Review for midterm exam (25 minutes)

Collect compositions

Day 8: Examen de mitad de semestre

Homework to be completed prior to Day 8

Entregar: Todos los ejercicios del Cuaderno de ejercicios y el Manual de laboratorio del Capítulo 3.
Repasar: Los Capítulos Preliminar al 3
Opcional: Las actividades en Internet y en el CD-ROM de los Capítulos Preliminar al 3

The exam should take the entire hour.

You may want to assign the web search activities for Chapter 3 to be done for the next class period (Day 9) for reentry of theme and structures, either as a full class assignment or as an extra credit opportunity.

Scripts for Chapter Listening Passages

Capítulo preliminar: Una conversación en la facultad

Ramón ¿Y cómo te va en la facultad?
Mónica ¡Ay! ¿No te dije? Creo que voy a cambiar de carrera.
Ramón **¿En serio?** ¿Qué pasa? ¿No... no te gusta la medicina?
Mónica No, creo que la medicina no es para mí.
Ramón **¡No me digas!**
Mónica Sí. Hace un año que... que estoy en medicina y la verdad es... no sé... creo que no me gusta. Tengo materias que no me interesan... y no sé. Me parece que estoy perdiendo el tiempo.
Ramón ¿Y... qué vas a hacer?
Mónica Mira. La opción que estoy considerando es estudiar derecho.
Ramón **¡No me digas!** ¿Derecho? ¿Abogada tú?
Mónica Sí, sí. ¿Por qué no? Me interesa mucho el derecho constitucional. Creo que es una carrera donde tengo más posibilidades. En este país hay tantos médicos que para... encontrar trabajo, pues es casi... casi imposible.
Ramón Sí, la verdad es que no se necesitan más médicos en las grandes ciudades y yo no quiero vivir en un pueblo. Pero, dime una cosa, y en la facultad de derecho, ¿te revalidan algunas de las materias de medicina?
Mónica No, no me revalidan nada. Ninguna de las materias que hice. Cero. Ni una. Tomé ocho materias: biología, anatomía y seis más, y no me revalidan ninguna. Es una lástima.
Ramón **¿En serio?** ¡Qué suerte tienes!
Mónica Sí, pero ¿qué puedo hacer? Tendré que **volver a empezar de cero**. Por suerte, por suerte, sólo he estado en medicina un año y no dos o tres años. ¿Te imaginas?
Ramón No, de verdad que no me lo imagino. Demasiado trabajo para mí. Y dime, ¿a qué edad vas a terminar la carrera?
Mónica Pues... tengo diecinueve... y se necesitan cinco años, así que a los... a los veinticuatro me recibo de abogada. ¿Qué crees? Y eso sí, esta vez no vuelvo a cambiar de carrera.
Ramón Estás segura, ¿no? Quiero tener una amiga abogada... puedo necesitar tu ayuda en cualquier momento. Pero bueno, mucha suerte.
Mónica Órale, pues.

Capítulo 1: Una cuestión de identidad

Pedro Discúlpame, Silvia. Te quería hacer una pregunta.
Silvia Sí, dime.
Pedro **Hace una hora que estoy** con esta solicitud para entrar a una universidad de California y **me llama la atención** la cantidad de categorías que hay: *Chicano/Mexican American, Latino, Latin American, Puerto Rican, Other Hispanic...* **Son unos pesados**. Esto es una ensalada de palabras. ¿Quién es qué? Dime, ¿quién es el "Mexican American"?
Silvia Bueno, el mexicoamericano es el ciudadano de los Estados Unidos que es descendiente de mexicanos, es decir, que sus padres o abuelos o bisabuelos eran mexicanos, y que se identifica con la cultura mexicana.
Pedro ¡Ah! O sea, que el mexicoamericano es ciudadano de los Estados Unidos, pero habla español.
Silvia Algunos hablan sólo inglés y otros hablan inglés y español.
Pedro Y el chicano, ¿quién es el chicano?

Silvia Bueno, chicano es una palabra que usan algunos mexicoamericanos para referirse a sí mismos, es decir, a gente de ascendencia mexicana, pero creo, creo que la palabra tiene una connotación política.

Pedro Política, ¿eh? Pues, entonces yo, ¿qué marco en esta solicitud?

Silvia Marca "Latin American".

Pedro Sí, ya sé que soy latinoamericano porque soy de Latinoamérica, pero latinoamericano también incluye a los brasileños porque ellos hablan portugués y el portugués es una lengua latina. Pues, yo quisiera poner chileno, pero marco "Latin American" y listo.

Silvia Y ¿sabes? Ya vas a aprender más cuando estés allí. Vas a ver que en la universidad no sólo asistes a clase; también participas en otras actividades como jugar al fútbol, cantar en el coro.

Pedro ¿Qué dices? ¿Cantar?

Silvia Sí, allí no es como aquí que cuando sales de clase tomas el autobús y te vas a tu casa.

Pedro O te vas a un bar a tomar algo con tus amigos... o adonde sea...

Silvia Exacto. Pero en cambio en los Estados Unidos, como todas las facultades están juntas en la ciudad universitaria, o el "campus", como se dice allí, hay muchas cosas para hacer. Es muy divertido porque generalmente te quedas en el "campus".

Pedro El "campus", ¿eh? No veo la hora de estar allí. Me parece que lo voy a pasar muy bien.

Capítulo 2: Un anuncio histórico

Radio Enrique Igles...

Hombre No, por favor.

Mujer Ponlo en el noventa y ocho. Siempre ponen música buena.

Anuncio En el año 711 los musulmanes, o moros, como los llamaban aquí en España, invadieron la Península Ibérica para llevar la palabra del Corán. 711, **año clave** en la historia de España.

Entre 1252 y 1284, con el rey Alfonso X, o Alfonso el Sabio, cristianos, moros y judíos pudieron explorar juntos la filosofía y las ciencias. 1252 a 1284, años clave.

En 1492 los Reyes Católicos, Fernando e Isabel, expulsaron a los moros de España y Cristóbal Colón llegó a América y empezó entonces la colonización de ese continente. 1492, año clave.

1898 España perdió sus últimas colonias: Cuba, Puerto Rico, Guam y las Islas Filipinas. 1898, año clave.

1936 La guerra civil española empezó y duró tres años. 1936, año clave.

1975 Después de casi 40 años de dictadura, Francisco Franco murió y se instituyó una monarquía parlamentaria. 1975, año clave.

Compren la serie de libros *Años clave en la historia de España.* El primer libro estará a la venta en todos los quioscos **el** próximo **lunes**. Una colección esencial para su biblioteca. El primer libro *De Altamira hasta los romanos,* **el lunes,** en su quiosco y todos **los lunes**, un nuevo libro de la serie *Años clave en la historia de España.*

Presentador ¡Ahora, lo que vosotros queréis, lo que vosotros esperáis, vosotros sabéis quiénes son...!

Capítulo 3: La leyenda del maíz

Bueno, hoy les voy a contar una historia, una leyenda, que es la leyenda del maíz. Es una leyenda tolteca. Los toltecas vivían en lo que hoy día es México. Bueno, **había una vez** en el cielo dos dioses, el Dios Sol y la Diosa Tierra, que tenían muchos hijos. Un día, uno de los hijos, que se llamaba Quetzalcóatl, les dijo a sus padres que quería ir a vivir a la Tierra y sus padres le dijeron que sí. Así que, con el permiso de sus padres, Quetzalcóatl bajó a vivir a la Tierra con los toltecas.

Los toltecas eran muy, muy pobres y, entonces, todas las noches Quetzalcóatl iba a una montaña y les pedía ayuda a sus padres, el Dios Sol y la Diosa Tierra. Y sus padres le enseñaron a obtener el oro, la plata, la esmeralda y el coral. Y con todo esto Quetzalcóatl construyó cuatro casas de coral con oro, plata y esmeraldas. Y entonces los toltecas ahora eran ricos, pero para Quetzalcóatl esto no era suficiente porque él quería algo más, algo útil para los toltecas; él quería darles algo para su futuro.

Una noche, Quetzalcóatl fue a la montaña a pedirles inspiración a sus padres, los dioses. Pero se quedó dormido y comenzó a soñar. Y en el sueño vio una montaña cubierta de muchas flores y, de repente, vio hormigas, muchas hormigas y pronto vio un hormiguero. En ese hormiguero entraban y salían muchas hormigas que llevaban algo, pero Quetzalcóatl no podía ver qué era.

Y ahí Quetzalcóatl se despertó y misteriosamente empezó a caminar hasta que llegó a una montaña preciosa cubierta de flores y allí **¿a que no saben** lo que vio? Sí, vio el mismo hormiguero que había visto en su sueño. No lo podía creer.

Y entonces como él era tan grande y la entrada del hormiguero era tan pequeña, les pidió a los dioses que lo convirtieran en hormiga para poder entrar en el hormiguero. Los dioses lo escucharon y lo convirtieron en hormiga y así Quetzalcóatl pudo entrar en el hormiguero y allí encontró el tesoro de las hormigas. ¿Cuál era el tesoro? ¿Qué era esta cosa tan valiosa? Eran cuatro granitos blancos. Quetzalcóatl tomó los cuatro granitos blancos y volvió a su pueblo pero no se los mostró a nadie. Los escondió muy, muy bien. ¿Dónde los puso para esconderlos? Los puso en la tierra.

No saben la sorpresa que se llevó una mañana **cuando** salió de su casa y vio unas plantas doradas, divinas, con hojas grandes y en el centro un fruto delicioso. Los dioses le habían dado algo más importante que el oro, la plata, el coral y la esmeralda. Le habían dado una planta. Sí, una planta: el maíz. Un cereal divino para la vida de los toltecas. Y colorín, colorado esta leyenda ha terminado.*

Capítulo 4: Entrevista a un artista cubano

Entrevistadora Bueno, Alex, primero quería preguntarte sobre el origen de tu familia.

Alex Pues como muchos cubanos, mi familia es de origen africano y de origen español. **Por parte de mi madre**, soy de origen español y soy africano por el lado de mi padre.

Entrevistadora ¿Y qué sabes de tu familia que llegó a Cuba?

Alex Pues, que el padre de mi abuela, es decir que mi bisabuelo era español, pero **por parte de mi padre** se remonta más atrás en la historia. No sé mucho, pero es algo que me gustaría investigar ya que existen archivos muy buenos en Trinidad sobre los esclavos que llegaron y sé que mis antepasados llegaron primero a Trinidad y luego fueron a Cuba.

Entrevistadora Ojalá que encuentres información; pero dime, si piensas en la influencia africana que ves a tu alrededor en Cuba, ¿qué influencias africanas podrías identificar?

Alex Bueno, obviamente se ve mucho en la música. Mira, uno de los instrumentos que sigue siendo popular hoy día es un tambor que se llama batá. La influencia africana también está en el baile y en la comida, pero en la comida hoy día está muy camuflada con la influencia española.

Entrevistadora ¿Camuflada?

Alex Sí, yo no te sé decir, por ejemplo, qué comida es típicamente africana porque ya está todo mezclado con lo español.

Entrevistadora Y **a pesar de que** está todo mezclado, en tu opinión, ¿existe la discriminación en la sociedad cubana?

Alex Pues, sí y no. El racismo en Cuba se ha convertido en algo que es tan parte de la vida normal que a veces la gente no se da cuenta, pero existe.

Entrevistadora Ah, sí, pues, ¿me podrías dar un ejemplo?

Alex Pues, por ejemplo, yo que soy de piel oscura, a veces estoy hablando con un cubano y si tenemos una conversación muy intelectual, esa persona a veces me dice "Pero, chico, tú no eres negro, eres blanco" como diciendo si eres inteligente, no puedes ser negro.

Entrevistadora ¿De veras?

Alex Sí, y la gente lo dice sin darse cuenta de lo que dice.

Entrevistadora Y en cuanto al tema de las parejas, ¿se mezclan?

Alex Sí, sí. Tú sabes que **a la hora de formar** pareja no se piensa en el color. Reconocemos que al final tú eres cubano y yo también, y somos todos iguales. Los matrimonios entre negros y blancos son muy comunes.

Entrevistadora Es decir que con el tiempo es posible que desaparezca esa discriminación.

Alex Sí, pero mira, yo te puedo seguir contando por horas y horas, pero para entender mejor la situación, te recomiendo que visites Cuba. Y es una buena idea que te quedes en una casa de familia para poder entender mejor cómo somos los cubanos. Es que las familias cubanas...

Capítulo 5: En esta mesa se habla español

Mujer Sabes que me encanta este restaurante cubano, es que siempre...

Mesero Aquí está su comida. A ver, ¿quién pidió moros y cristianos?

Hombre ¿Los moros y cristianos? ... Ah, son para mi esposa.

Mesero Bien. Y la ropa vieja, ¿para quién es?

Hombre La ropa vieja para mí.

Niño The chicken with fried plantains is for me.

Hombre No, niño. En español, vamos, habla español.

Niño But, papi...

Hombre Nada de peros. Es importante que seas bilingüe y si no hablas español...

Niño Bueno, bueno. Mesero, el pollo con plátano frito es para mí.

*Legend based on Otilia Meza, "La leyenda del maíz," *Leyendas del antiguo México: Mitología prehispánica* (México, D.F.: Edamex, 1985).

Mujer Chévere.
Mesero Buen provecho.
Hombre/Mujer Gracias.
Hombre Hmmmm, me encanta la comida cubana. ¡Qué sabrosa!
Niño Mami, mira a ese señor bailando el chachachá.
Mujer Pero ese señor no baila, ése mata cucarachas.
Hombre Tu abuelo sí que sabía bailar el chachachá... era el mejor que había.
Mujer Oye, Miguelito, quiero que te comas todo el plátano que tienes en el plato. ¿Me entiendes?
Niño ¿Comérmelo todo? Pero papi, no tengo mucha hambre.
Mujer Déjame probar un poquito. Hmmmm, ¡este plátano está delicioso!
Hombre Mira, niño, cómetelo todo.
Niño Bueno, está bien.
Mujer Y, por favor, put both hands on the table.
Niño ¡That's English! ¡Papá, mamá está hablando en inglés! ¿Por qué ella sí y yo no?
Mujer Lo siento, niño. Es verdad, pon las dos manos en la mesa.
Hombre ¿Y saben dónde se encontraron los primeros plátanos?
Mujer En Cuba, por supuesto.
Hombre No, en Cuba no. El plátano se originó en Asia. **¿Acaso no sabías?**
Mujer ¡En Asia! ¡Por favor! Miguelito, las dos manos en la mesa, ¿eh?
Hombre Pero es la verdad. Te lo digo en serio. Los primeros plátanos se encontraron en Asia y luego se plantaron en las Islas Canarias, que forman parte de España hoy día.
Mujer ¿En las Islas Canarias? ¿Y qué? ¿Entonces los españoles los llevaron de las Canarias al Caribe?
Hombre Así es. Ellos lo llevaron al Caribe en 1516.
Mujer Pero qué interesante. No tenía idea.
Niño Papi, **no tengo ganas de comer** más plátano.
Hombre Te digo que te comas todo el plátano.
Niño Bueno, me como uno más si tú dejas de **dar cátedra**. Mi plátano no viene ni de Asia ni de las Islas Canarias. Éste viene de la cocina **y punto.**

Capítulo 6: Nadie está inmune

Marcos ¿Leíste que Sting va a dar un concierto en favor de los derechos humanos?
Antonia No me digas. Me parece muy bien. Hace muchos años mi tío fue a un concierto que dio Sting en Mendoza en honor de las madres de **los desaparecidos**.
Marcos ¿Sting estuvo en Mendoza?
Antonia Sí, en 1988 durante la dictadura de Pinochet, por la censura le fue imposible tocar en Chile la canción "Ellas danzan solas", y entonces se fue a Mendoza a tocarla y lo interesante fue que 15.000 chilenos cruzaron la frontera para ir a escucharlo. Mi tío, que estuvo allí, me contó que Sting bailó con las madres en el escenario.
Marcos Sabía que Sting había escrito para las madres de los desaparecidos la canción "Ellas danzan solas", pero no sabía que ha-, que había estado en Mendoza.
Antonia ¡Cómo han cambiado las cosas! **Quién diría** que un día aparecería alguien como el juez español ese... ¿cómo se llama? Ah, sí, sí, Garzón. Aparecería Garzón y entonces Pinochet y otras personas como él sufrirían las consecuencias de sus actos.
Marcos Todavía no lo puedo creer. Me alegra que Pinochet, que fue responsable de la tortura y desaparición de miles de personas, y que personas como él, no sean inmunes a la justicia internacional. Pero, ¿cómo es la historia con Pinochet y el juez Garzón? Recuerdo que Pinochet estaba en Inglaterra...
Antonia Pues, sí, Pinochet ya no era dictador de Chile y estaba de visita en Inglaterra cuando el juez Garzón le pidió a Inglaterra su extradición a España. Pinochet decía que tenía inmunidad diplomática, pero ese juez español Garzón demostró que no era así.
Marcos Sí, pero al final no lo mandaron a España para juzgarlo sino que lo dejaron volver a Chile por problemas de salud, ¿no?
Antonia Así es, por estar enfermo lo mandaron a Chile, pero creo que la lección más importante del episodio es que ahora ningún gobernante va a pensar que puede hacer algo tan terrible como lo que ocurrió en nuestro país y **salirse con la suya** porque tarde o temprano le llegará su castigo.
Marcos Pero, lo que no recuerdo es cómo es posible que un juez español pueda juzgar a un chileno en otro país.
Antonia Bueno, es que el gobierno chileno no escuchó los reclamos de los familiares de los desaparecidos y, como algunos desaparecidos eran de ascendencia española, fueron a hacer el reclamo al gobierno español.
Marcos Ah sí, ahora recuerdo, si las víctimas son de ascendencia española, los criminales pueden ser juzgados en territorio español, ¿verdad?
Antonia Así es. Te digo que no es justo que llegue un gobernante y crea que puede hacer lo que quiere —matar a gente que no está de acuerdo con él— y que luego no se haga responsable de sus actos. Y los chilenos no somos los únicos. Esto ha pasado en otros países también... y no sólo de Latinoamérica.
Marcos Sí, sí, ya sé. Pero no hay duda que, después de muchos años, la situación política de los países latinoamericanos está ahora mucho más estable.

Capítulo 7: Unas vacaciones diferentes

Pablo ¿Y adónde vas a ir de vacaciones este verano?

María José Mm... ¿Sabes que no sé? La verdad es que no tengo ni idea qué quiero hacer este verano.

Pablo Pues, mujer, es lógico que no tengas idea. Has estado en tantos lugares que ya no te queda nada por conocer.

María José Bueno, no exageres. Es verdad que conozco un montón de sitios, pero todavía me queda mucho, mucho por conocer. Pero mm... quiero que... estas vacaciones sean, no sé, diferentes.

Pablo ¿Diferentes? ¿Diferentes en qué sentido?

María José Mm... no sé. Diferentes. Necesito ir a un lugar que sea tranquilo, donde no tenga que visitar catedrales, ni museos ni ruinas.

Pablo O sea, quieres unas vacaciones tranquilas, tranquilas. Y bueno. Entonces vete a un lugar que tenga playa.

María José ¿A la playa? No, no quiero ir a la playa. El verano pasado estuve en Huatulco en México, que es un lugar con playa, pero este verano busco un lugar donde haya más actividad, ¿me entiendes?

Pablo Más actividad, ¿eh? Pero no quieres visitar catedrales o museos.

María José No, esta vez no. ¡No quiero visitar ninguna catedral!

Pablo ¡Ah! ¿Sabes qué? **¡Ya sé!** Un amigo mío acaba de regresar de unas vacaciones en Ecuador.

María José ¿Ecuador? Mm... cuéntame, me interesa.

Pablo Bueno, resulta que hay una comunidad de... una comunidad de indígenas quichuas en un pueblito llamado Capirona.

María José Y, ¿qué voy a hacer yo en una comunidad de indígenas quichuas?

Pablo Bueno. Pues, mira. Espera que te cuente. Parece que los quichuas organizan un programa de ecoturismo en su pueblo.

María José ¿En serio? ¿Ecoturismo? ¿Y sabes en qué consiste el programa?

Pablo Creo que... creo que ellos organizan caminatas por la selva; y me parece que hacen demostraciones de cómo hacen sus canastos... y también se puede participar en una eh...en una minga.

María José ¿Minga? ¿Qué es una minga?

Pablo No estoy seguro, pero creo que en una minga los visitantes y la gente del lugar trabajan en algún proyecto comunitario o **algo así**.

María José ¿Como por ejemplo?

Pablo No sé. En realidad no me acuerdo. Pero, ¡ojo! El viaje no es fácil, ¿eh?... Solamente se puede llegar al pueblo en canoa o con una caminata de dos horas.

María José ¡Uf! ¡Qué ejercicio! Me tengo que poner en forma. Pero me parece interesantísimo. Ay, quisiera hablar con tu amigo.

Pablo Bueno, ¿sabes qué? Si quieres lo llamo y podemos salir a cenar juntos. ¿Te parece bien?

María José Ay, claro. **Desde luego.** Tengo miles de preguntas para hacerle.

Capítulo 8: Un trabajo en el extranjero

Entrevistador Hoy voy a entrevistar a dos jóvenes norteamericanos que han trabajado en el exterior para que nos cuenten cómo consiguieron el trabajo. Primero tenemos a Jenny Jacobsen, que estuvo enseñando inglés en España. ¿No es así, Jenny?

Jenny Así es.

Entrevistador Cuéntanos cómo hiciste para conseguir ese trabajo.

Jenny Bueno, yo tenía una maestría en enseñanza de español...

Entrevistador Ajá...

Jenny Y... mmmm... mandé mi curriculum a una escuela privada de inglés en Madrid. Tenía algunos amigos americanos en España que trabajaban allí y me habían dado la dirección del lugar.

Entrevistador Ajá...

Jenny Entonces, en enero me mandaron una solicitud; la llené y la devolví.

Entrevistador ¿Y tardaron mucho en contestarte?

Jenny No mucho. Creo que alrededor de mediados de marzo, ellos me entrevistaron en el congreso de TESOL que ese año fue en Chicago.

Entrevistador ¿Qué es el congreso de TESOL?

Jenny TESOL significa "Teachers of English to Speakers of Other Languages", o "profesores de inglés a hablantes de otros idiomas". Y es un congreso internacional que se hace o en los Estados Unidos o en Canadá y viene gente de todo el mundo para asistir al congreso y entrevistar a candidatos para profesores de inglés.

Entrevistador Pero, ¡qué interesante! Sigue, por favor.

Jenny Bueno, me fue muy bien en la entrevista. Entonces a las dos semanas me ofrecieron el puesto e inmediatamente me mandaron los papeles para sacar mi visa.

Entrevistador Y, ¿es difícil sacar visa para trabajar en España?

Jenny No es fácil y se necesita tiempo. Luego me fui a Madrid en septiembre y en esa escuela me dieron un entrenamiento de dos semanas para aprender a enseñar inglés.

Entrevistador Claro. Porque tú sabías enseñar español, pero nunca habías enseñado inglés, ¿verdad?

Jenny Correcto. Que uno hable inglés no quiere decir que uno sepa enseñarlo.

Entrevistador Es verdad.

Jenny Bueno. La experiencia fue realmente interesante. Al estar dando clases de inglés, conocí a mucha gente, me divertí **un montón** y, como puede ver, aprendí bastante español.

Entrevistador Ya lo creo. Pero dime, ¿y el sueldo? ¿Te alcanzaba para vivir?

Jenny Sí. Compartía un apartamento con una muchacha de Salamanca y el dinero me alcanzaba lo más bien. Nunca tuve problemas. Pero mucha gente también da clases particulares.

Entrevistador Y dime. ¿Hay muchos americanos enseñando inglés en España?

Jenny ¡Uf! Sí, hay cantidades.

Entrevistador Bueno, Jenny. Muchas gracias por haber compartido esta información con nosotros.

Jenny No. Por nada.

Entrevistador Y ahora estamos con nuestro segundo invitado de hoy, Jeff Stahley. Buenas tardes, Jeff.

Jeff Buenas tardes.

Entrevistador Tú también enseñaste inglés, ¿verdad?

Jeff Así es, pero no en Madrid como Jenny, sino en Medellín.

Entrevistador ¡Medellín, Colombia! ¿No era peligroso?

Jeff **No, en absoluto.** En realidad no tuve ningún problema.

Entrevistador ¿Y cómo hiciste para conseguir el trabajo en Colombia?

Jeff Bueno, pues yo me fui con visa de turista y una vez que estaba allí, la universidad me dio trabajo para enseñar inglés.

Entrevistador ¿Y cómo te dieron trabajo?

Jeff Bueno, la universidad quería contratarme y para poder enseñar, yo tenía que ser estudiante. Entonces tomé unos cursitos y así pude enseñar inglés. En vez de pagarme sueldo me dieron una beca. A mí **me daba igual** con tal de recibir dinero. También di clases particulares de inglés.

Entrevistador ¿Y cómo conseguiste los estudiantes para las clases particulares?

Jeff Bueno, hay tanta gente que quiere aprender inglés con americanos y tan pocos americanos allí que enseguida comencé a tener un montón de clientes.

Entrevistador ¿Y te pagaban bien?

Jeff ¡Uf! No sólo me pagaban bien, sino que como Jenny, conocí a mucha gente que me invitaba a su casa y salíamos juntos, hacíamos muchos programas juntos. En fin, realmente no era turista. Me sentía como en mi casa.

Entrevistador Y para finalizar. Dime, ¿qué consejos puedes darle a un norteamericano que quiera ir a enseñar inglés?

Jeff Pues... que tome algún curso corto para aprender a enseñar inglés antes de ir a otro país. Así puede tener muchas más posibilidades de trabajo.

Entrevistador Bien. Muchas gracias, Jeff, por charlar conmigo.

Jeff Fue un placer. Gracias.

Capítulo 9: Entrevista a una experta en artesanías

Locutor Bueno y hoy tenemos una invitada muy especial, María Gómez, oriunda de Ecuador. La Sra. Gómez nos va a hablar de un arte cuya perfección es admirada en todo el mundo: el famoso sombrero panamá. Sra. Gómez, buenos días y bienvenida a nuestro programa.

Sra. Gómez Muchas gracias a Ud. por invitarme.

Locutor Pues, cuéntenos un poco sobre los sombreros panamá.

Sra. Gómez Bueno. Pues... primero, yo quería explicar que estos sombreros tan famosos se hacen en Ecuador y no en Panamá como cree mucha gente.

Locutor Y entonces, ¿por qué se conocen como sombreros panamá si se hacen en Ecuador?

Sra. Gómez ¡Ja! Ocurre que desde hace tiempo los fabricaban en Ecuador, pero... pero los mandaban al resto del mundo desde Panamá y por eso comenzaron a llamarlos sombreros panamá. Los usaban personas como... como Teddy Roosevelt y el rey Eduardo VII de Inglaterra y por eso, con el tiempo, se pusieron muy de moda. Pero... recuerde Ud. que los mejores son los llamados Montecristi Finos, que están hechos en Montecristi, Ecuador, donde yo vivo, y no en Panamá.

Locutor ¡Pero qué curioso! Yo pensaba que eran de Panamá.

Sra. Gómez No, no, no. Los mejores son de mi pueblo, de Montecristi, Ecuador.

Locutor Bueno y, ¿por qué son tan particulares estos sombreros?

Sra. Gómez Pues porque los artesanos los hacen a mano con muchísimo cuidado. Usan paja para su fabricación, por supuesto, y... claro, sólo trabajan de noche.

Locutor ¡¿Trabajan de noche?! ¿A qué se debe eso?

Sra. Gómez Pues por la noche hace más fresco y de día, cuando hace calor, la transpiración del artesano puede echar a perder la paja porque... deja manchas.

Locutor Y, ¿cuánto tardan en hacer uno de estos sombreros?

Sra. Gómez Los buenos **les llevan** a los artesanos más o menos... más o menos dos meses, pero un sombrero verdaderamente fino lleva ocho meses.

Locutor ¿Ocho meses? Pero, **¡qué barbaridad!**

Sra. Gómez Sí, pues el trabajo hay que hacerlo con muchísimo cuidado y sólo quedan muy pocas personas que saben hacer buenos sombreros y todas son muy mayores. Debe haber... más o menos unas veinte personas. Así que dentro de muy pocos años, cuando estas personas ya no estén, no sé quién va a hacer los sombreros.

Locutor Entonces, probablemente este arte tan maravilloso desaparezca, ¿no?

Sra. Gómez Así es. Había una artesana que... que quería que su hija y su nieta aprendieran y pues... pues trató de enseñarles una vez, pero mmm... a ellas no les interesó y a ella **se le fueron las ganas de** enseñarles. Ud. ya sabe cómo son los jóvenes.

Locutor Sí, entiendo. Y... dígame una cosa, ¿cuánto cuesta un sombrero panamá?

Sra. Gómez Pues, depende. Yo sé que los distribuyen en algunas tiendas de Nueva York y Hawai y allí un sombrero bueno cuesta entre $350 y $750 dólares.

Locutor ¡Dios mío! No son baratos, ¿eh? ¿Y los mejores cuánto cuestan?

Sra. Gómez Los mejores se venden en unos diez mil dólares.

Locutor ¡Diez mil dólares! Pero, ¡qué **dineral**!

Sra. Gómez Sí, pero hay gente que aprecia la calidad del sombrero... que tiene el dinero y que paga... que paga ese precio. Por supuesto que los artesanos no ganan ni la mitad de eso. Pues Ud. sabe, hay muchos intermediarios; eh... el sombrero pasa por muchas manos hasta que llega al cliente y... y todos quieren sacar provecho del negocio.

Locutor Pero, de todas maneras, ¡es increíble!

Sra. Gómez Así es. ¡Es increíble!

Locutor Bueno, Sra. Gómez, se nos acabó el tiempo. Muchas gracias por venir a nuestro programa y compartir con nosotros esta información tan interesante.

Sra. Gómez De nada.*

Capítulo 10: ¡Que vivan los novios!

Locutora Queridos radioescuchas. Uds. han sintonizado KPGK, Radio Los Ángeles. Aquí les habla Dolores Alonso y bienvenidos a mi programa *Charlando con Dolores*. ¿Cómo están hoy? Quería comentarles que... que la semana pasada no estuve con Uds. porque fui a la boda de unos amigos. Y mientras estaba en la ceremonia, comencé a pensar en... en lo diferentes que son las bodas y las fiestas en otros países. ¿No creen? Pues... ése será el tema de hoy y... quisiera pedirles que nos llamen para contarnos cuáles son las tradiciones típicas de una boda en su país, señor, en su país, señora. ¿Qué les parece? Entonces, estamos a la espera de su llamada. Llámenos al 443-33-32. Sí, al 443-33-32. Aquí vamos con la primera llamada. Adelante por favor, díganos su nombre.

Susana Sí, me llamo Susana y soy de Argentina. Voy a casarme dentro de seis meses.

Locutora Felicitaciones, Susana.

Susana Gracias, y en mi boda habrá un pastel, por supuesto, y este pastel tendrá muchas cintas.

Locutora ¿Cintas en el pastel?

Susana Sí, tendrá como... como veinte cintas, más o menos. Las cintas tienen un dije cada una, o sea un adorno eh... una figurita de plástico que puede ser un elefante... una casa... una moneda.

Locutora ¿Es decir que el dije está dentro del pastel y sólo se ve la cinta?

Susana Así es. Entonces, todas las mujeres solteras... sólo las solteras, tomarán una cinta y estarán todas alrededor del pastel y cuando, y cuando yo diga ¡Ya! todas tirarán de la cinta y una de las cintas tendrá un anillo de boda... falso, de juguete, por supuesto. Y la que se saque el anillo es la que se casará el año que viene.

Locutora O sea, la persona que tiene la cinta con el anillo es la que se va a casar el año próximo.

Susana Sí.

Locutora Curioso. Es como coger el ramo de flores en este país. Pero, ¡qué bonita tradición! **¿No les parece?** ¿Y te vas a casar en los Estados Unidos?

Susana No, no, me voy a Argentina. Y primero está el casamiento por lo civil y dos días más tarde la... la ceremonia en la iglesia. Allá la ceremonia religiosa empieza a eso de las ocho, nueve, nueve y media de la noche. Y luego a la fiesta. ¡Es tan divertida! Comemos, bailamos hasta las seis de la mañana y generalmente después se les... se les sirve el desayuno a los invitados.

Locutora ¡El desayuno!

Susana Sí, café con medialunas o algo por el estilo.

Locutora ¡Desayuno después de la boda! ¡Qué increíble! Bueno... bien, Susana. Mucha suerte en tu boda. Y ahora, a otra llamada. Adelante, por favor.

Agustín Sí, me llamo Agustín y soy de México. Quería decirle que... que soy de un pueblo muy pequeño donde... donde hay gente que no tiene mucho dinero para gastar en una boda como la gente que vive en las ciudades que... que tiene dinero para todo. Las bodas son acontecimientos, son acontecimientos... ¿cómo le podría decir?... Son... son muy importantes en mi pueblo y para nosotros **mientras más vengan** a la boda, **mejor.** Invitamos a mucha, mucha gente, no sólo a nuestros **amigos íntimos,** ¿ve? Invitamos a amigos... primos... vecinos... Y algunas... algunas personas llevan la comida, otros llevan la bebida, otros llevan las mesas, otros las sillas...

Locutora Es decir que para muchos ese día es muy especial.

Agustín Sí, sí, muchos colaboran y hay mucha abundancia de comida y de bebida. Ayudándonos unos a otros no nos falta nada en absoluto.

*Some data taken from Harry Rosenholtz, "On Top," *Cigar Aficionado,* vol. 1, no. 4 (New York: M. Shanken Communication, 1993).

Locutora Este espíritu de comunidad es admirable. Gracias por su llamada. Y ahora, estimados radioescuchas, nos vamos a una pausa. Regresamos enseguida.

Capítulo 11: ¿Coca o cocaína?

Entrevistador Como boliviano, ¿nos podría explicar la diferencia entre la coca y la cocaína?

Boliviano Bueno la coca es una... es una hierba, una planta, como es una planta el café, como es una planta el té. La cocaína es la droga que a través de un proceso, a través de un proceso químico se extrae, se saca de la coca. La cocaína es como la cafeína es al café o cualquier droga que se saca de un elemento natural, de una cosa natural. Ehhhh... La diferencia es grande, es decir, la coca es una hoja verde que la mastican muchos habitantes de los países andinos, es decir Perú, Ecuador, Bolivia... mastican la coca como ehhh... en Estados Unidos hay gente que mastica tabaco, y es como tomar un café fuerte. Más o menos. Por otro lado, está la cocaína, que es un derivado químico de la coca. Que... bueno... Ésta es la parte ilegal. Es decir, por un lado hay que distinguir el uso tradicional, legal y correcto de la coca y por el otro el uso ilegal de la cocaína, que es un derivado de la coca. Eh... la coca como, como hierba, como planta o como el café o el té, como cualquier otro tipo de planta parecida, es consumida en los países andinos sin ningún tipo de restricción legal. Uno puede ir a un mercado y comprarse medio kilo de coca, por ejemplo, y consumirla. El consumo, en general está concentrado en las clases trabajadoras, que necesitan ese tipo de acompañante para aguantar jornadas de trabajo muy largas, jornadas continuas de trabajo sin dormir, etc. También es usada la coca, digo, entre, por ejemplo, estudiantes de la clase media... yo incluso como estudiante cuando tenía que escribir un trabajo muy largo, y tenía que trasnochar... quedarme despierto hasta muy tarde..., masticaba coca en vez de tomar tres cafés fuertes... masticaba coca o tomaba tres cafés fuertes... es una elección como cualquier otra hierba.

Entrevistador También es común que los turistas tomen coca, ¿verdad?

Boliviano Algunas ciudades andinas eh... al sur del Perú, pero sobre todo la capital de Bolivia, este... son muy altas. Es decir, La Paz queda a 3.800 metros sobre el nivel del mar y el aeropuerto de La Paz, una ciudad tan alta, queda más alto inclusive, 4.100 metros del nivel del mar. Entonces cualquier turista o persona que no está acostumbrada a esa altura cuando llega sufre una especie de mal que se llama soroche, que quiere decir, literalmente... es una palabra que quiere decir mal de la altura. Que es una especie de indisposición con dolor de cabeza, etcétera; depende eh... para... y esto dura... algunas personas no lo sufren, pero las personas que sí lo sufren cuando llegan a La Paz, eh... eso les dura como dos o tres días. Pero una de las formas de... de aliviar rápidamente este soroche, o mal de la altura, es tomar mate de coca y todo el mundo lo hace... es decir, todo el mundo lo recomienda. Es un mate, como puede ser un té, que consiste en agua hirviendo con unas hojas de coca. Uno toma eso y eso ayuda un poco para que se pase el mal de la altura.

Entrevistador Claro, y la gente que no entiende muy bien el tema se confunde entre la coca y la cocaína.

Boliviano Sí. El gobierno ha hecho campañas muy grandes para erradicar las plantaciones ilegales de coca, las plantaciones que se utilizan para la elaboración de la cocaína. Pero recuerde, la coca no es cocaína. Una vez, cuando la reina Sofía de España estuvo de visita por La Paz, como cualquier otro turista extranjero, tomó mate de coca. Y lo hizo **a propósito** diciendo que sabemos que esto no es una droga tal como se **pretende** convencer a la gente y entonces tomó un mate de coca porque estaba sufriendo soroche, mal de la altura, como todo extranjero que llega. Creo que **para dentro de diez años** el mundo ya habrá entendido la diferencia entre uno y otro.

Capítulo 12: Un poema

Locutora Buenas tardes, estimados radioescuchas. Estamos aquí hoy con otra edición del programa "Quiénes somos y hacia dónde vamos". Y para empezar el programa de hoy, quiero leerles un poema, un poema muy interesante que me mandó el hijo de una poeta. La autora es Raquel Valle Sentíes y el poema se llama "Soy Como Soy Y Qué". Comienzo.

(See Chapter 12, page 297, for poem.)

Y, ¿amigos? ¿les gustó? Llamen al programa para dar su opinión. Quiero que me digan lo que piensan. El teléfono es 888-956-1221.

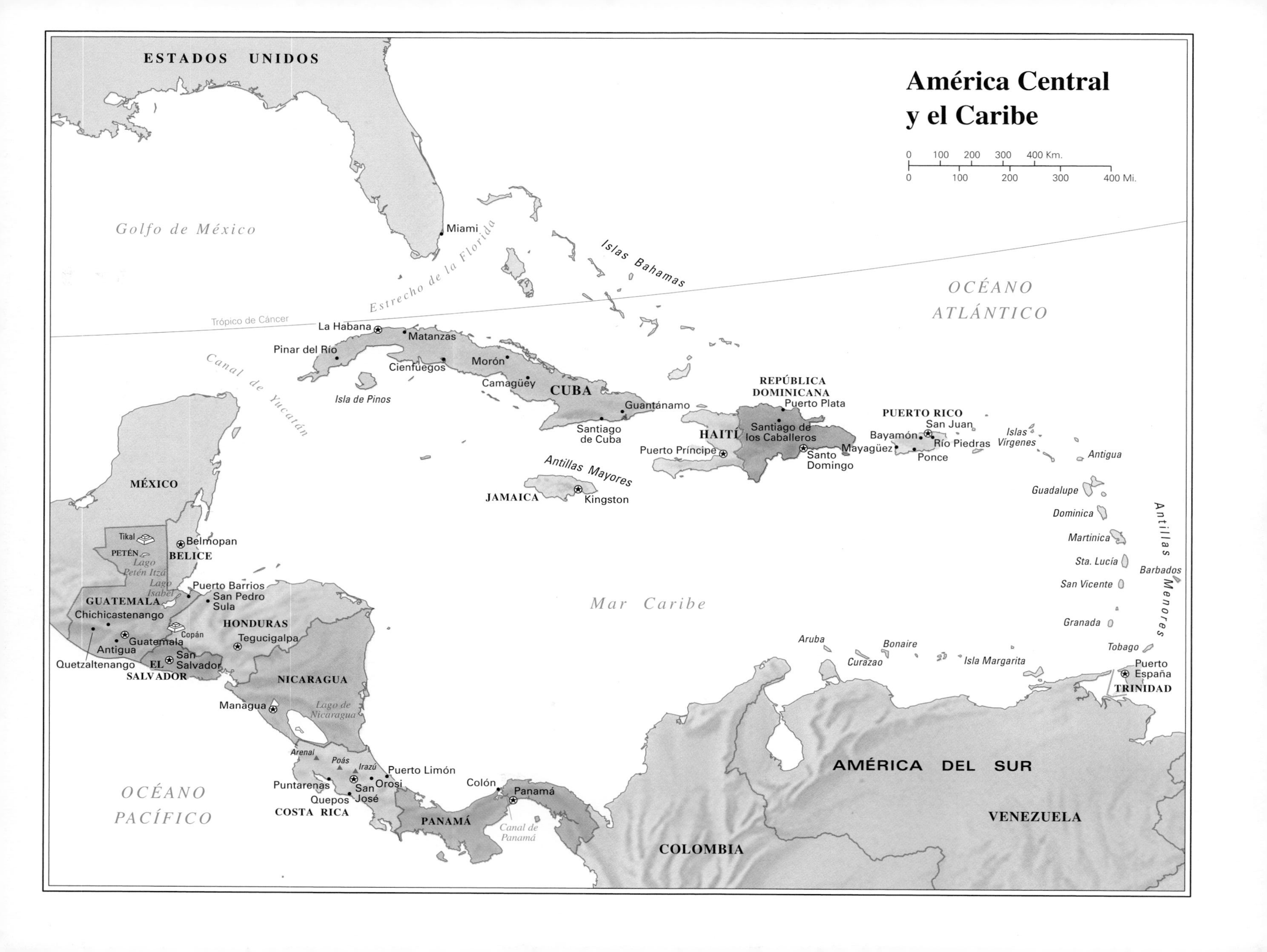

América Central
y el Caribe
0 100 200 300 400 Km.
0 100 200 300 400 Mi.
ESTADOS UNIDOS
Golfo de México
Miami
Estrecho de la Florida
Islas Bahamas
Trópico de Cáncer
OCÉANO
ATLÁNTICO
La Habana
Matanzas
Pinar del Río
Cienfuegos
Morón
Camagüey
CUBA
Isla de Pinos
Canal de Yucatán
Guantánamo
Santiago
de Cuba
REPÚBLICA
DOMINICANA
Puerto Plata
Santiago de
los Caballeros
HAITÍ
Puerto Príncipe
Santo
Domingo
PUERTO RICO
San Juan
Bayamón
Río Piedras
Mayagüez
Ponce
Islas
Vírgenes
Antigua
Antillas Mayores
JAMAICA
Kingston
MÉXICO
Tikal
PETÉN
Lago
Petén Itzá
Belmopan
BELICE
Lago
Isabel
Puerto Barrios
San Pedro
Sula
GUATEMALA
Chichicastenango
HONDURAS
Copán
Tegucigalpa
Guatemala
Antigua
San
Salvador
Quetzaltenango
EL
SALVADOR
NICARAGUA
Managua
Lago de
Nicaragua
Mar Caribe
Guadalupe
Dominica
Martinica
Sta. Lucía
Barbados
San Vicente
Granada
Antillas Menores
Tobago
Aruba
Bonaire
Curazao
Isla Margarita
Puerto
España
TRINIDAD
Arenal
Poás
Irazú
Puerto Limón
Puntarenas
Orosi
San
José
Quepos
COSTA RICA
Colón
Panamá
PANAMÁ
Canal de
Panamá
OCÉANO
PACÍFICO
AMÉRICA DEL SUR
VENEZUELA
COLOMBIA

FUENTES

Conversación y gramática

Third Edition

FUENTES

Conversación y gramática

Debbie Rusch
Boston College

Marcela Domínguez
Pepperdine University

Lucía Caycedo Garner
University of Wisconsin—Madison, Emerita

with the collaboration of

Donald N. Tuten Emory University
Carmelo Esterrich Columbia College Chicago

Houghton Mifflin Company Boston New York

Publisher: Rolando Hernández
Sponsoring Editor: Van Strength
Senior Development Editor: Sandra Guadano
Senior Project Editor: Rosemary R. Jaffe
Editorial Assistant: Rachel Zanders
Art and Design Manager: Gary Crespo
Senior Composition Buyer: Sarah Ambrose
Senior Photo Editor: Jennifer Meyer Dare
Manufacturing Manager: Karen Banks
Associate Marketing Manager: Claudia Martínez

Cover photography: Harold Burch Design, NYC.

Credits for texts, photographs, illustrations, and realia are found following the index at the back of the book.

Printed in the U.S.A.

Student Text ISBN: 0-618-46523-5

Instructor's Annotated Edition ISBN: 0-618-46524-3

Library of Congress Control Number: 2003116167

1 2 3 4 5 6 7 8 9-DOW-08 07 06 05 04

Preface Contents

To the Student

Fuentes: Conversación y gramática and *Fuentes: Lectura y redacción,* Third Edition, present an integrated skills approach to intermediate Spanish that develops both your receptive (listening and reading) and productive (speaking and writing) skills simultaneously, and also combines the skills in many of the activities you are asked to carry out. For instance, you may be asked to read a list of actions and mark those that you have done, then talk to a classmate to find out which he/she has done, and finally report orally or in writing on the experiences you have in common. In this way, you use multiple skills at once, as in real life, to develop your communicative skills in Spanish.

Learning Spanish also means developing an appreciation of the cultures that comprise the Hispanic world. In *Fuentes: Conversación y gramática* conversations, interviews, and other listening passages, as well as short readings expose you to information about diverse topics and Hispanic countries. You will also hear directly from Spanish speakers from numerous countries about their opinions, experiences, and individual perspectives in the **Fuente hispana** quotes that appear throughout the chapters. *Fuentes: Lectura y redacción*, the companion volume to *Fuentes: Conversación y gramática*, contains additional readings, as well as writing practice, coordinated with the topics and grammar of each chapter. The magazine and literary selections, as well as informational readings in *Fuentes: Lectura y redacción* are designed to further enrich your understanding of Hispanic cultures.

As you work with the *Fuentes* program, remember that learning a language is a process. This process can be accelerated and concepts studied can be learned more effectively if you study on a day-by-day basis. What is learned quickly is forgotten just as quickly, and what is learned over time is better remembered and internalized.

More important, envision yourself as a person who comprehends and speaks Spanish. Don't be afraid to take risks and make errors; it is part of the learning process. Finally, enjoy your study of the Spanish language and cultures as you progress through the course.

Study Tips for *Fuentes: Conversación y gramática*

The following study suggestions are designed to help you get the most out of your study of Spanish.

Tips for listening:

- Visualize the speakers in the listening passage.
- Listen for a global understanding the first time you hear the passage and listen for more specific information the second time, as indicated in the activities.
- Remember that you do not need to understand every word of each listening passage.

Tips for grammar study and activities:

- Prepare well before each class, studying a little every day rather than cramming the day before the exam.
- Focus on what you can do with the language or on what each concept allows you to express.
- Work cooperatively in paired and small-group activities.
- Do corresponding activities in the Workbook, on the CD-ROM, or on the Web when assigned or as additional practice.

Tips for vocabulary study:

- Pronounce words aloud.
- Study new words over a period of days.
- Try to use the new words in sentences that are meaningful to you.
- Do corresponding activities in the Workbook, on the CD-ROM, or on the Web when assigned or as additional practice.

An Overview of Your Textbook's Main Features

Fuentes: Conversación y gramática contains a preliminary chapter followed by 12 chapters.

The Chapter Opener identifies the thematic and functional goals of the chapter.

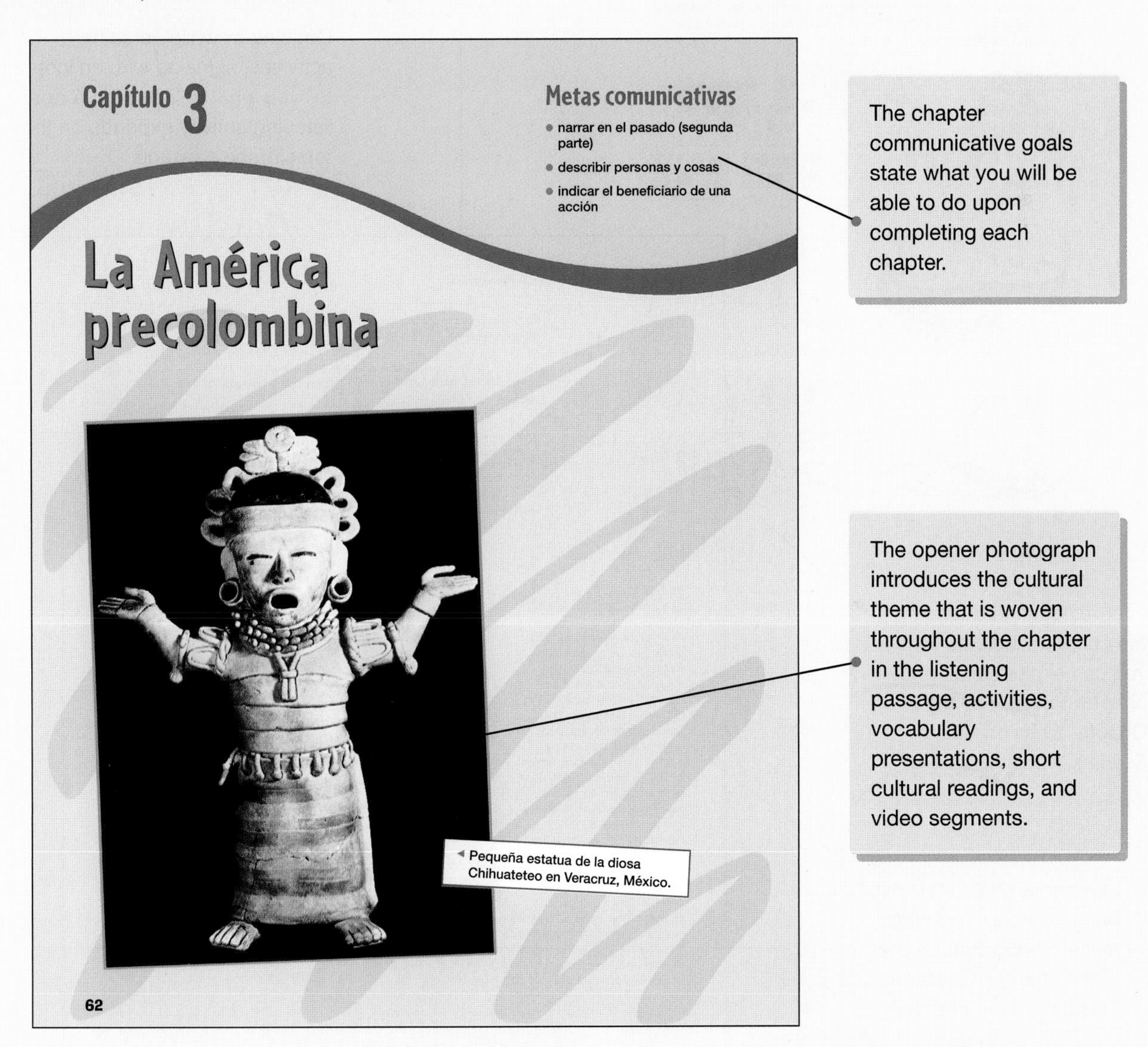

Integrated listening practice develops listening comprehension skills.

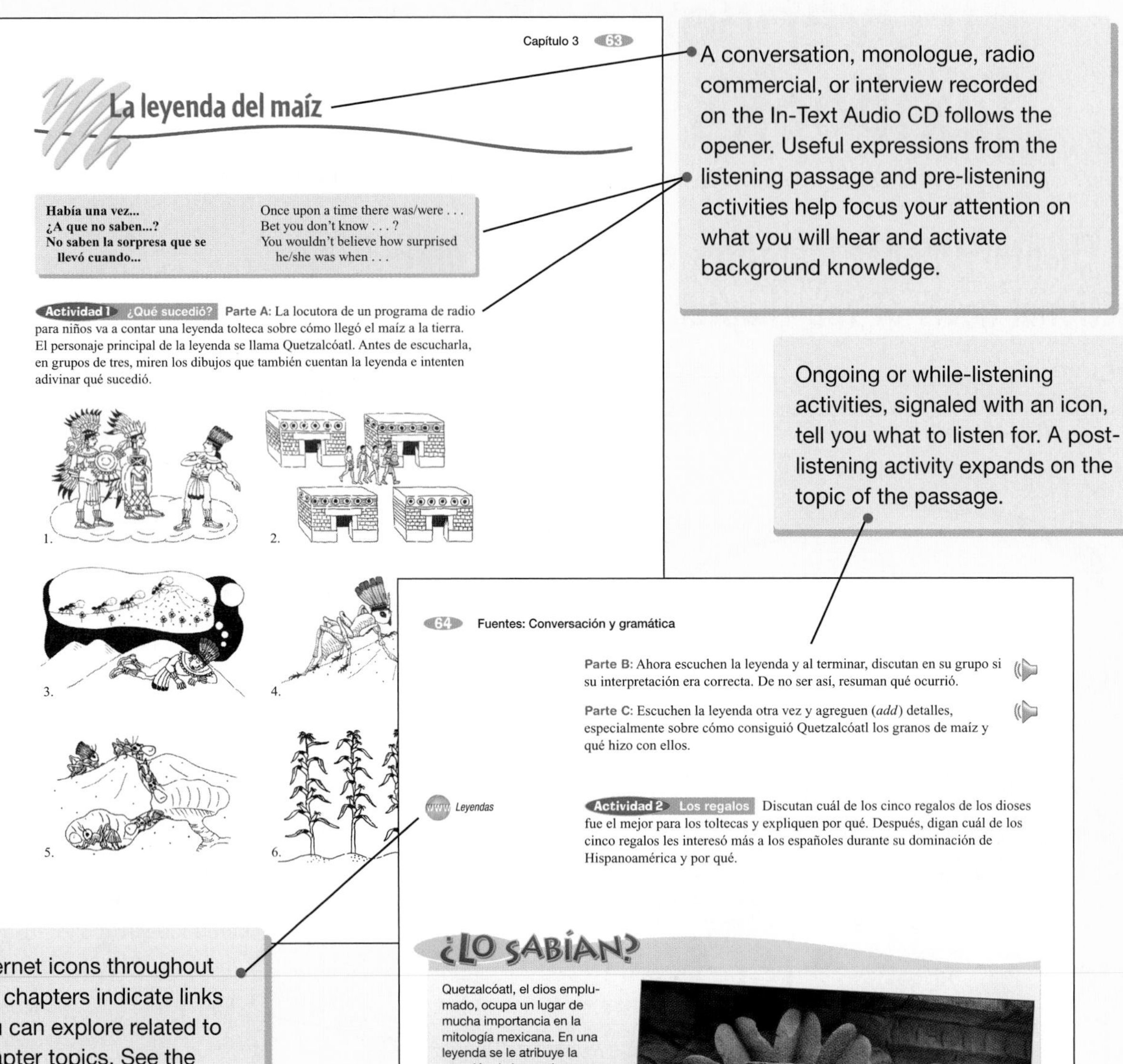

Capítulo 3 63

La leyenda del maíz

Había una vez...	Once upon a time there was/were . . .
¿A que no saben...?	Bet you don't know . . . ?
No saben la sorpresa que se llevó cuando...	You wouldn't believe how surprised he/she was when . . .

Actividad 1 ¿Qué sucedió? **Parte A:** La locutora de un programa de radio para niños va a contar una leyenda tolteca sobre cómo llegó el maíz a la tierra. El personaje principal de la leyenda se llama Quetzalcóatl. Antes de escucharla, en grupos de tres, miren los dibujos que también cuentan la leyenda e intenten adivinar qué sucedió.

1. 2. 3. 4. 5. 6.

64 Fuentes: Conversación y gramática

Parte B: Ahora escuchen la leyenda y al terminar, discutan en su grupo si su interpretación era correcta. De no ser así, resuman qué ocurrió.

Parte C: Escuchen la leyenda otra vez y agreguen (*add*) detalles, especialmente sobre cómo consiguió Quetzalcóatl los granos de maíz y qué hizo con ellos.

www Leyendas

Actividad 2 Los regalos Discutan cuál de los cinco regalos de los dioses fue el mejor para los toltecas y expliquen por qué. Después, digan cuál de los cinco regalos les interesó más a los españoles durante su dominación de Hispanoamérica y por qué.

¿LO SABÍAN?

Quetzalcóatl, el dios emplumado, ocupa un lugar de mucha importancia en la mitología mexicana. En una leyenda se le atribuye la creación de la raza humana. Se dice que descendió de la tierra de los muertos y encontró unos huesos, vertió (*shed*) su propia sangre sobre ellos y así creó a los seres humanos. También se dice que les enseñó a los habitantes de la tierra a tejer telas, a hacer mosaicos y a cortar y pulir el jade. Además inventó el calendario y les enseñó a los seres humanos la astronomía. Algunas leyendas cuentan que Quetzalcóatl era de color blanco y que tenía barba. Por eso, cuando Cortés llegó a México, Moctezuma, que era el líder azteca, creyó que había vuelto Quetzalcóatl y lo recibió amigablemente. Esto le facilitó a Cortés la conquista de México. Describe un personaje mitológico de gran importancia en el folclore de tu país.

▲ Cabeza de piedra del dios Quetzalcóatl en la antigua ciudad de Teotihuacán, que está en las afueras de la ciudad de México.

A conversation, monologue, radio commercial, or interview recorded on the In-Text Audio CD follows the opener. Useful expressions from the listening passage and pre-listening activities help focus your attention on what you will hear and activate background knowledge.

Ongoing or while-listening activities, signaled with an icon, tell you what to listen for. A post-listening activity expands on the topic of the passage.

Internet icons throughout the chapters indicate links you can explore related to chapter topics. See the Chapter Links on the *Fuentes* Website.

¿Lo sabían? readings expand on or provide information related to the cultural content of the chapter. Questions may ask you to compare your own culture with those you read about for a deeper understanding of cultural practices and perspectives.

Functional organization of grammar reflects the focus on communicative use of language in *Fuentes.*

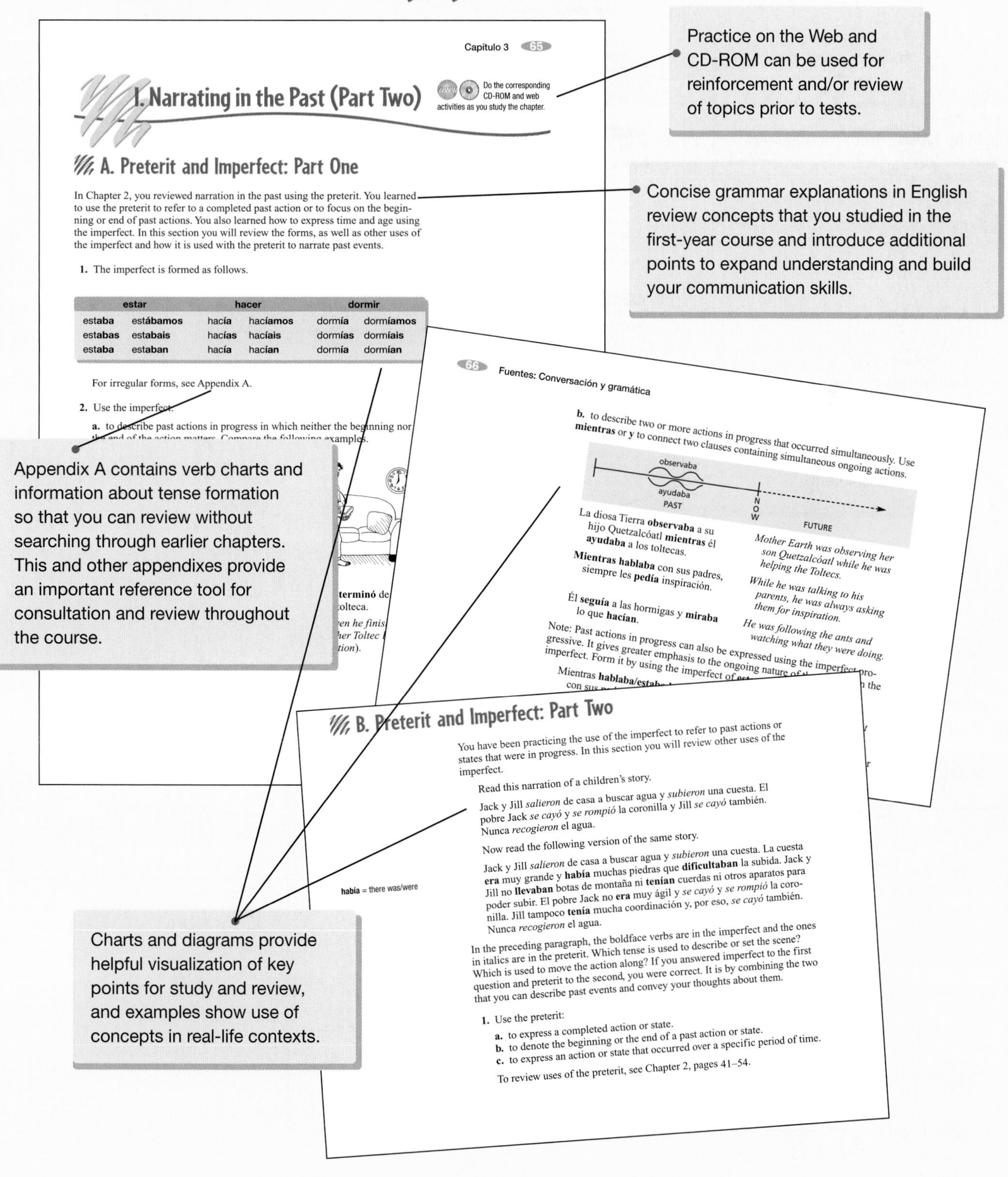

Capítulo 3 65

I. Narrating in the Past (Part Two)

Do the corresponding CD-ROM and web activities as you study the chapter.

A. Preterit and Imperfect: Part One

In Chapter 2, you reviewed narration in the past using the preterit. You learned to use the preterit to refer to a completed past action or to focus on the beginning or end of past actions. You also learned how to express time and age using the imperfect. In this section you will review the forms, as well as other uses of the imperfect and how it is used with the preterit to narrate past events.

1. The imperfect is formed as follows.

estar		hacer		dormir	
estaba	estábamos	hacía	hacíamos	dormía	dormíamos
estabas	estabais	hacías	hacíais	dormías	dormíais
estaba	estaban	hacía	hacían	dormía	dormían

For irregular forms, see Appendix A.

2. Use the imperfect:

a. to describe past actions in progress in which neither the beginning nor the end of the action matters. Compare the following examples.

66 Fuentes: Conversación y gramática

b. to describe two or more actions in progress that occurred simultaneously. Use **mientras** or **y** to connect two clauses containing simultaneous ongoing actions.

observaba
ayudaba
PAST
NOW
FUTURE

La diosa Tierra **observaba** a su hijo Quetzalcóatl **mientras** él **ayudaba** a los toltecas. — *Mother Earth was observing her son Quetzalcóatl while he was helping the Toltecs.*

Mientras hablaba con sus padres, siempre les **pedía** inspiración. — *While he was talking to his parents, he was always asking them for inspiration.*

Él **seguía** a las hormigas y **miraba** lo que **hacían**. — *He was following the ants and watching what they were doing.*

Note: Past actions in progress can also be expressed using the imperfect progressive. It gives greater emphasis to the ongoing nature of the ... imperfect. Form it by using the imperfect of esta...

Mientras **hablaba/estaba** ...

B. Preterit and Imperfect: Part Two

You have been practicing the use of the imperfect to refer to past actions or states that were in progress. In this section you will review other uses of the imperfect.

Read this narration of a children's story.

Jack y Jill *salieron* de casa a buscar agua y *subieron* una cuesta. El pobre Jack *se cayó* y *se rompió* la coronilla y Jill *se cayó* también. Nunca *recogieron* el agua.

Now read the following version of the same story.

Jack y Jill *salieron* de casa a buscar agua y *subieron* una cuesta. La cuesta **era** muy grande y **había** muchas piedras que **dificultaban** la subida. Jack y Jill no **llevaban** botas de montaña ni **tenían** cuerdas ni otros aparatos para poder subir. El pobre Jack no **era** muy ágil y *se cayó* y *se rompió* la coronilla. Jill tampoco **tenía** mucha coordinación y, por eso, *se cayó* también. Nunca *recogieron* el agua.

había = there was/were

In the preceding paragraph, the boldface verbs are in the imperfect and the ones in italics are in the preterit. Which tense is used to describe or set the scene? Which is used to move the action along? If you answered imperfect to the first question and preterit to the second, you were correct. It is by combining the two that you can describe past events and convey your thoughts about them.

1. Use the preterit:
   a. to express a completed action or state.
   b. to denote the beginning or the end of a past action or state.
   c. to express an action or state that occurred over a specific period of time.

To review uses of the preterit, see Chapter 2, pages 41–54.

Ample practice fosters communication skills.

A series of activities follows each topic so that you apply what you are learning, and a range of activity types—from more guided to more open—ensures numerous practice opportunities for mastery of concepts.

Frequent pair and group activities develop your oral communication skills with practice that encourages you to express your own ideas and opinions.

Open-ended activities that present and practice common phrases or rejoinders used in conversation also help improve your speaking ability and fluency.

Actividad 3 ¿Qué hacías? En parejas, túrnense para preguntarle a la otra persona sobre su pasado. Hagan preguntas como: **¿Qué hacías ayer a las 2:30 de la tarde? ¿Dónde estabas...?**

1. ayer a las 10:15 de la mañana
2. en esta época el año pasado
3. en junio hace dos años
4. a las 9:20 de la noche el sábado pasado
5. en noviembre del año pasado
6. en agosto del año pasado

Actividad 4 ... vecino en su apa...

► la señora ... Mientras ... jugaba/est...

1. el Sr. Pérez ...
2. el niño del 5...
3. la mujer del ...
4. la niña del 3...
5. la abuelita d...

Actividad 5 ... Esteban decidió ... casa inmediatam... adivina lo que ha...

► Enrique f... Enrique h...

1. Rosa fue co...
2. Carlos tenía ...
3. Antonio fue ...
4. Clara fue co...
5. Fernando y ...
6. Humberto fu...
7. Andrés lleva...
8. Laura e Isab... *brushes*).

¿LO SABÍAN?

Los primeros inmigrantes que llegaron a Hispanoamérica eran hombres que llegaban sin familia. Una vez allí, muchos tuvieron hijos con mujeres indígenas. El fruto de esas uniones tan tempranas en la historia poscolombina es el mestizo, que hoy en día forma una comunidad étnica predominante en muchos países hispanoamericanos, tales como Honduras (90%), El Salvador (90%), México (60%) y Colombia (58%). Di por qué en este país no hay tantos mestizos. Averigua cuántas personas hay en tu clase con antepasados indígenas de este país.

Actividad 8 Los mayas y los incas **Parte A:** En parejas, una persona es un/a arqueólogo/a que estudia a los mayas y la otra persona es un/a arqueólogo/a que se especializa en los incas. Lea cada uno solamente su información y úsenla para hablarle a su compañero/a.

Historia de los incas, mayas y aztecas

Los mayas
- habitar la península de Yucatán en el sur de México y en Centroamérica
- comer maíz, tamales, frijoles e insectos
- tener calendario, poder predecir los eclipses del sol y de la luna
- emplear una escritura jeroglífica con más de 700 signos

Los incas
- vivir en el sur de Colombia, Perú, Bolivia, Ecuador y el norte de Chile y Argentina
- tener una red de caminos excelente
- usar la piedra y el bronce
- hacer telas a mano, cerámica artística
- cultivar la papa y el maíz
- no tener escritura, todo transmitirse por tradición oral

Parte B: Ahora en grupos de cuatro, hablen de cómo vivían los indígenas de su país antes de que llegaran los europeos.

Actividad 9 La vida antes de la tecnología En grupos de tres, digan por lo menos una o dos cosas que hacía la gente cuando no existían los siguientes inventos. Luego, digan cuáles son las ventajas y desventajas de cada uno.

► Cuando no existía el disco compacto, la gente escuchaba música con grabadoras o estéreos. La calidad de la grabación no era...

1. el televisor
2. el avión
3. el plástico

Actividad 10 El barrio de tu infancia En parejas, describan cómo era su vida y el barrio donde vivían cuando eran niños, usando las siguientes ideas. Mientras escuchan sobre la vida de su compañero/a, reaccionen usando las siguientes expresiones y háganle preguntas para averiguar más información.

¡No me digas! /¿De veras?	El/La mío/mía también.
Yo también.	El/La mío/mía tampoco.
Yo tampoco.	¡Qué chévere! (Caribe)
	¡Qué lástima!

► Mi barrio era muy bonito porque tenía muchos árboles y era tranquilo.

barrio	rural, urbano, casas, edificios, tiendas, centros comerciales, parques
amigos	descripción física y personalidad, lugares favoritos para jugar, cosas que hacían juntos
vecinos	personas interesantes o raras
robos (*thefts*)	muchos, pocos
casa	moderna o vieja, color, número de habitaciones
habitación	número de camas, compartir con un/a hermano/a
pertenencias	cosas favoritas y por qué

Vocabulary practice builds a solid foundation for discussing chapter topics.

New vocabulary words and phrases are presented in thematic groups—such as adverbs of time, descriptive adjectives, food, the environment—to make learning easier. An illustration, **Fuente hispana** quote, or other material illustrates and/or shows selected words used in context.

II. Describing People and Things

A. Descripción física

el pómulo
los bigotes
la barbilla
el pelo lacio
la cara cuadrada
la mandíbula cuadrada

▸ Emiliano Zapata, mexicano (1879–1919)

Otras palabras

acogedor/a	welcoming, warm
atrevido/a	daring (*negative connotation*), nervy
caprichoso/a	capricious; fussy
cariñoso/a	loving, affectionate
celoso/a	jealous
espontáneo/a	spontaneous
holgazán/holgazana / perezoso/a	lazy
juguetón/juguetona	playful
malhumorado/a	moody, ill-humored
orgulloso/a	proud (*negative connotation*)
osado	daring (*positive connotation*)
tacaño/a	stingy, cheap
travieso/a	mischievous, naughty

tacaño/a = cheap (unwilling to spend money; describes people)

barato/a = cheap (inexpensive; describes goods and services)

To review other adjectives for describing people, see pp. 7, 8, and 12.

Annotations in the margin throughout the text provide study tips, helpful reminders, and additional cultural information.

¿LO SABÍAN?

En muchos países hispanos, con frecuencia la gente llama o se refiere a sus familiares, amigos o a su pareja usando palabras que en otras culturas pueden considerarse ofensivas. Por ejemplo, es común que los novios o una pareja casada se llamen **gordo** y **gorda** como términos de afecto, aunque las personas no pesen mucho. También es común que la gente les diga a sus amigos **flaco** o **flaca** como sobrenombre (*nickname*). Además en países como Colombia, Venezuela y Argentina se suele utilizar **negro** y **negra** como términos de afecto para una persona de tez morena. A menudo estas palabras se usan en diminutivo: **gordito, flaquito, negrita** y no son consideradas como insultos. Di si puedes usar estas palabras en inglés al hablarles a tus amigos o a tu novio/a.

Actividad 16 ¿Quién tiene esto? Parte A: Mira a tus compañeros y escribe el nombre de personas que tienen las siguientes características.

pelo lacio y largo	un tatuaje
un lunar en la cara	ojos color café
cara ovalada	pecas
una cicatriz	barba o bigotes
pelo rizado	cola de caballo o trenza(s)

Parte B: En grupos de tres, comparen sus observaciones.

Actividad 17 Lo positivo y lo negativo En grupos de tres, escojan tres adjetivos de la lista de la personalidad y digan qué es lo positivo y lo negativo de poseer esas características.

▸ Si una persona es muy, muy prudente cuando maneja, siempre va a llegar tarde, pero sí llegará porque no va a tener accidentes.

Activities reinforce the vocabulary presented so that you can increase your vocabulary and use it in a variety of contexts.

Parte B: Es común usar el presente en un relato histórico. Este uso del presente se llama presente histórico. En parejas, lean la historia de la Malinche otra vez. Luego cierren el libro y entre las dos personas cuenten la historia usando el pretérito y el imperfecto.

La Malinche

Do the corresponding CD-ROM and web activities to review the chapter topics.

¿LO SABÍAN?

El nombre de doña Marina con el tiempo se degeneró en Malinche. Hoy en día muchos mexicanos creen que la actitud de esa mujer al ayudar a los españoles fue un acto de traición. El término **malinche** se usa en México para referirse a una persona que prefiere lo extranjero a lo nacional o para una persona a quien se considera traidora. Sin embargo, muchas feministas han combatido este significado de la figura de la Malinche y la han revalorizado como una mujer de gran talento e inteligencia que supo sobrevivir a pesar de las condiciones adversas de su vida.

Vocabulario activo

Adverbios de tiempo

a menudo/con frecuencia/frecuentemente	*frequently*
de repente	*suddenly*
durante mi niñez	*during my childhood*
generalmente	*generally*
mientras	*while*
normalmente	*normally*
siempre	*always*
todos los días/domingos/meses/veranos/años	*every day/Sunday/month/summer/year*
una vez/dos veces/muchas veces	*once/twice/many times*

Descripción física

Forma de la cara	*Shape of the face*
cuadrada	*square*
ovalada	*oval*
redonda	*round*
triangular	*triangular*
la barbilla	*chin*
la mandíbula	*jaw*
el pómulo	*cheekbone*

Color de ojos	*Eye color*
azules	*blue*
claros	*light colored*
color café	*brown*
color miel	*light brown*
negros	*black*
pardos	*hazel*
verdes	*green*

Color y tipo de pelo/cabello	*Color and type of hair*
ser calvo/a	*to be bald*
ser pelirrojo/a o rubio/a	*to be a redhead or a blond/e*
tener cola de caballo/flequillo/trenza(s)	*to have a ponytail/bangs/braid(s)*
tener pelo castaño/canoso/negro	*to have brown/gray/black hair*
tener pelo lacio (liso)/ondulado/rizado	*to have straight/wavy/curly hair*
tener permanente	*to have a permanent*

At the end of each chapter, a **Vocabulario activo** list provides a wrap-up of vocabulary with translations to help you study more productively.

An emphasis on culture gives you insights into other ways of thinking and living, and...

Actividad 14 Una leyenda Al principio de este capítulo escuchaste una leyenda tolteca sobre el maíz. En grupos de tres, usen la imaginación para crear una leyenda sobre cómo apareció el búfalo en Norteamérica. Utilicen las siguientes ideas como guía.

- quién era el personaje principal de la leyenda
- qué hacía en su vida diaria
- qué quería para su gente
- qué ocurrió un día
- después de crear al búfalo, cómo lo empezaron a utilizar los seres humanos para mejorar su vida

Actividad 15 El encuentro **Parte A:** Lee lo que dijeron un colombiano y una venezolana sobre los aspectos positivos y negativos del encuentro entre los españoles y las culturas indígenas. Después contesta las preguntas de tu profesor/a.

Fuentes hispanas

"El principal aspecto positivo es que los europeos entendieron que el mundo era más grande, rico y diverso de lo que pensaban hasta ese momento; que había personas con una experiencia cultural totalmente diferente de la tradicional europea y se plantearon otra vez las características que formaban no sólo la cultura sino la humanidad en general.

El principal aspecto negativo es que la comprensión del mundo como más rico y diverso se hizo totalmente desde la perspectiva española y europea, sin darle oportunidad a la cultura indígena para manifestarse por sus propios medios; por eso, aunque se conoció la existencia de un "nuevo mundo", esta experiencia sirvió para que la cultura europea se entendiera a sí misma, pero no para entender a las culturas indígenas."

colombiano

"La conquista española trajo como consecuencia que diversas civilizaciones fueran exterminadas, los indígenas tuvieron que someterse al rey español, aprender un nuevo idioma y nuevas costumbres. Pero no todo fue malo pues de ese encuentro resultó el mestizaje étnico y cultural que existe en Latinoamérica. El ser mestizo forma parte de nuestra manera de ser y sentir. No somos blancos, ni negros, ni indios:

The **Fuente hispana** quotes, signaled by a tab on the edge of the page, provide a personalized view into Hispanic cultures and an opportunity to compare your experiences and ideas with those of Spanish speakers. About thirty speakers from nearly a dozen countries express their opinions and relate events and experiences on many of the text topics. The quotes may form part of an activity, introduce vocabulary, or appear in a **¿Lo sabían?** reading.

Capítulo 3 Los mayas

Antes de ver

Actividad 1 Indígenas de América Latina Antes de mirar un video sobre un grupo indígena de América Latina, habla sobre la siguiente información.

- grupos indígenas que habitan América Latina
- la zona con que los asocias
- algo sobre sus tradiciones o conocimientos

Mientras ves

Actividad 2 La cultura maya **Parte A:** Mira la primera parte del video sobre la cultura maya, hasta donde empieza a hablar el guía turístico, y busca información sobre los siguientes lugares.

- Mérida
- Tulum
- Chichén Itzá

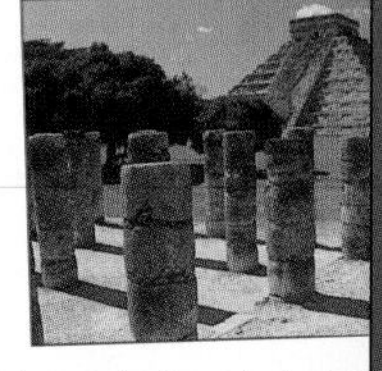

Parte B: Lee las siguientes preguntas y luego mira el resto del video para contestarlas.

1. ¿Quién era Kukulkán?
2. ¿Qué ocurre dos veces al año en su templo de Chichén Itzá?
3. Según el guía, ¿cómo desaparecieron los mayas?
4. ¿Cómo son físicamente los mayas?
5. ¿Por qué los jóvenes mayas se sienten avergonzados de ser mayas?

The **Videofuentes** video segments expand on the cultural theme of the chapter to give you added insights into Hispanic cultures. Filmed in Mexico, Spain, Argentina, and the United States, the varied segments include interviews, a short-subject film from Chile, and informative pieces related to music, historical events, agrotourism, and study abroad.

Pre-, ongoing, and post-viewing activities guide your viewing while reinforcing chapter vocabulary and functions as well as viewing and listening strategies.

Después de ver

Actividad 3 La revalorización En las últimas décadas se han empezado a apreciar más las culturas de los pueblos originales de América Latina. En grupos de tres, discutan las siguientes preguntas sobre las culturas indígenas de su país.

1. ¿Qué grupos indígenas existen hoy día en su país?
2. ¿Qué lugares indígenas se pueden visitar? ¿Han estado en alguno de ellos?
3. ¿Conocen a alguien de origen indígena? Si contestan que sí, ¿saben si habla o no el idioma de sus antepasados? Si eres de origen indígena, ¿hablas el idioma de tus antepasados?
4. ¿Qué grupos indígenas conservan su idioma?

Capítulo 4 La legendaria Celia Cruz

Antes de ver

► *La negra tiene tumbao* de Celia Cruz ganó en los Grammys Latinos de 2002.

La negra tiene tumbao = The black woman's got style

Los famosos Antes de ver un video sobre Celia Cruz, di cuántas personas de la primera lista conoces y si tienes CDs de algunas de ellas. Luego en grupos de tres, discutan la lista de ideas de la segunda columna.

Elvis Presley	• qué hicieron estas personas
Billie Holiday	• por qué fueron una leyenda en vida o después de su muerte
Jerry García	• qué talento tenían
Jim Morrison	• cómo se vestían para el escenario
Ella Fitzgerald	• cuáles eran sus innovaciones
Judy Garland	• edad de la gente que los escuchaba
Bill Haley	• qué aspectos tenían en común con otras personas famosas
Barry White	
Frank Sinatra	
John Lennon	

exposes you to the diversity of the Spanish-speaking world.

Student Components

Fuentes: Activities Manual

The Workbook portion of the Activities Manual allows you to practice the functional grammar and vocabulary presented in *Fuentes: Conversación y gramática* in order to reinforce what you learn in class as you progress through each text chapter. A Workbook Answer Key is also available at the request of your institution or instructor.

The Lab Manual section provides pronunciation and listening comprehension practice. The lab activities, coordinated with a set of recordings, can be done toward the end of each chapter and prior to any quizzes or exams.

Quia Online Activities Manual

The online version of the Activities Manual contains the same content as the print version in an interactive format that provides immediate feedback on many activities. The lab audio program is included in the online version.

In-Text Audio CD

Packaged with *Fuentes: Conversación y gramática,* the audio CD contains the listening selections at the beginning of the chapters so that you can listen to them outside of class.

Lab Audio CD Program

A set of recordings to accompany the Lab Manual portion of the Activities Manual contains pronunciation practice, listening comprehension activities based on structures and vocabulary presented in *Fuentes: Conversación y gramática,* and a final conversation dealing with the chapter theme. The CDs are available for purchase or can be used in your language lab. This audio program is the same as the recordings available in the online Activities Manual.

Fuentes Video

Videofuentes contains twelve video segments in a news-magazine format. Filmed in Mexico, Spain, Argentina, and the United States, the segments include interviews with the actor-comedian John Leguizamo and Elena Climent, a Mexican artist; a tribute to Celia Cruz; clips from a film by the Spanish director Pedro Almodóvar; a Chilean short-subject film; overviews of Mayan culture, the cultural heritage of Spain, nightlife in Madrid, agrotourism in northern Spain, and the "desaparecidos" and their children in Argentina.

The textbook, website, and CD-ROM provide a variety of related video-based activities for in-class and outside-class practice designed to promote cultural awareness and to help you reinforce your language skills.

Fuentes Multimedia CD-ROM 1.0

A series of exercises covering the structures and vocabulary presented in each chapter of *Fuentes: Conversación y gramática* is available to help you perfect language structures and verb forms while receiving immediate feedback. The exercises include listening, speaking, and writing practice, as well as activities based on clips from the *Fuentes* Video. The CD-ROM also includes a grammar reference, a Spanish-English glossary, and the complete video.

Fuentes: Website

The Website written to accompany the *Fuentes* program contains activities designed to give you further practice with structures and vocabulary as well as exercises about chapter topics that explore Spanish-language sites. Although the sites you will access are not written for students of Spanish, the tasks that you will be asked to do are. The site also includes activities based on feature films and a list of chapter-by-chapter links that can be used to explore additional cultural information on topics you have read about in *Fuentes: Conversación y gramática* and *Fuentes: Lectura y redacción.* You can access the site at http://college.hmco.com/languages/spanish/students.

Acknowledgments

The publisher and authors wish to thank the following reviewers for their feedback on the second edition of *Fuentes*. Many of their recommendations are reflected in the changes made in the new edition.

Sandra M. Anderson, College of DuPage
Jonathan F. Arries, College of William and Mary
Bárbara Ávila-Shah, University at Buffalo, State University of New York
Kimberly Boys, University of Michigan
Elizabeth Cure Calvera, Virginia Tech
Lola Chamorro, Brown University
Darrell J. Dernoshek, University of South Carolina-Columbia
Héctor Domínguez-Ruvalcaba, Denison University
Laura Fox, Grand Valley State University
Dennis C. Harrod, Syracuse University
Gillian Lord, University of Florida
Joanna (Joby) McClendon, St. Edward's University
Claudia Mejia, Tufts University
Deborah Mistron, Middle Tennessee State University
Mary E. O'Donnell, University of Iowa
Margaret M. Olsen, University of Missouri-Columbia
John T. Riley, Fordham University
Regina F. Roebuck, University of Louisville
Nohelia Rojas-Miesse, Miami University
Lilia D. Ruiz-Debbe, State University of New York at Stony Brook
Loreto Sánchez-Serrano, Johns Hopkins University
Carmen Schlig, Georgia State University
Jorge W. Suazo, Georgia Southern University
Dwight E. Raak TenHuisen, Calvin College
Mercedes Valle, Smith College
Maura Velázquez-Castillo, Colorado State University

A special word of appreciation is due Ramonita Marcano-Ogando, Mónica Velasco-González, and Joyce Martin of the University of Pennsylvania for their support of the program and their valuable input on the new edition.

We thank the following people for sharing their lives and thoughts by supplying us with information for the **Fuente hispana** feature. Through their words students will have the opportunity of seeing another very personal side of the Spanish-speaking world.

Helena Alonzo, Venezuela
Alexandre Arrechea, Cuba
Martín Bensabat, Argentina

Marcus Brown, Peru
Dolores Cambambia, Mexico
Fernando Cañete, Argentina
Bianca Dellepiane, Venezuela
Pedro Domínguez, Argentina
Viviana Domínguez, Argentina
Carmen Fernández Fernández, Spain
Fabián García, United States (Mexican-American)
Íñigo Gómez, Spain
María Jiménez Smith, Puerto Rico
Peter Neissa, Colombia
Bere Rivas de Rocha, Mexico
William Reyes-Cubides, Colombia
Ana Rodríguez Lucena, Spain
Mauricio Morales Hoyos, Colombia
Magalie Rowe, Peru
Lucrecia Sagastume, Guatemala
Víctor San Antonio, Spain
Mauricio Souza, Bolivia
Rosa Valdéz, United States (Mexican-American)
Alejandra Valdiviezo, Bolivia
Natalia Verjat, Spain
Alberto Villate, Colombia
María Elena Villegas, Mexico

Thank you to Raquel Valle Sentíes for the use of her poem, to Sarah Bartels for sharing her experience of walking the Inca Trail, to Jennifer Jacobsen and Jeff Stahley for their insight on teaching English abroad, to Catherine Wood Lange for information about her business Spanish course, to Hannah Nolan-Spohn for telling about her volunteer position while studying in Ecuador, and to Khandle Hedrick and Stephanie Valencia for supplying realia. A special thanks to Gene Kupferschmid for insightful comments and suggestions regarding different aspects of the program.

Thanks to Monie Scallon Mostaza, Miguel Jiménez, Carmen Fernández, Ann Merry, Olga Tedias-Montero, Liby Moreno Carrasquillo, Martha Miranda Gómez, Miguel Gómez, Rosa Maldonado Bronnsack, Alberto Dávila Suárez, Virginia Laignelet Rueda, Blanca Dávila Knoll, Jorge Caycedo Dávila, and André Garner Caycedo for their help in polling people for linguistic items of use today in the Spanish-speaking world.

We are extremely grateful to Nancy Levy-Konesky for her outstanding work writing and producing *Videofuentes* and to Frank Konesky and TVMAN/Riverview Productions, John Leguizamo, Elena Climent, Severino García, Nuria Miravalles, the Abuelas of Plaza de Mayo, Alberto Vasallo III, Tomás Moreno, Abel (Mayan guide), Patricia Sardo de Dianot, Ana María Pinto, Mercedes Meroño, Horacio Pietragalla Corti, and Buscarita Roa for participating in this project. We would also like to thank Telemundo for footage of their tribute to Celia Cruz, el deseo s.a. for allowing us to use clips from the Pedro Almodóvar film *Hable con ella*, and Rodrigo Silva Rivas and Aldo Aste Salbuceti for permission to show the short film *En la esquina*. Special thanks to Andrés Coppo, Stephanie Valencia, Nicole Gunderson, Sarah Link, the children who received awards at Fenway Park, and to our announcer Frances Colón for their participation in the video.

A very special thanks to Sandra Guadano for her insightful comments, her ability to get us to do our best, her gentle nudges to get all done on time, and her encouragement during the development phase. Thanks also to our production editor Rosemary Jaffe, the lady with the eagle eye, for her detailed approach to production, her clarity in instructions, and her dedication to making *Fuentes* the best it can be. We also thank all of the other people at Houghton Mifflin, from technology to marketing to sales, who have helped us along the way. Finally, thank you to our students for giving us feedback and for motivating us to do our best work.

D. R.
M. D.
L. C. G.

Contents

FUENTES

Conversación y gramática

Capítulo preliminar

La vida universitaria

Metas comunicativas

- presentarse y presentar a otros
- obtener y dar información sobre el horario de clases
- hablar de gustos
- describir a personas y clases
- expresar acciones futuras

▲ Jóvenes universitarias estudian en la biblioteca de una universidad de Santiago de Chile.

I. Introducing Yourself and Others

This chapter provides a quick review of some basics to allow you to hear students express themselves in class and to evaluate their aural comprehension and writing ability. This will help you determine early in the semester if any students are misplaced. Depending on the level of your class, spend more or less time on this and Ch. 1. Pick and choose or skip areas and activities where students perform well.

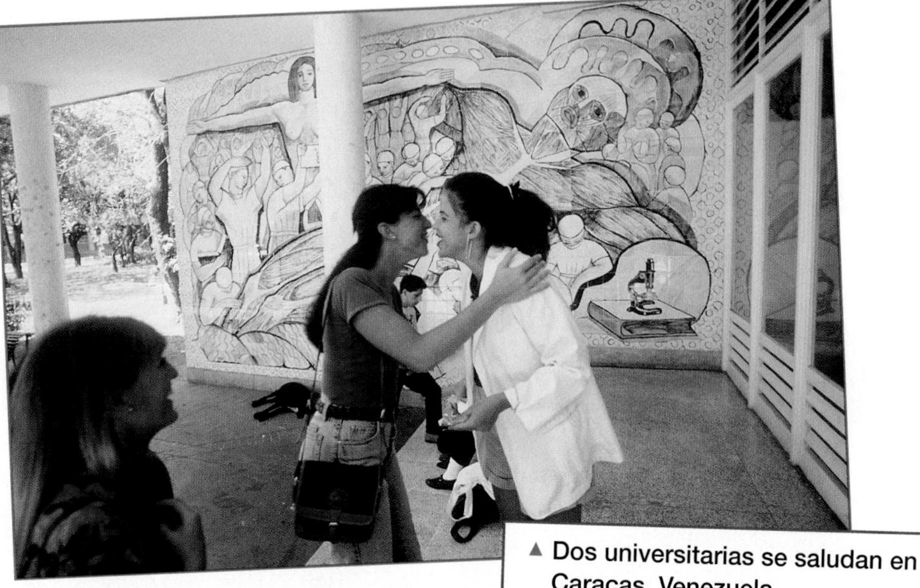

▲ Dos universitarias se saludan en Caracas, Venezuela.

Begin class by introducing yourself and asking individuals questions like those in Act. 1. Have individual students ask others some questions: **John, pregúntale a Carol de dónde es.**

Act. 1A: Have students fill in the question words and then check answers.

Primero and **tercero** drop the final **o** when they precede a masculine singular noun: **estoy en primer año.**

Actividad 1 ¡A conocerse! **Parte A:** Completa cada pregunta con la expresión interrogativa apropiada. Usa **cuál, cómo, de dónde, qué** o **cuántos.**

¿___Cómo___ te llamas?	Me llamo...
¿___Cuál___ es tu nombre?	Mi nombre es...
¿___Cuál___ es tu apellido?	(Korner.)
¿___Cómo___ se escribe (Korner)?	(Ka, o, ere, ene, e, ere.)
¿___Cuántos___ años tienes?	Tengo... años.
¿___De dónde___ eres?	Soy de (Chicago).
¿En ___qué___ año (de la universidad) estás?	En primero/segundo/ tercero/cuarto.
¿___Cuál___ es tu pasatiempo favorito?	Me gusta (jugar al tenis).

Act. 1B: Have students make six columns on a piece of paper, labeling them **(nombre, apellido, edad, origen, año, pasatiempo).** Next, have students mingle and interview at least three people.

Parte B: Ahora habla con un mínimo de tres personas para averiguar y escribir su información de la Parte A.

Parte C: Ahora, presenta a una de las personas de la Parte B.

▶ Les presento a Jessy Korner, es de Chicago y tiene 20 años. Está en su tercer año de la universidad. Le gusta jugar al tenis.

II. Obtaining and Giving Information About Class Schedules

Las materias académicas

Act. 2A: Practice words by working on pronunciation; stress pure vowel sounds. Set a time limit for students to mark their selections. This will encourage them to get on task quickly.

Actividad 2 Las materias de este semestre **Parte A:** Marca con una X las materias que tienes este semestre. Si tienes una materia que no aparece en la lista, pregúntale a tu profesor/a **¿Cómo se dice...?**

materias = **asignaturas**

Obvious cognates will be presented in thematic vocabulary lists throughout this text, and they will be translated only in the end-of-chapter vocabulary section.

_____ alemán
_____ álgebra
_____ antropología
_____ arqueología
_____ arte
_____ biología
_____ cálculo
_____ ciencias políticas
_____ computación
_____ comunicaciones
_____ contabilidad (*accounting*)
_____ ecología
_____ economía
_____ filosofía
_____ francés
_____ historia
_____ ingeniería
_____ lingüística
_____ literatura
_____ matemáticas
_____ mercadeo/marketing
_____ música
_____ negocios
_____ oratoria (*speech*)
_____ psicología
_____ química
_____ relaciones públicas
_____ religión
_____ sociología
_____ teatro
_____ trigonometría
_____ zoología

WWW *Universidades*

Internet references such as this indicate that you will find links to related sites on the *Fuentes* website.

computación = **informática** (en España)

Parte B: Ahora, en parejas, averigüen qué carrera (especialización) estudia la otra persona, qué materias tiene y alguna información sobre esas clases. Hagan las siguientes preguntas.

Act. 2B: Set up this portion by asking individuals **¿Tienes economía? ¿Tienes clase de cálculo?** (etc.) You may want to teach the verb **cursar** as in **¿Cursas matemáticas?** Form pairs, set a time limit, check by asking a few people what their partner studies.

¿Qué carrera estudias o no sabes todavía?
¿Tienes...?
¿Tienes clase de...?
¿Cuántos estudiantes hay en la clase de...?
¿Hay trabajos escritos (*papers*)?
¿Hay exámenes parciales?
¿Hay examen final?

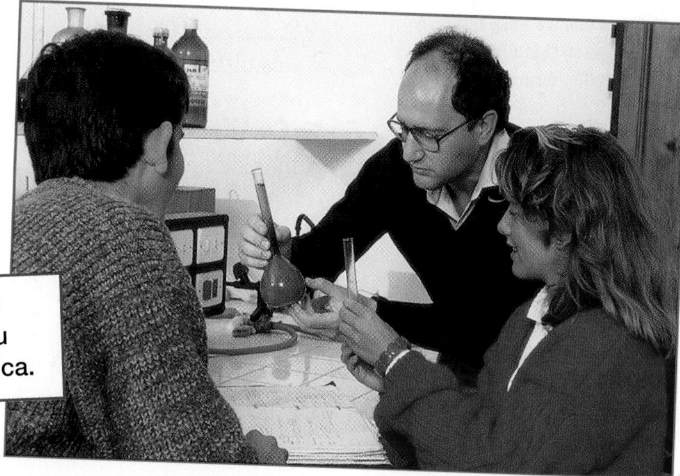

▶ Dos estudiantes españoles hacen experimentos con su profesor de química orgánica.

Most **¿Lo sabían?** sections are related to a topic raised or mentioned in the preceding activity or section. Upon reading the content, students learn more about the cultures of the Spanish-speaking world. Many of these sections end with a question to help students reflect on their own culture(s) to better make comparisons noting similarities as well as differences.

¿LO SABÍAN?

Al entrar en la escuela secundaria en algunos países, los estudiantes pueden elegir entre opciones diferentes: letras, ciencias, estudios técnicos, etc. Por ejemplo, si un estudiante quiere estudiar medicina, en la universidad, escoge la opción de ciencias. En la escuela secundaria, los estudiantes estudian muchas materias diferentes dentro de cada opción y luego, es común que entren directamente en una facultad como Derecho, Medicina, Geología o Filosofía y Letras. Por lo tanto, tienen que estar seguros de lo que quieren estudiar y, desde el comienzo, estudian materias relacionadas con su carrera. Para cambiar de carrera, muchas veces es necesario volver a empezar desde el principio. Generalmente se necesitan cinco años para completar la licenciatura. ¿Cuántos años necesitas para completar la licenciatura en tu país?

licenciatura = BA or BS degree

Actividad 3 Mi horario **Parte A:** Escribe rápidamente las materias que tienes, las horas de tus clases y el nombre del profesor / de la profesora de cada clase.

lunes, martes, miércoles, jueves, viernes. Abreviaturas = l/m/mier./j/v

materia				
día y hora				
profesor/a				

To tell time, use: **¿Qué hora es? Es la una. / Son las dos.**

To tell at what time something takes place: **¿A qué hora es? Es a la/s...**

Parte B: Completa cada pregunta con la palabra interrogativa necesaria.

¿___Qué___ materias tienes?
¿A ___qué___ hora es tu clase de...?
¿___Qué___ días tienes la clase de...?
¿___Cómo___ se llama el/la profesor/a? o, ¿___Quién___ es el/la profesor/a?

Act. 3A: If needed, practice telling time by asking questions: **¿A qué hora es la clase de español? ¿A qué hora es la primera clase de la universidad? ¿A qué hora es tu clase de... ? ¿A qué hora es el partido de fútbol americano contra... el sábado?** You may also want to ask about times for TV shows. Contrast with **¿Qué hora es?**

Explain the 24-hour clock.

Add the expressions **mediodía** and **medianoche** if you want.

Parte C: Ahora, con una pareja diferente a la de la actividad anterior, usen las preguntas de la Parte B para averiguar el horario de su compañero/a.

Act. 3B: Set up activity by asking individual students questions about their schedules. **¿A qué hora es tu clase de computación? ¿Qué días tienes la clase?** (etc.) Give students 30 seconds to fill in the question words and then check.

Act. 3C: Set up new pairs, set a time limit, begin the activity. When finished, have a few students report back to the class. Even though you may give students one minute to do a pair activity, they may take as many as three. Remember, the purpose of a time limit is to get them to get to work quickly.

III. Expressing Likes and Dislikes

Gustar and Other Verbs

1. To express likes and dislikes you can use the verb **gustar,** applying the following formula.

(A mí)	**me**	+	**gusta + el/la** + *singular noun*
(A ti)	**te**		**gusta** + *infinitive(s)*
(A Ud.)	**le**		**gustan + los/las** + *plural noun*
(A él)	**le**		
(A ella)	**le**		
(A nosotros)	**nos**		
(A vosotros)	**os**		
(A Uds.)	**les**		
(A ellos)	**les**		
(A ellas)	**les**		

The pronoun **mí** takes an accent, but the possessive adjective **mi** does not: **A mí me gusta esta clase. Mi hermano estudia aquí.**

Discuss your likes and dislikes about the university, your interests, and what bothers you. Do this in a conversational manner, interrupting occasionally to ask students if they have the same likes. **No me gusta comer en la cafetería..., pero me encanta comer en... ¿Dónde te gusta comer a ti?** Begin with **gustar,** but include other verbs while providing input.

Me **gusta** la clase de historia. — *I like history class.*

¿Te **gusta** hacer experimentos? — *Do you like to do experiments?*

(A ellos) Les **gusta** reunirse con amigos y trabajar juntos en proyectos.* — *They like to get together with friends and work on projects.*

Nos **gustan** las matemáticas. — *We like math.*

*Note: **Gusta,** the singular form of the verb, is used with one or more infinitives even if the infinitive is followed by a plural object.

2. An article is needed when **gustar** is followed by a noun. Notice in the following examples that you may use a possessive adjective **(mi, mis, tu, tus,** etc.) or a demonstrative adjective (**este, ese, aquel,** etc.) instead of an article before nouns.

Emphasize that **gustar** and verbs like it need an article or a possessive or demonstrative adjective when directly followed by a noun. **No me gusta la literatura.**

Me gusta **la** biología. — *I like biology.*

Me gustan **mis** clases este semestre, pero no me gusta estudiar mucho los fines de semana. — *I like my classes this semester, but I don't like to study much on weekends.*

A mis amigos y a mí nos gusta **esta** residencia estudiantil. — *My friends and I like this dorm.*

3. Other verbs used to express likes and dislikes that follow the same pattern as **gustar** are:

caer bien/mal	to like/dislike someone
importar	to matter
encantar	to really like
interesar	to interest
fascinar	to really like
molestar	to bother, to be bothered by

A los estudiantes no **les cae bien** la profesora de historia.*	*The students dislike the history professor. (The history professor is disliked by the students.)*
Me fascinan los libros que estudiamos en la clase de literatura comparada.	*I really like the books we study in my comparative literature class. (The books we study in my comparative literature class really fascinate me.)*
Nos importa sacar buenas notas.	*We care about getting good grades. (Getting good grades matters to us.)*
Al profesor Hinojosa **le molestan** los estudiantes que no vienen preparados a clase.*	*Professor Hinojosa is bothered by students who don't come to class prepared. (Students who don't come to class prepared bother Professor Hinojosa.)*

*Note:
1. **Me gusta la profesora de historia** might imply that you are attracted to the person. This is not the case with **Me cae bien la profesora de historia.**
2. Remember that **a** + **el** = **al: al profesor Hinojosa,** but **a la profesora Ramírez; al Sr. Vargas,** but **a los Sres. Vargas.**

Act. 4A: After students fill in the first column, check responses. Before doing Part B, go over the list in the third column and explain any new words.

Actividad 4 Práctica **Parte A:** Completa la primera columna con las palabras apropiadas.

A ____ nos		los colores de la universidad
A ____ me		trabajar los sábados
____ ____ Sra. Junco ____		las clases con muchos estudiantes
A ____ le		la mascota de la universidad
____ Uds. ____		las personas de la residencia
____ profesor ____	fascina/n	mi compañero/a de cuarto
____ mis amigos ____	cae/n bien	tomar un examen los viernes
____ ____ les	molesta/n	las personas falsas
____ Dr. Rodríguez ____		la gente que duerme en clase
____ Julia y ____ Pablo ____		oír música de los años 70
____ Laura y ____ ____ nos		la variedad de gente en esta universidad

Act. 4B: Call on individuals to create sentences. If errors occur, try to get the class to self correct.

Parte B: Ahora, forma oraciones usando un elemento de cada columna. Puedes añadir la palabra **no** si quieres. Luego comparte tus oraciones con la clase.

▶ A nosotros (no) nos molesta trabajar los sábados.

Actividad 5 Tus gustos **Parte A:** Lee las ideas incompletas que se dan a continuación y usa por lo menos cuatro de los siguientes verbos para indicar tus gustos: **fascinar, encantar, gustar, caer bien/mal, importar, interesar** y **molestar.**

Act. 5A: Assign as HW or allow 2 minutes to do it in class. Circulate and correct individual errors.

1. ______________ las clases fáciles.
2. ______________ mi profesor/a de...
3. ______________ mi horario de clases este semestre.
4. ______________ las clases con trabajos escritos y exámenes.
5. ______________ los exámenes finales para hacer en casa.
6. ______________ mis compañeros/as de cuarto o apartamento.
7. ______________ la gente que bebe mucho alcohol en las fiestas.
8. ______________ los profesores exigentes (*demanding*).
9. ______________ el costo de la matrícula (*tuition*).
10. ______________ participar en el gobierno estudiantil.
11. ______________ las fraternidades como ΩΣΔ.
12. ______________ (no) tener acceso al email de la universidad.

Although words such as **correo eléctronico** and **la red** exist, this text will use **email** and **Internet** since since these are the most commonly used terms by native speakers.

Parte B: Ahora, en parejas, háganse preguntas como las siguientes y den explicaciones para sus respuestas.

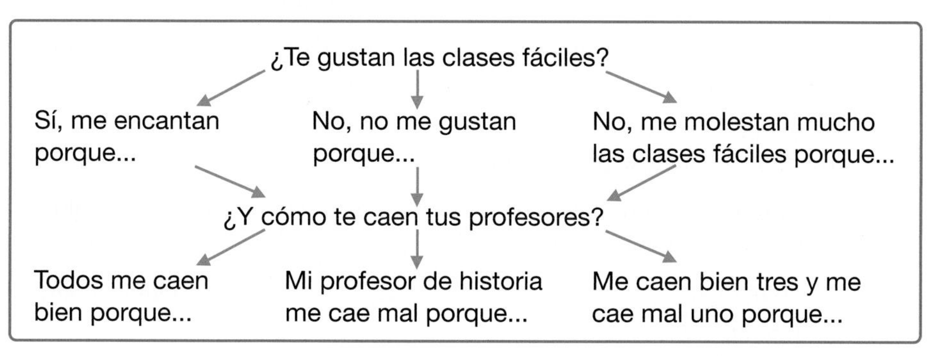

Act. 5B: Practice question formation and possible answers, set up pairs, set a time limit, and begin the activity. Check by asking some individuals about their partners' preferences. Ask questions like: **¿A Alan le fascinan los exámenes para hacer en casa? ¿Por qué? ¿A quién más le fascinan? Entonces, a Alan y a Jill...**

IV. Describing People, Places, and Things

Actividad 6 ¿Cómo es tu profe? **Parte A:** Piensa en un/a profesor/a que te cae bien este semestre y marca los adjetivos que describan mejor a esa persona.

To review adjective agreement, see Appendix C.

Act. 6A: Allow a moment for students to think of their professor. Set a time limit of one minute. If students have just started classes, you may want to suggest they think of a professor they've had before.

_____ admirable
_____ astuto/a
_____ atento/a (*polite, courteous*)
_____ brillante
_____ capaz (*capable*)
_____ cómico/a
_____ creativo/a
_____ divertido/a (*fun*)
_____ encantador/a (*charming*)
_____ estricto/a
_____ honrado/a (*honest*)
_____ ingenioso/a (*resourceful*)
_____ intelectual
_____ justo/a (*fair*)
_____ sabio/a (*wise*)
_____ sensato/a (*sensible*)
_____ sensible (*sensitive*)
_____ tranquilo/a

Act. 6B: Form pairs, model, set a time limit, and begin the activity. To check, have a few students share their findings.

Parte B: Ahora, habla con otra persona y descríbele a tu profesor/a.

▶ Me cae muy bien mi profesora de teatro porque es muy creativa y...

Parte C: En parejas, decidan cuáles son las cuatro cualidades más importantes en un profesor y por qué.

▶ Un profesor debe ser... porque...

Remember: use **ser** to describe what the professor and/or class are like.

Act. 7A: Assign as HW or allow a moment for students to do.

Actividad 7 Me molesta mucho **Parte A:** Marca los adjetivos que describen mejor la clase que menos te gusta este semestre y al profesor o a la profesora de esa clase. Piensa en la clase y las personas de esa clase.

_____ aburrido/a (*boring*)	_____ fácil
_____ cerrado/a (*narrow-minded*)	_____ grande
_____ conservador/a	_____ insoportable (*unbearable*)
_____ creído/a (*vain*)	_____ largo/a
_____ difícil	_____ lento/a (*slow*)
_____ enorme	_____ liberal
_____ exigente	_____ rígido/a

Act. 7B: When discussing information checked in Act. 7A, you may want to tell students to use a false name if they mention a professor in a negative context.

Parte B: Ahora, en parejas, quéjense de (*complain about*) la clase que menos les gusta sin mencionar el nombre del profesor / de la profesora.

▶ No me gusta nada mi clase de... porque es...
Me molesta la clase porque el profesor es...

Remember: use **estar** to say how the students in the class feel.

Act. 7C: **Ser** and **estar** + *adjective* will be formally presented in Chapter 3. Appendix B has a complete summary of their uses.

Parte C: Marquen y luego digan cómo están los estudiantes en una clase aburrida con un profesor malo y por qué.

_____ aburridos	_____ entretenidos (*entertained*)
_____ atentos (*attentive*)	_____ enojados
_____ distraídos (*distracted*)	_____ nerviosos
_____ dormidos	_____ preocupados

Expressing Future Actions

To express future actions, use: **voy, vas, va,** etc. + **a** + ***infinitivo.***

Actividad 8 Los planes En parejas, una persona habla sobre sus planes para este mes y el mes próximo y la otra persona le hace preguntas. Al terminar, cambien de papel. Aquí hay algunas ideas: **compras, trabajo, estudios, diversiones, deportes, viajes.** Cuando sea posible, expliquen por qué van a hacer esas actividades.

▶ El mes que viene voy a... porque..., ¿y tú?

Act. 8: Prior to doing Act. 8, state your plans for the next month or two to model the activity for students. Then form pairs and set a time limit of a minute or two. Make sure students understand that one person will talk about all his/her future plans before they switch roles. This will give students the possibility to say more than just a few phrases. When finished, have a few students report what their partners plan to do.

Actividad 9 La vida universitaria Teresa está en Buenos Aires, Argentina, y le escribe un email a su amigo Javier que vive en el D. F. Completa su mensaje con palabras lógicas. Usa sólo una palabra en cada espacio.

Note: Act. 9 and Act. 10 could be used as testing instruments to help determine if students are in the correct course. If you are using these activities to discern placement, you may want to photocopy them and allot class time to complete Act. 9. If you are not using this as a level check, Act. 9 could be assigned as homework. If you feel that a student may belong in a higher-level class, you may want to assign the person to write a short composition titled **Qué hiciste en tus últimas vacaciones** and/or have a brief oral interview with him/her with a focus on past narration. Fairly decent command of the preterit and imperfect will probably indicate that the student belongs in a higher level.

Para: jvelez@orale.com
De: khedrick@che.com
Tema: ¡Hola!
Fecha: 4 de abril de 2005

Querido Javier:
¿Cómo estás? Yo muy ___bien___, pero muy cansada porque acabo de empezar clases en la universidad y no tengo más vacaciones ___hasta___ julio. Como sabes, me tengo que levantar temprano porque ___trabajo___ durante el día en un banco y ___por___ la noche voy a clase. Por suerte, mi jefa es ___muy___ comprensiva y me permite salir del trabajo una hora antes. Entonces, voy a un bar enfrente de ___la___ universidad y mis compañeros y yo nos reunimos para estudiar para ___la___ clase de física. Es una clase muy difícil y no se pueden hacer muchas preguntas porque hay más de 100 estudiantes. El profesor es muy inteligente ___pero___ no es muy dinámico y por eso los estudiantes muchas veces ___están___ aburridos en su clase. Pero no todas mis clases son así; las otras materias que tengo son mucho mejores y aunque empiezan a las 8 de la noche y ___terminan___ a las 10, ___me___ caen bien los profesores que tengo. Bueno, luego cuando salgo de clase, tomo el autobús y llego a casa a ___las___ 10:30, pero no me acuesto hasta las 12. Como ves, mis días son muy largos, pero los fines de ___semana___ son muy buenos porque mis amigos y ___yo___ siempre organizamos alguna fiesta ___para___ divertirnos.
Bueno, escríbeme y cuéntame qué haces. Hace un mes ___que___ no me escribes y quiero que me cuentes un poco de ___tu___ vida.
Un abrazo,
Khandle

Una conversación en la facultad

1. Be sure students understand phrases in the screened box before listening to the conversation. Practice **¡No me digas!** and **¿En serio?** by asking **¿Quién estudia química?** Respond by saying **¡No me digas! Eres muy inteligente. / ¿En serio? Para mí la química es muy difícil.** Continue asking individuals similar questions. Have students repeat expressions.

2. Practice **volver a empezar de cero** by telling what you do if you're doing an experiment and you goof. Then ask students about similar situations.

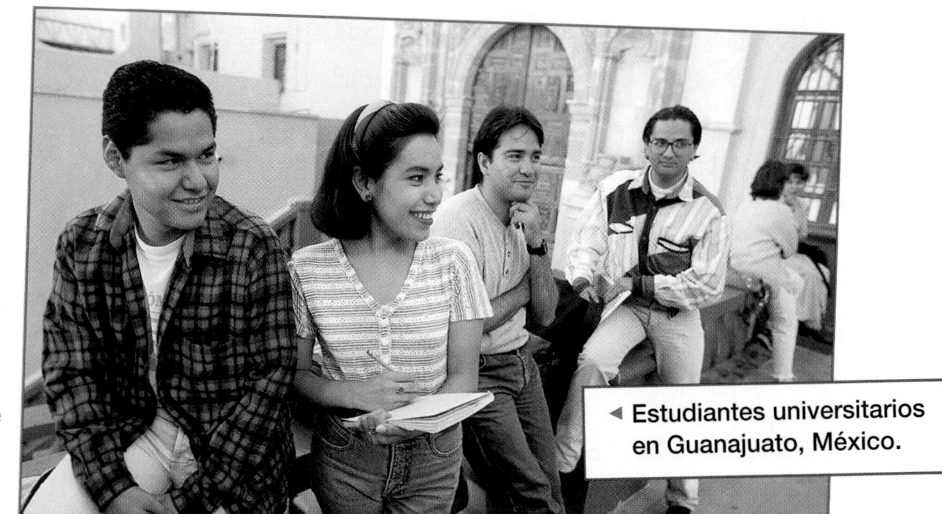

◂ Estudiantes universitarios en Guanajuato, México.

¿En serio?	Really?
¡No me digas!	Don't tell me! / You don't say! / Wow!
volver a empezar de cero	to start over again from scratch

Act. 10A: Set the scene for the conversation by reading the title, looking at the photo, and asking questions about its content. Read the first sentence in Act. 10A. Then give directions for the ongoing listening activity. Reassure students who have had little experience with listening comprehension that they need not understand every word. Tell them to focus on listening for the correct choice for each sentence. Stress the similarity between reading and listening for specific information. Play the conversation and check answers.

Act. 10B: Read through the items, play conversation, and check.

Act. 10B: Answers: 1. **b** 2. **b** 3. **a** 4. **b**

Actividad 10 La carrera de Mónica **Parte A:** Mónica es estudiante universitaria en Guanajuato, México, y le cuenta a Ramón cómo le va en sus estudios. Antes de escuchar la conversación, lee las siguientes ideas. Después escucha la conversación y marca las opciones correctas.

1. Mónica estudia...
   ____ derecho. ____ biología. __✓__ medicina.
2. Quiere estudiar...
   __✓__ derecho. ____ biología. ____ medicina.
3. Para terminar la carrera que ella quiere, se necesitan...
   ____ cuatro años. __✓__ cinco años. ____ seis años.
4. Mónica tiene...
   __✓__ 19 años. ____ 23 años. ____ 24 años.

Parte B: Ahora lee las preguntas y luego escucha la conversación otra vez para averiguar la información.

1. ¿Cuántas materias tuvo Mónica?
   a. 6 b. 8 c. 10
2. ¿Qué problema tiene ella al cambiar de carrera?
   a. Le revalidan pocas materias. b. Tiene que empezar desde cero. c. Tiene que cambiar de universidad.

(continúa en la página siguiente)

3. Cuando Mónica le cuenta a Ramón su problema, él le dice: "¡Qué suerte tienes!" ¿Qué significa este comentario en el contexto de la conversación?
   a. Que tiene mala suerte.   b. Que tiene suerte.   c. Que la suerte no existe.
4. ¿Qué título va a recibir Mónica después de cinco años?
   a. doctora   b. abogada   c. bióloga

Actividad 11 Comparaciones **Parte A:** En grupos de tres, discutan las siguientes preguntas sobre la educación universitaria en tu país.

1. ¿Cuántos años se necesitan para recibir una licenciatura?
2. ¿Cuáles de las siguientes licenciaturas puede recibir un estudiante?
   sociólogo   médico   profesor universitario de literatura
   ingeniero   abogado
3. Cuando un estudiante comienza la universidad, ¿sabe generalmente qué carrera va a estudiar?
4. ¿Qué ocurre si un estudiante decide cambiar de carrera?

Parte B: Ahora comparen el sistema universitario de este país con el sistema que describe Mónica y digan cuáles son los pros y los contras de cada sistema.

Act. 11B: More information on this topic can be found in **¿Lo sabían?** on page 4.

¿Lo sabían?

Cada cultura tiene su propio sentido del humor. Uno de los aspectos interesantes del humor de las personas de habla española es el uso de la ironía. Es común oír a una persona decir exactamente lo contrario de lo que piensa cuando el mensaje es obvio. En la conversación, Ramón dice que Mónica tiene suerte porque tiene que volver a empezar la carrera cuando es obvio que no tiene nada de suerte. De la misma manera, también se pueden oír frases como las siguientes:

- Al pasar frente a un edificio antiguo: ¡Qué moderno es!
- Al ver pasar a una persona muy alta: ¿Adónde va esa persona sin piernas?

Ahora, inventa oraciones irónicas para describir estos dibujos.

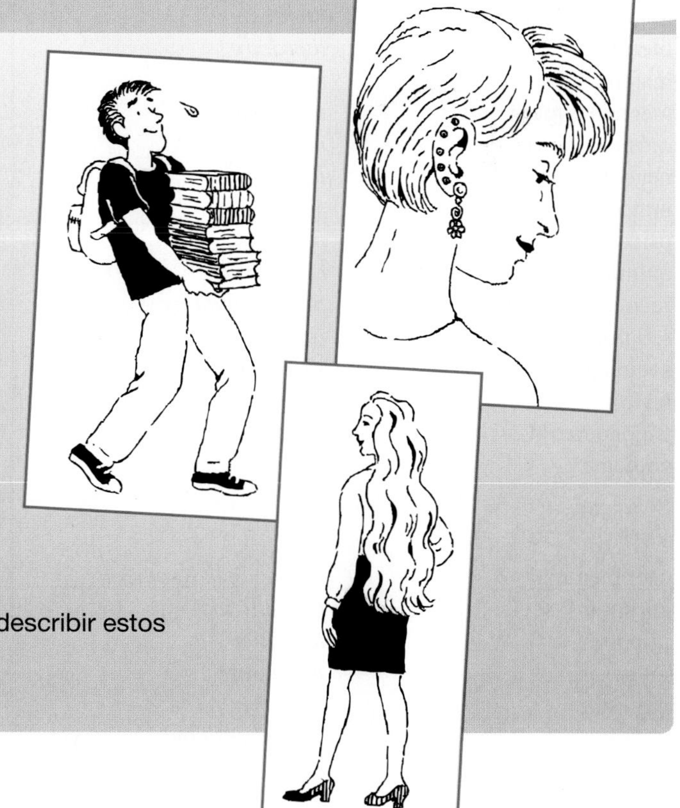

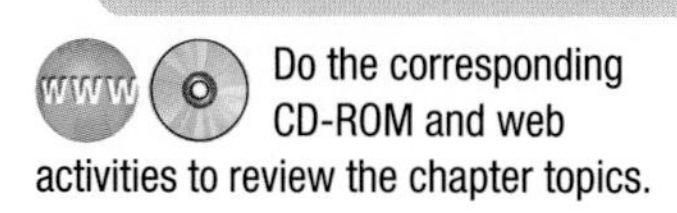

Do the corresponding CD-ROM and web activities to review the chapter topics.

Vocabulario activo

Las materias académicas

alemán	*German*
álgebra	*algebra*
antropología	*anthropology*
arqueología	*archeology*
arte	*art*
biología	*biology*
cálculo	*calculus*
ciencias políticas	*political sciences*
computación	*computer science*
comunicaciones	*communications*
contabilidad	*accounting*
ecología	*ecology*
economía	*economics*
filosofía	*philosophy*
francés	*French*
historia	*history*
ingeniería	*engineering*
lingüística	*linguistics*
literatura	*literature*
matemáticas	*mathematics*
mercadeo/marketing	*marketing*
música	*music*
negocios	*business*
oratoria	*speech*
psicología	*psychology*
química	*chemistry*
relaciones públicas	*public relations*
religión	*religion*
sociología	*sociology*
teatro	*theater*
trigonometría	*trigonometry*
zoología	*zoology*

Verbos como *gustar*

caer bien/mal	*to like/dislike someone*
encantar/fascinar	*to really like*
importar	*to matter*
interesar	*to interest*
molestar	*to bother, to be bothered by*

Adjetivos descriptivos

aburrido/a	*boring*
admirable	*admirable*
astuto/a	*astute, clever*
atento/a	*polite, courteous*
brillante	*brilliant*
capaz	*capable*
cerrado/a	*narrow-minded*
cómico/a	*funny*
conservador/a	*conservative*
creativo/a	*creative*
creído/a	*vain*
difícil	*hard*
divertido/a	*fun*
encantador/a	*charming*
enorme	*huge*
estricto/a	*strict*
exigente	*demanding*
fácil	*easy*
grande	*big*
honrado/a	*honest*
ingenioso/a	*resourceful*
insoportable	*unbearable*
intelectual	*intellectual*
justo/a	*fair*
largo/a	*long*
lento/a	*slow*
liberal	*liberal*
rígido/a	*rigid*
sabio/a	*wise*
sensato/a	*sensible*
sensible	*sensitive*
tranquilo/a	*calm*

Expresiones útiles

¿A qué hora es...?	*At what time is . . . ?*
¿En serio?	*Really?*
¡No me digas!	*Don't tell me! / You don't say! / Wow!*
la facultad	*school, college*
la licenciatura	*BA or BS degree*
la matrícula	*tuition*
el trabajo escrito	*paper*
volver a empezar de cero	*to start over again from scratch*

Vocabulario personal

In this section, you may write any new words you have learned in the chapter or in class that you want to remember, but that were not formally presented.

Learning Spanish is like learning to figure skate. Each year a skater adds a few moves to his/her routines, but never stops practicing and improving on the basics. As the skater progresses from doing a double axle to a triple axle, he/she must still polish technique. There are marks for both technical merit and artistic merit. Both must be worked on, and as the skater becomes better in the sport, actual progress is more and more difficult to perceive.

The process of learning a language is depicted in the cone below. In order to learn a foreign language, students must progress vertically as well as horizontally. As one proceeds vertically, one must also cover more distance horizontally. Progress is noted while moving vertically. This includes learning new tenses, object pronouns, etc. (or in skating, landing a new jump for the first time). Horizontal progress is not perceived as easily as vertical. Horizontal progress includes fine tuning what one has already learned by becoming more accurate, enlarging one's vocabulary, covering in more depth topics already presented in a beginning course, and gaining fluency. This progress is like improving scores for artistic merit or consistently skating cleaner programs than ever before. As you pursue your studies of Spanish, remember that progress is constantly being made.

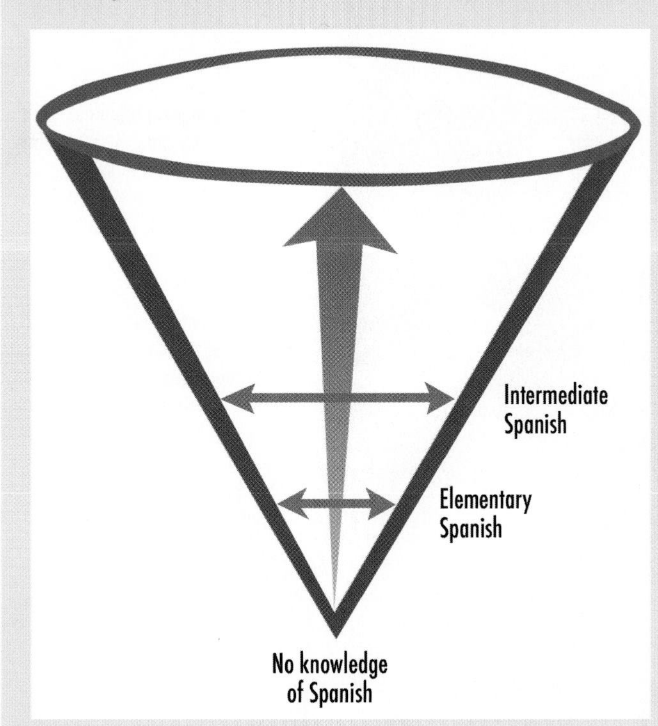

Capítulo 1

Nuestras costumbres

Metas comunicativas

- narrar en el presente y el futuro
- hablar sobre la vida nocturna
- evitar (*avoiding*) redundancias

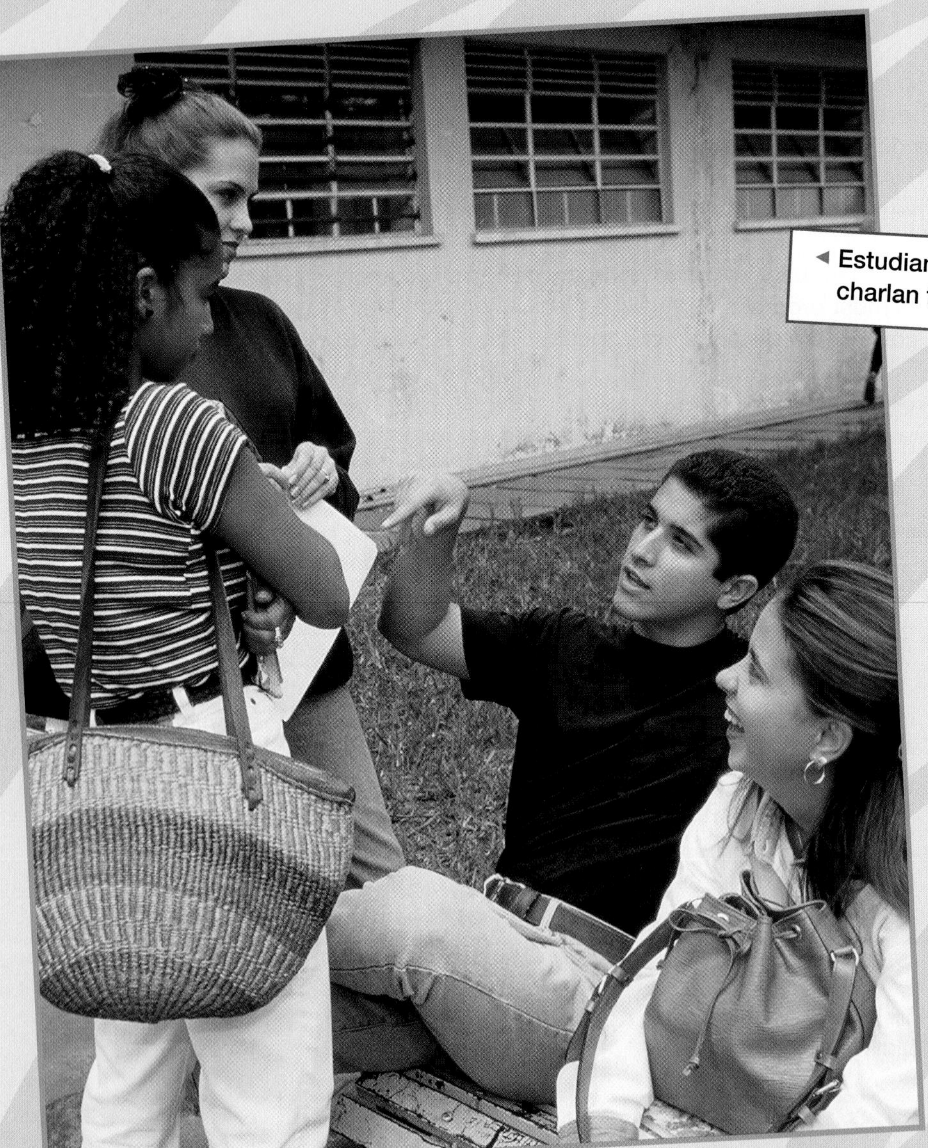

◂ Estudiantes venezolanos charlan fuera de clase.

Besides assigning grammar, vocabulary, and **¿Lo sabían?** the following activities may be prepared as HW: Act. 3A, Act. 4A, Act. 8A, Act. 11A, Act. 12A, Act. 13A, Act. 14B, Act. 15A, Act. 20A, Act. 21A, Act. 22, Act. 26A.

Activities for the chapter video episode are located in the **Videofuentes** section following Chapter 12. Show the chapter video episode at any point in the chapter that you see fit and do all or selected activities in class. Note: Content of the video supplements the cultural material in the chapter and activities reenter chapter grammar and vocabulary.

Una cuestión de identidad

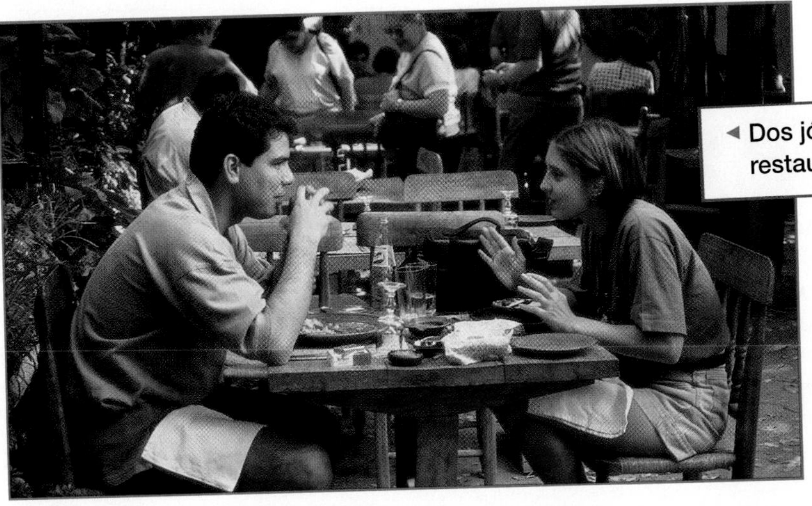

◄ Dos jóvenes almuerzan en un restaurante en Santiago de Chile.

FLR (*Fuentes: Literatura y redacción*) link: **Lectura 2:** Discusses terms such as **latino** and **hispano.**

Present the expressions by telling a story about someone you know. For example: **Hace diez años que tomo el autobús para venir aquí. Normalmente no pasa nada, pero últimamente hay un señor en el autobús que me llama la atención; porque habla y habla solo. Y a veces se pone a cantar en la autobús por la mañana cuando quiero dormir. Es un pesado. De verdad me molesta bastante. ¿Les llaman la atención algunas personas en esta ciudad? ¿Por qué?** Discuss the characteristics of people that can be **pesado/a.**

llamarle la atención	to catch someone's eye
ser un/a pesado/a	to be a bore
hace + *time expression* + **que** + *present tense*	to have been doing something for + *time expression*
Hace un año que vivo aquí.	I have been living here for one year.

Actividad 1 Términos **Parte A:** Los términos **chicano, mexicoamericano** y **latinoamericano** a veces provocan confusión. Decide qué características de la columna B pueden describir a cada uno de estos grupos. Es posible usar las características más de una vez.

Act. 1A: Prior to listening, have students do the matching and, when checking, justify responses.

A	B
chicano: a, c, d, f	a. es ciudadano norteamericano
mexicoamericano: a, c, d	b. es de Latinoamérica
latinoamericano: b, d, e	c. es de ascendencia mexicana
	d. habla español
	e. habla portugués
	f. tiene connotación política

El chicano

Internet references such as this indicate that you will find links to related sites on the *Fuentes* website.

Parte B: Pedro está en Chile y está completando una solicitud para ingresar a una universidad en los Estados Unidos. Le pregunta a su amiga Silvia, qué estudió allí, qué significan ciertos términos. Escucha la conversación y compara tu información de la Parte A con lo que dice Silvia.

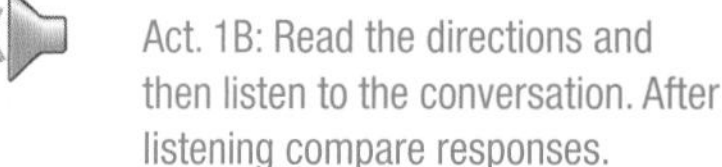

Act. 1B: Read the directions and then listen to the conversation. After listening compare responses.

Act. 2: Read questions aloud or allow time for students to read the questions silently, play the conversation, and check responses. After students have discussed the last question, read or discuss the information in the **¿Lo sabían?** that follows.

Actividad 2 Más información Antes de escuchar la conversación otra vez, lee las siguientes preguntas. Luego escucha la conversación para buscar la información necesaria.

1. ¿Qué problema tiene Pedro al completar la solicitud?
2. Después de escuchar la explicación de Silvia, ¿qué decide marcar Pedro?
3. Según la conversación, ¿en qué se diferencia una universidad de este país de una universidad de Latinoamérica?

Most **¿Lo sabían?** sections are related to a topic raised or mentioned in the preceding activity or section. Upon reading the content, students learn more about the cultures of the Spanish-speaking world. Many of these sections end with a question to help students reflect on their own culture(s) to better make comparisons noting similarities as well as differences.

¿LO SABÍAN?

En un país hispano, las facultades de una universidad pueden estar distribuidas por toda la ciudad. Los estudiantes asisten a clase en la facultad y luego se reúnen a estudiar o a charlar en el bar de la facultad o en los cafés cercanos. Las universidades generalmente no tienen tantos clubes como en los Estados Unidos, pero sí hay representantes de los partidos políticos que organizan reuniones o manifestaciones políticas. ¿Cómo es la vida de un universitario en este país? ¿Y de un universitario en un país hispano?

What it means to be Latino

Act. 3A: Assign reading as HW or have students speed read each response and ask questions to check comprehension after each. Speed reading will help train students not to worry about the meaning of every word and to read in chunks vs. word-by-word. You may want to tell students that people in Hispanic countries interpret the terms **hispanoamericano, latino**, etc., differently than the people in the United States. If you have heritage speakers in your class, ask what the terms mean to them.

Fuentes hispanas

Actividad 3 ¿Qué eres? **Parte A:** En este libro vas a leer sobre las experiencias y opiniones de hispanos de 20 a 50 años, que son de diferentes partes del mundo. Sus comentarios no se pueden generalizar para todos los hispanos; simplemente son la opinión de esa persona en particular. Lee lo que dicen una chica guatemalteca y una chica mexicana sobre su nacionalidad. Mira las preguntas y lo que respondieron.

¿Qué te consideras, guatemalteca/mexicana, hispana, latinoamericana, hispanoamericana, latina y por qué? ¿Qué significa cada término para ti? ¿Hay alguno que no signifique nada para ti?

"Bueno, depende de quién me lo pregunte, porque si es un europeo le digo hispanoamericana, pero si es alguien de habla hispana, definitivamente le digo guatemalteca. El término latinoamericano no me gusta porque regularmente te marginan por eso."

guatemalteca

"Yo soy mexicana, por el territorio en donde nací. Soy hispana, por la lengua que hablo. Soy latinoamericana por la unión de culturas en el pasado (la raíz de la lengua española y la mezcla con la cultura prehispánica). Soy hispanoamericana por la combinación de raíces españolas y americanas. Soy latina, por la secuencia de eventos que juntaron a todos los que vivimos desde Baja California Norte, hasta la Patagonia Argentina, desde Chile hasta la punta del Caribe, pasando por Yucatán y Brasil..."

mexicana

Parte B: En grupos de tres, utilicen las siguientes preguntas para hablar de su nacionalidad y el origen de su familia.

Act. 3B: Check by having a group sharing to find out about individual family traditions.

1. ¿Se consideran americanos, norteamericanos, italoamericanos, afroamericanos, francoamericanos, etc.? Y si son de Canadá, ¿se consideran Uds. norteamericanos, italocanadienses, etc.? ¿Sienten una conexión con personas de Inglaterra, Australia u otros países donde se habla inglés?
2. ¿Cuánto tiempo hace que su familia vive en este país?
3. Si sus padres o abuelos no son originalmente de un país de habla inglesa, ¿hablan el idioma de su país? ¿Lo entienden? ¿Hablan ellos inglés también?
4. ¿Cuáles son algunas costumbres y tradiciones que conservan del país de origen de su familia? Piensen en la música, la comida, las celebraciones especiales, etc.
5. ¿Por qué preguntan las universidades de los Estados Unidos en la solicitud de ingreso la raza y/o el origen étnico de los estudiantes?

I. Narrating in the Present

Do the corresponding CD-ROM and web activities as you study the chapter.

FLR (*Fuentes: Lectura y redacción*) link:
Lectura 1: Anuncios personales

A. Regular, Stem-Changing, and Irregular Verbs

To talk about what you usually do, you generally use the present tense. For information on how to form the present indicative (**presente del indicativo**), including irregular and stem-changing verbs, see Appendix A, pages 338–340.

Paulina y yo **caminamos** a la universidad todas las mañanas.	*Paulina and I walk to the university every morning.*
Ella **prefiere** tomar clases por la mañana, pero **sé** que a veces **trasnocha** y **falta** a clase.	*She prefers to take morning classes, but I know she sometimes stays up all night and misses class.*

Here is a list of verbs that you can use to talk about what you usually do.

-ar *verbs*

ahorrar (dinero/tiempo)	to save (money/time)
alquilar (videos)	to rent (videos)
charlar	to chat
cuidar (a) niños	to baby-sit
dibujar	to draw
escuchar música	to listen to music*
faltar (a clase/al trabajo)	to be absent (from class/work)
flirtear/coquetear	to flirt*
gastar (dinero)	to spend (money)
mirar (la) televisión	to watch TV*
pasar la noche en vela	to pull an all-nighter
pasear al perro	to walk the dog
probar (o → ue)	to taste; to try
sacar buena/mala nota	to get a good/bad grade
trasnochar	to stay up all night

Presentation of the present indicative tense: Provide comprehensible input by telling students what you do in a typical week. Interrupt your narrative to ask questions about what students do. Review basic verbs as needed.

Drill the present tense:
1. Practice new verbs by giving definitions and having students respond. T: **Le das dinero a alguien por usar algo durante un tiempo determinado.** Ss: **Alquilar.** Expand by asking questions like **¿Qué cosas alquila la gente?**
2. Have all students stand and ask them questions. When they answer, they can sit down.
3. In pairs, have students list things that business people and professors do on a typical weekend.

Cuido niños. (*Kids, anybody's kids.*) **Cuido <u>a</u> los niños de mi hermana.** (*Specific child/children*)

Flirtear from the English *to flirt,* is approved by the **Real Academia de la Lengua Española.**

Stem-changing verbs are followed by **ue, ie, i, u** in parentheses to show the stem change that takes place. Note that some **-ir** verbs have a second change, which is used when forming the preterit (**durmió, durmieron**) and the present participle (**durmiendo**).

*Notes:
1. **Flirtear** can take both male and female subjects while **coquetear** usually takes a female subject.
2. The verbs **mirar** (*to look at*) and **escuchar** (*to listen to*) only take **a** when they are followed by a person.

Mientras estudio, **escucho** música clásica.	*While I study, I listen to classical music.*
Siempre **escucho a** mi padre.	*I always listen to my father.*

-er *verbs*

devolver (o → ue)	to return (*something*)
escoger*	to choose
hacer investigación/dieta	to do research/to be on a diet
poder (o → ue)	to be able to, can
soler (o → ue) + *infinitive*	to usually do + *verb*
volver (o → ue)	to return

-ir *verbs*

asistir (a clase/a una reunión)	to attend (class/a meeting)
compartir	to share
contribuir*	to contribute
discutir	to argue; to discuss
mentir (e → ie, i)	to lie
salir* bien/mal (en un examen)	to do well/poorly (on an exam)
seguir* (instrucciones/a + alguien) (e → i, i)	to follow (instructions, someone)

Devolver is a transitive verb (it takes a direct object). Use it to say someone returns something somewhere: **Él va a devolver el suéter a la tienda. Volver** is an intransitive verb (it never takes a direct object). Use it to say someone returns somewhere: **Él va a volver a la tienda.**

Write **ja, ge, gi, jo, ju** on the board. Practice pronunciation and stress the relationship between spelling and pronunciation with the verb **escoger**.

*Note: Verbs followed by an asterisk in the preceding list have spelling changes or irregular forms. See Appendix A, page 339 for formation of these verbs.

The present tense can also be used to state what one is going to do or is doing at the moment.

(*phone conversation*)
—¿Qué haces? ¿Puedo ir a tu casa?
—Miro la tele, pero dentro de quince minutos voy al bar de la esquina a encontrarme con mi novia.

Remind students that the present indicative can also be used to refer to the future and actions in progress.

Actividad 4 Un conflicto familiar **Parte A:** Una madre tiene problemas con su hijo adolescente y le escribe a Consuelo, una señora que da consejos (*advice*) en Internet. Completa su email de la página 19, escogiendo el verbo apropiado para cada espacio en blanco. No repitas ningún verbo.

Act. 4A: Assign as HW and check in class. When finished checking, ask questions about content.

Parte B: En grupos de tres, comparen la familia de la madre desesperada con su propia familia. ¿Son iguales o diferentes?

- A mi madre también le molesta cuando mi hermano escucha música rap.
- Esos niños pequeños son perfectos, pero en mi familia no es así. Son muy mal educados. Asisten a clase, pero no escuchan a los maestros y no hacen la tarea.

Act. 4B: Form groups, set a time limit, and begin. When finished, ask a few groups to report back to the class.

almorzar
asistir
comer
dormir
hacer
mirar
regresar
sacar
ser
soler
tener

escuchar
faltar
flirtear
ir
jugar
mentir
sacar
ser
volver

asistir
comenzar
discutir
entender
estar
pedir
poner
trabajar
volver

pensar
querer
saber
ser
ser

Estimada Consuelo:

Estoy divorciada y tengo tres hijos: Carlos, Maricruz y Enrique, que tienen diez, once y dieciséis años respectivamente. Mis dos hijos menores son encantadores. Asisten a clase todos los días, sacan notas excelentes y almuerzan en el comedor de la escuela sin protestar. Por la tarde, regresan a casa, hacen la tarea y suelen preparar sándwiches porque tienen hambre. Luego comen mientras miran televisión y por la noche duermen como unos angelitos.

Mi hijo Enrique, en cambio, es muy rebelde. Está en la escuela secundaria, pero a veces falta a clase por la mañana. Y el chico me miente, pues me dice que va a clase, pero en vez de ir a clase, va a un parque con sus amigos y allí ellos juegan al fútbol y también flirtean con las chicas (a veces creo que estos chicos tienen demasiada testosterona). Luego, por la noche, él vuelve a casa muy tarde y escucha música rap a todo volumen en su habitación. Por supuesto estudia poquísimo y saca notas terribles en la escuela.

Yo comienzo mi día muy temprano porque tengo que estar en el trabajo a las ocho. Trabajo todo el día en una tienda de ropa y luego asisto a una clase de inglés en un instituto norteamericano. Por lo tanto, vuelvo a casa tarde después de un día largo y estoy muy cansada. A esa hora generalmente, Enrique pone esa música rap tan fuerte y yo le pido que baje el volumen, pero el muchacho no entiende que a mí me molesta. Entonces él y yo discutimos y todo termina muy mal.

Consuelo, ¿por qué mis hijos menores son tan buenos y mi hijo mayor es tan rebelde? Yo quiero a Enrique y todo el día pienso en soluciones posibles, pero no sé qué hacer.

Madre desesperada

Act 5: Encourage students to use the list of verbs that appears on pp. 17–18.

Actividad 5 Una clase aburrida En grupos de tres, digan qué hacen o no hacen generalmente los estudiantes cuando están en una clase que es aburrida. Mencionen un mínimo de cinco acciones.

Remember: Use **hace** + *time expression* + **que** + *present tense* to indicate how long an action has taken place. The action started in the past and continues in the present.

como/unas = aproximadamente

Act. 6: Set up pairs, practice forming questions and possible answers for the first two or three items, have students alternate asking questions, set a time limit, and begin. Check by asking a few questions.

Actividad 6 ¿Cuánto hace que...? En parejas, túrnense para entrevistarse y averiguar si la otra persona hace las actividades que siguen y cuánto tiempo hace que las hace. Sigan el modelo.

▶ A: ¿Estudias psicología?

B: Sí, estudio psicología. B: No, no estudio psicología.

A: ¿Cuánto (tiempo) hace que estudias psicología?

B: Hace (como/unas) tres semanas que estudio psicología.

ahorrar dinero	compartir apartamento/ habitación en una residencia estudiantil	asistir a esta universidad
esquiar	tocar un instrumento musical	trabajar
estudiar español	jugar al (*nombre de un deporte*)	hacer ejercicio
hablar otro idioma	charlar por Internet	? ? ?

Actividades de tiempo libre

Act. 7A: Go over possible questions: **¿Cuántas horas duermes los fines de semana? ¿En qué gastas dinero?** (etc.) Set up pairs by assigning interviewer and interviewee roles, make sure only interviewers have the book open, and begin. Then have them switch roles.

Actividad 7 Los fines de semana **Parte A:** En parejas, túrnense para entrevistarse y averiguar qué hacen los fines de semana. El/La entrevistado/a debe cerrar el libro. Sigan el modelo.

▶ —¿Qué prefieres hacer los fines de semana, comer en la universidad, pedir comida a domicilio o almorzar en...?
—Prefiero...

Preferir:
____ comer en la universidad ____ pedir comida a domicilio ____ almorzar y/o cenar afuera

Dormir:
____ 7 horas o menos ____ 8 horas ____ más de 8 horas

Gastar dinero en:
____ diversiones ____ comida ____ ropa ____ otras cosas

Asistir a:
____ conciertos ____ eventos deportivos ____ manifestaciones políticas
____ conferencias ____ estrenos (*premieres*) de películas ____ exhibiciones de arte

Gustarle:
____ trasnochar ____ hablar por teléfono ____ alquilar DVDs

Soler:
____ pasar la noche en vela ____ ir a fiestas ____ jugar al (nombre de un deporte)

Parte B: Ahora compartan la información que averiguaron con el resto de la clase para comparar lo que hacen los universitarios típicos.

Actividad 8 La puntualidad **Parte A:** Lee las siguientes preguntas sobre la puntualidad y mira las respuestas que dio un joven argentino. Luego escribe tus respuestas a estas preguntas.

Act. 8A: Assign as HW or set a brief time limit for Part A.

	un argentino	tú
1. Si invitas a amigos a cenar a tu casa, ¿para qué hora es la invitación y a qué hora llegan tus amigos?	"Es para las 9:00 y llegan a las 9:30/10:00."	
2. Si quedas en encontrarte con un amigo en un café a las 3:00, ¿a qué hora llegas?	"Llego a las 3:15."	
3. Si tienes una clase que empieza a las 10:00, ¿a qué hora llegas a la clase? ¿A qué hora llega tu profesor/a?	"Llego a las 10:05 y el profe llega a las 10:15. (Las clases son de dos horas.)"	
4. Si tienes una entrevista de trabajo a las 9:15, ¿a qué hora llegas?	"Llego a las 9:10."	
5. Si tienes cita con el médico a las 11:30, ¿a qué hora llegas? ¿A qué hora te ve el médico?	"Llego a las 11:30 y el médico me ve a las 12:00/12:30."	
6. Dentro de las normas de tu país y en tu opinión, ¿eres una persona puntual?	"Sí, soy bastante puntual."	

Parte B: Ahora compara tus respuestas con las de un/a compañero/a. Digan si sus respuestas son similares o no a las del argentino.

Act. 8B: After finishing the activity, talk about the concept of time as it relates to culture.

Actividad 9 ¿Qué hacen? **Parte A:** En grupos de tres, miren las listas de acciones de las páginas 17–18 y usen la imaginación para decir todo lo que hacen estas personas un día normal.

Act. 9A: Form groups, set up the activity, set a time limit, and begin. Have a group sharing when finished.

Parte B: Uds. tienen una bola de cristal y saben que la vida de estas cuatro personas se va a cruzar. Inventen una descripción lógica para explicar qué va a ocurrir. Comiencen diciendo: **La estudiante va a salir de su casa una noche y...**

Use **ir a** + *infinitive* to discuss future events.

Act. 9B: Use the same groups as in 9A, set up the activity, set a time limit, encourage students to use their imagination, and begin. When finished, call on a few individuals to describe how the people's paths will cross.

Act. 10: Form pairs and assign roles, allow a moment for each student to read his/her role, set a time limit, and begin. Option: Copy the role cards and hand them out to the students.

Actividad 10 Un conflicto en casa En parejas, una persona es el padre/la madre y la otra persona es el/la hijo/a. Cada persona debe leer solamente las instrucciones para su papel.

A

Padre/Madre

Tu hijo/a tiene 17 años y es un poco rebelde. A la derecha tienes una lista de cosas que hace que a ti no te gustan. Dile las cosas que hace y las cosas que tiene que hacer para cambiar su rutina. También hay algunas cosas de tu rutina que a tu hijo/a no le gustan y las va a comentar. Cuestiona lo que te dice. Empieza la conversación diciendo "Quiero hablar contigo".

Cosas que hace tu hijo/a

- faltar a clase
- tocar la batería (*drums*) constantemente
- trasnochar con frecuencia
- mentir mucho
- preferir andar con mala compañía
- sacar malas notas en la escuela
- dormir todo el fin de semana

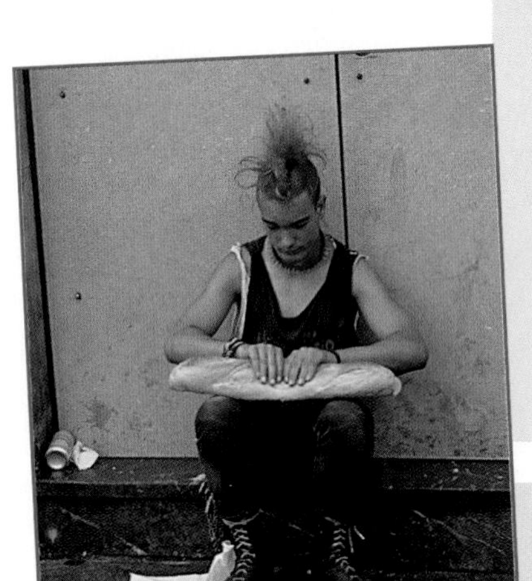

B

Hijo/a

Tu padre/madre observa cada movimiento que tú haces. Por eso tú decides observar las cosas que hace él/ella. A la derecha tienes una lista de cosas que hace tu padre/madre y que a ti no te gustan. Ahora tu padre/madre va a hablarte de las cosas que haces. Cuestiona lo que te dice y háblale de las cosas que él/ella hace que te molestan.

Cosas que hace tu padre/madre

- gastar mucho dinero en cosas innecesarias
- decir que está enfermo/a y faltar al trabajo cuando está perfectamente bien
- tocar el piano muy mal
- soler mirar *La rueda de la fortuna* en la tele
- contribuir demasiado dinero a UNICEF
- beber mucho los fines de semana
- fumar a escondidas detrás del garaje

When doing drills, personalize and adjust them to the needs of your class. Read the *Instructor's Guide* section of this text for further ideas.

Presentation of reflexive verbs: Provide input about your daily life. Contrast verbs that are reflexive with those that are not: **Una vez al mes lavo el auto y, claro, me ensucio y tengo que lavarme las manos y la cara.**

Remember: Definite articles (**el, la, los, las**) are frequently used with body parts.

B. Reflexive Constructions

1. To indicate that someone does an action to himself/herself, you must use reflexive pronouns (**pronombres reflexivos**). Compare the following sentences.

Me despierto a las 8:00 todos los días.	Todas las mañanas **despierto** a mi padre a las 8:00.
Mi padre **se baña** por la noche.	Mi padre **baña** a mi hermanito por la noche.
Mis hermanas siempre **se cepillan** el pelo por la mañana.	Mi hermana **cepilla** al perro una vez por semana.

In the first column on page 22, the use of reflexive pronouns indicates that the subject doing the action and the object receiving the action are the same. In the second column, subjects and objects are not the same. Therefore, reflexive pronouns are not used.

2. The reflexive pronouns are:

me acuesto	**nos** acostamos
te acuestas	**os** acostáis
se acuesta	**se** acuestan

For information on reflexive pronouns and their placement, see Appendix C, page 352.

3. Typical verbs that are used to describe your daily routine are:

acostarse (o → ue)
afeitarse (la barba/las piernas/etc.)
arreglarse (*to make oneself presentable*)
bañarse
cepillarse (el pelo/los dientes)
despertarse (e → ie)
desvestirse (e → i, i)
dormirse (o → ue, u)
ducharse
lavarse (el pelo/las manos/la cara/etc.)
maquillarse (*to put on makeup*)
peinarse
ponerse la camisa/la falda/etc.
prepararse (para)
probarse ropa (o → ue) (*to try on clothes*)
quitarse la camisa/la falda/etc.
secarse (el pelo/la cara/etc.)
sentarse (e → ie)
vestirse (e → i, i)

4. Here are some verbs that do not indicate actions performed upon oneself, but need reflexive pronouns in order for them to have the meanings listed here.

aburrirse (de)	to become bored (with)
acordarse (de) (o → ue)	to remember
caerse	to fall down
callarse	to shut up
darse cuenta (de)	to realize
despedirse (de) (e → i, i)	to say good-by (to)
divertirse (e → ie, i)	to have fun, to have a good time
enfadarse/enojarse	to get mad
equivocarse	to err, to make a mistake
interesarse (por)	to take an interest (in)
irse (de)	to go away (from), to leave
ocuparse (de)	to take care (of)
olvidarse (de)	to forget (about)
preocuparse (de/por)	to worry (about); to take care (of)
quejarse (de)	to complain (about)
reírse (de) (e → i, i)	to laugh (at)
sentirse (e → ie, i)	to feel

Drill reflexives:

1. Ask students to write down what time they usually get up every morning, and to ask each other questions in order to line themselves up from earliest to latest. Repeat for **acostarse**.

2. Have individuals or pairs of students act out sentences written on strips of paper. For example: **Me despierto. Me lavo el pelo. Despierto a mi hijo.**

3. Pair students and have them state what items of clothing they put on 1st, 2nd, 3rd, etc. **Primero me pongo la ropa interior, después me pongo las medias, después de ponerme las medias,** etc.

4. Contrast **dormir** and **dormirse** by acting them out. Then ask students **¿En qué clases te duermes? ¿Tu padre se duerme cuando mira la televisión? ¿Cuántas horas duermes cada noche?**

arreglar = to fix (*as in a car motor*)

arreglarse la cara = **maquillarse**

arreglarse el pelo = to fix one's hair

dormir = to sleep

dormirse = to fall asleep

Provide additional input by telling students about your workday. **Siempre tengo mucho trabajo. Me preocupo por mis clases, por eso las preparo bien antes de entrar en el aula. También me preocupo cuando un estudiante está ausente.** (etc.)

Drill:

1. Ask **¿En qué lugares te diviertes y en cuáles te aburres? ¿Te preocupas de entregar los trabajos a tiempo? ¿Te preocupas de llegar a clase a tiempo? ¿Y al trabajo?**

2. Give students a few situations and ask how they react: **Sacas B y crees que debes sacar A. ¿Te quejas o te callas?**

Do not confuse **sentirse** with **sentarse (e → ie) =** to sit down.

Act. 11A: Assign as HW and check in class. Ask questions on content.

Actividad 11 La respuesta de Consuelo **Parte A:** Completa el email que Consuelo le escribe a la madre desesperada de la Actividad 4. Elige el verbo y la forma apropiada para cada espacio en blanco.

afeitarse
despertarse
equivocarse
peinarse
vestirse

cepillarse
darse cuenta
levantarse
preocuparse
quejarse

aburrirse
divertirse
sentarse

Querida madre desesperada:

Yo también tengo un hijo adolescente y por eso entiendo muy bien su problema. Creo que no ___me equivoco___ si le digo que su hijo, como el mío, tiene malos hábitos: estoy segura que ___se despierta___ tarde por la mañana, no ___se peina___ y por eso tiene todo el pelo parado, no ___se afeita___ y a esta edad ya empieza a tener un poquito de pelo en la cara y tampoco ___se viste___ con ropa apropiada para ir a la escuela.

Nosotros como madres, ___nos preocupamos___ mucho por su apariencia física e inmediatamente les decimos qué deben hacer. Pero nuestros hijos ___se quejan___ de los consejos que les damos constantemente y en parte tienen razón. Pero ¿de qué modo puede Ud. ayudar a su hijo a independizarse? Hagan un plan entre los dos y digan qué cosas quiere cada uno: él debe ___levantarse___ temprano para ir a la escuela, pero si no quiere ___cepillarse___ el pelo, está bien. Si Ud. no le dice nada, estoy segura que él solo va a ___darse cuenta___ algún día que no está muy atractivo con el pelo parado.

También dice Ud. que su hijo no va a la escuela y estoy segura que ___se aburre___ y, por eso, prefiere ir al parque. Si su hijo ___se divierte___ con sus amigos, eso es importante porque un joven necesita pasarlo bien y estar con amigos. Pero Enrique tiene que aprender que en la vida hay obligaciones y diversiones y que las dos son importantes. Basta de tonterías y estupideces, nada de música rap a todo volumen. Su hijo necesita reglas y tiene que entender que todo comportamiento (*behavior*) tiene su consecuencia. Uds. deben ___sentarse___ y hablar para aclarar la situación de una vez por todas o ese chico nunca va a aprender a ser una persona responsable.

Le deseo mucha suerte,
Consuelo

Act. 11B: Form groups, pose the question, set a time limit, and begin. Check by calling on a few individuals to state their opinions.

Parte B: Consuelo cree que la comunicación entre la madre y su hijo es la mejor solución para ellos. En grupos de tres, comenten qué pueden hacer los padres para tener mejor comunicación con sus hijos.

▶ En mi opinión, los padres pueden... Deben... Tienen que...

Actividad 12 Tu rutina **Parte A:** En parejas, describan cuatro o cinco actividades de su rutina de la mañana y de su rutina de la noche. Usen verbos de la lista de la página 23 y mencionen algunos detalles adicionales. Sigan el modelo.

▶ Por la mañana yo me despierto a las 6:15, pero me levanto a las 6:45 y tomo café antes que nada. Después...

Act. 12A: Assign students to write their morning and evening routine or do in class. Encourage students to be as detailed as possible.

Parte B: Ahora díganse cuatro cosas que generalmente hacen los fines de semana y tres cosas que van a hacer este fin de semana.

▶ En general, los fines de semana me levanto tarde, pero este fin de semana voy a levantarme temprano porque...

Act. 12B: Call on a few individuals to check. Stress the correct placement of the reflexive pronoun.

Actividad 13 La salud **Parte A:** Completa la siguiente tabla sobre tu vida. Escribe tus iniciales en la columna apropiada.

Act. 13A: Either assign as HW or set a time limit for students to mark their answers.

	Siempre/Mucho	Generalmente	A veces	Nunca
soler comer frutas y verduras	______	______	______	______
despertarse tarde	______	______	______	______
dormirse con la tele encendida	______	______	______	______
escuchar música a todo volumen	______	______	______	______
practicar deportes	______	______	______	______
beber alcohol	______	______	______	______
fumar	______	______	______	______
cepillarse los dientes después de comer	______	______	______	______
pasar noches en vela	______	______	______	______
salir cuatro noches por semana	______	______	______	______
tener dolores de cabeza	______	______	______	______
preocuparse mucho por todo	______	______	______	______

Parte B: En parejas, entrevisten a la otra persona para ver si tiene una vida sana y escriban sus iniciales en la columna apropiada. Al escuchar la respuesta de su compañero/a reaccionen usando una de las expresiones que se presentan y averigüen más información. Sigan el modelo.

Act. 13B: Model the conversation with a few students and use the phrases to react to what was said whenever possible. Form pairs, set a time limit, and begin.

▶ —¿Fumas?
—Sí, fumo mucho. / No, nunca fumo. / etc.
—¡No me digas! ¿Por qué?
—Porque...

¡No me digas! /¿De veras?	*Really? / You're kidding.*
Yo también.	*I do too. / Me too.*
Yo tampoco.	*Neither do I. / Me neither.*
En cambio yo...	*Instead I . . . / Not me, I . . .*
¡Qué chévere! (*Caribe*)	*That's cool!*
¡Qué lástima!	*What a pity!*

sano/a = healthy

cuerdo/a = sane

Act. 13C: Ask a few people which of the two of them leads a healthier life. Have them justify their answers.

Parte C: Ahora, mira las respuestas y dile al resto de la clase si la otra persona lleva una vida sana. Justifica tu opinión.

▶ Liz (no) lleva una vida sana porque...

Act. 14A: Set up the activity, tell students to take notes if they want, set a time limit, and begin.

Actividad 14 ¿Cómo son Uds.? **Parte A:** En parejas, túrnense para entrevistar a la otra persona y así formar su perfil psicológico.

1. aburrirse con novelas románticas
2. divertirse solo/a o en compañía de otros
3. acordarse del cumpleaños de sus amigos
4. preocuparse por los demás (*others*)
5. sentirse mal si está solo/a
6. aceptar sus errores cuando se equivoca en la vida
7. olvidarse de ir a citas
8. interesarse por la salud de sus familiares

Act. 14B: Ask a few individuals about their partners. Ask them to justify their responses. This could be assigned as written HW.

Parte B: Ahora usen las siguientes palabras para describirle a la clase cómo es la persona que entrevistaron. Justifiquen su respuesta.

sociable, solitario/a
extrovertido/a, introvertido/a
despistado/a, despierto/a
considerado/a, egoísta

▶ Tom es una persona muy sociable porque...

Act. 15A: Assign as HW or do in class. Set a time limit and have students fill out the chart.

Actividad 15 Las reacciones **Parte A:** Primero, lee las siguientes situaciones. Segundo, elige uno de los adjetivos de la lista para describir cómo te sientes en cada situación y escríbelo en la primera columna. Después, pon una X en la segunda o la tercera columna para indicar si te callas o te quejas.

Adjetivos: **enojado/a, fatal, frustrado/a, impaciente, irritado/a, nervioso/a, preocupado/a,** etc.

	Me siento...	Me callo	Me quejo
si no me gusta el servicio de un restaurante	________	____	____
si una persona fuma en la sección de no fumar de un restaurante	________	____	____
si estoy en un avión y el niño que está detrás de mí me está molestando	________	____	____
si mi taxista maneja como un loco	________	____	____
si un profesor me da una nota que me parece baja	________	____	____
si alguien cuenta un chiste ofensivo	________	____	____
si mis vecinos ponen música a todo volumen	________	____	____
si no puedo matricularme en una clase	________	____	____

Parte B: En parejas, comparen y discutan sus respuestas. Justifiquen por qué se quejan o se callan. Usen las siguientes frases para reaccionar a los comentarios.

Act. 15B: Form pairs and model a discussion with a student. Have him/her give justifications.

No sirve para nada quejarse / No vale la pena quejarse...	*It's not worth it to complain . . .*
Vale la pena callarse porque...	*It's worth it to keep quiet, because . . .*
Tienes razón.	*You're right.*

Actividad 16 Un poco de imaginación En grupos de tres, imagínense que estas dos personas son sus amigos y contesten las preguntas que siguen.

Act. 16: Follow with a group sharing.

Follow-up: Have students bring in outlandish photos to discuss.

1. ¿Cómo se llaman y dónde trabajan?
2. ¿Qué hace el hombre para divertirse? ¿Y la mujer?
3. ¿Quién se divierte más?
4. ¿Dónde se aburren ellos?
5. ¿Se preocupan por su apariencia física?
6. ¿Se dan cuenta de los comentarios de los demás o no se preocupan por esas cosas?
7. ¿Cuál de los dos se interesa por la política? ¿Por qué?
8. ¿Cuál de los dos se olvida de pagar las cuentas a tiempo?

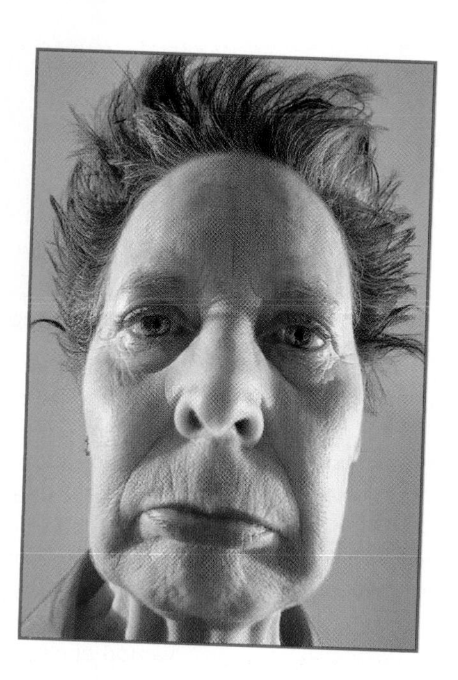

II. Discussing Nightlife

La vida nocturna

▸ Estudiantes de la Universidad Autónoma de México (UNAM) platican y planean qué van a hacer por la noche.

Ask questions about the content of the paragraph, incorporating the terms in bold whenever possible: **¿Qué pasa en algunas fiestas y por qué?**

Provide additional input by saying what you usually do.

"Cuando tenemos energía, salimos a escuchar música a algún bar o a cenar en un restaurante. Si salimos a un bar, escuchamos buena música, **pedimos algo de tomar** o de comer y salimos alrededor de las tres de la mañana. Si salimos a una fiesta, **pasamos tiempo** con gente que no vemos con frecuencia. A veces en algunas fiestas, nos aburrimos porque la música es mala o nadie **te saca a bailar.** Si salimos a cenar, pedimos buena comida, **platicamos**, nos divertimos y regresamos a nuestras casas a las doce de la noche. Los sábados si no salimos en la noche, vamos al cine a ver una película interesante; casi siempre son extranjeras, aunque a veces hay muy buenas películas mexicanas. Los domingos, **nos juntamos** siempre en los mismos lugares y **quedamos siempre a la misma hora** para tomar café y platicar sobre nuestras experiencias de la semana y estar siempre en contacto. A veces, para descansar después de una semana larga, es mejor alquilar una película, invitar a tus amigos y pedir pizza juntos."

mexicana

pedimos algo de tomar: we order something to drink
pasamos tiempo: we spend time, we hang out
te saca a bailar: asks you to dance
platicamos: we chat (*Mexico*)
nos juntamos / quedamos siempre a la misma hora: we get together / we always meet at the same time

ir a una disco (discoteca) / ir a bailar	
sacar a bailar a alguien	to ask someone to dance
pasar tiempo con alguien	to hang out with someone
pedir algo de tomar	to order something to drink
ir a un bar	to go to a bar, café
ir al cine	
ir a un concierto	
sacar/comprar entradas	to get/to buy tickets
sentarse en la primera/ segunda/última fila	
ir detrás del escenario	to go backstage
el revendedor	scalper
ir a los videojuegos	to go to the video arcade
dejar plantado/a a alguien	to stand someone up
ligar (España)	to pick someone up (at a club, bar, etc.)
pasar a buscar/recoger a alguien (por/en un lugar)	to pick someone up (at home, etc.)
pasear con el auto	to go cruising
quedar a una hora con alguien	to meet at an agreed upon time
reunirse/juntarse con amigos	to get together with friends
salir a dar una vuelta	to go cruising/for a ride / for a walk
tener un contratiempo	to have a mishap (*that causes one to be late*)

The verb **ligar** is never followed directly by a noun as a direct object. **Todas las noches Juan sale con sus amigos a ligar, pero nunca liga con nadie interesante.**

Actividad 17 Definiciones En parejas, túrnense para definir palabras o frases del vocabulario, pero no usen la palabra en su definición. Su compañero/a debe identificar la palabra o expresión.

Act. 17: Form pairs, allow one person to look at the vocabulary list while giving definitions. Switch partners halfway through. Check by calling on individuals to give a definition and have the class guess the word or phrase defined.

Actividad 18 Para divertirme... En grupos de tres, lean en la página 28 lo que hace una mexicana para divertirse por la noche y compárenlo con lo que hacen Uds.

El tiempo libre en México

Act. 18: Allow students a few moments to find similarities and differences. Have a group sharing. Note: there is no equivalent to "a Sunday brunch" in the Spanish-speaking world.

Actividad 19 Tu vida noctura En parejas, discutan las siguientes preguntas relacionadas con la vida nocturna.

Act. 19: When finished compare responses.

1. ¿Van a bailar y por qué? ¿Con qué frecuencia? ¿Sacan a bailar a otra persona o esperan que la otra persona los saque a bailar? ¿Por qué baila la gente?
2. ¿Les gusta ir a los bares? ¿Por qué? ¿Por qué se reúne la gente en los bares? ¿Por qué generalmente beben los jóvenes más que sus padres?
3. ¿Les compran las entradas a los revendedores el día del concierto o las compran con anticipación? ¿Cuánto cuesta normalmente una entrada? ¿Tienen a veces la oportunidad de ir detrás del escenario? ¿Qué hace la gente en un concierto de rock?
4. ¿Qué hacen si aceptan la invitación de alguien, pero después deciden no salir? ¿Y si alguien los está esperando en un lugar y Uds. tienen un contratiempo?

III. Obtaining and Giving Information

¿Qué? and ¿cuál?

Drill **qué/cuál:**

1. Provide answers and have students provide the questions: **Es el estudio de los animales y las plantas. / Mi número de teléfono es el 555 45 98.** (etc.)

2. Create a series of questions about Hispanic countries: **¿Cuál es la ciudad más grande de México? ¿Qué país de Centroamérica no tiene costa en el Caribe? ¿En qué país centroamericano el español no es el idioma oficial?** (etc.) Then put students in pairs and have them form questions. After they have formed questions, have each group pose one to the class as a whole.

3. Borrow caps (or another object) from students and have them answer questions. **¿Qué es una gorra? ¿Cuál es la gorra de John?**

1. In general, the uses of **qué** and **cuál** parallel English uses of *what* and *which,* except in cases where they are followed by **ser.**

¿**Qué** te ocurre?	*What's wrong? / What's the matter?*
¿**Qué** haces mañana?	*What are you doing tomorrow?*
¿**Cuál** le gusta más?	*Which do you like more?*
¿**Cuáles** de estos cantantes prefieren?	*Which of these singers do you prefer?*

Note: A noun can follow both **qué** and **cuál/es**, although **qué** + *noun* is more common: **¿Qué vestido te vas a poner esta noche?**

2. Use **qué** + **ser** to ask for a definition or for group classifications.

Definition	Group Classification
—¿**Qué es** dejar plantado a alguien?	—¿**Qué eres,** demócrata o republicano?
—Es quedar en encontrarte con una persona y esa persona no aparece.	—Ninguno de los dos. Soy del Partido Verde.

Note: The question **¿Qué es eso/esto?** is used to ask for the identification of an unknown object or action.

—**¿Qué es eso?**
—Es una quena. Es un instrumento musical que tocan en los Andes. (*identification*)

3. In all other instances not covered in points 1 and 2, use **cuál(es)** with **ser.**

¿**Cuál es** tu número de teléfono?	*What's your telephone number?* (*Which, of all the numbers in the world, is your phone number?*)
¿**Cuál es** tu dirección?	*What's your address?* (*Which, of all the addresses in the world, is your address?*)
¿**Cuáles son** tus zapatos?	*Which* (*of all the shoes*) *are your shoes?*

Compare the following questions.

—¿**Qué es** tarea?	—¿**Cuál es** la tarea?
—Tarea es un trabajo escrito que da el profesor para hacer en casa.	—La tarea para mañana es hacer las actividades 4 y 5 del cuaderno de ejercicios.

Notice that the question on the left is asking for a definition of what homework is while the one on the right is asking about a specific homework assignment.

Actividad 20 ¿Cuánto sabes? **Parte A:** Completa las siguientes preguntas sobre la cultura hispana con **qué** o **cuál/es.**

FLR link: **Lectura 3:** Deals with famous Hispanics.

Act. 20A: Have students complete the questions at home and check in class for accuracy.

1. ¿A ____qué____ hora almuerza la gente en España?
2. ¿____Cuál____ es un sinónimo de "pasarlo bien"?
3. ¿Con ____cuál____ de estas formas se despiden dos mujeres mexicanas jóvenes: un beso o un apretón de manos?
4. ¿____Qué____ es "tener un contratiempo"?
5. ¿____Qué/Cuáles____ películas ve más un mexicano: nacionales o extranjeras?
6. ¿____Qué____ significa ser hispano?
7. Se invita gente a una fiesta en Argentina a las diez de la noche. ¿A ____qué____ hora llegan los invitados?
8. ¿____Qué____ es una guayabera y en ____qué/cuáles____ países se lleva?
9. ¿____Cuál____ es el nombre de la mujer argentina que sirvió de inspiración para una obra de Broadway y una película con Madonna?
10. ¿____Cuáles____ son los dos países suramericanos que llevan el nombre de personajes históricos?
11. ¿____Qué____ es un "taco" en España? ¿Y en México?
12. ¿____Qué/Cuál____ moneda usan en México?
13. ¿____Cuál____ de las islas del Caribe es la más grande?
14. ¿____Cuál____ es la montaña más alta de América?

Parte B: En parejas, túrnense para hacer y contestar las preguntas anteriores. Si no saben la respuesta, digan **No sé. / No tengo idea. ¿Lo sabes tú?**

Act. 20B: Form pairs and have students alternate asking and answering questions. Check by asking each question. Answers are: 1. **a las 2:00 o más tarde** 2. **divertirse** 3. **un beso** 4. **cuando llegas tarde porque ocurre algo inesperado** 5. **extranjeras** 6. **Significa...** (*Answers will vary.*) 7. **a las 10:30, 11:00 o más tarde** 8. **una camisa, los países del Caribe y Centroamérica** 9. **Eva Perón** 10. **Bolivia (Bolívar), Colombia (Colón)** 11. **una mala palabra; algo que se come** 12. **el peso** 13. **Cuba** 14. **el Aconcagua en Argentina**. See the following **¿Lo sabían?**, **el Aconcagua** is the correct answer since the term **América** refers to the entire continent (**América** = North, Central, and South America) in Spanish.

¿LO SABÍAN?

En el mundo hispano y en la mayoría de los países del mundo, los estudiantes aprenden que hay cinco continentes y no siete como enseñan los libros de los Estados Unidos. Los cinco continentes son América, Europa, Asia, África y Oceanía. Por eso, en español normalmente no se habla de "las Américas" sino de "América" como un solo continente. Observa el uso de la palabra "América" en la pregunta 14 de la Actividad 20. Di cómo se traduce la siguiente oración que se podría escuchar en los Estados Unidos: *Mount McKinley is the tallest mountain in America*.

¿Lo sabían? Answer: **El monte McKinley es la montaña más alta de los Estados Unidos.**

IV. Avoiding Redundancies

Subject and Direct-Object Pronouns

Drill personal **a**:

1. Use a mirror to add humor and life to this presentation. Turn your back to your students and say what or who you see. **Veo a Brenda. Veo los zapatos de Lance. Lance, ¿son nuevos?** After a few examples, look at specific people and things and ask students **¿Qué/A quién veo?** Students respond.

2. Create a short narrative with different uses of **a**. Have students analyze why each **a** is or is not present. Uses to include are: **ir a** + *infinitive*; **ir a** + *art.* + *place*; verbs like **gustar**, and the personal **a.**

Read the following conversation and state what is unusual.

A: ¿Agustín invita a salir a Sara?
B: No, Agustín no invita a salir a Sara porque Agustín no conoce a Sara.
A: ¿Cuándo va a conocer a Sara Agustín?
B: No sé cuándo Agustín va a conocer a Sara.

Obviously there is a great deal of repetition in the conversation. Two ways of avoiding repetition are (1) substituting a subject pronoun (**yo, tú, Uds.,** etc.) for the subject or omitting the subject altogether and (2) substituting direct-object pronouns for direct-object nouns.

A: ¿Agustín invita a salir a Sara?
B: No, no la invita a salir porque él no la conoce.
A: ¿Cuándo va a conocerla?
B: No sé cuándo la va a conocer.

1. A direct object **(complemento directo)** usually receives the action of the verb directly. It answers the question *whom?* or *what?* Notice that when the direct object refers to a specific person or to a loved animal, the personal **a** precedes it.

No encuentro **las llaves.**	*I can't find the keys.*
No encuentro **a mi hijo.**	*I can't find my child.*
No encuentro **a mi perro.**	*I can't find my dog.*

You may want to explain the use of **a** with **tener** in cases other than possession, such as **Tengo a mi hermana en el hospital.**

Drill object pronouns:

1. Create redundant conversations like the one at the beginning of this section for students to fix.

2. Ask students whether they have certain items with them and have them answer using direct-object pronouns. T: **¿Tienes el carnet de estudiante contigo?** S: **Sí, lo tengo.** Possible items: **la chequera, la tarjeta de crédito, las llaves de tu coche/apartamento, el manual de ejercicios.**

Note: The personal **a** is not usually used after the verb **tener**: **Tengo una hermana.**

2. The direct-object pronouns are:

me	nos
te	os
lo, la	los, las

Sentences with direct objects	Sentences with direct-object pronouns
Anoto **el teléfono de la muchacha.**	**Lo** anoto.
Carlos ve **a su novia** dos veces por semana.	Carlos **la** ve dos veces por semana.
	Ella **me/te/os/nos** ve una vez por año.

Pobre Jaime, sus amigos quedan a una hora con él y no vienen, siempre **lo** dejan plantado.

3. Use direct-object pronouns:

a. before a conjugated verb

La ve dos veces por semana.
La quiere ver.
La va a ver.
La tiene que ver ahora.

b. after and attached to the infinitive

Quiere **verla.**
Va a **verla.**
Tiene que **verla** ahora.

You might mention **leísmo,** the use in Spain of **le/les** for **lo/los, la/las.** At this point, present as passive knowledge only.

Actividad 21 Miniconversaciones **Parte A:** Completa estas miniconversaciones con **a, al, a la, a los, a las,** o deja el espacio en blanco cuando sea necesario.

Remember:
a + el = al;
de + el = del.
This activity includes more uses of **a** besides the personal **a.** To review other uses, see Appendix E.

Act. 21A: Assign as HW and check in class. Have students analyze the different uses by making them justify their choices.

1. —¿Vas ____a____ cenar con Germán esta noche?
   —No, pero mañana sí.
2. —Buscamos ____a____ Felipe Yepes. ¿Sabe Ud. dónde está?
   —No tengo idea.
3. —¿Tus hijas continúan con sus clases de ballet?
   —Sí, pero tienen un problema, pues ____a____ ellas no les caen bien sus compañeritos.
4. —Todos los años visitamos ________ las islas del Caribe durante las vacaciones.
   —Y ¿este año no van ____a____ ir?
5. —¿Qué haces todos los días en el trabajo?
   —Escribo ________ cartas, mando ________ faxes, preparo ________ documentos y atiendo ____a (los)____ clientes.
6. —¿Puedes venir ____a____ mi casa esta tarde?
   —Me gustaría, pero tengo que pasear ____a____ Lulú, el perro de mi prima.
7. —¿Vas a ver ____al____ Sr. Loprete y ____a la____ Sra. Guerra esta tarde?
   —____A____ ella sí, pero ____a____ él no.

Act. 21B: Form pairs, allow students to select a mini-conversation (or assign one to each group), set a time limit, and check by having one or two groups present theirs to the class.

Parte B: En parejas, escojan una de las miniconversaciones y continúenla. Intenten crear una conversación de un mínimo de ocho líneas.

Actividad 22 En Los Ángeles La siguiente historia sobre un joven que vive en Los Ángeles contiene redundancias de sujeto y complemento directo que están en bastardilla (*italics*). Léela y después intenta reescribirla para que sea más aceptable.

EL DÍA DE LAS ELECCIONES

Información para todos los votantes

Una guía completa para nuevos y no tan nuevos votantes, incluso cómo empadronarse, cómo votar y cómo evaluar a los candidatos y sus plataformas

Soy de familia hispana, vivo en Los Ángeles con mis padres, mis hermanos y mi abuela. *Mi abuela* no habla inglés y por eso, cuando *mi abuela* necesita ir al médico, yo voy con *mi abuela.* Mientras el doctor examina *a mi abuela* para ver qué problema tiene, yo traduzco la con- 5 versación entre ellos. A veces es aburrido traducir *la conversación* porque mi abuela siempre tiene el mismo problema. Parece que *el problema* sigue *a mi abuela* por todas partes porque vamos al consultorio del doctor una vez por semana. Hay mucha gente mexicana en esta ciu- 10 dad y muchos saben inglés, otros estudian *inglés,* y otros no hablan *inglés* mucho. Sé que no es fácil aprender otro idioma y yo tuve suerte porque cuando era niño, aprendí *inglés* en la escuela y aprendí español en casa. Muchas personas, especialmente los mayores, que no hablan bien *inglés* tienen 15 miedo de participar activamente como ciudadanos. Por eso trabajo en un centro de votación que contrata a voluntarios. El centro entrena *a los voluntarios* durante un día y luego *los voluntarios* salen a hablar con la comunidad hispana sobre la importancia de votar. Vamos por lo general a supermercados adonde van muchos hispanos y le explicamos 20 a la gente que su voto cuenta y que es importante ejercer este derecho. Si no ejercen *este derecho* después no sirve protestar en contra del gobierno. Pronto va a haber elecciones locales y hay un candidato que no solamente tiene buenas ideas, sino que también tiene en cuenta los intereses de los hispanos. Por supuesto, yo pienso votar *a ese* 25 *candidato* porque vamos a beneficiarnos todos.

Act. 22: You may want to alert students that some italicized words will not be replaced, but simply deleted. If assigned as HW, have students peer edit each other's work. If done in class, students could work together. Answers will vary, so it may be good to have a few students read their versions. You may want to mention that **hispano** is the term preferred by some people of Hispanic origin to refer to themselves; others prefer **latino.** If you have heritage speakers in your class, ask what term they prefer. According to a survey in *Hispanic Magazine*, "Stereotypically, those who call themselves Hispanic are more assimilated, conservative, and young, while those who choose the term Latino tend to be liberal, older, and sometimes radical." (Source: From http://www.hispaniconline.com/magazine/BackIssues/2000/dec2000/polls/index.html; 11/29/2003, © Hispanic Publishing Group/HispanicOnline.com.)

Actividad 23 ¿Sabes quiénes...? En parejas, pregúntenle a su compañero/a si sabe qué grupo hispano hace las acciones que se indican. Sigan el modelo.

▶ decir la palabra "guagua" en vez de "autobús"
—¿Sabes quiénes dicen la palabra "guagua" en vez de "autobús"?
—Sí, la dicen los caribeños.

1. pronunciar la "ce" y la "zeta" como la "th" en inglés
2. usar el término "vos"
3. comer pan de muerto
4. decir "tacos"
5. generalmente no tener sangre indígena
6. decir la palabra "platicar" por "charlar"
7. tocar música con influencia de ritmos africanos

argentinos
caribeños (puertorriqueños, cubanos, dominicanos)
costarricenses
españoles
mexicanos

Act. 23: Answers: 1. **españoles** 2. **argentinos y costarricenses** 3. **mexicanos (para el Día de los Muertos)** 4. **españoles** 5. **españoles, caribeños (la mayoría de los indígenas se murieron por enfermedades) y argentinos (tienen el índice más bajo de indígenas en todo Suramérica)** 6. **mexicanos** 7. **caribeños**

Actividad 24 ¿Te pasan estas cosas? En parejas, averigüen si les pasan las siguientes cosas.

▶ —¿Te llaman por teléfono tus padres?

—Sí, me llaman mucho. —No, no me llaman nunca.

sus padres	llamarlo/la por teléfono visitarlo/la en la universidad
sus amigos	venir a visitarlo/la de otra universidad invitarlo/la a cenar criticarlo/la por algo
sus profesores	verlo/la fuera de las horas de oficina
su jefe	controlarlo/la mucho

Act. 24: Practice a few questions and possible answers. Form pairs, set a time limit, and begin.

Actividad 25 El jefe no nos escucha En grupos de tres, piensen en los jefes que han tenido y en otros jefes que conocen. Después, formen oraciones explicando cómo son los jefes en general. Sigan los modelos.

▶ Generalmente, no **nos ven** fuera de las horas laborales.

▶ Muchos de los jefes no **nos ven** fuera de las horas laborales, pero hay algunos que sí **nos ven**. Algunos incluso salen a tomar algo con nosotros.

1. escucharlos atentamente cuando Uds. hablan
2. respetarlos
3. conocerlos bien
4. considerarlos parte importante de la compañía
5. dejarlos salir temprano del trabajo en ocasiones especiales
6. invitarlos a tomar algo después del trabajo

Act. 25: Review phrases and words that are used to make generalizations: **algunos, pocos, normalmente, en general, generalmente, la mayoría,** etc. Write them on the board. Form groups of three, set a time limit, and begin. Compare groups' answers and try to reach a consensus.

Actividad 26 La primera salida **Parte A:** Lee lo que dicen un chico argentino y una chica mexicana sobre la primera vez que uno sale con alguien. Compara sus respuestas.

"En una primera salida típicamente el chico invita a la chica. Si él tiene auto, la pasa a buscar o si no, quedan en un lugar que puede ser un bar o un cine. La primera vez paga el chico porque es una cuestión social, pero hay muchos jóvenes que no tienen mucho dinero y a veces las chicas que no tienen mucho dinero **se aprovechan de** los chicos y salen con ellos sólo porque quieren salir. El chico muchas veces espera que ella le dé por lo menos un beso en la boca. En las próximas salidas generalmente pagan a medias y si se gustan, hay muchos más besos."

argentino

"Por tradición, el hombre se acerca e investiga sobre la mujer que le interesa. Por tradición, el hombre invita por primera vez después de platicar

◀ Pareja argentina.

Act. 26A: Option 1: Have students speed read each paragraph and follow with information questions. (You may want to project these paragraphs on an overhead.) Option 2: Have half the class read the first paragraph and half read the second, then form pairs and have each summarize what they have read for their partner.

Fuentes hispanas

se aprovechan de: they take advantage of

algunas veces con la mujer. Por tradición, el hombre la recoge en su casa y paga lo que sea que hagan (ir al cine, un café, una fiesta...). Por tradición, el hombre mantiene a su mujer y paga todos los gastos que tengan juntos. Hoy día hay mucha gente que no sigue las tradiciones porque no son muy prácticas. Entonces existen parejas que no dependen tanto de la diferencia de géneros. Así, a veces invita ella, a veces él o cada uno paga lo suyo."

mexicana

Act. 26B: Form groups, set a time limit, and begin. Check by having a group sharing and comparing the traditions in the United States with those in Mexico and Argentina.

Parte B: Ahora en grupos de tres, digan cómo es una primera salida en este país.

Do the corresponding CD-ROM and web activities to review the chapter topics.

Vocabulario activo

Verbos

-ar *verbs*

ahorrar (dinero/tiempo) — *to save (money/time)*
alquilar (videos) — *to rent (videos)*
charlar — *to chat*
cuidar (a) niños — *to baby-sit*
dibujar — *to draw*
escuchar música — *to listen to music*
faltar (a clase/al trabajo) — *to be absent (from class/work)*
flirtear/coquetear — *to flirt*
gastar (dinero) — *to spend (money)*
mirar (la) televisión — *to watch TV*
pasar la noche en vela — *to pull an all-nighter*
pasear al perro — *to walk the dog*
probar (o → ue) — *to taste; to try*
sacar buena/mala nota — *to get a good/bad grade*
trasnochar — *to stay up all night*

-er *verbs*

devolver (o → ue) — *to return (something)*
escoger — *to choose*
hacer investigación/dieta — *to do research/to be on a diet*
poder (o → ue) — *to be able to, can*
soler (o → ue) + *infinitive* — *to usually do + verb*
volver (o → ue) — *to return*

-ir *verbs*

asistir (a clase/a una reunión) — *to attend (class/a meeting)*
compartir — *to share*
contribuir — *to contribute*
discutir — *to argue; to discuss*
mentir (e → ie, i) — *to lie*
salir bien/mal (en un examen) — *to do well/poorly (on an exam)*
seguir (instrucciones/a + alguien) (e → i, i) — *to follow (instructions/someone)*

Verbos reflexivos

La rutina diaria

acostarse (o → ue) — *to lie down, go to bed*
afeitarse (la barba/las piernas/etc.) — *to shave (one's beard/legs/etc.)*
arreglarse — *to make oneself presentable*
bañarse — *to take a bath*
cepillarse (el pelo/los dientes) — *to brush (one's hair/teeth)*
despertarse (e → ie) — *to wake up*
desvestirse (e → i, i) — *to get undressed*
dormirse (o → ue, u) — *to fall asleep*
ducharse — *to take a shower*
lavarse (el pelo/las manos/la cara/etc.) — *to wash (one's hair/hands/face/etc.)*

maquillarse	*to put on makeup*
peinarse	*to comb (one's hair)*
ponerse + *item of clothing*	*to put on + item of clothing*
prepararse (para)	*to get ready (for)*
probarse ropa (o → ue)	*to try on clothes*
quitarse + *item of clothing*	*to take off + item of clothing*
secarse (el pelo/la cara/etc.)	*to dry (one's hair/face/etc.)*
sentarse (e → ie)	*to sit down*
vestirse (e → i, i)	*to get dressed*

Otros verbos que usan pronombres reflexivos

aburrirse (de)	*to become bored (with)*
acordarse (de) (o → ue)	*to remember*
caerse	*to fall down*
callarse	*to shut up*
darse cuenta (de)	*to realize*
despedirse (de) (e → i, i)	*to say good-by (to)*
divertirse (e → ie, i)	*to have fun, to have a good time*
enfadarse/enojarse	*to get mad*
equivocarse	*to err, to make a mistake*
interesarse (por)	*to take an interest (in)*
irse (de)	*to go away (from), to leave*
ocuparse (de)	*to take care (of)*
olvidarse (de)	*to forget (about)*
preocuparse (de/por)	*to worry (about); to take care (of)*
quejarse (de)	*to complain (about)*
reírse (de) (e → i, i)	*to laugh (at)*
sentirse (e → ie, i)	*to feel*

La vida nocturna

ir a una disco (discoteca) / ir a bailar	*to go to a disco / to go dancing*
sacar a bailar a alguien	*to ask someone to dance*
pasar tiempo con alguien	*to hang out with someone*
pedir algo de tomar	*to order something to drink*
ir a un bar	*to go to a bar, café*
ir al cine	*to go to the movies*
ir a un concierto	*to go to a concert*
sacar/comprar entradas	*to get/to buy tickets*
sentarse en la primera/segunda/última fila	*to sit in the first/second/last row*
ir detrás del escenario	*to go backstage*
el revendedor	*scalper*
ir a los videojuegos	*to go to the video arcade*
dejar plantado/a a alguien	*to stand someone up*
ligar (*España*)	*to pick someone up (at a club, bar, etc.)*
pasar a buscar a alguien (por/en un lugar)	*to pick someone up (at home, etc.)*
pasear con el auto	*to go cruising*
quedar a una hora con alguien	*to meet at an agreed upon time*
reunirse/juntarse con amigos	*to get together with friends*
salir a dar una vuelta	*to go cruising / for a ride / for a walk*
tener un contratiempo	*to have a mishap (that causes one to be late)*

Expresiones útiles

llamarle la atención	*to attract someone's attention*
ser un/a pesado/a	*to be a bore*
hace + (*time expression*) + que + *present*	*have been + -ing for (time expression)*
No sirve para nada quejarse / No vale la pena quejarse...	*It's not worth it to complain . . .*
Vale la pena callarse porque...	*It's worth it to keep quiet because . . .*
Tienes razón.	*You're right.*
¡No me digas! / ¿De veras?	*Really? / You're kidding.*
Yo también.	*I do too. / Me too.*
Yo tampoco.	*Neither do I. / Me neither.*
En cambio yo...	*Instead I . . . / Not me, I . . .*
¡Qué chévere! (*Caribe*)	*That's cool!*
¡Qué lástima!	*What a pity!*

Vocabulario personal

Capítulo 2

España: pasado y presente

Metas comunicativas

- narrar en el pasado (primera parte)
- hablar de cine
- decir la hora y la edad en el pasado

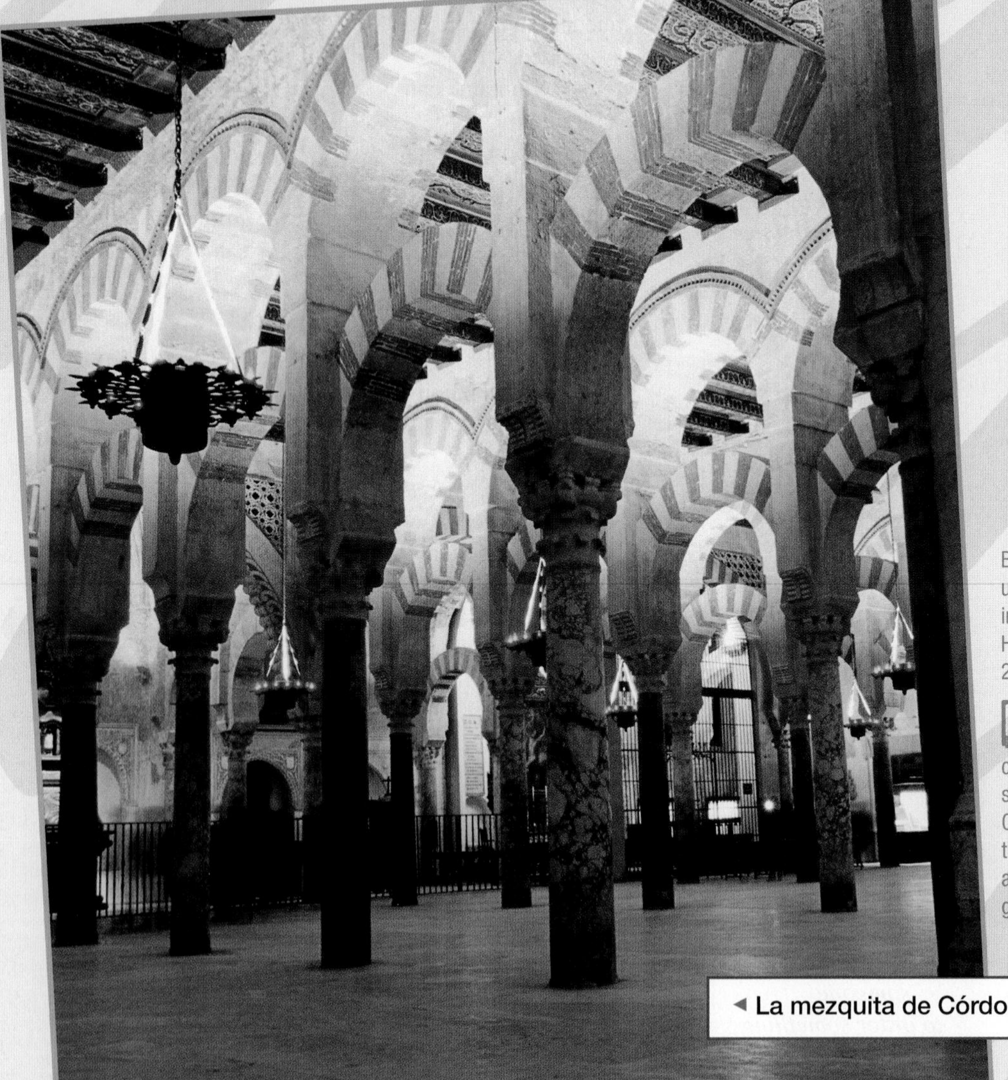

◄ La mezquita de Córdoba, España.

Besides assigning grammar, vocabulary, and **¿Lo sabían?**, the following activities may be prepared as HW: 3, 4, 5A and B, 7, 17A, 19, 22A, 24, 26 (involves research).

Show the chapter video episode at any point in the chapter that you see fit and do all or selected activities in class. Note: Content of the video supplements the cultural material in the chapter and activities reenter chapter grammar and vocabulary.

Un anuncio histórico

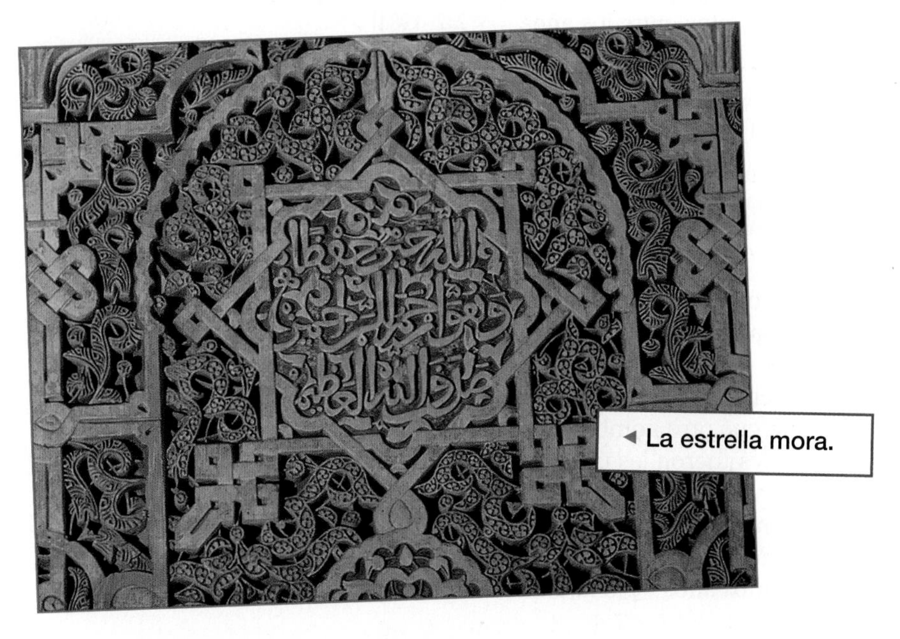

◄ La estrella mora.

Throughout this chapter, students will deal with historical facts presented through activities. Try to keep reviewing these facts in class warm-ups to give students a panoramic view of the history of Spain.

1. Practice **el** + *day* by telling students what they'll have to do for next Monday's/Tuesday's class. Ask what day an upcoming sports event or TV special will be.
2. Practice **los** + *day* by asking students what night certain TV shows are on or by asking them what days they have certain classes.
3. Practice **clave** by asking about key years in U.S. history. Tell students that **clave** is always singular (**los años clave).** You may also want to use other phrases like **palabra clave, ingrediente clave,** etc.

el lunes	on Monday
los lunes	on Mondays
(año) clave	key (year)

llave = key (*as in a car key*)

Actividad 1 Algo de historia **Parte A:** Antes de escuchar un anuncio comercial en la radio, habla sobre la siguiente información.

1. ciudades, países o zonas geográficas que relacionas con las siguientes religiones: el islam, el judaísmo y el catolicismo
2. religión que asocias con:
   - el *Tora*, la *Biblia*, el *Corán*
   - Mahoma, los reyes Fernando e Isabel de España, Maimónides
   - una iglesia, una sinagoga, una mezquita
3. año en que Colón llegó a América
4. tipo de gobierno que asocias con Francisco Franco (socialista, comunista, fascista, democrático)

Historia de España

Act. 1A: Inform students that Maimónides (1135–1204) was a Jewish physician and philosopher born in Spain.

Act. 1B: Before listening to the commercial, make sure students read the historical events. Check responses. Then, if you want, have students listen again and write the year each event took place; review large numbers prior to doing so. You could also practice large numbers by simply reading the numbers to the students as they wrote them after each event.

Parte B: Lee los siguientes acontecimientos de la historia española y luego, mientras escuchas el anuncio comercial, ponlos en orden cronológico.

__6__ Murió Franco y empezó la monarquía parlamentaria. [1975]
__1__ Los moros invadieron la Península Ibérica. [711]
__4__ España perdió sus últimas colonias. [1898]
__2__ Los judíos, los moros y los cristianos pudieron estudiar y trabajar juntos entre los años... [1252–1284]
__5__ Empezó la guerra civil. [1936]
__3__ Los Reyes Católicos expulsaron a los moros de la Península Ibérica. [1492]

Act. 2 Answers: 1. **moro** 2. **para llevar la palabra del Corán; Portugal y España** 3. **Alfonso X (el Sabio)** 4. **los Reyes Católicos** 5. **Cuba, Puerto Rico, Guam y las Islas Filipinas** 6. **781 años** 7. **406 años** 8. **36 años**

Actividad 2 Más información Escucha el anuncio comercial una vez más y contesta estas preguntas.

1. ¿Qué otro nombre se usa en España para musulmán?
2. ¿Por qué invadieron la Península Ibérica los musulmanes? ¿Sabes qué países forman esa península?
3. ¿Quién fue el rey español entre 1252 y 1284?
4. ¿Con qué otro nombre se conoce a Fernando y a Isabel?
5. ¿Cuáles fueron las últimas colonias que perdió España?
6. ¿Cuántos años estuvieron los moros en la Península Ibérica?
7. ¿Cuántos años duró la colonización española de América y la zona del Pacífico?
8. ¿Cuántos años duró la dictadura de Franco?

¿LO SABÍAN?

The marriage of Ferdinand and Isabel unified Aragon and Castilla. When the Moors were expelled in 1492, what we know today as modern Spain emerged. Catholicism was the religion of the state, and the publishing of the first grammar gave the Spanish language a sense of validity. It was the language and the religion that Columbus took with him to America.

Later in the chapter there will be a **¿Lo sabían?** on **el destape.**

destapar = to take the lid off

OTAN (Organización del Tratado del Atlántico Norte) = NATO

En el año 1492 ocurrieron tres acontecimientos de gran importancia, no sólo en la historia de España sino también en la historia mundial.

- Se publicó la primera gramática de la lengua española.
- Isabel y Fernando vencieron a los moros y expulsaron a los infieles, tanto moros como judíos, para tener en la península una sola religión, el catolicismo.
- La llegada de Colón a América marcó el principio del dominio y la colonización española en el Nuevo Mundo.

El año 1975 fue una fecha clave para la España moderna. Murió el general Francisco Franco y empezó el movimiento hacia la democracia con la institución de una monarquía parlamentaria bajo el rey Juan Carlos de Borbón. En el año 1977 se inició "el destape", un período de apertura, cambios sociales y una explosión de la libertad de expresión. En 1982 el país se unió a la OTAN y en 1986, España ingresó en la Comunidad Económica Europea (ahora la Unión Europea). ¿Cuál es la función de la OTAN? ¿En qué crees que se beneficia España al ser parte de la Unión Europea?

¡Viva el Rey!

Ya circula el euro

EL PRÍNCIPE FELIPE SE CASA CON UNA PERIODISTA

Do the corresponding CD-ROM and web activities as you study the chapter.

I. Narrating in the Past (Part One)

A. The Preterit

1. As you studied in previous Spanish courses, in order to speak about the past you need both the preterit **(pretérito)** and the imperfect **(imperfecto)**. This chapter will focus on the uses of the preterit and a few uses of the imperfect. In general terms, the preterit is dynamic and active and is used to move the narrative along while talking about the past. The preterit forms of regular verbs are as follows.

entr**ar**		perd**er***		viv**ir**	
entr**é**	entr**amos**	perd**í**	perd**imos**	viv**í**	viv**imos**
entr**aste**	entr**asteis**	perd**iste**	perd**isteis**	viv**iste**	viv**isteis**
entr**ó**	entr**aron**	perd**ió**	perd**ieron**	viv**ió**	viv**ieron**

*Note: **-ar** and **-er** stem-changing verbs do not have a stem change in the preterit. To review formation of the preterit and irregular forms, including **-ir** stem-changers, see Appendix A, pages 341–343.

2. Timelines can help you understand the uses of and relationships between different tenses. Examine the timelines as you read the examples.

Use the preterit:

a. to denote a completed state or an action.

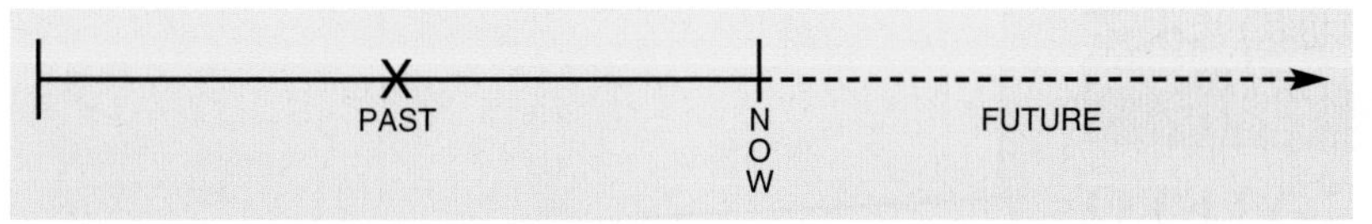

Los romanos **llegaron** a la Península Ibérica en el año 218 a. de C.	*The Romans arrived in the Iberian Peninsula in 218 B.C.*
Los romanos **construyeron** un acueducto en Segovia.	*The Romans built an aqueduct in Segovia.*

b. to express the beginning of a past action.

Los moros **comenzaron** la invasión en 711.	*The Moors began the invasion in 711.*
Cuando Pelayo ganó contra los moros en 718, **empezó** el período de la reconquista.	*When Pelayo won against the Moors in 718, the period of the Reconquest began.*

This chapter will focus on narrating events in the past, primarily using the preterit. Try to avoid questions or situations that necessitate use of past description and therefore the imperfect.

Presentation of the preterit: Provide input by telling students what you did last weekend or something that you did that bored you and something that you enjoyed. **El sábado pasado fui a... y me aburrí mucho, pero ayer vi... y me divertí un montón.** Elicit similar experiences from students.

Drill preterit forms:

1. Do a transformation drill. **Generalmente no miento, pero ayer...**
2. Ask students questions such as what movie they saw last week, what classes they had today/yesterday, and then ask: **¿A qué hora empezó? ¿A qué hora terminó? ¿Cuánto duró?**
3. Do a chain drill: **El fin de semana pasado el presidente...**
4. Have students tell you important events in movies they have seen. *Titanic:* **El barco chocó contra un témpano de hielo. La gente se murió.**
5. Practice reflexive forms by asking students about yesterday's morning or evening routine.

c. to express the end of a past action.

La dominación mora **terminó** en 1492. *Moorish domination ended in 1492.*

d. to express an action or state that occurred over a specific period of time. This time period is, many times, overtly expressed in the sentence.

La dominación mora **duró** 781 años. *Moorish domination lasted 781 years.*

Estuvieron en la península casi 800 años. *They were on the peninsula for almost 800 years.*

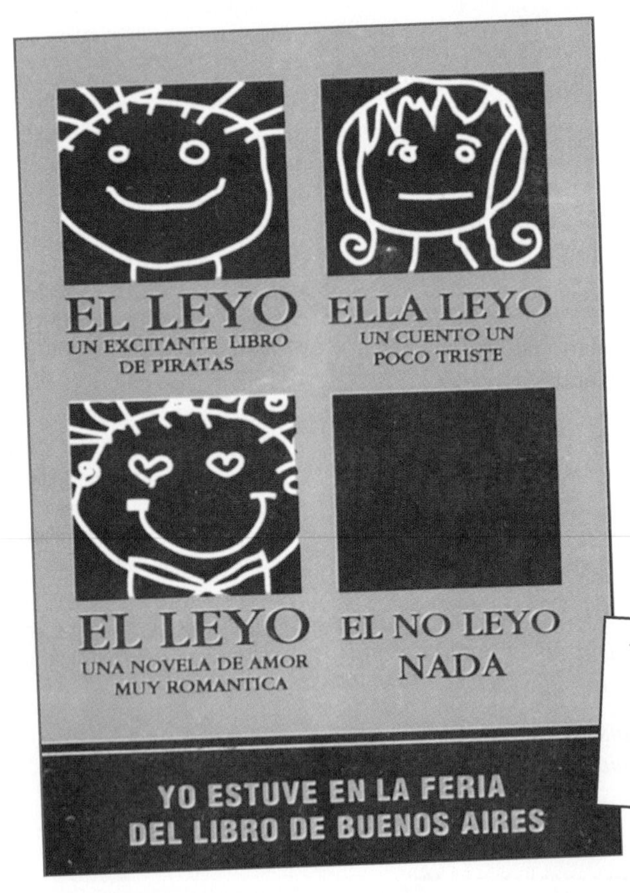

◄ Mucha gente no pone acentos en las mayúsculas porque las reglas de acentuación dicen que es opcional. Por eso dice aquí EL LEYO, y no ÉL LEYÓ. ¿Cuál fue el último libro que leíste tú?

Actividad 3 Analiza Examina las siguientes oraciones sobre la historia de España y la colonización del continente americano. Primero, subraya (*underline*) los verbos en el pretérito y segundo, indica cuál de los gráficos explica mejor el uso del pretérito en cada oración.

Act. 3: Can be assigned as HW. Prior to checking this activity, have students practice saying numbers. Then call on individuals to read sentences.

A. |———X———|- - - - - - - - ->

B. |———X. . . . .———|- - - - - - - - ->

C. |———. . . . .X———|- - - - - - - - ->

D. |———[X]———|- - - - - - - - ->

1. __D__ Isabel, junto con Fernando, gobernó una España unida desde 1492 hasta su muerte.
2. __B__ En 1502, empezó la colonización de las Antillas.
3. __A__ Isabel la Católica murió en Medina del Campo en 1504.
4. __D__ Desde 1510 hasta 1512, Juan Ponce de León fue gobernador de Puerto Rico.
5. __B__ En 1513, Juan Ponce de León inició la búsqueda de la Fuente de la Juventud en lo que hoy en día es la Florida.
6. __A__ En 1521, Hernán Cortés derrotó a los aztecas en la región que actualmente es México.
7. __A__ Francisco Pizarro capturó a Atahualpa, el último emperador inca, en 1532.
8. __C__ Pizarro completó la conquista del Imperio Inca en 1535.
9. __A__ Los españoles llegaron a lo que hoy día es Texas en 1720.
10. __B__ En 1769, los clérigos españoles comenzaron a fundar misiones en California para llevar la palabra de Dios a los indígenas.
11. __C__ En 1898 terminó la dominación española del continente americano.
12. __D__ Los españoles dominaron partes de Hispanoamérica y de los Estados Unidos durante más de cuatrocientos años.

To review large numbers, see Appendix G.

Actividad 4 El siglo XX Para aprender más sobre la España en el siglo XX, completa las siguientes oraciones con la forma correcta del verbo en el pretérito.

Act. 4: Assign as HW and check in class or do as a paired activity in class. When correcting, add additional information as you see fit.

Cuando los intelectuales huyen de un país por razones políticas, este éxodo se llama **fuga de cerebros**.

1. Durante y después de la guerra civil española, muchos intelectuales como los escritores Ramón Sender, Rafael Alberti y Francisco Ayala y músicos como Manuel de Falla y Pablo Casals ____salieron____ de España y ____vivieron____ en el exilio por no estar de acuerdo con el gobierno de Franco y por miedo de sufrir represalias por sus ideas. (salir, vivir)
2. En 1937 Picasso ____hizo____ el *Guernica*, un cuadro que conmemora la destrucción de un pueblo en el País Vasco en el norte de España. Desde 1939 hasta 1981 el Museo de Arte Moderno de Nueva York ____exhibió____ el cuadro. En 1981, seis años después del final de la dictadura de Franco, el cuadro ____volvió____ a España y ahora se lo puede ver en el Centro de Arte Reina Sofía en Madrid. (hacer, exhibir, volver)

s/z sound = za **ce** ci **zo** zu (empe**cé**, hi**zo**)

(continúa en la página siguiente)

Note: #3, students will research information on **La Pasionaria** in the last activity in the chapter. #6, Although Catalunya recognized stable gay relationships, the federal government did not. Thus this was a symbolic gesture on the part of the regional government.

The legalization of the Communist Party is representative of Spain's becoming a multiparty democracy.

la movida = nightlife in post-Franco Spain

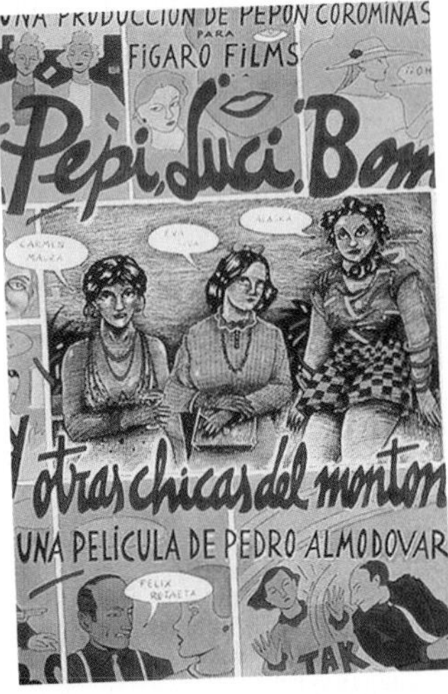

3. Dolores Ibárruri ___nació___ en Asturias en 1895. Los españoles la conocen como La Pasionaria, una famosa comunista española que ___dijo___ : "Antes morir de pie que vivir de rodillas". Durante la dictadura de Franco, ___se fue___ a vivir a la Unión Soviética donde ___pasó___ casi cuarenta años. ___Regresó___ a España en 1977, un mes después de la legalización del Partido Comunista Español. (nacer, decir, irse, pasar, regresar)
4. En mayo de 1976, ___apareció___ el periódico *El País*, un periódico que ___cambió___ la prensa española al permitir la libertad de palabra en la sección de opinión. (aparecer, cambiar)
5. En 1980, Pedro Almodóvar ___produjo___ la película *Pepi, Luci, Bom y otras chicas del montón* que ___mostró___ *"la movida"* de Madrid. La movida forma parte de la revolución cultural y sexual de la España posfranquista. (producir, mostrar)
6. Se ___legalizó___ el divorcio en 1981 y en 1985, el gobierno ___aprobó___ la ley del aborto pero sólo para casos muy especiales. En 1998, el gobierno regional de Cataluña ___aprobó___ la *Ley de Parejas de Cataluña* que ___reconoció___ la unión homosexual estable y les ___dio___ a los homosexuales todos los derechos que el gobierno regional le da a una pareja heterosexual. (legalizar, aprobar, aprobar, reconocer, dar)

El rey habló por televisión y otros militares que pensaban participar, no se levantaron. Después de horas de incertidumbre, la situación se resolvió y los militares que entraron en el Parlamento fueron detenidos.

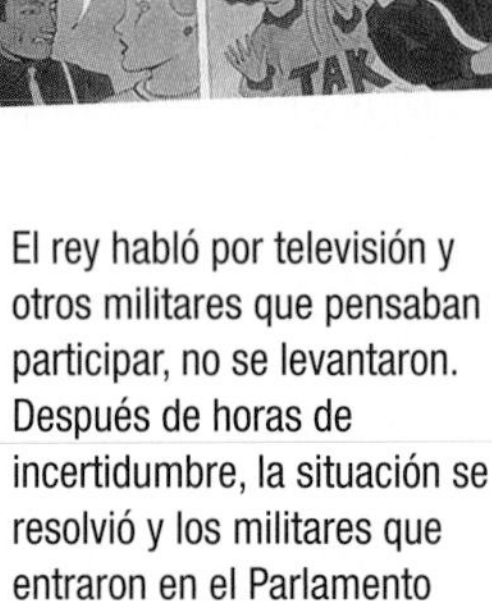

Act. 5: Assign Parts A and B as HW. Ask students what the effects of a successful coup could have been for Spain. Point out that for Spain membership in the EU was very important and would have been in jeopardy had the coup succeeded. Then, in class, discuss and do Parts B and C.

Actividad 5 Una historia personal **Parte A:** Lee lo que escribe un joven español sobre eventos históricos importantes que ocurrieron en las dos últimas décadas del siglo XX.

"El 23 de febrero de 1981: Este día es muy importante en la historia reciente de España porque un grupo de la Guardia Civil (similar a la policía) entró en el Parlamento con la intención de dar un golpe de estado. Por suerte no pudieron. Y además es mi cumpleaños.

El primero de enero de 1986: España entró en la Unión Europea. Sin duda fue una fecha muy importante en la historia de España porque marcó el fin del complejo de los españoles de ser un país atrasado con respecto a sus vecinos. La Unión Europea hoy les ofrece grandes posibilidades de trabajo y de convivencia a todos sus ciudadanos. Podemos viajar de un país a otro sin pasaporte y con la misma moneda y trabajar en cualquiera de los países de la Unión."

español

Parte B: Haz una lista de tres a cuatro acontecimientos históricos que tuvieron lugar durante tu vida hasta el año pasado, pero no escribas las fechas. Incluye por ejemplo: guerras, elecciones, muerte de personas famosas, accidentes graves (nucleares o desastres naturales como terremotos, erupciones volcánicas), actos de terrorismo, asesinatos, inventos, etc.

Parte C: Ahora, en parejas, háganse preguntas para ver si la otra persona sabe en qué año ocurrieron los acontecimientos que escribió cada uno.

▶ A: ¿En qué año fue la guerra con Iraq?
B: Fue en...
A: ¿En qué año no jugaron la Serie Mundial de béisbol?
B: No jugaron la Serie Mundial en...

Actividad 6 ¿Qué hiciste? **Parte A:** Marca en la primera columna las cosas que hiciste tú el fin de semana pasado. Después, en parejas, túrnense para preguntarle a su compañero/a si hizo las siguientes actividades el fin de semana pasado y marquen sólo las respuestas afirmativas en la segunda columna.

Act. 6A: Transition to Act. 6 by saying **Y este fin de semana, ¿leyeron alguna noticia importante sobre algo que ocurrió?** After students answer, tell them **Ahora vamos a hablar del pasado mucho más reciente y no tan serio. Vamos a hablar del fin de semana pasado.** Form pairs, set a time limit, and begin.

▶ —¿Miraste televisión el fin de semana pasado?

—Sí, miré televisión. —No, no miré televisión.

	Sí (yo)	Sí (mi compañero/a)
1. leer una noticia interesante	_____	_____
2. comer afuera y pedir un plato caro	_____	_____
3. conocer a alguien	_____	_____
4. dormir hasta muy tarde	_____	_____
5. hacer una llamada de larga distancia	_____	_____
6. jugar un deporte con pelota	_____	_____
7. alquilar un video	_____	_____
8. limpiar su cuarto	_____	_____
9. tocar un instrumento musical	_____	_____
10. pagar una cuenta	_____	_____
11. pensar en los próximos exámenes	_____	_____
12. decidir estudiar en vez de salir	_____	_____
13. ir a una fiesta	_____	_____
14. ver una película en el cine	_____	_____
15. vestirse con ropa elegante	_____	_____

Remember the following letter combinations when spelling preterit forms:

hard **c** sound = ca **que** qui co cu (to**qué**);

hard **g** sound = ga **gue** gui go gu (pa**gué**);

s/z sound = za **ce** ci **zo** zu (empe**cé**, hi**zo**).

Parte B: Ahora, cambia de pareja y cuéntale a otra persona algunas de las cosas que hiciste, algunas que hizo tu compañero/a y otras cosas que hicieron los dos.

Act. 6B: Change pairs, set a time limit. Check by asking who did what. You may want to highlight verbs with spelling changes that reflect pronunciation: **toqué, jugué, pagué.**

B. Narrating in the Past: Meanings Conveyed by Certain Verbs

Note: Verbs with changes in meaning will be recycled in the next two chapters when narrating and describing in the past are contrasted.

Drill changes in meaning:

1. Find out if students know anybody in the Foreign Language Department/the president of the university. Then ask **¿Cuándo lo/la conociste?**

2. Find out when students met their roommate/best friend.

3. In pairs, have students tell three things they had to do yesterday or last week. **¿Qué tuviste que hacer ayer/la semana pasada?**

4. Do a chain drill: **Anoche se cortó la luz y por eso no pude...**

5. Tell students they have a spoiled brother and their parents left them in charge of him last weekend. Have them say what the child refused to do. **No quiso estudiar. No quiso desayunar. No quiso bañarse.**

In Spanish, certain verbs may convey a different meaning in the preterit than they do in the present when translated into English. The meaning conveyed by the preterit in Spanish reflects the nature of the preterit itself, in that it moves the narration along by indicating a completed action or the beginning or end of an action.

	Present	Preterit
conocer (**a** + *person*)	to know (*someone or someplace*); to be acquainted with	met for the first time/began to know (*someone or someplace*)
saber (+ *information*)	to know (*something*)	found out (*something*)

Cuando Colón **supo** que a los portugueses no les interesaba su viaje, se fue a España. — *When Columbus found out that the Portuguese weren't interested in his trip, he went to Spain.*

En 1486 **conoció a** los Reyes Católicos en Córdoba. — *In 1486 he met the Catholic Kings in Cordoba.*

	Present	Preterit
no querer (+ *infinitive*)	not to want (*to do something*)	refused and didn't (*do something*)
no poder (+ *infinitive*)	not to be able (*to do something*)	was/were not able and didn't (*do something*)

Los portugueses **no quisieron** financiar las ideas de Colón; por eso **no pudo** hacer su viaje. — *The Portuguese refused to finance Columbus' ideas; that is why he couldn't make the trip.*

	Present	Preterit
tener que (+ *infinitive*)	to have to (*do something*)	had to and did (*do something*)

Colón **tuvo que** ir a España para pedir dinero. — *Columbus had to go to Spain to ask for money.*

Act. 7: Assign as HW and check in class or do as a paired activity in class.

Actividad 7 Este semestre Habla de la siguiente información sobre el principio de este semestre.

1. Nombra a tres personas a quienes conociste el primer día de clases.
2. ¿Cuándo supiste los nombres de tus profesores, el semestre pasado o al principio del semestre?
3. ¿Intentaste entrar en una clase y no pudiste? Si contestas que sí, ¿cuál fue?
4. ¿Cuáles son dos cosas que tuviste que hacer cuando llegaste a la universidad?

Actividad 8 ¿Qué tal la fiesta? En parejas, usen las siguientes ideas para contarle a su compañero/a sobre la última fiesta a la cual asistieron.

1. cómo supiste de la fiesta
2. adónde fuiste
3. quién organizó la fiesta
4. cómo fuiste (caminaste, fuiste en metro/coche)
5. una persona a quien conociste
6. quiénes más asistieron
7. qué sirvieron para beber/comer
8. tres cosas que hiciste
9. si lo pasaste bien o mal
10. si sueles ir a muchas fiestas

Act. 8: You may want to instruct students to take notes so that they'll be prepared in the check phase when you have students report back about their partner's party. Then when checking, ask them about the party their partner attended.

C. Indicating When Actions Took Place: Time Expressions

Practice time expressions:

1. Ask **¿Cuándo fuiste al gimnasio/a la piscina/al laboratorio? ¿A qué hora te despertaste/desayunaste/almorzaste? ¿Cuánto tiempo hace que llamaste a tus padres?**

2. Ask about events in the news, Spanish history, or history in general. **¿Cuándo se murió Francisco Franco? ¿Cuándo se inventó el teléfono? ¿Cuándo fue la última vez que los Packers ganaron el Superbowl? ¿Y la primera vez?**

1. To move the narration along in the past, use adverbs of time and other expressions of time that tell when an action took place. Some common expressions include:

de repente	suddenly
a las tres/cuatro/etc.	at three o'clock/four o'clock/etc.
anoche	last night
anteanoche	the night before last
ayer	yesterday
anteayer	the day before yesterday
el lunes/fin de semana/mes/año/siglo pasado	last Monday/weekend/month/year/century
la semana/década pasada	last week/decade
en (el año) 1588	in (the year) 1588
en el 98	in '98

Anteanoche miré una película sobre la guerra civil española. — *The night before last I saw a movie about the Spanish Civil War.*

Esta guerra empezó **en 1936.** — *This war started in 1936.*

2. To express how long ago an action took place, use one of the following formulas.

Hace + *period of time* + **(que)** + *verb in the preterit*
Verb in the preterit + **hace** + *period of time*

Que is frequently omitted in speech except when asking questions.

¿Cuánto tiempo **hace que** los europeos **probaron** el chocolate? — *How long ago did Europeans try chocolate?*

Hace casi cinco siglos (**que**) los europeos **probaron** el chocolate por primera vez.

Los europeos **probaron** el chocolate por primera vez **hace casi cinco siglos.**

Europeans tried chocolate for the first time almost five centuries ago.

3. Use the following expressions with the preterit tense to denote how long an action occurred:

desde... hasta...	from . . . until . . .
por...* años/semanas/horas	for . . . years/weeks/hours
durante...* años/semanas/horas	during . . . years/weeks/hours

El dominio español de Hispanoamérica duró **desde finales del siglo XV hasta finales del siglo XIX.**

The Spanish dominance of Hispanic America lasted from the end of the 15th century until the end of the 19th century.

*Note: It is common to specify a time period with or without **por** or **durante.**

España dominó Hispanoamérica **por/durante 406 años.**

España dominó Hispanoamérica **406 años.**

Act. 9: Practice questions stressing that some questions are about the past and others about the present. Instruct students to ask one question of one student and then to move on to avoid bunching. Another option is to form two concentric circles and have the inner circle move to the right after asking and answering a question. Also encourage them to ask the questions out of order.

Actividad 9 Averigua Usa la siguiente información para hacerles preguntas a tus compañeros sobre el presente y el pasado. Escribe sólo el nombre de los que contesten que sí.

▶ —¿Asististe a un concierto de música rap el fin de semana pasado?

—Sí, asistí a un concierto. (escribe el nombre de la persona)

—No, no asistí a ningún concierto.

	Nombre
ir a la oficina de un profesor el semestre pasado	________
tener cuatro materias este semestre	________
elegir una clase fácil el semestre pasado	________
darse cuenta de algo importante la semana pasada	________
hacer ejercicio ayer durante 30 minutos	________
faltar al trabajo anteayer	________
dejar de salir con alguien el mes pasado	________
hacer experimentos en un laboratorio todas las semanas	________
sentirse muy cansado/a al principio del semestre	________
generalmente discutir con su compañero/a de habitación (o novio/a, esposo/a o un pariente)	________
tener un/a estudiante de posgrado como profesor/a el semestre pasado	________
pasar una noche en vela el semestre pasado	________

Actividad 10 **¿Qué hizo?** En parejas, túrnense para contar lo que Uds. creen que hizo su profesor/a ayer. Usen cada una de estas expresiones de tiempo en cualquier orden: **ayer, primero, después, más tarde, luego, por la tarde, durante dos horas, a las cinco, por la noche.** Tachen (*Cross out*) las expresiones al usarlas.

Act. 10: Form pairs and instruct students to be inventive. Check by calling on individuals to tell different parts. When finished, tell them what you really did.

Actividad 11 **¿Cuánto hace?** En parejas, túrnense para preguntarse cuánto hace que hicieron las siguientes cosas y averiguar más información sobre cada una.

Act. 11: Form pairs, practice questions, and begin activity. You may want to remind students of the fact that **que** is often omitted in everyday speech.

► A: ¿Cuánto tiempo hace que fuiste al cine con un amigo?
B: Hace tres días que fui al cine. / Fui al cine anteanoche.
A: ¿Qué viste?
B: ...

1. alquilar un video bueno
2. invitar a alguien a cenar
3. conducir por lo menos dos horas
4. enojarse con alguien
5. ir a otra ciudad
6. venir a esta universidad
7. olvidarse de algo importante
8. faltar a una clase
9. gastar más de cien dólares en algo
10. hacer una locura (*something crazy*)

D. Indicating Sequence: Adverbs of Time

In order to narrate a series of actions, it is necessary to use words that indicate when the actions occurred in relation to other actions. The following words and phrases are used to express sequence.

Practice adverbs of time:

Do a chain drill: **El sábado antes de levantarse, Cameron Díaz leyó una revista en la cama. Tan pronto como se levantó...** (etc.)

antes	before
antes de + *infinitive*	before *verb* + -ing
primero	first
más tarde/luego	later/then
después	later/then/afterwards
después de + *infinitive*	after *verb* + -ing
tan pronto como/en cuanto	as soon as
inmediatamente	immediately
enseguida	at once
finalmente	finally
al terminar	after finishing

Preposition + infinitive: después **de** volver

Enseguida may be written as one word or two: **en seguida.**

Note: When sequencing events use **más tarde, luego,** and **después.** Only use **entonces** to indicate a result and not to indicate "later" or "afterwards". **Estaba cansada y entonces (por eso) me fui a dormir.**

Act. 12: Form pairs, set up activity, set a time limit, and begin. Check by having two students perform for the class.

Actividad 12 Un día terrible En parejas, creen una historia sobre el día terrible que tuvo un amigo de Uds. usando las expresiones de la columna A en el orden en que aparecen y las acciones de la columna B en orden lógico.

A	B
1. Esta mañana...	ponerse dos medias de diferente color
2. En cuanto...	salir de la casa tarde
3. Luego...	llegar a clase con la ropa mojada de sudor (*soaked with sweat*)
4. Después...	entrar en la ducha / quemarse con agua caliente
5. Más tarde...	levantarse tarde
6. Tan pronto como...	correr a clase cansadísimo/a
7. Enseguida...	tomar el autobús equivocado
8. Finalmente...	bajar del autobús / caerse

Act. 13: Model activity by telling students in detail what you did yesterday morning. Form groups, set a time limit, and begin. Have a few people report back. As they report back, focus on the difference between **después** and **después de** by posing questions to the class using these terms or by using faded cues **Tiffany se cepilló los dientes después de...** vs. **Tiffany se duchó y después...**

Actividad 13 Tu día, ayer En grupos de tres, cuéntenle a sus compañeros con muchos detalles qué hicieron ayer. Usen palabras como: **primero, luego, más tarde, después de** + *infinitivo*.

WWW *La arquitectura española*

Actividad 14 Sus vacaciones **Parte A:** Lee esta parte del diario de un turista sobre las vacaciones que tomó en Granada y luego responde a las preguntas de tu profesor/a.

... por la mañana subí la calle hacia la Alhambra, un castillo moro increíble. Al llegar, por todas partes había gitanas que querían venderme flores; todo era muy caótico pero luego entré en la Alhambra —un lugar donde había vivido un sultán con su harén— y eso era otro mundo. Primero visité las diferentes salas decorada cada una con diseños geométricos y escritura árabe; algunas veces había poemas en las paredes. Pero lo que más me impresionó fue el constante sonido del agua. Había agua por todas partes como en el Patio de los Leones. Luego visitamos los baños y un guía nos explicó que en el siglo XIV había baños y que los moros tenían agua fría, agua caliente y agua perfumada. Después de salir de la Alhambra, pensé en que el sultán se bañaba mientras que los europeos podían pasar un año sin bañarse —si no me equivoco, creo que los europeos, o sea los cristianos, asociaban el acto de bañarse con ser pagano, o sea no creer en Dios...

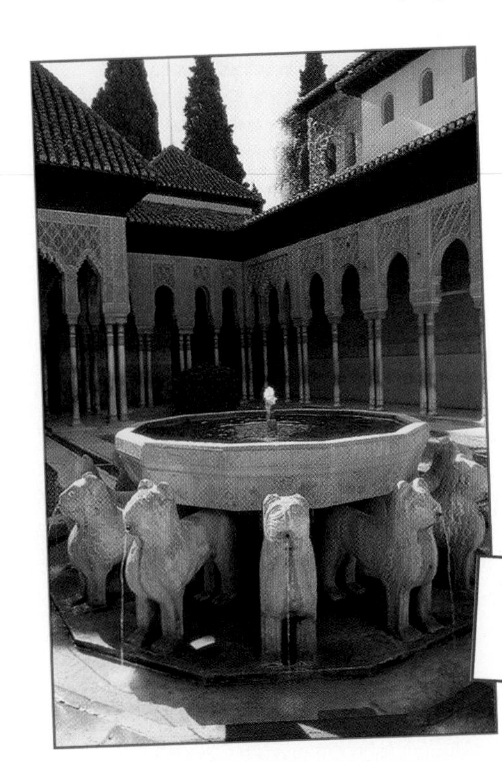

El Patio de los Leones en la Alhambra, un palacio moro en Granada, España.

Act. 14A: Allow time for students to read the paragraph on Granada and then ask comprehension questions. Note: a short walk from the Alhambra and a little higher up is the Generalife, a summer palace of the Moors. The cathedral of Granada houses the tombs of Ferdinand and Isabel.

Parte B: En parejas, usen las siguientes ideas para contarle a su compañero/a sobre sus últimas vacaciones. Recuerden usar palabras como: **primero, luego, después, después de** + *infinitivo*.

adónde fuiste	cuánto costó	qué cosas hiciste
cuánto tiempo estuviste	cómo viajaste	a quién conociste
con quién fuiste	qué lugares visitaste	

Al escuchar sobre las vacaciones de su compañero/a, reaccionen usando una de estas expresiones.

Para expresar sorpresa:	**¡Por Dios! ¡Por el amor de Dios!**
Para comentar positivamente sobre algo:	**¡Qué bueno! ¡Qué divertido!**
Para pedir más información:	**¿Y después qué? Cuéntame más.**

Act. 14B: Form pairs, set a time limit, and begin. Have a few tell about their vacations while the class asks questions and reacts.

E. Past Actions That Preceded Other Past Actions: The Pluperfect

When narrating in the past, you frequently refer to an action that preceded another action in the past. Spanish uses the pluperfect tense (had + *past participle*) to express an action that occurred before another. To form the pluperfect tense (**pluscuamperfecto**), use a form of the verb **haber** in the imperfect + *past participle.*

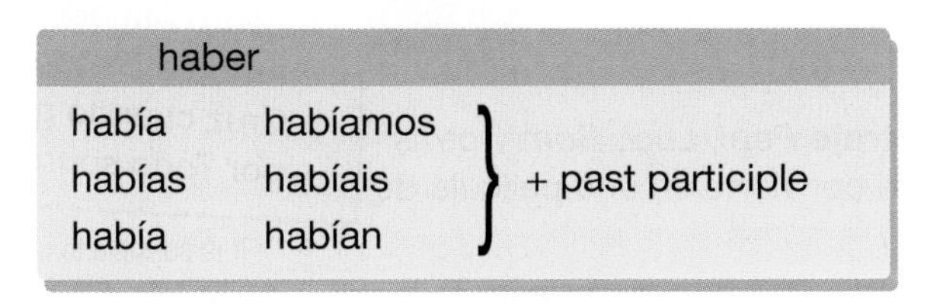

haber		
había	habíamos	+ past participle
habías	habíais	
había	habían	

To review the formation of past participles, see page Appendix A, pages 348–349. Common irregulars include: **abierto, dicho, hecho, visto.**

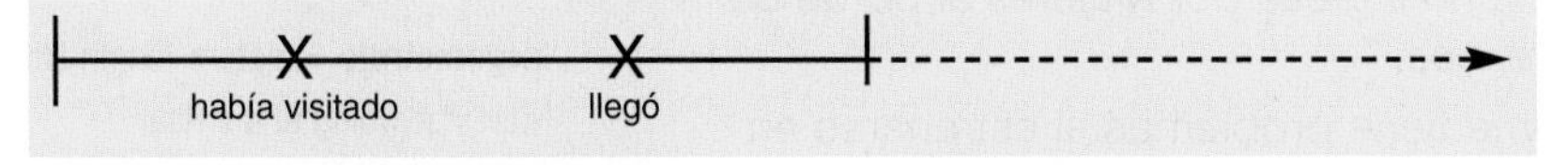

Leif Ericsson ya **había visitado** América cuando **llegó** Colón.	*Leif Ericsson had already visited America when Columbus arrived.*

Note: **Ya** is frequently used before the pluperfect to emphasize that an action had *already* occurred before another took place.

E. Practice the pluperfect:

1. Make a list of things that students do before starting the university. Items may include: **tomar exámenes de A.P., visitar la universidad, hablar con su consejero/a académico/a, conocer a su compañero/a de cuarto, recibir su número de teléfono, recibir su dirección de correo electrónico, abrir una cuenta en el banco,** etc. Have students say what they had done before entering the university.

2. Use two or three famous people your students know well and have them tell you what they had done prior to doing something else: **Cuando J Lo empezó a salir con Ben Affleck, ya... Cuando Hillary Clinton ganó las elecciones para ser senadora del estado de Nueva York, ya...** (etc.)

Note: The past participle always ends in **-o** when it is part of a verb phrase.

Act. 15: Set up activity by having students construct the questions, set a time limit, and begin. Check by asking a few questions.

Actividad 15 ¿Ya habías...? En parejas, háganse preguntas sobre su pasado. Sigan el modelo.

► viajar a Europa / terminar la escuela secundaria
—¿Ya habías viajado a Europa cuando terminaste la escuela secundaria?
—Sí, fui con mis padres en 2003. / —No, ...

1. sacar la licencia de manejar / empezar el tercer año de la escuela secundaria
2. aprender a leer / empezar el primer grado de la primaria
3. vivir en el mismo lugar toda la vida / venir a estudiar aquí
4. ver una película de Almodóvar / tomar esta clase

Act. 16: Ask students if they have seen any of Almodóvar's movies. Discuss the significance of his work in post-Franco Spain and use it as a lead in to the **¿Lo sabían?** reading about the **destape** that follows.

Actividad 16 La vida de Pedro Almodóvar **Parte A:** Pedro Almodóvar, cineasta español, pasó su infancia y su juventud bajo la dictadura de Franco. Es uno de los representantes del destape cultural que ocurrió después de la muerte de Franco. Lee su información biográfica para responder a las preguntas de tu profesor/a.

▲ Pedro Almodóvar (centro) con Antonio Banderas y Penélope Cruz cuando ganó el Oscar por *Todo sobre mi madre.*

Pedro Almodóvar	
1949	Nace* en Calzada de Calatrava, España, durante la dictadura de Francisco Franco.
1965	A los 16 años llega a Madrid justo después de cerrarse la Escuela Oficial de Cine.
1965–1980	Consigue trabajo en una compañía telefónica donde se queda por 12 años. Filma **cortometrajes** con una cámara de 8 mm. En 1975 muere Franco.
1980	Hace su primer **largometraje** *Pepi, Luci, Bom y otras chicas del montón* que se convierte en una película de culto entre los españoles.
1984	Su película *¿Qué he hecho yo para merecer esto?*, una comedia negra, recibe aclamación mundial.
1988	Recibe una nominación para el Oscar a la mejor película de habla no inglesa por *Mujeres al borde de un ataque de nervios*.
1989	Su película *Átame* tiene problemas al estrenarse en los EE.UU. *La Motion Picture Association of America* la califica con "X". Almodóvar y otros artistas empiezan un proceso legal contra la MPAA y logran que la MPAA establezca una nueva clasificación, la de "NC17".
2000	Gana el Oscar a la mejor película de habla no inglesa por *Todo sobre mi madre.*
2003	Gana el Oscar al mejor **guion** original por *Hable con ella.*

* It is possible to use the present tense instead of the preterit to narrate in the past. This is called the **presente histórico**.

cortometraje = film "short"

largometraje = feature-length film

Note: According to the Real Academia de la Lengua Española, since **guion** is a monosyllabic word that does not have a homonym (as do **él/el** or **sí/si**), it does not need a written accent. Since this rule is relatively new, you may want to alert students that they may see it spelled **guión** or **guion**.

guion = script (screenplay)

Parte B: Ahora usa la siguiente información para formar oraciones sobre su vida. ¡Ojo! Algunos verbos deben estar en el pretérito y otros en el pluscuamperfecto.

▶ Franco subir al poder / nacer Almodóvar
Franco ya había subido al poder cuando nació Almodóvar.

1. llegar a Madrid / la Escuela Oficial de Cine cerrarse
2. morir Franco / hacer *Pepi, Luci, Bom y otras chicas del montón*
3. recibir aclamación mundial / recibir una nominación para el Oscar a la mejor película de habla no inglesa por *Mujeres al borde de un ataque de nervios*
4. la MPAA darle una clasificación de "X" a *Átame* / la MPAA establecer la clasificación de "NC17"
5. ganar el Oscar al mejor guion original / ganar el Oscar a la mejor película de habla no inglesa

Before reading, ask students what they think **destape** might be. Remind them of the meaning of the word and that this period occurred after almost 40 years of dictatorship. Set a time limit for students to read the description and ask comprehension questions when finished. Ask students to use adjectives to describe the tone.

¿LO SABÍAN?

Después de la muerte de Franco, España pasó por una época llamada "el destape". Pedro Almodóvar dirigió, escribió y actuó en películas durante esa época. ¿Exactamente qué fue el destape? Para saber, lee lo que dice una madrileña.

"El destape efectivamente, fue una época muy curiosa que empezó en el 75, año de la muerte de Franco. Se legaliza en la Semana Santa de 1976 el Partido Comunista. Se aprueba la Constitución en el 78. La represión existente en vida de Franco deja de existir, y pasamos a una política abierta y permisiva. Surgieron muchas revistas con orientaciones muy diversas que escribían sin censura, algo que era totalmente nuevo para muchos españoles. Dentro de estas revistas estaban las que hablaban un poco de todo, política, cotilleos, economía y sexualidad (algo impensable) e incluían cantidad de fotos de chicas ligeras de ropa o en *topless* (destapadas). Todos los artículos que acompañaban estas fotos hablaban de "la liberación de la mujer", "de que las españolas éramos retrógradas", "de cómo vivían las europeas (nosotras al parecer no lo éramos) suecas, francesas, alemanas", etc. La "movida madrileña", equiparable en su concepto al "destape", fue un movimiento de libertad y bullicio que llenó las calles hasta las madrugadas, y que se trasladaba de un barrio a otro, que llenó de asombro a las personas conservadoras, y que resultó ser una expresión de una cultura joven y sin censura. Fue como la fiebre, una fuerte subida y después todo volvió a la normalidad."

española

Act. 17A: Transition into Act. 17 by telling students that **el destape** was an important event in this person's life. Show your **línea de la vida** on an overhead and tell them that these are important personal events in your life. Only include important dates. Encourage students to ask you what happened on those dates. Set a time limit and have them write down their own life lines. If this portion is assigned as HW, show yours the day you give the assignment to prepare students to do their own.

Actividad 17 La línea de tu vida **Parte A:** En la siguiente línea marca un mínimo de cinco años importantes de tu vida. Algunas posibilidades son: el año en que naciste, el año en que recibiste un premio o tu equipo ganó una competencia, el año en que trabajaste por primera vez. Marca los años, pero no escribas qué hiciste esos años.

Act. 17B: Form pairs and set a time limit.

Parte B: En parejas, muéstrense su línea y pregúntense sobre las fechas importantes de su vida. Usen expresiones como: **¿Qué pasó en...?, ¿En qué año (terminaste la escuela secundaria)?, ¿Ya habías... cuando...?**

Act. 17C: Give students a minute to write one or two sentences about their partner. Call on a few people to check.

Parte C: Ahora hablen de la vida de su compañero/a diciendo oraciones como la siguiente.

▶ Ella ya **había estudiado** un poco de español cuando **fue** a México por primera vez.

II. Discussing Movies

El cine

El cine

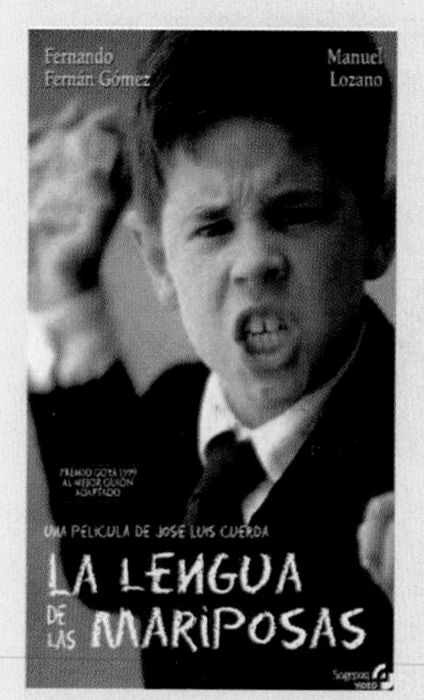

Ficha técnica

La lengua de las mariposas

España, 1999

Castellano, color, 94 minutos

Clasificación moral: Todos los públicos

Drama

Director: José Luis Cuerda

Actores: Fernando Fernán Gómez (Don Gregorio), Manuel Lozano (Moncho), Uxía Blanco (Rosa), Gonzalo Martín Uriarte (Ramón), Alexis de los Santos (Andrés), Guillermo Toledo (O'lis)

Guion: Rafael Azcona y José Luis Cuerda, basado en la novela *¿Qué me quieres, amor?* de Manuel Rivas

Producción: Mónica Martínez, Myriam Mateos

Fotografía: Javier Salmones

Música: Alejandro Amenábar

Sinopsis: Moncho (Manuel Lozano), un niño, que en 1936, a los ocho años asiste a la escuela primaria por primera vez. La historia ocurre en un pueblo de la provincia de Galicia y coincide con el comienzo de la guerra civil española. A medida que avanza el año escolar, Moncho forma una relación especial con su maestro (Fernando Fernán Gómez), el profesor que nunca les pega a los estudiantes, que le enseña a Moncho sobre el mundo, la vida y la importancia de que las mariposas tengan la lengua en forma de espiral. Pero el 18 de julio de ese año las cosas cambian para siempre cuando empieza la guerra civil española.

Clasificación moral = Rating

This film was rated "**Todos los públicos**" in Spain, but received a rating of R in the U.S. and 18A in Canada.

See note on **guion** at the bottom of p. 52.

Palabras relacionadas con el cine

el argumento	plot
la banda sonora	sound track
la clasificación moral	rating
las colas/los trailers	previews
la crítica	critique
el/la crítico/a de cine	movie critic
el estreno; estrenarse	premiere/opening; to premiere
el género	genre
de ciencia ficción	
comedia	
de espionaje	spy movie
documental	
drama	
infantil	
melodrama	
las películas mudas	silent films
el papel de...	the role of . . .
hacer el papel del malo	to play the role of the bad guy
el personaje	character
el premio	award
producir	to produce
el vestuario	costumes

El cine

1. Give definitions and have students provide the terms: **Ebert escribe esto. ¿Qué son PG, R, X? Cuando vas al cine y ves una película la primera noche que la dan, vas al...** (etc.)

2. Have students classify old movies by genre. *Bowling for Columbine, E.T., Agente 007 contra el Dr. No, Aladino, Psicosis, Casablanca,* etc.

El personaje is always masculine: **Me gustó el personaje que hizo Penélope Cruz en *Todo sobre mi madre.***

Otras palabras relacionadas con el cine

el actor/la actriz
la actuación
actuar
el/la director/a
los efectos especiales
filmar
la fotografía
el/la productor/a

Frases relacionadas con el cine

dar una película	to show a movie
seguir / estar en cartelera	to still be showing / "Now playing"
ser muy hollywoodense	to be like a Hollywood movie
ser una película taquillera	to be a blockbuster

Actividad 18 Definiciones En parejas, una persona debe dar definiciones y la otra persona tiene que adivinar qué palabra o frase es. Usen frases como: **Es la persona que..., Es un tipo de película en que..., Es el lugar donde...,** etc.

Act. 18: Set up by giving a few examples, form pairs, set a time limit, and begin. When finished, have a few students give definitions for the class.

Act. 19: Assign as HW or do in class. Follow up by asking about movies based on historical events. Many films are based on or loosely based on history. In *La lengua de las mariposas* one can see the different factions of the Spanish Civil War in a fictitious town in Galicia. Other movies that are based on real events include *Romero* (about the assassination of Archbishop Romero in El Salvador), *Missing* (about the assassination of an American reporter in Chile during the Pinochet coup), *El Norte* (about problems in Guatemala that drove illegal immigration to the U.S.), and *The Mission* (about Jesuit missions in South America and the first encounters with the indigenous people). Ask students about other films like these that they might know (*Bowling for Columbine, Schindler's List, The Pianist,* etc.)

Actividad 19 La película Mira la ficha técnica de la película *La lengua de las mariposas* en la página 54 y contesta estas preguntas.

1. ¿Quién dirigió la película?
2. ¿Quiénes son los protagonistas?
3. El guion no fue original, sino adaptado. ¿Adaptado de qué?
4. ¿Dónde se filmó la película y cuándo se estrenó?
5. ¿De qué género es?
6. ¿Ganó algún premio?
7. Lee la sinopsis. ¿Te gustaría ver esta película? ¿Por qué sí o no?

Actividad 20 El género En grupos de tres, piensen en las películas que están dando ahora mismo y hagan lo siguiente.

1. Clasifíquenlas por género.
2. Comenten si las bandas sonoras son buenas, malas o no son de importancia.
3. Comenten sobre la reacción de los críticos.
4. Nombren una película que vieron últimamente que no es un éxito de taquilla pero que vale la pena ver.
5. Comenten si todas las películas taquilleras son muy hollywoodenses o no.

Act. 21: If the Oscars have not occurred and nominations have not yet been made, simply do the activity. If the nominees are out, but the awards have not yet been given, you may want to provide students with a list of the nominees to decide. If the Oscars just occurred, tell students they were not in agreement and have them create their own list. When finished have a group sharing. As students mention their favorite films, react if you know that a Latino actor played a role. Then ask students to mention actors from Spanish-speaking countries. Some Spanish-speaking actors include: Antonio Banderas, Javier Bardem, and Penelope Cruz (Spain); Benicio del Toro (Puerto Rico); Salma Hayek (Mexico).

Actividad 21 Los Oscars En grupos de cinco, decidan qué películas o personas deben recibir el Oscar este año en las siguientes categorías.

1. la mejor película
2. la mejor dirección
3. el mejor actor
4. la mejor actriz
5. el mejor guion original/adaptado
6. los mejores efectos especiales
7. el mejor vestuario

Act. 22: Prior to doing the activity, describe your favorite movie as an example and then either do it in pairs in class or assign it as HW and have students discuss the film with a partner the next day. When giving a synopsis, you may want to use present tense to avoid problems with preterit vs. imperfect in the description (**Es una película sobre una familia que vive en...**).

Actividad 22 Mi favorita **Parte A:** Piensa en tu película favorita. Después, prepárate para hablar de esa película con otra persona para convencerla de que debe alquilar la película o ir a verla si todavía sigue en cartelera. Piensa en lo siguiente y prepárate para dar una pequeña sinopsis de la película.

el/la director/a; los protagonistas
la banda sonora; la fotografía
si el guion está basado en un hecho real, una novela, un cuento, etc.
dónde la filmaron y en qué año se estrenó
si recibió alguna nominación o premio

Parte B: En parejas, hable cada uno de su película favorita.

III. Stating Time and Age in the Past

The Imperfect

You saw how the preterit is used to move the narrative along. In this section you will see how the imperfect sets the background or scene for past events. Time and age, in a broad sense, help provide background information.

Drill **time** and **age** in the past:

1. In pairs, have students quickly ask each other **¿Qué hora era cuando te acostaste anoche?** and **¿Qué hora era cuando sonó el despertador esta mañana?** Have a few groups report back their findings. Find out who slept the least and the most.

2. Write on the board world events that happened during students' lifetimes, or brainstorm a list: **Clinton ganó la presidencia (1996). Linda McCartney murió (1998). Los Broncos de Denver ganaron el Superbowl (1999). La princesa Diana y la Madre Teresa murieron (1997).** Then, ask how old students were when these events occurred.

1. To tell time in the past, use **era/eran** + *the time.*

A: ¿Qué hora **era** cuando empezó la película?	*What time was it when the movie started?*
B: **Era** la una y cuarto.	*It was a quarter after one.*
A: ¿Qué hora **era** cuando terminó?	*What time was it when it ended?*
B: **Eran** las tres y pico.	*It was a little after three.*

2. To state someone's age in the past, use a form of the verb **tener** in the imperfect + *age.*

Pedro Almodóvar **tenía 16 años** cuando se mudó a Madrid.	*Pedro Almodóvar was 16 when he moved to Madrid.*

The word **años** is necessary when expressing age: **Pedro Almodóvar tenía 16 años.** *Pedro Almodóvar was 16 (years old).*

Actividad 23 ¿Qué hiciste el viernes pasado? **Parte A:** Mira la lista de acciones y tacha las cosas que no hiciste el viernes pasado.

Act. 23A: Explain premise and set a time limit for students to cross out items.

levantarte	estudiar
ducharte	hacer ejercicio
desayunar	ver una película
asistir a tu primera clase	cenar
almorzar	reunirte con amigos
volver a casa	acostarte

Parte B: En parejas, intercámbiense las listas. Pregúntenle a su compañero/a qué hora era cuando hizo las cosas de la lista que no están tachadas. Miren el modelo e intenten variar sus preguntas.

Act. 23B: Practice asking and answering questions, form pairs, set a time limit, and begin. Check by asking individuals a few questions.

▶ —¿Qué hora era cuando te levantaste? / —¿A qué hora te levantaste?

—Eran las ocho y media cuando me levanté. / —Me levanté a las ocho y media.

Act. 23C: Check when finished to compare eating times, movie times, etc.

Parte C: Lean el siguiente párrafo que describe lo que hizo un joven español de 26 años el viernes pasado y comparen las horas a las que Uds. y él hicieron acciones similares.

▶ Se levantó a las 9, pero yo me levanté a las...

Fuente hispana

"Eran las 9:00 a. m. cuando me desperté el viernes. Me duché y desayuné tranquilamente y después empecé a estudiar para una asignatura. Eran las 11:30 cuando cogí el coche y conduje a la universidad para asistir a una hora de clase. Luego volví a casa a eso de la 1:00, encendí el ordenador y leí el correo electrónico. Era la 1:45 cuando preparé la comida. Comí solo y después de comer, leí el periódico en el sofá y luego dormí un poco. Eran las 5:00 cuando empecé a estudiar otra vez y estudié hasta las 8. Entonces me preparé para ir a nadar y fui a nadar por media hora. Eran las 9:15 cuando volví a casa y entonces mi familia y yo cenamos. Luego fui al cine con unos amigos. La película empezó a las 10:30. Al salir de la película tomamos una cerveza en un bar. Allí hablamos un rato y después se fue cada uno a su casa. Eran las 2:00 de la mañana cuando llegué a casa."

español

Act. 24: May be assigned as HW. Do as a whole-class activity or in pairs. If in pairs, have students switch roles when finished. Check by focusing on some questions: which student has the youngest father, how many were 17 when they graduated from high school, and how many were 18, etc.

Actividad 24 Tenía... Contesta estas preguntas sobre ti y tu familia.

1. ¿Cuántos años tenían tus padres cuando se conocieron? ¿Dónde se conocieron?
2. ¿Cuántos años tenía tu madre cuando tú naciste? ¿Y tu padre?
3. ¿Tienes un/a hermano/a menor? ¿Cuántos años tenías cuando nació?
4. ¿Tienes un/a hermano/a mayor? ¿Cuántos años tenía cuando tú naciste?
5. ¿Tienes un/a hijo/a o un/a sobrino/a? ¿Cuántos años tenías tú cuando nació?
6. ¿Cuántos años tenías cuando te graduaste de la escuela secundaria?
7. ¿Cuántos años vas a tener al terminar tus estudios universitarios?

Act. 25: Form pairs assigning A and B roles. Have all A's cover B's table and vice versa, and make sure they don't peek! Practice asking a few questions. Check by asking how old explorers were when they died or when certain events took place.

Actividad 25 La historia de la conquista En parejas, una persona cubre el cuadro A y la otra persona cubre el cuadro B de la página 59. Háganse preguntas para intercambiar la siguiente información y completar su cuadro sobre personajes famosos de la conquista.

a. cuándo nacieron
b. dónde nacieron
c. qué cosas importantes hicieron
d. cuántos años tenían cuando hicieron algunas de esas cosas
e. cuándo murieron y qué edad tenían cuando murieron

▶ A: ¿Cuándo nació Ponce de León?
B: Nació en... ¿Cuándo murió Ponce de León?
A: Murió en...

◀ Grabado al aguafuerte del inca Atahualpa a los pies de Francisco Pizarro.

A

	Fechas	Nacionalidad	Datos importantes
Juan Ponce de León	________–1521	________	________, fundar San Juan, ________
Américo Vespucio	1451–________	italiano	________, hacer expediciones a América del Sur y América Central desde 1497 hasta 1503
Álvaro Núñez Cabeza de Vaca	1490–________	________	ser explorador, explorar el suroeste de los Estados Unidos y llegar al Golfo de California, ________
Francisco Pizarro	1471–________	________	ser líder de la conquista del Perú desde 1530 hasta 1535

B

	Fechas	Nacionalidad	Datos importantes
Juan Ponce de León	1460–________	español	ser gobernador de Puerto Rico desde 1510 hasta 1512, ________, explorar la Florida en 1513
Américo Vespucio	1451–1512	________	ser explorador, hacer expediciones a ________ y ________
Álvaro Núñez Cabeza de Vaca	________–1557	español	ser explorador, ________ y ________, ser gobernador de Paraguay desde 1541 hasta 1542
Francisco Pizarro	________–1541	español	________

Actividad 26 Los famosos Busca en Internet la siguiente información sobre uno de los famosos de la lista. Ven preparado/a para presentarle esta información al resto de la clase.

- dónde nació
- cuándo murió
- cuántos años tenía cuando murió
- qué hizo

Andrés Segovia (guitarrista)
La Pasionaria (una de las líderes del partido comunista español)
Ernest Hemingway (escritor —busca información sobre lo que hizo en España)
Federico García Lorca (dramaturgo, poeta)
Manuel de Falla (compositor de música clásica)
Isabel la Católica (reina de España)
Torquemada (inquisidor)
Maimónides (filósofo y médico judío)

Act. 26: Assign specific people to individual students based on their interests if possible. Use people from the list or others of your choosing. In class, form groups and have students inform the others about their person.

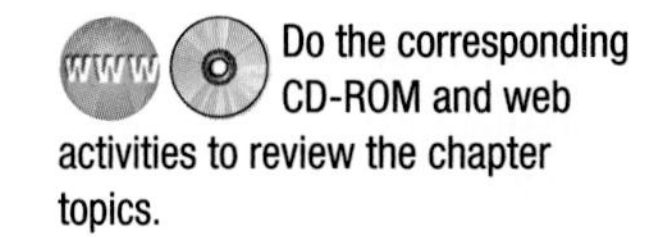

Do the corresponding CD-ROM and web activities to review the chapter topics.

Vocabulario activo

Expresiones de tiempo

de repente — *suddenly*
a las tres/cuatro/etc. — *at three o'clock/four o'clock/etc.*
anoche — *last night*
anteanoche — *the night before last*
anteayer — *the day before yesterday*
ayer — *yesterday*
la semana/década pasada — *last week/decade*
el lunes/fin de semana/mes/año/siglo pasado — *last Monday/weekend/month/year/century*
en (el año) 1588 — *in (the year) 1588*
en el 98 — *in '98*

desde... hasta... — *from . . . until . . .*
durante... años/semanas/horas — *during . . . years/weeks/hours*
por... años/semanas/horas — *for . . . years/weeks/hours*

Palabras para indicar secuencia

al terminar — *after finishing*
antes — *before*
antes de + *infinitive* — *before verb + -ing*
después — *later/then/afterwards*
después de + *infinitive* — *after verb + -ing*
enseguida — *at once*
finalmente — *finally*
inmediatamente — *immediately*
luego/más tarde — *later/then*
primero — *first*
tan pronto como/en cuanto — *as soon as*

El cine

el actor/la actriz — *actor/actress*
la actuación — *acting*
actuar — *to act*
el argumento — *plot*
la banda sonora — *sound track*
la clasificación moral — *rating*
las colas/los trailers — *previews*
la crítica — *critique*
el/la crítico/a de cine — *movie critic*
el/la director/a — *director*
los efectos especiales — *special effects*
estrenarse — *to premiere*
el estreno — *premiere/opening*
filmar — *to film*
la fotografía — *photography*
el género — *genre*
- comedia — *comedy*
- de ciencia ficción — *science fiction*
- de espionaje — *spy movie*
- documental — *documentary*
- drama — *drama*
- infantil — *children's movie*
- melodrama — *melodrama*
- las películas mudas — *silent films*

el guion — *script*
el papel de... — *the role of . . .*
- hacer el papel del malo — *to play the role of the bad guy*

el personaje — *character*
el premio — *award*
producir — *to produce*
el/la productor/a — *producer*
el vestuario — *costumes*

Frases relacionadas con el cine

dar una película — *to show a movie*
seguir / estar en cartelera — *to still be showing / "Now playing"*
ser muy hollywoodense — *to be like a Hollywood movie*
ser una película taquillera — *to be a blockbuster*

Expresiones útiles

(año) clave	*key (year)*
hacer una locura	*to do something crazy*
el lunes	*on Monday*
los lunes	*on Mondays*
ya	*already*
Cuéntame más.	*Tell me more.*
¡Por Dios! ¡Por el amor de Dios!	*My gosh/God!*
¡Qué bueno!	*That's great!*
¡Qué divertido!	*How fun!*
¿Y después qué?	*And then what?*

Vocabulario personal

Capítulo 3

La América precolombina

Metas comunicativas

- narrar en el pasado (segunda parte)
- describir personas y cosas
- indicar el beneficiario de una acción

May be assigned: Grammar, vocabulary, **¿Lo sabían?,** Act. 4, 5, 6, 7, 12A, 21A, 25A, 27, 28, 31A. The following activities can be read in class (Act. 11A and Act. 15A) and the second part can be prepared orally at home to retell in class the next day. This allows students to have time to think (Act. 11B and Act. 15B).

Show the chapter video episode at any point in the chapter that you see fit and do all or selected activities in class. Note: Content of the video supplements the cultural material in the chapter and activities reenter chapter grammar and vocabulary.

◄ Pequeña estatua de la diosa Chihuateteo en Veracruz, México.

La leyenda del maíz

Había una vez...	Once upon a time there was/were . . .
¿A que no saben...?	Bet you don't know . . . ?
No saben la sorpresa que se llevó cuando...	You wouldn't believe how surprised he/she was when . . .

Practice expressions: Write them on the board and tell students an abridged version of a well-known fairy tale such as **Ricitos de oro y los tres ositos,** using the expressions. Then have them repeat all expressions with key points of the fairy tale. Use the concept of a fairy tale as an introduction to legends. Ask students to describe the characteristics of each before doing Act. 1.

Actividad 1 **¿Qué sucedió?** **Parte A:** La locutora de un programa de radio para niños va a contar una leyenda tolteca sobre cómo llegó el maíz a la tierra. El personaje principal de la leyenda se llama Quetzalcóatl. Antes de escucharla, en grupos de tres, miren los dibujos que también cuentan la leyenda e intenten adivinar qué sucedió.

Act. 1A: Form groups of three, give instructions, set a time limit, and begin. Check by having a few groups relate their stories. Correctness of story line is not an issue; accept all possibilities. The purpose is to make predictions prior to listening.

1.

2.

3.

4.

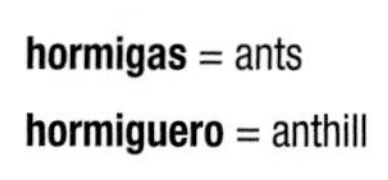
hormigas = ants
hormiguero = anthill

5.

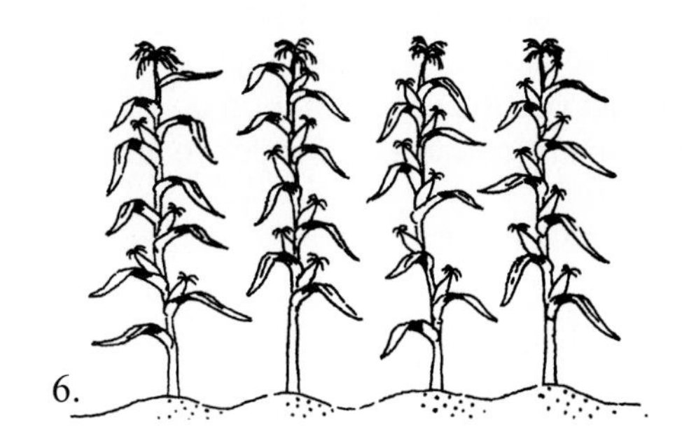
6.

Act. 1B: Play legend, next have students compare their predictions with the legend in groups, and then have groups share what they understood.

Act. 1C: Play legend and pause at various points asking questions to recreate the entire story with details.

Parte B: Ahora escuchen la leyenda y al terminar, discutan en su grupo si su interpretación era correcta. De no ser así, resuman qué ocurrió. 

Parte C: Escuchen la leyenda otra vez y agreguen (*add*) detalles, especialmente sobre cómo consiguió Quetzalcóatl los granos de maíz y qué hizo con ellos. 

 *Leyendas*

Act. 2: Have students state what the five presents were: **coral, oro, plata, esmeraldas y maíz.**

Actividad 2 Los regalos Discutan cuál de los cinco regalos de los dioses fue el mejor para los toltecas y expliquen por qué. Después, digan cuál de los cinco regalos les interesó más a los españoles durante su dominación de Hispanoamérica y por qué.

¿LO SABÍAN?

Quetzalcóatl, el dios emplumado, ocupa un lugar de mucha importancia en la mitología mexicana. En una leyenda se le atribuye la creación de la raza humana. Se dice que descendió de la tierra de los muertos y encontró unos huesos, vertió (*shed*) su propia sangre sobre ellos y así creó a los seres humanos. También se dice que les enseñó a los habitantes de la tierra a tejer telas, a hacer mosaicos y a cortar y pulir el jade. Además inventó el calendario y les enseñó a los seres humanos la astronomía. Algunas leyendas cuentan que Quetzalcóatl era de color blanco y que tenía barba. Por eso, cuando Cortés llegó a México, Moctezuma, que era el líder azteca, creyó que había vuelto Quetzalcóatl y lo recibió amigablemente. Esto le facilitó a Cortés la conquista de México. Describe un personaje mitológico de gran importancia en el folclore de tu país.

▲ Cabeza de piedra del dios Quetzalcóatl en la antigua ciudad de Teotihuacán, que está en las afueras de la ciudad de México.

Paul Bunyan is one possible choice as a mythological character.

I. Narrating in the Past (Part Two)

Do the corresponding CD-ROM and web activities as you study the chapter.

A. Preterit and Imperfect: Part One

In Chapter 2, you reviewed narration in the past using the preterit. You learned to use the preterit to refer to a completed past action or to focus on the beginning or end of past actions. You also learned how to express time and age using the imperfect. In this section you will review the forms, as well as other uses of the imperfect and how it is used with the preterit to narrate past events.

1. The imperfect is formed as follows.

estar		hacer		dormir	
est**aba**	est**ábamos**	hac**ía**	hac**íamos**	dorm**ía**	dorm**íamos**
est**abas**	est**abais**	hac**ías**	hac**íais**	dorm**ías**	dorm**íais**
est**aba**	est**aban**	hac**ía**	hac**ían**	dorm**ía**	dorm**ían**

For irregular forms, see Appendix A.

2. Use the imperfect:

a. to describe past actions in progress in which neither the beginning nor the end of the action matters. Compare the following examples.

Drill actions in progress:

Do a short chain drill: Have one student say what he/she was doing yesterday at 8:15 P.M. Have the next student repeat what the first student was doing, what he/she was doing, and so on. Every four or five students start over with a new time.

Ayer a las siete **leía** otra leyenda tolteca.

Yesterday at seven he was reading another Toltec legend (action in progress, start or end of action not important).

Ayer a las siete **terminó** de leer otra leyenda tolteca.

Yesterday at seven he finished reading another Toltec legend (end of an action).

Drill actions in progress with **mientras:**

Do a completion drill: Tell your students they have a lazy roommate. **Ayer mientras yo limpiaba la casa, él/ella...**

b. to describe two or more actions in progress that occurred simultaneously. Use **mientras** or **y** to connect two clauses containing simultaneous ongoing actions.

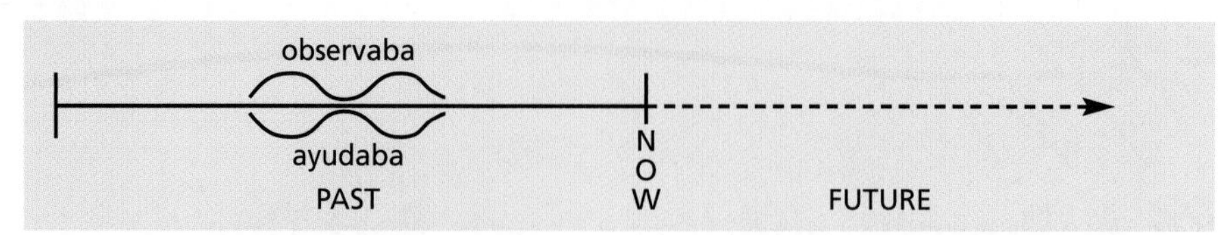

La diosa Tierra **observaba** a su hijo Quetzalcóatl **mientras** él **ayudaba** a los toltecas.	*Mother Earth was observing her son Quetzalcóatl while he was helping the Toltecs.*
Mientras hablaba con sus padres, siempre les **pedía** inspiración.	*While he was talking to his parents, he was always asking them for inspiration.*
Él **seguía** a las hormigas y **miraba** lo que **hacían**.	*He was following the ants and watching what they were doing.*

Note: Past actions in progress can also be expressed using the imperfect progressive. It gives greater emphasis to the ongoing nature of the action than the imperfect. Form it by using the imperfect of **estar** + *present participle.*

Mientras **hablaba/estaba hablando** con sus padres, **pensaba/estaba pensando** cómo ayudar a los toltecas.	*While he was talking to his parents, he was thinking about how to help the Toltecs.*

Drill interrupted actions in progress:

Brainstorm four or five actions in progress and list them on the board. Then assign one to each pair of students and ask them to provide an interesting interruption. **Me bañaba cuando un pato entró por la ventana y empezó a nadar en la bañera.**

Hand pairs of students slips of paper and have them act out individual sentences for the class. **Caminaba por la calle cuando alguien me robó el dinero. Alguien tocó a la puerta y el perro ladró. Tocaba el piano cuando el teléfono sonó.** (etc.)

c. to describe an action in progress in the past that was interrupted by another action. Use the preterit for the interrupting action and **cuando** to connect the two clauses. Compare the following sentences.

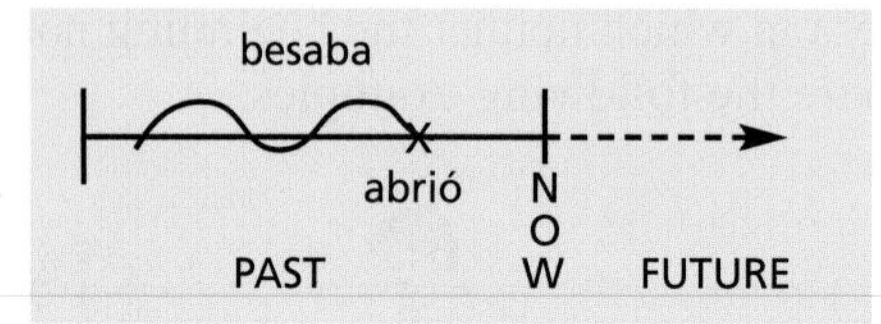

besó
abrió
PAST
NOW
FUTURE

Quetzalcóatl **besaba/estaba besando** a su novia **cuando** su padre **abrió** la puerta.	Quetzalcóatl **besó** a su novia y su padre abrió la puerta.
Quetzalcóatl was kissing his girlfriend (action in progress) when his father opened the door (interrupting action). [Ok, so it wasn't part of the real legend . . .]	*Quetzalcóatl kissed his girlfriend and his father opened the door. (First Quetzalcóatl kissed her, then his father opened the door.)*
Cuando Quetzalcóatl **entró** al hormiguero, las hormigas **trabajaban/estaban trabajando** como locas.	**Cuando** Quetzalcóatl **entró** al hormiguero, **tomó** los cuatro granitos y **se escapó.**
When Quetzalcóatl entered the anthill (interrupting action), the ants were working like crazy (action in progress).	*When Quetzalcóatl entered the anthill (onset of an action), he took the four grains (completed action) and escaped (completed action).*

Actividad 3 ¿Qué hacías? En parejas, túrnense para preguntarle a la otra persona sobre su pasado. Hagan preguntas como: **¿Qué hacías ayer a las 2:30 de la tarde? ¿Dónde estabas...?**

1. ayer a las 10:15 de la mañana
2. en esta época el año pasado
3. en junio hace dos años
4. a las 9:20 de la noche el sábado pasado
5. en noviembre del año pasado
6. en agosto del año pasado

Act. 3: Practice question asking and some possible answers. Form pairs, set a time limit, and begin. Have students alternate asking questions. Check by asking a few students about their partners' activities.

Actividad 4 Acciones simultáneas En parejas, digan qué hacía cada vecino en su apartamento e inventen lo que hacía su pariente mientras tanto.

▶ la señora del 3º B / hablar por teléfono, / su hija / ? ? ?
Mientras la señora del 3º B hablaba/estaba hablando por teléfono, su hija jugaba/estaba jugando en el baño con el lápiz de labios.

1. el Sr. Pérez del 1º B / mirar televisión, / su esposa / ? ? ?
2. el niño del 5º A / hacer la tarea, / su hermana / ? ? ?
3. la mujer del 7º C / dar a luz (*give birth*) en su casa, / su esposo / ? ? ?
4. la niña del 3º B / tocar el piano, / su profesora de piano / ? ? ?
5. la abuelita del 4 º A / dormir, / sus nietos traviesos (*mischievous*) / ? ? ?

Act. 4: Assign as HW. Prior to checking, review ordinal numbers. Check or do in class, having students create other possible endings for the sample sentence. Encourage originality. Form pairs, set a time limit, and begin. Check by calling on volunteers.

Actividad 5 La fiesta de último momento A las ocho de la noche, Esteban decidió hacer una fiesta. Llamó a sus amigos y les dijo que fueran a su casa inmediatamente, así, tal y como estaban. Lee cómo fue cada persona y adivina lo que hacía cuando llamó Esteban.

▶ Enrique fue con pantalones cortos, camiseta y pesas.
Enrique hacía ejercicio/estaba haciendo ejercicio cuando llamó Esteban.

1. Rosa fue con pijamas.
2. Carlos tenía solamente parte de los bigotes.
3. Antonio fue con una guía de televisión.
4. Clara fue con una toalla solamente.
5. Fernando y Marcos llevaban delantales de cocina y cucharas de madera.
6. Humberto fue con el pelo mojado y un secador de pelo.
7. Andrés llevaba sólo un zapato.
8. Laura e Isabel fueron con pintura en la cara y con brochas (*paint brushes*).

Act. 5: Option 1: Assign as HW and check in class. Option 2: Do in pairs in class and follow with a check.

Act. 6: Assign as HW or do in class. Make sure students understand that box A contains actions in progress interrupted by actions from box B. Model activity, form pairs, set a time limit, and begin. Have students share their sentences with the class.

Actividad 6 Situaciones En parejas, combinen las acciones de la caja A con las acciones de la caja B para contar qué les ocurrió a diferentes personas de su clase de español cuando estaban haciendo ciertas cosas. Finalmente digan qué hicieron estas personas después. Sigan el modelo.

▶ afeitarse cortarse la luz

John se afeitaba cuando se cortó la luz y por eso usó su afeitadora manual para terminar de afeitarse en el auto.

A	B	C
1. ducharse 2. caminar por la calle 3. manejar por la autopista 4. cocinar un huevo en el microondas 5. bajar las escaleras 6. pasear al perro	morder a una persona explotar caerse ver a su novio/a con otro/a chocar con otro carro acabarse el agua caliente	¿Qué hizo/hicieron después?

B. Preterit and Imperfect: Part Two

FLR link: Lectura 1

You have been practicing the use of the imperfect to refer to past actions or states that were in progress. In this section you will review other uses of the imperfect.

Read this narration of a children's story.

Jack y Jill *salieron* de casa a buscar agua y *subieron* una cuesta. El pobre Jack *se cayó* y *se rompió* la coronilla y Jill *se cayó* también. Nunca *recogieron* el agua.

Now read the following version of the same story.

había = there was/were

Jack y Jill *salieron* de casa a buscar agua y *subieron* una cuesta. La cuesta **era** muy grande y **había** muchas piedras que **dificultaban** la subida. Jack y Jill no **llevaban** botas de montaña ni **tenían** cuerdas ni otros aparatos para poder subir. El pobre Jack no **era** muy ágil y *se cayó* y *se rompió* la coronilla. Jill tampoco **tenía** mucha coordinación y, por eso, *se cayó* también. Nunca *recogieron* el agua.

In the preceding paragraph, the boldface verbs are in the imperfect and the ones in italics are in the preterit. Which tense is used to describe or set the scene? Which is used to move the action along? If you answered imperfect to the first question and preterit to the second, you were correct. It is by combining the two that you can describe past events and convey your thoughts about them.

1. Use the preterit:

a. to express a completed action or state.
b. to denote the beginning or the end of a past action or state.
c. to express an action or state that occurred over a specific period of time.

To review uses of the preterit, see Chapter 2, pages 41–54.

2. Use the imperfect:

a. to set the scene or background of a story. In Chapter 2 you learned how to set the scene by stating the time an action occurred, or by telling the age of a person. A past scene can also be set by describing people, places, and things or by describing ongoing emotions and mental states.

Eran las once de la noche y **había** luna llena.	*It was eleven o'clock at night and there was a full moon.*
El hormiguero **estaba** en la colina y **había** hormigas y flores por todas partes.	*The anthill was on a hill and there were ants and flowers all over the place.*
Quetzalcóatl **tenía** tanto sueño que no podía quedarse despierto.	*Quetzalcóatl was so tired that he couldn't stay awake.*
Tenía sólo veintitantos años, pero siempre hacía más de lo que sus padres **esperaban.**	*He was only twenty something, but he always did more than his parents expected.*

b. to describe habitual actions in the past.

Todos los días Quetzalcóatl **iba** a la montaña y les **rezaba** a sus padres, los dioses.	*Every day Quetzalcóatl went up/used to go up to the mountain and prayed to his parents, the gods.*
Durante el día **pasaba** el tiempo con los toltecas. **Trabajaba** y **comía** con ellos, pero sentía que les faltaba algo.	*During the day he spent/used to spend time with the Toltecs. He worked/used to work and ate/used to eat with them, but he felt that they were lacking something.*

c. to describe actions in progress (see p. 65–66).

Look at the following time expressions and decide which are generally followed by a verb in the imperfect. The answer is at the bottom of the page.

a. siempre
b. a menudo
c. con frecuencia
d. una vez
e. todos los días
f. dos veces
g. de repente
h. durante mi niñez
i. muchas veces

Always use the verb **soler** in the imperfect when talking about the past since it is only used to describe past habitual actions. It can be translated as *used to* and is followed by an infinitive. **Quetzalcóatl solía ir a la montaña por la noche.**

Iba a + *infinitive*, and verbs like **saber** and **conocer** will be presented in Chapter 4.

Drill setting the scene and habitual actions in the past:

1. Have students tell what time they got up this morning, what the weather was like when they walked to class, who was sitting in the classroom when they arrived, etc.

2. Have students tell you what they usually did when they were in high school. Option: Expand by having students say whether or not they do the same things now. **Iba a clase todos los días, pero ahora sólo voy a clase tres veces por semana.**

3. Ask students what people used to do before having access to the Internet. Provide leading questions if needed. **¿Iban más a menudo a la biblioteca? ¿Cómo se comunicaba la gente?**

Answer: a, b, c, e, h, i

Act. 7: Assign as HW and check in class. Ask comprehension questions after checking.

Actividad 7 Cómo vivían los aztecas Para enterarte sobre la vida de los aztecas, completa este párrafo con el pretérito o el imperfecto de los verbos indicados.

comenzar
ser
hablar
adorar
hacer
tener, asemejarse

construir
ver

pensar
fundar
estar
llegar
unirse
contar
perder
morirse
traer

La civilización azteca ___comenzó___ en México doscientos años antes de la Conquista. El gobierno que tenían los aztecas ___era___ una monarquía elegida y la lengua que ___hablaban___ era el náhuatl. Esa civilización ___adoraba___ a una multitud de dioses y sus líderes religiosos ___hacian___ muchos sacrificios humanos. ___Tenían___ numerosos templos que ___se asemejaban___ a las pirámides de Egipto.

Los aztecas ___construyeron___ su capital Tenochtitlán en una isla porque un día uno de sus líderes religiosos ___vio___ en ese preciso lugar un águila en un cacto devorando una serpiente, y ___pensó/pensaron___ que se cumplía la profecía hecha por un dios. Los aztecas ___fundaron___ esa capital en 1428. El imperio ___estaba___ unido por la fuerza y no por la lealtad (*loyalty*); por eso cuando Cortés ___llegó___, algunas ciudades descontentas con los líderes ___se unieron___ a él en contra del imperio azteca. En el siglo XVI, la sociedad azteca, que ___contaba___ con ocho millones de habitantes, ___perdió___ más de la mitad de la población ya que muchísimos ___se murieron___ de viruela, una enfermedad que ___trajeron___ del Viejo Mundo los españoles.

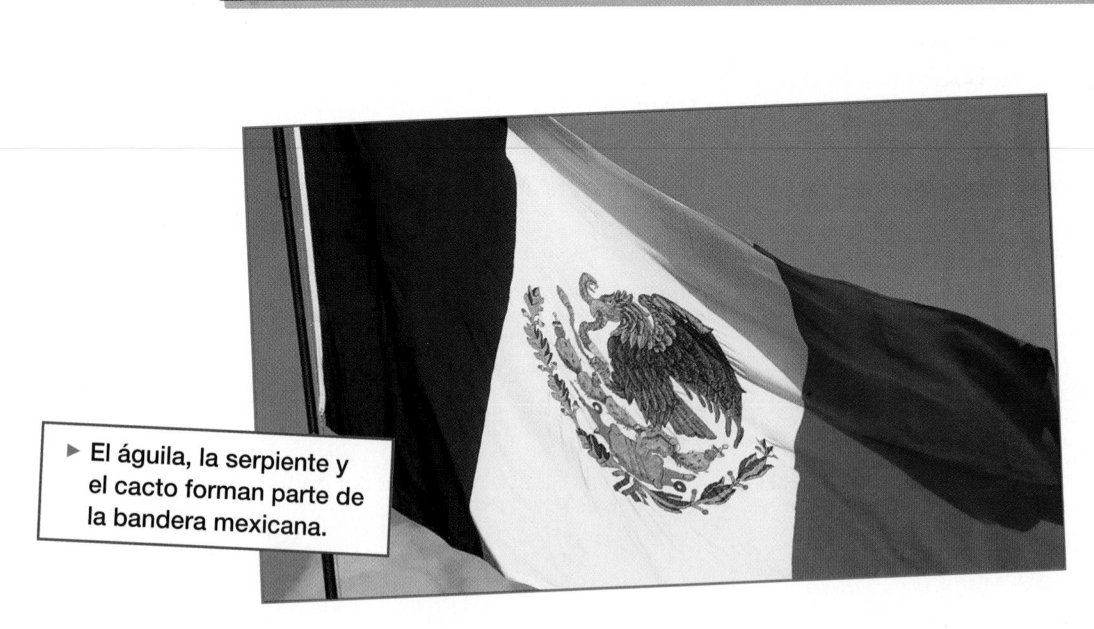

▸ **El águila, la serpiente y el cacto forman parte de la bandera mexicana.**

¿LO SABÍAN?

Los primeros inmigrantes que llegaron a Hispanoamérica eran hombres que llegaban sin familia. Una vez allí, muchos tuvieron hijos con mujeres indígenas. El fruto de esas uniones tan tempranas en la historia poscolombina es el mestizo, que hoy en día forma una comunidad étnica predominante en muchos países hispanoamericanos, tales como Honduras (90%), El Salvador (90%), México (60%) y Colombia (58%). Di por qué en este país no hay tantos mestizos. Averigua cuántas personas hay en tu clase con antepasados indígenas de este país.

Actividad 8 Los mayas y los incas **Parte A:** En parejas, una persona es un/a arqueólogo/a que estudia a los mayas y la otra persona es un/a arqueólogo/a que se especializa en los incas. Lea cada uno solamente su información y úsenla para hablarle a su compañero/a.

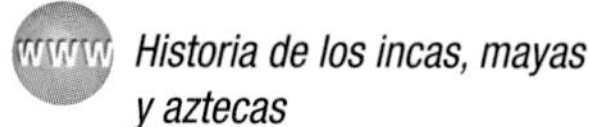

Historia de los incas, mayas y aztecas

Los mayas

habitar la península de Yucatán en el sur de México y en Centroamérica

comer maíz, tamales, frijoles e insectos

tener calendario, poder predecir los eclipses del sol y de la luna

emplear una escritura jeroglífica con más de 700 signos

Los incas

vivir en el sur de Colombia, Perú, Bolivia, Ecuador y el norte de Chile y Argentina

tener una red de caminos excelente

usar la piedra y el bronce

hacer telas a mano, cerámica artística

cultivar la papa y el maíz

no tener escritura, todo transmitirse por tradición oral

Act. 8A: Form pairs assigning the Inca or Maya data. Allow a moment for students to read their data individually. Tell them to use the maps in the inside covers of the book to show their partner where the Incas/Mayas lived as they exchange information. Check by asking questions like **¿Quiénes tenían un calendario?** Bring in pictures of Inca and Mayan ruins or artwork.

Parte B: Ahora en grupos de cuatro, hablen de cómo vivían los indígenas de su país antes de que llegaran los europeos.

Act. 8B: Combine pairs into groups of four. Supply any additional vocabulary they may need such as **tiendas, cazar, arcos y flechas, pescar.** As a wrap-up, have groups share with the rest of the class.

Actividad 9 La vida antes de la tecnología En grupos de tres, digan por lo menos una o dos cosas que hacía la gente cuando no existían los siguientes inventos. Luego, digan cuáles son las ventajas y desventajas de cada uno.

► Cuando no existía el disco compacto, la gente escuchaba música con grabadoras o estéreos. La calidad de la grabación no era...

1. el televisor
2. el avión
3. el plástico
4. la electricidad
5. la computadora

Act. 9: Have students continue the example. Then form groups of three, encourage them to be creative, set a time limit, and begin. Check by calling on volunteers.

Act. 10: Have one partner speak about his/her childhood until you tell him/her to stop. Next the other partner should speak. This is meant to encourage students to continue talking instead of finishing quickly. Partners should ask questions of each other to get details about the description and should react using the expressions in this activity, most of which were introduced in Ch. 1. Form pairs, set a time limit, and begin. Check by asking questions like **¿Quién vivía en un barrio urbano? ¿Quién compartía su dormitorio? ¿Te gustaba compartir el dormitorio con tu hermano? ¿Por qué?**

Actividad 10 El barrio de tu infancia En parejas, describan cómo era su vida y el barrio donde vivían cuando eran niños, usando las siguientes ideas. Mientras escuchan sobre la vida de su compañero/a, reaccionen usando las siguientes expresiones y háganle preguntas para averiguar más información.

¡No me digas! /¿De veras?	El/La mío/mía también.
Yo también.	El/La mío/mía tampoco.
Yo tampoco.	¡Qué chévere! (Caribe)
	¡Qué lástima!

▶ Mi barrio era muy bonito porque tenía muchos árboles y era tranquilo.

barrio	rural, urbano, casas, edificios, tiendas, centros comerciales, parques
amigos	descripción física y personalidad, lugares favoritos para jugar, cosas que hacían juntos
vecinos	personas interesantes o raras
robos (*thefts*)	muchos, pocos
casa	moderna o vieja, color, número de habitaciones
habitación	número de camas, compartir con un/a hermano/a
pertenencias	cosas favoritas y por qué

Act. 11A: Assign reading as HW or do in class. After reading, ask comprehension questions.

Actividad 11 ¿Qué hacían tus padres? **Parte A:** Una muchacha mexicana describe cómo era la vida de sus padres cuando tenían la edad que ella tiene ahora. Lee con cuidado la descripción.

"Mi mamá trabajaba en una tienda departamental, en el departamento de ropa y le gustaba salir con sus amigas a caminar por el centro y platicar en las cafeterías. Veía a mi papá sólo los fines de semana porque él trabajaba en una ciudad diferente y venía cada fin de semana a ver a sus padres y, por supuesto, a mi mamá. Él era comerciante en esa época y se casaron cuando él tenía 24 años y ella 21. A ellos les gustaba ir de vacaciones a ciudades coloniales como Oaxaca y a la playa en Veracruz o Acapulco. Los fines de semana salían al cine, o días de campo, también iban a conciertos de cantantes de boleros. A mi papá le gusta bailar, pero no a mi mamá, así que raramente iban a clubes nocturnos. Cuando tuvieron a su primera hija, tenían parejas de amigos con hijos pequeños, y salían con ellos porque se mudaron juntos a la ciudad donde trabajaba mi padre y estaban lejos de la familia de ambos."

mexicana

Act. 11B: Do as HW or orally in class. Have students compare what their parents did with what the narrator's and their classmates' parents did.

Parte B: En parejas, describa cada uno la vida de sus propios (*own*) padres usando las siguientes ideas como guía. Luego compárenla con la de los padres de la muchacha mexicana de la Parte A.

actividades: estudiar, dónde trabajar	qué hacer en su tiempo libre durante el día, durante la noche
con quién /dónde vivir	adónde ir de vacaciones
tener hijos	

Actividad 12 ¿Cómo eras cuando naciste? **Parte A:** Lee las siguientes ideas para tratar de recordar información que sabes sobre tu nacimiento. Si hay algo que no sabes, usa la imaginación.

Act. 12A: Assign as HW and encourage students to invent information they don't know or to call their parents to find out the truth.

- ser gordo/a
- ser grande / prematuro/a
- tener la cabeza en forma de cono
- tener mucho/poco pelo
- tener una mancha de nacimiento
- tener cólicos
- comer bien/mal
- mamar o tomar fórmula
- nacer por parto natural o por cesárea
- cuánto tiempo / durar el parto
- haber complicaciones
- a qué hora / nacer
- dónde / tener lugar el parto
- cuánto tiempo / estar tu madre y tú en el hospital

Parte B: En parejas, háganse preguntas para averiguar sobre el nacimiento de la otra persona.

Act. 12B: Form pairs, set a time limit and begin. When finished, find out which mother had the longest delivery, who was colicky, etc.

Actividad 13 En el cielo Unos animales están en el cielo contando cómo murió cada uno. Cada animal trata de impresionar a los otros con su cuento. En grupos de tres, usen la imaginación para completar lo que dijo cada uno y después compartan sus respuestas con la clase.

Act. 13: Elicit names of animals in Spanish. Then form groups, set a time limit, and begin. Encourage originality of responses. Option: Assign each group a different animal and have them create a full story about what happened.

Act. 14: Through question and answer, have students retell the legend they heard about the origin of corn. Form groups of three and instruct them to construct a legend about the buffalo. Ask them to take notes, but not to write the entire story out. When finished, have some groups share their legends with the class.

Actividad 14 Una leyenda Al principio de este capítulo escuchaste una leyenda tolteca sobre el maíz. En grupos de tres, usen la imaginación para crear una leyenda sobre cómo apareció el búfalo en Norteamérica. Utilicen las siguientes ideas como guía.

- quién era el personaje principal de la leyenda
- qué hacía en su vida diaria
- qué quería para su gente
- qué ocurrió un día
- después de crear al búfalo, cómo lo empezaron a utilizar los seres humanos para mejorar su vida

Actividad 15 El encuentro **Parte A:** Lee lo que dijeron un colombiano y una venezolana sobre los aspectos positivos y negativos del encuentro entre los españoles y las culturas indígenas. Después contesta las preguntas de tu profesor/a.

Act. 15A: Assign reading as HW or do in class. Ask comprehension questions: **¿Qué aspecto positivo mencionó el colombiano? ¿Y el aspecto negativo? Según la venezolana, ¿cómo sufrió el indígena por ese encuentro de culturas? Ella habla del ser mestizo. ¿Qué es ser mestizo y por qué es tan importante para ella?**

"El principal aspecto positivo es que los europeos entendieron que el mundo era más grande, rico y diverso de lo que pensaban hasta ese momento; que había personas con una experiencia cultural totalmente diferente de la tradicional europea y se plantearon otra vez las características que formaban no sólo la cultura sino la humanidad en general.

El principal aspecto negativo es que la comprensión del mundo como más rico y diverso se hizo totalmente desde la perspectiva española y europea, sin darle oportunidad a la cultura indígena para manifestarse por sus propios medios; por eso, aunque se conoció la existencia de un "nuevo mundo", esta experiencia sirvió para que la cultura europea se entendiera a sí misma, pero no para entender a las culturas indígenas."

colombiano

"La conquista española trajo como consecuencia que diversas civilizaciones fueran exterminadas, los indígenas tuvieron que someterse al rey español, aprender un nuevo idioma y nuevas costumbres. Pero no todo fue malo pues de ese encuentro resultó el mestizaje étnico y cultural que existe en Latinoamérica. El ser mestizo forma parte de nuestra manera de ser y sentir. No somos blancos, ni negros, ni indios: somos una raza mixta, nueva, que combina tradiciones muy diversas. Aunque tenemos muchos nexos con España, los latinos somos únicos, diferentes y tenemos así una manera muy particular de ver la vida."

venezolana

Act. 15B: Do as HW or orally in class. Analyze the type of language and structures used by **el colombiano** and **la venezolana**. Form groups of three, set a time limit, and begin. When finished, have a group sharing and list the positive and the negative on the board in two columns.

Parte B: En grupos de tres, digan los aspectos positivos y negativos del encuentro entre los europeos que llegaron a este país y las culturas indígenas. Luego compartan sus ideas con el resto de la clase.

¿LO SABÍAN?

Después de la llegada de los colonizadores españoles, la vida de los indígenas cambió para siempre. Muchos de ellos murieron porque sus cuerpos no resistían las enfermedades extrañas de los europeos. Otros fueron matados por los colonizadores. En Perú en 1572, los españoles arrestaron y mataron a Tupac Amaru, el último inca, delante de la catedral de Cuzco y enfrente de miles de personas. En 1780, Tupac Amaru II, un descendiente del último inca, lideró un levantamiento inca contra los españoles, pero fracasó y lo mataron también delante de la catedral de Cuzco.

La época de la colonización terminó, pero el avance de la modernización amenaza con hacer desaparecer las costumbres de los indígenas y es por eso que esa lucha continúa. A principios del siglo XX, Emiliano Zapata luchó en México por las tierras que los ricos les habían confiscado a los campesinos (indígenas y mestizos). Hoy día la indígena guatemalteca Rigoberta Menchú va de país en país hablando de los problemas de su gente, algunos tan básicos como la escasez de agua potable en los pueblos más remotos. Y en Bolivia, personas como Evo Morales, cocalero y político, trabajan dentro del sistema democrático para que el gobierno de la nación escuche la voz de los indígenas y ellos puedan controlar mejor su propio futuro. Hoy día, ¿los indígenas de este país continúan luchando por sus derechos?

Indígenas hoy día

You may want to inform students that the Zapatista movement in Chiapas is named after Emiliano Zapata. You may also want to tell students that the deceased rapper's mother changed his name at a young age to Tupac Amaru Shakur after the Inca chief. You may explain that being a **cocalero** (a coca farmer) has nothing to do with drugs. The coca plant forms part of the culture of the area. This will be further discussed in Chapter 11.

II. Describing People and Things

A. Descripción física

▸ Emiliano Zapata, mexicano (1879–1919)

1. Use pictures of magazines to point out items.

2. Use students as models and discuss characteristics.

3. Use word association: **Salvador Dalí / bigotes, Lucille Ball / pelirroja**,etc.

4. Ask students if they have any scars or tattoos and where.

5. Form pairs, tell them to study the other person's face, then have them sit back-to-back to describe each other. Tell them to be as specific as possible.

6. Show pictures of famous people and have students describe them. You may want to teach the term **rubia de farmacia.** Then have students give adjectives to describe the personality of the famous people. You may also want to have them describe the personality traits of characters they may have played.

7. If you want, explain the difference between **ser orgulloso/a** (*negative connotation*) and **estar orgulloso de** (*positive connotation*).

Forma de la cara

ovalada oval
redonda round
triangular triangular

Color de ojos

azules blue
claros light colored
color café brown
color miel light brown
negros black
pardos hazel
verdes green

Color y tipo de pelo/cabello

tener pelo castaño/canoso/negro to have brown/gray/black hair
ser pelirrojo/a o rubio/a to be a redhead or a blond/e
tener permanente to have a permanent
tener pelo ondulado/rizado/ lacio (liso) to have wavy/curly/straight hair
ser calvo/a to be bald
tener cola de caballo/ flequillo/trenza(s) to have a ponytail/bangs/braid(s)

Piel

blanca light-skinned
morena dark-skinned
trigueña olive-skinned

Señas particulares

la barba beard
la cicatriz scar
los frenillos braces
el hoyuelo dimple
el lunar beauty mark
las patillas sideburns
las pecas freckles
el tatuaje tattoo
ser peludo to be hairy
tener cuerpo de gimnasio to be buff
tener brazos fornidos to have muscular arms

B. Personalidad

All of the following adjectives are used with the verb **ser** when describing personality traits.

Cognados obvios

idealista **paciente** **prudente**
impulsivo/a **pesimista** **realista**
optimista

Otras palabras

acogedor/a	welcoming, warm
atrevido/a	daring (*negative connotation*), nervy
caprichoso/a	capricious; fussy
cariñoso/a	loving, affectionate
celoso/a	jealous
espontáneo/a	spontaneous
holgazán/holgazana / perezoso/a	lazy
juguetón/juguetona	playful
malhumorado/a	moody, ill-humored
orgulloso/a	proud (*negative connotation*)
osado	daring (*positive connotation*)
tacaño/a	stingy, cheap
travieso/a	mischievous, naughty

tacaño/a = cheap (unwilling to spend money; describes people)

barato/a = cheap (inexpensive; describes goods and services)

To review other adjectives for describing people, see pp. 7, 8, and 12.

¿LO SABÍAN?

En muchos países hispanos, con frecuencia la gente llama o se refiere a sus familiares, amigos o a su pareja usando palabras que en otras culturas pueden considerarse ofensivas. Por ejemplo, es común que los novios o una pareja casada se llamen **gordo** y **gorda** como términos de afecto, aunque las personas no pesen mucho. También es común que la gente les diga a sus amigos **flaco** o **flaca** como sobrenombre (*nickname*). Además en países como Colombia, Venezuela y Argentina se suele utilizar **negro** y **negra** como términos de afecto para una persona de tez morena. A menudo estas palabras se usan en diminutivo: **gordito**, **flaquito**, **negrita** y no son consideradas como insultos. Di si puedes usar estas palabras en inglés al hablarles a tus amigos o a tu novio/a.

Actividad 16 ¿Quién tiene esto? **Parte A:** Mira a tus compañeros y escribe el nombre de personas que tienen las siguientes características.

Act. 16A: Allow a short period of time for Part A.

pelo lacio y largo	un tatuaje
un lunar en la cara	ojos color café
cara ovalada	pecas
una cicatriz	barba o bigotes
pelo rizado	cola de caballo o trenza(s)

Parte B: En grupos de tres, comparen sus observaciones.

Act. 16B: When finished have a group sharing. As a follow-up, have students name famous people that have these features.

Actividad 17 Lo positivo y lo negativo En grupos de tres, escojan tres adjetivos de la lista de la personalidad y digan qué es lo positivo y lo negativo de poseer esas características.

► Si una persona es muy, muy prudente cuando maneja, siempre va a llegar tarde, pero sí llegará porque no va a tener accidentes.

Act. 17: As a group, use the example and find other positive and negative points about being **prudente**. Form groups and begin. Check by asking the class about certain adjectives.

Act. 18A: Discuss the image of the Marlboro man as an example of the type of person Madison Ave. wanted to portray in advertisements in decades past. Then ask them what Madison Ave. looks for today. Form pairs, set a time limit, and begin. When finished, have a group sharing.

Actividad 18 La persona ideal **Parte A:** En parejas, describan cómo son físicamente el hombre y la mujer ideales que aparecen en los anuncios comerciales de este país. Mencionen también tres adjetivos que describan su personalidad.

Parte B: Ahora lean las siguientes descripciones que hacen una mexicana y un peruano sobre la persona ideal. Compárenlas con las descripciones que hicieron Uds.

Act. 18B: Do comparisons as a class or as a group. Particularly note the references to height.

"El hombre ideal que aparece en los anuncios comerciales de México es alto (más de 1 metro 75), de complexión atlética (cuerpo de gimnasio), tiene espalda ancha y brazos fornidos (hmmmm), es moreno, por supuesto, de ojos más bien claros, color miel, cabello oscuro y bien peinado. No es muy peludo de la cara, tiene labios gruesos, mandíbula cuadrada, **pómulos resaltados** y nariz recta."

high cheekbones

mexicana

"Pues la mujer ideal tiene piel blanca o canela (durante el verano), es delgada pero con curvas. Mide 1 metro 70. Tiene pelo castaño u oscuro, preferiblemente lacio. La boca es chica, la **nariz respingada**, los ojos claros y la cara delgada."

turned up nose

peruano

Act. 19: To begin this activity, bring in a picture of yourself at this age and set up the activity by describing yourself. Allow students 30 seconds to select the adjectives. Form pairs, set a time limit, and begin. In the check phase find out who has changed the most.

Actividad 19 ¿Cómo eras de adolescente? En parejas, escojan tres adjetivos que describan su propia personalidad cuando tenían 14 años, tres que describan cómo eran físicamente y díganselos a la otra persona. Díganle también si en la actualidad tienen o no esas características.

► Cuando yo era adolescente era muy celoso porque..., pero ahora... Físicamente, tenía...

Act. 20A: Answers: Madonna, Jack Nicholson. Form pairs, encourage students to be creative. Have a group sharing when finished. Note: High school pictures of celebrities are easily found on the Internet.

Actividad 20 Los famosos **Parte A:** Las siguientes son fotos de personas famosas que fueron tomadas cuando estaban en la secundaria. ¿Quiénes son? En parejas, cada uno seleccione una de las fotos y después diga cómo era físicamente esa persona.

Parte B: En parejas, cada persona mira la foto de una persona hispana famosa cuando era muy joven y describe cómo era esa persona y qué hacía un día típico. Luego comenten cómo son esas personas ahora y qué hacen.

Act. 20B: Encourage students to use their imagination to describe what these people used to do on a typical day and what they do now.

◂ Christina Aguilera.

◂ Ricky Martin del grupo *Menudo*.

C. Describing: *Ser* and *estar* + Adjective

To describe, you can use **ser** and **estar** followed by adjectives. The following rules will help you remember when to use which.

1. Use **ser** + *adjective* when you are describing the *being*, that is, when you are describing physical, mental, or emotional characteristics you normally associate with a person, or physical characteristics you associate with a thing.

Pablo **es** tan **alto** como su padre.	*Pablo is as tall as his father.*
Su hermana **es** una persona **inteligente.**	*His sister is an intelligent person.*
La esposa de Pablo **es** (**una persona**) muy **celosa.** Él no puede ni mirar a otra mujer.	*Pablo's wife is (a) really jealous (person). He can't even look at another woman.*
Su apartamento **es** (**un lugar**) **muy moderno.**	*His apartment is (a) very modern (place).*

Drill **ser** and **estar:**

1. Bring in pictures and ask **¿Cómo es? ¿Cómo está hoy?**

2. Contrast meaning by having students finish sentences like **Cindy Crawford es una mujer bonita porque... Hoy ella está bonita porque... / Los tamales mexicanos son buenos porque... Estos tamales están buenos porque...**

2. Use **estar** + *adjective* when describing the *condition* or *state of being* of a person, place, or thing.

Nosotros **estamos cansados** de estar en la playa.	*We are tired of being at the beach.*
El agua **está muy fría.**	*The water is very cold.*
Mi padre siempre **está enojado** con alguien de la familia.	*My father is always mad at someone in the family.*

Students may associate **siempre** with the use of **ser.** Stress that this is erroneous.

Siempre is frequently used with **estar. Siempre está preocupado/borracho/enfermo/**etc.

3. Use prominent people and places in the news. Adjust these examples to today's news: **¿Cómo es Martha Stewart? ¿Cómo está Martha Stewart después de todos los problemas? / ¿Cómo era Christopher Reeve (Superman) antes de su accidente? ¿Cómo es físicamente después de su accidente? ¿Cómo está de ánimo?**

3. Adjectives that are normally used with **ser** to describe the characteristics of a person or thing may be used with **estar** to indicate a change of condition.

ser + *adjective* Being	estar + *adjective* Change of Condition
Mi marido **es (un hombre) muy cariñoso.**	**Estás muy cariñoso hoy**, ¿qué pasa?
My husband is (a) very affectionate (man).	*You are really affectionate today; what's up? (Possible implication: You are usually not that way . . . are you trying to get something from me?)*
Eres (una persona) muy elegante.	Me encanta tu corbata, **estás muy elegante.**
You are (a) very elegant (person).	*I love your tie; you look especially elegant.*
El gazpacho **es** una sopa española **fría.**	Camarero, esta sopa **está fría.**
Gazpacho is a cold Spanish soup.	*Waiter, this soup is cold.*

Drill **ser** and **estar:**

Contrast meaning by having students finish these sentences: **No me gusta ese video porque (es aburrido). / Los niños no saben qué hacer hoy y (están aburridos). // Haces mucho ruido y el niño ahora (está despierto). / La niña aprende todo enseguida; (es despierta). // Me gusta este sándwich; (está bueno). / Me gustan los sándwiches de esa cafetería porque (son buenos).** (etc.)

4. Some adjectives convey different meanings, depending on whether they are used with **ser** or **estar**. Remember that **ser** is used to describe the *being* and **estar** the *condition* or *state of being.*

ser + *adjective* Being	estar + *adjective* Condition or State of Being
La película **era aburrida.**	Nosotros **estábamos aburridos.**
The movie was boring.	*We were bored.*
Soy listo.	**Estoy listo.** Vamos.
I'm smart.	*I'm ready. Let's go.*
La maestra dice que el niño **es muy despierto.**	El niño **está despierto** y quiere jugar.
The teacher says the child is very alert.	*The child is awake and wants to play.*
El mango **es bueno** porque tiene muchas vitaminas.	El mango **está muy bueno**; quiero más.
Mango is good because it has a lot of vitamins.	*The mango tastes really good (today); I want some more.*
Es viva y nadie se aprovecha de ella.	**Está viva.** Llamemos a una ambulancia.
She's smart/sharp and no one takes advantage of her.	*She's alive. Let's call an ambulance.*

está muerta = she's dead

Actividad 21 Ser o estar **Parte A:** Las siguientes son partes de anuncios comerciales. Complétalos usando **ser** o **estar.**

Act. 21A: Assign as HW and check in class.

1. Mi esposo ____es____ muy cariñoso. Siempre me regala algo romántico para el día de San Valentín.
2. No vengo más a este restaurante. Esta sopa ____está____ fría.
3. Finalmente encontré al amor de mi vida. ____Es____ acogedora, osada y espontánea.
4. De adolescente, ____era____ gordo porque me encantaba comer.
5. —Tienes que cerrar los ojos.
   —Ya, ____estoy____ lista... ¡Huy! ¡Un anillo!
6. Son las doce de la noche y mi niña ____está____ despierta y no quiere dormir.
7. Ellas ____son____ muy vivas. Siempre saben divertirse con muy poco dinero.
8. La película que vimos ____era____ muy aburrida y con tantas interrupciones comerciales parecía que nunca iba a terminar.
9. El plato cubano ropa vieja ____es____ caliente y muy adecuado para estos días de invierno.

Parte B: En parejas, escojan uno de los anuncios comerciales y desarróllenlo (*develop it*).

Actividad 22 Impresiones equivocadas En parejas, Uds. trabajan para una empresa y por primera vez asisten a una fiesta con sus compañeros de trabajo. Se sorprenden porque algunas personas están mostrando un aspecto de su personalidad que nunca se ve en la oficina. Reaccionen a las descripciones. Sigan el modelo.

Act. 22: Set up the premise of the activity by saying that people can act differently in different settings. Read the model. Form pairs and encourage them to gossip. Check by saying you weren't at the party last night and ask about it. Students should respond by saying **Marta es optimista, pero anoche...**

▶ Marta Ramos: secretaria; siempre le encuentra el lado positivo a las cosas, pero esta noche no es así porque su novio está bailando con otra.

Marta es tan..., pero, ¡qué increíble! Esta noche está muy...

1. Jorge Mancebo: jefe de personal; siempre lleva corbata y habla poco; esta noche lleva una cadena de oro; está bailando cumbia con la cocinera.
2. Cristina Salcedo: trabaja en relaciones públicas; siempre habla con todos y escucha sus problemas; esta noche está sentada sola en un rincón mirando al suelo y tomando Coca-Cola.
3. Paulina Huidobro: jefa de producción; nunca sonríe y siempre le ve el lado negativo a todo; esta noche tiene una sonrisa de oreja a oreja y está besando apasionadamente a Juan Gris, el jefe de ventas.

Actividad 23 Sus compañeros En parejas, hablen de la personalidad de tres compañeros de la clase por lo menos y digan cómo creen que se sienten ellos hoy.

Act. 23: Form pairs and encourage students to be creative with their responses.

▶ Craig es muy cómico e hiperactivo. Hoy está preocupado porque se peleó con su novia.

Act. 24: Assign roles and explain the conflict. Have students read their role card. Set a time limit and begin. Have a few students act this out for the class, switch to a new student playing the role each time one of the expressions is used correctly.

Actividad 24 Un conflicto escolar En parejas, una persona lee las instrucciones para el papel A y la otra para el papel B. Al hablar usen las siguientes expresiones.

Me parece que...	It seems to me that . . .
Creo que...	I think that . . .
En mi opinión...	In my opinion . . .
Es decir... **O sea...**	That is . . .
Ud. me dice que...	You are telling me that . . .

A

Tu hijo de ocho años es muy bueno y obediente. Hoy te dijo que la maestra no lo quiere y lo trata muy mal y por eso recibe malas notas. Estás muy enojado/a y ahora tienes una cita con su maestra. Explícale la situación y háblale de la personalidad de tu hijo.

B

Eres maestro/a y hay un estudiante de ocho años que tiene muchos problemas de comportamiento (*behavior*) y ahora viene el padre o la madre a hablarte. Explícale cómo es su hijo y cómo se comporta últimamente.

D. Describing: The Past Participle as an Adjective

Provide input by describing what you see in the room. **Los alumnos están sentados y estoy parado/a delante de la clase. Los libros están abiertos. Las ventanas están cerradas y la puerta está abierta. La tarea está escrita en la pizarra...** (etc.)

Drill past participles as adjectives:

1. Give sentences and have students state the result: **Me siento, ahora... Abro la puerta, ahora...** (etc.)

2. In pairs, one student gives the infinitive and the other gives the participle. Or provide two numbered lists so students quiz each other. Provide answers with the lists to ensure accuracy.

3. Create a crime scene by turning over a desk, putting a jacket over it, etc. Have students describe it using past participles.

Emphasize that these differ from past participles in verb phrases (**había hecho**) because they are adjectives and thus agree in number and gender with the noun they modify.

1. Use **estar** + *past participle* to indicate the result caused by an action.

Action	Result
Los padres **se preocupaban** porque sus hijos no sacaban buenas notas en la escuela.	**Estaban preocupados.** *They were worried.*
Pablo **pone** la mesa para comer.	La mesa **está puesta.** *The table is set.*

2. The past participle functions as an adjective and agrees in gender and number with the noun it modifies.

El poll**o** está servid**o.**
Las cam**as** están hech**as.**

3. Some irregular past participles that are frequently used as adjectives include:

abrir → abierto/a	poner → puesto/a
escribir → escrito/a	resolver → resuelto/a
hacer → hecho/a	romper → roto/a
morir → muerto/a	

To review formation and a more complete list of irregular past participles, see Appendix A, pages 348–349.

Actividad 25 En una discoteca **Parte A:** Completa estas conversaciones que escuchas en una discoteca, usando **estar** + *el participio pasivo* (*past participle*) de los siguientes verbos.

abrir	envolver	romper
descomponerse	hacer	vestirse
disponerse		

Act. 25A: Assign as HW and check in class.

1. —El sistema de sonido de esta discoteca __está descompuesto__.
   —Entonces, salgamos de aquí y vamos a tomar algo al café de la esquina.
2. —Hace cinco minutos yo __estaba dispuesta__ a sacar a bailar a ese chico.
   —¿Y qué ocurrió? ¿Por qué no bailaron?
3. —Mira a esas dos muchachas.
   —Sí, __están vestidas__ con ropa ridícula.
4. —Perdón, pero creo que necesitas dejar de bailar.
   —Pero, ¿por qué?
   —Es que tus pantalones __están rotos__.
5. —Estoy convencida de que ella es una persona muy cerrada.
   —¿De veras? Ayer __estaba abierta__ a nuevas ideas.
6. —Vamos, abre el regalo.
   —Pero, ¿qué es? Y ¿por qué __está envuelto__ en papel de periódico?
7. —Mira los tatuajes que lleva ese hombre y los va a tener para toda la vida.
   —No te preocupes. __Están hechos__ con tinta lavable. Después de bañarse, van a desaparecer.

Parte B: En parejas, escojan una de las conversaciones y continúenla.

Act. 25B: Form pairs and have the students pick the conversation themselves, or assign different conversations to different groups. Check by having some groups perform for the class.

Actividad 26 La escena La puerta del vecino estaba abierta. Uds. entraron en el apartamento y esto es lo que vieron. Describan lo que vieron y saquen conclusiones para explicar qué ocurrió.

Act. 26: This can be done as a full class activity, in groups, or in pairs. Check by getting a complete description and then some possible conclusions as to what happened.

III. Indicating the Beneficiary of an Action

The Indirect Object

FLR link: Lectura 3

Drill indirect-object pronouns:

1. Do a substitution drill: T: **Te escribió una carta. (A ellos)** S: **Les escribió una carta a ellos.** T: **A mí.** S: **Me escribió una carta a mí.**

2. Ask students **¿Quién te escribe mensajes electrónicos? Y tú, ¿a quién le escribes mensajes electrónicos? ¿Quién te manda mensajes interesantes? ¿Te mandan chistes? Al principio del año académico, ¿qué cosas les ofrecen a los estudiantes las tiendas y restaurantes de esta ciudad? ¿Y las grandes compañías nacionales, también les hacen ofertas interesantes? ¿Cuál es la mejor cosa que te ofrecieron este año?**

1. In Chapter 1 you saw that a direct object answers the questions *what* or *whom*. An indirect object normally answers the questions *to whom* or *for whom*. In the sentence "I gave a gift to my friend," "a gift" is *what* I gave (direct object), and "my friend" is the person *to whom* I gave the gift (indirect object).

2. If a sentence has an indirect object, it almost always needs an indirect-object pronoun. As you saw with the verb **gustar,** the indirect-object pronouns are:

me	nos
te	os
le	les

Mi amiga Dolores hace investigaciones en el Amazonas y no tiene teléfono, por eso **le** escribí una carta.	*My friend Dolores is doing research in the Amazon and doesn't have a telephone; that's why I wrote a letter to her.*
Le escribí una carta **a Dolores.***	*I wrote a letter to Dolores.*
Les compré un regalo **a Marcos y a Ana.***	*I bought a present for Marcos and Ana.*
Me compraste ese regalo **a mí,** ¿no?*	*You bought that present for me, didn't you?*

*Note: A prepositional phrase introduced by **a** can be used to provide clarity, or simply for emphasis.

Use either the indirect-object pronoun or a prepositional phrase introduced by **para** but not both in the same sentence. **Compré una camisa para mi padre. Le compré una camisa (a mi padre).**

Mí has an accent when it is a prepositional pronoun: **detrás de mí, a mí, para mí,** etc. **Mi** without an accent is a possessive adjective: **Mi madre es peruana.**

3. Use the following pronouns after the preposition **a.**

a **mí**	a **nosotros/as**
a **ti**	a **vosotros/as**
a **Ud.**	a **Uds.**
a **ella**	a **ellas**
a **él**	a **ellos**

No lo podía creer... Viviana **me** dio un regalo **a mí**.	*I couldn't believe it. Viviana gave me a present. (Emphasis)*

4. Place indirect-object pronouns:

a. before a conjugated verb

Le escribo una postal a mi hermano.
Le había escrito una postal antes de irme de Ecuador.
Le escribí una postal ayer.
Le quiero escribir una postal.
Le estoy escribiendo una postal.

b. after and attached to the infinitive or the present participle

Quiero **escribirle** una postal.
Estoy **escribiéndole*** una postal.

*Note the need for an accent. To review accent rules, see Appendix F, pages 358–359.

Actividad 27 ¿Quién besó a quién? En parejas, miren el dibujo y decidan cuáles de las siguientes oraciones describen la escena.

Act 27: Assign as HW or do in class. Answers: 2, 3, 5, 6, 8, 10.

1. Le dio ella un beso a él.
2. Él le dio un beso a ella.
3. Le dio un beso a ella.
4. Le dio un beso ella.
5. Le dio un beso.
6. Le dio un beso él.
7. Ella le dio un beso a él.
8. Le dio él un beso a ella.
9. Le dio un beso a él.
10. A ella le dio un beso.

Actividad 28 El regalo Usa pronombres de complemento indirecto para completar la historia sobre un episodio que le sucedió a un joven chileno durante un viaje.

Act. 28: Assign as HW and check in class.

Hace un mes mi hermano y yo fuimos de vacaciones a Oaxaca, México, una región que tiene hoy día un millón de indígenas. Allí ____les____ compramos a mis padres un jarrón de cerámica negra, típica de la región, para su aniversario de boda. Pusimos el regalo cuidadosamente en una caja y lo facturamos (*checked it in*) en el aeropuerto. Por desgracia, cuando llegamos a Santiago, nos dimos cuenta de que el jarrón estaba roto. Entonces fuimos directamente a la oficina de reclamos donde ____me/nos____ pidieron la queja (*complaint*) por escrito. Yo ____le____ escribí una carta al gerente de la aerolínea en ese aeropuerto. Poco después, el gerente ____me/nos____ envió un carta por correo expreso disculpándose por lo que había pasado. En la carta él ____me/nos____ hizo muchas preguntas sobre el contenido de la caja y su valor en dólares norteamericanos. ¡Qué fastidio! Como yo no ____le____ pude contestar todas las preguntas, ____le____ pregunté a mi hermano que siempre lo sabe todo o, por lo menos, cree que lo sabe todo. Luego el gerente ____me/nos____ ofreció el dinero que habíamos gastado, pero nosotros ___le___ explicamos enfáticamente que no queríamos el dinero, sólo queríamos el recuerdo que les habíamos comprado a nuestros padres. A la semana siguiente recibimos otra carta del gerente que nos dejó boquiabiertos y en la que ___nos___ proponía otra idea: ___nos___ daba gratis (a nosotros) dos pasajes a Oaxaca, México, para nuestros padres. Nos fascinó la idea e inmediatamente ___le___ informamos que aceptábamos su oferta. ¡Valió la pena escribir tantas cartas y ser tan perseverantes!

parientes = relatives

padres = parents

Act. 29A: Form pairs and begin. When some groups have finished, have all groups change roles.

Actividad 29 Parientes típicos o atípicos **Parte A:** En parejas, entrevístense para obtener respuestas a las siguientes preguntas y así averiguar si la otra persona tiene parientes típicos o atípicos.

1. ¿Te regalan ropa pasada de moda o ropa de moda?
2. ¿Te dan mucha comida?
3. ¿Te pellizcaban (*pinch*) la mejilla cuando eras niño/a?
4. ¿Les daban muchos consejos a tus padres sobre cómo educarte cuando eras niño/a?
5. ¿Les ofrecen a otros parientes y a ti trabajos horribles en su compañía o su tienda durante los veranos?
6. ¿Les muestran a Uds. fotos o videos aburridísimos de la familia?
7. ¿Le dicen a la gente cuánto dinero ganan? Si contestas que sí, ¿le mienten sobre la cantidad?
8. Cada vez que te ven, ¿te dan dinero?
9. ¿Les piden dinero a tus padres?
10. ¿Te cuentan historias aburridas sobre su juventud?

Act. 29B: Have students tell each other why their families are typical or atypical. Tell them to give examples from their partners' answers to support their opinions. When finished, ask a few people about their partners' families.

Parte B: Ahora, díganle a su compañero/a si tiene una familia típica o atípica y defiendan su opinión.

▶ En mi opinión, tus parientes son atípicos porque te regalan...

Act. 30A: Practice question formation if needed and some possible responses. Review time expressions if needed (**hace tres días..., el año pasado**, etc.). Form pairs and begin. Have students alternate asking questions.

Actividad 30 ¿Cuándo fue la última vez que...? **Parte A:** En parejas, túrnense para preguntarle a la otra persona cuándo fue la última vez que hizo las actividades de la lista.

▶ A: ¿Cuándo fue la última vez que le compraste flores a una persona?

B: Hace un mes les compré flores a mis padres.	B: Nunca le compro flores a nadie.
↓	↓
A: ¿Por qué les compraste flores?	A: ¿Por qué nunca le compras flores a nadie?
↓	↓
B: Porque era su aniversario.	B: Porque no me gusta regalar flores.

1. comprarle flores a una persona
2. hablarles a sus padres sobre su novio/a
3. escribirle una carta de amor a alguien

(continúa en la página siguiente)

4. regalarle algo a un/a amigo/a
5. escribirle un poema a alguien
6. decirle a alguien "te quiero"
7. mandarle a alguien una tarjeta virtual cómica o cursi

Parte B: Ahora digan cuándo fue la última vez que alguien les hizo a Uds. las acciones de la Parte A.

Act. 30B: When they are finished, call on individuals to report back.

▶ Hace cinco meses que alguien me regaló flores. / Mi hermana me regaló flores hace cinco meses. / Nadie me regala flores nunca.

Actividad 31 La historia de la Malinche **Parte A:** Lee el párrafo sobre un personaje importante de la historia de México y contesta la pregunta que le sigue.

Act. 31A: Assign as HW and check in class. Ask some questions on content to ensure comprehension.

Malinalli es la hija de un noble indígena y sabe hablar maya y también náhuatl, el idioma azteca. Cuando se muere su padre, su madre **la** vende y un grupo de indígenas la compra. Este grupo, a su vez, se la vende a otro grupo de indígenas. Después de la batalla de Tabasco, estos indígenas **le**
5 dan un regalo a Cortés: Malinalli. Él **la** bautiza y **le** pone el nombre de Marina. Aguilar, un español que sabe maya, **le** enseña español. Durante un período de seis años ella se convierte en compañera, intérprete, enfermera y amante de Cortés, y **le** enseña a Cortés a llevarse bien con los indígenas. **Lo** ayuda a formar una alianza con los tlaxcalas, archienemi-
10 gos de los aztecas, para derrotar el imperio de Moctezuma. Doña Marina, como **la** llaman los conquistadores, es indispensable tanto para los españoles como para los tlaxcalas. El gran conquistador y doña Marina tienen un hijo juntos y Cortés se queda con ella hasta que no **la** necesita más. Luego doña Marina pasa a ser propiedad de uno de sus capitanes.
15 Después de su separación de Cortés, esta mujer tan importante en la conquista de México pasa a ser anónima. Hoy día se la conoce con el nombre de la Malinche.

¿A quiénes se refieren las palabras en negrita?

a. **la** en la línea 2 ___Malinalli___
b. **le** en la línea 4 ___Cortés___
c. **la** en la línea 5 ___Malinalli___
d. **le** en la línea 5 ___Malinalli___
e. **le** en la línea 6 ___Malinalli___
f. **le** en la línea 8 ___Cortés___
g. **lo** en la línea 9 ___Cortés___
h. **la** en la línea 11 ___Malinalli___
i. **la** en la línea 13 ___doña Marina___

▶ En el mural *La alianza de Cortés*, de Desiderio Hernández Xochitiotzin, aparecen Moctezuma, Hernán Cortés y la Malinche.

Act. 31B: Discuss the use of the historical present. Assign pairs and have students rewrite the paragraph in the past. Encourage them to defend their choices in each case. Check when finished.

Follow up: Ask students if they know of any other similar stories in history (e.g., Sacajawea who helped Lewis and Clark, Benedict Arnold who sold out to the British).

 *La Malinche*

  Do the corresponding CD-ROM and web activities to review the chapter topics.

Parte B: Es común usar el presente en un relato histórico. Este uso del presente se llama presente histórico. En parejas, lean la historia de la Malinche otra vez. Luego cierren el libro y entre las dos personas cuenten la historia usando el pretérito y el imperfecto.

¿LO SABÍAN?

El nombre de doña Marina con el tiempo se degeneró en Malinche. Hoy en día muchos mexicanos creen que la actitud de esa mujer al ayudar a los españoles fue un acto de traición. El término **malinche** se usa en México para referirse a una persona que prefiere lo extranjero a lo nacional o para una persona a quien se considera traidora. Sin embargo, muchas feministas han combatido este significado de la figura de la Malinche y la han revalorizado como una mujer de gran talento e inteligencia que supo sobrevivir a pesar de las condiciones adversas de su vida.

Vocabulario activo

Adverbios de tiempo

a menudo/con frecuencia/frecuentemente — *frequently*
de repente — *suddenly*
durante mi niñez — *during my childhood*
generalmente — *generally*
mientras — *while*
normalmente — *normally*
siempre — *always*
todos los días/domingos/meses/veranos/años — *every day/Sunday/month/summer/year*
una vez/dos veces/muchas veces — *once/twice/many times*

Descripción física

Forma de la cara — ***Shape of the face***
cuadrada — *square*
ovalada — *oval*
redonda — *round*
triangular — *triangular*

la barbilla — *chin*
la mandíbula — *jaw*
el pómulo — *cheekbone*

Color de ojos — ***Eye color***
azules — *blue*
claros — *light colored*
color café — *brown*
color miel — *light brown*
negros — *black*
pardos — *hazel*
verdes — *green*

Color y tipo de pelo/cabello — ***Color and type of hair***
ser calvo/a — *to be bald*
ser pelirrojo/a o rubio/a — *to be a redhead or a blond/e*
tener cola de caballo/flequillo/trenza(s) — *to have a ponytail/bangs/braid(s)*
tener pelo castaño/canoso/negro — *to have brown/gray/black hair*
tener pelo lacio (liso)/ondulado/rizado — *to have straight/wavy/curly hair*
tener permanente — *to have a permanent*

Piel	*Skin*
blanca	*light-skinned*
morena	*dark-skinned*
trigueña	*olive-skinned*

Señas particulares	*Identifying characteristics*
la barba	*beard*
los bigotes	*mustache*
la cicatriz	*scar*
los frenillos	*braces*
el hoyuelo	*dimple*
el lunar	*beauty mark*
las patillas	*sideburns*
las pecas	*freckles*
el tatuaje	*tattoo*
ser peludo	*to be hairy*
tener cuerpo de gimnasio	*to be buff*
tener brazos fornidos	*to have muscular arms*

Descripción de la personalidad

acogedor/a	*welcoming, warm*
atrevido/a	*daring (negative connotation)*
caprichoso/a	*capricious; fussy*
cariñoso/a	*loving, affectionate*
celoso/a	*jealous*
espontáneo/a	*spontaneous*
holgazán/holgazana	*lazy*
idealista	*idealistic*
impulsivo/a	*impulsive*
juguetón/juguetona	*playful*
malhumorado/a	*moody, ill-humored*
optimista	*optimistic*
orgulloso/a	*proud (negative connotation)*
osado/a	*daring (positive connotation)*
paciente	*patient*
perezoso/a	*lazy*
pesimista	*pessimistic*
prudente	*prudent*
realista	*realistic*
tacaño/a	*stingy, cheap*
travieso/a	*mischievous, naughty*

Expresiones útiles

¿A que no saben...?	*Bet you don't know . . . ?*
Creo que... / En mi opinión...	*I think that . . ., In my opinion . . .*
El/La mío/mía también.	*Mine too.*
El/La mío/mía tampoco.	*Mine either.*
Es decir... / O sea...	*That is . . .*
Había una vez...	*Once upon a time there was/were . . .*
Me parece que...	*It seems to me that . . .*
No saben la sorpresa que se llevó cuando...	*You wouldn't believe how surprised he/she was when . . .*
Ud. me dice que...	*You are telling me that . . .*

Vocabulario personal

Capítulo 4

Llegan los inmigrantes

Metas comunicativas

- hablar de la inmigración
- hablar de la historia familiar
- narrar y describir en el pasado (tercera parte)
- expresar ideas abstractas y sucesos no intencionales

May be assigned: Grammar, vocabulary, **¿Lo sabían?,** Act. 7, Act. 8, Act. 9A, Act. 12A, Act. 13, Act. 16, Act. 17, Act. 19A, and Act. 20A. The following activities can be read in class (Act. 11A, Act. 15A, and Act. 27A) and the second part can be prepared orally at home to retell in class the next day. This allows students to have time to think (Act. 11B, Act. 15B, and Act. 27B).

Show the chapter video episode at any point in the chapter that you see fit and do all or selected activities in class. Note: Content of the video supplements the cultural material in the chapter and activities reenter chapter grammar and vocabulary.

◄ *Escena de mestizaje*, Miguel Cabrera. México, 1763, Museo de América, Madrid.

Entrevista a un artista cubano

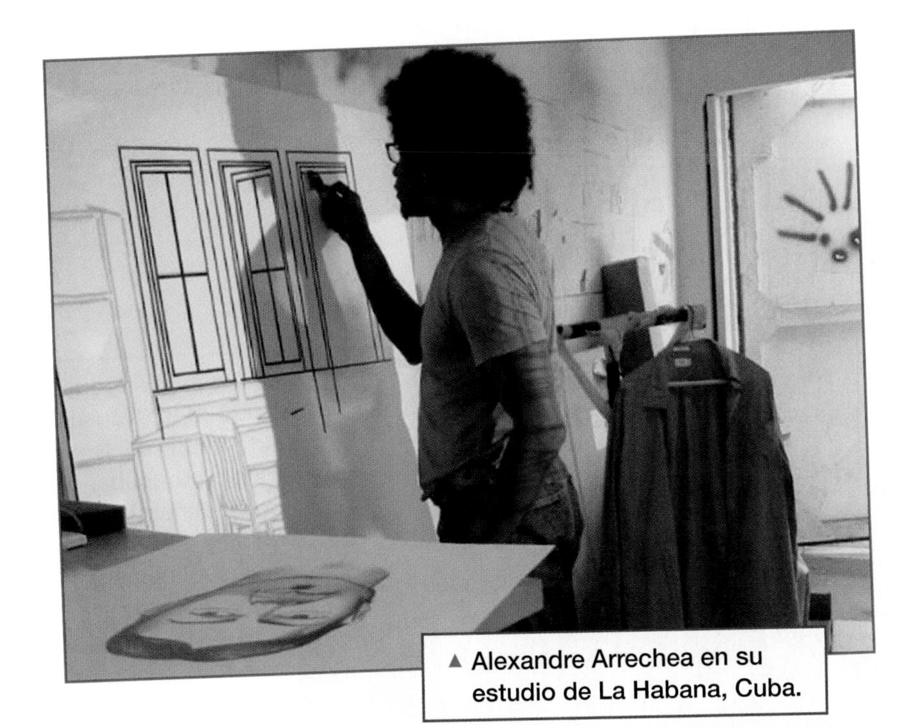

▲ Alexandre Arrechea en su estudio de La Habana, Cuba.

 **FLR** link: **Lectura 1**

Practice expressions by discussing your family background (it may also relate to an immigration story). As you tell it, incorporate the phrases. For example: **Por parte de mi madre soy de origen italiano y por parte de mi padre soy de origen alemán.** Ask students about their background. Then say **A pesar de que mis abuelos hablaban alemán, mi padre no sabía ni una palabra.** Ask them about their parents and grandparents. Ask them why they picked Spanish to study by saying **A la hora de empezar a estudiar un idioma, ¿por qué escogiste español?**

por parte de (mi, tu, etc.) **padre/madre**	*on my father's/mother's side*
a pesar de que	*even though*
a la hora de + *infinitivo*	*when the time comes to + infinitive*

Many speakers omit the possessive adjective and say **por parte de madre/padre.**

Actividad 1 La influencia de los inmigrantes Piensa en los diferentes grupos de inmigrantes que hay en este país y dónde se puede ver su influencia. Da ejemplos específicos.

Act. 1: Encourage students to think about immigrant groups in your geographic area. Have students think of food items, music, words that have entered our vocabulary, architecture, etc.

Actividad 2 La entrevista **Parte A:** Vas a escuchar una entrevista con Alexandre Arrechea, un artista cubano. Mientras escuchas, anota la siguiente información. 

1. origen de su familia
2. un ejemplo de influencia africana
3. un ejemplo de racismo

Act. 2A: Read through the items, listen to the conversation, and check.

Act. 2B: Option 1: Play the conversation and ask questions. Option 2: Play a portion of the conversation, pause it, ask a few questions, and repeat the process.

Parte B: Escucha la entrevista otra vez para contestar estas preguntas. 

1. ¿Qué tipo de trabajo tuvieron sus antepasados de origen africano?
2. ¿Por qué dice el artista que la influencia africana en la comida cubana está camuflada?
3. ¿A qué se refiere el comentario "Tú no eres negro, eres blanco"?
4. En cuanto a las parejas, ¿hay muchos matrimonios entre diferentes grupos étnicos?
5. Alex le sugiere a la entrevistadora que visite Cuba. ¿Dónde le recomienda que se quede para entender mejor a la gente?

◂ *La jungla*, Wifredo Lam (1902–1982), Museo de Arte Moderno, Nueva York. Este pintor cubano, de ascendencia africana, china y europea, muestra en sus pinturas la influencia africana.

Prior to reading, have students predict what percentage of African slaves that came to the Americas came to the United States.

¿LO SABÍAN?

Cuando los conquistadores llegaron al continente americano, usaron inicialmente a los indígenas para los trabajos pesados, pero con el tiempo muchos empezaron a morirse de enfermedades que traían los españoles. Los españoles comenzaron a darse cuenta que los indígenas también se resistían a servir a los conquistadores. Es en parte por esa falta de mano de obra que comenzó el tráfico de esclavos de África hacia el Nuevo Mundo. Aunque llegaron esclavos a todo el continente, el 38,2% fue a Brasil, el 7,3% a Cuba y solamente el 4,6% llegó a los Estados Unidos. Hoy día, en Cuba, la influencia africana se encuentra en la música, el baile, la comida y en la cultura en general. Hasta en la religión que practican algunos cubanos, que se llama santería, se ve esta fusión de culturas al combinar a dioses africanos con santos de la religión católica.

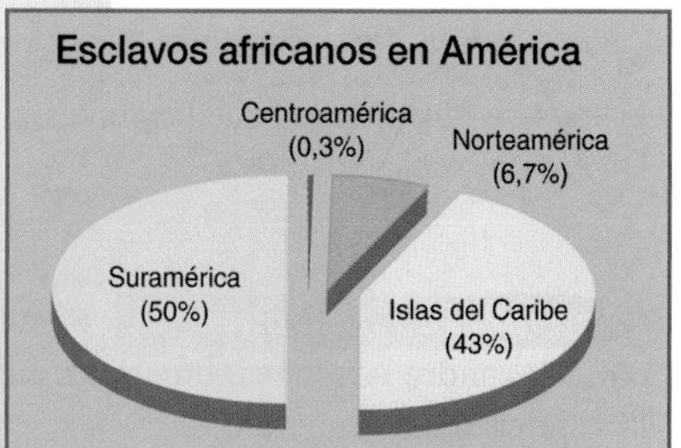

(Fuente: The African Presence in the Americas 1492–1992, Schomburg Center for Research in Black Culture, The New York Public Library. http://www.si.umich.edu/CHICO/Schomburg/text/migration7big.html.)

Actividad 3 En los Estados Unidos En grupos de tres, hablen de los inmigrantes africanos que llegaron a los Estados Unidos. Digan cuándo y por qué vinieron y dónde se ve su influencia hoy día.

I. Discussing Immigration

Do the corresponding CD-ROM and web activities as you study the chapter.

La inmigración

In this chapter students will be discussing their family histories. Have them get information from parents/grandparents ahead of time regarding family stories dealing with immigration, moves from one state/city/house to another, etc. If students have no immigration stories in their own families, encourage them to interview others.

Introduce immigration vocabulary by discussing your own family history or that of someone you know. As you tell your story, interrupt frequently to see if students had something similar happen in their family. For example: **Mis bisabuelos maternos son oriundos de Italia**. Ask a few individuals **¿Son oriundos de Italia tus bisabuelos? Mi abuela era bilingüe**. Then ask an individual **¿Tu abuela era bilingüe?**

▲ Pedro Domínguez y sus hermanos. Buenos Aires, Argentina, 1926.

"Mi madre es argentina y mi abuela también, pero mis bisabuelos maternos eran italianos. Mi abuelo materno emigró de Casablanca, Marruecos, cuando tenía 18 años. A lo largo de este capítulo voy a contar la historia de inmigración de mi padre.

Mi padre llegó por barco a Buenos Aires, Argentina, desde España en 1925 cuando tenía dos años. Eran nueve en total: Mi abuelo, mi abuela y sus siete hijos. Todos **eran oriundos de** Cáceres en la región de Extremadura e iban a Argentina a **hacerse la América** y **en busca de nuevos horizontes** porque la situación en España no era muy buena y América prometía más oportunidades de triunfar. Era una familia **de pocos recursos**, pero llegaron con algo de dinero y mi abuelo **tenía mucha iniciativa.** Él era comerciante en España y cuando llegó a Buenos Aires abrió una camisería, una tienda donde hacía camisas a medida."

Marcela, argentina

Fuente hispana

Many people of Italian, Spanish, and even North African and Middle Eastern origin emigrated to Argentina in the 20th century. So, this may be considered a typical Argentine family.

were originally from

to seek success in America / in search of new opportunities (horizons)

low income

he had a lot of initiative

MUSEO DEL INMIGRANTE

Certificado de arribo a América

ISAAC BENSABAT
de Nacionalidad ESPAÑOLA
procedente de STA. CRUZ DE TENERIFE,
llegó a BUENOS AIRES
el 7 de Junio de 1907
en el buque CAP. VERDE

Sus datos de origen son : EDAD : 58 años
Estado Civil : CASADO
Profesión : COMERCIANTE
Religión : CATOLICA

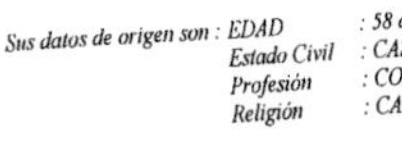

La información consignata fue obtenida por el C.E.M.L.A. según los registros de Embarque de inmigrantes de la Dirección Nacional de Población y Migración. No obstante este Certificado no tiene validez para realizar cualquier trámite administrativo, judicial o de otra indole.

Line

Casa FOA

Personas

el/la bisabuelo/a	great grandfather/grandmother
el/la descendiente	descendant
el/la emigrante	
el/la esclavo/a	slave
el/la extranjero/a	foreigner
el/la inmigrante	
el/la mestizo/a	
el/la mulato/a	
el/la pariente lejano/a	distant relative
el/la refugiado/a político/a	political refugee
el/la residente	
el/la tatarabuelo/a	great, great grandfather/grandmother

Otras palabras relacionadas con la inmigración

la ascendencia	ancestry
la discriminación, discriminar a alguien	
emigrar, la emigración	
el extranjero	abroad
hacer algo contra su voluntad	to do something against your will
hacerse ciudadano/a	to become a citizen
inmigrar, la inmigración	
la libertad	freedom
el orgullo	pride
recibir a alguien con los brazos abiertos	to receive someone with open arms
sentir nostalgia (por)	to be homesick; to feel nostalgic (about)
sentirse rechazado/a	to feel rejected
ser bilingüe/trilingüe/políglota	
ser mano de obra barata/gratis	to be cheap/free labor
ser una persona preparada	to have an education
tener incentivos	
tener prejuicios contra alguien	to be prejudiced against someone
tener título	to have an education/a degree
tener un futuro incierto	to have an uncertain future

Act. 4: Give one or two definitions as examples. Allow time for students to define 6–7 words each. Form pairs, set a time limit, and begin. Check by having individuals give definitions for the class to guess.

Actividad 4 Definiciones En parejas, miren la lista de palabras sobre la inmigración y túrnense para definir una palabra o frase sin usarla en su definición. La otra persona debe adivinar qué palabra o frase es.

Act. 5: Tell students that the charts show detailed immigration to some countries only. This is only a small picture of immigration to Latin America. In the last century there was a great deal of immigration surrounding the World Wars especially from all parts of Western and Eastern Europe.

Actividad 5 ¿Quiénes llegaron? Latinoamérica ha recibido gente de todas partes del mundo. En parejas, una persona debe mirar la tabla A y la otra la tabla B. Luego háganse preguntas para completar su tabla sobre los diferentes inmigrantes que llegaron.

WWW *Los inmigrantes*

Act. 5: Set up pairs highlighting the fact that each has information that the other needs. Model a question with one student. Set a time limit and begin. Eliminate questions from the last column if time is limited.

A

nacionalidad y épocas importantes de emigración	adónde fueron y por qué	condiciones en su país de origen	otros datos
alemanes ???	Chile – el gobierno (ofrecerles) tierra	???	• (ser) gente preparada – artesanos, (tener) título universitario
chinos 1849–1874	???	???	• ??? • (trabajar) bajo condiciones infrahumanas
italianos ???	Argentina – (trabajar) en las fábricas y en ???	• ??? • en el norte (haber) interés en hacerse la América	• (haber) dos hombres por cada mujer emigrante
judíos al final del siglo XIX	???	• (huir) de la pobreza y el antisemitismo en Rusia	???

B

nacionalidad y épocas importantes de emigración	adónde fueron y por qué	condiciones en su país de origen	otros datos
alemanes 1846–1851	???	(haber) problemas políticos (especialmente para la clase media con ideas liberales) y (haber) una crisis agrícola	???
chinos ???	Perú – (trabajar)	• (haber) sobrepoblación en China	• ??? • casi todos (ser) hombres • hoy día 2 millones de peruanos (ser) de sangre china
italianos 1880–1914	Argentina – ??? y trabajar en la agricultura	• en el sur (haber) sobrepoblación y pobreza • ???	???
judíos ???	Argentina – (haber) tolerancia religiosa después de independizarse de España	???	• Argentina (ser) hoy el octavo país del mundo en números de judíos

You may want to tell students that Japanese emigrated mainly to Peru in search of work between 1899 and 1923 when the Japanese government passed less strict laws to emigrate. During WWII, Peru sent Japanese to internment camps in the United States. Today, Japan is Peru's third largest trade partner.

¿Lo sabían?

En el año 1965 cuando la situación económica en Corea estaba en crisis y puesto que países como Paraguay y Argentina ofrecían incentivos para inmigrantes, un número de ciudadanos coreanos optó por inmigrar a esos países y con el tiempo les empezó a ir bien económicamente. Aunque los niños de estos inmigrantes asistían a escuelas locales donde se mezclaban con los niños del lugar, las familias coreanas vivieron apartadas y muchas nunca se integraron culturalmente al país al que llegaron. Desafortunadamente, cuando los países receptores entraron en un período económico difícil, algunas personas culparon a los coreanos de tener éxito con sus negocios cuando otros estaban perdiendo trabajo en el sector industrial. Por eso, algunos de esos inmigrantes decidieron irse del país que en un momento los había recibido con los brazos abiertos. ¿Conoces casos en la historia de tu país cuando un aumento de xenofobia ha coincidido con una crisis económica?

Act. 6A and B: You may also assign different immigrant groups and then have the class report. After doing Act. 6, ask students questions about different groups of Hispanics in the U.S.: Spanish **conquistadores**, before the Treaty of Guadalupe (1848); Mexicans (Southwest); Cubans, 1959–post Castro (Florida); Puerto Ricans, post WWII to work in industry (East Coast cities); 20th century, Mexicans to work in agriculture (California, Texas); many other countries because of political/economic situation in their countries.

Actividad 6 El mosaico de razas **Parte A:** Todos los países tienen inmigrantes de diferentes partes del mundo. En grupos de tres, mencionen cuáles son los principales grupos de inmigrantes que vinieron a este país.

Parte B: Ahora discutan las siguientes ideas sobre los italianos.

- cuándo vinieron
- por qué vinieron
- cuál era la situación en su país
- cómo llegaron a este país
- si fueron recibidos con los brazos abiertos
- qué idioma hablaban
- qué educación tenían
- si hubo discriminación una vez que llegaron aquí
- en qué partes del país se establecieron

▲ Shakira, la famosa cantante colombiana de raíces sirio-libanesas, bailando la danza del vientre.

Actividad 7 Un pariente En parejas, lean otra vez la descripción de Marcela en la página 93 sobre cómo llegó su padre a Buenos Aires. Luego, cuéntenle a su compañero/a cómo llegó un/a pariente o un/a conocido/a a este país.

There are Syrians and Lebanese throughout Latin America and many major cities have groups such as **Club Libanés Potosino** (**San Luis de Potosí, México**), **Club Colombo Libanés** (**Bogotá**), **Club Sirio Libanés** (**Buenos Aires**), **Centro Sirio Venezolano** (**Puerto la Cruz**), **Club Sirio Unido** (**Santiago, Chile**), etc., that frequently sponsor sports teams as well as cultural events. Carlos Menem, the ex-president of Argentina, is of Syrian descent and his parents were Sunni Muslims. Menem converted to Catholicism as a teenager.

Act. 7: Students can talk about a family member or relate a story about a friend or a relative of a friend. You may want to assign this as homework since students might have to contact family or friends to gather information.

II. Expressing Past Intentions, Obligations, and Past Knowledge

Preterit and Imperfect (Part Three)

1. To express a past plan that did not materialize, use the imperfect of **ir** + **a** + *infinitive*. This construction can be used to give excuses.

Mi bisabuelo **iba a ir** a los EE.UU. en el Titanic, pero se enfermó y fue unas semanas más tarde en otro barco.

My great grandfather was going to go to the U.S. on the Titanic, but he got sick and went some weeks later on another ship.

Iba a mudarse al norte, pero hacía mucho frío en esa región y por eso no fue.

He was going move to the north, but it was very cold in that region and that's why he didn't go.

2. Because the imperfect and the preterit express different aspects of the past, they may convey different meanings with certain verbs when translated into English. In these cases the imperfect emphasizes the ongoing nature of the state while the preterit emphasizes the onset or end of an action. These verbs or verb phrases include:

	Imperfect	Preterit
conocer (**a** + *person*)	knew (someone or some place); was acquainted with	met/began to know (someone or some place)
saber (+ *information*)	knew (something)	found out (something)
no querer (+ *infinitive*)	didn't want (to do something)	refused and didn't (do something)
no poder (+ *infinitive*)	was/were not able (to do something)	was/were not able and didn't (do something)
tener que (+ *infinitive*)	had to (do something), was supposed to (do something) but didn't necessarily do it	had to and did (do something)

Discuss with the students what you did last summer. Start by saying what you were going to do (**iba a** + *inf.*) but didn't do. Then ask them what they were going to do, but didn't last summer. Continue talking about your summer and saying whom you met (**conocí a...**). Ask them whom they met. Then tell them something you learned last summer that was of interest to you (**supe...**). Continue this process to provide comprehensible input contrasting uses of the preterit and imperfect with verbs like **querer, poder, saber,** etc.

Drill changes in meaning:

1. Ask questions like: **¿A quién de esta clase conocías antes de empezar el semestre? ¿Cuándo lo/la conociste? ¿A qué deporte sabías jugar cuando eras niño/a? ¿Cuándo fue tu último examen? ¿Cuándo supiste la nota?**

2. Have students tell things they did not want to do when they were children. **No quería estudiar. No quería levantarme. No quería hacer la tarea.** Then have them tell something they refused to do (and didn't do) as children: **No quise estudiar piano.**

3. Have students tell things they weren't able to do when they were 2, 15, etc. **No podía vestirme solo/a. No podía manejar porque todavía no tenía licencia.**

4. Have students tell you two things they had to do and didn't, and then two things they had to do and did. Then, in pairs, have them discuss and amplify: S1: **Tuve que ir al banco.** S2: **¿Por qué?** S1: **Porque no tenía ni un centavo.**

It is normal for students to have only limited use of preterit–imperfect distinctions with these verbs at this level.

Josef Hausdorf **no podía** vivir más en su país y por eso emigró con su familia a Chile.	*Josef Hausdorf couldn't live in his country any more so he emigrated with his family to Chile.*
Su hijo Hans **no quería** irse a Chile porque **no quería** despedirse de los amigos y no **conocía** a nadie allá.	*His son Hans didn't want to go to Chile because he didn't want to say good-by to his friends and he didn't know anyone over there.*
Hans **tenía que** despedirse de su mejor amigo Fritz, pero fue a su casa y no estaba.	*Hans had to say good-by to his best friend Fritz, but he went to his house and he wasn't there.*
Al final **no pudo** decirle adiós en persona así que le escribió una carta.	*In the end he wasn't able (didn't manage) to say good-by to him in person so he wrote a letter.*
Al llegar al puerto, Hans **supo** que había otros niños en el barco a Chile.	*When he arrived at the port, Hans found out there were other kids on the ship to Chile.*
Conoció a más de quince niños la primera noche y para el segundo día ya **sabía** todos los nombres.	*He met fifteen kids the first night and by the second day he already knew all their names.*

Act. 8: Assign as HW and check in class or do as an in-class activity. As a lead into this activity, tell students five different things you were going to do but didn't last weekend and state what problem came up and what you did instead. Before they begin, ask students to look at the list of problems and say which are completed actions, which are actions in progress, and which are states and whether they need the preterit or the imperfect. Encourage connected discourse by having students expand on the problems they had.

Actividad 8 Tenía todas las buenas intenciones Ayer tus amigos y tú iban a hacer muchas cosas, pero todos tuvieron diferentes problemas. Usa la siguiente información para decir cuáles eran sus intenciones, por qué no las llevaron a cabo y qué hicieron después.

▶ Paul y yo íbamos a esquiar en el lago, pero no pudimos prender el motor del bote y por eso nos quedamos allí tomando el sol y nadando un poco.

Intenciones	Problemas	
1. hacer un picnic	no tener estampilla	
2. ir a una fiesta	llover	
3. comprar el libro de trigonometría	estar cansados	
	invitarte a una fiesta	¿Qué ocurrió después?
4. estudiar para el examen	no haber más en la librería	
5. jugar un partido de tenis	no tener el carnet de estudiante	
6. sacar un libro de la biblioteca	quedarse dormidos	
7. pagar la cuenta de la luz por correo		

Actividad 9 Miniconversaciones **Parte A:** Diferentes personas en la cafetería de la universidad hablan del fin de semana pasado. Completa las conversaciones con el pretérito o el imperfecto de los verbos indicados.

Act. 9A: Assign as HW and check in class. Note, for #5, **no podía** indicates the person never even tried.

1. —Me presentaron al novio de María, pero yo ya lo ___conocía___ muy bien. (conocer)
   —¿Dónde lo habías conocido?
   —Es mi ex novio.
2. —Pedro ___tenía que___ llamar al dentista para cancelar la cita. (tener que)
   —¿Y lo llamó o no?
   —Se olvidó por completo porque la cita era un sábado.
3. —El sábado fui a una fiesta.
   —¿___Conociste___ a alguna persona interesante? (conocer)
   —Sí, ___conocí___ a una muchacha encantadora. (conocer)
4. —Ayer en la fiesta, mi novio ___no quería___ bailar conmigo. (no querer)
   —¿Y bailaste con otro?
   —Cuando vio que yo iba a bailar con otro, vino rápidamente y bailamos hasta las cinco de la mañana. Hoy ___no pude___ ponerme mis zapatos favoritos porque me duelen mucho los pies. (no poder)
5. —¡Qué contento te ves!
   —Sí, cuando era niño ___no podía___ hablar con mi abuelito mexicano, pero gracias a esta clase de español, el fin de semana pasado finalmente tuvimos una plática de una hora y ___supe___ por él que mi tatarabuela era huichola y mi tatarabuelo español. (no poder, saber)

Huicholes are indigenous people in Mexico who are descendent from the Aztecs and are related to the Hopi indians of Arizona.

6. —¿Por qué no fuiste a la fiesta el sábado?
   —___Tuve que___ estudiar y ahora estoy muy preparado para el examen. (tener que)
7. —Ayer Carlos me preguntó si me había quedado en casa el sábado por la noche.
   —¿Y le dijiste la verdad?
   —Al principio no ___sabía___ qué decirle, pero finalmente sí, le dije que había ido al cine con mis amigos. (saber)
8. —¿Por qué no se reunió Rosa con el grupo ayer para trabajar en el proyecto?
   —Su novio estaba enfermo, así que ella ___tuvo que___ cuidarlo todo el día. (tener que)
9. —Finalmente llegaron mis padres de Guatemala.
   —Deben estar muy contentos tus padres de ver a sus nietos.
   —Sí y no, porque mis niños, que hablan inglés todo el día, ___no___ les ___quisieron/quieren___ hablar en español. (no querer)

Parte B: En parejas, escojan una de las conversaciones y continúenla. Mantengan una conversación por lo menos de diez líneas usando el pretérito y el imperfecto dentro de lo posible.

Act. 9B: Form pairs, set a time limit, and begin.

Act. 10: Tell students they can choose from the list or use other actions of their choice.

Actividad 10 La semana pasada En parejas, digan tres cosas que tenían que hacer y que no hicieron la semana pasada y por qué. Luego digan tres cosas que sí tuvieron que hacer. Piensen en cosas como las siguientes.

dejar una clase
hacer fotocopias
comprar...
llamar a sus padres/un amigo
estudiar para la clase de...
devolver un video
mandar un email a...
pagar la cuenta de luz/gas/etc.
limpiar su apartamento/habitación
empezar a escribir un trabajo

Actividad 11 Un cambio radical **Parte A:** Lee la siguiente historia de lo que ocurrió cuando el padre de Marcela llegó a Argentina.

internado = boarding school

In the case of Marcela's grandfather's children, the schooling was free of charge due to his circumstances.

"Después de cuarenta días en barco con siete niños —la más pequeña de un añito— la familia de mi padre llegó a Argentina. Mis abuelos **no conocían a nadie** y **no sabían dónde iban** a vivir. Por suerte, otro español los ayudó y encontraron un lugar en la capital. Lamentablemente, al mes de llegar a Argentina, se murió mi abuela y mi abuelo se quedó solo con siete hijos. Entonces **tuvo que poner** a sus hijas en un internado de monjas y a los hijos en un internado de curas. Al principio los niños **no querían ir** a la escuela, pero finalmente lo aceptaron. Los dos únicos que se quedaron en casa por un tiempo fueron la hija menor que tenía un año y mi padre que tenía dos años y medio."

Marcela, argentina

Parte B: En grupos de tres, hablen sobre una vez que Uds. se mudaron a un lugar nuevo, empezaron a asistir a una escuela nueva o fueron a un campamento durante el verano. Expliquen los problemas que tuvieron, qué tuvieron que hacer para hacer nuevos amigos y también hablen de las cosas que no querían hacer porque se sentían incómodos.

Act. 11A: Option 1: Allow a few moments for students to read the paragraph and ask comprehension questions to make sure students comprehend the content. Option 2: Read to them, stopping after Marcela states that her grandmother died, leaving her grandfather with seven children just one month after arriving in Argentina. Encourage them to create a story saying what happened next. Then read what actually happened.

Act. 11B: Option 1: Form groups and have students tell their stories. Give each person two minutes to tell their story; encourage others to interrupt if need be to ask for clarification. As they tell their stories, walk around and listen. When finished have one or two tell their stories for the class. Option 2: Do 11A and assign 11B as HW to prepare a story orally to tell the next day in class.

¿LO SABÍAN?

Cuando una persona va a vivir a otro país, generalmente pasa por lo que se llama el choque cultural. Este proceso consiste de cuatro etapas diferentes y la duración de cada una varía de persona a persona. La primera etapa es la llamada luna de miel, en la que el recién llegado se siente encantado con el lugar y todo le resulta novedoso y atractivo. La segunda etapa es la del rechazo, cuando el individuo se siente incómodo con todo lo que esté conectado con la cultura a la que ha llegado; se cuestiona por qué está allí y se aísla de su entorno. A medida que pasa el tiempo, la persona comienza a aceptar las nuevas costumbres y a adaptarse para la supervivencia diaria. Algunas personas se quedan en esa tercera etapa, pero por lo general, muchas van más allá y se integran a la cultura: celebran las tradiciones del lugar, comen sus comidas y tienen amigos de esa cultura. ¿Has pasado un período largo en otro país? Si contestas que sí, ¿pasaste por alguna etapa del choque cultural?

III. Expressing Abstract Ideas

Lo + Adjective and *lo que*

 **FLR** link: **Lectura 2**

Introduce **lo** and **lo que** by telling students **Lo interesante de la clase…, Lo que me gusta de esta clase es…, Lo que no me gusta es…** Then ask a few students to give their opinions about their classes or the university.

1. Use the word **lo**, followed by a masculine singular adjective, to express abstract ideas.

Lo bueno es que muchos inmigrantes logran integrarse a la sociedad.	*The good (part/thing/point) is that many immigrants manage to integrate into society.*
Lo triste son los individuos que discriminan a estos inmigrantes.*	*The sad (part/thing) are the individuals who discriminate against these immigrants.*

*Note: Just as in English, since **individuos** is plural, so is the verb that precedes it.

2. **Lo que** is used to express *the thing that* or *what,* whenever *what* is not a question word.

Lo que les interesaba era no perder contacto con la familia.	*What/The thing that they were interested in was not losing contact with their family.*
¿Qué dices? **Lo que** propones es absurdo.	*What are you saying? What/The thing that you propose is absurd.*

Act. 12A: Assign as HW or do in class. Do as full class activity, having individual volunteer responses. Assign viewing of the movie *Romero* or *Frida* as extra credit.

Actividad 12 Libros y películas **Parte A:** Vamos a ver cuánto sabes de libros y películas. Intenta combinar ideas de las tres columnas y empieza cada oración con **lo** + *adjetivo.*

▶ trágico *Romero* asesinar / al arzobispo
Lo trágico de la película *Romero* fue que asesinaron al arzobispo.

interesante	*Psicosis*	Hester Prynne / tener / un hijo ilegítimo
trágico	*Frida*	él / enamorarse / de Dulcinea
increíble	*ET*	quemarse / la ciudad de Atlanta
escandaloso	*Bambi*	morirse / su madre
terrible	*La letra escarlata*	esconderse / en el armario
cómico	*El Quijote*	los dos / suicidarse
triste	*Lo que el viento se llevó*	él / atacarla / en la ducha
romántico	*Romeo y Julieta*	sufrir / un accidente de tráfico horrible

Parte B: Ahora menciona otras películas o libros y di qué fue lo interesante/ horrible/increíble/cómico, etc.

Act. 13: Assign as HW or do in class. Encourage students to talk about major news events or Hollywood. Also encourage them to say why in each case.

Act. 14: Form groups of three, set a time limit, and begin. Transition to Act. 15 by saying **Vamos a ver lo que le pasó a la familia de Marcela.** Ask them a few questions to see what they remember: **¿Cuántos hijos tenía el abuelo de Marcela? ¿Qué pasó un mes después de llegar a Buenos Aires?** Then do Act. 15.

Actividad 13 El año pasado En parejas, díganle a la otra persona qué fue lo mejor, lo peor, lo terrible, lo que les fascinó, lo que les molestó y lo que les interesó del año pasado.

▶ Lo molesto / Lo que me molestó del año pasado fueron los nuevos programas de la televisión... todos los reality shows... prefiero la ficción.

Actividad 14 Tu universidad En grupos de tres, discutan las siguientes ideas sobre su universidad.

lo que les divierte
lo que les gusta
lo que les molesta
lo que proponen para mejorarla

Act. 15A: After students read the paragraph, ask comprehension questions. Explain that playing the lottery is popular in Spain and that prizes can be quite large. Through question/answer make sure students realize that Marcela's grandfather's wife died and his friend in Spain won the lottery at about the same time.

Actividad 15 Lo triste fue que... **Parte A:** Lee el siguiente episodio de la familia de Marcela y responde a las preguntas de comprensión de tu profesor.

mercería = notions shop

"Antes de emigrar a Argentina, mi abuelo tenía una mercería en Cáceres y al lado había una zapatería. Todos los meses, el dueño de la zapatería y mi abuelo jugaban juntos a la lotería. **Lo triste** fue que al mes de irse mi abuelo con toda su familia a Argentina, el dueño de la zapatería se sacó 'la grande'. Mi abuelo supo esto como un año más tarde porque en esa época era muy difícil comunicarse a larga distancia. **Lo irónico** fue que mi abuelo se fue a Argentina para hacerse la América y su amigo que se quedó en España fue el que se hizo millonario."

Marcela, argentina

Act. 15B: Option 1: Allow a short time period for students to think about their own stories. Form pairs, have students tell their own stories. Option 2: Do 15A on one day and assign 15B to be prepared at home orally to tell in class.

Parte B: En parejas, hablen de momentos de su vida o de la vida de alguien que conozcan y digan qué fue **lo triste, lo cómico, lo trágico, lo irónico,** etc.

IV. Expressing Accidental or Unintentional Occurrences

Unintentional *se*

1. To express accidental or unintentional occurrences, use the following construction with **se** and an *indirect-object pronoun*.

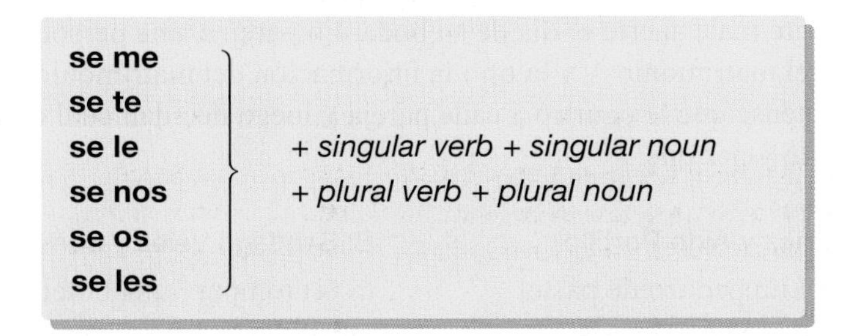

Se nos cayó la **computadora.**	*We dropped the computer.*
Se le perd**ieron** las **llaves.**	*He/She/You lost the keys.*
Se le perd**ieron** las **llaves** (a María).*	*María lost the keys.*
(A María) **se le** perd**ieron** las **llaves.**	

*Note: A phrase introduced by **a** + *noun/pronoun* can be used to provide clarity or emphasis of the indirect-object pronoun (**me, te, le, nos, os, les**). It can be placed at the beginning or end of a sentence.

2. Compare the following sentences, one involving an intentional occurrence and the other an unintentional one.

Intentional Occurrence	Unintentional Occurrence
El otro día me enfadé con mi novio y **quemé su foto** para no tener ningún recuerdo de él.	El otro día prendí una vela cerca de la foto de mi novio y me fui; cuando volví **se me había quemado la foto.**
The other day I got mad at my boyfriend, and I burned his picture so as not to have any reminder of him.	*The other day I lit a candle near my boyfriend's picture and I left. When I returned, the picture had burned.*

Start fumbling through a wallet and say **¡Ay! Se me acabó el dinero.** Then look all over for your pen (have it behind your ear) and say **Se me perdió el bolígrafo.** Look in your book bag and say **Se me olvidaron sus papeles en mi oficina.** Knock something off the desk and say **Se me cayó...** (etc.) When finished, say **Soy un desastre hoy. ¡Qué mala suerte!**

Note that the singular and plural nouns function as subjects of the verbs in this construction even though they are placed after the verb.

Review **lo** + *adjective* and introduce unintentional **se** constructions by saying **Lo maravilloso para Christa McAuliffe fue que NASA la escogió para volar en el transbordador (*shuttle*), pero lo trágico para ella y su familia fue que a NASA se le explotó el transbordador. A NASA se le explotaron dos transbordadores, el primero en 1986 y el segundo en 2003.**

Compare accidental occurrences vs. planned ones. Compare a recent arson in the area to a fire that happened by accident. Compare **Carlos quemó la casa** and **Se le quemó la casa a Víctor.** Ask students for which person they feel sorry.

Drill unintentional **se:**

Hand out cards and have students mime the sentences for the class to guess. For example: **Se le quemó el pastel. Se les cayeron las botellas. Se le rompió la taza. Se le perdió la llave. Se les acabó el agua.**

3. The following list presents verbs commonly used with this construction.

acabar/terminar	**Se me acabó** el dinero. No tengo ni un centavo.
caer	**Se le cayeron** dos platos al suelo (a Jorge).
descomponer	**Se me descompuso** el televisor y me costó 250 pesos arreglarlo.
olvidar	(A ella) Siempre **se le olvidan** las llaves del carro.
perder	Tu tía me contó que **se te perdió** el perrito.
quedar	**Se me quedaron** los anteojos en casa.
quemar	¡Qué mala suerte! **Se nos quemó** la cena.
romper	**Se les va a caer** el estéreo y **se les va a romper.**

Descomponer (*some countries in Hispanic America*) = **averiar** (*Spain*)

Act. 16: Emphasize that the indirect-object pronouns already indicate who the affected person is so that students say **Se le rompió el** (not **su**) **vestido.** Assign as HW or do in class. Form pairs and have students tell each other what happened to the couples. When finished ask the class which couple had the worst luck.

Actividad 16 La boda Dos parejas que se casaron la semana pasada tuvieron bastante mala suerte el día de su boda. En parejas, una persona mira la información del matrimonio A y la otra la información del matrimonio B. Después, cuéntense qué le ocurrió a cada pareja y luego decidan cuál creen que tuvo peor suerte y por qué.

A: Clara Gómez y Aldo Portillo

(a ella) caer / un pedazo de pastel de boda / en el vestido
(a él) romper / la cremallera (*zipper*) de los pantalones
(a ellos) quedar / los pasaportes en la casa / el avión salir sin ellos / empezar / su luna de miel un día tarde
(a él) perder / las tarjetas de crédito el segundo día de la luna de miel
(a él) perder / el anillo de matrimonio

B: Santiago Vélez y Sara Sosa

(a él) romper / una botella de champaña
(a ella) caer / el anillo de matrimonio en el lavabo
(a ellos) olvidar / los pasajes de avión en la casa
(a ellos) acabar / la gasolina camino al aeropuerto / el avión salir / sin ellos
(a ella) perder / las maletas

Act. 17: Assign as HW and check in class. Encourage students to be creative when giving responses.

Actividad 17 Excusas por llegar tarde Mañana cinco policías van a llegar tarde al trabajo para protestar contra los sueldos bajos. Escribe las cinco excusas que van a dar por llegar tarde, usando la construcción con el **se** accidental. Empieza las oraciones con frases como: **Una policía va a decir que... / Un policía va a explicar que...**

Actividad 18 La pregunta inocente En las culturas hispanas los niños ponen el diente debajo de la almohada y el Ratoncito Pérez les deja dinero. Antes de mirar la caricatura, contesta las siguientes preguntas.

1. Cuando eras pequeño, ¿dónde ponías los dientes cuando se te caían?
2. ¿Alguien te traía algo? Si contestas que sí, ¿quién y qué te traía?
3. ¿Qué parte de la computadora asocias con la palabra "ratón"?

V. Narrating and Describing in the Past

Summary of Preterit and Imperfect

Look at how the preterit and imperfect are used to talk about the past as you read this brief summary of Marcela's father's childhood in Argentina.

Preterit	Imperfect
	• **Setting the scene** (1) "Después de la muerte de mi abuela, mi abuelo **estaba** solo y **tenía** muy poco dinero para mantener a sus siete hijos.
• **Completed action** (2) Por eso un día **puso** a sus hijos en un internado.	• **Time and age** (3) Mi padre **tenía** siete años cuando empezó la escuela. **Eran** las ocho de la mañana cuando llegó a su primer día de clase.
	• **Action or state in progress** (4) **Le gustaba** ir a la escuela porque sus hermanos **estaban** allí.
	• **Habitual or repeated action** (5) Luis, hermano mayor de mi padre, siempre **se escapaba** de la escuela.
• **Action in progress interrupted** (6) Un día mientras Luis **se escapaba** por una ventana, un cura lo **vio** y **llamó** a mi abuelo para decirle que Luis ya no podía volver a la escuela.	
• **Beginning/end of action** (7) Mi padre **terminó** de estudiar a los 12 años y **empezó** a trabajar con mi abuelo porque la familia necesitaba dinero.	• **Intention** (8) Mi padre **iba a estudiar** hasta los 18, pero la familia necesitaba dinero.
• **Action over specific period of time** (9) Así que mi padre **asistió** a la escuela sólo cinco años.	• **Simultaneous ongoing actions** (10) Mientras los hijos **trabajaban**, las hijas **preparaban** la comida y **lavaban** y **planchaban** la ropa. • **Ongoing emotion or mental state** (11) Mi abuelo **no sentía** nostalgia por su país pues **estaba** contento de estar en un lugar con tantas oportunidades."

FLR link: **Lectura 3**

You may tell a story yourself (preferably about immigration) and have students analyze uses of each verb. Then switch to giving them the verb in a phrase and having them give you the correct form. Or, simply move on and do the activities that follow the summary.

Act. 19A: Assign as HW.

Actividad 19 Siempre hay una primera vez **Parte A:** Piensa en una de las siguientes situaciones y completa la tabla.

¿Cuándo fue la primera vez que...
diste o recibiste un beso?
viajaste en avión o en tren?
manejaste un coche y estabas solo/a?

Circunstancias				Lo que ocurrió
Edad	Lugar	Tiempo	Emociones	

Act. 19B: Prior to telling stories, stress that to describe the circumstances one needs to use the imperfect and to say what happened one needs to use the preterit. Form pairs and encourage students to react to what they hear. Listen as they tell their stories and have one or two students retell their stories for the class.

Parte B: Ahora, en parejas, cuéntenle la historia a la otra persona y háganse preguntas para averiguar más información. Para reaccionar a la historia de su compañero/a usen las siguientes expresiones.

¡Qué horror!	How terrible/horrible!
¡Qué cursi!	How tacky!
¡Qué genial!	How great!
Lo pasaste bien/mal, ¿eh?	You had a good/bad time, right?
Te cayó bien/mal, ¿eh?	You liked/disliked him/her, right?
¡Caray!	Geeze!
Fuiste de Guatemala a Guatepeor.	You went from bad to worse. (*play on words in Spanish*)
No puede ser. / No te creo.	That can't be true. / I don't believe you.

Act. 20A, B, and C: Even though Acts. 19 and 20 are similar the purpose is to ensure ample creative practice with preterit and imperfect while encouraging extended discourse in a controlled setting. Follow instructions for 19A and B. You may want to do 19A and B on one day and 20A, B, and C on the next day.

Actividad 20 Una historia interesante **Parte A:** Piensa en una de las siguientes situaciones y completa la tabla para prepararte a contar la historia.

- una vez que hiciste algo malo y tus padres te pillaron (*caught you*)
- la ocasión en que conociste a tu primer/a novio/a
- una fiesta sorpresa a la cual asististe
- tu primer día de universidad
- la peor salida con alguien

Circunstancias				Lo que ocurrió
Edad	Lugar	Tiempo	Emociones	

Parte B: Ahora, en parejas, cuéntenle la historia a la otra persona y háganle preguntas para averiguar más información. Tomen apuntes sobre la historia de tu compañero/a porque luego van a contarle su historia a otra persona.

Parte C: Ahora cambien de compañero/a y usen sus apuntes para contarle la historia que acaban de escuchar.

Actividad 21 La historia de Canelo: un perro fiel En parejas, miren los siguientes dibujos que cuentan la historia verídica (*true*) de un hombre enfermo que necesitaba diálisis y que no tenía a nadie excepto a su perro Canelo. Expliquen qué ocurrió usando el pretérito y el imperfecto.

Act. 21: Form pairs, set a time limit, and begin. Check by having students tell the story in a chain-like fashion.

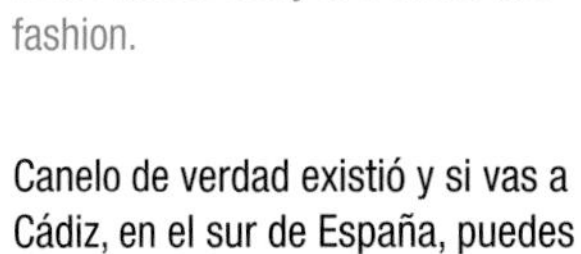
Canelo de verdad existió y si vas a Cádiz, en el sur de España, puedes visitar la calle Canelo, leer la placa en su honor y ver su estatua.

Todos los días...

Pero un día....

Lamentablemente...

Una mañana...

Pero al día siguiente...

Unos meses después...

Lo increíble fue que...

Al día siguiente...

Pero una noche, doce años después, cuando...

Finalmente...

Actividad 22 Armemos una historia En parejas, cada uno mire una de las siguientes listas de palabras y luego, inventen juntos una historia integrando las palabras. Deben turnarse para usar las expresiones de su lista en el orden que prefieran. Al usar una expresión, táchenla (*cross it out*). Comiencen la historia con la siguiente oración:

Manuela había llegado a los Estados Unidos hacía dos semanas y no hablaba inglés...

Act. 22: You may want to photocopy the lists so that each person does not see the other's list.

A

un día	Lo que siempre
pero entonces	Lo cómico fue que
conoció	mientras
tenía que	sentía nostalgia

B

finalmente	de repente
ya sabía	no quería
por suerte	se le cayó
Lo triste fue que	se sentía rechazada

Act. 23: Form groups of three, set a time limit, and begin. When finished have different groups tell their stories and vote on the best.

Actividad 23 La foto misteriosa En grupos de tres, miren la siguiente foto y usen la imaginación y la guía de ideas para inventar una historia sobre lo que ocurrió.

- cómo era la vida de esta persona, de qué país había emigrado, qué tenía que hacer un día típico, qué sabía hacer, a qué persona importante conocía
- qué ocurrió un día y por qué, qué hora era, a quién conoció, qué iba a hacer pero no pudo, qué tuvo que hacer ese día
- al final qué pasó

VI. Discussing the Past with Present Relevance

The Present Perfect

So far in this text you have used the indicative mood in the preterit, the imperfect, and the pluperfect to discuss past occurrences. In this chapter, you will use the present perfect **(pretérito perfecto)** to expand your ability to discuss past experiences.

1. You can use the present perfect to discuss events that have taken place in the past and are relevant either to the present or to past events and actions that might be repeated or continued in the present.

—¿Quieres alquilar *El Norte*?	*Do you want to rent* El Norte*?*
—No. **He visto** esa película cuatro veces.	*No. I've seen that movie four times.* (It is probably very fresh in the speaker's mind now. When the action occurred is not important.)
—Gregory Nava, el director de *El Norte*, **ha dirigido** varias películas de mucho éxito.	*Gregory Nava, the director of* El Norte, *has directed several successful movies.* (And may do so again.)

2. Use the present perfect with the expression **alguna vez** to ask the question, *Have you ever. . .?*

¿Alguna vez **has visitado** el pueblo donde nació tu bisabuelo?	*Have you ever visited the town where your great grandfather was born?*

3. The present perfect is formed by using a form of **haber** in the present indicative + *past participle.*

haber		
he	hemos	+ past participle
has	habéis	
ha	han	

To review past participle formation, see page Appendix A, pages 348–349.

Drill present perfect:

1. Have students mention important inventions and discoveries that have taken place in the last 50 years. **Han inventado los teléfonos celulares. Han encontrado una solución para...**

2. Find out if they are adventurous or not by asking questions like **¿Has nadado sin traje de baño alguna vez?** Find out if students are liars or honest. **¿Les has mentido a tus padres alguna vez sobre adónde fuiste con el coche?**

3. Ask students whether they have already done the following things: **¿Ya han desayunado/almorzado/cenado? ¿Ya han hecho la cama? ¿Ya han hecho ejercicio?**

Generally, only the first letter of a movie title is capitalized and words indicating directions **(norte, sur,** etc.) are written with lowercase letters. In the movie title *El Norte* the *N* is intentionally capitalized as if it were a country.

Present = relevance in the present

Perfect = perfective or completed action

aún = todavía

aun = hasta (*even*)

Phrases like **Ya terminé** and **Ya comí** are frequently used in Latin America and the northwest of Spain. Phrases like **Esta mañana me he levantado a las siete** are frequently used in parts of Spain instead of the preterit since it is common to use the present perfect to refer to events in the near past, particularly those that occurred earlier that day.

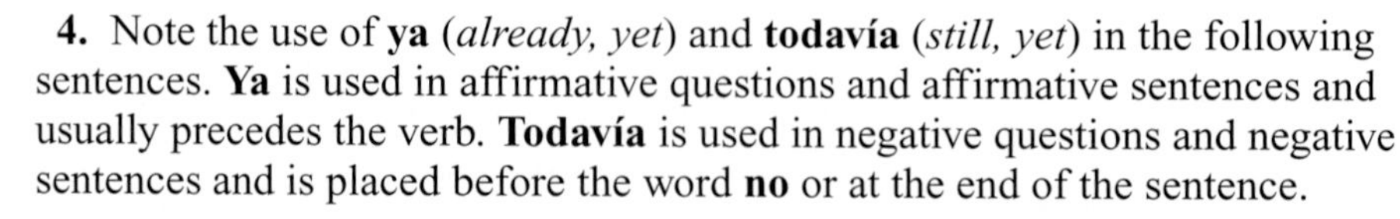

4. Note the use of **ya** (*already, yet*) and **todavía** (*still, yet*) in the following sentences. **Ya** is used in affirmative questions and affirmative sentences and usually precedes the verb. **Todavía** is used in negative questions and negative sentences and is placed before the word **no** or at the end of the sentence.

—¿**Ya** has terminado?	*Have you already finished? / Have you finished yet? / Did you finish yet?*
—Sí, **ya** he terminado.	*Yes, I've already finished.*
—¿**Ya** has comido?	*Have you eaten already? / Have you eaten yet? / Did you eat yet?*
—No, **todavía no** he comido nada. / No, **no** he comido nada **todavía.**	*No, I haven't eaten anything yet. / No, I still haven't eaten anything.*
—¿**Todavía no** has llamado a tu bisabuelo?	*Haven't you called your great grandfather yet?*
—No, **no** lo he llamado **todavía.**	*No, I haven't called him yet.*

 *Fusión de culturas*

Act. 24: Ask follow-up questions. If students have visited their relatives' home towns in other countries, ask them to tell a bit more about the experience. If they have attended a festival of another culture, ask if anything seemed strange or interesting to them. If someone dated someone from a different culture, ask if there were any problems or funny misunderstandings based on cultural differences. (etc.)

Actividad 24 Tu familia **Parte A:** Hazles preguntas a tus compañeros para averiguar quién ha hecho las siguientes cosas.

1. ver el árbol genealógico de su familia
2. hacer investigación sobre su familia en Internet
3. visitar el sitio en Internet de la isla de Ellis
4. ir a otro país donde viven/vivieron parientes suyos
5. estudiar la lengua de sus tatarabuelos
6. sentirse discriminado por su raza, sexo, religión, orientación sexual
7. asistir a un festival de otra cultura
8. salir con alguien de otra nacionalidad

Parte B: Ahora comparte tus respuestas con el resto de la clase.

Act. 25: You may want to point out to students that **ha habido** in the first example is singular since it is the present perfect equivalent of **hay** in the present: *there is/are* = **hay**, *there was/were* = **había/hubo**, *there has/have been* = **ha habido.**

Act. 25: Option 1: Assign pessimist/optimist roles. Tell students they can use the list of changes or invent some of their own. Check by asking for a few events in each category. Option 2: If needed, brainstorm events that occurred in the last year and make two lists on the board (only use infinitives in the lists). Students can then use items in this student-generated list as cues.

Actividad 25 Cambios En grupos de cuatro, dos de Uds. son personas muy pesimistas y las otras dos son muy optimistas. Mencionen tres o cuatro de los cambios sociales y políticos más importantes que han ocurrido en los últimos doce meses. Pueden usar la lista de cambios que se presenta a continuación. Sigan los modelos.

▶ (pesimista) Este año ha habido muchos robos en esta ciudad.

▶ (optimista) Este año hemos creado más programas sociales.

haber más/menos personas sin trabajo
crear más/menos programas para reducir la violencia en el hogar
aumentar/reducir la contaminación
haber más/menos escándalos políticos
haber más/menos atentados terroristas
mejorar/empeorar el nivel de la enseñanza primaria y secundaria
tener más/menos accidentes de avión
aumentar/reducir el nivel de pobreza

Actividad 26 Y este semestre, ¿qué? En parejas, pregúntenle a la otra persona si ha hecho las siguientes actividades este semestre. La persona que responde debe explicar su respuesta. Sigan el modelo.

Act. 26: Ask students if they plan ahead or leave things until the last moment. Then form pairs and have them do the activity. You may want to alter items to reflect what students are doing at this time of year at your school. This may include buying tickets to a concert, a sporting event, etc.

▶ —¿Ya has tomado un examen?

—Sí, ya he tomado un examen. Tuve uno...

—No, todavía no he tomado ningún examen. Tengo uno...

1. hablar con su consejero/a
2. ir a la oficina de su profesor/a de español
3. elegir las materias para el próximo semestre
4. decidir con quién(es) va a vivir el año que viene
5. encontrar un lugar para vivir el año que viene
6. solicitar un trabajo para el verano

Actividad 27 Recuerdos **Parte A:** Todos tenemos un recuerdo triste, traumático, raro o gracioso. Lee la siguiente historia y decide si la situación fue triste, traumática, rara o graciosa. Luego intenta explicar el uso del pretérito y del imperfecto en esta historia.

The narrator starts by saying **He celebrado mi cumpleaños de muchas formas diferentes...** You may want to start your story by saying **He** + *past participle* to say what you have done and then tell your listener about that special event that you remember. For example, **He ido muchas veces de mi pueblo a Charleston, pero...**

He celebrado mi cumpleaños de muchas formas diferentes, pero recuerdo en particular ese 15 de febrero. El día que cumplí mis ocho añitos, fui con mis padres y mis abuelos a una cafetería al aire libre y allí yo estaba sentada en una silla al lado de las escaleras. Como estábamos de vacaciones en Torremolinos, yo pensé que no me iban a dar tarta, cuando de repente mi madre me dijo: "¿Quieres acompañarme a la pastelería para comprarte la tarta?" Al escuchar a mi madre, me levanté con mucho entusiasmo, y justo cuando el camarero bajaba las escaleras mi cabeza dio contra su bandeja. Oí un ruido horrible y todo se le cayó encima al pobre camarero: la chaqueta del señor ya no era blanca, sino que estaba cubierta de Coca-Cola, café y helado y había vasos rotos por todas partes. Empecé a llorar, pero por suerte, el señor no se enojó y no tuvimos que pagar nada. Todavía recuerdo ese día cada vez que veo la chaqueta blanca de los camareros.

cake = **tarta** (*Spain*), **torta/pastel** (*Hispanic America*)

Act. 27A: Could be assigned to read at home. Ask comprehension questions to make sure students understand what happened. You may want to have a few act out the scene.

Parte B: En parejas, túrnense para contar situaciones tristes, traumáticas, raras o graciosas usando el pretérito y el imperfecto. Incluyan muchos detalles. Usen estas ideas como guía.

- cuántos años tenías
- cómo eras
- dónde estabas
- adónde fuiste y con quién
- qué hacías
- qué ocurrió
- cómo te sentiste después

Act. 27B: Option 1: Form pairs and have students tell their stories. Option 2: Do Act. 27A one day and assign 27B to be done orally the next day.

Do the corresponding CD-ROM and web activities to review the chapter topics.

Vocabulario activo

La inmigración

Personas

el/la bisabuelo/a	*great grandfather/ grandmother*
el/la descendiente	*descendant*
el/la emigrante	*emigrant*
el/la esclavo/a	*slave*
el/la extranjero/a	*foreigner*
el/la inmigrante	*immigrant*
el/la mestizo/a	*mestizo (indigenous and European)*
el/la mulato/a	*mulatto (black and European)*
el/la pariente lejano/a	*distant relative*
el/la refugiado/a político/a	*political refugee*
el/la residente	*resident*
el/la tatarabuelo/a	*great, great grandfather/ grandmother*

Otras palabras relacionadas con la inmigración

la ascendencia	*ancestry*
buscar nuevos horizontes	*to look for new horizons*
la discriminación	*discrimination*
discriminar a alguien	*to discriminate against someone*
emigrar, la emigración	*to emigrate, emigration*
el extranjero	*abroad*
hacer algo contra su voluntad	*to do something against your will*
hacerse ciudadano/a	*to become a citizen*
hacerse la América	*to seek success in America*
inmigar, la inmigración	*to immigrate, immigration*
la libertad	*freedom*
el orgullo	*pride*
recibir a alguien con los brazos abiertos	*to receive someone with open arms*
sentir nostalgia	*to be homesick; to feel nostalgic (about)*
sentirse rechazado/a	*to feel rejected*
ser bilingüe/trilingüe/ políglota	*to be bilingual/ trilingual/a polyglot*
ser mano de obra barata/ gratis	*to be cheap/free labor*
ser oriundo/a de (+ *ciudad o país*)	*to be originally from (+ city or country)*
ser una persona de pocos recursos	*to be a low-income person*
ser una persona preparada	*to have an education*
tener incentivos	*to have incentives*
tener iniciativa	*to have initiative, drive*
tener prejuicios contra alguien	*to be prejudiced against someone*
tener título	*to have an education/a degree*
tener un futuro incierto	*to have an uncertain future*

Verbos que se usan con la construcción se + pronombre de complemento indirecto

acabar/terminar	*to run out (of)*
caer	*to fall*
descomponer	*to break down*
olvidar	*to forget*
perder	*to lose*
quedar	*to leave behind*
quemar	*to burn*
romper	*to break*

Expresiones útiles

a la hora de + *infinitivo*	*when the time comes to + infinitive*
a pesar de que	*even though*
¡Caray!	*Geeze!*
Fuiste de Guatemala a Guatepeor.	*You went from bad to worse.*
Lo pasaste bien/mal, ¿eh?	*You had a good/bad time, right?*
No puede ser. / No te creo.	*That can't be true. / I don't believe you.*
por parte de mi padre/madre	*on my father's/ mother's side*
¡Qué cursi!	*How tacky!*
¡Qué genial!	*How great!*
¡Qué horror!	*How terrible/ horrible!*
Te cayó bien/mal, ¿eh?	*You liked/disliked him/her, right?*

Vocabulario personal

Capítulo 5

Metas comunicativas

- influir, sugerir, persuadir y aconsejar
- dar órdenes directas e indirectas
- hablar de hábitos alimenticios
- informar y dar instrucciones

Los Estados Unidos: Sabrosa fusión de culturas

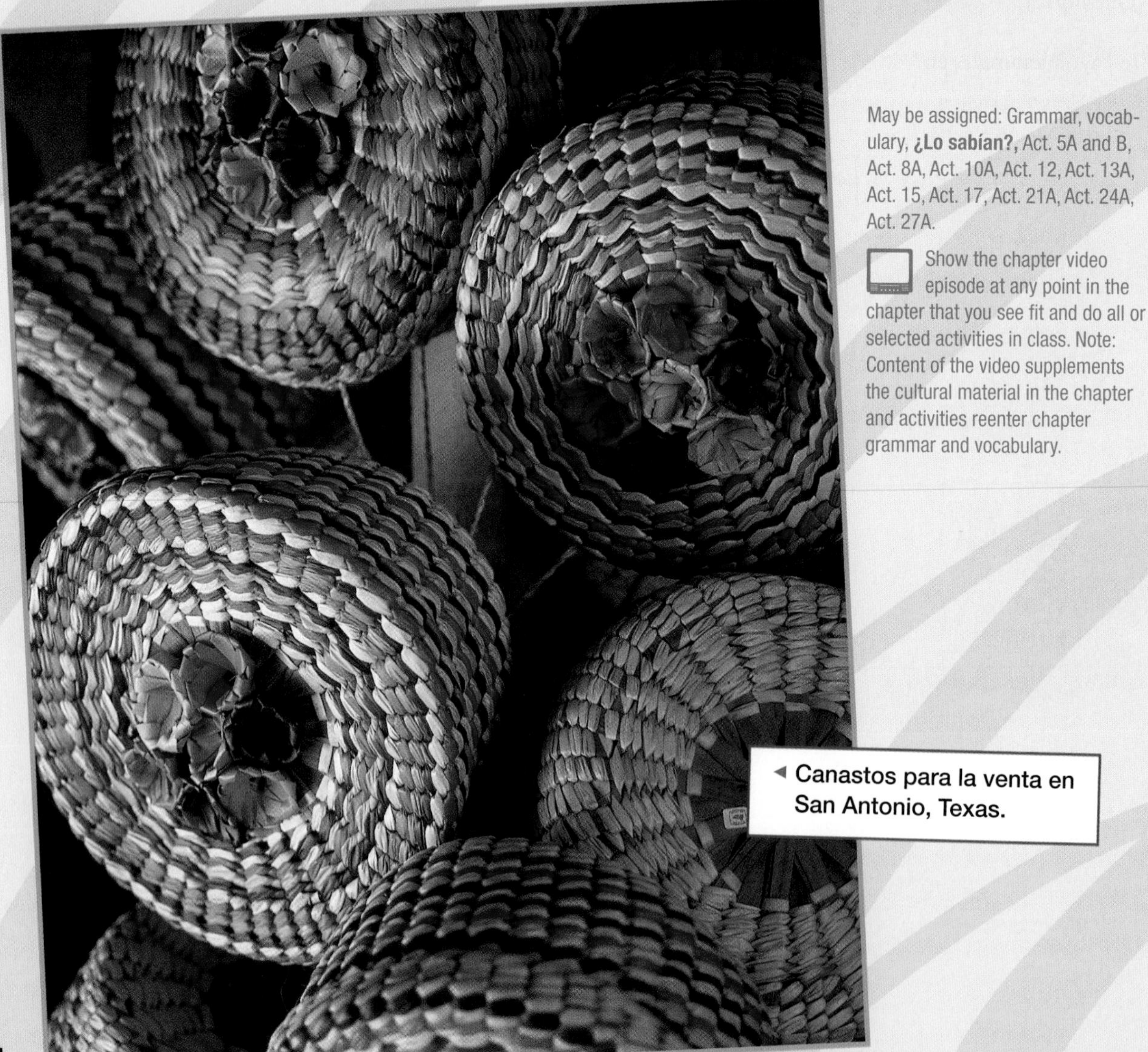

◂ Canastos para la venta en San Antonio, Texas.

May be assigned: Grammar, vocabulary, **¿Lo sabían?,** Act. 5A and B, Act. 8A, Act. 10A, Act. 12, Act. 13A, Act. 15, Act. 17, Act. 21A, Act. 24A, Act. 27A.

Show the chapter video episode at any point in the chapter that you see fit and do all or selected activities in class. Note: Content of the video supplements the cultural material in the chapter and activities reenter chapter grammar and vocabulary.

En esta mesa se habla español

tener ganas de + *infinitive*	to feel like + *ing*
¿Acaso no sabías?	But, didn't you know?
dar cátedra	to lecture someone (on some topic)
... y punto.	. . . and that's that.

catedrático/a = university professor

Practice expressions: Write them on the board and tell a story about eating chicken with mole poblano and explain that mole is a sauce made with chocolate. End by saying **Tengo ganas de comer pollo con mole.** Have students repeat. Ask students what they feel like eating now. Then tell them that chocolate came from America and ask **¿Acaso no sabían?** Ask individuals so that they hear the question a number of times. Then lecture them about the origin of chocolate (cacao seeds found in the New World/Indians drank it bitter/conquistadores took it to Spain/mixed it with sugar/etc.). Say **No debo dar cátedra, ¿verdad?** End presentation by telling them a bit more and say **Pues, todo esto es verdad, y punto.**

You may want to teach the Caribbean expression **chévere** that appears in the conversation.

Actividad 1 La comida y su origen **Parte A:** Una familia está en los Estados Unidos almorzando en un restaurante hispano. Antes de escuchar su conversación, nombra platos típicos que conozcas de España, México y Cuba. También nombra tipos de música que asocias con esos países.

Parte B: Ahora mientras escuchas la conversación, marca los adjetivos que describan la conversación y luego, di qué problemas tienen los padres con el niño.

_✓_ graciosa
___ estimulante
_✓_ informativa
___ tranquila
___ romántica
___ agresiva
_✓_ inesperada
___ tensa

Act. 1A: If students cannot name foods, you might list some and have them guess the country of origin: Spain — **paella, fabada** (a thick bean soup), **cocido** (stew with garbanzos), **gazpacho**, **flan**; Mexico — **tamales, mole poblano** (a thick chili sauce that is made with chocolate), **quesadillas**, **tacos**; Cuba — **ropa vieja** (shredded beef stew), **tostones** (fried green plantains), **plátano frito** (fried ripe plantain), **moros y cristianos** (black beans and rice). Music includes: **flamenco**, Spain; **mariachi**, Mexico; **chachachá, mambo, salsa,** etc., Cuba.

Act. 1B: Read through the list of adjectives and play the conversation. Discuss answers and have students justify responses.

Lo afrocubano

Act. 2: Read through the items first and play the conversation. Check when finished.

When referring to how he dances, the woman says that he looks like he is killing cockroaches (stomping around) vs. dancing.

Actividad 2 En el restaurante Lee las siguientes oraciones y complétalas mientras escuchas la conversación otra vez.

1. La familia pidió ___moros y cristianos___, ___ropa vieja___ y ___pollo con plátano frito___ para comer.
2. Estos platos son de ___Cuba___. (país)
3. El niño no quiere hablar ___español___. (idioma)
4. Hay un señor que está bailando el ___chachachá___ y no es buen bailarín.
5. El plátano es original de ___Asia___. (continente)
6. Los españoles llevaron el plátano al Caribe desde ___las Islas Canarias___ (lugar) en ___1516___. (año)
7. Los padres quieren que el niño ponga las ___manos___ en la mesa.
8. Según el niño, el plátano viene de la ___cocina___.

¿LO SABÍAN?

El Tratado de Guadalupe Hidalgo

Note: The Adams-Onís Treaty was signed in 1819, but was not implemented until 1821 when Florida became part of the United States.

Por más de dos siglos los españoles exploraron y ocuparon gran parte del territorio de lo que hoy son los Estados Unidos, especialmente la Florida y el suroeste. Entre 1810 y 1821, España perdió sus posesiones en Norteamérica. México comenzó su guerra de independencia en 1810 y finalmente logró su independencia en 1821. Ese mismo año España le vendió la Florida a los Estados Unidos. Luego en 1848 por el Tratado de Guadalupe Hidalgo, México le cedió a los Estados Unidos un gran territorio que hoy es conocido como el "Southwest". Los norteamericanos se encontraron allí con una población ya establecida que no hablaba inglés y que se integró a la cultura estadounidense a través de las sucesivas generaciones. Algunos, sin embargo, conservaron su lengua y sus tradiciones a través de las generaciones.

Hoy día hay en los Estados Unidos alrededor de 40 millones de hispanos sin contar los 3,8 millones que viven en la isla de Puerto Rico, pero no se puede suponer que porque son hispanos todos hablan español. Como ocurre con los inmigrantes que hablan otros idiomas, muchos hispanos de segunda y subsiguientes generaciones empiezan a perder el español. Debido a que los hispanos se encuentran rodeados del inglés, este idioma también influye en el español que hablan muchos. Es común oír a hispanos que alternan entre el español y el inglés dentro de una misma conversación y con frecuencia lo hacen inconscientemente. ¿Qué palabras del español usas al hablar inglés?

Siglos XVII y XVIII

Territorio inglés
Territorio francés
Territorio español

You may want to discuss a few aspects of Spanish and/or English use in the United States. Past immigrants (e.g., Germans, Italians) preserved their language only over a few generations. Will this happen to Hispanics? Perhaps not. Reasons: First, in the Southwest, Spanish was not an immigrant language since the territories first belonged to Spain and Mexico. Second, the Spanish-speaking population is larger and increasing, and due to the proximity to the United States, there is a constant influx of immigrants from Mexico and Central America. Third, communications are better: Internet, television, music, travel for business or pleasure, etc.

Borrowed words related to foods are **flan, paella, tamale,** etc., and those related to the West are **rodeo, bronco,** etc. Some expressions have been anglicized such as *vamoose* from **vámonos**. Other terms enter the lexicon due to use in movies such as *Hasta la vista, baby.*

Actividad 3 La influencia culinaria **Parte A:** En grupos de tres, intenten decir cuáles de estos alimentos conocían los indígenas del continente americano antes de 1492 y cuáles conocían los europeos. Si no están seguros, traten de adivinar. Sigan el modelo.

▶ Antes de 1492 los europeos ya conocían..., pero los indígenas no lo/la/los conocían.

1. la papa
2. los productos lácteos (*dairy*)
3. el tomate
4. el chocolate
5. el chile
6. el trigo (*wheat*)
7. el maíz
8. el azúcar

Parte B: Después de comparar sus respuestas con el resto de la clase, digan cómo influyeron estos productos en la dieta italiana, irlandesa y mexicana.

▶ En México, usan el queso (producto lácteo) para preparar chiles rellenos.

Act. 3A: Form groups, encourage students to support their answers and to take guesses, set a time limit, begin, and check. Answers: 1. **América** 2. **Europa** 3. **América** 4. **América** 5. **América** 6. **Europa** 7. **América** 8. **Europa** (desde Asia)

Act. 3B: Do as a class activity. Answers: **italiana: tomate, irlandesa: papa, mexicana: productos lácteos.** Follow by asking students about other cuisines. Students may know that chocolate is native to the Americas, but point out that sugarcane came from Asia and dairy products came to the Americas from Europe. Sweet milk chocolate as we know it today didn't exist prior to 1492.

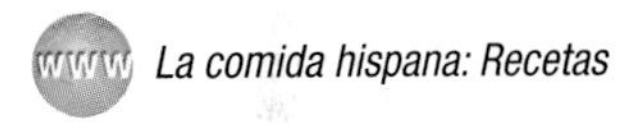
La comida hispana: Recetas

¿LO SABÍAN?

La variedad de comida hispana que se puede encontrar en los Estados Unidos es representativa de las diversas culturas hispanas que viven en este país. La comida mexicana con sus tortillas, tacos y chile ya es parte también de la dieta norteamericana. Sin embargo, no se debe olvidar que así como los conquistadores llevaron de México a España el chocolate, el aguacate, el tomate y el maíz, entre otros productos, también llevaron a México productos lácteos como el queso y la costumbre de freír los alimentos. Hoy día está muy de moda la comida tex mex que es una combinación de ingredientes de Texas y del norte de México. Entre las comidas más populares se encuentran platos como el chile con carne y las fajitas. ¿Qué otras comidas de origen hispano has probado?

Como consecuencia del impacto de la mezcla de culturas, tanto las compañías norteamericanas como las extranjeras ofrecen comidas para gustos diversos en los supermercados de los Estados Unidos.

FLR link: **Lectura 1**

Another example of the fusion of cultures are pigeon peas (**gandules**) that were introduced in the Caribbean by African slaves and are a staple of the Puerto Rican diet.

Transition to Act. 4 by saying **Ummmm, huelen bien los tamales.** Then talk about in what situations one might hear that phrase and the implied message it might contain (**¡Quiero uno!**).

Act. 4: This activity is intended to help students realize the many ways language is used to influence the actions of others, and to get them ready for studying this function of the subjunctive. Form pairs and do the first item, then check and vote on the best one. Continue this process for the others.

Actividad 4 Las implicaciones En la conversación que escucharon, la mujer le dice al niño que el plátano está delicioso. Dado el contexto, lo que la mujer probablemente implica es "Debes comértelo". Hay muchas maneras de influir en las acciones de otra persona. Por ejemplo: si eres una persona muy perezosa y hay una ventana abierta y tienes frío, puedes usar varios métodos directos e indirectos para lograr que otra persona se levante y cierre la ventana.

Directos

Por favor, ¿podrías cerrar la ventana?
Debes cerrar las ventanas cuando hace frío.
Tienes que cerrar la ventana... hace frío.

Indirectos

¿No tienes frío? Te vas a enfermar.
¿De dónde viene esa corriente de aire? ¡Qué frío!

En parejas, formen oraciones que muestren maneras directas e indirectas para lograr que otra persona haga estas acciones.

1. preparar café
2. sacar a pasear al perro
3. lavar los platos
4. no cambiar de canal de televisión constantemente

I. Influencing, Suggesting, Persuading, and Advising

Do the corresponding CD-ROM and web activities as you study the chapter.

A. The Present Subjunctive

In Spanish, the indicative (**el indicativo**) and the subjunctive (**el subjuntivo**) are two verbal moods. So far in this text, you have been using the indicative mood in asking questions, stating facts, and describing. The subjunctive mood can be used in sentences that express influence, doubt, emotion, and possibility. This chapter will focus on the use of the subjunctive to express influence and give advice.

1. The present subjunctive endings are as follows.

habl**ar**		com**er**		sal**ir**	
que habl**e**	habl**emos**	que com**a**	com**amos**	que salg**a**	salg**amos**
habl**es**	habl**éis**	com**as**	com**áis**	salg**as**	salg**áis**
habl**e**	habl**en**	com**a**	com**an**	salg**a**	salg**an**

To review the formation of the present subjunctive, see Appendix A, pages 345–346.

2. To express influence over other people's actions or to give advice, you can use the following construction.

Independent clause	que	Dependent clause
subject 1 + verb of influence (indicative)	que	subject 2 + verb (subjunctive)

(Yo)	quiero	que	(Uds.)	vengan mañana.
I	*want*		*you*	*to come tomorrow.*
Ellos	prefieren	que	Marc Anthony	cante salsa.
They	*prefer*	*that*	*Marc Anthony*	*sing salsa.*

Notice that the independent clause has a subject and a verb expressing influence, and the dependent clause has a different subject that may or may not carry out an action.

3. Use these verbs to express influence or give advice.

esperar (*to hope*) insistir en preferir (ie, i) querer (ie)

me/te/le/etc. + aconsejar / exigir (*to demand*) / pedir (i, i) / proponer (*to propose*) / recomendar (ie) / rogar (ue) (*to beg*) / sugerir (ie, i) / suplicar (*to implore*)

Me aconsejan que pruebe el plátano frito. — *They advise me to try the fried plantain.*

Les rogamos que bajen la música. — *We beg them to lower the music.*

Notice that the indirect-object pronouns (**me, te, le**, etc.) refer to the person being advised/begged/etc. and not to the person doing the advising/begging/etc.

4. Compare the following sentences and notice that if there is no influence expressed toward another person, an infinitive follows the main verb and there is no dependent clause introduced by **que.**

Two Subjects: Subjunctive	One Subject: No Subjunctive
Él prefiere que tú vengas mañana.	**Él prefiere ir** mañana.
Quiero que ella vaya a la fiesta.	**Quiero ir** a la fiesta.

Drill the subjunctive:

When drilling forms, have students conjugate forms with the word **que** to reinforce the use of the subjunctive in dependent clauses: **que hable, que hables,** etc.

1. Elicit from students and write on the board actions in the infinitive they want their instructor to do: **hablar en inglés, no dar tarea, preparar una comida en clase, dar buenas notas,** etc. Then have them tell you what they want you to do by saying **Queremos que Ud. hable...** (etc.)

2. Do a transformation drill: Tell students they are nagging parents and have to tell members of the family what to do. Write on the board: **Quiero que / Es necesario que /** etc. T: **Debes preparar la comida** (point to one of the expressions on the board). S: **Quiero que prepares la comida.** T: **Debes poner la mesa** (point to another expression). S: **Es necesario que pongas la mesa.**

3. Have students say things parents tell teenagers to do or not to do when they go to a party. **No quiero que bebas.**

Drill subjunctive with impersonal expressions: Have students give advice to a classmate on how to throw a successful party / get an "A" in Spanish / impress a date. **Es importante que invites a mucha gente. Es buena idea que tengas buena música.** (etc.)

5. To express influence or give advice in an impersonal way, you may use an impersonal expression such as **es bueno** or **es necesario.**

Independent clause	que	Dependent clause
Impersonal expression (indicative)	**que**	Subject + verb (subjunctive)

Es importante *It's important*	**que** *that*	(Uds.) *you*	**presten** atención. *pay attention.*
Es necesario *It's necessary*	**que** *that*	(tú) *you*	**pongas** la mesa. *set the table.*

6. Use the following impersonal expressions in the affirmative or the negative to express influence in an impersonal way.

(no)	+	es aconsejable	(*it's advisable*)
		es buena/mala idea	
		es bueno/malo	
		es importante	
		es mejor	(*it's better*)
		es necesario	
		es preferible	(*it's preferable*)

7. Compare the following sentences and notice that an infinitive follows the impersonal expression when no specific person is mentioned.

Subject in Dependent Clause: Subjunctive	No Subject in Dependent Clause: No Subjunctive
Es mejor que (Ud.) vuelva mañana.	**Es mejor volver** mañana.
Es preferible que prepares las papas ahora.	**Es preferible preparar** las papas ahora.

Act. 5A and B: Assign as HW. Check Part A in class asking why students selected subjunctive or infinitive forms.

Act. 5B: Check by calling on individual students to share a wish. If not assigned, give students a moment to think of sentences or to jot one or two down. Then call on individual students.

Act. 5C: Have students list groups, try to get a variety such as ethnic and religious groups, as well as blondes, computer nerds, etc. Form groups of three, set a time limit, and have them share ideas. When finished, have a group discussion that highlights the dangers of stereotyping.

Actividad 5 Dos deseos **Parte A:** Un periódico local publicó los deseos que tienen dos hispanos que viven en los Estados Unidos. Completa los deseos de la página 121 usando el infinitivo o el presente del subjuntivo de los verbos que se presentan.

Parte B: Ahora, pide algunos deseos para ti y tu familia para el próximo año. Usa expresiones como: **Quiero..., Quiero que mi padre...**

Parte C: En grupos de tres, mencionen los estereotipos que existen en los Estados Unidos sobre diferentes grupos (hombres blancos, mujeres asiáticas, deportistas, etc.) y expliquen si alguna vez alguien ha hecho comentarios de este tipo sobre Uds. y qué quieren que sepa la gente que hace esa clase de comentarios.

dominar	En primer lugar, yo quiero que mi hijo ___domine___ el inglés porque es
saber	importante ___saber___ inglés para triunfar en este país, pero a la vez
hablar, leer	espero que también ___hable___, ___lea___ y
escribir	___escriba___ español. Es decir, quiero que mi hijo
ser	___sea___ bilingüe. También es importante que
ser	___sea___ bicultural y, para entender su otra cultura, la cultura
saber	puertorriqueña, es importante que ___sepa___ el idioma de la isla.
comunicarse	También es necesario que el niño ___se comunique___ con sus abuelos que
poder	viven allí y no hablan inglés y yo también quiero ___poder___ hablar con él en ese idioma. Espero que los maestros no solamente le
enseñar	___enseñen___ inglés sino también español.

Jorge Ramos

estereotipar	Mi deseo es muy simple: Espero que la gente ___estereotipe___ cada vez menos. Estoy un poco cansada de escuchar decir cosas como que a los hispanos no
trabajar	les gusta ___trabajar___, que prefieren dormir la siesta y que nunca son
darse	puntuales. Es necesario que la gente ___se dé___ cuenta de que no es
generalizar	verdad y que no es bueno ___generalizar___ de esa manera por el
hacer	comportamiento de unos pocos. Prefiero que la gente no ___haga___ comentarios ni positivos ni negativos.

Tina Olmos

Actividad 6 El compañero de cuarto En parejas, díganle a la otra persona qué cualidades son importantes y qué cualidades no son importantes en un/a compañero/a de cuarto o apartamento.

▶ Para mí, es importante que mi compañero/a no ponga música a todo volumen.

ser ordenado/a	no usar mis cosas sin permiso
saber cocinar	tener mucho dinero
no fumar	pagar las cuentas a tiempo
no hacer mucho ruido	no llevar muchos amigos a casa
ser hombre/mujer	no hablar mal de otros
no mirar la televisión a toda hora	? ? ?

Transition to Act. 6 by asking **¿Conoces a alguien que estereotipe mucho? ¿Tu compañero/a de cuarto estereotipa?** Then ask what they look for in a roommate and do the activity.

Act. 6: Before setting up pairs and doing the activity, practice a few possible responses: **Es importante que sea ordenado, que sepa cocinar,** etc.

Transition to Act. 7 by asking **¿Quién mira la televisión con mucha frecuencia? ¿Miran Oprah? ¿Dr. Phil? ¿Cristina?** You may want to explain that Cristina is a TV show similar to Oprah's. Introduce the activity by saying **Bueno, ahora Uds. están en *"El show de Silvina,"* un programa similar a los de Cristina y Oprah.**

Act. 7: Read the quotes with students and discuss possible reasons for these statements. Then form pairs and have them give advice. Check by sharing advice with the class. Transition to Act. 8 by saying, **Cristina Saralegui, la Oprah latina, es una hispana famosa de origen cubano. Otra hispana famosa es Dolores Huerta.**

Act. 8A: Part A recycles the preterit and imperfect. Assign as HW or do in class. Discuss the use of the **presente histórico** briefly.

Answers: **Nació, dejó, se mudó, tenía, tenía, pudo/podía vivir, nacieron, obtuvo, participó, se dedicaba a inscribir, organizaba, terminó trabajando, murió, nombraron**

Actividad 7 Padres hispanos, hijos rebeldes Uds. están en televisión en *El show de Silvina*, un programa como el de Oprah Winfrey. El tema del programa de hoy es "Padres hispanos, hijos rebeldes". Éste es un tema de interés en la comunidad hispana ya que muchos padres tienen conflictos cuando sus hijos comienzan a relacionarse con niños y adolescentes de otras culturas de este país y a rebelarse contra las tradiciones familiares. Las siguientes son algunas de las cosas que dicen los padres y los hijos.

Comentarios de los padres

"Mi niña es una rebelde. Nunca llega a casa a la hora que le digo."
"Mi hijo siempre lleva la misma gorra (*cap*). Nunca se la quita."
"Ahora anda con unos que no respetan a los mayores."

Comentarios de los hijos

"Mamá no habla inglés bien."
"Odio hablar español en público."
"A los 18 años me voy a ir de la casa."

En parejas, Uds. son psicólogos invitados al programa de Silvina. Piensen en las citas (*quotes*) anteriores al preparar por lo menos tres consejos para darles a padres e hijos hispanos.

▶ Es importante que Uds. aprendan a escuchar a la otra persona.
▶ Les recomiendo que conozcan a los amigos de sus hijos.

Actividad 8 "Sí, se puede" **Parte A:** Lee esta biografía de Dolores Huerta y cámbiala al pasado usando el pretérito y el imperfecto.

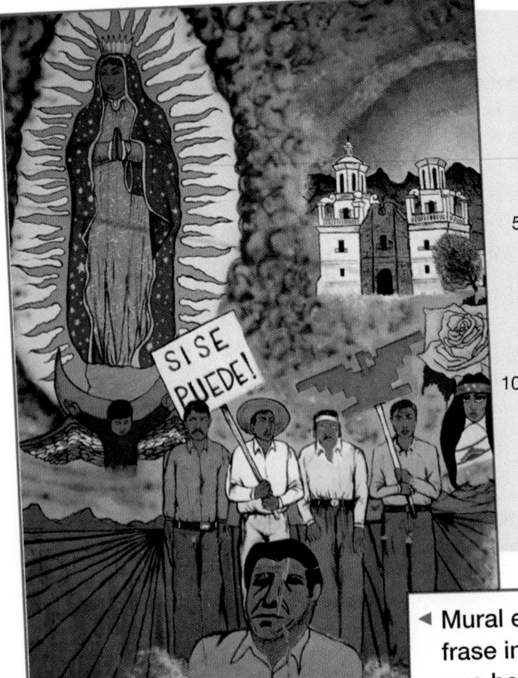

Dolores Huerta

Nace en Nuevo México en 1930, y cuando deja la casa de sus padres, se muda con su madre, dos hermanos y su abuelo a Stockton, California, donde tiene parientes. Puesto que su madre tiene un restaurante y un hotel, puede vivir con cierta comodidad. Después de su primer matrimonio, durante el cual nacen dos hijas, obtiene un título universitario. Después de la Segunda Guerra Mundial, participa en un grupo que se dedica a inscribir a la gente para votar y organiza clases de ciudadanía; finalmente termina trabajando como la mano derecha de César Chávez en la organización y administración del sindicato de trabajadores agrícolas *United Farm Workers* y cuando muere Chávez, la nombran presidenta del sindicato. Hoy día continúa trabajando para el sindicato y es defensora de los derechos del campesino y de la mujer.

◀ Mural en Tucson, Arizona con la frase inventada por Dolores Huerta que hoy día es el lema (*slogan*) de la *United Farm Workers Union.*

Parte B: Muchos inmigrantes, especialmente de México y Centroamérica, trabajan en los campos agrícolas de los Estados Unidos. Sus hijos, muchos nacidos en los Estados Unidos, viajan con ellos de granja en granja y de escuela en escuela. Formen oraciones con las siguientes frases para hacer una lista de deseos que organizaciones como *United Farm Workers* hacen para los campesinos.

Act. 8B: Check by calling on individuals.

▶ La organización *United Farm Workers* espera que los granjeros…

1. darles viviendas adecuadas
2. no emplear a niños
3. no usar insecticidas dañinos como bromuro de metilo (*methyl bromide*)
4. pagarles un sueldo apropiado
5. ofrecerles seguro médico
6. cooperar económicamente con las escuelas donde estudian los niños
7. no tener reglas que exploten a los trabajadores

¿LO SABÍAN?

César Chávez nació en 1927 en Yuma, Arizona, y con su familia, trabajó en muchos campos de California. Junto con su hermano, asistió a 37 escuelas diferentes hasta que terminó el octavo grado y luego, en vez de continuar sus estudios, siguió trabajando en el campo para ayudar a su familia. Ya mayor, y al igual que Dolores Huerta, comenzó a trabajar motivando a la gente a votar. Chávez era un hombre pacífico que luchaba día y noche sin violencia por los campesinos. De vez en cuando hacía ayunos (*fasts*) como forma de protesta pues pensaba que la gente podía conservar el respeto y la dignidad y fortalecer su espíritu si intentaba que se hiciera justicia sin violencia. Chávez murió en 1993 a unas pocas millas de donde había nacido, pero su espíritu vive en la organización de *United Farm Workers* y sus logros como el seguro médico, el establecimiento de un plan de pensiones para los trabajadores y su constante vigilancia sobre los insecticidas ayudaron y ayudarán a muchas familias.

United Farm Workers

Transition to Act. 9 by saying women such as Dolores Huerta were mothers and also worked outside the home. In the second half of the 20th century there have been changes in the role of women and men. Then do Act. 9A.

Act. 9A: Part A recycles the imperfect and prepares students for Part B, which requires the subjunctive. When finished, spot check a few items.

Actividad 9 Las exigencias de la sociedad **Parte A:** En grupos de tres, digan si eran los hombres o las mujeres los que hacían las siguientes labores en las familias típicas de la televisión de los años 60 ó 70, como la familia Brady del programa *The Brady Bunch*.

▶ Generalmente, cocinaban las mujeres.

labores domésticas: cocinar, limpiar el baño, lavar los platos, sacar la basura, cortar el césped, pasar la aspiradora
trabajo: trabajar tiempo completo, trabajar horas extras
niños: cuidarlos, bañarlos, darles de comer, llevarlos a la escuela, hablar con sus maestros, disciplinarlos, participar en sus actividades deportivas

Act. 9B: After finishing, compare a few answers with those from Part A to see how roles have changed (or stayed the same). Follow up by separating the class into groups and having students make statements: **En general, los hombres quieren que su esposa trabaje.**

Parte B: En grupos de tres, usen la lista de la Parte A para comentar qué espera la sociedad norteamericana actual que hagan los hombres y las mujeres después de casarse. Usen expresiones como: **La sociedad le exige a la mujer que..., espera que el hombre..., quiere que...**

▶ La sociedad le exige al hombre que tenga trabajo y le exige a la mujer que...

Act. 9C: When comparing, ask the students to also comment on whether or not these two Mexican-Americans agree or not on the topic. Are they stereotyping or simply making observations?

Fuentes hispanas

Parte C: Ahora lean lo que dicen dos jóvenes mexicoamericanos de primera y segunda generación sobre lo que se espera del hombre y de la mujer. Luego comparen esas opiniones con las que discutieron en la Parte B.

"En la sociedad mexicana se espera que sea el hombre el que trabaja fuera de la casa y la mujer dentro, pero cuando llegan a los Estados Unidos las cosas cambian. Aquí la sociedad le exige a la mujer que trabaje fuera de la casa y también dentro, pero el hombre mexicano que viene aquí no quiere hacer los quehaceres domésticos pues teme ser **un mandilón.**"

un mandilón: a man wrapped around his wife's little finger

mexicoamericana de primera generación

"Las mujeres mexicanas que llegan a este país saben cocinar y atender al esposo, hacen los quehaceres de la casa y también trabajan fuera de la casa. En cambio, las mexicanas de segunda generación no saben ni quieren hacer nada. Creo que es porque sus papis les dan todo y yo quiero una mujer que me atienda, y que, como yo, trabaje dentro y fuera de la casa. Por supuesto, en la casa yo voy a contribuir lavando los platos, haciendo la comida a veces y llevando a los niños a la escuela."

mexicoamericano de segunda generación

B. Giving Indirect Commands and Information: *Decir que* + Subjunctive or Indicative

Drill **decir que** + *subjunctive* or *indicative:*

1. Have students imagine that they are giving indirect commands to a child who is not listening: T: **Te lo debes comer todo.** S: **Te digo que te lo comas todo.** T: **Te debes acostar.** S: **Te digo que te acuestes.**

1. To give indirect commands, you can use a form of the verb **decir** in the independent clause followed by **que** and a verb in the subjunctive in the dependent clause.

Tu madre **te dice que pruebes los chiles rellenos.**	*Your mom is telling you to try the chiles rellenos.*
Les dice que estén más abiertos a otras culturas.	*He's telling them to be more open to other cultures.*

Notice how you can use this construction to express impatience or emphasize a point when someone does not heed your desires.

—Ayúdame... esta caja es muy pesada.	*Help me . . . this box is very heavy.*
—Sí, sí... espera.	*OK, OK . . . wait.*
—¡**Te digo que me ayudes**!	*I'm telling you to help me!*

tell to (do something) → subjunctive

2. To give information instead of commands, use the verb **decir** in the independent clause followed by **que** and a verb in the indicative in the dependent clause.

Tu madre **dice que** siempre **comes** toda la comida. ¡Qué bueno eres!	*Your mom says that you always eat all your food. You're so good!*
Ella **dice que está** ocupada con los niños.	*She says that she's busy with the kids.*

say/tell that → indicative

2. Tell students that a husband and wife have argued and are not talking to each other. Their child is reporting what the other says. **Va a nevar.** → **Dice que va a nevar. / Debes llevar chaqueta.** → **Dice que lleves chaqueta. / Juan y Clara vienen a cenar a las 9:00.** (etc.)

Actividad 10 ¿Qué dijo? **Parte A:** Estás tomando un café en un bar y escuchas las siguientes conversaciones. Complétalas según el contexto, con el indicativo o el subjuntivo del verbo que está entre paréntesis.

Act. 10A: Assign as HW and check in class asking students to explain their choices.

1. —Yo probé ropa vieja y es un plato de Cuba.
   —No estoy muy segura de eso.
   —Te digo que ropa vieja ___es___ un plato cubano. (ser)
2. —¿Qué tarea dio el profesor de cocina hoy?
   —Dice que ___vayamos___ a Internet y que ___busquemos___ más recetas vegetarianas. (ir, buscar)
3. —Estoy cansadísima.
   —Siempre, te digo que no ___bailes___ tanto, pero nunca me escuchas. (bailar)
4. —¿Conoces algún restaurante bueno cerca de aquí?
   —Me dicen que ___hay___ uno que tiene comida mexicana auténtica cerca del congreso. (hay)
5. —Perdón. ¿Puede hablar más despacio? Soy extranjero (*foreigner*).
   —Digo que la panadería se ___cierra___ a las 13:30. (cerrar)
6. —No puedo bailar merengue. Es muy difícil.
   —Te digo que ___tomes___ unas clases y vas a ver qué rápido aprendes. (tomar)

Parte B: En parejas, escojan una de las conversaciones y continúenla.

Actividad 11 La reunión de voluntarios **Parte A:** En parejas, B llegó tarde a una reunión sobre trabajo voluntario en la comunidad y A se tuvo que ir antes del final de la reunión. Usen los apuntes que tomaron para explicarle a la otra persona qué ha dicho la coordinadora. También usen expresiones como: **La coordinadora dice que nosotros hablemos... La coordinadora dice que hay trabajos...**

Act. 11A: Form pairs, explain premise of activity, model with a student, set a time limit, and begin. Check by calling on individuals.

A
- nosotros: comenzar trabajando con otro voluntario
- haber muchos trabajos diferentes
- nosotros: dedicarle tres horas semanales al trabajo
- nosotros: notificar si no podemos venir

B
- nosotros: pensar si tenemos tiempo
- su oficina preparar a los voluntarios
- nosotros: no descuidar los estudios
- nosotros: elegir el trabajo que vamos a hacer

Act. 11B: If your university offers opportunities to volunteer with Latinos in the area or has service trips over Spring Break to Spanish-speaking countries, you may want to mention them at this time.

Parte B: Ahora contesten estas preguntas.

1. ¿Hacen Uds. algún tipo de trabajo voluntario?
2. ¿Qué trabajo voluntario se puede hacer a través de su universidad? ¿Cuál prefieren y por qué?
3. ¿Hay programas patrocinados por su universidad en otros países? ¿Cuáles son?

II. Giving Direct Commands

A. Affirmative and Negative Commands with *Ud.* and *Uds.*

Drill **Ud.** and **Uds.** commands:

1. Do a transformation drill around the context of a doctor's office: T: **Deben venir mañana.** S: **Vengan mañana.**

2. Do a transformation drill with object pronouns also around the context of a doctor's office: T: **Coma dulces.** S: **No los coma.** T: **Beba alcohol.** S: **No lo beba.**

3. Have students give commands to prepare for their first year in college / for a trip / for an interview, etc.

You already know a number of ways to express influence over another person's actions. Some are more direct than others.

Quiero que Ud. venga mañana.
Le digo que venga mañana.
Ud. tiene que venir mañana.
Es mejor que Ud. venga mañana.
Ud. debe venir mañana.
¿Por qué no viene Ud. mañana?

1. The most direct way to get someone to do something is by giving a command (**una orden**). When giving an affirmative or negative command to someone you address in the **Ud.** or **Uds.** form, use the subjunctive form of the verb.

Venga (Ud.)* mañana.	*Come tomorrow.*
Vayan (Uds.)* ahora mismo.	*Go right now.*
No toquen eso; está caliente.	*Don't touch that; it's hot.*

*Note: Subject pronouns are rarely used with commands, but if they are, they follow the verb.

2. Object pronouns (reflexive, direct, or indirect) follow and are attached to affirmative commands; they precede verbs in negative commands.

Affirmative Commands	Negative Commands
Pruébenlo, está muy rico.	No **lo prueben,** está horrible.
Dígamelo todo... quiero saber todos los detalles.	No **me lo diga,** prefiero no saber nada.
Levántese.	No **se levante.**

To review accent rules, see Appendix F, pages 358–359.

Actividad 12 Para bajar el colesterol Una doctora le dice a un paciente lo que necesita hacer para bajar el colesterol. Cambia las sugerencias a órdenes.

Act. 12: If assigned as HW, check in class. You can have students role play this activity. The patient can give excuses for not wanting to do what the doctor orders.

1. Ud. tiene que hacer una dieta estricta.
2. No puede comer huevos.
3. Su esposa y Ud. no deben comer en restaurantes.
4. Necesita hacer ejercicio por lo menos tres veces por semana.
5. Ud. y su esposa deben salir a caminar juntos.
6. Es mejor evitar (*avoid*) la carne.
7. Debe venir a verme dentro de tres meses.
8. Necesita hacerse otro examen de colesterol antes de venir.

Actividad 13 La clase de salsa **Parte A:** El paciente de la actividad anterior decide tomar una clase de salsa como parte de su actividad física semanal. En parejas, completen las instrucciones que les dio el profesor a los estudiantes el primer día de clase.

Act. 13A: Assign as HW and check in class.

El paso hacia atrás

1. ___Pongan___ la punta del pie derecho en el suelo. No ___cambien___ el peso y no ___muevan___ el pie izquierdo. (Poner, cambiar, mover)
2. En el segundo tiempo, ___lleven___ el pie derecho hacia atrás y ___cambien___ el peso a la pierna derecha. No ___muevan___ el pie izquierdo. (llevar, cambiar, mover)
3. ___Cambien___ el peso a la pierna izquierda. No ___muevan___ la pierna derecha. (Cambiar, mover)
4. ___Lleven___ el pie derecho hacia el centro y ___cambien___ el peso hacia la pierna derecha. No ___muevan___ el pie izquierdo. (Llevar, cambiar, mover)

El paso hacia adelante

5. ___Hagan___ exactamente lo mismo pero hacia adelante y con el pie opuesto. (Hacer)

Parte B: Ahora pongan un CD de salsa y practiquen los pasos.

Act. 13B: Bring in salsa music and have students try to dance. If someone in the class is a good dancer, have him/her give commands and instructions.

 *Música hispana*

¿LO SABÍAN?

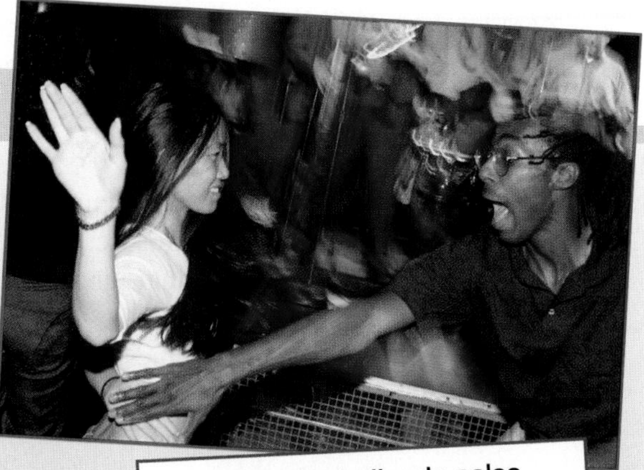

▲ Una pareja bailando salsa en El Flamingo en Nueva York.

La música y los bailes típicos varían de un país hispano a otro. En España, por ejemplo, el flamenco, de origen principalmente árabe, es uno de los bailes tradicionales mientras que en Cuba son populares la rumba, el chachachá y el mambo. La salsa, a pesar de lo que se cree comúnmente, se originó en Nueva York entre los inmigrantes cubanos y puertorriqueños y no en Cuba o Puerto Rico. Entre los músicos famosos se encuentran Celia Cruz (cubana, 1925?–2003), conocida como "la Reina de la Salsa" y Tito Puente (1923–2000), percusionista que nació en Harlem de familia puertorriqueña y que combinó elementos del jazz americano con la música caribeña y los ritmos africanos. Pero la música latina más popular dentro de los Estados Unidos es la norteña que combina ritmos mexicanos, como la ranchera, con música popular en los Estados Unidos como la polka. Entre los conjuntos norteños más famosos está el de Ramón Ayala y sus Bravos del Norte. Además existen artistas que primero se hicieron famosos cantando en español y luego hicieron el "crossover" al cantar en inglés para el mercado norteamericano. En esta categoría se destacan cantantes como Shakira, Enrique Iglesias y Ricky Martin. ¿Conocen a otros cantantes que hagan "crossover"?

Bring in music to play if time allows to show different styles. Or play music before class starts over a period of days.

Actividad 14 Problemas y soluciones Dos personas acaban de llamar a un programa de radio para contar sus problemas. Lee sus problemas y dales órdenes (*commands*) y sugerencias a estas personas para que los solucionen.

Act. 14: Have students close their books and listen while you read the first problem to the class or have one student read it out loud. Then give students a minute to think of solutions. Follow by having a group sharing. Follow the same procedure for the second problem.

Follow-up: Create or assign students to create more problems to role play in class the next day. Use as a warm-up activity, having the class suggest solutions.

Llamada no. 1

"Mi vecino es insoportable. Se levanta temprano y se pone a bailar salsa. Hace un ruido fatal. Hablé con él, pero dice que hace ejercicio porque necesita bajar el colesterol, que está en su casa y que nadie puede decirle lo que debe hacer."

Llamada no. 2

"Mi esposo está loco. Desde que el doctor le dijo que debe hacer ejercicio para bajar el colesterol no para un momento. Ahora baila salsa todo el día, por la mañana se levanta temprano y empieza chaca, chaca chaca chaca, chaca chaca, chacachá. Me insiste en que yo vaya a su clase de salsa también. Pero yo no sé bailar. Estoy harta (*fed up*) y no sé qué hacer."

B. Affirmative and Negative Commands with *tú* and *vosotros*

1. When giving commands to people you address using **tú,** follow these rules.

Affirmative **tú** Commands	Negative **tú** Commands
Third Person Singular of the Present Indicative	**No** + Subjunctive **tú** Form

Cierra la puerta.	**No cierres** la puerta.
Siéntate aquí.	**No te sientes** aquí.
Cuéntame el problema.	**No me cuentes** el problema, ya sé qué pasa.
Explícalo mejor.	**No lo expliques** más.

Remember that object pronouns follow and are attached to affirmative commands, and precede verbs in negative commands.

2. Irregular affirmative **tú** command forms include:

	Affirmative Commands	Negative Commands
decir	**Di** la verdad.	No digas nada.
hacer	**Haz**lo.	No hagas eso.
ir(se)	**Ve**te de aquí.	No te vayas.
poner	**Pon** los vasos en la mesa.	No pongas los codos en la mesa.
salir	**Sal** inmediatamente.	No salgas.
ser	**Sé** bueno.	No seas malo.
tener	**Ten** cuidado, está caliente.	No tengas miedo, el perro es bueno.
venir	**Ven** aquí.	No vengas todavía.

3. When giving commands to people you address using **vosotros**, follow these rules. Remember: the **vosotros** form is only used in Spain.

Affirmative **vosotros** Commands	Negative **vosotros** Commands
Delete **r** from the Infinitive and Substitute **d**	**No** + Subjunctive **vosotros** Form

Habladme en voz alta.	**No me habléis**.
Corred.	**No corráis**.
Abridlo.	**No lo abráis**.

Reflexive Verbs Delete the **r** from the Infinitive and Add **os**	**No** + Subjunctive **vosotros** Form

Levantaos.	**No os levantéis.**

The affirmative **tú** and **vosotros** commands are the only commands that do NOT use the subjunctive form.

You may want to mention that in Spain, colloquially, infinitives are often used as affirmative **vosotros** commands: **¡Venir y sentaros!**

Drill **tú** commands:

1. Have students give physical commands to their classmates such as **levántate, escribe tu nombre en el papel, dame cinco dólares.**

2. Have students contradict what you say to a student: T: **Tom, di la verdad.** Ss: **No digas la verdad.** T: **Habla conmigo.** Ss: **No hables con ella.** T: **Dame lo que tienes en la mano.** Ss: **No le des lo que tienes en la mano.** (etc.)

Conoce los secretos del agua

Procura comer muchos vegetales y frutas, la mayoría contienen hasta un 80% de agua.

- Utiliza siempre productos de belleza con alto contenido hídrico.
- Hazte una sauna en casa, deja correr el agua caliente de la ducha hasta que el baño se llene de vapor, desnúdate y deja que tu cuerpo absorba la humedad.
- Durante el invierno mantén el humificador en la habitación, porque la calefacción es el peor enemigo de la belleza.
- Si quieres un secreto de las bellezas de Hollywood, aquí te lo damos: toma a diario y en ayunas un vaso de agua tibia con jugo de limón. Aseguran que es una de las fuentes de la eterna juventud.

▲ ¿Haces algunas de estas cosas?

Remember: Place the object pronoun before the verb in a negative command and after and attached to an affirmative command.

Act. 15: Assign as HW and check in class. Discuss significance of each line and act out if needed to ensure comprehension. Ask them which order they like best and why. Repeat in the **Uds.** form, or the **vosotros** form if desired.

Actividad 15 Un fax El siguiente es un fax incompleto que alguien recibió en su trabajo. Complétalo con las órdenes apropiadas correspondientes a la forma de **tú**.

31-3-2005 16:25 P. 01

Instrucciones para las personas que no quieren trabajar

I. No ___lo confieses___ nunca. (confesarlo)

II. ___Espera___ sin impaciencia la orden de trabajo; no ___la busques___. (Esperar, buscarla)

III. No ___molestes___ a los que trabajan. (molestar)

IV. ___Adopta___ una postura especial para dar la impresión de que estás ocupado. (Adoptar)

V. Amas el trabajo bien hecho, por eso, ___déjalo___ para los compañeros más calificados. (dejarlo)

VI. Si te vienen ganas de trabajar, ___siéntate___ y ___espera___ a que se te pasen. (sentarse, esperar)

VII. No ___te sientas___ culpable al recibir el primer sueldo. (sentirse)

VIII. Hay más accidentes en el trabajo que en las cafeterías: ___ve___ a la cafetería a menudo. (ir)

IX. El trabajo consume; el descanso no: ¡___Ten___ cuidado! ___Haz___ lo menos posible. (Tener, Hacer)

Conclusión:

El trabajo es una cosa buena. No ___seas___ egoísta y ___déjalo___ para los demás. (ser, dejarlo)

Act. 16: Form pairs, set a time limit, and begin. Check by asking each group to read their best two. A commandment that will most probably come up will be related to eating something sweet. As a follow-up you may want to ask students why we find comfort in sweet things. To transition to Act. 17, ask whom people can see if they have emotional problems. Then transition to the work social workers do and move on to the next activity.

Actividad 16 Los cuatro mandamientos para un amigo triste En parejas, Uds. tienen un amigo que siempre está triste y deciden escribirle una lista de **cuatro mandamientos** (*commandments*) para ayudarlo a ser feliz. Intenten ser graciosos. Pueden usar el estilo de la Actividad 15 como guía.

▶ No salgas con personas más tristes que tú. Debes salir con personas más alegres.

Actividad 17 La asistente social y su caso Una asistente social les da órdenes a miembros de una familia porque no escuchan sus consejos. Cambia las siguientes sugerencias a órdenes con la forma para **tú, Ud.** o **Uds.** según a quién le esté hablando ella.

Act. 17: If assigned as HW, check in class.

▶ Felipe, debes limpiar tu habitación.
Felipe, limpia tu habitación.

1. Uds. deben escuchar a su hijo.
2. Juan, es importante que te comuniques con tus padres.
3. Uds. no deben pelearse delante de sus hijos.
4. Muchachos, Uds. tienen que ir a la escuela todos los días.
5. Señor, tiene que darles consejos a sus hijos.
6. Muchachos, no deben acostarse tarde.
7. Lucía, no debes desobedecer las órdenes de tus padres.
8. Muchachos, deben hacer un esfuerzo por hablar el idioma de sus padres.
9. Todos deben gritar menos y escuchar más.
10. Ignacio, debes venir a verme el mes que viene.

Desobedecer is conjugated like **conocer**.

Actividad 18 Órdenes implícitas **Parte A:** Mira el siguiente cuadro sobre la oración **Hace frío** y las órdenes que están implícitas en las tres situaciones.

Act. 18A: As in Act. 4 in this chapter, this activity is meant to make students think about the richness in meaning of a single phrase. Have students focus on the use of informal or formal commands, depending on the interlocutors. After examining the model, **Hace frío**, ask for other possible situations and meanings.

Oración	Quién a quién	Dónde	Orden implícita
Hace frío.	un jefe a su empleado	en una oficina	Apague el aire acondicionado.
	un instructor de esquí a otro	en la montaña	Ponte el anorak.
	un amante a su pareja	en un coche aparcado	Dame un beso.

Parte B: Ahora en grupos de tres, completen las cajas en blanco del segundo cuadro. Recuerden poner una orden bajo la columna "Orden implícita".

Act. 18B: You may want to do each sentence individually, setting a brief time period and then having the groups share responses. Continue this process with each.

Oración	Quién a quién	Dónde	Orden implícita
Tengo hambre.	un niño a su padre	en un carro en la autopista	Dame comida. / Para en un restaurante.
	un hombre a su esposa	en su casa	Prepárame la comida. / Ve a comprar algo para comer.
Dentro de cinco minutos los atiendo.	un mesero a los clientes	en un restaurante	No me molesten. / No me miren constantemente.
Esta sopa está fría.	una suegra a su nuera	en casa de la nuera	Cocina mejor. / Prepara bien la comida que le sirves a mi hijo.
	un hijo a sus padres / un cliente a un mesero	en un restaurante	No me den sopa. / Tráigame otra sopa. / Caliéntela.

Mention the importance of certain items in the economy of some countries. For example, coffee is important in the economies of Guatemala, El Salvador, and Colombia. Ecuador is the largest exporter of bananas in the world. Argentina is famous for the quality of its meat. Chile is an exporter of fine wine and fruit, and Spain exports fruit, especially Valencia oranges, and olive oil.

Discussing Food

La comida

FLR link: **Lectura 3**

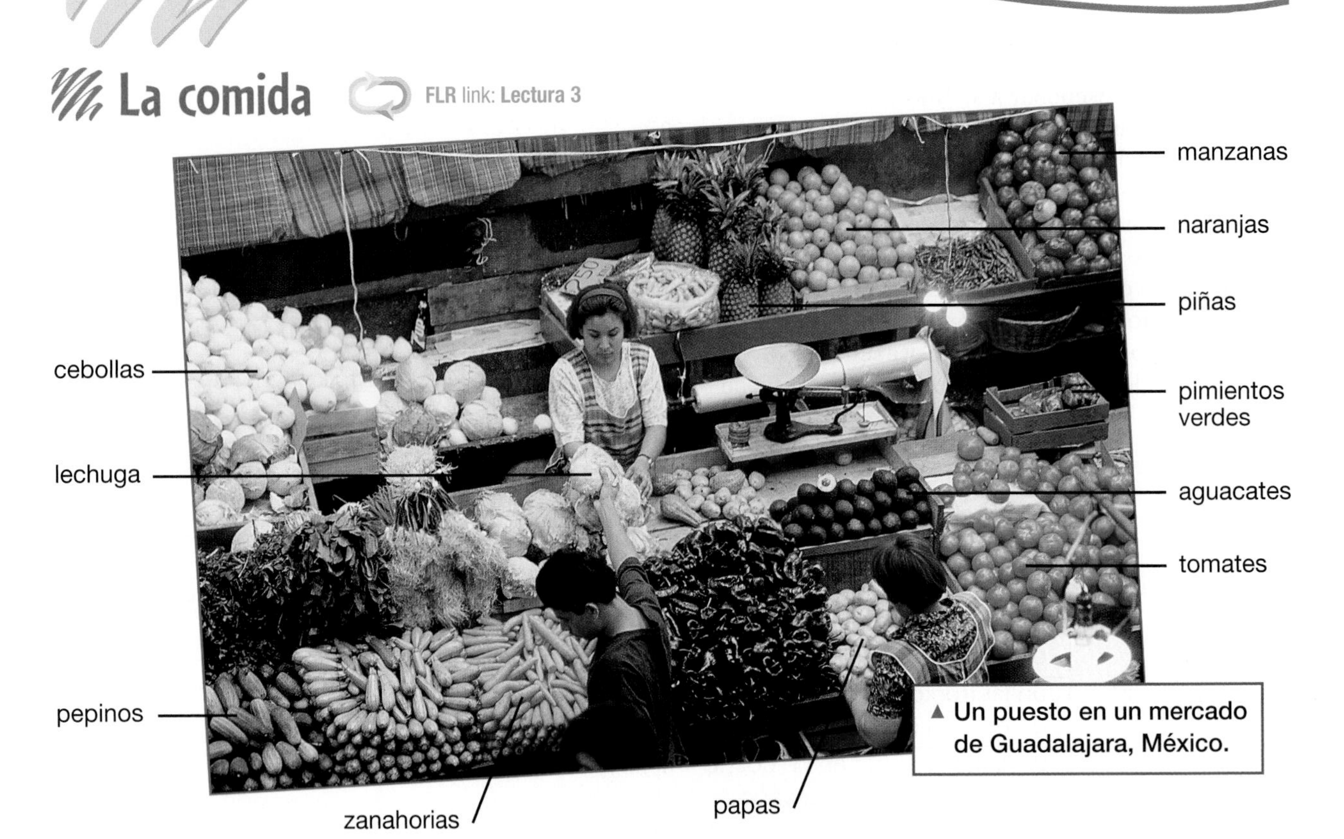

▲ Un puesto en un mercado de Guadalajara, México.

For more food items see Appendix G, p. 360.

camarones (*Latinoamérica*) = **gambas** (*España*)

durazno (*Latinoamérica*) = **melocotón** (*España*)

arvejas (*partes de Latinoamérica*) = **guisantes** (*España*)

papas (*Latinoamérica*) = **patatas** (*España*)

maní (*Latinoamérica*) = **cacahuetes** (*España*), **cacahuates** (*México*)

Carnes: cerdo (*pork*), cordero (*lamb*), cochinillo (*roast suckling pig*), solomillo (*filet mignon*), ternera (*veal*)
Pescado: anchoas, atún, lenguado (*sole*), merluza (*hake*), sardinas
Mariscos: calamares, camarones (*shrimp*), langostinos (*prawns*), mejillones (*mussels*), ostras
Fruta: durazno (*peach*), pera, sandía (*watermelon*)
Verduras: berenjena (*eggplant*), brócoli, maíz
Legumbres: arvejas (*peas*), frijoles (*beans*), garbanzos (*chick peas*), lentejas (*lentils*)
Embutidos: salchicha
Cereales: arroz
Dulces: flan, pastel (*cake; pie*)
Frutos secos: almendras, maní (*peanuts*)
Productos lácteos: crema
Bebidas: agua mineral con o sin gas, vino, jugo (*juice*)
Productos: congelados (*frozen*), enlatados, frescos
Platos: el aperitivo, el primer plato, el segundo plato, el postre, el café

Actividad 19 Me encanta **Parte A:** En parejas, digan qué comidas de la lista en la página 132 les encantaba comer y cuáles no les gustaban para nada cuando eran niños.

Parte B: Ahora digan cuáles de las comidas que mencionaron comen ahora.

Actividad 20 Congelados, enlatados o frescos En parejas, decidan a qué categoría(s) pertenecen los siguientes productos. Luego añadan dos productos más en cada categoría.

1. pollo
2. berenjena
3. jamón
4. ajo
5. arvejas
6. langostinos
7. maíz
8. anchoas

Productos		
Enlatados	Congelados	Frescos

Actividad 21 ¿Qué comiste? **Parte A:** Haz una lista de todo lo que comiste ayer y di cuándo lo comiste.

▶ A las ocho comí cereal con leche y un plátano.
A las diez comí una barra de chocolate—un Snickers.

Parte B: En parejas, lean lo que comieron una española y una mexicana y comparen lo que comieron ellas con lo que comieron Uds. También comparen el horario de las comidas. ¿Quién comió comidas más saludables? ¿Quién almorzó más temprano? Etc.

◂ **Un desayuno típico en España es café con leche, zumo de naranja, tostadas, mantequilla y mermelada. Se comen las tostadas con cuchillo y tenedor y no con las manos.**

zumo (*España*) = **jugo** (*Latinoamérica*)

Act. 19A: This activity recycles the use of the imperfect for habitual and repetitive actions.

Act. 20: You can **dar cátedra** after checking this activity. Possible information includes: **En los países de habla española es común preparar la mayoría de la comida con productos frescos. Las verduras se compran frescas y no enlatadas o congeladas. Después de comprar la carne, no es común congelarla, o sea, se prepara ese día o al día siguiente. Tanto las sopas como los guisados se suelen hacer en casa y algunas veces se usa una olla de presión** (*pressure cooker*) **para no pasar todo el día cocinando.**

Act. 21A: This could be assigned as HW. In class, have students share what they ate yesterday.

Act. 21B: Besides comparing what was eaten and the times, discuss the types of foods: high in fat vs. low fat, fresh vs. processed, at home vs. out, etc. Since students tend to eat a "strange" diet, ask them to compare what the Mexican and Spaniard ate with what they would have eaten on a typical day when they lived at home vs. in a dorm. Ask Heritage speakers if their family eats any traditional dishes at home.

café con leche = café con mucha leche caliente (se sirve en taza normal, normalmente se toma por la mañana y no después de comer)

carne guisada = stew

cortadito = un café expreso con un poquito de leche (se sirve en taza pequeña, se toma después de comer o por la tarde)

cañas = glasses of beer

tortilla = *omelet (Spain)*

mayonesa (*Latinoamérica*) = **mahonesa** (*España*)

"Ayer desayuné una tostada, un par de galletas y un **café con leche**. Sobre las 11:30 entré en un bar y me tomé un café con un croissant y a eso de la una, empecé a preparar la comida. De primer plato hice mahonesa para acompañar unos espárragos, de segundo, una **carne guisada** con patatas y zanahorias y de postre, sandía y melocotón. Me puse a comer alrededor de las dos y media y claro, para terminar, me tomé un **cortadito**. Por la tarde fui de compras con mi madre y a las 7:30 paramos en un bar donde tomamos un aperitivo. Pedimos unas **cañas** y el camarero nos dio unas patatas fritas y aceitunas para picar, pero teníamos hambre y pedimos una ración de gambas al ajillo para compartir. Dejé a mi madre en su casa, y al volver a la mía me encontré con un amigo y paramos en otro bar donde tomé una Coca-Cola y compartimos un pincho de **tortilla**. Por la noche, más o menos a las once me preparé dos huevos fritos con una loncha de jamón y un poco de queso. De postre me comí un poco más de la sandía mientras miraba la tele."

española

chilaquiles = tortillas con salsa y queso

café = café expreso

"El sábado desayuné a las nueve de la mañana **chilaquiles** con frijoles, cóctel de frutas y jugo de naranja. Comí a las tres de la tarde crema de brócoli, pechuga de pollo asada con ensalada de verduras y un pastelito de postre. Cené a las nueve de la noche un vaso de leche."

mexicana

Act. 22A: Form groups, set a time limit, and begin. As they work, try to move them along by announcing how much longer they have.

Actividad 22 El menú **Parte A:** En grupos de tres, Uds. trabajan en una compañía de servicio de comidas. Su profesor/a es un/a cliente y les pide que le planeen el menú para una cena importante. Planeen qué van a servir de aperitivo, de primer y segundo plato y de postre. Saben lo siguiente sobre los invitados.

Diego Maldonado: Es vegetariano.
Alicia Carvajal: Le fascina todo tipo de carne.
Germán Martini: Tiene alergia a los camarones y a los langostinos y está a dieta, por eso prefiere comida de pocas calorías.
Lucrecia Hernández: Tiene buen paladar, le gusta absolutamente todo.

En España se toma el aperitivo antes de comer en casa o en un bar. Consta de un trago (una Coca-Cola, una cerveza, un Cinzano, etc.) y, a veces, algo pequeño para picar como aceitunas o un platito de papas fritas. Se suele tomar los fines de semana. En otros países es común tomar el aperitivo sólo en ocasiones especiales.

Act. 22B: Have different groups read their menus and pick the one that you like the best to cater the dinner. You may want to interrupt to ask the caterers specific questions.

Parte B: Ahora denle las sugerencias del menú perfecto a su profesor/a y estén preparados para explicar por qué eligieron ese menú. Usen expresiones como **De aperitivo le recomendamos que sirva..., También le sugerimos que ofrezca...**

Act. 23A and B: Form pairs, set a time limit, and begin. Then tell students to change roles, set a new time limit, and begin. When finished, have students do Part B. Check by taking a poll dealing with junk food and cooking ability of class members.

Actividad 23 Gustos personales **Parte A:** En parejas, entrevístense para averiguar sus preferencias alimenticias.

1. ¿Te gusta la comida de otros países? ¿Cuál es tu plato favorito? ¿Cuál es el país de origen de esa comida?
2. ¿Prefieres la comida casera o la de restaurante?
3. ¿Cuándo fue la última vez que comiste fuera y qué comiste?
4. ¿Qué platos comías con mucha frecuencia cuando eras niño/a?

(continúa en la página siguiente)

5. ¿Cuántas veces por día comes?
6. ¿Comes mientras miras televisión o mientras lees algo?
7. ¿Comes muchas porquerías (*junk food*) o comida rápida?
8. ¿Te gusta cocinar? Si contestas que sí, ¿quién te enseñó? ¿Qué platos cocinas?

Parte B: Ahora díganle a la otra persona si tiene buenos hábitos alimenticios, basando su opinión en las respuestas de la Parte A. Si no tiene buenos hábitos, denle consejos.

▶ No tienes buenos hábitos alimenticios porque... Te aconsejo que...

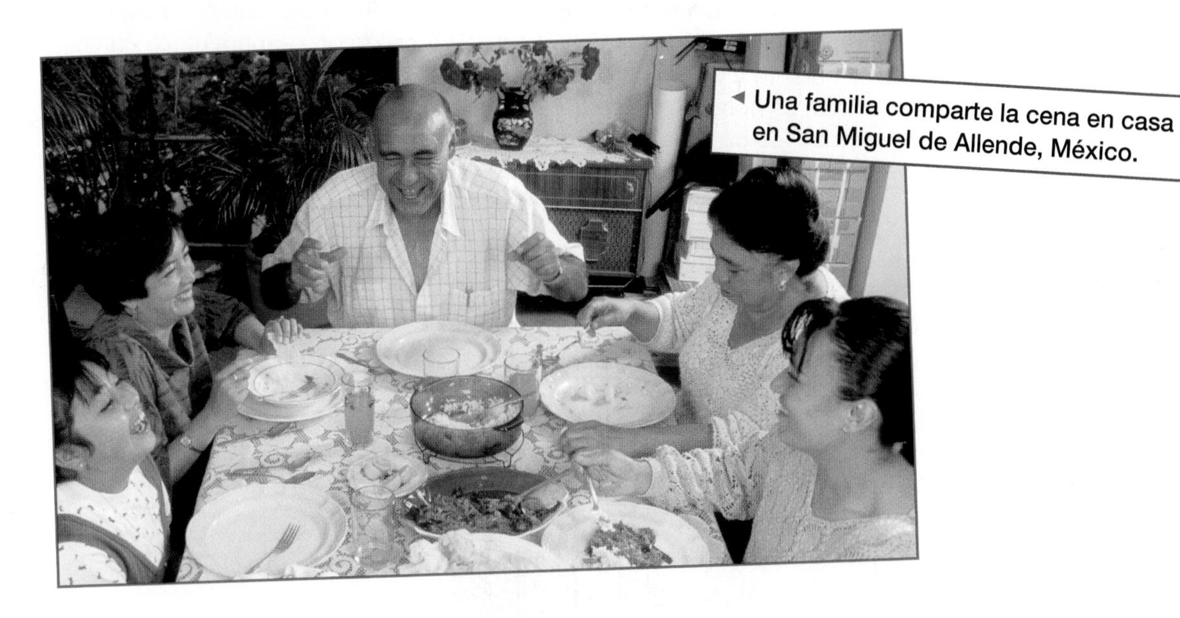

◀ Una familia comparte la cena en casa en San Miguel de Allende, México.

Actividad 24 Los modales de la mesa **Parte A:** Usa las siguientes ideas para decir órdenes que normalmente oyen los niños hispanos o los de tu país a la hora de comer.

Act. 24A: May be assigned as HW and checked in class.

1. poner las dos manos en la mesa
2. poner la mano que no usas debajo de la mesa
3. empujar los frijoles con el cuchillo
4. no apoyar los codos en la mesa
5. dejar el cuchillo y tomar el tenedor con la otra mano al comer
6. tomar sólo un pedazo de pan para comerlo y no todo el pan
7. no levantarse de la mesa inmediatamente después del postre

Parte B: En parejas, decidan cuáles de las órdenes anteriores se oyen en tu país y cuáles se oyen en un país hispano.

Act. 24B: Commands typically heard in a Hispanic household include: 1, 3, 4, 6 (bread should be broken into bite-size pieces as you eat), 7 (after eating, it is common to sit and talk for a while - **sobremesa**). Commands typically heard in the U.S.: 2, 4, 5.

 *Etiqueta y modales en la mesa*

If you want, you may provide additional information about eating habits: **Normalmente no se le da el salero a otra persona en la mano porque eso trae mala suerte. Es mejor ponerlo enfrente de la persona que lo pidió. Se toma el café al final de la comida después del postre. Este café normalmente es un café expreso solo o con un poco de leche (un cortado) y no se repite.**

¿LO SABÍAN?

Los modales de la mesa varían en todo el mundo. Lo que es apropiado en un lugar, puede ser descortés en otro. En la mayoría de los países de habla española, se considera buena educación siempre tener las dos manos en la mesa, no levantar mucho los brazos al cortar la comida y empujar con la ayuda de un pedazo de pan o del cuchillo para poner la comida en el tenedor. El pan se rompe con la mano en trocitos pequeños a medida que se come.

Después de comer el postre, viene la sobremesa que consiste en conversar mientras se toma el café. Por eso si uno espera mesa en un restaurante y ve a un grupo de personas que acaban de terminar de comer, es posible que se queden un rato más sólo para charlar. Sólo cuando los clientes piden la cuenta —se considera mala educación llevarla a la mesa sin que la pidan— uno sabe que se preparan para irse. ¿Qué hace la gente en un restaurante en tu país cuando termina de comer el postre?

Act. 25: Read the quotes to the students, form groups, have them discuss them for a moment, and then have a group discussion on the topic.

Fuentes hispanas

Actividad 25 A discutir En grupos de tres, lean las siguientes citas relacionadas con la comida y coméntenlas.

"En la mesa se descubre la educación de cualquier persona. Si quieres saber si un hombre o una mujer tiene buenos modales, invítalo a comer: si no sabe comportarse, pues fuera de la mesa será peor, te lo aseguro."

—Pedro Vargas Ponce
Director de la Escuela Superior de Protocolo, Venezuela

"Comer no es sólo una actividad biológica; es también algo social, cultural. La comida es un momento muy especial en el que de algún modo se manifiestan actitudes esenciales ante la vida."

—José Fernando Calderero
Autor de* Los buenos modales de tus hijos mayores*, España

III. Informing and Giving Instructions

Impersonal and Passive *se*

1. When giving information or instructions in situations where the person doing the action is not important, you may use the following construction with **se.**

se	+	*third person singular of verb*		
		third person singular of verb	+	*singular noun*
		third person plural of verb	+	*plural noun or series of nouns*

Se come bien en esta casa.	*People/They/You eat well in this house.* (No noun follows the verb; therefore the verb is singular.)
Se estudia mucho en esta universidad.	*People/They/You study a lot at this university.*
En España, **se usa aceite** de oliva para cocinar.	*Olive oil is used to cook in Spain.* (In everyday English: People/They/You use olive oil to cook in Spain.)
Se comen quesadillas en México.	*Quesadillas are eaten in Mexico.* (In everyday English: People/They/You eat quesadillas in Mexico.)
Se añaden sal y pimienta.	*Salt and pepper are added.*
Primero, **se calientan las verduras** y luego **se añade el arroz.**	*First, the vegetables are heated and then the rice is added.* (In everyday English: People/They/You heat the vegetables and then add the rice.)

The following is a rhyme that is said to children at the table so that they will have good manners.

En la mesa no se canta,
ni tampoco se dan gritos,
ni se juega con las cosas,
ni se ponen los coditos.

FLR link: **Lectura 2**

For simplicity at this level, no distinction is made between impersonal and passive **se.** The passive voice will be presented in Chapter 9.

You may want to tell your students that **deber, poder, soler,** and **tener que** are pluralized before an infinitive when the object is plural: **Primero se tienen que hervir las papas.**

Drill the **se** construction:

1. Give directions to make your favorite dish and have students change verbs, using **se.** T: **Para hacer una quesadilla necesito queso y tortillas.** Ss: **Se necesitan...** T: **Primero** (cutting gesture) **corto el queso en pedacitos.** Ss: **Se corta...** T: **Luego en una sartén...**

2. Ask students questions about food on campus. **¿Se come bien en la cafetería? ¿Qué se come? ¿Qué se prepara? ¿Con qué se preparan los mejores/peores sándwiches?**

3. Have the whole class give directions on how to make a typical American dish like chocolate chip cookies. Provide vocabulary as needed.

2. The following verbs related to food preparation are frequently used with the **se** construction.

añadir to add
bajar/subir el fuego to lower/raise the heat
calentar (ie) to heat
echar to pour; to put in
freír (i, i) to fry
hervir (ie, i) to boil
mezclar to mix

Act. 26: Try to pair upperclassmen with freshmen so that they actually learn about the university. Check by comparing responses from different pairs.

Actividad 26 Información para novatos En parejas, contesten estas preguntas sobre actividades estudiantiles de su universidad. Usen la construcción con **se** en las respuestas.

1. ¿Dónde se come bien?
2. ¿Dónde se estudia?
3. ¿Cuándo se estudia?
4. ¿Se estudia mucho o poco?
5. ¿Adónde se va los fines de semana para divertirse?
6. ¿Dónde se vive el primer año? ¿Y el último año?
7. Normalmente, ¿a qué hora se va a la primera clase?

Act. 27A: Assign as HW or do in class. Check. You may want to mention that Puerto Rico does not use the metric system due to influences from the U.S.

www *La comida hispana: Recetas*

Actividad 27 Una receta **Parte A:** Completa las instrucciones para una receta típica de Puerto Rico, usando la construcción con **se**. Atención: gandules y habichuelas son tipos de frijoles (*beans*).

calabaza = pumpkin
sofrito = combination of lightly fried ingredients
puerco = pork
dorados = golden
espese = it thickens

(limpiar) Se limpian las habichuelas. (lavar) Se lavan dos veces en agua fría y (dejar) se dejan en agua durante una noche. (quitar/hervir) Se quita el agua. Se hierven 8 tazas de agua en una olla. (añadir) Se añaden las habichuelas y la calabaza. (dejar) Se dejan hervir a fuego moderado por una hora hasta que las habichuelas estén casi blandas.

Mientras tanto, (preparar) se prepara el sofrito. En una cacerola (calentar) se calienta el aceite. A fuego lento (freír) se fríe el puerco curado y el jamón hasta que estén dorados. (bajar) Se baja el fuego a muy bajo, y (freír) se fríen ligeramente la cebolla, los pimientos, el ajo, el cilantro y el orégano por 10 minutos.

Cuando las habichuelas están casi blandas, (pisar) se pisa la calabaza con un tenedor y (añadir) se añade la mezcla al sofrito. (añadir) Se añaden la salsa de tomate y la sal. (poner) Se pone todo a hervir y (cocinar) se cocina sin tapar, a fuego moderado, por una hora hasta que espese al gusto.

Habichuelas puertorriqueñas
(**8** porciones)
1 libra de gandules o habichuelas
8 tazas de agua
3/4 de libra de calabaza, pelada y cortada en pedacitos
1 cucharada de aceite vegetal
1 pedazo (**2** onzas) de puerco curado (tocino grueso)
2 onzas de jamón
1 cebolla, picada
1 pimiento verde, picado
2 pimientos rojos, picados
1 cucharada de cilantro, picado
1/4 de cucharadita de orégano, espolvoreado
1 diente de ajo
1/4 de taza de salsa de tomate
2 cucharaditas de sal

Parte B: Ahora, dale instrucciones detalladas a tu profesor/a para preparar un sándwich de mantequilla de maní y mermelada.

Act. 27B: Do as a full class activity. Bring in ingredients and carry out students' commands to the letter, do not assume anything: if they say **ponga la mermelada en el pan,** put the jar of jelly on the bread. This will force them to be very specific in their commands.

Actividad 28 Música y comida La música y la comida son parte importante de la cultura de un país. En parejas, completen el cuadro y luego formen oraciones usando la construcción con **se** para decir en qué país se consumen las siguientes comidas y se escucha la siguiente música.

▶ tomar fabada, una sopa
En España se toma fabada, una sopa. / No estoy seguro/a, pero creo que se toma fabada en España.

	Comidas y bebidas	Música
Cuba		
España	tomar fabada,	
México		
Argentina		
Perú		

Comidas y bebidas

servir arroz con gandules
usar salsa picante
preparar gazpacho (una sopa fría)
servir asado (*barbecue*)
comer mole
beber Inca Cola
freír plátano
hacer tortillas de maíz
comer tortillas de huevos
beber sangría
comer ropa vieja

Música

tocar música andina
bailar el flamenco
componer tangos
bailar el mambo
tocar música de mariachis
bailar el chachachá
tocar la gaita (*bagpipe*)

Ask students ¿Dónde se dicen "tacos" en vez de comerlos?

Act. 28: **Fabada** is a thick soup from Asturias, the base of which is fava beans.

Act. 28: Answers may include: Cuba: **moros y cristianos, plátano, ropa vieja**; **rumba, mambo, chachachá;** España: **gazpacho, tortilla de huevos, sangría; flamenco, gaita** (in Galicia, Spain); México: **salsa picante, mole** (a thick chili sauce that is made with chocolate), **tortillas de maíz; mariachis;** Argentina: **asado; tangos;** Perú: **Inca Cola; música andina.** Question: **España, tacos** = swear words.

Young people usually listen to **rock nacional o de otros países** instead of **flamenco, mariachis, tango y música andina.**

◀ Ernie Acevedo toca congas con el Conjunto Imagen en la ciudad de Nueva York.

Act. 29: Explain any menu item unknown to the students. Note: The Cuban **tortilla** is an omelet.

You may want to photocopy the menu and the role cards and put the expressions to use on a screen using an overhead projector. This will allow you to do the activity with books closed. Form four groups: all the children, all the waiters, all husbands, and all wives. Have them discuss the types of things they will do and say in the role play. When finished, set up groups containing people that play the four different roles or, if you don't have an even number, have one group with two diners and a waiter. Set a time limit and begin. As a check you may want to have some groups act out the conversation for the rest of the class, or you may ask the waiters what their clients ordered, and the clients how the waiters behaved.

Actividad 29 En el restaurante puertorriqueño En grupos de cuatro, lea cada uno solamente uno de los siguientes papeles y prepárense para representarlo. También miren el menú.

A

Eres camarero/a en un restaurante puertorriqueño. No te gusta tu trabajo para nada, por lo tanto eres muy antipático/a con los clientes. Ahora llega una familia al restaurante. Prepárate para darles algunas sugerencias del menú de bajo contenido graso (♥). Usa expresiones como: **Le sugiero/recomiendo que pruebe... La ensalada se prepara con... ¿Quiere algo de primer plato?** La familia va a estar en la mesa y tú apareces en la escena para tomar el pedido, servir la comida, darles alguna mala noticia o hacerles algún comentario negativo. Usa alguna de las expresiones que aparecen al final de la actividad.

B

Estás en un restaurante puertorriqueño con tu esposa e hijo/a. Tu hijo/a tiene muy malos modales en la mesa y siempre estás atento para corregirlo/a. Tú tienes el colesterol alto, pero te encantan las comidas de alto contenido graso. Pídele sugerencias al camarero o a la camarera. Usa expresiones como: **¿Qué me sugiere/recomienda? ¿El pollo se prepara con (mucho aceite/ajo)? ¿Con qué viene la carne?** Usa alguna de las expresiones que aparecen al final de la actividad.

C

Estás en un restaurante puertorriqueño con tu esposo y tu hijo/a. Tu esposo tiene el colesterol alto y le gusta mucho comer comidas de muchas calorías. Tienes que asegurarte de que él pida comida de bajo contenido graso y que no coma mucho. Tú eres vegetariana y tienes un hambre atroz. Pídele sugerencias al camarero o a la camarera. Usa expresiones como: **¿Qué me sugiere/recomienda? ¿La tortilla de papas se prepara con (mucho aceite)?** Usa algunas de las expresiones de la siguiente lista.

D

Estás en un restaurante puertorriqueño con tus padres y estás muy aburrido/a y no tienes mucha hambre. También tienes muy malos modales en la mesa. Te gusta, por ejemplo, poner los codos en la mesa para llamar la atención de tu padre. Actúa diferentes modales inaceptables en una mesa hispana. A tus padres les gusta comer y tu rol es comentar sobre sus hábitos alimenticios y los tuyos usando algunas expresiones de la siguiente lista.

Buen provecho.	Enjoy your meal.
ser de buen comer	to have a good appetite
tener un hambre atroz	to be really hungry
querer repetir	to want a second helping
estar satisfecho/a **no poder más**	to be full

Borinquen

Restaurante puertorriqueño

Especialidades de la casa	
Camarones a la criolla	$9.95
♥ Arroz con pollo	$6.50
Bistec con cebollas	$6.95
Fricasé de ternera	$6.50
♥ Arroz con gandules	$5.75
(con plátano frito)	$6.75
Lechón asado con yuca frita	$7.00
Carne guisada de res	$7.95
♥ Pescado del día con papas	$9.25
♥ Pollo al ajo con verduras	$6.95
Pechuga de pollo rellena de plátano maduro	$7.95
Arroz blanco y habichuelas	$3.00
Mofongo	$1.50
Tostones	$1.50
Pasteles	$1.50
Plátanos maduros	$1.50

Ensaladas	
♥ Ensalada mixta	$3.00
♥ Ensalada de tomate	$1.50
♥ Ensalada verde	$1.50
Sopas	
♥ Habichuelas negros	$2.00
Pollo	$2.00
Asopaos de Pollo, Camarones, Mariscos	$7.95
Postres	
Flan de coco	$1.95
Coco rallado con queso	$2.50
Dulce de papaya con queso	$2.50
Bebidas	
Agua mineral	$1.00
Cerveza	$2.50
Jugos tropicales	$1.50
Batida de mango	$2.00
Café	$1.00

Debido a la influencia de los Estados Unidos en Puerto Rico, los puertorriqueños usan punto en vez de coma cuando escriben números: Puerto Rico 8.95, el resto de los países de habla española 8,95.

lechón asado = roast suckling pig

mofongo = plantain side dish

tostones = fried plantain chips

asopaos = thick soup similar to gumbo

Do the corresponding CD-ROM and web activities to review the chapter topics.

Vocabulario activo

Verbos para expresar influencia

aconsejar	*to advise*
esperar	*to hope*
exigir	*to demand*
insistir en	*to insist*
pedir (i, i)	*to ask (for)*
preferir (ie, i)	*to prefer*
proponer	*to propose*
querer (ie)	*to want*
recomendar (ie)	*to recommend*
rogar (ue)	*to beg*
sugerir (ie, i)	*to suggest*
suplicar	*to implore*

Expresiones impersonales para expresar influencia

es aconsejable	*it's advisable*
es buena/mala idea	*it's a good/bad idea*
es bueno/malo	*it's good/bad*
es importante	*it's important*
es mejor	*it's better*
es necesario	*it's necessary*
es preferible	*it's preferable*

La comida

Carnes	*Meat*
el cerdo	*pork*
el cochinillo	*roast suckling pig*
el cordero	*lamb*
el solomillo	*filet mignon*
la ternera	*veal*

Pescado	Fish
las anchoas	*anchovies*
el atún	*tuna*
el lenguado	*sole*
la merluza	*hake*
las sardinas	*sardines*

Mariscos	Seafood
los calamares	*calamari, squid*
los camarones/las gambas (*Spain*)	*shrimp*
los langostinos	*prawns*
los mejillones	*mussels*
las ostras	*oysters*

Fruta	Fruit
las aceitunas	*olives*
el aguacate	*avocado*
el durazno/el melocotón (*Spain*)	*peach*
la manzana	*apple*
la naranja	*orange*
la pera	*pear*
la piña	*pineapple*
la sandía	*watermelon*

Verduras	*Vegetables*
la berenjena	*eggplant*
la cebolla	*onion*
la lechuga	*lettuce*
el maíz	*corn*
la papa/la patata (*Spain*)	*potato*
el pepino	*cucumber*
el pimiento (verde/rojo)	*(green/red) pepper*
el tomate	*tomato*
la zanahoria	*carrot*

Legumbres	*Legumes*
las arvejas/los guisantes (Spain)	*peas*
los garbanzos	*garbanzos (chick peas)*
las lentejas	*lentils*

Embutidos	*Types of Sausages*
la salchicha	*sausage*

Cereales	*Cereals*
el arroz	*rice*

Dulces	***Sweets***
el flan	*custard*
el pastel	*cake; pie*
el pastelito	*pastry*
Frutos secos	***Dried fruit***
las almendras	*almonds*
el maní	*peanuts*
las nueces	*nuts*
Productos lácteos	***Dairy products***
la crema	*cream*
Edulcorante	***Sweeteners***
el azúcar	*sugar*
la sacarina	*saccharine*
Bebidas	***Drinks***
el agua mineral	
con gas	*sparkling water*
sin gas	*mineral water*
el café	*espresso*
el café con leche	*coffee with milk (coffee with lots of hot milk)*
el cortado	*espresso with a touch of milk*
el vino	*wine*
Productos	***Products***
congelados	*frozen*
enlatados	*canned*
frescos	*fresh*
Platos	***Dishes, courses (in a meal)***
el aperitivo	*appetizer*
el primer plato	*first course*
el segundo plato	*second course*
el postre	*dessert*
el café	*coffee*

Verbos relacionados con la comida

añadir	*to add*
bajar el fuego	*to lower the heat*
calentar (ie)	*to heat*
freír (i, i)	*to fry*
hervir (ie, i)	*to boil*
mezclar	*to mix*
subir el fuego	*to raise the heat*

Expresiones útiles

Buen provecho.	*Enjoy your meal.*
ser de buen comer	*to have a good appetite*
tener un hambre atroz	*to be really hungry*
querer repetir	*to want a second helping*
estar satisfecho/a / no poder más	*to be full (have enough to eat)*
¿Acaso no sabías?	*But, didn't you know?*
dar cátedra	*to lecture someone (on some topic)*
tener ganas de + *infinitive*	*to feel like + ing*
... y punto	*... and that's that*

Vocabulario personal

Capítulo 6

Metas comunicativas

- expresar emociones, sentimientos y opiniones sobre el presente, pasado y futuro
- expresar duda, emoción o negación sobre el presente, pasado y futuro
- hablar de política
- expresar causa, propósito y destino

Nuevas democracias

Meta adicional

- formar oraciones complejas

▲ Ciudadanos chilenos exigen saber dónde están sus familiares que desaparecieron durante la dictadura de Pinochet.

May be assigned: Grammar, vocabulary, **¿Lo sabían?,** Act. 4A, Act. 6A, Act. 8A, Act. 9, Act. 14A, Act. 18A, Act. 19A, Act. 26, Act. 27A, Act. 29, Act. 30A.

Show the chapter video episode at any point in the chapter that you see fit and do all or selected activities in class. Note: Content of the video supplements the cultural material in the chapter and activities reenter chapter grammar and vocabulary.

Nadie está inmune

los desaparecidos	missing people
quién diría	who would say
salirse con la suya	to get his/her way

▲ Sting cantó "Ellas danzan solas" para las madres y esposas de los desaparecidos en Buenos Aires, Argentina.

Practice expressions: Write the three expressions on the board. Practice the expressions by giving students background information to help them understand the conversation. While looking at the photo on page 144, stress that the children and spouses of these people are **desaparecidos que un día estaban con sus familias y que al día siguiente no porque el gobierno se los llevó y sus familias nunca los volvieron a ver.** Continue by saying **Quién diría que esto podría pasar, pero durante años esos militares o gobiernos militares se salieron con la suya—o sea, que hicieron lo que querían cuando querían.** You could go on and ask if certain U.S. presidents **se salieron con la suya** (Nixon/Watergate, Reagan/Iran-Contra, Clinton/Monica/Whitewater, George W. Bush/la guerra con Iraq).

FLR link: **Lectura 1**

Note: **Los desaparecidos** has become almost a proper name applied to people that disappeared in the **Cono Sur** during the dictatorships of the 70s and 80s.

Students can read both Spanish and English lyrics of **"Ellas danzan solas"** / "They Dance Alone" online.

Act. 1A: Do this in small groups or as a full group activity.

Act. 1B: Allow students a moment to read through the items. Play the CD, correct. Play the CD twice if needed.

Mendoza es una ciudad en Argentina al lado de los Andes y cerca de la frontera con Chile.

Actividad 1 La situación política **Parte A:** Antes de escuchar a dos chilenos hablar sobre mucha gente que desapareció en Chile durante el gobierno militar del general Pinochet, identifica las siguientes cosas.

- dos países hispanos, aparte de Chile, que han tenido gobierno militar
- un país hispano que hoy día tiene un gobierno estable
- dos factores que pueden causar inestabilidad económica en una democracia
- músicos o actores que han dado un concierto o hecho un anuncio en favor de los derechos humanos o en contra del abuso de los mismos

Parte B: Lee las siguientes oraciones y luego escucha la conversación para completarlas.

1. En ___1988___ (año) Sting dio un concierto en Mendoza, Argentina, en honor de ___los desaparecidos___.
2. Durante el gobierno militar de Chile torturaron y desaparecieron ___miles de___ personas.
3. Pinochet, el ex dictador chileno, estaba de viaje en ___Inglaterra___ cuando el juez español Garzón le pidió a ese país su extradición.
4. Algunas de las víctimas de Pinochet eran de ascendencia ___española___.
5. Al final, el dictador Pinochet no fue encarcelado por sus crímenes por estar ___enfermo___.

Act. 2: Play CD again and ask students the questions in this activity. Note: When Pinochet returned to Chile from England after suffering international humiliation, he was placed under "house arrest" (**arresto domiciliario**).

Actividad 2 Más datos Escucha la conversación otra vez para responder a las siguientes preguntas.

1. ¿Por qué fueron 15.000 chilenos al concierto de Sting en Mendoza, Argentina?
2. Sting escribió una canción dedicada a las madres y esposas de los chilenos desaparecidos. ¿Por qué crees que la llamó "Ellas danzan solas"?
3. ¿A qué se refiere la chica cuando dice que los gobernantes no van a salirse con la suya?
4. ¿Por qué decidieron los familiares de los desaparecidos hacer el reclamo a España?
5. Pinochet creía que tenía inmunidad diplomática, pero Garzón no opinaba lo mismo. Después de lo que ocurrió en Inglaterra, ¿va a ser más fácil o más difícil para los violadores de derechos humanos visitar otros países?

 *Desaparecidos*

Other countries like Argentina, Uruguay, and Guatemala also had large numbers of **desaparecidos;** Argentina had more than 30,000 during **la guerra sucia.** Just as the Chilean women did the cueca, the Argentine mothers to this day go every Thursday to the Plaza de Mayo in front of the **Casa Rosada** (a government building) to demand an explanation for their missing children to make sure these horrors are not repeated (**Nunca más**).

The movie *La historia oficial* deals with this issue of the **desaparecidos** in Argentina and could be assigned as extra credit.

¿LO SABÍAN?

Durante la dictadura de Pinochet en Chile entre el 11 de septiembre de 1973 y 1990 desaparecieron o murieron más de 3.000 personas. Entre ellos había estudiantes, trabajadores de fábricas, artistas y profesionales que fueron torturados y asesinados por disentir del gobierno. La forma pacífica que encontraron las madres y esposas de los desaparecidos para expresar su protesta era bailar la cueca frente a una estación de policía. Éste es un baile típico de Chile que es lento y se baila en pareja, pero en esas ocasiones las mujeres llevaban en su pecho la foto del familiar desaparecido y bailaban con un compañero invisible. Cuando el cantante Sting se enteró de la situación en Chile, se conmovió por lo ocurrido, escribió una canción en honor de esas mujeres y la llamó "Ellas danzan solas". La canción imitaba en parte el ritmo de la cueca.

Act. 3: If students do not challenge each other's responses, play devil's advocate just to get some discussion going. For example: You may state that some people say that the death penalty is a violation of human rights, especially in the case of a 17-year-old offender or someone with a low I.Q. You may state that there is a difference in wealth between rich and poor, but all can be rich if they work hard, quit crying, get working, etc.

Actividad 3 La situación aquí En grupos de tres, digan si están de acuerdo con estas ideas sobre su país y justifiquen sus respuestas.

1. La situación económica de este país está cada día mejor.
2. Cada vez hay más gente de clase media y menos gente de clase baja.
3. No existe la violación de los derechos humanos en este país.
4. Hay muchos actos de violencia.

I. Expressing Feelings, Emotions, and Opinions about Present, Future, and Past Events

 Do the corresponding CD-ROM and web activities as you study the chapter.

A. The Present Subjunctive

1. In Chapter 5, you learned how to use the subjunctive to make suggestions, persuade, influence, and give advice. The subjunctive can also be used to express feelings, emotions, and opinions about another person's actions or about a situation in the present or future as in the following construction.

Independent Clause	que	Dependent Clause
Subject 1 + *verb of emotion* (indicative)	**que**	Subject 2 + verb (subjunctive)

(Yo)	estoy contento de	que	(Uds.)	puedan votar.
I	*am happy*	*that*	*you*	*can vote.*
(Él)	tiene miedo de	que	(ella)	no lo defienda mañana en la corte.
He	*is afraid*	*that*	*she*	*will not defend him in court tomorrow.*

2. Use these verbs to express emotion.

esperar	to hope
estar contento/a (de)	to be happy
estar triste (de)	to be sad
lamentar	to lament, be sorry
sentir (ie, i)	to be sorry
temer	to fear
tener miedo (de)	to be afraid
alegrarle (a alguien)*	to be glad, happy
darle pena (a alguien)*	to feel sorry
molestarle (a alguien)*	to be bothered
sorprenderle (a alguien)*	to be surprised

Ella está contenta de que haya una democracia estable. — *She is happy that there is a stable democracy.* (present situation)

Les da* pena que el vicepresidente esté enfermo. — *They feel sorry that the vice president is sick.* (present situation)

Drill subjunctive with feelings and opinions:

1. Write **Es fantástico que..., Lamento que..., Me alegra que...** on the board. Tell students they are instructors and have to express feelings about their students. Give cues like **estudiar mucho, no hacer la tarea, ir al laboratorio.** S: **Me alegra que Uds. estudien mucho.**

2. Tell students that they suffer from **agorafobia** (fear of open or public spaces) and have them brainstorm things they fear about crowds: **gente robarme, alguien hablarme, gente tocarme, alguien mirarme.** Then have students express their fears: **Temo que la gente me robe. Tengo miedo (de) que alguien me hable por la calle.** Now have them say things they fear about going outside: **Temo caerme y romperme una pierna.** (etc.)

3. Have students express their feelings about other classmates' behavior or about upcoming local, campus, or national events. **Me alegra que intentes hablar español. Es malo que tengas tres novios.** (etc.)

You may want to explain the difference between **Me sorprendo de tu habilidad** where **me** is a reflexive pronoun and **yo** is the implied subject, and **Me sorprende tu habilidad** where **me** is an indirect object and **tu habilidad** is the subject. The same applies for **alegrarse de** and **alegrarle** and other similar verbs.

You may want to explain that in some countries (such as Mexico) **darle pena** means *to feel ashamed.*

Nos molesta* que el gobierno no ayude a todos los ciudadanos.	*It bothers us that the government doesn't help all citizens.* (present situation)
¿Te alegra* que el pueblo vote por ese candidato en las próximas elecciones?	*Are you glad that the people will vote for that candidate in the next elections?* (future situation)

*Note: These verbs function like **gustar** and they are always singular when followed by a clause introduced by **que.**

You may want to inform students that expressions such as **lamentar, molestarle** can also be used with only one subject followed by the subjunctive although an infinitive is more common: **Lamentamos que no podamos ir** vs. **Lamentamos no poder ir.**

3. Compare the following sentences and notice that when the emotions are not expressed toward another person, an infinitive follows the main verb, and there is no dependent clause introduced by **que.**

Two Subjects: Subjunctive	One Subject: No Subjunctive
Ella teme que el gobierno no reaccione con diplomacia.	**Ella teme no reaccionar** con diplomacia.
Les molesta que yo nunca **participe.**	**Les molesta participar** en política.
Sentimos que no puedas ir a la manifestación.	**Sentimos no poder ir** a la manifestación.

4. To express feelings or emotions in an impersonal way about somebody's present or future situation, you may use an impersonal expression such as **es fantástico** or **es lamentable.**

Independent Clause	**que**	Dependent Clause
Impersonal expression (indicative)	**que**	Subject + verb (subjunctive)

Es fantástico	que	Chile	**tenga** un gobierno democrático.
It's wonderful	*that*	*Chile*	*has a democratic government.*
¡Qué pena	que	(tú)	no **vengas** mañana!
What a shame	*that*	*you*	*aren't coming tomorrow!*

5. Use the following impersonal expressions.

es bueno/malo	
es fantástico	
es horrible/terrible	
es lamentable	
es maravilloso	
es una lástima/pena	it's a shame
es raro	it's strange
es una vergüenza	it's a shame/shameful
¡Qué bueno...!	How good . . .!
¡Qué lástima/pena...!	What a shame . . .!
¡Qué sorpresa...!	What a surprise . . .!
¡Qué vergüenza...!	How shameful . . .!

6. Compare the following sentences and notice that an infinitive follows the impersonal expression when no specific person is mentioned.

Subject in Dependent Clause: Subjunctive	No Subject in Dependent Clause: No Subjunctive
Es maravilloso que puedas votar.	**Es maravilloso poder** votar.
Es una vergüenza que ese gobernante sea corrupto.	**Es una vergüenza ser** corrupto.
¡Qué lástima que no tengamos elecciones este año!	**¡Qué lástima no tener** elecciones este año!

7. The word **ojalá** (*I hope*) comes from the Arabic meaning *may Allah grant.* The verb that follows **ojalá** is always in the subjunctive form. **Que** is optional.

Ojalá (que) tengamos paz en el mundo.	*I hope that we have peace in the world.*

Remember that because of the Moorish influence in Spain, there are many Arabic words in Spanish such as **algodón** and **álgebra.**

Actividad 4 La política laboral **Parte A:** Dos oficinistas están hablando sobre el aumento de sueldo (*salary raise*) en su oficina. Elige el verbo y la forma apropiada del presente del subjuntivo o el infinitivo para completar la conversación.

Act. 4A: Assign as HW and check in class.

Marta Me sorprende que nuestros jefes no le ____den____ un aumento de sueldo a Carlos el mes que viene. (dar)

Ernesto ¿Qué dices? ¿Cómo lo sabes?

Marta Me contó nuestra jefa. Es una lástima que él no ____reciba____ aumento como nosotros. Ojalá que la jefa ____cambie____ de idea. (recibir, cambiar)

Ernesto Mira, mujer. Me alegra que la jefa ____reconozca____ el trabajo que nosotros hacemos y lamento que la empresa no le ____dé____ a Carlos el aumento. Pero tú sabes que él no trabaja tanto como los demás. Es bueno que las cosas ____sean____ justas. (reconocer, dar, ser)

Marta ¡Qué increíble! Es lamentable ____oír____ este tipo de comentario de tu parte. (oír)

Ernesto ¿A qué te refieres?

Marta ¡Qué pena que tú no ____intentes____ ser objetivo y que no ____puedas____ hacer un comentario imparcial sobre un colega! Dices eso sobre Carlos porque no toleras que él ____sea____ mejor trabajador que tú. Y punto. (intentar, poder, ser)

Parte B: En parejas, usen la conversación entre Ernesto y Marta como ejemplo, pero cámbienla para hablar de un estudiante de la escuela secundaria que no va a recibir una beca (*scholarship*) el año que viene y por eso no va a poder ir a la universidad.

Act. 4B: Form pairs, explain the premise, and model the first two sentences: **—Me sorprende que la universidad no le dé la beca a Carlos. —Pues, ¿por qué te sorprende?** Set a time limit and begin. When finished, have two groups model their conversations.

Transition to next activity by saying **Me molesta mucho que muchos padres les paguen los estudios a sus hijos cuando esos estudiantes faltan a clase, no estudian, etc. Vamos a ver qué cosas les molestan a Uds.**

Act. 5: Form groups of three, model possible answers, set a time limit, and begin. Check by finding out which items are the most and least bothersome. Expand by asking students what other behavior bothers them.

Actividad 5 Me molesta En grupos de tres, usen la lista para decir cuatro o cinco cosas que les molestan o no de otras personas. Digan si les molestan mucho, un poco o nada y expliquen por qué.

▶ Me molesta mucho que una persona siempre esté contenta porque...

ser inmadura	hablar con la boca llena
fumar cerca de ti	no compartir sus cosas
quejarse constantemente	pedir dinero prestado
masticar (*chew*) chicle y hacer ruido	opinar de política sin fundamentos (*facts*)
hablar mal de otros	votar a un candidato sólo por ser carismático
mentir mucho	???
criticar al gobierno, pero no votar	
dar consejos	

Act. 6A: Assign as homework or model activity with the first sentence, showing possible responses; set a brief time limit and begin.

Act. 6B: Form pairs, model by asking for a student's opinion on the first situation and ask the student to qualify his/her answer. Set a time limit and begin. Check by finding out which they found **lamentable, raro,** etc.

Transition to the next activity by using the example of an unworthy student getting a scholarship to the university, and state that not all goes according to our wishes. Then tell them they have an opportunity to tell the university what they want, and do Act. 7.

Actividad 6 ¿Lamentables o raras? **Parte A:** Lee las ocho situaciones siguientes y marca si son buenas, lamentables o si son raras o no.

a. es bueno
b. es lamentable
c. es raro
d. no es raro

1. _____ un hombre / gastar / mucho dinero en ropa
2. _____ una persona desconocida / pedirte / dinero para el autobús
3. _____ un hombre / ser / víctima de acoso (*harassment*) sexual
4. _____ tu ex novio/a / salir / con tu mejor amigo/a
5. _____ tus amigos / criticar / a tu pareja
6. _____ un esposo / quedarse / en casa con los niños y / no trabajar
7. _____ una persona / no pagar / los impuestos (*taxes*)
8. _____ un estudiante no muy trabajador / recibir / una beca importante

Parte B: Ahora en parejas, túrnense para dar su opinión sobre estas situaciones y expliquen por qué piensan así.

▶ (No) Es raro que un hombre gaste mucho dinero en ropa porque generalmente a los hombres (no) les interesa la ropa.

Act. 7: Discuss problems at your university by asking questions: **¿Hay suficientes residencias para todos los estudiantes? ¿Son bonitas? ¿Cuesta demasiado o es barato vivir en una residencia?** Write phrases on the board to prompt students to vary their sentences: **es importante, insistir en, esperar, es necesario, es aconsejable, le/s aconsejar, le/s recomendar**, plus the word **QUE** in big letters. Form pairs, set up the activity, set a time limit, and begin. Encourage students to include real problems on campus. Check by playing the role of a dean and having them inform you of their desires.

Actividad 7 La universidad y sus prioridades Tu universidad y su política afectan tu vida de estudiante universitario y por eso crees que se necesitan cambios. En parejas, miren la lista de la página 151 y elijan dos puntos de cada categoría. Luego escriban oraciones para expresar su opinión y decirles a las autoridades de la universidad qué cambios son necesarios.

▶ Es lamentable que no haya facultad de estudios afrocaribeños. Es necesario que Uds. abran esa facultad.

Facultades

abrir una nueva facultad de...
contratar a más profesores para la facultad de...
tener más ayudantes de cátedra (*teaching assistants*)
prestar más atención a las evaluaciones de los profesores que hacen los estudiantes
poner en Internet las evaluaciones que hacen los estudiantes

Remember: **facultad** = academic department (Math) or school (Law)

Vivienda y transporte

construir más residencias para estudiantes
edificar apartamentos para estudiantes de cuarto año
construir apartamentos baratos para estudiantes casados o con hijos
aumentar/implementar un sistema de autobuses gratis
ofrecer más lugares para estacionar (*park*)
bajar el precio de las residencias y las comidas

Tecnología

comprar más computadoras
incluir más videos y computadoras en el laboratorio de idiomas
darles a los estudiantes un programa de correo electrónico más moderno
modernizar los laboratorios de ciencias

Act. 8A: Have students read the information in class or as HW and then question them about the content.

Actividad 8 Las elecciones en Perú **Parte A:** Así como participar en la política de la universidad hace que se produzcan cambios, votar en las elecciones para presidente también genera cambios. Lee lo que explica un peruano sobre el voto en Perú.

"En Perú el voto es obligatorio, como en varios países de Latinoamérica, pero cuando no nos gustan los candidatos que se presentan, tenemos la opción de votar en blanco. Ese tipo de voto se usa como señal de protesta y los políticos lo tienen muy en cuenta. A diferencia de los Estados Unidos donde un tercer candidato, como Ross Perot o como Ralph Nader, puede afectar el resultado de una elección, en Perú, un candidato necesita el 50% de los votos más un voto para ganar. Pero si nadie obtiene ese porcentaje, se realiza una segunda vuelta o segunda elección entre los dos candidatos con el mayor número de votos. Lo bueno es que entonces todo el pueblo puede reevaluar su voto y volver a votar."

peruano

Fuente hispana

Voting is obligatory in a majority of countries in Latin America. The **voto en blanco** is also common throughout the region and results are announced. When voting is obligatory, it is common to deny services at a government office to someone that doesn't vote or not to allow the person to carry out any government business (e.g., sell a house) without paying a fine. As students compare the Peruvian election process with the one in their country, have them state what happens in their country: in the U.S., for example, there are primary elections that serve to determine the Republican and Democratic candidates, but a third, fourth, etc., candidate from another party can run on the ballot in November. In other countries, like Peru, there are many candidates, but a run-off election takes place if no one receives over 50% of the votes in the first elections.

El voto en blanco

Parte B: En grupos de tres, expliquen si han votado en el pasado y especifiquen en qué elecciones. Luego den su opinión sobre el voto obligatorio, el voto en blanco y la segunda votación en Perú. ¿Creen que pueda existir una segunda votación en este país algún día? Usen expresiones como: **Me alegro de que... porque..., Espero que..., Tengo miedo de que..., Me sorprende que...**

Act. 8B: When finished, have a group sharing.

B. The Present Perfect Subjunctive

Drill present perfect subjunctive:

List expressions like **es lamentable, me molesta, qué terrible, me sorprende, qué vergüenza,** etc., on the board. Tell students they are parents who arrive home and find their house is a mess. Ask them what they would tell their child or children (the instructor or a student could play the role of the child). **Es lamentable que no hayas lavado los platos.** (etc.)

1. As you learned before, when expressing present feelings or emotions about another person's actions or about a situation, in the present or future, you use the present subjunctive in the dependent clause. Look at the following sentences made by a man who has not seen his lover in a while and is anxiously waiting for her.

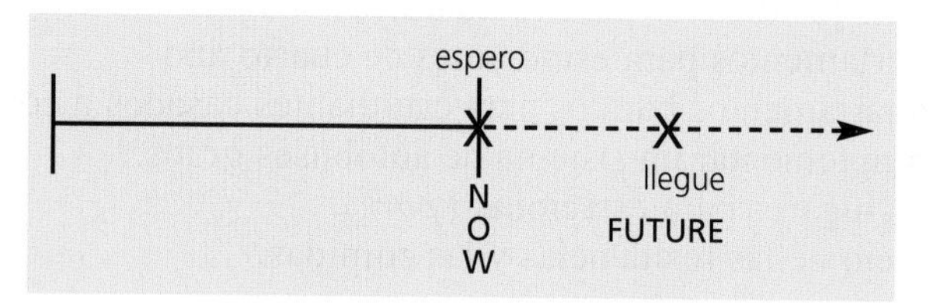

Espero que el vuelo de LanChile **llegue** pronto. — *I hope that the LanChile flight arrives/will arrive soon.*

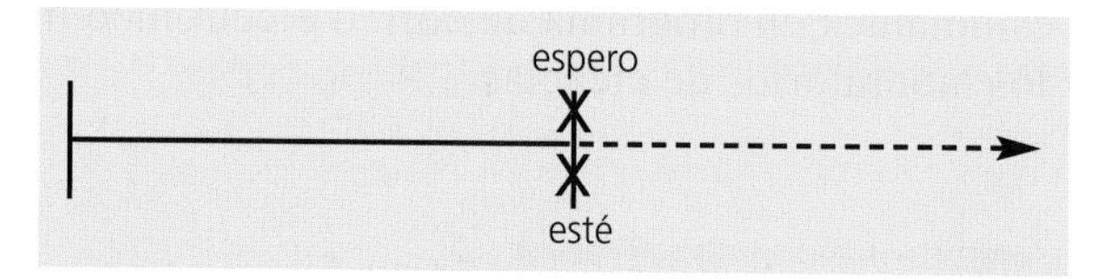

Espero que Rosa **esté** en ese vuelo. — *I hope that Rosa is on that flight.*

2. When expressing present feelings or emotions about something that has already occurred, use the present perfect subjunctive (**pretérito perfecto del subjuntivo**) in the dependent clause.

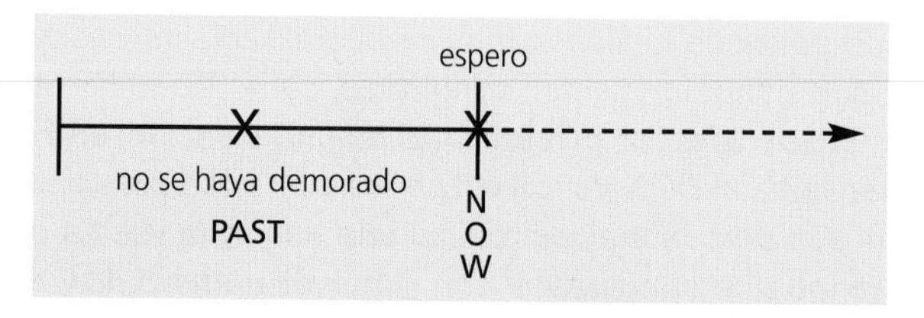

Espero que el avión no **se haya demorado.*** — *I hope that the plane hasn't had any delays.*

¡Qué bueno que ella **haya encontrado** un pasaje económico! — *How good that she (has) found a cheap ticket!*

Me sorprende que hayan puesto a Rosa en primera clase. — *It surprises me that they (have) put Rosa in first class.*

*Note: In a verb phrase, past participles (e.g., **demorado**) always end in **-o.** Also note that object pronouns (**me, lo, le, se,** etc.) are placed before **haya.**

3. The present perfect subjunctive is formed by using the present subjunctive form of the verb **haber** + *past participle.*

To review irregular past participles, see Appendix A, page 349.

haber		
haya	hayamos	+ *past participle*
hayas	hayáis	
haya	hayan	

Actividad 9 Carta a una hija Un padre le escribe una carta a su hija que está en otro país. Completa esta parte de la carta con la forma apropiada del presente del subjuntivo, del pretérito perfecto del subjuntivo o con el infinitivo de los verbos que se presentan.

Act. 9: Assign as HW and check in class.

8 de noviembre

Querida Gabriela:

(estar) Espero que ___estés___ bien. Toda la familia te echa de menos. Sí, finalmente se acabaron las elecciones. Es una pena que tú no (poder) ___hayas podido___ escuchar el discurso del nuevo presidente porque estuvo sensacional. Él dijo que es necesario (tener) ___tener___ paciencia, pero que las cosas van a cambiar. Es maravilloso que el domingo pasado los ciudadanos (elegir) ___hayan elegido___ a alguien del P.R.U. después de años de un gobierno opresivo. Por mi parte, estoy contento de que el país (tener) ___tenga___ este nuevo presidente. Ahora es importante (tomar) ___tomar___ conciencia de la situación del país y que nosotros (hacer) ___hagamos___ algo para que la situación mejore. Lamento que tú no (estar) ___estés___ aquí en este momento histórico tan importante.

(acordarse) Ojalá que ___te hayas acordado___ de ir al consulado a votar el domingo pasado. Me olvidé de decírtelo antes. Como sabes, creo que el voto es un derecho que todos tenemos que ejercer.

Act. 10A: Call on individuals to hear their reactions.

Actividad 10 Las elecciones **Parte A:** La tabla muestra el porcentaje de la población estadounidense que, de acuerdo a la edad, votó en las elecciones presidenciales. Reacciona a la información con frases como: **Es lamentable que..., Me sorprende que..., Es interesante que...,** etc.

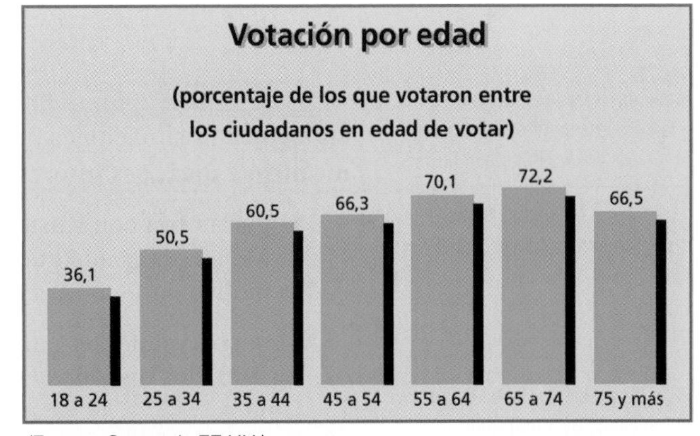

(Fuente: Censo de EE.UU.)

Parte B: En parejas, usen la imaginación para pensar en las cinco excusas más comunes que tuvieron muchos americanos para no votar en las últimas elecciones.

▶ No sabían dónde ir para votar.

Act. 10B: Compare students' responses to the U.S. Census' conclusion as to why people didn't vote: **estaban muy ocupados el 20,9%; estaban enfermos o tuvieron una emergencia el 14,8%; no tenían interés el 12,2%; estaban de viaje, otro motivo el 10,2%; no les gustaban los candidatos el 7,7%; no quisieron votar el 7,5%; tuvieron problemas para inscribirse el 6,9%; se les olvidó votar el 4%; era un inconveniente el 2,6%; tenían problemas de transporte el 2,4%; hacía mal tiempo ese día el 0,6%.** Note: the statistics given are from the presidential elections in the year 2000. (Fuente: U.S. Census Bureau, Current Population Survey, November 2000.)

Act. 10C: Encourage students to be creative and to stress that if more vote, more is done for the group that votes.

Parte C: En parejas, discutan qué pueden hacer el gobierno o los partidos políticos para que haya más participación de los ciudadanos. Usen frases como: **Es posible que…, Sugiero que…, Deben…, Tienen que…, Es necesario que…, Les aconsejo que…,** etc.

¿LO SABÍAN?

A la hora de las elecciones, los candidatos para la presidencia de los Estados Unidos tienen muy en cuenta a la población hispana ya que, con unos 40 millones, es la minoría más grande de este país. El votante hispano tiende a ser conservador en asuntos sociales, pero en general, apoya a aquellos candidatos que suelen ser liberales. Aunque, como grupo de votantes, existe una tendencia entre los latinos a inclinarse hacia el partido demócrata, también hay grupos que suelen votar por los republicanos como los cubano-americanos cuyos votos, especialmente en el estado de Florida, fueron de gran importancia en las elecciones presidenciales del año 2000.

Hoy día, los políticos organizan campañas para atraer el voto latino y algunos de ellos dan discursos y hacen debates en español. También tienen páginas Web en español y hacen propaganda en Univisión y Telemundo.

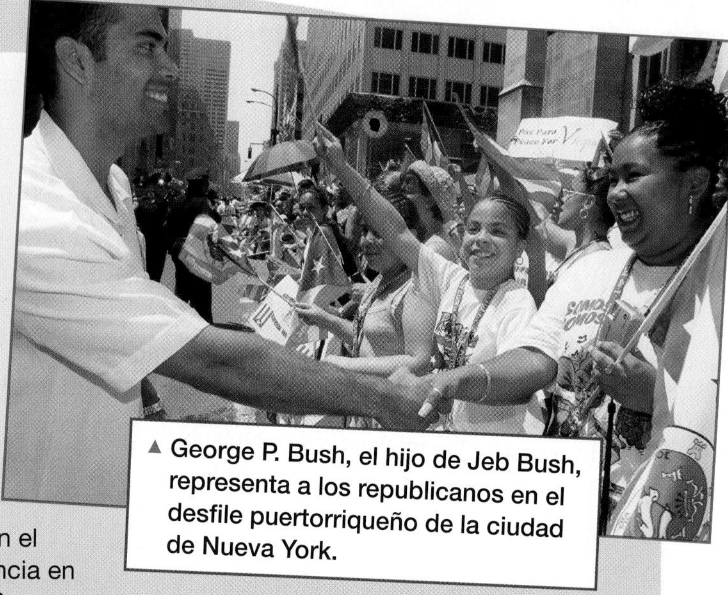

▲ George P. Bush, el hijo de Jeb Bush, representa a los republicanos en el desfile puertorriqueño de la ciudad de Nueva York.

WWW *Las páginas Web de los partidos norteamericanos en español*

President George W. Bush received a large percentage of the Cuban American vote in Florida in the 2000 elections, more than other recent Republican presidential candidates (280,000 or about 75%). Although most thought Bush would carry the Cuban-American vote, some feel that the large percentage can be traced to one issue: the return of Elián González (a young Cuban boy) to the island by Janet Reno, Clinton's Attorney General.

Act. 11: After checking the activity, use **Perón** as a lead-in to the **¿Lo sabían?** that follows.

Actividad 11 Acontecimientos importantes Expresa tu opinión sobre las siguientes situaciones del pasado con frases como: **es lamentable que..., me alegra que..., es interesante que...**

► guerra fría con Rusia / terminar
Me alegra que la guerra fría con Rusia haya terminado porque no hay motivo para pelear con ese país.

1. México / venderles California a los Estados Unidos
2. En 2003 los hispanos / convertirse en la minoría más grande de los Estados Unidos
3. España / sufrir una guerra civil entre 1936 y 1939
4. Violeta Chamorro / ser la primera mujer presidente de Nicaragua
5. Óscar Arias (ex presidente costarricense) / ganar el Premio Nobel de la Paz
6. Perón (ex presidente argentino) / quemar iglesias

¿LO SABÍAN?

Históricamente, la influencia de la Iglesia católica en los países hispanos ha sido muy importante. Esto se debe a que, en gran parte, la población es católica, aunque muchos no vayan regularmente a la iglesia. Con frecuencia, la Iglesia ha hecho oír su opinión en las decisiones gubernamentales. Por ejemplo, en Argentina, en 1954, la Iglesia estaba en contra del presidente Perón debido a la corrupción y represión que ejercía su gobierno. Perón decidió entonces quemar varias iglesias para acallar su protesta. En El Salvador, se dice que el gobierno fue el responsable del asesinato del arzobispo Romero en 1980, así como de seis curas jesuitas en 1989, quienes trabajaban en contra de la opresión que ejercía el gobierno sobre el pueblo. Di cuánta influencia tienen los diferentes grupos religiosos en la política de tu país.

You may want to discuss the rising number of Evangelists in Hispanic countries. It may be interesting to note that even though the government was burning churches in Argentina, the law required the president to be Catholic.

Use the last sentence as a topic of discussion. Ask students to be specific and to give examples from history. For example: in the 1950s, the term "In God we trust" was added to the currency in the United States in response to attitudes against the Cold War. This will recycle narrating in the past.

Actividad 12 El año pasado **Parte A:** En parejas, miren la siguiente lista de acciones. Cada uno escoja dos temas para hablar en detalle sobre su vida durante el año pasado.

Act. 12A and B: Allow students a moment to think about what they will say, form pairs, set a time limit, and begin.

1. aprender español
2. conseguir un buen trabajo
3. poder practicar deportes
4. preocuparte seriamente por tus estudios
5. hacer amigos nuevos
6. mirar mucha televisión
7. conocer bien a tus profesores
8. hacer un viaje a otro país
9. empezar a/dejar de salir con alguien
10. ver un documental sobre...

Parte B: Ahora miren la lista otra vez y expresen emociones sobre aspectos de su vida. Expliquen también las consecuencias que esos aspectos tienen hoy día en su vida. Usen expresiones como: **Es una lástima que..., Es fantástico que...**

► ir a fiestas
Es una lástima que no haya ido a más fiestas porque me encantan y ahora que tengo clases más difíciles y un trabajo no tengo mucho tiempo.

Actividad 13 Los jubilados **Parte A:** En parejas, uno de Uds. es don Rafael, un jubilado que está haciendo una revisión de su vida, y la otra persona es su amiga doña Carmen. Después de que Uds. lean la biografía de Rafael, debe hablar de las cosas que lamenta de su pasado usando expresiones como: **¡Qué lastima que...!, Es triste que...** Doña Carmen debe hacerle ver a don Rafael el lado positivo usando expresiones como: **¡Qué bueno que...!, Es maravilloso que...** Pueden inventar detalles.

Act. 13A: Form pairs and assign roles. Stress that don Rafael will complain about his life while doña Carmen will find the positive points in it. Set a time limit and begin.

Rafael Legido, 75 años, jubilado

Cuando era joven, sus padres ofrecieron pagarle los estudios universitarios, pero no quiso estudiar. En vez de estudiar, fue a trabajar de cajero en un banco. Después de muchos años, llegó a ser subgerente del banco. En su trabajo, conoció a la mujer con la cual se casó. No tuvieron hijos. Sus compañeros de trabajo jugaron juntos a la lotería y ganaron 10 millones de dólares. Él no quiso jugar.

Act. 13B: Have students read doña Carmen's biography and have don Rafael find the positive in her life. Check by having a pair role play for the class. As a follow-up you may want to ask students if they would like to be **Miss** or **Mister Universo** and ask them about the problems some contestants have with **anorexia, esteroides,** and **autoestima.**

Parte B: Ahora, Carmen hace una revisión negativa de su vida y Rafael trata de hacerle ver el lado positivo.

Carmen Ramos, 77 años, jubilada

Llegó a ser Miss Chile. Nunca usó su fama para luchar contra el abuso de menores o la pobreza de su país. No se casó con el amor de su vida porque él no tenía dinero. En cambio, se casó con un millonario, pero no tuvo un matrimonio feliz. Tuvo seis hijos. Nunca les dedicó mucho tiempo a sus hijos, más bien pasó su tiempo viajando.

II. Discussing Politics

Noticias del día

La política

Student groups exist in a number of Latin American governments. They are advisory in nature, but provide a place for student concerns to be heard and for young people to get training to become future politicians.

▸ Manifestantes obreros y estudiantiles protestan contra el aumento del presupuesto militar en Colombia.

"El **activismo** político y social es una faceta más de la vida estudiantil universitaria de América Latina. Diariamente, antes de empezar clases, entre clases y después de ellas, los estudiantes se reúnen en cafeterías cerca de las universidades para charlar y es frecuente debatir la situación política y social del país. El mantenerse al tanto de lo que está sucediendo no se considera una tarea sino un deber ciudadano, un **compromiso** social.

Pero la participación sociopolítica no sólo es el discutir los **sucesos** del momento sino también la intervención en **huelgas** o **paros** nacionales y en **protestas** y **manifestaciones** públicas para que se realicen cambios en el sistema que afectan **el bienestar común**. Tan importantes son la valoración y el consenso estudiantil para la vida política de un país en Latinoamérica que en algunos países la Cámara y el Senado tienen representantes de la juventud."

colombiano

activism
commitment
events
strikes / work stoppages
protests / demonstrations
the common good

Cognados obvios

el abuso, abusar
la corrupción
la democracia, democrático/a
la dictadura, el/la dictador/a
la eficiencia/ineficiencia
la estabilidad/inestabilidad
la influencia, influir* en
la protección, proteger
la protesta, protestar

*Note: irregular verb

To refer to the two major U.S. political parties use **el partido demócrata** and **el partido republicano.**

For irregular verbs, see Appendix A, page 339.

Drill political vocabulary:

1. Have students take turns giving definitions of the words. Model the drill by giving definitions and have the class shout out responses. Next form pairs, set a time limit, and begin.

2. Ask students questions about world history using the words on the list. For example: **¿Francia apoyó a los EE.UU. en la guerra contra Iraq? ¿Había libertad de prensa en España bajo la dictadura de Franco? En el año 2000, ¿influyó Ralph Nader en el resultado de las elecciones presidenciales?** (etc.)

Otras palabras

el acuerdo	agreement (pact)
estar de acuerdo	to be in agreement
llegar a un acuerdo	to reach an agreement
la amenaza, amenazar	threat, to threaten
el apoyo, apoyar	support, to support
el asunto político/económico	political/economic issue
la campaña electoral	political campaign
la censura, censurar, censurado/a	censorship, to censor, censored
el golpe de estado	coup d'état
la igualdad/desigualdad	equality/inequality
la inversión, invertir (ie, i)	investment, to invest
la junta militar	military junta
la libertad de palabra/prensa	freedom of speech/the press
la política	politics
el político/la mujer política	politician
el pueblo	the people
respetar/violar los derechos humanos	to respect/to violate human rights
el soborno	bribe
el/los suceso(s)	the event(s); current event(s)

el soborno = la mordida (*México*)

Este chiste es de un argentino llamado Quino. Él hace un comentario sobre la política de su país. ¿Crees que el comentario sea válido para tu país? ¿Por qué?

Act. 14 A and B: Have students do reading in class or as HW. Ask comprehension questions. Make students be specific; if they cannot mention specific events, be ready with a list of items that students at your university have done at the university, local, state, or national level. Once you have jarred their memory, have them explain what occurred.

Actividad 14 La voz de los jóvenes **Parte A:** Mira la sección de vocabulario de la página 156 y lee otra vez lo que dice un colombiano sobre la participación de los jóvenes en la política de América Latina.

Parte B: En grupos de tres, comparen lo que dice el colombiano con lo que pasa en su universidad o en su país. ¿Hablan de política los estudiantes? Comenten sobre la participación o falta de participación de los estudiantes de su universidad y den ejemplos específicos de su participación reciente.

Actividad 15 La democracia y la dictadura En parejas, digan cuáles de las siguientes palabras asocian Uds. con la dictadura y cuáles con la democracia y por qué. Es posible asociar la misma palabra con las dos.

▶ Una joven deposita su voto en una urna electoral en Guazapa, El Salvador.

amenazas
gran número de robos (*thefts*)
campaña electoral
censura
soborno
corrupción
ineficiencia
violaciones de derechos humanos
libertad de prensa
alto número de manifestaciones

Act. 15: Form pairs, set a time limit, and begin. Check by asking the class to categorize each one and to justify responses. The following items can be associated with a **dictadura: amenazas, censura, soborno, corrupción, violaciones de derechos humanos.** The following with a **democracia: gran número de robos, campaña electoral, corrupción, ineficiencia, libertad de prensa, alto número de manifestaciones.** Some students may say that censorship and bribes are present in both and they would be correct, but these are normally higher in a dictatorship.

Act. 16: While setting up the activity, stress that some ideas will need present subjunctive and others present perfect subjunctive. You may want to have students expand upon some answers.

The movie *Missing* deals with the overthrow of Allende in Chile and could be assigned as extra credit.

Actividad 16 Situación política en Hispanoamérica Da tu opinión sobre los siete siguientes ejemplos de la situación política y social en Hispanoamérica y explica por qué piensas así. Usa expresiones como: **(no) me sorprende, es una lástima, es bueno/malo, me da pena.**

▶ Un juez español pidió la extradición de un militar argentino para juzgarlo en España.
Me alegra que un juez español haya pedido la extradición de un militar argentino para juzgarlo porque...

1. Rigoberta Menchú, indígena guatemalteca, ganó el Premio Nobel de la Paz.
2. Existe discriminación racial en Hispanoamérica.
3. La CIA ayudó al general Pinochet a subir al poder en Chile con un golpe de estado.
4. Hay mucha desigualdad económica en Hispanoamérica.

(continúa en la página siguiente)

5. Han muerto muchos políticos en Colombia por hacerles frente (*stand up to*) a los narcotraficantes.
6. Los militares tienen mucha influencia en algunos gobiernos hispanoamericanos.
7. El voto en blanco ganó por mayoría en las elecciones de legisladores de la ciudad de Buenos Aires en 2002.

Act. 17: Do topics 1 and 2. Try to generate some discussion when supporting opinions. Topics 3, 4, and 6 may lead to good discussion (e.g., **Tenemos que reducir la demanda, no eliminar el suministro (oferta) de drogas.** vs. **Tenemos que eliminar el suministro y entonces no va a haber demanda de drogas.**)

Actividad 17 ¿Intervenir? Di si es bueno o no que un país intervenga en otros países y defiende tu opinión. Usa expresiones como: **(No) Es buena idea que un país... porque..., Me molesta que un país... porque...**

▶ ayudar a educar a los analfabetos
Es buena idea que un país ayude a educar a los analfabetos de otros países porque si más gente sabe leer, creo que esos países van a necesitar menos ayuda en el futuro.

1. darles ayuda económica para mejorar su infraestructura
2. venderles armas y entrenar a los militares
3. ayudar a combatir el tráfico de drogas
4. tolerar la violación de los derechos humanos
5. mandarles medicamentos y construir hospitales
6. ayudar a proteger el medio ambiente
7. abrir fábricas y crear fuentes de trabajo
8. contribuir a la campaña electoral de algunos candidatos
9. mandar espías (*spies*)
10. ayudar cuando hay desastres naturales

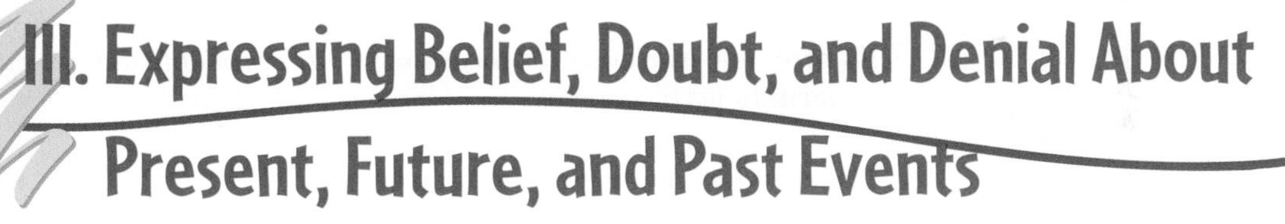

III. Expressing Belief, Doubt, and Denial About Present, Future, and Past Events

FLR link: **Lectura 2**

1. To express doubt or denial about a situation or someone's actions (even your own) in the present, future, or past, use the following subjunctive construction.

Independent Clause	que	Dependent Clause
Subject 1 + *verb of doubt* (indicative)	**que**	Subject 1 or 2 + verb (subjunctive)

(Yo)	no creo	que	(ellos)	reformen la constitución.
I	*don't think (believe)*	*that*	*they*	*will reform the constitution.*
(Yo)	dudo	que	(yo)	puedo ganar las elecciones.
I	*doubt*	*that*	*I*	*can win the elections.*

When expressing an opinion, native speakers generally use **(no) creer**; therefore **(no) pensar** has intentionally been excluded. Likewise, **no negar** and **negar** have been excluded because they are not normally used in Spanish except in expressions like **No lo niego.**

If you want, inform students that in readings they may see the indicative used after statements with **no creer** and questions with **creer.** It is also heard colloquially.

Drill subjunctive to express doubt or denial:

1. Tell students they are very skeptical individuals and have them react to what you say about their university. T: **Todos los profesores son excelentes.** S: **Dudo que todos los profesores sean excelentes.** T: **La universidad va a reducir el costo de la matrícula.** S: **No creo que la universidad reduzca el costo de la matrícula.** (etc.)

2. Have some students brag about their future and have others react. S1: **En 2010 voy a tener dos millones de dólares.** S2: **Dudo que en 2010 tengas mucho dinero.**

3. Have them express certainty or doubt about current news. T: (*name of a politician*) **ha recibido donaciones ilegales.** S1: **Es verdad que ha recibido donaciones ilegales porque...** S2: **No creo que haya recibido donaciones ilegales porque...**

You may want to review **quizás** and **tal vez** + *subjunctive.*

2. To express belief or certainty about an action or situation, use the indicative in the dependent clause. Compare and contrast the following expressions and examples.

Expressions of Doubt: Subjunctive	Expressions of Belief or Certainty: Indicative
no estar seguro/a (de) **no creer** **¿creer?** **dudar**	**estar seguro/a (de)** **creer**
No estamos seguros de que hayan actuado incorrectamente.	**Estamos seguros de que ellos han actuado/actuaron** incorrectamente.
¿Crees que el presidente tenga una buena política exterior?	**Creo que el presidente tiene** una buena política exterior.
No creo que (yo) vote en las elecciones.*	**Creo que voy a votar** en las próximas elecciones.*

*Note: Remember that the subject of the independent and dependent clauses can be the same in sentences with expressions of certainty, doubt, and denial.

3. To express doubt or denial about a situation or someone's actions, you may also use an impersonal expression followed by a dependent clause with a verb in the subjunctive.

Es posible que ellos **ganen** las elecciones.	*It's possible that they will win the election.*
Es probable que nosotros **hayamos perdido** las elecciones.	*It's probable that we have lost the election.*

4. Use the following impersonal expressions.

es imposible	**(no) puede ser**	
es improbable	**no es evidente**	
(no) es posible	**no es obvio**	it's not obvious
(no) es probable	**no es verdad/no es cierto**	it isn't true

5. Compare the following sentences and notice that an infinitive follows the impersonal expression when no specific person is mentioned.

Subject in Dependent Clause: Subjunctive	No Subject in Dependent Clause: Infinitive
Es imposible que ganen con esa política exterior.	**Es imposible ganar** con esa política exterior.
No es probable que ella haya perdido las elecciones sólo por no tener el apoyo de los sindicatos.	**No es posible perder** las elecciones sólo por no tener el apoyo de los sindicatos.

6. The following impersonal expressions indicate certainty and, therefore, take the indicative in the dependent clause.

es cierto	it's true	**es verdad**	
es evidente		**está claro**	
es obvio	it's obvious	**no cabe duda (de)**	there is no doubt
es seguro	it's certain		

Doubt or Denial Expressed: Subjunctive	Certainty Expressed: Indicative
No es verdad que los partidos políticos **tengan** mucho dinero.	**Es verdad que** los partidos políticos **tienen** mucho dinero.
No es evidente que haya corrupción en todos los gobiernos.	**Es evidente que hay** corrupción en todos los gobiernos.

Actividad 18 Un candidato a presidente **Parte A:** Un candidato presidencial está preparando su discurso final antes de las elecciones. Complétalo con la forma apropiada de los verbos correspondientes.

Act. 18A: Assign as HW and correct in class.

Querido pueblo:
Mañana son las elecciones y llega el momento de la decisión final. Si Uds. me eligen como líder del país, pueden estar seguros de que ___voy___ a hacer todo lo que prometí durante la campaña electoral. Ya sé que es imposible ___complacer___ a todos los ciudadanos, que hay gente que no cree que yo ___me haya preocupado___ por sus problemas en el pasado y que duda que yo ___haya pensado___ en el pueblo cuando era senador. Lo niego (*deny*) categóricamente. No es verdad que a mí no ___me interesen / me hayan interesado___ sus problemas y se lo voy a demostrar a todos. Les prometo ___prestar___ atención a todas sus necesidades. Yo quiero trabajar por el país, pero creo que todos ___tenemos___ que poner nuestro granito de arena para que el país progrese. Mis colaboradores y yo creemos que ___debemos___ empezar a actuar ya mismo. No cabe duda de que el país ___necesita___ un cambio inmediato. Pueblo querido: ¡Mañana triunfaremos!

ir
complacer
preocuparse
pensar
interesarse
prestar
tener
deber
necesitar

Parte B: Ahora en grupos de tres, expresen su opinión sobre los políticos en general usando frases como: **(No) Creo que..., (No) Estoy seguro (de) que..., Dudo que...**

Act. 18B: Form groups and have students give opinions. You may want to have students describe specific scandals to illustrate their point. Transition to the next activity by asking them if they themselves are **honrados.**

▶ Dudo que muchos políticos se preocupen por los niños de este país porque ellos no votan.

prestar atención al medio ambiente	cumplir sus promesas
hacer lo que quiere la gente	interesarse por las grandes empresas
preocuparse por los pobres	ser honrados

Act. 19A: Assign as HW or do in class.

Act. 19B: Model by showing a list of items you claim you have done (some true, some false). Have students say which ones they think are false: **Dudo que Ud. haya..., No creo que Ud. haya...**, etc. After doing all items, tell them which are true or false. Form pairs, set a time limit, and instruct students to read their sentences to each other and to react saying if they think they are true or false. Check by asking some students to say one or two things from their list and having the class react.

Actividad 19 ¿Mentira o verdad? **Parte A:** ¡Vas a decir mentiras! Escribe una lista de cinco cosas que hiciste en el pasado, pero algunas deben ser mentira.

Parte B: En parejas, escuchen lo que dice su compañero/a y decidan si es verdad o no.

▶ —Me gradué de la escuela secundaria cuando tenía dieciséis años.

—Dudo que te hayas graduado de la escuela secundaria cuando tenías dieciséis años.

—Creo que es verdad porque eres muy inteligente.

Act. 20: Form pairs, model the activity stressing the need to justify responses. Check by calling on individuals and encourage debate when there is a difference of opinion.

Actividad 20 Opiniones sobre la historia En grupos de tres, den su opinión sobre los siguientes sucesos usando expresiones como: **(No) Creo que... porque..., Dudo que..., No cabe duda que...**

1. Oswald actuó solo en el asesinato de Kennedy.
2. Michael Jordan fue el mejor jugador de la historia del basquetbol.
3. Bill Clinton aspiró el humo cuando fumó mariguana.
4. O. J. mató a Nicole Brown Simpson y a Ron Goldman.
5. Mark McGwire fue el mejor bateador de la historia del béisbol.

Act. 21: Introduce this activity by discussing the impact of television and other sources of the media on public opinion. Form pairs, model the activity, set a time limit, and begin. Check by having students determine the most and least important items.

Actividad 21 Un político con éxito En parejas, elijan las cinco características más importantes para que un político tenga éxito. Usen expresiones como: **(no) es importante, (no) es necesario, (no) es posible.**

▶ Es importante que el político aparezca con niños en las fotos.

▶ No es posible que tenga éxito si no habla bien.

ser honrado/a
besar a los bebés
tener buena apariencia física
tener dinero para su campaña electoral
creer en Dios
ser buen/a padre/madre
tener título universitario
tener buen sentido del humor
estar casado/a
serle fiel a su esposo/a
estar en buen estado físico
? ? ?

Act. 22: Form pairs (to spice this up, you may want to place liberals with conservatives, an apathetic student with an activist, etc.), model the activity, set a time limit, and begin. Check by having individuals state and support opinions.

Actividad 22 El futuro En parejas, discutan el futuro de su país bajo un presidente liberal o conservador. Usen expresiones como: **(No) Creo que..., (No) Estoy seguro/a de que...**

▶ aumentar los impuestos
—Creo que un presidente liberal va a aumentarle los impuestos a la clase alta.

—No creo que sea verdad porque...

—Creo que tienes razón porque...

1. mejorar la situación económica del país
2. contribuir más a las causas de los pobres

3. ofrecer una mejor educación para los niños
4. luchar contra el terrorismo
5. invertir (*invest*) más dinero en investigaciones de enfermedades mortales
6. reducirles los impuestos a los ciudadanos de la clase media
7. aumentarles los impuestos a las empresas
8. proteger el medio ambiente (*environment*)
9. ofrecerles ayuda económica a los estudiantes universitarios
10. combatir la violencia

IV. Forming Complex Sentences

The Relative Pronouns *que* and *quien*

As you progress in your study of Spanish, using relative pronouns **(pronombres relativos)** in your speech and writing will improve your fluency. Compare these two narrations in English.

Dick and Jane are friends. They have a dog. The dog's name is Spot. Spot runs fast.	Dick and Jane, who are friends, have a dog (that's) named Spot, that runs fast.

As you can see, relative pronouns are important to connect shorter sentences in order to avoid repetition. They help make speech interesting to listen to and give prose richness and variety.

Drill **que** and **quien**:

1. Ask about the plot of famous movies. ***Romeo y Julieta* es sobre una pareja que está enamorada y muere.** (etc.)

2. Have students say what people in different occupations do. **Un arquitecto o una arquitecta es una persona que diseña apartamentos. Un aeromozo o una aeromoza es alguien que...** (etc.)

3. Give pairs of students incomplete sentences and have them add information. **El presidente, ..., es muy carismático.** (*Name of famous person*), **..., siempre miente.**

1. When you want to give crucial or essential information that describes a noun, you may introduce it with **que** (*that/which/who*). Note that omitting essential information changes the meaning of the sentence.

Remember to use **que** for essential information even when referring to people.

En los países hispanos, las personas **que estudian inglés** tienen mejores oportunidades de trabajo.	*In Hispanic countries, the people who/that study English have better job opportunities.* (only the people who study English)
Cursé una clase de geografía social **que me interesaba mucho.**	*I took a social geography class which/that interested me a lot.*
El cuadro ganador fue pintado por un niño **que sólo tenía cuatro años.**	*The winning painting was painted by a child who/that was only four years old.*

Quien(es) is generally preferred in writing to give nonessential information about people.

You may want to remind students that, as in English, **quien/es** is preferred after prepositions when referring to people: **La chica de quien te hablé es mi prima.** If needed, write on the board incomplete sentences such as **Ésa es la muchacha de..., Ése es el hombre con..., Ése es el restaurante en....** etc.

2. When you want to give nonessential information in a sentence, you may introduce it with **que** or **quien(es)** for people, and **que** for things. In writing, you must set off the nonessential information with commas, and in speaking you must make a brief pause right before and after it. Note that nonessential information may be omitted from a sentence without changing the meaning of the sentence itself. Compare the following sentences.

La maestra fue con algunos niños a la playa. Los niños, **que/quienes** sabían nadar, se metieron en el agua en cuanto llegaron.	*The teacher went with some kids to the beach. The kids, who knew how to swim, got in the water as soon as they arrived.* (All the kids knew how to swim, all the kids got in the water.)
La maestra fue con algunos niños a la playa. Los niños **que** sabían nadar se metieron en el agua en cuanto llegaron. Los otros hicieron castillos de arena.	*The teacher went with some kids to the beach. The kids who knew how to swim got in the water as soon as they arrived. The others made sand castles.*

Act. 23: Have a contest between groups to see how many people students can identify.

Transition to the next activity by asking students which of the people in the previous activity came to the U.S. to live (Carlos Santana, Sammy Sosa, Antonio Banderas, Celia Cruz, Gloria Estefan). Then talk about the problems they may have had learning English.

Actividad 23 Identifica a hispanos famosos En parejas, túrnense para identificar al mayor número posible de hispanos famosos usando pronombres relativos.

▶ Isabel Allende es la escritora chilena que escribió *Mi país inventado*.

Carlos Santana	Hernán Cortés	Gloria Estefan
La Malinche	Ricky Martin	Celia Cruz
Sammy Sosa	Cameron Díaz	Gabriel García Márquez
Juan Domingo Perón	Antonio Banderas	Isabel la Católica

Act. 24A and B: This activity practices circumlocution. Set up activity by posing as a foreigner and asking what an *infomercial* is; then form pairs while assigning roles, set a time limit, and begin. When a few groups finish the first part, stop the class and have all switch roles. Check by having some individuals explain what some items are.

Actividad 24 ¿Qué es eso? **Parte A:** Al llegar a un país nuevo los estudiantes extranjeros siempre tienen problemas con palabras y costumbres que no entienden. En parejas, una persona es un/a extranjero/a que no entiende algunas cosas y la otra persona le explica los significados. Usen pronombres relativos en las respuestas. Sigan el modelo.

▶ —¿Qué es un *banjo*?
—Es un instrumento que generalmente tiene cinco cuerdas (*strings*) y que se usa en la música country.

1. Fui a una fiesta con un amigo y me dijo que él iba a ser el *designated driver*. ¿Qué significa eso?
2. Entiendo qué significan *right* y *way*; pero, ¿qué significa *right of way*?
3. ¿Qué es *voice mail*?

Parte B: Ahora, cambien de papel.

1. Voy a ir a un partido de fútbol americano de los Cowboys y todo el mundo dice que tengo que ver a las *cheerleaders*. ¿Qué son *cheerleaders*?
2. ¿Qué es *big hair*?
3. El otro día en la televisión, una persona dijo que había asistido a la *school of hard knocks*. ¿Qué significa eso?

Actividad 25 ¿Dónde los sentamos? Todas las noches, durante la Feria del Libro, los Duques de Manzanares ofrecen una cena para escritores. El duque, quien es mayor, no oye bien, por eso suele decir que sí a todo y siempre se sonríe. La duquesa es una persona que cuando uno le habla siempre cambia de tema. En parejas, decidan dónde van a sentar a los escritores para poder tener una cena agradable.

Los Duques van a estar en los dos extremos de la mesa. A continuación tienen ciertos datos de los invitados para que puedan decidir. Usen expresiones como: **Dudo que..., No creo que..., Teresa Guzmán, que/quien es.., debe sentarse..., Ella escribió un libro que..., Pon a... al lado de... porque...**

Act. 25: Read directions and ask questions to ensure comprehension. Have students use the drawing in the book or create their own on a separate sheet of paper. Form pairs; encourage them to use relative pronouns in their discussion. Inform them that there is no one correct solution and that they must be able to justify their seating plan. Check by having one or two pairs give and justify their solution. This activity should take at least 10 minutes.

Teresa Guzmán
líder de una organización feminista
fuma mucho
es muy cómica
le gusta participar en una buena discusión
libro: *Madres en la política*

Josefina Santos
senadora ultraderechista
quiere ayuda económica para su país
se ríe con facilidad
suele beber mucho y contar chistes verdes (*dirty jokes*)
libro: *Capitalismo: El opio de la gente*

Ernestina Villarreal
periodista
le fascina todo
es asmática y no tolera el humo del cigarrillo
libro: *Entrevistas escandalosas*

Paolo
modelo internacional
hace fotos con y sin ropa
es muy egoísta
no le gusta la política, sólo quiere paz en el mundo
libro: *Cambie el cuerpo con sólo diez minutos de ejercicio por día*

Alfredo Vargas
representante de Amnistía Internacional
tiene fama de ser mujeriego (*womanizer*)
libro: *Presos políticos*

José María Hidalgo
experto en el medio ambiente
es serio, le gusta hablar de ciencia
libro: *Fluorocarbonos: Un peligro constante*

V. Indicating Cause, Purpose, and Destination

Por and para

 **FLR** link: **Lectura 3**

Remember to use prepositional pronouns after **por** and **para** when needed: **mí, ti, Ud., él/ella, nosotros/as, vosotros/as, Uds., ellos/as.**

If needed, review other uses of **por** and **para: por dos años** (duration), **te doy $100 por la impresora** (exchange), **para mí** (opinion).

Drill **por** and **para:**

1. Ask students of other instances where artists or entertainers donated time or money for a cause. Examples include: Whoopi Goldberg, Robin Williams, Billy Crystal – Comic Relief for the homeless; Bono – AIDS in Africa; Jimmy Carter – Habitat for Humanity; Doctors – Doctors Without Borders; etc.

2. Have students finish work-related sentences: **Mi padre tiene una gran empresa y yo trabajo ___ él. Hoy mi hermana está enferma y quiere que yo trabaje ___ ella. Muchas personas trabajan ___ vivir, y otras viven ___ trabajar.**

3. Have students tell you why they have chosen their course of studies and what they want to be able to do in the future.

1. Use **por:**

a. to express *on behalf of, for the sake of*, or *instead of*

Acepto este premio **por** mi padre que murió durante la Guerra Sucia. — *I accept this award for* (*on behalf of*) *my father who died during the Dirty War.*

Debes hacerlo **por** el bienestar común. — *You should do it for* (*for the sake of*) *the common good.*

Ayer trabajé **por** mi tío.* — *Yesterday I worked for* (*instead of*) *my uncle.*

*Note: Compare this sentence with **Ayer trabajé para mi tío.** *Yesterday I worked for my uncle.* (He is my boss.)

b. to indicate movement *through* or *by*

Caminé **por** el congreso. — *I walked through the Congress.*

Pasé **por** el congreso. — *I went by the Congress.*

c. to express reason or motivation

La congresista va a tomar licencia **por** estar embarazada. — *The congresswoman is going to take a maternity leave.* (The pregnancy is the reason she is taking her leave.)

Por el golpe de estado en 1973, los chilenos vivieron años de mucha inseguridad. — *Because of the coup d'état in 1973, the Chileans lived years of much insecurity.*

2. Use **para:**

a. to express physical or temporal destination

Después del terremoto, el gobierno mandó medicinas **para** las víctimas. — *After the earthquake, the government sent medicine for the victims.* (physical destination)

El lunes, el presidente sale **para** la zona del terremoto. — *On Monday, the president leaves for the earthquake zone.* (physical destination)

Deben tener listo el discurso presidencial **para** mañana, ¿verdad? — *They should have the presidential speech ready for tomorrow, right?* (temporal destination)

b. to express purpose

Ella trabaja como voluntaria en el congreso **para** poder tener experiencia en la política. — *She works as a volunteer in Congress to be able to have experience in politics.*

Este programa de computación es **para** realizar gráficos tridimensionales. — *This computer program is for making three-dimensional graphs.*

Estudia **para** (ser) diplomática. — *She's studying to be a diplomat.*

Note: **Por** and **para** are prepositions, therefore, verbs immediately following them need to be in the infinitive form.

After having studied these uses of **por** and **para,** compare the following sentences and analyze the reasons for using **por** or **para** in each case.

El presidente sale mañana **para** la zona del terremoto.
The president is leaving tomorrow for the earthquake zone.

Va a pasar cinco horas viajando **por** los pueblos más afectados.
He is going to spend five hours traveling through the hardest hit towns.

Lo va a hacer **para** darles esperanza a las víctimas.
He is going to do this to give hope to the victims.

Lo va a hacer **por** ser su responsabilidad.
He is going to do this because it is his responsibility.

Actividad 26 Intenciones Elige un itinerario de la primera columna y el lugar de paso lógico de la segunda para formar la ruta completa de cada viaje. Consulta los mapas de este libro si es necesario. Sigue el modelo.

Act. 26: Assign as HW and check in class. Answers: Lima: Cuzco; Madrid: Zaragoza; ciudad de México: Taxco; La Paz: Cochabamba; Buenos Aires: Córdoba; Santiago: Valparaíso; Medellín: Cali; Guatemala: Antigua

▶ Washington → Miami / Atlanta
Mañana salgo de Washington **para** Miami y pienso pasar **por** Atlanta.

Inicio del viaje → destino final

Lima → Machu Picchu
Madrid → Barcelona
la ciudad de México → Acapulco
La Paz → Sucre
Buenos Aires → Salta
Santiago → Viña del Mar
Medellín → Popayán
Guatemala → Chichicastenango

Lugar de paso

Taxco
Córdoba
Zaragoza
Valparaíso
Antigua
Cali
Cochabamba
Cuzco

Act. 27A: Assign as HW and check in class. At the time of publication of this textbook, there was an Internet site with this address: cacerolazo.com. At this site one could listen to recordings of **cacerolazos.** A humorous point: In Venezuela a CD was made that contained the sound of a **cacerolazo,** so that all people had to do was put in the CD, turn up the volume, and open a window.

Actividad 27 Los cacerolazos **Parte A:** Lee la historia sobre un tipo de protesta muy popular en Latinoamérica y completa los espacios con **por** o **para.**

En Chile durante el gobierno de Allende, se empezó un tipo de protesta llamada "el cacerolazo". Espontáneamente, algunas madres de familias salieron a las calles con sus ollas, sartenes y cucharas y empezaron a hacer ruido ___para___ llamarle la atención al gobierno por la falta general de comida. Los cacerolazos, como los famosos "sit-ins" de los años 60 en los Estados Unidos, eran una manera no violenta ___para___ luchar ___por___ el bien del pueblo. La idea chilena era sencilla: las mujeres caminaban ___por___ las calles y plazas de las ciudades haciendo ruido. Hoy día lo hacen mujeres y hombres ___para___ conseguir lo que quieren del gobierno o ___para___ protestar por una situación específica. A través de los años, las cacerolas se convirtieron en símbolo de protesta ___para___ el pueblo latinoamericano. También hay sitios en Internet que usan cacerolas como iconos y si hay cacerolazos, muchas veces, anuncian la hora y el lugar ___por___ Internet.

▲ Venezolanos participan en un cacerolazo para protestar contra el presidente.

Parte B: En grupos de tres, hablen de diferentes problemas al nivel internacional, nacional, estatal o local y digan qué hace la gente para que los gobernantes oigan sus quejas.

Act. 27B: If any events have happened recently at your university, ask questions about what students did to make their voices heard.

Act. 28: Do as a whole class activity or as a paired activity and check by calling on volunteers to explain each conversation. 1A: Person receives a car as a present. 1B: She was to bring the car—a chore, an assignment, a task—and he did it for her. 2A: They are the boyfriend's shoes and she is taking them to him. 2B: She is wearing high heel shoes because her boyfriend is tall.

Actividad 28 ¿Qué ocurre? Lee los siguientes pares de miniconversaciones y piensa en el contexto de cada situación (quiénes hablan, qué ocurre) para explicar en qué se diferencia cada par de situaciones.

1. A. —¡Querido! ¡Tengo una sorpresa!
   —¡Un carro! ¿Lo trajiste para mí? Muchas gracias.
1. B. —¡Querido! ¡Tengo una sorpresa!
   —¡El carro! ¿Lo trajiste por mí? Muchas gracias.

2. A. —¿Adónde vas con esos zapatos?
   —Los llevo para mi novio; tiene una fiesta y necesita ir elegante.
2. B. —¿Adónde vas con esos zapatos?
   —Los llevo por mi novio; él es muy alto.

Actividad 29 Motivos y propósitos Habla de los motivos y propósitos de cada una de las siguientes situaciones, formando oraciones con una frase de la primera columna y una de la segunda. Debes encontrar dos posibilidades para cada frase de la primera columna: una con **por** para indicar el motivo de la acción y otra con **para** para indicar el propósito.

▶ La familia llegó a casa a las nueve **por** el tráfico que había.
La familia llegó a casa a las nueve **para** ver su programa de televisión favorito.

Personas y hechos

1. Romeo y Julieta se suicidaron
2. El presidente subió al poder
3. Ralph Nader empezó a investigar productos
4. Nike usa en sus anuncios a muchos deportistas
5. El gobierno norteamericano participa en el Tratado de Libre Comercio (*TLC*)

Motivos y propósitos

a. haber prometido cambios radicales
b. las oportunidades de trabajo que crea
c. vender sus productos
d. estar unidos en la muerte
e. el fraude que hay en los anuncios
f. la fama que tienen entre los jóvenes
g. mejorar la situación económica
h. proteger al consumidor
i. amor
j. aumentar las exportaciones a México y Canadá

Act. 29: May be assigned as HW and checked in class. Call on individuals for possible responses.
1. **para estar unidos en la muerte / por amor** 2. **para mejorar la situación económica / por haber prometido cambios radicales** 3. **por el fraude que hay en los anuncios / para proteger al consumidor** 4. **para vender sus productos / por la fama que tienen entre los jóvenes** 5. **para aumentar las exportaciones a México y Canadá / por las oportunidades de trabajo que crea**

Actividad 30 Debate sobre la pena de muerte **Parte A:** La pena de muerte es un tema de mucha controversia. Lee las siguientes ideas y complétalas con **por** o **para** si hay espacio en blanco. Luego marca si las oraciones están a favor (AF) o en contra (EC) de la pena de muerte.

	AF	EC
1. La pena de muerte se implementa ____para____ prevenir más asesinatos.	✓	
2. La violencia genera violencia.		✓
3. Los asesinos pasan ____por____ un juicio (*trial*) justo antes de ser condenados a muerte.	✓	
4. La ejecución no es nada más que un asesinato legalizado.		✓
5. La ejecución es necesaria ____para____ aliviar el sufrimiento de los familiares de la víctima.	✓	
6. El dicho "ojo ____por____ ojo, diente ____por____ diente" se debe poner en práctica.	✓	
7. En países donde no existe la pena de muerte hay menos asesinatos.		✓
8. ____Por____ miedo a la pena de muerte, los criminales matan menos.	✓	
9. No podemos tener la pena de muerte ____por____ el bien de la sociedad. Somos un país civilizado.		✓
10. Es muy costoso darles a los criminales cadena perpetua (*life imprisonment*).	✓	

(continúa en la página siguiente)

Act. 30A: You may want to assign this as HW and check in class.

Countries with no death penalty in the western hemisphere include: Canada, Colombia, Costa Rica, the Dominican Republic, Ecuador, Honduras, Nicaragua, Panama, Paraguay, Uruguay, and Venezuela. All countries in the European Union, which includes Spain, oppose the death penalty. The following countries allow the death penalty in special cases only (such as violations of human rights): Argentina, Bolivia, Chile, El Salvador, Mexico, and Peru. These countries have the death penalty: Cuba, Guatemala, and the United States (38 states yes, and 12 no). (Fuente: Amnesty International, http://www.deathpenaltyinfo.org.)

	AF	EC
11. Matar al asesino no es una solución ___para___ los familiares de la víctima.		✓
12. La pena de muerte es más humana que la cadena perpetua.	✓	
13. ___Para___ la gente pobre es difícil tener buena representación en la corte.		✓
14. Se puede llegar a ejecutar a personas que son inocentes.		✓

Act. 30B: Encourage students to incorporate some of the statements from Part A in their argument and to supplement with arguments of their own.

Do the corresponding CD-ROM and web activities to review the chapter topics.

Parte B: Ahora en grupos de cuatro, dos personas van a debatir a favor y dos personas en contra de la pena de muerte. Pueden usar sus propias ideas y las ideas de la Parte A para defender su postura.

Vocabulario activo

Verbos para expresar emoción

alegrarle (a alguien)	*to be glad, happy*
darle pena (a alguien)	*to feel sorry*
esperar	*to hope*
estar contento/a (de)	*to be happy*
estar triste (de)	*to be sad*
lamentar	*to lament, be sorry*
molestarle (a alguien)	*to be bothered*
sentir (ie, i)	*to be sorry*
sorprenderle (a alguien)	*to be surprised*
temer	*to fear*
tener miedo (de)	*to be afraid (of)*

Expresiones impersonales para expresar emoción

es bueno	*it's good*
es fantástico	*it's great*
es horrible	*it's horrible*
es lamentable	*it's a shame, lamentable*
es una lástima	*it's a shame*
es malo	*it's bad*
es maravilloso	*it's wonderful*
es una pena	*it's a shame*
es raro	*it's strange*
es terrible	*it's terrible*
es una vergüenza	*it's a shame, shameful*

¡Qué bueno...!	*How good . . .!*
¡Qué lástima...!	*What a shame . . .!*
¡Qué pena...!	*What a shame . . .!*
¡Qué sorpresa...!	*What a surprise . . .!*
¡Qué vergüenza...!	*How shameful . . .!*

Verbos para expresar duda y certeza

(no) estar seguro/a (de)	*(not) to be sure*
(no) creer	*(not) to think, believe*
dudar	*to doubt*

Expresiones impersonales para expresar duda, certeza y negación

no cabe duda	*there is no doubt*
(no) es cierto	*it is (isn't) true*
es claro	*it's clear*
(no) es evidente	*it's (not) evident*
es imposible	*it's impossible*
es improbable	*it's improbable*
(no) es obvio	*it's (not) obvious*
(no) es posible	*it's (not) possible*
(no) es probable	*it's (not) probable*
(no) es verdad	*it's (not) true*
(no) puede ser	*it can(not) be*

Palabras relacionadas con la política

abusar	*to abuse*
el abuso	*abuse*
el activismo	*activism*
el acuerdo	*agreement (pact)*
estar de acuerdo	*to be in agreement*
llegar a un acuerdo	*to reach an agreement*
la amenaza	*threat*
amenazar	*to threaten*
apoyar	*to support*
el apoyo	*support*
el asunto político/económico	*political/economic issue*
el bienestar común	*the common good*
la campaña electoral	*political campaign*
la censura	*censorship*
censurado/a	*censored*
censurar	*to censor*
el compromiso	*commitment*
la corrupción	*corruption*
la democracia	*democracy*
democrático/a	*democratic*
los derechos humanos	*human rights*
respetar/violar los derechos humanos	*to respect/violate human rights*
la desigualdad	*inequality*
el/la dictador/a	*dictator*
la dictadura	*dictatorship*
la eficiencia	*efficiency*
la estabilidad	*stability*
el golpe de estado	*coup d'état*
la huelga	*strike*
la igualdad	*equality*
la ineficiencia	*inefficiency*
la inestabilidad	*instability*
la influencia	*influence*
influir en	*to influence something*
la inversión	*investment*
invertir (ie, i)	*to invest*
la junta militar	*military junta*
la libertad de palabra/prensa	*freedom of speech/the press*
la manifestación	*demonstration*
el paro	*work stoppage*
el partido demócrata	*Democratic party*
el partido republicano	*Republican party*
la política	*politics*
el político/la mujer política	*politician*
la protección	*protection*
proteger	*to protect*
la protesta	*protest*
protestar	*to protest*
el pueblo	*the people*
el soborno	*bribe*
el/los suceso(s); los sucesos del momento	*the event(s); current events*

Expresiones útiles

el/la ayudante de cátedra	*teaching assistant*
la beca	*scholarship*
los desaparecidos	*missing people*
quién diría	*who would say*
salirse con la suya	*to get his/her way*

Vocabulario personal

Capítulo 7

Metas comunicativas

- afirmar y negar
- describir lo desconocido
- describir acciones que están por ocurrir
- hablar del medio ambiente y del turismo de aventura
- evitar la redundancia

Nuestro medio ambiente

▲ Grupo de ecoturistas cruza el lago Carhuacocha en los Andes peruanos.

May be assigned: Grammar, vocabulary, **¿Lo sabían?**, Act. 7, Act. 8A, Act. 9A, Act. 10A, Act. 14A, Act. 15A, Act. 16A, Act. 20A and B, Act. 21, Act. 23A, Act. 24, Act. 28B.

Show the chapter video episode at any point in the chapter that you see fit and do all or selected activities in class. Note: Content of the video supplements the cultural material in the chapter and activities reenter chapter grammar and vocabulary.

Unas vacaciones diferentes

Ecoturismo

Practice expressions: Write them on the board and use them as you try to make a paper airplane in front of the class. Make mistakes and elicit help from the class: **Voy a hacer un avión de papel. ¿Pueden ayudarme?** Point to the board and have them say **desde luego.** They give commands to help you make one correctly. Continue having problems and get a student to do one. **Necesito tu ayuda, ¿puedes hacerlo tú?** (After observing a student, say) **Ah, ¡ya sé!** Start making the plane and ask students **¿Algo así?** Transition to talking about trips by asking **¿Adónde quieres que te lleve este avión?** S:... T: **En mis últimas vacaciones fui a...**

¡Ya sé!	I've got it!
algo así	something like that
desde luego	of course

◂ Indígenas quichuas preparan terrazas para el cultivo en Latacunga, Ecuador.

Act. 1A: Call on students to tell where they went and categorize trips into different types on the board: **playa y sol, montañas y esquí, negocios, aventuras, viajes culturales,** etc.

Act. 1B: Read items with students, play the conversation, and check.

Note: The Incas worked cooperatively in **mingas** when the Spaniards arrived. Upon entering Cuzco a sign read **Ama Sua, Ama Quella, Ama Lulla** (*don't lie, don't steal, don't be lazy*). The work ethic was so strong that the penalty for laziness was death. The Spaniards destroyed the **mingas** and used the natives as forced labor. But this institution did not die and is still practiced today in parts of the Andes.

Actividad 1 Viajando se aprende **Parte A:** Antes de escuchar la conversación, menciona los tres últimos lugares adonde fuiste de vacaciones, di qué hiciste en cada viaje y cómo lo pasaste.

Parte B: Ahora vas a escuchar una conversación en la cual María José habla con Pablo sobre sus próximas vacaciones. Primero lee las siguientes oraciones y luego, mientras escuchas, marca si son ciertas (**C**) o falsas (**F**).

1. __F__ María José no conoce muchos lugares.
2. __F__ Ella quiere ir a un lugar donde pueda visitar catedrales.
3. __F__ El verano pasado estuvo en Venezuela.
4. __C__ Un amigo de Pablo estuvo en Ecuador.
5. __F__ A María José no le interesa ir a Ecuador.

Actividad 2 Los detalles Primero, lee las siguientes preguntas y después escucha la conversación otra vez para contestarlas.

1. ¿Qué grupo indígena vive en Capirona, Ecuador?
2. ¿En qué consiste el programa que organizan?
3. ¿Qué es una minga?
4. ¿Cómo se llega al pueblo?
5. ¿Por qué crees que le interesa este viaje a María José?

Act. 2: Read all questions, listen to the conversation, and check. Or, read one question at a time, listen to the conversation until the question is answered, pause, and check. Answers: 1. **quichua** 2. **ecoturismo (caminatas, demostraciones)** 3. **un proyecto comunitario** 4. **en canoa y caminando** 5. **Es algo nuevo.**

Act. 3: Form groups, set a time limit, and have a group sharing. Follow up by seeing if anyone in the class has ever taken this type of trip or any out-of-the-ordinary trip. If so, have him/her explain what it was like.

Ask students if they are aware of any groups on their own campus that offer this type of opportunity. Bring in brochures if available. Ask if they know of other organizations that do similar work.

Do the corresponding CD-ROM and web activities as you study the chapter.

Actividad 3 Opiniones En grupos de tres, discutan qué es lo peligroso, lo divertido y lo beneficioso de hacer un viaje de ese tipo.

¿Lo sabían?

Si te interesan los viajes educativos donde puedes trabajar como voluntario, hay muchas organizaciones que preparan grupos para viajar a regiones del mundo donde se necesita ayuda. Una de ellas es "Amigos de las Américas", que recluta a gente joven para trabajar en proyectos de salud en pueblos rurales de América Latina. En Internet también se encuentran sitios como **www.volunteerabroad.com** que ofrecen una innumerable lista de organizaciones, muchas sin fines de lucro, que organizan proyectos humanitarios. ¿Conoces o has participado en otros viajes como los que ofrecen estos grupos?

I. Discussing Adventure Travel and the Environment

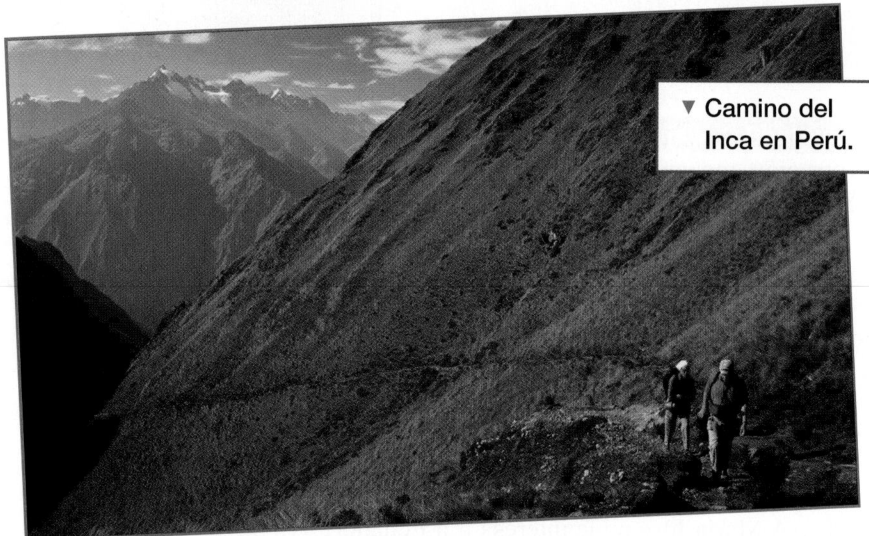

▼ Camino del Inca en Perú.

Have students read the paragraph, and ask them if they camp and what gear they have. Show pictures of the Camino del Inca.

You may want to mention the following terms used in some countries: **carpa = tienda de campaña; bolsa de dormir = saco de dormir.**

"Mi padre y yo hicimos el Camino del Inca que termina en Machu Picchu hace un par de años. Pisamos las mismas piedras y cruzamos los mismos puentes que construyeron los incas antes de la llegada de los españoles. Para hacer este viaje de cuatro días por las montañas de Perú, hay que estar en buen estado físico y hay que llevar algunas cosas. Por ejemplo, no es necesario llevar **tienda de campaña** ni comida ni cacharros para preparar la comida porque eso lo llevan los porteadores (asistentes). No hace falta llevar **mapa** para seguir el camino porque un guía siempre acompaña al grupo, pero sí es necesario tener **saco de dormir, linterna,**

repelente contra insectos y también es buena idea llevar **una navaja suiza.** Otra cosa de suma importancia es un buen **protector solar** porque a esas alturas el sol puede ser superfuerte. Los porteadores son los que llevan las **mochilas** y, por consideración hacia ellos, es buena idea llevar pocas cosas. También se debe llevar una cámara con muchos rollos porque se puede sacar un sinnúmero de fotos y si la cámara es digital, es importante tener **pilas** extras."

norteamericana

pilas = batteries
batería = car battery

Sports related vocabulary:

1. Mime other sports for students to name. Provide names of sports students don't know. Basic sports are presented in Appendix G.
2. Have students categorize the sports from most dangerous to least.
3. Have students interview each other to see how many of the sports they have done. Make a contest out of it to see which pair wins.
4. Ask students to name two sports they would never participate in and ask why. Have them complete this formula to do so: **No me gustaría hacer... porque...**

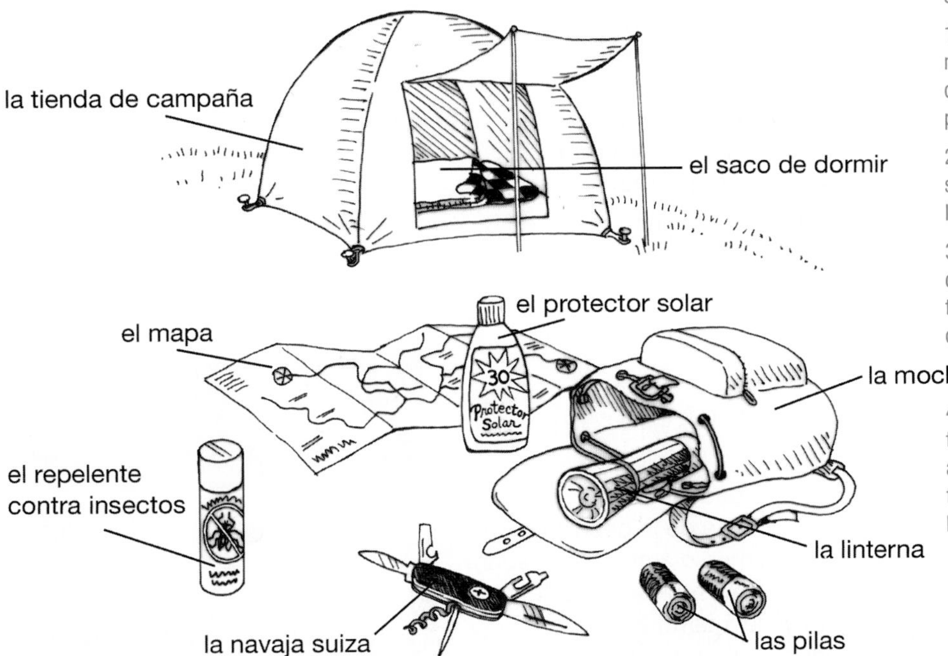

Deportes

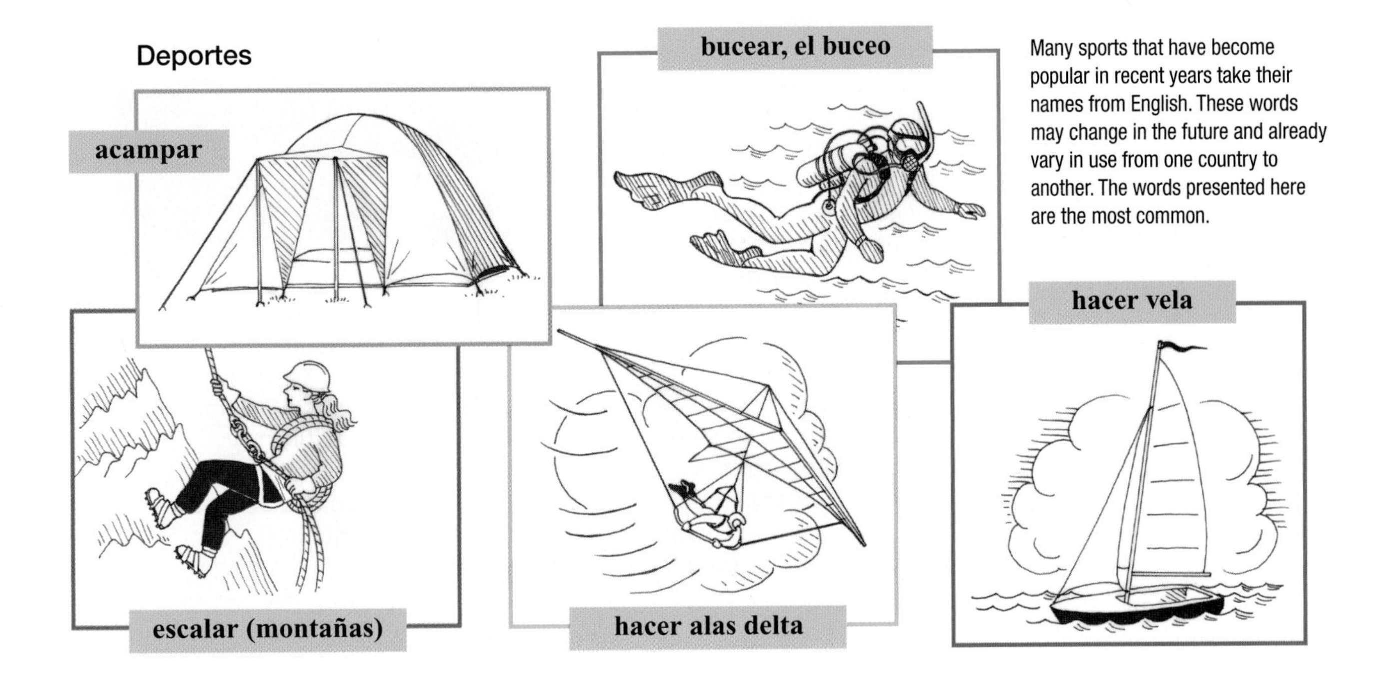

Many sports that have become popular in recent years take their names from English. These words may change in the future and already vary in use from one country to another. The words presented here are the most common.

You may also see the word **piragua** for *kayak*.

hacer rafting = **hacer navegación de rápidos** (*Costa Rica*)

For more words related to the environment, see Appendix G.

Contaminante = **contaminador/a** are both adjectives and can also be used as nouns. **Contaminación** = **polución,** but the former is preferable.

 *El reciclaje*

 **FLR** link: **Lectura 1**

Environmental vocabulary:

1. Ask students what is done at the university to conserve energy. Then ask what more should be done (**La universidad debe..., Es importante que la universidad...,** etc.).

2. Ask how many students have a Walkman in class. Ask if the batteries are rechargeable or not.

3. Ask **¿Qué quiere el gobierno que hagan los ciudadanos para conservar el medio ambiente? ¿Qué quiere la gente que haga el gobierno?**

4. In pairs, have students take turns giving definitions and guess the words defined using terms related to adventure travel and the environment. Have them use phrases like: **Es la acción de..., Es una cosa que se usa para...**

Refer students to Appendix G for basic vocabulary relating to the environment.

hacer esquí nórdico/alpino/acuático, kayak, rafting, senderismo/trekking, snorkel, snowboard, surf
montar a caballo/en bicicleta de montaña

El medio ambiente

la conservación, conservar	conservation, to conserve
la contaminación, contaminante, contaminar	pollution, contaminating, to contaminate/pollute
los desechos, desechable, desechar	rubbish, disposable, to throw away
el desperdicio, desperdiciar	waste, to waste
la destrucción, destruir	destruction, to destroy
el efecto invernadero	greenhouse effect
la extinción, extinguirse	extinction, to become extinct
la preservación, preservar	
la protección, proteger	
recargable, recargar	rechargeable, to recharge
la reducción, reducir	
la restricción, restringir	

¿LO SABÍAN?

En la actualidad, casi todo el mundo está consciente de la necesidad de proteger el medio ambiente, cuidar nuestra tierra y reciclar. Esta toma de conciencia también ha despertado interés por hacer viajes de ecoturismo, es decir, viajes donde uno está en contacto con la naturaleza y aprende sobre ella. En Latinoamérica, además de Costa Rica donde gran parte del país está destinado al ecoturismo, hay numerosos lugares que son frecuentados por ecoturistas. Entre ellos están: las Islas Galápagos de Ecuador para ver la flora y fauna, el Parque Tayrona en Colombia para explorar la selva, la laguna de Scammon en México para ver ballenas y los glaciares de la Patagonia en Argentina. Otro tipo de actividad que comienza a ser popular es el viaje de turismo rural. En estos viajes el visitante visita una finca o una casa rural y aprende a hacer productos locales como comida, bebidas o artesanías. Di si te gustaría hacer ecoturismo o turismo rural. ¿Conoces lugares para hacer ese tipo de viajes?

▲ Estudiante en un viaje de ecoturismo cerca de Iquitos, Perú.

Actividad 4 Los viajes En grupos de tres, hagan una lista de cosas que se necesitan para hacer las siguientes actividades y compártanla con la clase.

1. acampar un fin de semana
2. una caminata de un día por la montaña
3. un viaje de una semana por la selva
4. un viaje en bicicleta, en verano, durante quince días

Act. 4 and 5: Form groups of three and keep same groups for both activities, set a time limit, and begin. Encourage students to incorporate other vocabulary they know. Have students justify their choices.

Actividad 5 Categorías En grupos de tres, túrnense para nombrar por lo menos cuatro deportes que pertenecen a las siguientes categorías. Pueden incluir palabras de la lista de vocabulario y otras que Uds. sepan.

1. deportes acuáticos
2. deportes en los cuales los participantes usan zapatos especiales
3. deportes que se practican en el aire
4. deportes que se practican cuando hace frío
5. deportes que se practican cuando hace calor
6. deportes baratos
7. deportes caros

Actividad 6 Actividades peligrosas **Parte A:** En grupos de tres, discutan las siguientes preguntas.

1. ¿Practican algún deporte peligroso?
2. ¿Qué deportes peligrosos se pueden practicar en la ciudad donde viven o cerca de allí?
3. ¿Por qué creen que algunas personas disfrutan de deportes peligrosos como escalar montañas o bucear en cuevas del Caribe?

Parte B: Hay gente que dice que todos los deportes son peligrosos. Cuente cada uno un accidente que tuvo mientras practicaba un deporte. Si no tuvieron ninguno, hablen de un accidente que tuvo alguien que conozcan.

Act. 6A and 6B: To practice vocabulary do Part A; to practice connected discourse do Part B. Use same groups of three as in previous activities. Check by finding out what dangerous sports people practice, why some do, why some don't, if they would like to, etc.

Actividad 7 Cuidemos el mundo en que vivimos En grupos de tres, discutan las siguientes preguntas.

1. ¿Qué cosas desperdician Uds.? ¿Escriben en un solo lado del papel? ¿Dejan las luces encendidas? ¿Pueden nombrar cinco cosas que Uds. pueden hacer para reducir el desperdicio de recursos naturales?
2. ¿Qué productos destruyen la capa de ozono? ¿Podemos usar otros productos que contaminen menos? ¿Cuáles son?
3. ¿Cuántos animales que están en peligro de extinción pueden nombrar? ¿Por qué están en peligro? ¿Podemos hacer algo para detener su extinción?
4. Muchas veces los desechos de un lugar se tiran en otro. ¿Creen que sea apropiado, por ejemplo, que el estado de Nueva York tire su basura en Tennessee? ¿Por qué sí o no?
5. ¿Qué se puede usar en los carros en lugar de gasolina? ¿Y en lugar del gas, qué se puede usar para calentar las casas?
6. Muchos lugares tienen restricciones sobre el nivel de emisiones tóxicas que producen los carros. ¿Creen Uds. que todos los países deban tener ese tipo de leyes? ¿Tiene el estado o el país donde Uds. viven algunas restricciones?

Act. 7: Could be assigned as HW to form a solid base for discussion. Option 1: Form groups, have all groups discuss answers, then have a group sharing. Option 2: Form groups, have them answer one question at a time having a group sharing after each. Option 3: Assign two questions to each group to discuss (in a class of 20 to 25 students, each set should be answered by at least two groups). Have groups report back to the class with their responses.

Act. 8A and 8B: Assign Act. 8A as HW. Ask students questions to ensure comprehension of Part A. Start by asking them how many pairs of tennis shoes/caps/pairs of earrings/ etc. they own to get them to think about the theme. Encourage creativity while doing Part B.

Fuente hispana

Actividad 8 Los recursos naturales **Parte A:** Lee lo que dice un argentino sobre los recursos naturales de Latinoamérica y explica de qué manera no intencional recicla la gente.

> "En muchos países latinoamericanos se usan menos recursos naturales que en países como los Estados Unidos porque la gente, que en general tiene menos dinero, compra menos y por lo tanto consume menos. Esto incluye la compra de comida, de ropa, de objetos de diversión y recreación como CDs, artículos de deportes, etc., y también energía. Mucha gente consume menos gasolina porque usa el transporte público o tiene carros pequeños que consumen menos. Y cuando algo se rompe, como un televisor, una radio o un secador de pelo, es más económico llevarlo a arreglar que comprar uno nuevo. Esto se debe a que la mano de obra es barata y a que algunos de esos productos son importados, así que pueden tener tarifa de importación y, por eso, son generalmente caros. Entonces en Latinoamérica muchas veces se recicla no necesariamente de manera consciente sino porque resulta más práctico y económico y así al consumir menos logran conservar más."
>
> ***argentino***

Parte B: Ahora en grupos de tres, preparen por lo menos cinco recomendaciones para hacerle a la clase sobre qué pueden hacer en su vida diaria para consumir menos recursos naturales. Miren la lista de ideas que se presenta y al hablar, usen expresiones como: **Les recomendamos que..., Les aconsejamos que...**

▶ Les recomendamos que vayan menos a las tiendas para no ver tantas cosas atractivas y comprar tantas cosas innecesarias.

cosas que se compran todos los días
cantidad de plástico/papel que se usa para empacar las cosas
gas/electricidad/agua/gasolina
cantidad de comida que se compra
compras innecesarias
compras por catálogo/Internet
productos desechables
compra de libros versus biblioteca
uso innecesario del carro
comerciales en la tele, el periódico y la radio
propaganda por correo (catálogos, ofertas del supermercado, etc.)

Act. 9A: Assign as HW. Have students mark their reactions to these statements. Poll the class as to their responses and be attentive to what positions students take. Use this knowledge to better form the groups for the debate in Part B. Have students say **Estoy seguro de que..., Es posible que..., No creo que...** to recycle the subjunctive when expressing their opinions.

Actividad 9 Ecoturismo, ¿peligro o no? **Parte A:** Lee las siguientes oraciones y marca tu opinión usando esta escala:

1 = estoy seguro/a 2 = es posible 3 = no lo creo

1. _____ La sola presencia del ser humano destruye el medio ambiente.
2. _____ Para llegar a lugares remotos hay que usar medios de transporte que contaminan el ambiente.
3. _____ Para tomar conciencia del valor de la naturaleza, hay que ver las zonas remotas y vírgenes con los propios ojos.
4. _____ El dinero que gastan los turistas se puede usar para la conservación de las áreas silvestres.
5. _____ Después de hacer un viaje de ecoturismo, los participantes tienen un papel más activo en el movimiento verde: reciclan más, compran productos que contaminan menos e intentan cambiar las leyes de su país para proteger el medio ambiente.

6. _____ Los controles de un gobierno nunca van a ser suficientemente estrictos para controlar los problemas que puede traer el ecoturismo.
7. _____ El contacto con los turistas cambia para siempre la vida de las personas de una región.
8. _____ Los ecoturistas nunca tiran basura ni hacen nada para destruir el lugar que visitan.
9. _____ La presencia constante de grupos de turistas no es natural y por eso, crea un desequilibrio (*imbalance*) en el área.

Parte B: Algunos creen que el ecoturismo es beneficioso porque así la gente aprende a apreciar y preservar la naturaleza. Otros creen que el mismo ecoturismo ayuda a destruir el medio ambiente. Formen grupos de cuatro, con dos a favor y dos en contra, y preparen un debate sobre este tema. Pueden usar las ideas mencionadas en la Parte A y expandirlas e inventar otras razones para apoyar su postura. Al debatir usen las siguientes expresiones.

Act. 9B: Form groups for a debate. Allow students a few minutes to prepare arguments.

Para estar de acuerdo	Para no estar de acuerdo	Para interrumpir
Estoy de acuerdo.	No estoy de acuerdo.	Pido la palabra.
Seguro.	No estoy de acuerdo del todo.	Perdón, pero...
Sin duda alguna.	De ningún modo.	¿Me dejas terminar?
Opino como tú.		

II. Affirming and Negating

In this section you will review commonly used affirmative and negative expressions, and specifically how negative expressions are used.

Drill affirmative and negative expressions:

1. Have students contradict what you say. T: **Siempre reciclo el plástico.** S: **No, Ud. no recicla el plástico nunca.** T: **Tengo muchos amigos. / Con frecuencia voy al teatro. / Conozco a todo el mundo.** / etc.

2. Tell students they are very naive about politics and have them deny what you say: T: **Algunas personas del gobierno son corruptas.** S: **No es verdad. Ninguna persona es corrupta.** T: **Todos dicen mentiras. / Jamás se preocupan por los ciudadanos. / Todo es un caos.** / etc.

1. Here is a list of common affirmative and negative expressions.

Affirmative Expressions	Negative Expressions
todo everything **algo** something	**nada** nothing, (not) anything
todos/as everyone **todo el mundo** everyone **muchas/pocas personas** many/few people **alguien** someone	**nadie** no one
siempre always **muchas veces** many times **con frecuencia / a menudo** frequently **a veces** sometimes **una vez** once	**nunca / jamás** never

2. Two common ways to create sentences with negative expressions in Spanish are:

Remember: If you use **no** before the verb, use a negative word after the verb.

no + *verb* + *negative word*
negative word + *verb*

—¿Te ayudó la Sra. López?	*Did Mrs. López help you?*
—¿Ayudarme? Esa mujer **no** me **ayuda jamás.** / Esa mujer **jamás** me **ayuda**.	*Help me? That woman doesn't ever help me / never helps me.*
—¿Quiénes fueron a la reunión de negocios?	*Who went to the business meeting?*
—**No fue nadie.** / **Nadie fue.**	*Nobody went.*
—¿Funciona?	*Does it work?*
—No, **no funciona nada** en esta oficina. / No, **nada funciona.***	*No, nothing works in this office.*

*Note: **Nada** can only precede the verb when it is the subject.

3. When **nadie** and **alguien** are direct objects, they must be preceded by the personal **a.**

—¿Viste **a alguien**?	*Did you see anyone?*
—**No, no** vi **a nadie.**	*No, I didn't see anyone.*

Compare the previous sentences with the following ones in which **nadie** and **alguien** are the subject.

Ayer **no** vino **nadie. / Nadie** vino ayer.	*Nobody came yesterday.*
Alguien derramó una sustancia tóxica en el río.	*Somebody spilled a toxic substance in the river.*

4. To talk about indefinite quantity in affirmative sentences and questions use the following adjectives and pronouns.

Affirmative Adjectives	Affirmative Pronouns
algún/alguna/algunos/algunas + *noun*	**alguno/alguna/algunos/algunas**

Creo que hay **algunas tiendas de campaña** en rebaja.	*I think that there are some tents on sale.*
—¿Sabes que los chicos se fueron a hacer vela? ¿**Alguno** te llamó para avisarte?	*Do you know that the kids went sailing? Did any one (of them) call you to let you know?*
—Sí, pero preferí quedarme en casa.	*Yes, but I preferred to stay at home.*

5. To talk about indefinite quantity in negative sentences, use the following adjectives and pronouns.

Negative Adjectives	Negative Pronouns
ningún/ninguna + *singular noun*	**ninguno/a**

The plural form **ningunos/as** is seldom used except with plural nouns such as **pantalones** and **tijeras** (*scissors*): No tengo **ningunos pantalones** limpios.

No hay **ningún centro de reciclaje** en mi barrio.	*There aren't any recycling centers in my neighborhood.*
—¿Reciclaste **algunas** revistas?	*Did you recycle any magazines?*
—No, no reciclé **ninguna.**	*No, I didn't recycle any.*

Negative questions with **ningún/ninguno/a** are not high frequency and will therefore not be presented at this point.

6. It is common to use the pronouns **ninguno** and **ninguna** with a prepositional phrase beginning with **de: Ninguno de mis amigos** se droga.

Actividad 10 Conversaciones ecológicas **Parte A:** Completa las siguientes conversaciones relacionadas con la ecología usando palabras afirmativas o negativas.

Act. 10A: Assign as HW and correct in class.

1. —No, gracias. No necesito ___ninguna___ bolsa. Traje tres de mi casa para toda la compra.
   —Bien.
2. —¿Hay ___algo___ que podamos hacer para detener la deforestación? ¡Mira este lugar!
   —Sí, es terrible, pero no sé qué se puede hacer.
3. —¿___Alguien___ de tu familia desperdicia el agua?
   —Sí, mi hermano se da duchas de 25 minutos.
4. —¡Qué horror! Hay 50 personas y ___nadie/ninguna___ se preocupa por reciclar el papel que se usa en este lugar.
   —Estoy totalmente de acuerdo. Debemos hablar con ___todos/alguien___ para resolver este problema.
5. —No compro árboles de Navidad de verdad ___nunca___ porque tengo uno de plástico.
   —Yo también, y aunque parezca mentira, se ve bien bonito.
6. —¿Oyes ___algún___ ruido?
   —No, no oigo ___nada/ninguno___. ¡Qué placer! Me encanta el silencio de este lugar.

Parte B: Ahora, en parejas, digan dónde creen que tiene lugar cada conversación y de qué hablan. Usen oraciones como: **Es posible que ellos estén en... y creo que están hablando sobre...**

Act. 10B: Form pairs, set a time limit, and begin. Encourage imagination in responses.

Act. 11A: Form pairs, model the activity, set a time limit, and begin. Check by asking: **¿Hay alguien que a menudo monte en bicicleta?** (etc.)

Actividad 11 ¿Con qué frecuencia? **Parte A:** En parejas, túrnense para averiguar con qué frecuencia hace su compañero/a las siguientes actividades. Marquen las respuestas en la tabla. Sigan el modelo.

▶ —¿Con qué frecuencia montas en bicicleta?
—Monto en bicicleta a veces.

	jamás	a veces	a menudo
1. montar en bicicleta	_____	_____	_____
2. comprar verduras orgánicas	_____	_____	_____
3. hacer deportes al aire libre	_____	_____	_____
4. usar transporte público	_____	_____	_____
5. vestirse con ropa de algodón	_____	_____	_____
6. reciclar latas (*cans*) de bebidas	_____	_____	_____
7. hacer ecoturismo	_____	_____	_____
8. contribuir con dinero a organizaciones que protegen el medio ambiente	_____	_____	_____

Act. 11B: Model use of the imperfect in the second part of the activity. Set a time limit and begin. Check by having a group sharing. Encourage connected discourse with **pero, en cambio, por un lado/por otro lado,** etc., by having students form sentences like: **Ahora jamás monto en bicicleta, en cambio montaba mucho en bicicleta cuando estaba en la escuela secundaria.**

Parte B: Repitan la actividad, pero ahora con referencia a sus años de la escuela secundaria.

Act. 12A: Form pairs, explain the premise, and allow one minute for students to mark their predictions.

Actividad 12 ¿Conoces a tu compañero? **Parte A:** Escojan una pareja, y luego sin consultar a su compañero/a, marquen las cosas de la siguiente lista que creen que tiene su compañero/a en la habitación o apartamento.

_____ discos compactos de Elvis
_____ un osito de peluche (*teddy bear*)
_____ cuadros de arte moderno
_____ un póster de un animal en peligro de extinción
_____ un saco de dormir
_____ guías de turismo
_____ fotos de su familia
_____ videos de películas de acción
_____ una bicicleta
_____ un instrumento musical

Act. 12B: Model the exchanges, set a time limit, and begin. Check by saying: **Creo que Jack tiene fotos de su familia. ¿Es verdad?** Expand activity by having students predict what you have in your home.

Parte B: Ahora, hablen con su compañero/a para confirmar sus predicciones. Sigan el modelo.

▶ —Creo que tienes algunos discos compactos de Elvis.

—Es verdad, tengo tres.

—Te equivocas, no tengo ninguno. / No tengo ningún disco compacto de Elvis.

Actividad 13 ¿Cómo es tu familia? En parejas, usen la siguiente lista de ocupaciones para averiguar sobre la familia de su compañero/a. Sigan el modelo.

▶ A: ¿Hay algún piloto en tu familia?

B: Sí, hay una mujer piloto.

A: ¿Quién es?

B: Mi hermana y trabaja para Mexicana.

B: No, no hay ningún piloto. / No, no hay ninguno.

1. político
2. plomero
3. vendedor
4. artista
5. enfermero
6. arquitecto
7. cartero
8. ecologista
9. carpintero

Act. 13: Before starting, you may want to have students say masculine and feminine forms of the occupations presented (**la mujer plomero/la plomero,** etc.). Then model the activity, form pairs, set a time limit, and begin. Check by asking about a few professions. For example, find out who has an artist in the family and ask about the type of artwork done.

plomero = **fontanero** (*España*)

III. Describing the Unknown

The Subjunctive in Adjective Clauses

1. As you have already learned, the subjunctive can be used in sentences to express influence, emotion, doubt, and denial. Additionally it can be used to describe a person, animal, or thing that you are looking for or want and that may or may not exist. Study the following examples.

May or May Not Exist	Exists
Subjunctive	Indicative
Buscamos una persona **que organice** programas de reciclaje. *We are looking for someone who organizes recycling programs.* (There may or may not be such a person.)	Buscamos a la persona **que organiza** programas de reciclaje. *We are looking for the person who organizes recycling programs.* (We know this person exists.)
Tengo que encontrar un abogado **que haya estudiado** derecho del medio ambiente. *I have to find a lawyer who has studied environmental law.* (Might exist, might find one.)	Conozco a un abogado **que estudió** derecho del medio ambiente. *I know a lawyer who studied environmental law.* (Exists.)
Buscamos un lugar **donde no haya** mucha contaminación. *We are looking for a place where there isn't much pollution.* (Might exist, we might find it.)	Sabemos de un lugar **donde no hay** mucha contaminación. *We know of a place where there isn't much pollution.* (Exists, we can take you there.)

Drill subjunctive in adjective clauses:

1. Do a chain drill: **Busco un profesor de matemáticas/un abogado/un amigo que sea...** Then, have students describe a professor they have. S: **Tengo un profesor de matemáticas que es...**

2. Have students complete the phrase **Quiero unas vacaciones que...**

When describing a person that you are looking for or want and that may or may not exist, the personal **a** is not used (compare the first two sentences in each column).

Many native speakers use the preterit instead of the present perfect in sentences like **Conozco a un abogado que estudió/ha estudiado las leyes ecológicas.**

Drill subjunctive with negation:

Tell students they are whiners. Have them complain about the university: **No hay ninguna clase que sea fácil.** (etc.)

Notice that sometimes you must use **donde** instead of **que** to talk about places. This use parallels English.

2. The subjunctive is also used in dependent adjective clauses to emphatically describe something that, according to the speaker, does not exist. Note the following construction.

no + *verb* + *negative word* + **que** + *subjunctive*

No encuentro nada que me **guste.**	*I can't find anything that I like.*
No hay ningún profesor que dé poca tarea.	*There is no professor that gives a small amount of homework.*

3. The *personal **a*** is only used in sentences with dependent adjective clauses if they contain **alguien** or **nadie**.

—¿Conoces **a alguien** que sepa hacer vela?	*Do you know anyone who knows how to sail?*
—No, no conozco **a nadie** que sepa hacer vela.	*No, I don't know anyone who does.*

Act. 14A: May be assigned as HW. If done in class, give instructions, and allow one minute to complete.

Actividad 14 El lugar ideal **Parte A:** En el mundo hay una gran variedad de lugares para vivir. Mira la siguiente lista y marca con una X las tres características más importantes para ti.

_____ nevar mucho/poco
_____ ofrecer una variedad de restaurantes étnicos
_____ tener escuelas buenas
_____ estar cerca de las montañas
_____ ser un centro urbano
_____ haber alquileres bajos
_____ haber muchas/pocas actividades culturales
_____ estar cerca del agua
_____ tener temperaturas moderadas
_____ estar en el campo
_____ ser un lugar tranquilo
_____ convivir gente de diferentes razas y culturas
_____ estar poco contaminado
_____ haber poca delincuencia
_____???

Act. 14B: Form pairs, model possible sentences, point out the use of the indicative in **Conozco un lugar que...**, set a time limit, and begin. Correct by trying to have the class agree on the most and least important.

Parte B: En parejas, díganle a su compañero/a las características que buscan Uds. en un lugar para vivir. Usen expresiones como: **Busco un lugar que/donde..., Quiero vivir en un lugar que/donde...** Después, digan si conocen un lugar que tenga esas características. Usen **(No) Conozco un lugar que/donde...**

Act. 15A: May be assigned as HW.

Actividad 15 El medio ambiente **Parte A:** Mira la siguiente información y di qué se necesita hacer para proteger el medio ambiente. Usa frases como: **Necesitamos..., Se necesita/n..., Queremos tener...** Sigue el modelo.

▶ personas / recoger / basura de la calle
Se necesitan personas que recojan basura de la calle.

1. fábricas / no tirar / desechos a los ríos
2. más científicos / hacer / estudios para encontrar nuevas fuentes de energía
3. más organizaciones / proteger / las especies de animales que están en peligro de extinción

4. alcaldes / construir / zonas verdes en las ciudades
5. carros / emitir / menos gases tóxicos
6. compañías / construir / paneles de energía solar baratos para las casas
7. supermercados / no envolver / absolutamente todo en plástico
8. gente / no desperdiciar / recursos naturales

Parte B: En grupos de tres, organicen las ideas anteriores de la más importante a la menos importante. Estén listos para justificar el orden que han elegido. Usen expresiones como: **Lo más importante es que..., También es importante que...**

Act. 15B: Model with a student. Begin by asking him/her which is the most important. Then disagree and begin to argue your point. Form groups of three, set a time limit, yet allow time for students to argue and to come to an agreement. Check by calling on groups to find out which they listed as the most important and which was the least. Try to get the class to agree at least on these two.

¿LO SABÍAN?

- Suramérica pierde el 1% de los bosques cada año.
- En el sur de Chile hay conejos con cataratas y ovejas con córneas inflamadas, posiblemente por el agujero en la capa de ozono.
- La urbanización de América Latina crece más rápidamente que en ninguna otra parte del mundo. En la actualidad el 78% de la población vive en zonas urbanas.
- En América Latina se encuentra el 40% de todas las especies de los bosques tropicales del mundo.
- Centroamérica, con sólo el 0,5% de la superficie emergida (*land*) del planeta, tiene el 7% de la biodiversidad del planeta.
- Colombia tiene el 10% de las especies de flora y fauna del mundo.

¿Lo sabían?: Ask students which of the facts surprises them the most and which is the most tragic.

Actividad 16 ¿Qué piensas? **Parte A:** Completa estas ideas sobre tu universidad con la forma correcta del verbo indicado. Después, marca con una X las oraciones con las que estás de acuerdo y con una O aquéllas con las que no estás de acuerdo.

1. _____ No hay ningún estudiante que _____quiera_____ estudiar muchas horas por día. (querer)
2. _____ No hay ninguna cafetería en esta universidad que _____sirva_____ buena comida. (servir)
3. _____ No conozco a ningún profesor que _____llegue_____ tarde a clase. (llegar)
4. _____ No hay ningún profesor que _____dé_____ exámenes finales fáciles. (dar)
5. _____ No hay nadie en esta universidad que _____copie_____ en los exámenes. (copiar)

Parte B: En grupos de tres, compartan y justifiquen sus opiniones.

Act. 16A: Assign as HW. Correct subjunctive forms in class.

Act. 16B: Form pairs and have students compare responses. Check student opinions for each question by a show of hands. If they are in disagreement, ask some to support their opinions.

Note: In countries like Chile, Peru, and Argentina they say **Los profesores toman exámenes y los estudiantes los dan.** In many other countries these verbs are reversed.

Act. 17A: Option 1: Inform students they are to ask one question of one person, answer a question themselves, and then move on to another person. Option 2: Form two concentric circles and have students ask one question of one person, answer a question themselves, and then the inner circle moves clockwise to the next person. The outer circle stays in place. Note: In both options, if students answer affirmatively, the person interviewing them writes their name.

Greenpeace en España

Act. 17B: Have students return to their seats. Form pairs, model the activity, set a time limit, and begin. Check by seeing which pair had the most affirmative responses.

Actividad 17 Una encuesta **Parte A:** Entrevista a tus compañeros para ver si hay alguien que haga algunas de las siguientes actividades. Si alguien responde afirmativamente, escribe su nombre en la columna de la derecha. Sigue el modelo.

▶ —¿Apagas las luces al salir de tu habitación?

—Sí, las apago. —No, no las apago.

1. reciclar papel ____________
2. tener un carro que gaste poca gasolina ____________
3. usar pilas recargables ____________
4. darse duchas de cinco minutos o menos ____________
5. comprar bombillas de luz de larga duración ____________
6. ser miembro de un grupo ecológico como Greenpeace ____________

Parte B: En parejas, túrnense para averiguar si su compañero/a tiene a alguien en su lista que haga las actividades anteriores.

▶ —¿Hay alguien en tu lista que apague las luces?

—Sí, Cindy las apaga. ¿Y tú? ¿Hay alguien en tu lista que...?

—No, no hay nadie que las apague. ¿Y tú? ¿Hay alguien en tu lista que...?

Act. 18: Have students practice some questions, form pairs, set a time limit, and begin. Check by asking a few questions. Note: Warren Miller is a producer of ski movies.

Actividad 18 ¿Conoces a alguien que...? En parejas, túrnense para decir si conocen a alguien que haya hecho las siguientes cosas. Sigan el modelo.

▶ A: ¿Conoces a alguien que haya nadado en el río Amazonas?

B: No, no conozco a nadie que haya nadado en el Amazonas.

B: Sí, conozco a alguien.

A: ¿Quién es y cuándo lo hizo?

B: Mi hermano nadó en el Amazonas el año pasado.

1. ir a un país de Suramérica
2. escalar los Andes
3. hacer rafting
4. ver una película de esquí de Warren Miller
5. cruzar el Atlántico en barco
6. hacer alas delta
7. saltar con una cuerda bungee
8. ? ? ?

Act. 19: Form pairs, instruct them to read only their role, have them sit back-to-back to simulate a phone conversation, set a time limit, and begin. Check by having two people carry out the role play for the class.

Actividad 19 Un lugar de vacaciones En parejas, una persona quiere ir de vacaciones y llama a una agencia de viajes para que le recomienden un lugar. El/La agente de viajes le da algunas sugerencias. Lea cada uno un papel y luego mantengan una conversación telefónica.

Cliente

Éstas son algunas de las características que buscas en un lugar de vacaciones: al lado del mar, tranquilo, económico, temperatura no mayor de 30 grados. Usa expresiones como: **Busco un lugar que..., Quiero un lugar donde...**

30 grados centígrados = 86 Fahrenheit

Agente de viajes

Averigua qué tipo de lugar busca el/la cliente y luego recomiéndale y descríbele uno de los siguientes lugares. Usa expresiones como: **Le recomiendo que..., Le aconsejo que..., Este lugar es...**

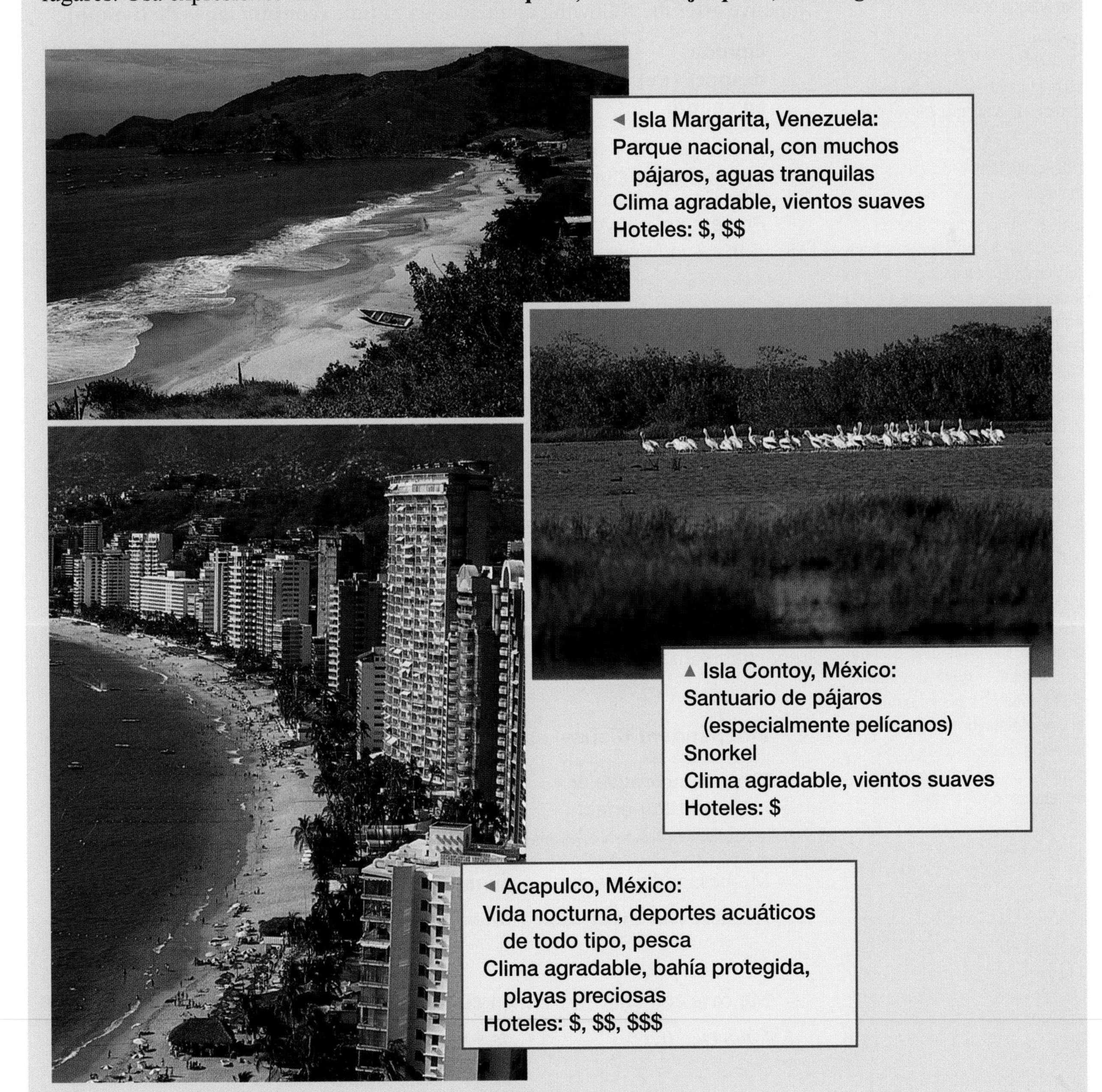

◄ Isla Margarita, Venezuela:
Parque nacional, con muchos pájaros, aguas tranquilas
Clima agradable, vientos suaves
Hoteles: $, $$

▲ Isla Contoy, México:
Santuario de pájaros (especialmente pelícanos)
Snorkel
Clima agradable, vientos suaves
Hoteles: $

◄ Acapulco, México:
Vida nocturna, deportes acuáticos de todo tipo, pesca
Clima agradable, bahía protegida, playas preciosas
Hoteles: $, $$, $$$

IV. Expressing Pending Actions

The Subjunctive in Adverbial Clauses

A conjunction is a word that links two actions or states.

FLR link: **Lectura 2**

Point out that the subject of the dependent and independent clauses may be the same or different.

Drill subjunctive in adverbial clauses:

1. List conjunctions of time on the board. Pair students and tell them to give ridiculous endings to the following sentences: **Me voy a casar con ella... (cuando yo tenga 90 años). Voy a hacer la tarea de español... Me voy a dejar crecer el pelo...**

2. Contrast pending and habitual actions by having students complete the following: **Generalmente hago la tarea..., pero hoy voy a hacer la tarea...**

3. Have students complete these sentences with the correct form of the verb **llegar** and then finish the sentences in a creative manner: **De pequeño, todos los días cuando ___ a casa... / Aquí en la universidad, todos los días cuando ___ al colegio mayor** (**al apartamento/a casa**)**... / Esta noche cuando ___ al colegio mayor** (**al apartamento/a casa**)**...**

1. When you want to talk about *pending* actions or states use the present subjunctive after the following conjunctions of time **(conjunciones de tiempo).**

cuando	when	**hasta que**	until
después (de) que	after	**tan pronto como**	as soon as
en cuanto	as soon as		

Independent Clause	Dependent Adverbial Clause
Present indicative or **ir a** + *infinitive*	Conjunction of time + Subjunctive

Me voy a casar con él	**cuando**	un astronauta **llegue** a Plutón.
I'll marry him	*when*	*an astronaut lands on Pluto.* (pending action)
Quiere asociarse a un grupo ecológico	**en cuanto**	**tenga** dinero.
She wants to join an ecological group	*as soon as*	*she has money.* (pending state)

2. In contrast, when you want to talk about states or habitual or completed actions, use the indicative in the dependent clause because you are merely *reporting* something that *happened* or *usually happens.*

Independent Clause	Dependent Adverbial Clause
Present indicative or Preterit/Imperfect	Conjunction of time + Indicative

Me besa todos los días	**cuando**	**llego** de la oficina.
He kisses me every day	*when*	*I arrive from the office.* (habitual)
Me casé con ella	**en cuanto**	**terminé** los estudios.
I married her	*as soon as*	*I finished my studies.* (completed)

Compare the following sentences.

Pending actions	Habitual or completed actions
Ella va a llamar a sus padres **tan pronto como llegue.**	Ella llamó a sus padres **tan pronto como llegó.**
She's going to call her parents as soon as she arrives.	*She called her parents as soon as she arrived.* (completed)
Después de que almorcemos, queremos caminar por el parque.	**Después de que almorzamos,** generalmente caminamos por el parque.
After we have lunch, we want to walk in the park.	*After we have lunch, we generally walk in the park.* (habitual)

3. Después de and **hasta** without the word **que** are prepositions, not conjunctions, and are followed directly by an infinitive.

Después de terminar mis estudios, voy a hacer ecoturismo en las Islas Galápagos.

After finishing my studies, I am going to take an ecotour of the Galápagos Islands.

Actividad 20 El futuro está en nuestras manos **Parte A:** Lee el siguiente comentario sobre el medio ambiente que publicó en Internet un ecologista y complétalo con el infinitivo o con la forma apropiada del indicativo o del subjuntivo de los verbos que aparecen en el margen.

Act. 20A: Assign as HW and check in class. Have students explain each choice.

Gran parte de los habitantes de esta ciudad están conscientes de que hay que proteger el medio ambiente y esperamos que cuando nuestros hijos ___tengan___ su propia familia, todavía disfruten de agua limpia y aire puro. Cada uno de nosotros puede hacer algo por el futuro de nuestros hijos. (tener)

En nuestra ciudad, muchos ciudadanos llevan un carrito o sus propias bolsas para los comestibles cuando ___van___ al supermercado. (ir) Otros reciben bolsas de plástico en el supermercado, pero después de ___usar___ las bolsas, las reciclan utilizándolas como bolsas de basura. (usar) Sin embargo, no vamos a solucionar el problema del desperdicio de plástico hasta que todos los ciudadanos ___usen/usemos___ carritos o ___reciclen/reciclemos___ las bolsas. (usar, reciclar)

Hace muchos años, cuando nosotros ___sacábamos___ la basura de los edificios, ésta se quemaba en incineradores. (sacar) Hoy en día, en algunos edificios, cuando la gente ___tira___ la basura, ésta se pasa por una compactadora de basura. (tirar) Las asociaciones de vecinos tienen que empezar a ahorrar dinero y tan pronto como _____ahorren_____ (ahorrar) lo suficiente, deben comprar compactadoras. Es necesario hacerlo para salvar el futuro de nuestros hijos.

Generalmente, cuando alguien _____compra_____ (comprar) bebidas en el supermercado, deja un depósito que luego se le entrega en cuanto _____devuelve_____ (devolver) sus envases. No obstante, todavía se ven botellas rotas en la calle; pero hasta que todos no _____estén/estemos_____ (estar) conscientes de estos problemas, no vamos a poder solucionarlos.

La contaminación ambiental causada por los carros es muy peligrosa. Para combatirla hay ciertos días de la semana cuando sólo los que tienen placa que termina en número par _____pueden_____ (poder) salir a la calle y hay otros días cuando sólo pueden salir los que tienen placa impar. Muchas familias, sin embargo, no quieren cooperar y si tienen dos carros se aseguran de que uno tenga número par y el otro impar. Así que cuando el ambiente _____sufre_____ (sufrir), ellos no. Hasta que todos no _____obedezcan_____ (obedecer) esta ley, no vamos a tener una ciudad con aire puro.

Obedezcamos is also correct here.

Prometo que no vamos a dejar de trabajar por esta causa hasta que _____gocemos_____ (gozar) de agua limpia y aire puro. Es importante que trabajemos juntos. Es nuestra obligación. Se lo debemos a nuestros hijos.

Act. 20B: May be assigned as HW. Check by calling on individuals and comparing their answers to those of the rest of the class. Write on the board **Actividades constructivas/ Actividades destructivas**. Each time you poll the class, place a mark in the appropriate column according to the practices of the majority.

Parte B: Compara la información que dio el ecologista con tus costumbres.

1. Cuando vas al supermercado, ¿llevas bolsas? ¿Tienes carrito propio para no tener que usar bolsas? ¿Pides bolsas de plástico o de papel? ¿Las reciclas? ¿Qué hiciste ayer para reciclar?
2. ¿Devuelves las botellas a la tienda, las reciclas o las tiras a la basura? ¿Qué haces con las latas de gaseosa (*soda*) vacías?
3. ¿Qué malas costumbres de gente que tú conoces afectan el medio ambiente?

► Muchas personas prefieren llevar su propia bolsa de la compra. Un mercado al aire libre en Montevideo, Uruguay.

Actividad 21 En una reunión de Mundo Verde Estás en una fiesta con miembros de Mundo Verde, una organización que se dedica a proteger el medio ambiente. Sólo oyes partes de las conversaciones, pero puedes imaginar el resto. Completa estas frases de forma lógica.

1. Los bosques van a estar en mejores condiciones después de que...
2. Va a seguir agrandándose (*grow larger*) el agujero en la capa de ozono hasta que...
3. En un supermercado que hay a la vuelta de mi casa, las gaseosas son caras pero devuelven parte del dinero cuando...
4. La contaminación causada por las fábricas va a reducirse en cuanto...
5. Si piensas comprar un coche usado, tienes que hacerle un control de emisión tan pronto como...

www *La ecología*

Act. 21: Assign as HW and check in class. Ask for different possible responses to the same item.

Actividad 22 Tu vida actual y tus planes futuros En parejas, túrnense para hacerse las siguientes preguntas. Al contestar, usen las expresiones que están entre paréntesis.

▶ —¿Cuándo vas a ir a visitar a tu familia? (en cuanto)
—En cuanto termine el semestre.

1. Generalmente, ¿cuándo haces la tarea para esta clase? (después de que)
2. ¿Cuándo sales con tus amigos? (después de)
3. ¿Cuándo vas a comprar un carro nuevo? (en cuanto)
4. ¿Cuándo miras televisión? (cuando)
5. ¿Hasta cuándo vas a vivir en el lugar donde vives ahora? (hasta que)
6. ¿Cuándo vas al cine? (cuando)
7. ¿Cuándo te levantas? (tan pronto como)
8. ¿Cuándo vas a ver a tus padres? (después de que)

Pending → Subjunctive
Completed, habitual → Indicative

Act. 22: Form pairs, model the activity, and check by calling on a few individuals. For additional practice, in pairs, have students tell their partner three things they plan to do when/after/as soon as the semester ends. Follow up by having individuals report their partners' plans.

Actividad 23 ¿Verdad o mentira? **Parte A:** ¡Vas a mentir! Escribe cuatro cosas que piensas hacer, usando las ideas que se presentan. Algunas cosas deben ser mentira y otras deben ser verdad. Usa las palabras **cuando, después de que, en cuanto** y **tan pronto como** en tus oraciones.

▶ terminar la clase de hoy
Después de que termine la clase de hoy, voy a alquilar una película en español.

tu jefe / pagarte
empezar las vacaciones
tener mucho dinero
graduarte de la universidad
conseguir tu primer trabajo permanente
? ? ?

Parte B: En parejas, compartan sus planes con su compañero/a y decidan si son verdad o mentira. Usen frases como: **Dudo que..., No creo que..., Sí, creo que..., Es posible que...**

Act. 23A: Assign as HW.

Act. 23B: Model this activity by telling students your future plans while they react to the truthfulness of your statements. After doing all items, tell them which are true or false. Form pairs, set a time limit, and begin. Check by calling on a few individuals to state their plans and have the class react.

V. Avoiding Redundancies

Double Object Pronouns

Never use **me lo, me la,** etc., with verbs like **gustar** since the noun following the verb is not a direct object, but rather the subject of the verb.

Indirect-object pronouns

me	**nos**
te	**os**
le	**les**

Direct-object pronouns

me	**nos**
te	**os**
lo, la	**los, las**

1. In Chapters 1 and 3 you reviewed the use of direct- and indirect-object pronouns. When you use both in the same sentence, the indirect-object pronoun precedes the direct-object pronoun. The chart on the right shows all possible combinations of indirect- and direct-object pronouns.

me lo, me la, me los, me las
te lo, te la, te los, te las
se lo, se la, se los, se las
nos lo, nos la, nos los, nos las
os lo, os la, os los, os las
se lo, se la, se los, se las

—¿Quién **te** mandó **flores**?
—José Carlos **me las** mandó.
José Carlos sent them to me.

—¿**Me** puedes explicar **el problema**?
—Ya **te lo** expliqué.
I already explained it to you.

Remember: Indirect-object pronoun before direct-object pronoun.

Have students recite the combinations of object pronouns as if they were a poem: Line 1: **Me lo, me la, me los, me las** Line 2: **te lo,** etc.

FLR link: **Lectura 3**

Drill double object pronouns:

1. Tell students that they are very impatient people and have them answer rudely to your requests. T: **¿Me puedes dar la tarea?** S1: **Ya se la di.** T: **¿Me puedes explicar el ejercicio?** S2:...T: **¿Me puedes prestar tu libro?** (etc.)

2. Tell students that they are procrastinators and have them promise to do different tasks now. T: **¿Le explicaste la tarea a Jean?** S: **Ahora mismo voy a explicársela.**

3. Threaten students with things you are going to do and have them tell you not to do them. T: **Voy a decirle a tu novio que te vi con otro hombre.** S: **No se lo diga.** T: **Voy a mostrarles tu foto de cuando eras niño/a a tus amigos. Voy a darle tu teléfono al decano.** (etc.)

2. Note that the indirect-object pronouns **le** and **les** become **se** when followed by the direct-object pronouns **lo, la, los,** or **las.**

—¿**Le** regalaste **la corbata** a tu padre?
—Sí, **se la** regalé ayer.

3. Review the following rules you learned for placement of object pronouns.

Before a Conjugated Verb or a Negative Command	After and Attached to Infinitives, Present Participles, and Affirmative Commands
Siempre **se lo digo.**	
Se lo dije.	
¿Quieres que yo **se lo diga?**	
Se lo voy a decir. (**voy** = conj. verb)	Voy a **decírselo.*** (**decir** = inf.)
Se lo estoy diciendo. (**estoy** = conj. verb)	Estoy **diciéndoselo.*** (**diciendo** = pres. part.)
¡No **se lo digas**! (**no digas** = neg. command)	**¡Díselo!*** (**di** = aff. command)

*Note: Remember the use of accents. To review accent rules, see Appendix F.

Actividad 24 El regalo anónimo Lee la siguiente conversación y contesta la pregunta que le sigue.

Act. 24: Assign as HW and check in class by having students compare responses with a partner.

Marcos: ¿Y estas flores?
Ignacio: **Se** las mandaron a mi hermano Juan.
Marcos: ¿Quién?
Ignacio: No tengo la menor idea. En este momento mi hermano **le** está
5 preguntando a su novia Marisol por teléfono.
Marcos: Mira, aquí entre las flores hay una tarjeta.
Ignacio: A ver. Dáme**la** que quiero leerla.
Marcos: ¿Qué dice?
Ignacio: "Ojalá que te gusten. **Te las** mando para tu cumpleaños. Espero
10 verte esta noche." Pero, ¿quién escribió esto?
Juan: [Cuelga. (*He hangs up.*)] ¡Oigan! Marisol dijo que ella no **me las** envió.
Marcos: Vamos, dinos quién es. Confiésa**noslo.** ¿Quién es tu admiradora secreta?

¿A qué o a quién se refieren los siguientes pronombres de complemento directo e indirecto?

1. línea 2, **se** ___Juan___
2. línea 4, **le** ___Marisol___
3. línea 7, **la** ___tarjeta___
4. línea 9, **te** y **las** ___Juan, flores___
5. línea 12, **me** y **las** ___Juan, flores___
6. línea 13, **nos** y **lo** ___Marcos e Ignacio (nosotros), quién le mandó flores___

Actividad 25 ¿Quién? En parejas, una persona le hace preguntas sobre su vida a la otra. La que contesta debe usar pronombres de complemento directo e indirecto cuando sea posible. Cuando terminen, cambien de papel.

Act. 25 and 26: Practice questions and possible responses, form pairs, set a time limit, and begin. Check by asking partners questions to practice **se lo/la,** etc.

▶ quién te deja mensajes graciosos en el contestador
—¿Quién te deja mensajes graciosos en el contestador?

—Nadie me los deja. —Mi amigo Paul me los deja.

1. quién te envía correo electrónico
2. quién te manda flores
3. a quién le mandas correo electrónico
4. quién te da regalos que te gustan
5. quién te da regalos que no te gustan
6. a quién le das consejos amorosos

Actividad 26 La vida universitaria En parejas, túrnense para hacerse preguntas sobre su vida universitaria. Al contestar deben usar pronombres de complemento directo e indirecto cuando sea posible.

1. si alguien le prestó el dinero para la universidad
2. si recibió una beca al graduarse de la escuela secundaria
3. si la universidad le ofreció una beca
4. quién le da consejos para seleccionar las materias
5. dónde estudió español por primera vez
6. cuándo va a terminar su carrera
7. quién le explica las materias difíciles
8. cuál de sus amigos lo/la ayuda más

Act. 27A and B: Model the activity with a student, form pairs, set a time limit, and begin. Then have Bs ask questions. Check by having students say what their partners didn't do and what excuse they gave.

Actividad 27 Vamos a acampar **Parte A:** En parejas, Uds. están preparándose para ir a acampar juntos. El/La estudiante A mira sólo la columna A, y B mira sólo la columna B. El/La estudiante A debe preguntarle a B si hizo las cosas que tenía que hacer. Si B no las hizo, A debe darle órdenes para que las haga. Sigan el modelo.

► A: ¿Le diste las llaves del apartamento al vecino?

B: Sí, se las di. Desde luego.

B: No, no se las di.
↓
A: ¿Por qué no se las diste?
↓
B: Porque...
↓
A: Pues dáselas.

A check mark indicates that you completed the task.

A	B
Esto es lo que tenía que hacer tu compañero/a hoy:	Esto es lo que tenías que hacer hoy:
☐ poner la navaja en la mochila	☐ poner la navaja en la mochila
☐ mandarle el dinero al Sr. Gómez para la reserva del camping	☑ mandarle el dinero al Sr. Gómez para la reserva del camping
☐ darle a un amigo un número de teléfono en caso de emergencia	☐ darle a un amigo un número de teléfono en caso de emergencia
☐ comprar las pilas para la linterna	☑ comprar las pilas para la linterna

Parte B: Ahora el estudiante B mira la columna B y le pregunta a A si hizo las cosas que tenía que hacer y le da órdenes si no las hizo.

A	B
Esto es lo que tenías que hacer hoy:	Esto es lo que tenía que hacer tu compañero/a hoy:
☑ darle el código de la alarma del apartamento a tu padre	☐ darle el código de la alarma del apartamento a su padre
☐ pedirle el mapa topográfico a tu prima	☐ pedirle el mapa topográfico a su prima
☐ poner el protector solar en la mochila	☐ poner el protector solar en la mochila
☑ limpiar los sacos de dormir	☐ limpiar los sacos de dormir

Actividad 28 Costa Rica **Parte A:** Vas a leer parte de un folleto que escribió el gobierno costarricense sobre Costa Rica. Antes de leer y en parejas, completen el siguiente gráfico sobre Costa Rica. Si no saben, traten de adivinar.

Costa Rica

Act. 28A: Do not assign as HW since some students will read ahead to get the answers. It is important that they guess so that they learn to apply their own knowledge of the world when reading. Do NOT have a group sharing when finished.

Geografía	Clima	Flora y fauna	Deportes
Gobierno	**Historia**	**Composición étnica**	**Nivel de vida actual**

Parte B: Lean esta parte del folleto y después contesten las preguntas que le siguen.

Act. 28B: Assign as HW. Prior to reading you may want to do some prediction using the headings of the different sections. Encourage students to read the questions first and scan for answers. Tell students they are not expected to understand every word. Set a time limit. Have them work together after a certain point to compare responses. When finished, call on individuals to respond.

Imagínense un pequeño país lleno de asombrosos bosques tropicales, un sinnúmero de playas, donde la persona con la que probablemente va a encontrarse es con su yo interior; un clima variado (más fresco en las montañas y cálido en las playas), una fascinante vida silvestre y un ambiente hogareño le permitirán tener una idea básica de Costa Rica. Detengámonos ahora en su gente: su cultura es una refrescante mezcla de tradiciones europeas, americanas y afrocaribeñas, pulida por más de cien años de educación gratuita y una democracia estable. Alguien dijo una vez que para el resto del mundo, Costa Rica es como un parque nacional: un lugar donde aquello que se valora es preservado. Es una pequeña maravilla.

Belleza y aventura

Un escritor de viajes americano dijo que Costa Rica "ofrece más belleza y aventura por acre que cualquier otro lugar en el mundo". Los viajeros salen de Costa Rica sintiendo que no sólo han visto mucho, sino que han hecho cosas nuevas. Las caminatas, la pesca, el "snorkeling", el buceo, la navegación de rápidos, el ir en kayak y el

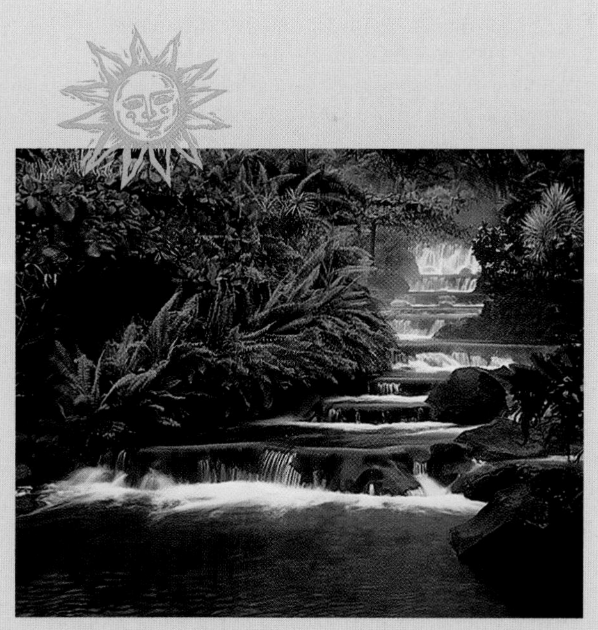

▲ Aguas termales de Tabacón en Costa Rica.

"surfing", se ubican entre las actividades favoritas. Las caminatas probablemente se ubican en primer lugar debido a que hay tanto que ver en Costa Rica, desde sus paisajes naturales, pasando por aves, mariposas, hasta tortugas que vienen a desovar. Costa Rica es reconocida por pescadores experimentados en todo el mundo debido a los récords mundiales en pesca de sábalo, róbalo y pez vela. La navegación de rápidos ha ido aumentando en popularidad como una manera excitante pero segura de experimentar la naturaleza. Los amantes de este deporte saben que en Costa Rica pueden encontrar corrientes confiables durante todo el año. Para cualquiera de estas actividades resulta fácil encontrar proveedores y guías profesionales. Muchos de ellos cuentan con la representación de mayoristas y agentes en los Estados Unidos y Canadá, entre otros.

Diversidad

Costa Rica es un puente biológico entre América del Norte y América del Sur. Esto explica la increíble diversidad de su flora y fauna, como también el flujo constante de especies emigrantes. Más pequeño que el Lago Michigan, el territorio costarricense cuenta con tres cadenas montañosas y más de doce zonas climáticas. Usted podrá manejar desde el Caribe hasta el Pacífico en un día, visitar un volcán y disfrutar de una gran variedad de paisajes. Hay más de 600 millas de playa que le permitirán descansar del bullicio de la gente.

Una naturaleza espléndida

Costa Rica goza de reconocimiento internacional por sus Parques Nacionales. Incluyen impresionantes volcanes, bosques, llanuras, escenarios de anidamiento de aves y desove de tortugas, arrecifes de coral y virtualmente cualquier forma de naturaleza que usted espera encontrar en el Trópico.

- Costa Rica posee más de 800 especies de aves, más de lo que se encuentra en toda Norte América.
- Tiene unas 1.200 especies de orquídeas.
- 8.000 especies de plantas de mayor evolución.
- El 10% de todas las mariposas del mundo y más mariposas de las que existen en todo el continente africano.
- Más quetzales que cualquier otro país en el mundo.
- Más de 150 especies de frutas comestibles.*

*Éstos y otros datos tomados de *Costa Rica, the traveler's choice* de Rex Govorchin.

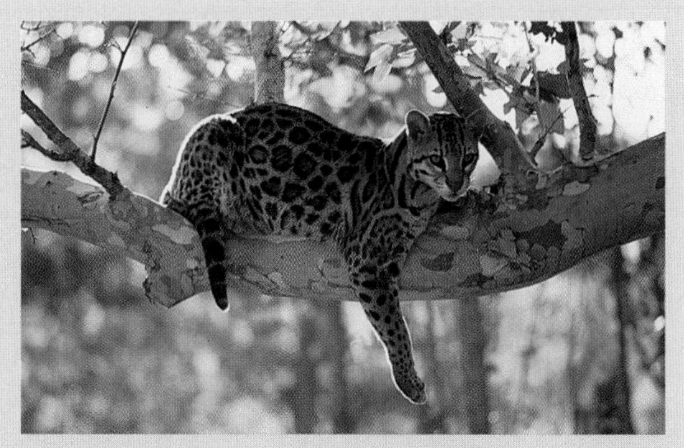

▲ Un ocelote descansa en el árbol de un parque nacional en Costa Rica.

Nación pacífica y culta

Cristóbal Colón, suponiendo la existencia de muchísimo oro, bautizó estas tierras con el nombre de Costa Rica. Luego resultó que la mayoría del oro ya había sido convertido en joyería por los indígenas. Sin poseer el atractivo que generan las minas de oro y plata, Costa Rica permaneció relativamente aislada y despoblada durante 400 años. Todos, incluso el gobernador español, tenían que producir su propia comida. Esto condujo a que Costa Rica tuviera una sociedad relativamente igualitaria de pequeños agricultores. Las cosas comenzaron a cambiar durante el siglo XIX, cuando el café de Costa Rica comenzó a exportarse a Europa. La recién independiente sociedad costarricense adquirió los beneficios de la civilización, tales como educación, desarrollo político, ferrocarriles y energía eléctrica, sin muchos de los trastornos inherentes a la misma. Cien años más tarde, Costa Rica posee el nivel de alfabetización más elevado de Latinoamérica, un alto promedio de esperanza de vida y una Orquesta Sinfónica de clase mundial. Un 25% de su territorio lo constituyen las áreas de conservación y no posee un ejército, a diferencia del resto de los países americanos.

After this brochure was written, Panama disbanded its army.

1. ¿Cómo es el clima de Costa Rica?
2. ¿Qué puedes decir de la flora y fauna?
3. ¿Cómo crees que sea físicamente el costarricense típico?
4. ¿Cuál es el tamaño de Costa Rica?
5. ¿Hay muchos ríos en Costa Rica? ¿Cómo lo sabes?
6. ¿Qué deportes acuáticos se pueden practicar en Costa Rica? ¿Dónde se pueden practicar?
7. ¿Cuál es un deporte muy popular y por qué?
8. ¿Qué te gustaría hacer en Costa Rica?
9. ¿Cómo es el nivel de vida de Costa Rica? ¿Puedes compararlo con el de los otros países centroamericanos?
10. ¿Hace algo el gobierno para conservar el medio ambiente?
11. Obviamente el gobierno escribió este folleto para gente de habla española, pero ¿a quién crees que se dirija principalmente? ¿Cómo lo sabes? (Hay tres pistas en el texto.)

Parte C: En parejas, vuelvan a mirar su gráfico de la Parte A y comparen sus respuestas con lo que aprendieron al leer. ¿Tenían la información correcta? Ahora, hagan un gráfico semejante con los datos que aprendieron al leer. Después, decidan qué datos son los más sorprendentes. Al hablar, usen expresiones como: **Me sorprende mucho que Costa Rica..., Es interesante que...**

Parte D: Ahora, imagínense que Uds. van a pasar una semana en Costa Rica. Hagan una lista de lo que van a hacer cada día. Usen expresiones como: **Busco un lugar que/donde..., por eso quiero que nosotros...; Después de que... podemos...; Lo que prefiero...**

Answer to question 11: Hispanics in the U.S. and Canada. The three clues are: **agentes en los Estados Unidos y Canadá, 600 millas** (instead of **kilómetros en EE.UU.**) and comparison with **Lago Michigan.**

Act. 28C: Form pairs and instruct students to only include in the graph what they learned in the reading. When finished have a group sharing to see how much they learned as a class.

Act. 28D: Give instructions, set a time limit, and begin. Check by having two students carry out the conversation.

Do the corresponding CD-ROM and web activities to review the chapter topics.

Vocabulario activo

Expresiones afirmativas y negativas

a menudo / con frecuencia	*frequently*
a veces	*sometimes*
algo	*something*
alguien	*someone*
algún/alguna/os/as + *noun*	*a, some, any*
alguno/a/os/as	*one, some*
jamás/nunca	*never*
muchas/pocas personas	*many/few people*
muchas veces	*many times*
nada	*nothing, (not) anything*
nadie	*no one*
ningún/ninguna + *singular noun*	*not any*
ninguno/a	*not any, none, no one*
siempre	*always*
todo	*everything*
todo el mundo / todos/as	*everyone*
una vez	*once*

Conjunciones de tiempo

cuando	*when*
después (de) que	*after*
en cuanto / tan pronto como	*as soon as*
hasta que	*until*

Los viajes de aventura

El equipo	*Equipment*
la linterna	*flashlight*
el mapa	*map*
la mochila	*backpack*
la navaja suiza	*Swiss army knife*
la pila	*battery*
el protector solar	*sunblock*
el repelente contra insectos	*insect repellent*
el saco de dormir	*sleeping bag*
la tienda de campaña	*tent*

Actividades	*Activities*
acampar	*to go camping*
bucear	*to scuba dive*
el buceo	*scuba diving*
escalar (montañas)	*to climb (mountains)*
hacer	
alas delta	*to hang-glide*
esquí nórdico/alpino/acuático	*to cross country/downhill/water ski*
kayak	*to go kayaking*
rafting	*to go rafting*
senderismo/trekking	*to go hiking*
snorkel	*to go snorkeling*
snowboard	*to snowboard*
surf	*to surf, go surfing*
vela	*to sail, go sailing*
montar a caballo	*to ride a horse*
montar en bicicleta de montaña	*to ride a mountain bike*

El medio ambiente

la conservación	*conservation*
conservar	*to conserve*
la contaminación	*pollution*
contaminante	*contaminating*
contaminar	*to contaminate, pollute*
desechable	*disposable*
desechar	*to throw away*
los desechos	*rubbish*
desperdiciar	*to waste*
el desperdicio	*waste*
la destrucción	*destruction*
destruir	*to destroy*
el efecto invernadero	*greenhouse effect*
la extinción	*extinction*
extinguirse	*to become extinct*
la preservación	*preservation*
preservar	*to preserve*
la protección	*protection*
proteger	*to protect*
recargable	*rechargeable*
recargar	*to recharge*
la reducción	*reduction*
reducir	*to reduce*
la restricción	*restriction*
restringir	*to limit, restrict*

Expresiones útiles

algo así	*something like that*
de ningún modo	*no way*
desde luego	*of course*
¿Me dejas terminar?	*Will you let me finish?*
(No) estoy de acuerdo.	*I (don't) agree.*
No estoy de acuerdo del todo.	*I don't completely agree.*
Opino como tú.	*I'm of the same opinion.*
Perdón, pero...	*Excuse me, but. . .*
Pido la palabra.	*May I speak?*
Seguro.	*Sure.*
Sin duda alguna.	*Without a doubt.*
¡Ya sé!	*I've got it!*

Vocabulario personal

Capítulo 8

Metas comunicativas

- expresar posibilidad, tiempo, propósito y restricción
- hablar sobre el trabajo
- expresar selección y negación
- contar lo que dijo alguien
- describir acciones recíprocas

Hablemos de trabajo

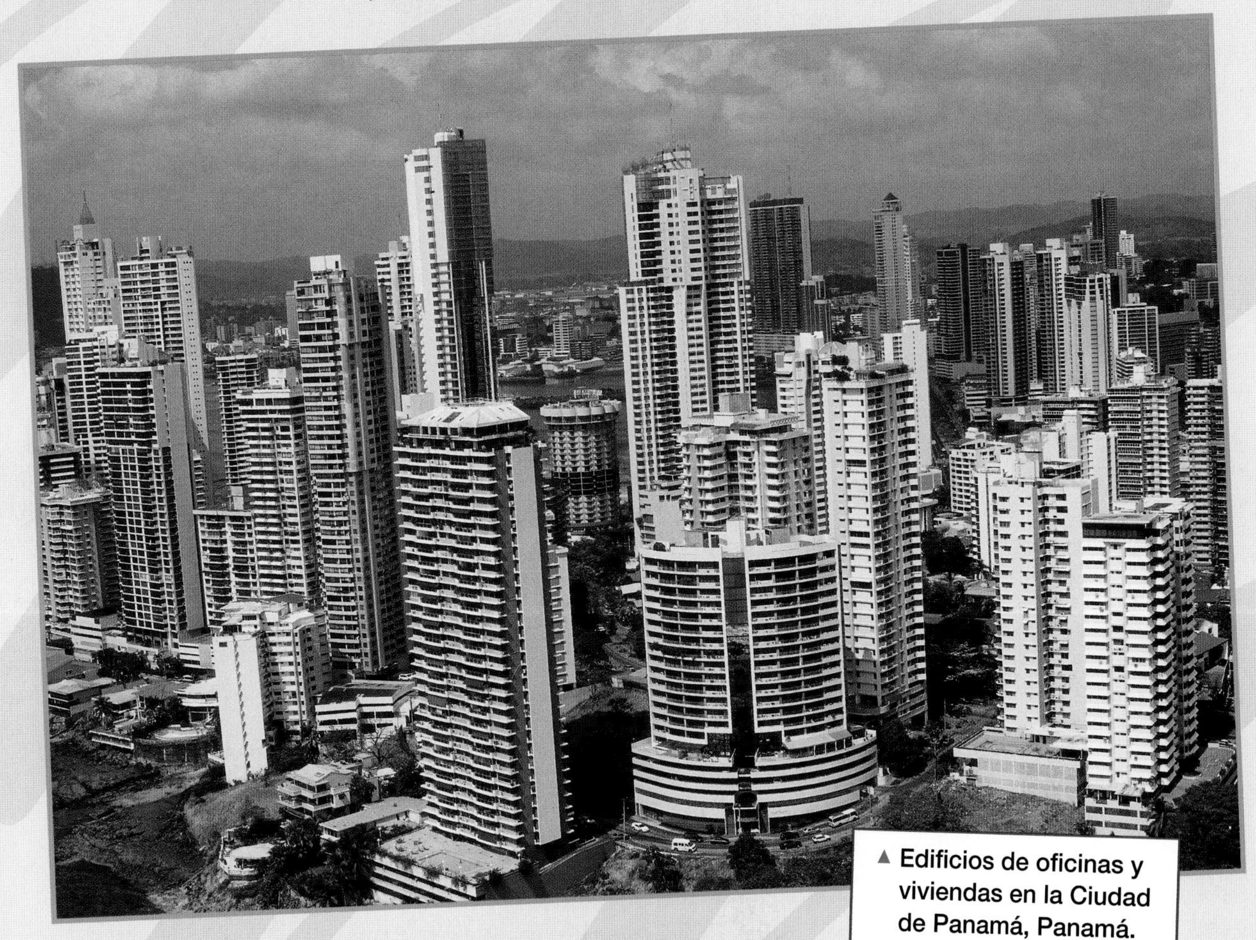

▲ Edificios de oficinas y viviendas en la Ciudad de Panamá, Panamá.

May be assigned: Grammar, vocabulary, **¿Lo sabían?**, Act. 6A, Act. 11A, Act. 12, Act. 17, Act. 19, Act. 21, Act. 24A.

Show the chapter video episode at any point in the chapter that you see fit and do all or selected activities in class. Note: Content of the video supplements the cultural material in the chapter and activities reenter chapter grammar and vocabulary.

Un trabajo en el extranjero

Practice expressions: Write them on the board. Practice them by creating a context. Use **me da igual** by asking **¿Te molesta o te da igual recibir cosas innecesarias por correo?** Use **un montón** by saying **Antes me daba igual porque recibía poco, pero ahora me mandan un montón de cosas. ¿Alguien recibe un montón de...?** (etc.) Tell students **No me molesta en absoluto cuando recibo cosas gratis por correo, como champú o cereales.** Ask individuals **¿A ti te molesta...?** prompting them to answer **No, en absoluto** by pointing to the board. Transition to discussing work by saying **Me molesta mucho recibir tantas cosas, pero es una manera de promocionar productos y ganar dinero. ¿Dónde piensas trabajar cuando termines los estudios?** S:... T: **Vamos a escuchar una entrevista con dos norteamericanos que trabajaron en el exterior.**

FLR link: **Lectura 2**

un montón	a lot
No, en absoluto.	No, not at all.
darle igual (a alguien)	to be all the same (to someone), to not care

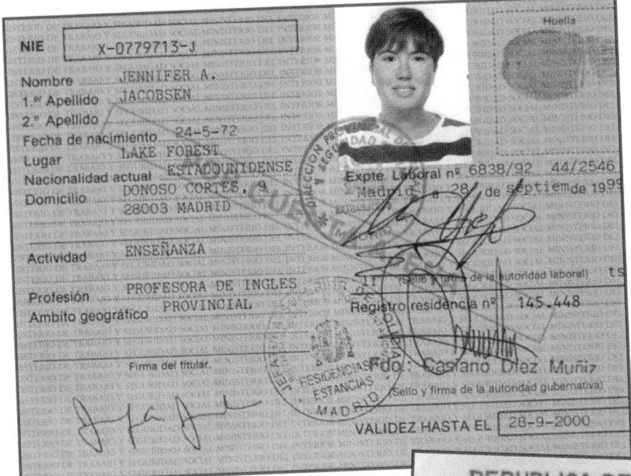

Act. 1: After group work, find out who knows people who have worked abroad. Follow up by finding out how much they know about those jobs. If you worked abroad as a teacher of English as a Foreign Language, discuss your experience after doing the listening comprehension.

Actividad 1 Trabajar fuera del país Vas a escuchar a dos americanos hablar en una entrevista de radio sobre cómo consiguieron trabajo en el extranjero. Antes de escucharlos, en grupos de tres, discutan las siguientes preguntas y luego compartan sus respuestas con el resto de la clase.

1. ¿Conocen a alguien que haya trabajado en el extranjero? Si contestan que sí, ¿qué hizo esa persona? ¿Cómo consiguió el trabajo?
2. ¿Les gustaría trabajar en el extranjero? Si contestan que sí, ¿qué tipo de trabajo les gustaría tener? ¿Adónde les gustaría ir?

Actividad 2 Las entrevistas **Parte A:** Lee la lista de ideas y después, mientras escuchas la primera entrevista, toma apuntes sobre estos temas.

1. país en el que trabajó la persona
2. tipo de trabajo que tuvo
3. estudios que había hecho antes
4. cómo consiguió el trabajo
5. si el dinero que ganaba le alcanzaba para vivir

Parte B: Ahora lee esta lista de ideas y después, mientras escuchas la segunda entrevista, toma apuntes sobre estos temas.

1. país en el que trabajó la persona
2. tipo de trabajo que tuvo
3. cómo consiguió el trabajo
4. lo beneficioso del trabajo para esta persona
5. consejo que les da esta persona a los que quieran hacer lo mismo

Actividad 3 Una comparación Di en qué se asemejan y en qué se diferencian la situación de Jenny y la de Jeff. Escucha las entrevistas otra vez si es necesario.

Act. 2A: Have students read the items, play the interview first, and check responses. If students are unable to answer an item, just skip it and continue checking other responses. Then play the interview again and stop after the missed item is answered.

Act. 2A: Answers: 1. **España** 2. **enseñanza de inglés** 3. **maestría en enseñanza de español** 4. **mandó una solicitud a una escuela privada y la entrevistaron en TESOL** 5. **sí**

Act. 2B: Follow the same procedure as in 2A. Answers: 1. **Colombia** 2. **enseñanza de inglés** 3. **una universidad le dio el trabajo** 4. **conoció a mucha gente** 5. **tomar un curso para aprender a enseñar inglés antes de ir**

Act. 3: Read the directions and play the interviews again if needed. Option 1: Have students as a class compare Jeff's and Jenny's experiences. Option 2: Form pairs to make comparisons, set a time limit, and begin. When finished, have a group sharing.

Follow-up: If you have worked abroad, have students interview you about your experience and have them compare Jenny's and Jeff's experiences with yours.

He aquí algunos consejos para conseguir trabajo como profesor de inglés en el extranjero.

- Tomar en la universidad una clase o más sobre la pedagogía de la enseñanza de inglés como segunda lengua o como lengua extranjera.
- Ir al congreso de TESOL (*Teachers of English to Speakers of Other Languages*) al que asisten alrededor de 10.000 personas y adonde van en busca de profesores muchas escuelas, institutos y universidades. Es aconsejable solicitar puesto en estas instituciones antes de marzo para asegurarse una entrevista en el congreso.
- Buscar en Internet academias de inglés en el país que te interesa. Un buen sitio para encontrar este tipo de información es **www.eslcafe.com**.
- Al llegar a un país, se pueden conseguir estudiantes particulares poniendo anuncios en los periódicos o en algunas librerías, pero otro método eficaz es pedirles información a amigos o a maestros de escuela primaria.

Add any other tips and advice you may have.

I. Discussing Work

Do the corresponding CD-ROM and web activities as you study the chapter.

El trabajo

"Soy profesora en una universidad de Boston y doy un curso que se llama *Español para negocios*. Algunos de mis estudiantes hacen **pasantías** en bancos internacionales, en **empresas** de publicidad que se especializan en el mercado hispano, en televisión y radio, y también en organizaciones sin fines de lucro. En esas pasantías trabajan **medio tiempo** mientras estudian y ganan un pequeño **sueldo** aunque no reciben ni **seguro médico** ni otros **beneficios.** Lo que sí obtienen es **experiencia laboral** que pueden incluir en su **curriculum** y también pueden obtener una buena **carta de recomendación** y mejorar así las oportunidades de conseguir un buen trabajo."

profesora de Español para negocios

internships
companies
part time
salary / health insurance
benefits / work experience
CV (curriculum vitae), resumé
letter of recommendation

A one-page resumé is not frequently used in Spanish-speaking countries.

En busca de trabajo

los avisos clasificados	classified ads
completar una solicitud	to fill out an application
contratar/despedir (i, i) a alguien	to hire/fire someone
entrevistarse (con alguien)	to be interviewed (by someone)
estar desempleado/a / estar sin trabajo	to be unemployed
la oferta y la demanda	supply and demand
solicitar un puesto/empleo	to apply for a job
tomar cursos de perfeccionamiento/ capacitación	to take continuing education/ training courses

estar desempleado/a, estar sin empleo = **estar en (el) paro** (*España*)

El empleo

aumentar/bajar el sueldo	to raise/lower the salary
el pago mensual/semanal	monthly/weekly pay
la renta/los ingresos	income
el salario mínimo	minimum wage
trabajar tiempo completo	to work full time

el alquiler = the rent

Note: **sueldo** = salary; **salario** = wages (hourly pay)

Los beneficios

el aguinaldo	end-of-the-year bonus
los días feriados	holidays
la guardería (infantil)	child care center
la licencia por maternidad/ paternidad/enfermedad/ matrimonio	maternity/paternity/sick/ wedding leave
el seguro dental/de vida	dental/life insurance

el aguinaldo = **la paga extraordinaria** (*España*)

Tell students to imagine that they each had a perfect job and left it to come to the university. Have them brag about what benefits they received, how much they earned, and how they got the job. This will review narration in the past while practicing new items.

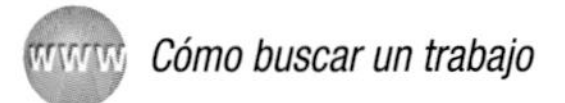
Cómo buscar un trabajo

Actividad 4 Quiero un trabajo Usa el vocabulario sobre el trabajo y di qué se necesita hacer para conseguir un trabajo.

Actividad 5 Los beneficios En grupos de tres, discutan cuáles son los beneficios que puede ofrecer una empresa. Luego pónganse de acuerdo para ponerlos en orden de importancia y justifiquen su orden. Comiencen diciendo **¿Cuáles son algunos de los beneficios que...?**

Act. 5: Form groups, model the activity, and begin. Check by having groups say the most and least important benefits and justify their responses.

Look at the AIESEC website and ask **¿Qué tipos de trabajos o pasantías puede ofrecer una compañía como Procter & Gamble en Venezuela?** Make a list and then ask them if they would qualify for any of these.

Actividad 6 Las pasantías **Parte A:** La mitad de la clase debe buscar información en su universidad sobre qué oportunidades hay para hacer pasantías. La otra mitad tiene que buscar información de organizaciones que ofrecen pasantías en el extranjero. Para la próxima clase deben estar listos para hablar de diferentes posibilidades.

Parte B: En grupos de cuatro, hablen de lo que encontraron sobre las pasantías.

Act. 6A: Assign as HW. Have half of the students go to the Internship office in your institution to find out what they offer or to check university websites. Have the other half research on the Internet internship possibilities abroad.

Act. 6B: Form groups of four with two students having researched each topic. Set a time limit and begin. Have a group sharing when finished and see if any people in the class may be interested in pursuing internships, particularly abroad. Bring in a guest speaker on this subject if possible.

Actividad 7 Historia laboral En grupos de tres, discutan las siguientes preguntas.

1. ¿Han trabajado alguna vez?
2. ¿Han tenido o tienen trabajo de tiempo completo con beneficios? Si contestan que sí, ¿qué beneficios recibieron? ¿Seguro médico? ¿Seguro dental? ¿Aguinaldo? ¿Vacaciones pagadas? ¿Licencia por maternidad? ¿Por matrimonio?
3. ¿Han trabajado medio tiempo? ¿Han trabajado sólo durante los veranos? Si contestan que sí, ¿recibieron algunos beneficios?
4. ¿Cuál es el mejor o el peor trabajo que han tenido? Descríbanlo y expliquen por qué fue bueno o malo.
5. Cuando nacieron, ¿estaba empleada su madre? Si contestan que sí, ¿dejó el puesto? ¿Le dieron licencia por maternidad? ¿Volvió a trabajar? ¿Trabajó tiempo completo o medio tiempo? ¿Existía la oportunidad de pedir licencia por paternidad? Si contestan que sí, ¿la pidió su padre?

Act. 7: Form groups of three. Have students take turns posing questions. If there are students who have never worked, ask them to ask the questions and take notes to report back to the class. Check by having a group sharing.

Act. 8: Model the activity by setting the scene and conducting an entire interview with a student. Ask questions like **¿Ha usado computadora antes? ¿Ha trabajado con el público? ¿Qué idiomas extranjeros sabe?** (etc.) Remind students they should use the **Ud.** form. Prior to beginning, you may want to have them brainstorm some questions. Form pairs, assigning roles of interviewer and job applicant. When finished, ask a few students if they will employ their partner and why.

Actividad 8 La entrevista de trabajo En parejas, una persona va a entrevistar a la otra para el puesto de recepcionista de un hotel usando la información que aparece a continuación. El trabajo es de tiempo completo durante el verano y medio tiempo durante el año escolar. El/La candidato/a debe contestar diciendo la verdad sobre su experiencia y su preparación. El/La entrevistador/a debe decidir si va a darle el puesto a esta persona o no. Escuchen primero mientras su profesor/a entrevista a otro/a estudiante y después entrevisten a su pareja.

Responsabilidades y requisitos

tener buena presencia	tener experiencia con el público
saber llevarse bien con otros empleados	ser organizado
usar computadoras	tener conocimiento de uno o dos idiomas extranjeros
contestar al teléfono	
ser capaz de resolver conflictos	trabajar días feriados

Act. 9: Do as a whole class activity or in pairs or small groups. Check by asking students' opinions. Encourage business students to get involved in the discussion.

Actividad 9 ¿Qué opinas? Di si estás de acuerdo o no con las siguientes ideas y por qué.

1. Todas las empresas deben tener guardería.
2. Debe haber más cursos de capacitación para los desempleados.
3. Es justo que las empresas bajen los sueldos para no tener que despedir a algunos empleados.
4. Si una empresa tiene que despedir a unos empleados, éstos deben ser los últimos que se han contratado.
5. Todo empleado de tiempo completo debe tener seguro médico y un mes de vacaciones pagadas cada año.

Act. 10A: Have one student be the group secretary and take notes about their aspirations. This information may be useful while doing Part B.

Actividad 10 La oferta y la demanda **Parte A:** En grupos de cuatro, analicen sus posibilidades de empleo en el futuro. Para hacerlo, apunten la siguiente información para cada miembro del grupo.

- el puesto que quiere tener
- dónde prefiere tener ese trabajo
- cuánto dinero quiere ganar
- la oferta y la demanda de ese trabajo en el mundo, en este país, en diferentes regiones del país o en ciudades específicas
- el efecto de la oferta y la demanda sobre el sueldo que va a poder ganar

Act. 10B: Check by listing on the board easy-to-find jobs and those that will be harder to land as perceived by the class.

Parte B: Basándose en las respuestas de la Parte A, decidan quién tiene las mejores posibilidades de conseguir el puesto que busca y quién creen que va a tener más dificultades y por qué.

¿LO SABÍAN?

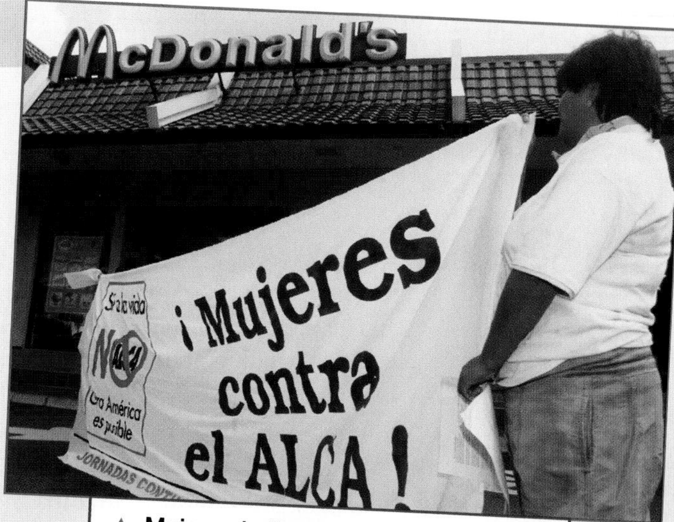

▲ Mujeres indígenas protestan contra el ALCA frente a un McDonalds en Ecuador. Muchas personas creen que este acuerdo va a beneficiar sólo a las grandes empresas.

En los últimos años, grandes y numerosos cambios económicos han ocurrido en los países latinoamericanos. Esto se debe en parte a la intervención de grupos como el FMI (el Fondo Monetario Internacional) y tratados como el Mercosur, el ALCA y el Tratado de Libre Comercio (*NAFTA*) que fomentan el comercio entre países. También se debe a una nueva generación de tecnócratas y políticos que han obtenido títulos de posgrado en universidades norteamericanas como Harvard y M.I.T. y han vuelto a sus países a poner en práctica los nuevos conocimientos obtenidos en el extranjero. Ellos opinan que para que la situación de sus países mejore, éstos deben formar parte de la economía mundial. La conexión entre los Estados Unidos y las otras naciones del hemisferio tanto como las relaciones económicas entre los países latinoamericanos mismos pueden cambiar para siempre las relaciones comerciales en el continente.

Mira estos anuncios que han aparecido en periódicos de diferentes países y que muestran esta interdependencia y di si has pensado trabajar en otro país. ¿Cómo crees que puedas usar el español en tu futuro empleo?

Cherche photographe pour travailler au Méxique et aux Etats-Unis. 5 ans d'expérience, parlant espagnol et anglais. Envoyez CV et dix de vos meilleures photos à l'attention de Mme. Nathalie Drouglazet, Intercommunications S.p.A., 74 Rue de la République, 75014 Paris.

ALCA = Acuerdo de Libre Comercio de las Américas (*Free Trade Area of the Americas*)

Cercasi venditore di computers con Laurea in Informatica. 3 anni di esperienza, milite esente, desideroso di viaggiare, necessaria conoscenza di francese e inglese. Contattare Dott. Barello al numero: 011-65.68.378.

Relaciones públicas. Se busca Licenciado en Ciencias de la Comunicación, con buena redacción y óptimo dominio del inglés para empresa internacional. Mandar curriculum a **Martínez y Asociados**. Bulnes 3233. Capital Federal 1425. Oficina de personal.

WWW *Pro and Con of Trade Agreements*

Ask students how many have studied or are planning on studying abroad. Discuss the importance of this in building relations between nations. Have students find words similar to English or Spanish in the Italian and French ads.

II. Expressing Restriction, Possibility, Purpose, and Time

The Subjunctive in Adverbial Clauses

FLR link: **Lectura 1**

Drill subjunctive in adverbial clauses:

To remember the conjunctions, memorize the acronym **ESCAPAS.**

E **en caso (de) que**
S **sin que**
C **con tal (de) que**
A **antes (de) que**
P **para que**
A **a menos que**
S **siempre y cuando**

1. Write the acronym **ESCAPAS** and the following incomplete sentences on the board: **Siempre hago la tarea... / Voy a trabajar en el extranjero...** Have students finish each sentence in as many ways as possible: **para que el profesor esté contento, sin que nadie me ayude.** (etc.)

In Chapter 7, you studied the use of the subjunctive with conjunctions of time to express pending actions. In this chapter, you will study conjunctions that express restriction, possibility, purpose, and time.

1. The following adverbial conjunctions are followed by the subjunctive.

Restriction:	**siempre y cuando / con tal (de) que**	provided that
	a menos que	unless
	sin que	without
Possibility:	**en caso (de) que**	in the event that, if
Purpose:	**para que**	in order that, so that
Time:	**antes (de) que**	before

Podemos comenzar el proyecto **siempre y cuando** la jefa lo **autorice.** — *We can start the project provided that the boss authorizes it.*

Voy a cancelar la reunión **en caso de que** el jefe **no pueda** venir. — *I'm going to cancel the meeting if the boss can't come.*

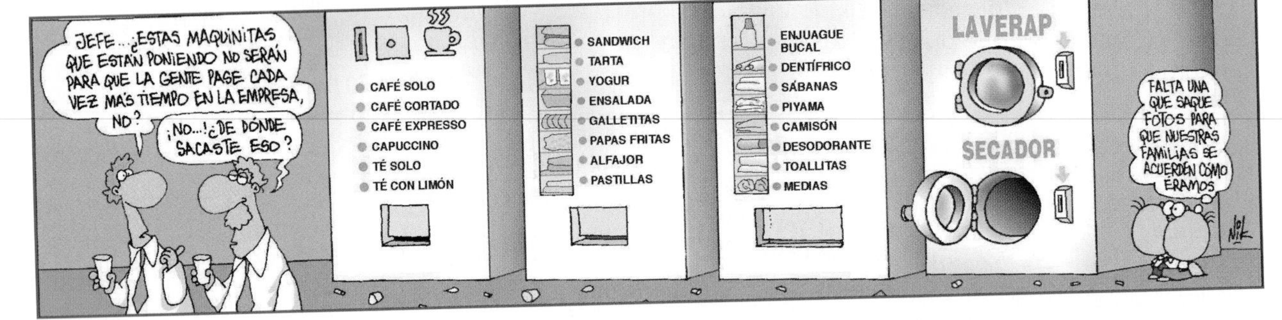

2. Have students finish ideas about American politics: **El gobierno cobra impuestos para que..., Los políticos hacen campañas electorales antes de que..., Ellos reciben donaciones sin que...**

3. Contrast with prepositions followed by infinitives: **El presidente habla sin..., Los políticos besan a los bebés para...**

2. If there is no change of subject, an infinitive follows the preposition **sin, para,** and **de** (in phrases like **antes de, con tal de, en caso de**).

Two Subjects: Conjunction + Subjunctive	One Subject: Preposition + Infinitive
Mi hermano trabaja día y noche **para que su familia pueda** vivir bien.	**Mi hermano** trabaja **para poder** vivir bien.
Yo pienso hacerlo **sin que nadie** me **oiga.**	**Yo** pienso hacerlo **sin molestar** a nadie.
En caso de que Juan se enferme, Diana va a hablar con su jefe.	**En caso de enfermarse, Juan** va a hablar con su jefe.

Los empleados van a reunirse **antes de que la jefa** les **hable** sobre los nuevos beneficios laborales.

Los empleados van a reunirse **antes de hablar** con la jefa sobre los beneficios laborales.

Carmen va a aceptar ese trabajo **con tal (de) que** le **den** muchos días de vacaciones.

Carmen va a aceptar ese trabajo **con tal de tener** muchos días de vacaciones.

3. The conjunctions **a menos que** and **siempre y cuando** are always followed by the subjunctive whether or not there is a change of subject in the dependent clause.

You may want to inform students that **en caso de que** and **con tal de que** can also be used with only one subject and are followed by the subjunctive.

Ellos van a buscar un regalo esta tarde **a menos que** (**ellos**) no **tengan** tiempo. — *They are going to look for a present this afternoon unless they don't have time.*

(Nosotros) Podemos terminar el proyecto **siempre y cuando** (**nosotros**) **tengamos** el dinero. — *We can finish the project provided that we have the money.*

Act. 11A: Assign as HW and check in class.

La licencia por paternidad también existe en muchos países hispanos.

Actividad 11 Beneficios laborales **Parte A:** Completa la siguiente explicación sobre los beneficios laborales que existen en Argentina con la forma apropiada de los verbos que se presentan.

(tener) Argentina ofrece algunos beneficios para que el trabajador ___tenga___ cierta protección económica. Uno de estos beneficios es la licencia por matrimonio, gracias a la cual si alguien se casa, puede faltar al trabajo por doce días sin que su jefe le ___compute___ esas faltas. (computar) En caso de que un empleado ___esté___ enfermo, le puede dar licencia por enfermedad; (estar) y en caso de ___estar___ embarazada, una mujer tiene derecho de pedir licencia por maternidad. (estar) El número de días que estos trabajadores pueden faltar depende de la gravedad del caso. Cuando un trabajador se siente mal, no puede faltar sin ___llamar___ a su trabajo ese mismo día. (llamar) El jefe se encarga entonces de mandar a un médico a la casa del empleado para que lo ___examine___, (examinar) ___diagnostique___ y ___pase___ un informe a la empresa. (diagnosticar, pasar)

Los empleados reciben dos aguinaldos, cada uno equivalente a medio mes de sueldo. Las empresas les pagan a sus trabajadores ese dinero extra para que ellos ___disfruten___ mejor de la Navidad y de las vacaciones de invierno en julio o agosto. (disfrutar)

Antes de ___despedir___ a un empleado, un jefe tiene que mandarle un telegrama a su casa diciéndole que va a quedar cesante después de un mes. (despedir) A partir de ese momento y durante su último mes, el empleado va a trabajar seis horas por día en vez de ocho y generalmente usa esas dos horas diarias para ___buscar___ otro trabajo. (buscar) Por lo general, el empleador no tiene problemas siempre y cuando ___haga___ lo que le indica la ley: pagarle al empleado el sueldo de su último mes, un sueldo mensual por cada año que trabajó en la empresa, más las vacaciones que no tomó y parte del aguinaldo. (hacer)

Act 11B: Have a group sharing when finished. Try to utilize students who are studying business related fields and may be more aware of American business practices.

The average American changes jobs seven times in his or her lifetime.

Parte B: En parejas, discutan las siguientes preguntas.

1. ¿Ofrecen las empresas de este país los mismos beneficios?
2. ¿Les sorprenden algunos de estos datos? ¿Por qué?
3. ¿Les parece que estos beneficios son buenos para las empresas? ¿Y para los empleados?

¿LO SABÍAN?

Los beneficios laborales que recibe un empleado varían de país en país. En Uruguay, por ejemplo, un beneficio importante son las vacaciones. Un empleado puede recibir veinte días laborales de vacaciones después del primer año de trabajo y un día más por cada cuatro años adicionales de trabajo. Antes de irse de vacaciones, el empleador debe darle un bono que consta del 45 por ciento del sueldo diario por cada día de vacaciones, es decir, que si un empleado gana cincuenta pesos por día y toma veinte días de vacaciones, recibirá un bono de 450 pesos y, además, su sueldo. Di en qué ocasiones recibe el empleado bonos en este país.

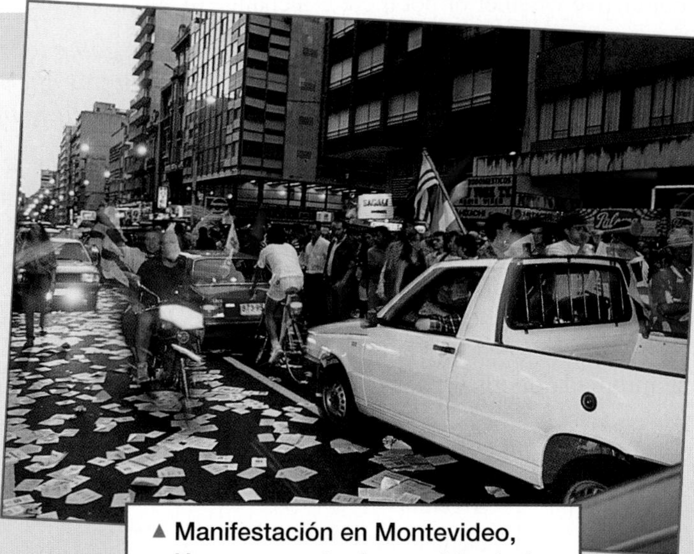

▲ Manifestación en Montevideo, Uruguay, contra los sueldos bajos.

Act. 12: May be assigned as HW. Check answers by calling on individuals.

Actividad 12 Derechos y obligaciones laborales Trabajas en la oficina de Recursos Humanos de una empresa y estás a cargo de redactar algunos de los derechos y obligaciones de los empleados. Completa las siguientes reglas.

Los empleados...

no deben hacer llamadas personales a larga distancia en el trabajo a menos que...

pueden llegar tarde algunas veces siempre y cuando...

pueden trabajar en su casa una vez por semana en caso de que...

si hacen llamadas a larga distancia desde su casa, deben apuntar la fecha, la hora y el nombre de la persona para que...

no deben usar papel con membrete (*letterhead*) de la compañía a menos que...

no deben trabajar horas extras sin...

pueden navegar por Internet para...

Actividad 13 ¿Le digo la verdad? **Parte A:** A veces es problemático decidir cuándo se le debe decir la verdad a alguien. En parejas, lean las siguientes situaciones laborales y hagan oraciones completas con las opciones que se dan. Luego decidan cuál es la mejor solución en cada caso. Estén listos para defender su opinión.

Act. 13A: If needed, go through items and practice possible responses. Form pairs, encourage students to discuss responses and to justify their choices. Option 1: Do and then check items one by one. Option 2: Do all items at once and check when one or two groups finish.

You may want to have pairs role play the different situations.

1. Un empleado oyó rumores de que el jefe iba a despedir a un compañero de trabajo. ¿Qué debe hacer? (No) Debe decírselo a su compañero...
   a. para que / su compañero / comenzar a / buscar otro trabajo
   b. a menos que / él / poder / confirmar el rumor
   c. antes de que / el jefe / decírselo
2. Un empleado ve accidentalmente el recibo de sueldo de un compañero que tiene el mismo puesto que él. Se da cuenta de que el sueldo de su compañero es mejor. Debe hablar con su jefe...
   a. para / recibir / el mismo sueldo
   b. sin que / su compañero / saberlo
   c. en caso de que / el empleado / creer / que es injusto
3. Una empleada trabaja para una empresa que fabrica carros. Encontró un defecto en el diseño de un carro nuevo que puede causar muchos accidentes. Sin embargo, rectificar este problema puede costar muchísimo dinero y el primer carro va a salir a la venta el mes que viene. (No) Debe...
   a. hablar con su jefe para que / él / estar / informado
   b. decir nada a menos que / alguien / preguntarle algo
   c. informar anónimamente a una organización protectora de los consumidores para que / la empresa / cambiar / el diseño
4. Una empleada trabaja con su cuñado, pero él no hace su trabajo; por eso ella tiene el doble de trabajo. Debe...
   a. decirle algo a su esposo para que / él / hablar / con su hermano
   b. explicarle la situación a su jefe siempre y cuando / él / prometer / no decirle nada al cuñado
   c. negarse a hacer el trabajo de su cuñado a menos que / esto / afectar / la producción de la empresa
5. Cada vez que un empleado le da una buena idea a su jefa, ella va al presidente de la empresa y se atribuye la idea. Por eso el presidente piensa que la creatividad de esta mujer es esencial para la empresa. El empleado debe...
   a. hacer una cita con el presidente para explicarle todo antes de que / la jefa / contarle / otras ideas
   b. mandarle emails a su jefa con copias a otras personas / para que / los demás / saber / de quién son las ideas
   c. consultar con un abogado a menos que / ella / dejar de / robarle las ideas

▼ Ministros de Paraguay y Nicaragua dialogan en una reunión del ALCA en Miami.

Parte B: ¿Alguna vez tuviste un problema grave en el trabajo como los de la sección anterior? ¿O sabes de alguien que haya estado en una situación muy desagradable en el trabajo? En parejas, cuéntense qué problema tuvieron en el trabajo o qué le pasó a un/a amigo/a y cómo lo resolvieron.

When doing Act. 14, you may want to have students look at this photo when discussing appropriate business attire.

Act. 14A: Ask comprehension questions, such as: **¿Debes hablar de las relaciones entre los Estados Unidos y México? ¿Es aconsejable llevar guayabera a una oficina?**

Actividad 14 Los mexicanos y los negocios **Parte A:** Un hombre de negocios norteamericano va a ir a México en un viaje de negocios y recibe la siguiente información de una colega sobre cómo comportarse con los mexicanos. Lee la información y luego contesta las preguntas de tu profesor/a.

Sé que se va a México y quería darle algunas recomendaciones para que las tenga en cuenta a la hora de hacer negocios con los mexicanos
Clara González

Cómo dirigirse a la gente

Los títulos profesionales son muy importantes en el protocolo mexicano. Use los términos **doctor, profesor, ingeniero, abogado, licenciado, contador** y **arquitecto** seguido del apellido al hablar con estos profesionales para mostrar respeto.

Vestimenta

- A mucha gente de negocios le causa una buena impresión que otros lleven ropa de diseñadores y puede llevarla siempre y cuando sea de colores oscuros como gris o azul marino.
- En caso de que tenga una comida informal, no se puede llevar guayabera—camisa liviana que se usa afuera de los pantalones. Esto está bien en el Caribe, pero normalmente no en México.

Temas de conversación

Para que le cause buena impresión a sus clientes mexicanos, es importante poder hablar de México y de sus lugares famosos, de la cultura y de la historia mexicana. También, si comenta sobre fútbol nacional o internacional, va a ser bien recibido. En caso de que ya conozca bien a la persona, es buena idea preguntar por la familia. Si no la conoce todavía, hágale preguntas sobre ella. Obviamente, también se habla del trabajo, pero no al principio de la conversación.

Temas que hay que evitar

Para que no tenga problemas, es aconsejable que evite hablar de política y de religión.

Comportamiento

- Al hablar, la gente está físicamente más cerca uno de otro que en los EE.UU. Se considera descortés alejarse de la persona con la que uno habla.
- Los hombre mexicanos son cálidos y por lo general establecen contacto físico con otro hombre ya sea tocándole los hombros o tomando el brazo del otro.
- En caso de que un mexicano lo invite a su casa, no hable de negocios. La invitación es simplemente social y quizás para establecer un primer contacto.

Parte B: En parejas, ahora decidan cuáles son los tres consejos más importantes que leyeron y por qué. Justifiquen sus respuestas diciendo **Es importante que... para que..., a menos que...**

Parte C: Ahora en grupos de tres, preparen un mínimo de cinco ideas sobre cómo debe comportarse un hombre/una mujer de negocios mexicano/a que va a venir a este país. Incluyan expresiones como: **para (que), sin (que), en caso de (que), a menos que, siempre y cuando.**

Act. 14B: Call on individuals for responses.

Act. 14C: Form groups, set a time limit, and begin. When finished, have a group sharing and decide on which are the most important items.

Actividad 15 Lo perfecto **Parte A:** Una empresa hizo un concurso de diseños para el coche perfecto y el siguiente es uno de los posibles ganadores. Mira el coche y después termina las siguientes oraciones que se presentan.

1. Hay una cafetera con una cantidad ilimitada de café para que...
2. Hay un paraguas en caso de que...
3. Hay una cámara de video en la parte trasera del carro y un televisor adelante para que...
4. Con un periscopio el conductor puede ver el tráfico sin...
5. El asiento del conductor vibra para...
6. Las llantas traseras son enormes en caso de que...
7. Hay una pajita que va de la cafetera al conductor para que...

pajita = straw = **popote** (*México*), **pitillo** (*Colombia*)

Act. 15A: Call on individuals to give each answer.

Parte B: En parejas, miren el siguiente dibujo del sofá perfecto y descríbanlo usando expresiones como: **para (que), sin (que), en caso de (que), a menos que.** Sigan el modelo.

▶ El sofá tiene un/a... para que...

Act. 15B: Form pairs, set a time limit, and begin. Check by asking different groups what certain items are for. As a follow-up ask students to invent **la canoa/computadora/bicicleta perfecta** and to explain the invention to the class using **a menos que, para (que), en caso de (que), sin (que).**

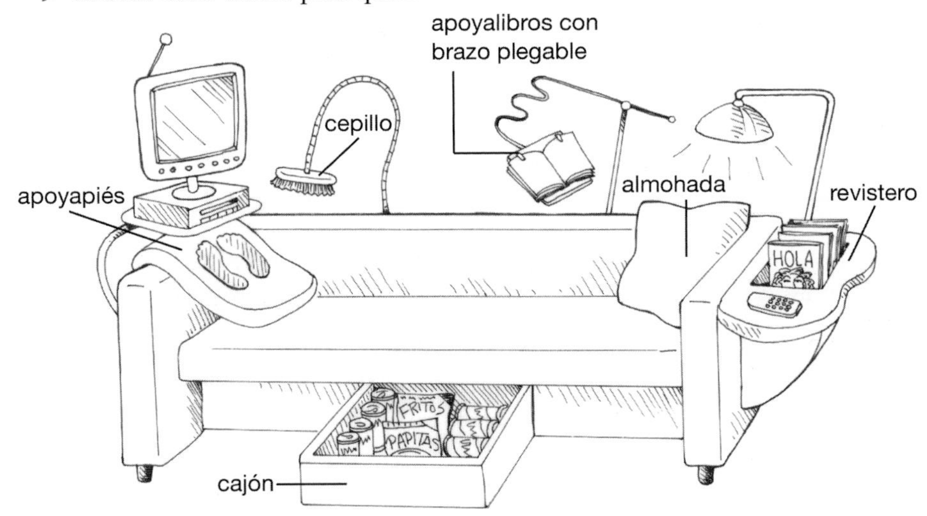

Actividad 16 Reacción en cadena En grupos de tres, inventen una historia con una de las ideas de la siguiente lista. Formen cinco oraciones en cadena (*chain sentences*) con expresiones como: **para que, sin que, en caso de que, a menos que, siempre y cuando.** Creen las oraciones de la siguiente manera: la última idea de una oración se convierte en la primera idea de la oración siguiente. Sigan el modelo.

▶ ir a Guatemala
A: Antes de que yo vaya a Guatemala, mis padres tienen que darme dinero.
B: Mis padres van a darme dinero siempre y cuando saque buenas notas.
C: No voy a sacar buenas notas a menos que estudie mucho.
etc.

1. conseguir un buen trabajo
2. comprar un perro
3. el/la profesor/a de español estar contento/a

Act. 16: Write conjunctions or the **ESCAPAS** acronym on the board. Then model a chain with the class. T: **Voy a ir de vacaciones siempre y cuando mis padres me den dinero.** S: **Mis padres van a darme dinero para que yo pueda divertirme.** S: **Me voy a divertir con tal de que venga mi amiga Emily.** (etc.) Form groups of three, set a time limit, and begin. When finished, do a chain using volunteers from the whole class.

III. Reporting What Someone Said

FLR link: **Lectura 3** can be used to practice reported speech.

Reported Speech

Reported speech: You may want to point out that these Spanish patterns are similar to those used in English.

Drill reported speech:

1. Make statements about your activities and have students report them. Vary tenses and examples. Although the presentation emphasizes introductory phrases in the preterit, include present-tense examples to ensure students understand the concept and similarity to English.

2. Have students report something that a friend/roommate told them this week. Have them report a news item.

Some common introductory phrases in the preterit are: **dijo que, explicó que, añadió que, preguntó qué/cuándo/si, contestó que, respondió que, comentó que.**

When an introductory phrase in the present is used, the reporting verb doesn't change tense: **Vi un accidente terrible. Dice** (introductory verb → present) **que vio** (reporting verb) **un accidente terrible.**

Some common introductory phrases in the present are: **dice que, explica que, pide que, comenta que.**

1. Telling or reporting what someone said is called reported speech **(estilo indirecto)**. Look at the following exchange.

Pedro **¿Vas a ir** a la reunión con los representantes de Telecom?
Teresa Sí. **¿Y tú?**
Pedro **No, no voy a ir** porque **me invitaron** a una exposición de productos nuevos de Nokia.

Now look at a report of what was said.

Pedro le preguntó a Teresa si **iba a ir** a la reunión con los representantes de Telecom. Ella le respondió que sí y le preguntó a Pedro si él **iba a ir.** Él dijo que **no** porque lo **habían invitado** a una exposición de productos nuevos de Nokia.

2. Study the combinations in the following examples showing how to report what was said when the reporting verb is in the preterit.

Estilo directo	Estilo indirecto (verbo introductorio en pretérito)
Narración en el presente	**Imperfecto**
—**Asiste** a clase todos los días.	Dijo que **asistía** a clase todos los días.
Narración en el futuro	
—**Vamos a ir** más tarde.	Le comentó que **iban a ir** más tarde.
Narración en el pasado con el imperfecto	
—**Tomaba** clases de dibujo.	Nos explicó que **tomaba** clases de dibujo.
Narración en el pasado sin el imperfecto	**Pluscuamperfecto**
—¿**Has hecho** la escultura?	Le preguntó si **había hecho** la escultura.
—Sí, la **terminé** hace dos días.	Le respondió que la **había terminado** la noche anterior.
—Nunca **había trabajado** con alguien tan rápido.	Añadió que nunca **había trabajado** con alguien tan rápido.

Actividad 17 ¿Qué dijeron? Cambia esta conversación del estilo directo al indirecto. Sigue el modelo.

▶ Mauricio le preguntó a Virginia qué iba a hacer esa noche.

▶ Ella le contestó que...

Mauricio	¿Qué vas a hacer esta noche?
Virginia	Tengo una reunión de trabajo.
Mauricio	¿Qué pasó?
Virginia	No terminamos el proyecto, por eso tenemos que quedarnos en la oficina.
Mauricio	¿Han tenido muchos problemas?
Virginia	Sí, hemos tenido algunos, pero esta noche vamos a terminar. Si quieres, podemos ir al bar de la esquina de casa a las once para tomar un café.

Act. 17: Assign as HW and check in class. Suggest that they use a variety of expressions: **dijo que, explicó que, añadió que, preguntó qué/cuándo/si, contestó que, respondió que**. Answers: **iba a hacer, tenía, había pasado, no habían terminado, tenían que quedarse, habían tenido, habían tenido, iban a terminar, quería, podían ir.**

Actividad 18 La desaparición de un compañero En parejas, una persona es un/a estudiante universitario/a y la otra persona es un/a detective de la policía. Lean sólo el papel que les corresponde.

Act. 18: Form pairs assigning the roommate and detective's roles. Tell students to look at their role only, allow time for them to study their parts and formulate some questions or responses, and begin the activity. Check by calling on individuals to relate what was said.

El/La estudiante universitario/a

Hace dos días que tu compañero/a de cuarto salió del cuarto y no volvió. Ésta fue la última conversación que tuviste con él/ella.

Antonio/a	¡Qué cansado/a estoy! He estado todo el día con el proyecto de física para la clase del profesor López y finalmente lo terminé.
Tú	Pensé que nunca ibas a terminar... trabajaste 12 horas en ese proyecto.
Antonio/a	Estoy muerto/a. Ahora voy a ir al cine para distraerme.
Tú	¿Qué película vas a ver?
Antonio/a	Creo que la última de Benicio del Toro.
Tú	Ah sí, la están dando en el cine que está cerca de aquí.
Antonio/a	Sí, la función empieza a las 8:00, así que pienso estar en casa a las 10:30. ¿Quieres ir conmigo?
Tú	No, gracias. Voy a encontrarme con unos amigos para cenar.

Ahora vas a hablar con un/a detective. Contesta sus preguntas usando el estilo indirecto.

▶ Me dijo que estaba muy cansado/a.

El/La detective

Un/a estudiante universitario/a te llama para decirte que hace dos días que su compañero/a de cuarto no aparece por la residencia. Hazle preguntas.

1. qué decirle su compañero/a antes de irse
2. por qué estar cansado/a
3. decirle a Ud. adónde ir
4. informarle a Ud. a qué hora volver
5. él/ella invitarlo/a a Ud.
6. qué explicarle Ud. que ir a hacer

Empieza la conversación preguntándole **¿Qué le dijo su compañero/a antes de irse?**

Act. 19: Assign as HW or do in class. Form pairs and allow time for each member of the pair to read one of the two stories. Then have students tell each other the story. You may want to model the first sentence or two as a class to get them off to a good start.

Historia 1: Un amigo me contó que se consideraba una persona muy respetuosa y que nunca había sido irrespetuoso con nadie. Añadió que el miércoles pasado tenía una entrevista de trabajo a las ocho de la mañana y que su reloj despertador no había sonado...

Historia 2: Mi amigo Marcos me contó que el otro día su jefe les había mandado un email a él y a Fernanda con la siguiente información: Dijo que ellos tenían que terminar el proyecto ese día y entregárselo al Sr. Covarrubias que lo necesitaba con urgencia...

Actividad 19 Dos historias cómicas En parejas, cada persona lee una de las siguientes historias y luego se la cuenta a su compañero/a usando el estilo indirecto.

Historia 1

"Me considero una persona muy respetuosa y nunca he sido irrespetuoso con nadie. Pero el miércoles pasado tenía una entrevista de trabajo a las ocho de la mañana y mi reloj despertador no sonó. Me desperté a las ocho menos cuarto, salté de la cama, me vestí y salí de casa corriendo. Estaba muy nervioso porque sabía que iba a llegar tarde. Iba en mi carro y al llegar al lugar, vi que un auto estaba por estacionar en el único lugar que había. Pero yo estaba desesperado y tomé el lugar. La mujer del otro carro estaba furiosa, pero yo entré corriendo al edificio donde tenía la entrevista. Me recibió la secretaria, esperé unos minutos y pasé a la oficina para la entrevista. Qué sorpresa cuando vi entrar a la mujer a quien yo le robé el último lugar para estacionar. Voy a comprarme dos despertadores para no llegar tarde a citas importantes y para no hacer cosas desesperadas."

Empieza diciendo: Un amigo me contó que...

Historia 2

El otro día mi jefe nos mandó un email con la siguiente información:

> "Queridos Fernanda y Marcos:
> Hoy tenemos que terminar el proyecto y entregárselo al Sr. Covarrubias que lo necesita con urgencia."

El Sr. Covarrubias es insoportable, le encanta trabajar y nos obliga a trabajar tanto como él. Pero yo tengo esposa e hijos y también quiero pasar tiempo con ellos. Por eso, me molestó mucho recibir ese email y para descargarme, le escribí un email a mi jefe que también opina que ese señor es muy molesto:

> "Ese hombre me tiene harto. Estoy seguro que está solo en la vida y no tiene otra cosa que hacer. Lo único que hace es trabajar. Tengo una idea: voy a presentarle a mi hermana. Así va a interesarse menos por el trabajo."

El único problema fue que en vez de hacer clic en "contestar", hice clic en "contestar a todos", sin saber que mi jefe nos había mandado el email a Fernanda, a mí Y AL SR. COVARRUBIAS. A los cinco minutos recibí un email del Sr. Covarrubias que decía: "Quiero conocerla".

Empieza diciendo: Mi amigo Marcos me contó que...

Actividad 20 **¿Alguna vez?** En grupos de tres, háganse las siguientes preguntas para hablar de diferentes situaciones personales.

1. ¿Alguna vez te has vuelto a encontrar con un vecino o un amigo de tu niñez? ¿Qué te preguntó? ¿Qué te contó de su vida? ¿Qué le contaste tú?
2. Cuando estabas en la escuela secundaria, ¿tuviste novio/a alguna vez? ¿Qué le dijiste para comenzar el noviazgo?
3. ¿Alguna vez alguien te ha ofrecido en su casa una comida que te disgustaba mucho? ¿Qué le dijiste?
4. ¿Alguna vez has rechazado la invitación de alguien con una mentira? ¿Qué le dijiste?
5. ¿Alguna vez le has dicho a alguien una verdad muy difícil de aceptar? ¿Qué le dijiste?

Act. 20: Form groups of three, model responses to a few questions, and begin. Check by asking about #4. Expand by asking students if it is OK to tell a lie. If they say yes, ask when. Ask if they have ever lied to protect someone and what they said. Encourage connected discourse.

IV. Expressing Choice and Negation

O... o, ni... ni, ni siquiera

1. When you want to say *either. . . or*, use **(o)... o.** When you want to express *neither. . . nor*, use **(ni)... ni.**

To review rules on negating, see Chapter 7, pages 179–181.

Drill **(o)... o, (ni)... ni:**

Esta noche quiero ir (**o**) al cine **o** a un restaurante.	*I want to go (either) to the movies or to a restaurant tonight.*
Trabajé tanto hoy que esta noche **no** quiero ir (**ni**) al cine **ni** a un restaurante.	*I worked so hard today that I don't want to go to the movies or to a restaurant.* (literally, I worked so hard today that I don't want to go neither to the movies nor to a restaurant.)
Ni Carlos ni Perla me han llamado.*	*Neither Carlos nor Perla has called me.*

Remember to use the double negative when **ni** follows the verb in phrases beginning with **no**.

Have students discuss their plans for this week: **Este fin de semana voy (o) a... o... , Esta noche quiero (o)... o... , El sábado no quiero (ni)... ni...**

*Note: When subjects are preceded by **ni... ni...**, or **(o)... o...** the verb is plural.

2. To express *not even,* use **ni** (**siquiera**).

Ni (**siquiera**) mi novia me entiende.	*Not even my girlfriend understands me.*
No recibí **ni** (**siquiera**) un centavo por el trabajo.	*I didn't even receive a penny for the work.*

Act. 21: Encourage students to be creative with their responses. Accept all plausible answers that are not contradicted in the text.

Actividad 21 Lectura entre líneas Lee primero la siguiente conversación y después contesta las seis preguntas que le siguen para reconstruir lo que crees que ocurrió. Hay muchas posibilidades; por eso, usa la imaginación al contestar, pero basa tus respuestas en la conversación. Intenta usar **ni... ni** y **o... o** al hablar.

Lola Por fin has llegado. ¿Sabes algo?
Verónica Nada. Y tú no te has movido, sigues al lado del teléfono.
Lola No sé qué hacer. Ni ha llamado ni ha dejado una nota... ¡Nada!
Verónica ¡Qué raro que no haya dado ninguna señal de vida!
Lola Han pasado tres días.
Verónica ¿Ha llamado él a Víctor?
Lola Ni siquiera a él. No ha llamado ni a Víctor ni a nadie.
Verónica ¿Has llamado a la policía?
Lola No. Todavía no he hecho nada. O lloro pensando en alguna tragedia o me enfado pensando que está divirtiéndose por ahí y que no se ha preocupado ni siquiera por avisar.
Verónica ¿Qué vas a hacer cuando vuelva?
Lola O lo voy a abrazar... o lo voy a matar.

1. ¿Cuál de estas palabras describe mejor los sentimientos de Lola: desesperada, interesada o preocupada?
2. ¿De quién hablan las mujeres: un esposo, un amante, un hijo o un amigo? ¿Por qué crees eso?
3. ¿Qué crees que haya hecho Verónica en las últimas dos o tres horas?
4. ¿Es Víctor una persona importante en la vida del hombre misterioso? ¿Cuál es la importancia de las palabras **ni siquiera** en la frase, **Ni siquiera a él**? ¿Quién puede ser Víctor?
5. ¿Dónde está el hombre misterioso y qué está haciendo?
6. ¿Va a llamar el hombre? ¿Va a volver? Si vuelve, ¿qué va a pasar?

Act. 22: Encourage students to go beyond the items listed and to make up other sentences about their future jobs.

Actividad 22 Tu futuro En parejas, miren las siguientes listas y decidan qué lugares y tipo de trabajos van a ser parte de su futuro y cuáles no. Usen las siguientes ideas u otras originales y sigan el modelo.

▶ Me gustaría vivir o en... o en..., pero no quiero estar ni en el campo ni...

Lugar para vivir

pueblo pequeño	norte	Europa	Suramérica
sur	campo	medio oeste	afueras de una ciudad
Alaska	Hawai	ciudad	noreste

Lugar de trabajo

oficina	al aire libre	escuela	empresa pequeña
hospital	laboratorio	casa	negocio de mi familia

Un trabajo relacionado con...

construcción	ventas	salud	investigación
educación	turismo	política	administración

¿LO SABÍAN?

Algunas personas tienen pocas posibilidades de elegir lo que van a hacer en la vida por haber nacido en una familia pobre con poco acceso a la educación y al dinero. Desde hace unos años ha surgido una manera innovadora para ayudar a esas personas o, más bien, para que se ayuden ellas mismas. Lee lo que explica una peruana sobre lo que pasa en su país.

▲ **Mujeres peruanas que recibieron un microcrédito. En sus reuniones toman asistencia y deciden cómo utilizar el dinero en sus microempresas.**

Fuente hispana

"Existen en el mundo los llamados bancos éticos que son organizaciones que buscan ayudar a la gente necesitada a la vez que les brindan beneficios a sus inversores. El sistema de estos bancos consiste en dar microcréditos a familias pobres en países en vías de desarrollo, en especial a las mujeres porque son ellas las que, por lo general, tienen menos acceso a la educación y al trabajo y quienes, en algunos casos, son jefe de familia. Se forman así los bancos comunales que consisten en grupos de diez a treinta mujeres que se encargan de seleccionar un comité de administración. Estas mujeres reciben préstamos con un interés muy bajo que cada una destina a diferentes microempresas como, por ejemplo, la venta de comida y la manufactura y venta de ropa. El grupo de mujeres se apoya en sus microempresas y en el pago del préstamo en cuotas."

peruana

The **asistencia** page is where they take attendance for meetings (**p = presente, t = tarde, f = falta**). The **cuenta interna** page is the official booking system.

www *El microcrédito*

V. Describing Reciprocal Actions

Se/Nos/Os + Plural Verb Forms

Drill reciprocal forms:

Call a pair of students up to the front of the class and give them a slip of paper with instructions on it to act out. The class then says what they are doing. Change pairs after a couple of actions. Examples include: **Uds. se miran. Se abrazan. / Una persona mira hacia la puerta y la otra mira hacia las ventanas. / Él le besa la mano. Se hablan. / Una persona habla con el/la profesor/a y la otra persona escucha la conversación.** (etc.) You may want to add more difficult items. For example: **Se hablan, pero no se escuchan.**

1. The pronouns **se, nos,** and **os** may be used to describe actions that people do *to themselves:* **Ella se ducha.** Another use of these pronouns is to describe actions people do *to each other* or *to one another*. These are called *reciprocal actions*. Compare the following sentences and drawings.

Él **se baña.**
He's bathing (himself).

Los trillizos de la familia Peñalver **se bañan.**
The Peñalver triplets are bathing one another.

Se llaman por teléfono con frecuencia.	*They call each other frequently.*
Nos peleamos como perros y gatos.	*We fight like cats and dogs.*
Vosotros **os** lleváis muy bien.	*You get along very well.*

2. Note the ambiguity in meaning of the following sentence.

Ellos **se miraron.** { *They looked at themselves.* / *They looked at each other.* }

Tell students they can drop the articles in the expressions without affecting the meaning. If the article is used in the first part of the expression, it must be used in the second half.

To avoid ambiguity or to add emphasis, it is common to include the phrase **el uno al otro** and its feminine and plural forms **la una a la otra/los unos a los otros/las unas a las otras.** The definite articles are optional.

Después de hacer su última oferta, los dos negociantes **se miraron** intensamente **(el) uno a(l) otro.**	*After making their last offer, the two negotiators looked intensely at each other.*
Los empleados **se ayudan (los) unos a (los) otros** con el nuevo programa de computadoras.	*The employees help one another with the new computer program.*

When there is a masculine and a feminine, use the masculine form: **Él y ella se miraron (el) uno a(l) otro.**

3. Verbs that are often used with a specific preposition use the same prepositions to clarify a reciprocal action.

Se despidieron (la) una **de** (la) otra.	*They said good-by to each other.*
Se pelearon (el) uno **con** (el) otro.	*They fought with each other.*
Se rieron (los) unos **de** (los) otros.	*They laughed at one another.*

Actividad 23 La interacción En parejas, digan cómo se comportan Uds. con diferentes personas o cómo se comportan ciertas personas entre ellas y por qué, combinando una frase de la primera columna y una frase de la segunda.

Act. 23: Follow-up: To practice **os** you can have students interview one another by asking questions: **¿Tu madre y tú os escribís con frecuencia?** Stress that in Spanish, as in English, it is considered unacceptable to say **yo y mi madre** instead of **mi madre y yo.**

mi novio/a y yo	no dirigirse la palabra
mi padre/madre y yo	llevarse bien/mal
mis padres	(no) entenderse
mi hermano/a y yo	amarse
mis primos	(no) pelearse
mi perro/gato y yo	besarse
mi abuelo/a y mi madre	escribirse emails
mi compañero/a de cuarto y yo	
mi ex novio/a y yo	

Actividad 24 Un guion de telenovela **Parte A:** Completa esta parte del guion de una telenovela, usando pronombres de complemento directo o indirecto y pronombres reflexivos y recíprocos.

Remember: Direct-object pronouns are **me, te, lo, la, nos, os, los, las** and indirect-object pronouns are **me, te, le, nos, os, les.**

Act. 24A: Assign as HW and check in class.

Él ___le___ entrega una flor a ella y ella ___la___ huele (*smells*) y sonríe. Ella ___le___ toma la mano (a él). ___Se___ miran uno a otro con mucha intensidad y (ellos) ___se___ besan. En ese momento entra otra mujer. Ella ___los___ mira (a ellos) con asombro, pero ellos no ___la___ ven hasta que ella ___los___ comienza a insultar. Él ___le___ pone una mano sobre la boca y ___la___ intenta calmar. (Ella) no ___se___ calla. Las dos mujeres ___se___ siguen mirando. La primera mujer ___le___ explica a la otra quién es. Todos ___se___ ríen aliviados. Al final, todos ellos ___se___ abrazan.

Parte B: Ahora en grupos de cuatro, representen el guion que acaban de completar. Uno de Uds. debe leerlo mientras los otros tres actúan.

Act. 24B: Have all groups practice and then have one group present it for the class. If groups of four aren't possible, form some groups of five and have one work as the director. As a follow-up ask them to write a new description to act out. Assign one person to be the group secretary; allow sufficient time. Circulate and make corrections as needed. Have each secretary read the description as the group performs.

Act. 25A: Before doing the activity, review relevant business vocabulary. Then form groups of four assigning two to Pair A and two to Pair B, explain the roles of each pair, have them read their role cards, and allow a few minutes for them to prepare.

Actividad 25 No nos entendemos **Parte A:** En grupos de cuatro, formen dos parejas (Pareja A y Pareja B). Todos Uds. trabajan para la empresa MicroTec. Lean solamente el papel para su pareja y prepárense para la discusión.

Pareja A

Uds. son representantes del sindicato (*labor union*) de MicroTec y deben crear una lista de beneficios laborales para los empleados. En los últimos años la empresa ha reducido los beneficios y ahora Uds. los consideran miserables y un insulto a su trabajo.

Pareja B

Uds. son representantes de la dirección de MicroTec y deben crear una lista de beneficios laborales para los empleados. Obviamente quieren empleados felices, pero también quieren ahorrarle dinero a la empresa. En los últimos años, Uds. han reducido los beneficios BASTANTE para no tener que despedir a ningún empleado.

Act. 25B: Allow a few minutes for the negotiations. Check by asking what the different groups agreed to do.

Parte B: Ahora los representantes del sindicato y la dirección deben discutir los beneficios laborales e intentar llegar a un acuerdo. Usen expresiones como: **Queremos..., Insistimos en..., a menos que..., para (que)...** Usen también las expresiones de las siguientes listas.

Para estar de acuerdo total o parcialmente

En eso coincidimos.
Coincidimos en parte.
Opino como Ud.
¡Cómo no!

Para no estar de acuerdo

No exactamente.
No, en absoluto.

Para interrumpir

Yo quisiera decir...
Déjenme hablar.
¿Puedo decir algo?
Escúcheme/Escúchenme.
Un momentito.

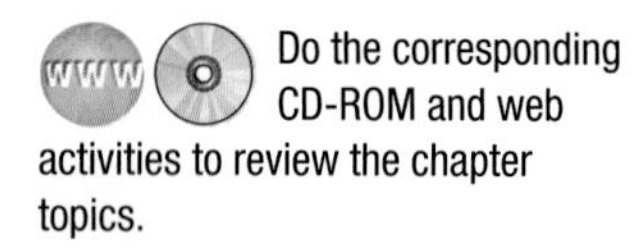

Do the corresponding CD-ROM and web activities to review the chapter topics.

Vocabulario activo

Conjunciones adverbiales

En caso (de) que	*in the event that, if*
Sin que	*without*
Con tal (de) que	*provided that*
A menos que	*unless*
Para que	*in order that, so that*
Antes (de) que	*before*
Siempre y cuando	*provided that*

Palabras relacionadas con el trabajo

los avisos clasificados	*classified ads*
la carta de recomendación	*letter of recommendation*
completar una solicitud	*to fill out an application*
contratar a alguien	*to hire someone*
el curriculum (vitae)	*CV, resumé*
despedir (i, i) a alguien	*to fire someone*
entrevistarse (con alguien)	*to be interviewed (by someone)*
estar desempleado/a / estar sin trabajo	*to be unemployed*
la experiencia laboral	*work experience*
hacer una pasantía	*to do an internship*
la oferta y la demanda	*supply and demand*
las referencias	*references*
solicitar un puesto/empleo	*to apply for a job*
tomar cursos de perfeccionamiento/ capacitación	*to take continuing education/ training courses*

El empleo

aumentar/bajar el sueldo	*to raise/lower the salary*
la empresa	*company*
los ingresos/la renta	*income*
el pago mensual/semanal	*monthly/weekly pay*
el salario mínimo	*minimum wage*
el sueldo	*salary*
trabajar medio tiempo/ tiempo completo	*to work part/full time*

Los beneficios

el aguinaldo	*end-of-the year bonus*
los días feriados	*holidays*
la guardería (infantil)	*child care center*
la licencia	*leave (of absence)*
por enfermedad	*sick leave*
por maternidad	*maternity leave*
por matrimonio	*wedding leave*
por paternidad	*paternity leave*
el seguro médico/dental/ de vida	*health/dental/life insurance*

Expresiones útiles

darle igual (a alguien)	*to be all the same (to someone)*
un montón	*a lot*
ni... ni	*neither. . . nor*
ni (siquiera)	*not even*
o... o	*either. . . or*
el uno al otro/la una a la otra	*each other*
los unos a los otros/las unas a las otras	*one another (more than two people)*
Coincidimos en parte.	*We partially agree.*
¡Cómo no!	*Of course!*
Déjenme hablar.	*Let me speak.*
En eso coincidimos.	*We agree on that.*
Escúcheme/Escúchenme.	*Listen to me.*
Un momentito.	*Wait a minute.*
No, en absoluto.	*No, not at all.*
No exactamente.	*Not exactly.*
Opino como Ud.	*I think the same way you do.*
¿Puedo decir algo?	*May I say something?*
Yo quisiera decir...	*I would like to say. . .*

Vocabulario personal

Capítulo 9

Metas comunicativas

- expresar influencia, emociones y reacciones en el pasado
- hablar sobre arte
- cambiar el enfoque de una oración

Metas adicionales

- usar el infinitivo
- usar frases de transición

Es una obra de arte

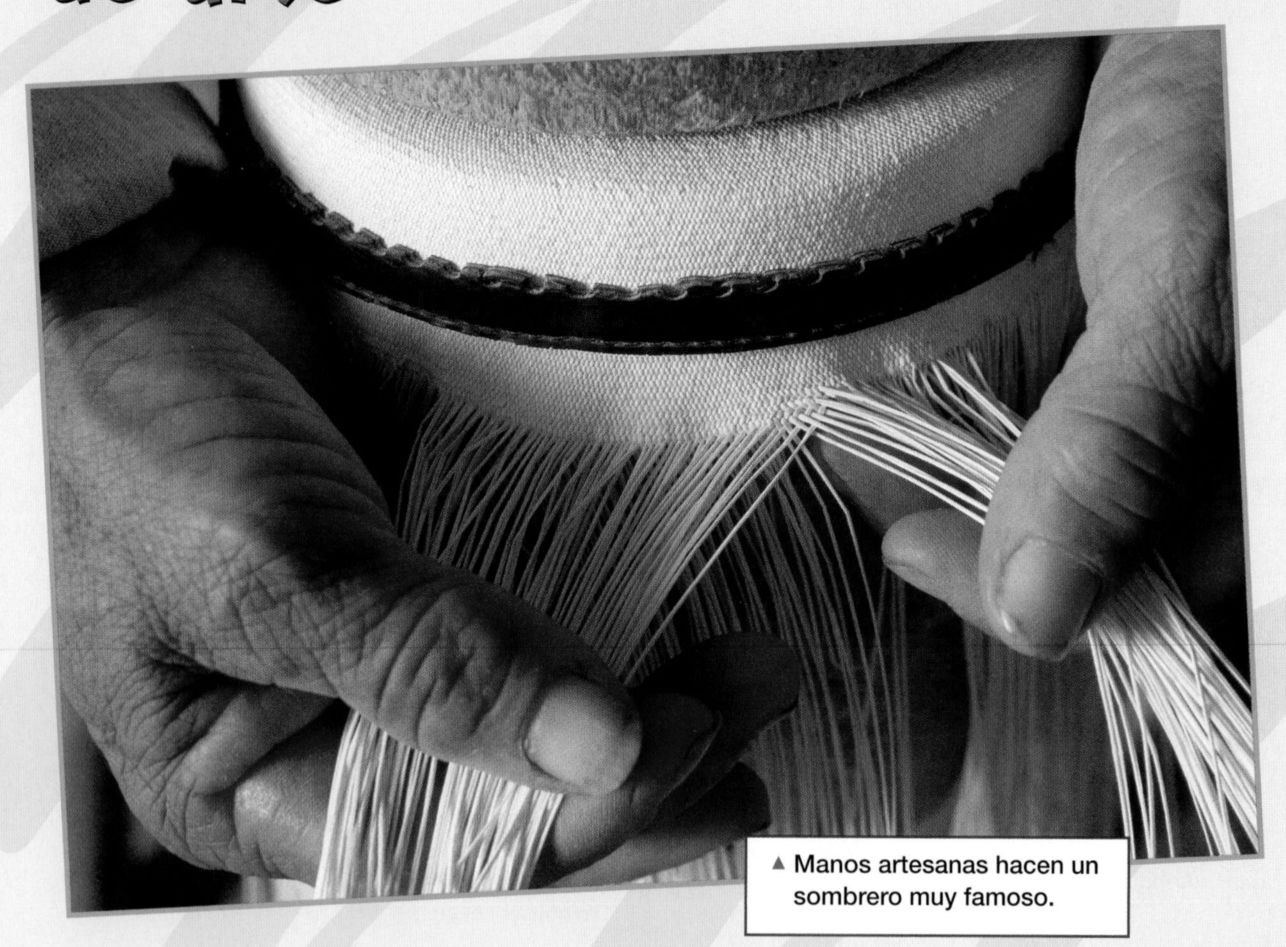

▲ Manos artesanas hacen un sombrero muy famoso.

May be assigned: Grammar, vocabulary, **¿Lo sabían?**, Act. 9, 13A, Act. 14A, Act. 24, Act. 25, Act. 26.

Show the chapter video episode at any point in the chapter that you see fit and do all or selected activities in class. Note: Content of the video supplements the cultural material in the chapter and activities reenter chapter grammar and vocabulary.

Entrevista a una experta en artesanías

llevarle (a alguien) dos/tres meses	to take (someone) two/three months
¡Qué barbaridad!	Wow! (Literally, What a barbarity!) (*negative connotation*)
se me fueron las ganas de + *infinitive*	I didn't feel like + *verb* + *ing* anymore
un dineral	a great deal of money

Actividad 1 El sombrero **Parte A:** El locutor de un programa de radio entrevista a una experta acerca de un sombrero muy famoso. Antes de escuchar la entrevista, mira la foto que aparece en esta página y la foto de la página 222 y usa la imaginación y la lógica para intentar contestar las siguientes preguntas.

1. ¿Sabes cómo se llama ese tipo de sombrero?
2. ¿Quiénes hacen esos sombreros?
3. ¿Dónde crees que los hagan?
4. ¿Cuánto tiempo lleva hacer un sombrero bueno? ¿Y uno muy bueno?
5. ¿Dónde se venden y cuánto cuestan?

Parte B: Ahora, para confirmar tus predicciones, escucha la entrevista. Busca también la respuesta a las siguientes preguntas.

1. ¿En qué momento del día se hacen esos sombreros y por qué?
2. ¿Quiénes reciben la mayor parte del dinero de la venta de los sombreros?

Actividad 2 La interpretación En la entrevista, la Sra. Gómez le comenta al locutor del programa que la hija y la nieta de una artesana no están interesadas en continuar esta tradición porque "Ud. ya sabe cómo son los jóvenes". ¿Qué quiere decir con esa frase?

Practice expressions by creating a context: Write expressions on the board. Tell about a real or fictitious person who has been an artist for the last ten years: **Hace diez años que pinta... pero antes trabajaba en una corporación y ganaba un dineral. Cuando dejó su trabajo, la gente decía "¡Qué barbaridad!"** (etc.) Explain how it was a good move because **se le fueron las ganas de ir a la oficina, pero le llevó mucho tiempo tomar esa decisión.** End the story, then continue to practice expressions by asking questions such as in which professions people earn **un dineral.**

Act. 1A: Refer students to the photos of the hat when answering these questions. They are not expected to give correct answers. Wild guesses are fine.

Act. 1B: Play the interview and go over questions in 1A again and the questions in 1B. Answers for 1A: 1. **sombrero panamá** 2. **aproximadamente veinte personas mayores** 3. **en Ecuador** 4. **dos meses** (**los buenos**), **ocho meses** (**los mejores**) 5. **Nueva York y Hawai; US $350–$750** (**los buenos**), **US $10.000** (**los mejores**). Answers for 1B: 1. **por la noche pues la transpiración puede echar a perder la paja** 2. **los intermediarios**

Act. 2: Whole class activity or pairs. Encourage opinions about the loss of arts with the passing of generations. Ask students what their favorite dish is that their grandmother or grandfather prepares and if they know the recipe. This may help spark discussion at a more personal level.

Los sombreros panamá

¿Lo sabían?

▲ Bolsas otavaleñas.

Entre los artesanos de Hispanoamérica se destacan los otavalos, un grupo indígena de Ecuador que produce mantas y telas. En 1966, los otavalos abrieron su primera tienda propia y sólo doce años después ya tenían setenta y cinco tiendas. Hoy en día, se dedican a la exportación de sus productos a otros países, especialmente a Europa, Canadá y los Estados Unidos. Por ser tan industriosos y buenos comerciantes, se considera a los otavalos como uno de los grupos indígenas más prósperos de Hispanoamérica. ¿Puedes mencionar artesanías que se hacen en tu país y explicar quiénes las hacen?

www *Los otavalos*

While discussing artisans and their work, you may want to focus on how they are frequently exploited by vendors and on the existence of organizations that ensure the artisans, particularly in third world nations, will receive a larger portion of the monies. Ask what **artesanía** is produced in the U.S.: Native American beadwork (**artesanías con cuentas**), Kachina dolls, birch bark canoes (**canoas de corteza de abedul**), Amish quilts, etc. Many artisans also produce tools or items related to farming, cooking, or other such activities.

I. Discussing Art

www Do the corresponding CD-ROM and web activities as you study the chapter.

El arte

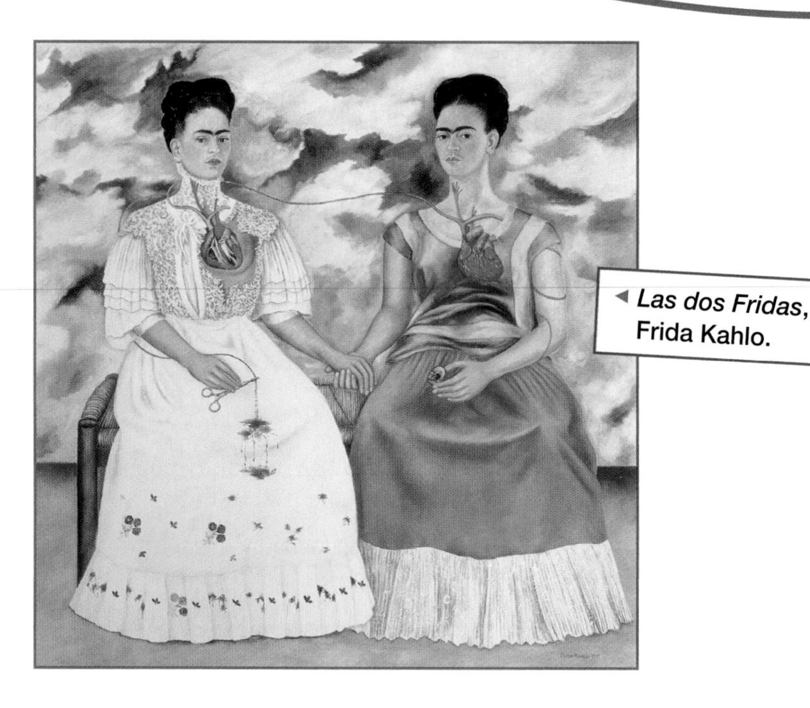

◀ *Las dos Fridas*, Frida Kahlo.

Fuente hispana

masterpieces — source of inspiration — self-portrait

"No entiendo mucho de arte, pero hay algunas **obras maestras** que me encanta ver una y otra vez. Entre ellas están el *Guernica* del pintor español Picasso y *Las dos Fridas* de la mexicana Frida Kahlo. Para el primero, **la fuente de inspiración** fue el ataque aéreo a una ciudad de España y el otro es **un autorretrato** de una artista que tuvo un accidente muy grande de niña que la afectó durante toda la vida. Ambas pinturas son muy tristes, pero tienen una energía increíble. Por lo general, **las naturalezas muertas** me aburren porque me parecen siempre muy parecidas unas a otras y **las obras abstractas** no las entiendo y no las puedo **interpretar**."

venezolana

still lifes
abstract works
to interpret

La obra de arte

la imagen	
el paisaje	landscape
la reproducción	
el retrato	portrait
la burla, burlarse de...	mockery, to mock/joke (make fun of)
expresar	
glorificar	to glorify
el mensaje	message
la sátira	satire
el símbolo, el simbolismo, simbolizar	

Apreciación del arte

la censura, el censor, censurar	
la crítica; el crítico; criticar	critique; critic; to critique, to criticize
la interpretación	

Expresiones para hablar de un cuadro

¿Qué te parece (este cuadro)?	What do you think (about this painting)?
No tiene ni pies ni cabeza.	I can't make heads or tails of it.
No tiene (ningún) sentido para mí.	It doesn't make (any) sense to me.
Qué maravilla.	How marvelous.
Qué horrible.	How horrible.
(No) Me conmueve.	It moves/doesn't move me.
Me siento triste/contento/a al verlo.	I feel sad/happy when I see it.
Ni me va ni me viene. / Ni fu ni fa.	It doesn't do anything for me.

El arte, when singular, generally takes masculine adjectives: **el arte moderno.** When plural, it takes feminine modifiers: **las bellas artes.**

Algunos movimientos artísticos: abstracto, barroco, cubismo, impresionismo, realismo.

Basic art vocabulary is presented in Appendix G.

Review basics (**pincel, escultura, esculpir, dibujar, la escena, pintar, mural**) or expand vocabulary depending on level or class interest (**primer plano, fondo, artesano**).

Actividad 3 Categorías Asocia las siguientes personas o instituciones con un mínimo de tres palabras de la lista de vocabulario y explica por qué elegiste esas palabras.

1. un crítico
2. una artista
3. el gobierno
4. una actriz
5. un comediante
6. una universidad

Act. 3: Whole class activity or pairs. Accept any association students give as long as they can justify the more obscure choices.

Act. 4: Whole class activity or pairs. Answers: **blanco = pureza; rojo = violencia/pasión; calavera = muerte; cruz = religión; paloma = paz; verde = esperanza.**

Actividad 4 Los símbolos Las obras de arte están llenas de símbolos y mensajes. Habla del simbolismo en el arte combinando un símbolo con un concepto.

▶ El color blanco representa/simboliza... porque...

Símbolos	Conceptos
el color blanco	la muerte
el color rojo	la esperanza
una calavera	la religión
una cruz	la paz
una paloma (*dove*)	la pureza
el color verde	la violencia, la pasión

calavera

Actividad 5 ¿Qué te parecen? En parejas, miren todas las obras de arte que hay en este capítulo y usen las expresiones que se presentan en la sección de arte para hablar de los cuadros. Expliquen por qué hacen esos comentarios.

Act. 6: With books closed, see if students can say where the painters mentioned in the activity are from; say the name of the work and see if they can say who painted/sculpted it. Then have students open their text. Form groups of three, explain the premise of the activity, and begin. All students are not expected to know all responses. Check by having volunteers say where they think the works of art are located. If possible, bring in pictures of the works mentioned.

La Mona Lisa también se llama *La Gioconda*.

Act. 6: Answers: ***El David*/Galería de la Academia; *La piedad*/el Vaticano; *La vista de Toledo*/Museo Metropolitano; *La maja vestida*/El Prado; *Guernica*/Centro Reina Sofía; *La Mona Lisa*/El Louvre; *El pensador*/Museo Rodin; *Hispanoamérica*/La Universidad de Dartmouth.**

Actividad 6 ¿Dónde están? En grupos de tres, digan dónde están las siguientes obras maestras. Usen expresiones como: **Estoy seguro/a de que..., la obra maestra de** (*nombre del artista*), **está en... / Sé que no... /** (**No**) **es posible que... /** (**No**) **creo que...**

Obra maestra	Lugar
El David / Miguel Ángel	la Galería de la Academia en Florencia
La piedad / Miguel Ángel	el Museo Rodin en París
La vista de Toledo / El Greco	la Universidad de Dartmouth en New Hampshire
La maja vestida / Goya	el Centro Reina Sofía en Madrid
Guernica / Picasso	el Louvre en París
La Mona Lisa / da Vinci	el Museo Metropolitano en Nueva York
El pensador / Rodin	el Vaticano
Hispanoamérica / Orozco	el Museo del Prado en Madrid

Using the last item in Act. 6, discuss Orozco as a muralist as a lead-in to this reading. Bring photos of murals to give students an idea of the topics and style of these murals. To expand, ask if there are any murals at the university or in their city and what their contents are.

¿LO SABÍAN?

En 1923, un grupo de artistas mexicanos que habían vivido bajo la dictadura de Porfirio Díaz y habían pasado por un período revolucionario cuando eran estudiantes de arte, formaron un sindicato de pintores y escultores. Entre ellos estaban los famosos muralistas Diego Rivera, David Alfaro Siqueiros y José Clemente Orozco. Debido a que este sindicato apoyaba el papel revolucionario del nuevo gobierno, éste les ofreció a los pintores diferentes muros (*walls*) de la ciudad y de edificios públicos para que hicieran pinturas sobre ellas. Así comenzó el movimiento llamado *Muralismo*, el primero de la historia que desarrolló temas sociopolíticos en la pintura.

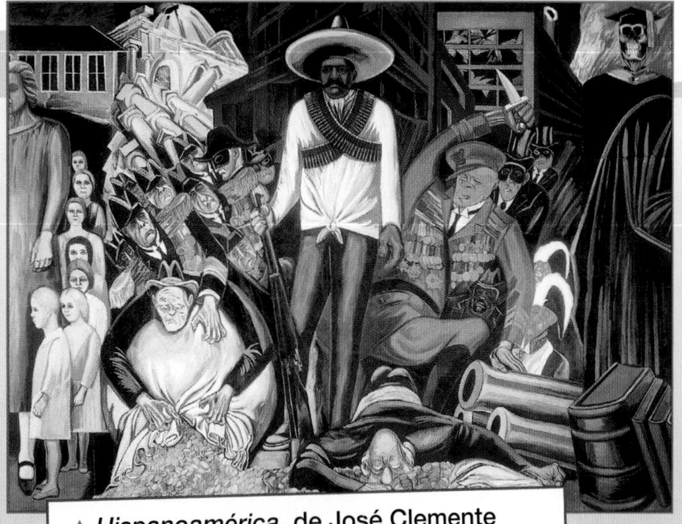

▲ *Hispanoamérica*, de José Clemente Orozoco, se encuentra en la Universidad de Dartmouth en New Hampshire.

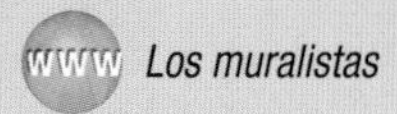 *Los muralistas*

Actividad 7 El arte en California Mucha gente cree, erróneamente, que el arte de los artistas mexicoamericanos en los Estados Unidos ha recibido influencia del arte hispanoamericano en general. La mayor influencia que se encuentra en el arte mexicoamericano es la de los muralistas mexicanos. En parejas, comparen el siguiente mural de una artista chicana con el del **¿Lo sabían?** Usen palabras de la lista de vocabulario para decir en qué se parecen y en qué se diferencian.

Act. 7: Encourage students to use their powers of observation in this discussion of themes. *La ofrenda* features Dolores Huerta, a leader of United Farmer Workers Union (she was discussed in Chapter 5). Yreina Cervantez (1952–) is a painter, printmaker, and teacher born in Kansas and raised near San Diego.

◀ Parte del mural *La ofrenda*, Yreina Cervantez.

¿LO SABÍAN?

 *Murales en Los Ángeles*

Algunas ciudades de los Estados Unidos poseen una gran cantidad de murales. Una de estas ciudades es Los Ángeles.

"La ciudad de Los Ángeles posee una colección de más de mil murales. Algunos de ellos son de los años 20 cuando creció la ciudad y eran realizados en edificios públicos como cines y correos. Durante los años 40, la ciudad les encargó murales a los artistas como una forma de crear trabajo después de la Gran Depresión. Hacia fines de los 80, se comenzó un proyecto de comisionar murales tratando de retomar la tradición muralista mexicana. Ya que muchos de los murales que posee la ciudad están en lugares al aire libre como la pared externa de algún edificio o debajo de algún puente en una autopista, éstos se ven afectados por el sol y la contaminación ambiental y, como consecuencia, se deterioran. Se necesita entonces la intervención de un grupo de restauradores, gente que se ocupa de limpiar y reconstruir las partes deterioradas. Luego de horas y horas de trabajo intenso, se cubre el mural con una capa de protección antigrafiti. De ese modo, si alguien trata de pintarlo con grafiti otra vez, esta pintura se quitará con mucha facilidad."

argentina, restauradora de murales en Los Ángeles

In order to prepare for this activity, use the chapter links given on the *Fuentes* website or do your searches in Spanish. Instead of just searching for Frida Kahlo, add a Spanish word to your search such as **pintura, accidente, cuadro**, etc. or use a search engine like Google and then select "Spanish Language."

Act. 8: *Guernica* is in the Museo Centro de Arte Reina Sofía in Madrid. *Las dos Fridas* is in the Museo de Arte Moderno in Mexico City.

Actividad 8 La historia tras el cuadro En la introducción a esta sección de arte, una venezolana menciona que algunas de sus obras favoritas son *Guernica* y *Las dos Fridas*. Para la próxima clase debes traer una foto de *Guernica* (el otro cuadro está en la página 224). También debes buscar la siguiente información y prepararte para explicar qué quería cada artista que entendiéramos al mirar su obra.

- qué ocurrió en la ciudad de Guernica, España
- qué accidente tuvo Frida Kahlo
- en qué ciudades se encuentran hoy día estas obras de arte

Act. 9: Could be assigned as HW and/or done in class in pairs. Encourage students to be as specific as possible in their answers. Check by asking for different opinions. Question 5: Some famous American logos are the Nike swoosh, the CBS eye, and the NBC peacock.
Note: **el grafiti** = **la pintada** (*Spain*).

Actividad 9 ¿Qué es realmente arte? En parejas, discutan estas preguntas sobre el arte.

1. ¿Cuál es la diferencia entre arte y artesanía?
2. Cuando un niño hace un dibujo, ¿se considera arte?
3. ¿Cuál es la diferencia entre un grafiti y un mural? ¿Conocen a alguien que haya pintado grafiti? ¿Cómo era el grafiti y dónde lo pintó?
4. Muchos artistas de tiras cómicas (*comic strips*) usan sátira o se burlan de algo, pero existen periódicos que censuran esas tiras cómicas y no las publican. ¿Cuándo y por qué creen que los periódicos hacen eso? ¿Cuál es su tira cómica favorita y por qué?

(continúa en la página siguiente)

5. Otro tipo de arte es el diseño gráfico. Las empresas gastan un dineral en crear sus logotipos (*logos*). ¿Qué logotipos les gustan? ¿Simbolizan algo en especial? Miren los logotipos que se presentan aquí y digan qué simbolizan y qué promocionan.

Actividad 10 El arte en la ropa Camiseta, un par de jeans y zapatos de tenis es la vestimenta más común que llevan los jóvenes de hoy. En parejas, averigüen qué tipo de mensajes tienen las camisetas que Uds. generalmente llevan. Sigan el modelo.

► —¿Tienes alguna camiseta que tenga una imagen simbólica?

—Sí, tengo una con la paloma de la paz de Picasso.

—No, no tengo ninguna que tenga una imagen simbólica.

1. tener una imagen simbólica
2. tener un mensaje político o ecológico
3. glorificar la universidad, un equipo deportivo, etc.
4. criticar algo directamente
5. hacer sátira de algo
6. tener una obra de arte
7. tener algo gracioso

Act. 10: If students are wearing T-shirts, start by commenting on their content. If you have different T-shirts, bring them in and comment on them. Before beginning the activity, you may want to have students quickly jot down what T-shirts they own. After introducing the theme, form pairs and check by seeing what types of T-shirts people own.

Actividad 11 La comunicación El artista suele querer transmitir algo a los que ven su obra y, de hecho (*in fact*), el arte se usa muchas veces para contar una historia. En parejas, miren el siguiente cuadro y digan qué historia quiere contar el artista.

Act. 11: Form groups. Check by discussing students' responses. In *Mujeres de Tehuantepec* one can see the influence of cubism on Tamayo's art, which the artist combines with his Mexican roots.

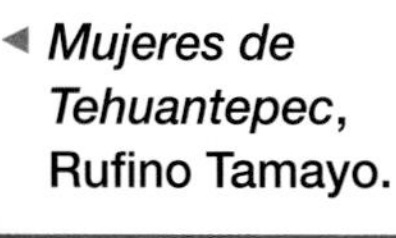
◄ ***Mujeres de Tehuantepec*, Rufino Tamayo.**

Act. 12: Form groups of three and have students discuss their impressions. When finished, have a give-and-take of perceptions between groups.

Actividad 12 Críticos de arte En grupos de tres, miren el cuadro que está abajo y después discutan las siguientes ideas.

1. su reacción al mirar el cuadro
2. por qué tienen esa reacción
3. todos los detalles que hay en el cuadro: la luz, las sombras, las figuras, las líneas diagonales y las curvas, los colores
4. cuál creen que haya sido la fuente de inspiración de la artista
5. cuál es el mensaje de este cuadro

▲ *Sueño y premonición*, María Izquierdo (México).

Before reading this **¿Lo sabían?** ask students to tell you all the famous artists they can name. Do this as a class shout-out and write the names on the board. Without telling the students what you are doing, put men on one side of the board and women on the other. The latter list should be quite short. Without further comment, have them read the information. You may want to show works by the artists mentioned.

¿Lo sabían?

Durante muchos siglos las artes estuvieron dominadas por los hombres. En general, ellos eran quienes las patrocinaban (*sponsored*) y quienes tenían fama mundial. Actualmente se reconocen las contribuciones de las artistas también. Entre las más conocidas de Hispanoamérica se encuentran las mexicanas Frida Kahlo (1907–1954) y María Izquierdo (1902–1955), que lograron reconocimiento gracias a su conexión con Diego Rivera. Otras artistas conocidas en la actualidad son Lidy Prati (1921–) y Liliana Porter (1941–), ambas argentinas, la venezolana Marisol (1930–), la colombiana Ana Mercedes Hoyos (1942–) y la cubana Ana Mendieta (1948–1985). Intenta nombrar alguna artista norteamericana famosa del pasado o del presente. ¿Qué sabes sobre ella?

II. Expressing Past Influence, Emotions, and Other Feelings and Reactions

The Imperfect Subjunctive

In previous chapters you learned many uses of the subjunctive:

Chapter 5: influencing, suggesting, persuading, and advising
Chapter 6: expressing feelings, emotions, opinions, belief, and doubt
Chapter 7: describing the unknown and expressing pending actions
Chapter 8: expressing restriction, possibility, purpose, and time

In this chapter you will learn how to express all of the preceding uses, but in reference to the past. In the interview you heard, the Panama hat expert used the imperfect subjunctive when she discussed an artisan's past desire that her daughter and granddaughter learn to make the hats: **"Había una artesana que quería que su hija y su nieta *aprendieran* [este arte]."**

1. To form the imperfect subjunctive (**imperfecto del subjuntivo**), use the third person plural of the preterit, drop the **-ron** ending, and add the following subjunctive endings. To review formation of the preterit, see Appendix A, pages 341–343.

pagar → paga~~ron~~		**poder → pudie~~ron~~**		**pedir → pidie~~ron~~**	
pagar**a**	pagá**ramos**	pudier**a**	pudié**ramos**	pidier**a**	pidié**ramos**
pagar**as**	pagar**ais**	pudier**as**	pudier**ais**	pidier**as**	pidier**ais**
pagar**a**	pagar**an**	pudier**a**	pudier**an**	pidier**a**	pidier**an**

Note: There is an optional form, frequently used in Spain and in some areas of Hispanic America, in which you substitute **-se** for **-ra;** for example: **pagara = pagase; pidiéramos = pidiésemos.**

2. Once you have determined that a subjunctive form is needed, you must decide which of the following forms to use.

present subjunctive	**que compre, que compres,** etc.
present perf. subjunctive	**que haya comprado, que hayas comprado,** etc.
imperfect subjunctive	**que comprara, que compraras,** etc.

FLR link: **Lectura 3**

Review uses of present subjunctive.

Drill the imperfect subjunctive:

1. Make statements about the present and have students change them to the past: **Busco un novio que sea inteligente... Quiero que su familia me conozca. Debe saber que estoy enojada sin que yo se lo diga. Dudo que encuentre una persona así. No hay nadie que sea así.** (etc.)

2. Have students state what they wanted or hoped for about the university before they came, based on cues such as **las clases son fáciles, hay pocos exámenes, los profesores son excelentes, los libros son baratos.** Ss: **Esperaba que las clases fueran fáciles.** (etc.)

3. Have students finish ideas about when they were in high school: **Siempre dudaba que..., Buscaba novios/as que..., Quería que mis amigos..., No había ningún estudiante que...** Contrast with indicative: **Había estudiantes que...**

You may want to point out it is possible to use the imp. subj. instead of the pres. perf. subj. when using the present tense in the independent clause, if the action referred to in the dependent clause is in the distant past: **Mucha gente duda que Cristóbal Colón fuera italiano.**

Use the following guidelines to determine which form is needed.

a. As you studied in previous chapters, when the verb in the independent clause refers to the present or the future, you use the present subjunctive in the dependent clause to refer to a present or future action or state.

	Independent Clause Present/Future	Dependent Clause Present Subjunctive (Present/Future Reference)
Influencing: Chapter 5	Mi jefe **va a querer** *My boss is going to want*	que yo **trabaje** en su estudio de arte. *me to work in his art studio.*
Indirect commands: Chapter 5	**Te dice** *He's telling you*	que **traigas** las esculturas. *to bring the sculptures.*
Feelings: Chapter 6	**Me alegra** *I'm glad*	que el museo **abra** temprano. *that the museum opens early.*
Unknown: Chapter 7	**Buscamos** un diseño *We are looking for a design*	que **sea** moderno. *that is modern.*
Pending actions: Chapter 7	**Quiero vender** mi cuadro *I want to sell my painting*	**en cuanto termine** de pintarlo. *as soon as I finish painting it.*
Time: Chapter 8	¿**Vas a reescribir** el contrato *Are you going to rewrite the contract*	**antes de que lleguen?** *before they arrive?*

b. As you studied in Chapter 6, when the verb in the independent clause refers to the present and the dependent clause refers to a past action or state, you use the present perfect subjunctive in the latter.

	Independent Clause Present	Dependent Clause Present Perfect Subjunctive (Past Reference)
Doubt: Chapter 6	**Es probable** *It's probable*	que el artesano **haya visto** ese cuadro. *that the artisan has seen the painting.*
Feelings: Chapter 6	No **me sorprende** *It doesn't surprise me*	que **hayan censurado** tu cuadro. *that they have censored your painting.*

c. When the verb in the independent clause is in a past tense and the dependent clause refers to a past action or state, use the imperfect subjunctive in the dependent clause.

	Independent Clause Past	Dependent Clause Imperfect Subjunctive (Past/Past Pending Reference)
Influencing: Chapter 5	Ella me **aconsejó** *She advised me*	que **comprara** esa reproducción. *to buy that reproduction.*
Doubt: Chapter 6	Nosotros **dudábamos** *We doubted*	que la pintura **fuera** auténtica. *that the painting was authentic.*
Unknown: Chapter 7	**Quería** un sombrero panamá *I wanted a Panama hat*	que no **costara** un dineral. *that didn't cost a fortune.*

Estudió muchísimo *She studied a lot*	**para que** la **admitieran** en la escuela de Bellas Artes *so that they would admit her to the School of Fine Arts.*	Purpose: Chapter 8
Le **iba a hablar** *I was going to talk to him*	**cuando** él **llegara** a casa. *when he arrived home.*	Pending Action: Chapter 7

Act. 13A: Assign as HW and check in class. If possible, bring a photo of *The Family of Carlos IV* by Goya.

Museo del Prado

Actividad 13 El arte del pasado **Parte A:** Lee la siguiente información sobre el arte en España y elige el verbo y la forma correcta del imperfecto del subjuntivo para completar cada espacio en blanco.

admirar
aprender
comenzar
hacer
parecer
pintar
representar
tener
utilizar

Antes de la Primera Guerra Mundial (1914–1918), existía en España el llamado arte oficial. El rey contrataba pintores para su corte y les indicaba lo que quería que ellos ___hicieran/pintaran___. En general, antes de que el artista ___comenzara/hiciera___ su trabajo, se hacía un contrato en el cual se especificaba quiénes aparecerían en la pintura y qué estilo y materiales se esperaba que el pintor ___utilizara___. No había muchos pintores famosos que ___tuvieran___ la oportunidad de expresar sus propias ideas, ya que el artista seguía el estilo de la corte. Dos excepciones fueron Diego Velázquez (1599–1660) y Francisco de Goya (1746–1828) que lograron expresarse y, a la vez, complacer a sus reyes al hacer lo que éstos querían que ellos ___hicieran/pintaran___. Velázquez retrató no sólo a la familia real, sino también a los bufones (*buffoons*) de la corte. Entre sus obras famosas se encuentra *Las meninas.* Goya se hizo famoso por el realismo de sus retratos de la familia real, en los cuales no hizo nada para que los miembros de la familia ___parecieran___ físicamente más atractivos de lo que en realidad eran. Uno de sus cuadros más conocidos es *La familia de Carlos IV.*

Había también, por otro lado, un arte llamado religioso comisionado por la Iglesia. Ésta contrataba a artistas para que ___representaran/pintaran___ escenas de la Biblia. Casi siempre estas escenas eran descriptivas y dramáticas y con ellas la Iglesia buscaba que el pueblo ___aprendiera___ el contenido de las Sagradas Escrituras.

Después de la Segunda Guerra Mundial (1939–1945), hubo en España una reacción contra lo oficialmente establecido y los artistas querían que la gente ___admirara___ su individualismo. Es así como aparecieron múltiples estilos de pintura que más tarde se llevaron al continente americano donde influyeron en los diversos estilos artísticos.

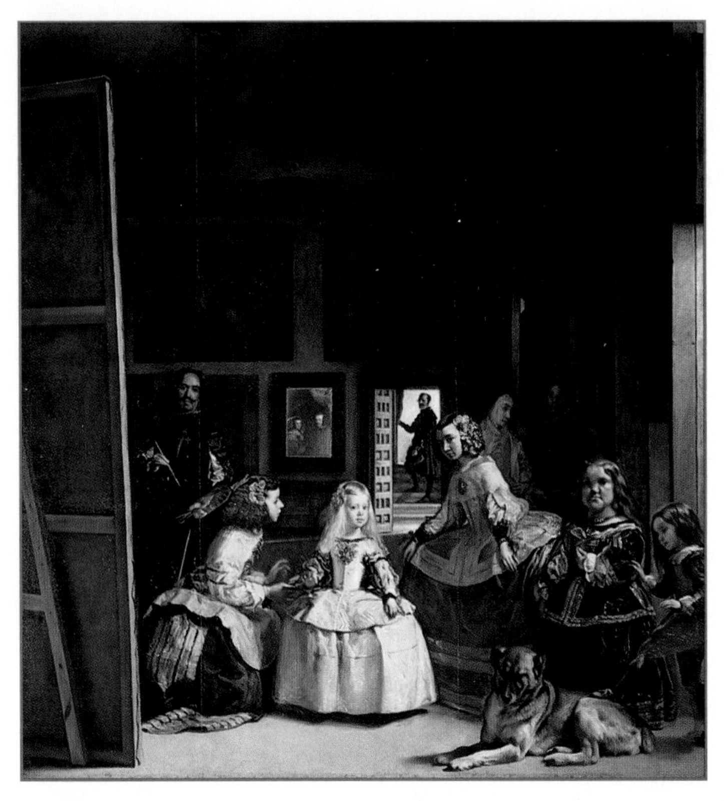

Parte B: En parejas, miren el cuadro de Velázquez, *Las meninas*, y contesten estas preguntas.

1. ¿A cuántas personas pintó Velázquez en este cuadro?
2. ¿Pueden encontrar al artista en el cuadro? ¿Hacia dónde mira?
3. Sabiendo que Velázquez pintó a los reyes y a la Infanta (*Princess*) Margarita en el cuadro, ¿puedes encontrarlos?
4. ¿Quiénes quería el pintor que fueran las personas principales, la infanta o los reyes?
5. ¿Pueden encontrar a los bufones?
6. ¿Es una pintura estática o hay movimiento?
7. ¿Pueden deducir algo sobre la vida diaria del palacio real?

Act. 13B: Form pairs, set a brief time limit, and check by calling on individuals. You may want to bring in photos of some works by Goya and Velázquez, especially *Las meninas* (in the Prado Museum in Madrid). It measures 125 3/16 inches in height by 108 1/8 inches in width. All but one character in the painting have been identified by art historians. The young child in the center is the Princess Margarita. There are two dwarfs at the right. The reflections of Felipe IV and his second wife, María Ana de Austria, can be seen in the mirror in the center of the painting. Velázquez is looking out of the painting at the king and queen who are observing the scene being painted.

Act. 14A: Assign as HW and check in class.

Act. 14B: Model by discussing possibilities for the first sentence or two. Form pairs, set a time limit, and begin. Check by calling on a few volunteers to discuss a few sentences.

Actividad 14 Se oyó en un museo **Parte A:** Estás en un museo y escuchas las siguientes frases que dicen algunas personas que están a tu alrededor. Complétalas con el presente del subjuntivo, el pretérito perfecto del subjuntivo o el imperfecto del subjuntivo de los verbos entre paréntesis.

1. Me alegré de que IBM me ___contratara___. (contratar)
2. Nos rogó que lo ___hiciéramos___ lo antes posible. (hacer)
3. Dudo que ayer ella los ___haya convencido___. (convencer)
4. Sentí mucho que tú no ___pudieras___ ir al picnic. (poder)
5. Les recomendé que ___vinieran___ a las doce. (venir)
6. Quiero que mañana tú ___invites___ a los Ramírez a comer en el mejor restaurante. (invitar)
7. ¿Crees que nosotros ___vendamos___ algunos en la exhibición de mañana? (vender)
8. La policía dice que no hay nadie que lo ___haya visto___. (ver)
9. Lo hizo sin que tú ___estuvieras___ presente. (estar)
10. Ella no iba a descansar hasta que la ___terminara___. (terminar)

Parte B: Ahora, en parejas, usen la imaginación y creen un contexto para cinco o seis de las frases. El contexto debe contener la siguiente información.

- quién la dijo
- a quién se la dijo
- en referencia a qué

Usen expresiones como: **Es posible/probable que se la haya dicho... a... porque...**

Actividad 15 Las exigencias de nuestros padres **Parte A:** Cuando Uds. estaban en la escuela secundaria, probablemente escuchaban muchas exigencias de sus padres. En parejas, túrnense para decir si éstas eran o no algunas de las exigencias de sus padres. Para formar oraciones, combinen una frase de la primera columna con una de la segunda. Sigan el modelo.

Act. 15A: As a review, point out the use of the imperfect for describing habitual actions in the past. If practice is needed before beginning, have students simply form sentences or questions using any logical verb from the first column and a phrase from the second. Then form pairs, model the activity, and begin. Check by finding out what was the number one item about which parents were concerned.

▶ exigirle / volver a casa temprano

—¿Te exigían tus padres que volvieras a casa temprano?

—Sí, mis padres me exigían que volviera a casa temprano.

—No, mis padres no me exigían que volviera a casa temprano.

preferir	(no) poner la música a todo volumen
insistir en	sacar buenas notas en la escuela
esperar	(no) andar con malas compañías
exigirle	hacer la cama
recomendarle	(no) ver mucha televisión
prohibirle	(no) pelearse con su hermana/o
pedirle	(no) beber alcohol
(no) querer	(no) consumir drogas
	(no) hacerse tatuajes
	? ? ?

Parte B: En parejas, hablen de las exigencias que les hacen sus padres ahora. ¿Son iguales a las que les hacían cuando estaban en la secundaria o diferentes? Usen oraciones como: **Cuando era menor me exigían que..., pero/y ahora insisten en que...**

Act. 15B: Model possible sentences, form pairs, and begin. Check by asking what parents say and list the advice on the board in three columns: **muy válido, válido, absurdo.**

Actividad 16 Era importante que... Di qué cosas de la siguiente lista eran o no importantes para ti cuando tenías diez años. Usa expresiones como: **(no) interesarle, (no) querer, (no) ser importante.**

Remember: if you have no change of subject, use the infinitive.

Act. 16: First, have students say what things are important for ten-year-olds. Then, form pairs, model the activity, set a time limit, and begin. Check by polling students: **¿A cuántos de Uds. les interesaba que sus amigos fueran populares? ¿Es más o menos importante que sus amigos sean populares ahora que cuando eran menores?**

▶ tus amigos / ser / populares
Cuando tenía diez años, me interesaba que mis amigos fueran populares.

1. tener muchas cosas
2. tus amigos / respetarte
3. llevar ropa de moda
4. tus padres / estar / orgullosos de ti
5. cuidar el físico
6. fumar
7. tus maestros / no darte / mucha tarea
8. tener muchos amigos
9. tus hermanos / no tocar / tus cosas
10. ? ? ?

Act. 17: Do in groups of three or as a whole class activity.

Actividad 17 Tus amigos de la secundaria En grupos de tres, digan qué tipo de amigos querían tener y tenían cuando estaban en la escuela secundaria. Pueden usar las siguientes ideas. Sigan el modelo.

▶ Tenía amigos que no consumían drogas.

▶ Buscaba amigos que fueran cómicos.

(no) hablar mal de ti	(no) tener carro
(no) practicar deportes	(no) chismear (*gossip*)
(no) tener mucho dinero	(no) estudiar mucho
(no) vivir cerca de ti	(no) ser divertidos
(no) gustarles fumar	???

Act. 18: Have students glance at phrases in the text and brainstorm good and bad things a boss wants employees to do. Set up the premise, form pairs, and begin. Check by asking for examples of what good and bad bosses do.

Actividad 18 Los mejores y los peores En parejas, terminen estas frases para hablar de los mejores y peores trabajos que han tenido.

Los trabajos terribles	**Los trabajos fantásticos**
El/La jefe/a siempre quería que nosotros...	El/La jefe/a siempre quería que nosotros...
Nos exigía que...	Nos exigía que...
Nos prohibía que...	Nos prohibía que...
Me molestaba que mi jefe/a...	Me encantaba que mi jefe/a...
Siempre hacía/decía... para que...	Siempre hacía/decía... para que...

Act. 19: Form pairs or do as a whole class. Expand by asking students to create other similar sentences. Encourage students to engage in connected discourse.

Actividad 19 Creencias del pasado Forma oraciones para expresar las creencias falsas que tenía la gente en el pasado y contrástalas con lo que se sabe ahora. Sigue el modelo.

▶ no creer / el insecticida DDT / causar / problemas para el ser humano
—En el pasado la gente no creía que el insecticida DDT causara problemas para el ser humano.
—Es verdad, pero ahora sabemos que...

1. no creer / el asbesto / ser / peligroso para el ser humano
2. estar segura / la tierra / ser / plana
3. creer / el consumo de muchas proteínas / ser / bueno para la salud
4. no creer / la cocaína / ser / una droga
5. dudar / el hombre / poder / volar

Act. 20A: Encourage students to make guesses about the content of the painting and its artist. Check by asking individuals their opinion. They may disagree with each other. Encourage people to justify their responses. Remember: there are no right or wrong responses, only opinions.

Actividad 20 La hipótesis del cuadro **Parte A:** En grupos de tres, miren el cuadro de la página 237 y contesten las preguntas para formar una hipótesis sobre su contenido y su historia.

1. ¿Es una escena estática o hay movimiento? Den ejemplos para justificar su respuesta.
2. ¿En qué año más o menos creen Uds. que el/la artista haya pintado el cuadro?
3. ¿De qué país creen que sea este cuadro?

4. ¿Creen que lo haya pintado un hombre o una mujer? ¿Por qué?
5. La persona que pintó el cuadro usaba modelos al pintar. Para encontrar sus modelos, ¿buscaba personas que fueran de la alta sociedad, de la clase media, de la clase baja o personas marginadas de la sociedad? Justifiquen su respuesta.
6. ¿Quién es la figura central del cuadro? ¿Cómo era? ¿Qué hacía un día normal?
7. ¿Qué quería el/la artista que sintiéramos al ver esta escena: tristeza, orgullo, felicidad, melancolía? ¿Algo más? Justifiquen su respuesta.

Parte B: Ahora escuchen la información que les va a dar su profesor/a sobre el cuadro para ver qué adivinaron de la Parte A.

Act. 20B: Inform students about the painting *Las alegrías*: Julio Romero de Torres; Córdoba, Spain (1874–1930); became famous when his painting *Vividoras del amor* was censored for being immoral (a scene in a brothel); he frequently used gypsy women as models for his work. Gypsies were considered **marginados.** In *Las alegrías*, painted in 1917, the symbol of the Andalusian soul is expressed through flamenco. The main character is the Catalán gypsy, Julia Borrull; the woman clapping is a gypsy from Córdoba, as is the guitar player. Romero's paintings and his own image have been used on stamps and prior to the euros on the 100 peseta bill.

Actividad 21 Interpretación de un cuadro **Parte A:** Mira el cuadro de la página 238 y lee qué dijo un colombiano al verlo. Luego prepárate para hablar de la información que aparece después de la descripción.

Botero

"Me acuerdo del día en que visité el Museo Nacional de los Estados Unidos en Washington, D.C. Fui con unos parientes que me estaban visitando y por accidente nos metimos donde se estaban exponiendo los óleos del pintor colombiano Fernando Botero.

Lo que estaba viendo en ese momento me fascinó. Parecía que el maestro había pintado a mi familia. Allí, en el lienzo, claramente podía yo ver a mi papá vestido de modo muy conservador; a mi tío, el coronel, quien era miembro del ejército colombiano, que resplandecía con sus medallas e imponía una sensación de firmeza; a mi primo, el cura, quien había estudiado en Roma y decían que iba ser arzobispo dentro de muy poco tiempo, lo había pintado como una figura humilde y sencilla. Mi madre, a quien Botero había pintado en el centro del cuadro, estaba bien vestida y mantenía una expresión serena, pero a la misma vez aburrida; a la izquierda del cuadro, estaba mi abuela, quien sostenía a mi hermana menor. Mi abuela era idéntica a mi papá. Mi hermana sentada sobre mi abuela, se veía bellísima, pero también tenía esa mirada aburrida que mantenía mi mamá. Podía ser que ya se hubieran dado cuenta de los límites que la sociedad les estaba imponiendo. Yo también estaba en ese cuadro insolente, el pintor me había colocado detrás de todos, medio escondido porque yo era el escándalo de la familia. Mi padre quería que yo fuera abogado o

Act. 21A: Ask students the name of the painting, the artist, and where the painting is located. Then allow time to read the description, and finally have students discuss the two points presented. Have them describe the seven persons the Colombian saw in the painting. Note: This is a true account of a Colombian's reaction to the painting. You may want to discuss how Botero's painting and the commentator's family reflect some of the major factions of Colombian society.

médico, pero en cambio, yo salí del país y me fui a los Estados Unidos a estudiar literatura.

Y al fondo del cuadro, Botero había pintado la gran cordillera de los Andes, algo que me hacía falta aquí en Washington D.C., porque todo era plano en esta ciudad. Salí del museo queriendo agradecerle a Botero por haberle mostrado al mundo una parte de mi identidad colombiana."

colombiano

1. Describe otro elemento del cuadro, algo que no menciona el colombiano.
2. Explica de qué modo muestra el cuadro la identidad colombiana del hombre que lo describe.

◄ ***La familia presidencial*, Fernando Botero.**

Act. 21B: After finishing, you may want to have a group role play the situation for the rest of the class.

Parte B: Ahora en grupos de tres, haga uno el papel del joven colombiano y los otros dos el papel de los padres y representen el día en que el hijo les dice a sus padres que se va a estudiar literatura a los Estados Unidos.

Parte C: En parejas, imaginen que están en una galería de arte y ven el siguiente cuadro que les recuerda a su familia. Escojan quiénes son Uds. en el cuadro y describan qué sintieron al ver el cuadro y qué miembros de su familia estaban presentes. Miren la descripción del colombiano como referencia.

◄ ***La tamalada*, Camen Lomas Garza, mexicoamericana (1948–).**

III. Shifting the Focus in a Sentence

The Passive Voice

FLR link: **Lectura 2**

Drill passive voice:

Have students change the following ideas to passive voice: **La galería va a exponer las obras de Botero. Los expertos publicaron una crítica. El gobierno censuró la escultura. El gobierno patrocina a artistas jóvenes.** (etc.)

Many sentences you have dealt with up to this point have been in the active voice (**la voz activa**). That is to say that the subject (agent or doer of the action) does something to someone or something (the object of the action).

Botero pintó *La familia presidencial.*
Botero painted The Presidential Family.

Examine the following active sentences containing *subject + verb + object.*

Active Voice

Subject (Agent)	Action	Object
Siqueiros *Siqueiros*	pintó *painted*	muchos murales. *many murals.*
La prensa *The press*	ha publicado *has published*	las críticas de la exhibición. *the critiques of the exhibition.*
La ciudad *The city*	va a construir *is going to build*	un museo de esculturas. *a sculpture museum.*

1. The passive voice (**la voz pasiva**), which in Spanish is mainly found in writing, is used to place emphasis on the action and the receiver of the action instead of the doer of the action: *The movie was panned by the critics.* In Spanish, as in English, the passive construction is formed by reversing the word order and changing the form of the verb according to the following formula.

Passive Voice

Object (Passive Subject)	ser + *past participle*	por	Agent
Muchos murales *Many murals*	**fueron** pintad**os** *were painted*	por *by*	Siqueiros. *Siqueiros.*
Las críticas *The critiques*	**han sido** publicad**as** *have been published*	por *by*	la prensa. *the press.*
Un museo de esculturas *A sculpture museum*	**va a ser** construid**o** *is going to be built*	por *by*	la ciudad. *the city.*

Note: The past participle agrees in gender and in number with the object of the action. To review past participle formation see Appendix A, pages 348–349.

2. Compare the following active and passive sentences.

Active	Passive
La gente aclamó la obra de Picasso.	La obra de Picasso **fue aclamada** (por la gente).
El gobierno va a censurar esa pintura.	Esa pintura **va a ser censurada** (por el gobierno).
La galería vendió el cuadro en un millón de pesos.	El cuadro **fue vendido** en un millón de pesos (por la galería).

Note: In many passive sentences it is possible to omit the agent (the phrase with **por**) when it is obvious, irrelevant, a secret, or unknown.

In Spanish, the passive voice isn't frequently used in the present. It is preferable to use the **se** construction instead.

3. To express an idea where the doer of the action is not important, it is more common to use the **se** + *singular/plural verb* construction. To review, see Chapter 5, pages 137–138.

Se critica a Botero con frecuencia.	*Botero is criticized frequently.*
Se exhiben cuadros fantásticos en esa galería.	*Great paintings are exhibited in that gallery.*

Act. 22: Instruct students that some of the sentences are false, but that first they're going to turn the sentences into the passive voice. Do one by one calling on individuals. Then, as a class or in pairs, ask them to decide if the sentences are true or false and to correct the false. Check responses. Answers: 1. **falso: los moros** 2. **cierto** 3. **falso: los incas** 4. **cierto** 5. **falso: Orozco/Siqueiros/Rivera**/etc. 6. **cierto**

Actividad 22 ¿Ciertas o falsas? Pon estas oraciones sobre el arte y la arqueología en la voz pasiva y después decide si son ciertas o falsas. Corrige las falsas.

1. Los romanos construyeron La Alhambra en Granada.
2. Velázquez pintó el cuadro *Las meninas*.
3. Los aztecas construyeron Machu Picchu.
4. Frank O. Gehry diseñó el Museo Guggenheim Bilbao.
5. Salvador Dalí pintó muchos murales en México.
6. María Izquierdo pintó *Sueño y premonición*.

Act. 23: Do as a whole class activity. Encourage students to guess if they don't know. Answers: **La canción "Suerte" fue grabada por Shakira. / La vacuna contra la polio fue creada por J. Salk. / La película *Hable con ella* fue dirigida por P. Almodóvar. / La quinta sinfonía fue compuesta por Beethoven. / El cuadro *Guernica* fue pintado por P. Picasso. / La teoría de la relatividad fue desarrollada por A. Einstein. / La novela *La casa de los espíritus* fue escrita por I. Allende. / El metal radio fue descubierto por P. y M. Curie.**

Actividad 23 Acontecimientos importantes Forma oraciones con la voz pasiva usando palabras de las tres columnas. Si no estás seguro/a, adivina.

► El primer email — mandar — Ray Tomlinson en 1971

El primer email fue mandado por Ray Tomlinson en 1971.

La canción "Suerte" ("*Whenever Wherever*")	componer	Pierre y Marie Curie
La vacuna contra la polio	crear	Pablo Picasso
La película *Hable con ella*	desarrollar	Shakira
La quinta sinfonía	grabar	Pedro Almodóvar
El cuadro *Guernica*	dirigir	Alberto Einstein
La teoría de la relatividad	descubrir	Isabel Allende
La novela *La casa de los espíritus*	pintar	Jonas Salk
El metal radio	escribir	Beethoven

IV. Using the Infinitive

Summary of Uses of the Infinitive

During this course you have used the infinitive in a variety of situations. The following rules will help you review the different uses.

1. Use an infinitive:

a. after verbs such as **querer, necesitar, desear, soler,** and **poder**

Quiero ir a la exhibición de Botero. — *I want to go to Botero's exhibition.*

Ella **desea tener** una escultura de él y luego **invitar** a todos sus amigos para que la vean. — *She wants to have a sculpture by him and then invite all her friends to see it.*

b. after **tener que** and **hay que**

Tengo que escribir una crítica sobre ese cuadro. — *I have to write a critique of that painting.*

No hay que ser rico para ir a un museo. — *You don't have to be rich to go to a museum.*

c. after impersonal expressions such as **es posible** or **es necesario** when there is no specific subject mentioned

No es posible pintar bien sin recibir instrucción previa. — *It's not possible to paint well without receiving previous instruction.*

d. directly after a preposition

Después de pintar por muchos años, Ernesto fue finalmente aceptado en el mundo del arte. — *After painting for many years, Ernesto was finally accepted in the art scene.*

No puedes entrar a la exhibición **sin tener** invitación. — *You can't enter the exhibition without having an invitation.*

e. after **al**

Al ver el cuadro, Marisel sintió nostalgia por su familia y su pueblo. — *Upon seeing the painting, Marisel felt nostalgic about her family and her village.*

f. when a verb is the subject of the sentence

Note that the use of the definite article **el** is optional.

(El) Expresar lo que uno siente es a veces necesario. — *Expressing what one feels is sometimes necessary.*

Drill use of the infinitive:

1. Have students make a list about their activities tonight: 1. what they have to do (**tener que / hay que**) 2. what they should do (**deber**) 3. what they like to do (**gustar**) 4. what they want to do (**querer/ desear**) 5. what they can do (**poder**). When finished with the lists, ask them what they actually will do tonight (**ir a**).

2. Have students finish these sentences: **Después de terminar el *Guernica*, Picasso... Antes de empezar a pintar el cuadro *Las meninas*, la infanta y el perro...** Continue, by changing names of works and artists. It is best to bring in a copy of the work to show when asking the question.

3. Have students finish these sentences: **Ir a museos es bueno para... Pintar un cuadro es bueno para... Al ver *Las dos Fridas*, yo...**

Spanish: *preposition + infinitive* (**después de obtener**)

English: *preposition + gerund* (*after getting*)

To review verbs like **gustar,** see pp. 5–6.

2. The infinitive also functions as the subject after verbs that follow the pattern of **gustar.**

A Carlos no le **gusta vender** ni **regalar** sus obras de arte.	*Carlos doesn't like selling nor giving away his works of art.*

Act. 24: Assign as HW or do in class.

Actividad 24 Ideas sobre el arte Completa estas ideas sobre el arte con el infinitivo y otras palabras necesarias.

1. Si quieres interpretar una obra de arte es imprescindible...
2. Para... lo que pinta un artista a veces es necesario... el contexto histórico.
3. Un artista se expone a la crítica al...
4. Un restaurador a veces no puede...
5. ... un cuadro y... una crítica es fácil, pero pintar una obra maestra es muy difícil.
6. Muchos artistas ganan poco dinero por...
7. Antes de... una obra de arte, es importante... y también se debe...

Act. 25: This could be assigned as HW or done in class in small groups or in pairs. Students pick one of the events or you could assign them. When finished, have students read their message to the class or collect and correct.

Actividad 25 Mensajes informativos En grupos de tres, Uds. son locutores de una emisora de radio y tienen que escribir una serie de mensajes cortos para informarle al público sobre las múltiples oportunidades que hay para ver arte en su ciudad. Al escribir los mensajes integren diferentes usos del infinitivo cuando sea posible. A continuación hay una lista de cinco eventos a los que la gente puede asistir este mes.

¿Qué?	¿Dónde?
La historia en cuadros – La historia de Latinoamérica 1492–1800, representación cronólogica.	Museo de la Ciudad
Tú también puedes ser escultor – Oportunidad para gente entre cinco y ochenta años para trabajar con las manos y crear una obra de arte.	Museo del Barrio
CIEN – Exhibición multimedia de fotografías en blanco y negro de 100 personas el día que cumplieron los 100 años. Cada foto viene acompañada de una narración de la persona misma.	La sala de exhibiciones en el Banco de la República
Los murales del barrio – Una visita a un barrio donde vamos a explorar los murales hechos por jóvenes de la ciudad. Algunos van a estar allí para hablar con nosotros sobre sus obras.	Lugar de encuentro: La puerta del Museo del Barrio Sábado, 20 marzo a las 13:00
Invenciones – prácticas, graciosas, ingeniosas e inútiles – Exhibición de invenciones de aparatos que se pueden encontrar en una casa para ayudarnos a hacer las tareas domésticas.	Museo de Ciencias

▶ ¿Quieren **tener** una vida más fácil? ¿No les gusta **tener** que **atarse** los zapatos todos los días? No importa, una máquina puede **hacerlo.** Deben **visitar...**

V. Using Transitional Phrases

Expressions with *por*

Por is frequently used in transitional phrases that help to move a conversation or a narrative along. The following list contains common expressions with **por.**

por casualidad	by chance
por cierto	by the way
por ejemplo	for example
por eso / por esa razón	that's why, for that reason
por lo general	in general
por lo menos	at least
por un lado... por el otro / por una parte... por la otra	on one hand . . . on the other
por otro lado / por otra parte	on the other hand
por (si) las dudas / por si acaso / por si las moscas	just in case
por lo tanto / por consiguiente	therefore
por supuesto	of course

Drill expressions with **por:**

Have students complete sentences: **Mañana voy a traer un paraguas... ¿Han visto mis anteojos...? Por un lado, es bueno estudiar un poco todos los días, ... Necesito... cuatro voluntarios para un juego.**

Actividad 26 Miniconversaciones **Parte A:** Completa las siguientes conversaciones usando expresiones con **por.**

Act. 26: Could be assigned as HW or done in class. Other answers are possible.

1. —¿Adónde vas con esos prismáticos (*binoculars*)?
   —Los llevo ___por si las moscas___. Sé que tenemos asientos en la séptima fila, pero quiero ver bien a los actores.
2. —___Por un lado___, me gusta esta escultura, pero ___por el otro___, me parece carísima.
   —Entonces no la compres.
3. —Me fascinan las canciones de Ricky Martin.
   —___Por cierto/Por casualidad___, ¿escuchaste su última canción? Es excelente.
4. —¿Has visto mi flauta ___por casualidad___?
   —Creo que la vi en la mesa de la cocina, debajo del periódico.
5. —Esta exhibición me parece malísima; ___por lo tanto___, me voy.
   —Espérame, espérame que quiero ver algunos cuadros más.
6. —¿Cuánto crees que cueste esa obra de arte?
   —No estoy seguro, pero debe costar ___por lo menos___ 100.000 pesos.

Parte B: Ahora en parejas, escojan una de las conversaciones y continúenla.

Act. 28: Discuss briefly censorship of art, books, songs, ideas, etc., for political or moral reasons. Ask students to give examples of items that have been banned. Examples include: Christmas decorations in public places; songs and prayer in public schools; the teaching of the theory of evolution; *The Adventures of Huckleberry Finn; Catch 22*; some plays by Shakespeare; etc. Refer students to: (1) the **quena,** which was banned in Chile in the 1970s due to its use in music frequently associated with Allende's government and which was a symbol of freedom and self-determination; (2) Alicia Alonso, a world-acclaimed Cuban ballerina, who was at the peak of her career during the Castro regime, and could not enter the U.S. since she supported Castro.

Divide the class into two groups and inform them of the side they are to support. Tell them to disregard their personal opinions and to argue intensely for the side of the issue to which they are assigned. This may avoid people having to choose sides and thus expose their own personal views. Allow time for each side to prepare. Have a debate.

Actividad 27 Los comentarios En parejas, digan qué piensan sobre cada una de las siguientes ideas usando por lo menos tres expresiones con **por** para cada situación.

▶ Las artesanías no son arte.
Por lo general eso es lo que piensa mucha gente y **por eso** no aprecia el trabajo de los artesanos. Pero **por otro lado,** ...

1. El grafiti es arte.
2. Hay censura artística en este país.
3. Algún día van a desaparecer los libros.

Actividad 28 ¿Censura o no? Muchos gobiernos patrocinan (*sponsor*) las artes, pero siempre existe la posibilidad de la censura. El arte provoca reacciones y también controversia y, por lo tanto, existe un sector del público que quiere establecer controles sobre el dinero que gasta el gobierno en las artes. Ha habido ocasiones en que gente con dinero le paga a un artista para hacer arte público. En 1933, Nelson Rockefeller contrató a Diego Rivera, el muralista mexicano, para pintar un mural en una de las paredes del Centro Rockefeller en Nueva York. Al pintar el cuadro, Rivera incluyó un retrato de Vladimir Lenin. A Rockefeller no le gustó y le pidió a Rivera que cambiara la cara de Lenin por la de un individuo desconocido. Rivera rechazó la idea y Rockefeller lo despidió y destruyó el mural para que no se viera. Divídanse en dos grupos para debatir esta idea:

> Los gobiernos no deben patrocinar obras de arte que la mayor parte de la población no acepta.

Cada grupo tiene cinco minutos para preparar su argumento, uno a favor o y el otro en contra. Su profesor/a va a moderar el debate.

▶ Diego Rivera pinta un mural en el edificio RCA del Centro Rockefeller en Nueva York.

▲ La quena: instrumento prohibido en Chile durante la dictadura de Pinochet.

◀ Alicia Alonso, bailarina y coreógrafa cubana. Se prohibió su entrada en los Estados Unidos durante casi todo el régimen de Castro por apoyar su gobierno.

Do the corresponding CD-ROM and web activities to review the chapter topics.

Vocabulario activo

La obra de arte

el autorretrato — *self-portrait*
la burla — *mockery*
burlarse de — *to mock, make fun of*
expresar — *to express*
fuente de inspiración — *source of inspiration*
glorificar — *to glorify*
la imagen — *image*
el mensaje — *message*
la naturaleza muerta — *still life*
la obra abstracta — *abstract work*
la obra maestra — *masterpiece*
el paisaje — *landscape*
la reproducción — *reproduction*
el retrato — *portrait*
la sátira — *satire*
el simbolismo — *symbolism*
simbolizar — *to simbolize, signify*
el símbolo — *symbol*

Apreciación del arte

el censor — *censor*
la censura — *censorship; censure*
censurar — *to censor; to censure*
la crítica — *critique*
criticar — *to critique; to criticize*
el crítico — *critic*
la interpretación — *interpretation*
interpretar — *to interpret*

Expresiones para hablar de un cuadro

¿Qué te parece (este cuadro)? — *What do you think (about this painting)?*
No tiene ni pies ni cabeza. — *I can't make heads or tails of it.*
No tiene (ningún) sentido para mí. — *It doesn't make (any) sense to me.*
Qué maravilla. — *How marvelous.*
Qué horrible. — *How horrible.*
(No) Me conmueve. — *It moves/doesn't move me.*
Me siento triste/contento/a al verlo. — *I feel sad/happy when I see it.*
Ni me va ni me viene. / Ni fu ni fa. — *It doesn't do anything for me.*

Expresiones con *por*

por casualidad — *by chance*
por cierto — *by the way*
por ejemplo — *for example*
por eso / por esa razón — *that's why, for that reason*
por lo general — *in general*
por lo menos — *at least*
por lo tanto / por consiguiente — *therefore*
por un lado... por el otro / por una parte... por la otra — *on one hand . . . on the other*
por otro lado / por otra parte — *on the other hand*
por (si) las dudas / por si acaso / por si las moscas — *just in case*
por supuesto — *of course*

Expresiones útiles

un dineral — *a great deal of money*
llevarle (a alguien) + *time period* — *to take (someone) +* time period
¡Qué barbaridad! — *Wow!* (literally, *What a barbarity!*) (*negative connotation*)
se me fueron las ganas de + *infinitive* — *I didn't feel like +* verb + ing *anymore*

Vocabulario personal

Capítulo 10

Metas comunicativas

- discutir temas sociales
- expresar acciones futuras
- expresar condiciones, dar consejos y pedir que alguien haga algo
- expresar probabilidad
- hacer hipótesis sobre el presente y el futuro

Las relaciones humanas

▲ Una pareja charla en un parque de Viña del Mar, Chile.

May be assigned: Grammar, vocabulary, **¿Lo sabían?**, Act. 6A, Act. 6B, Act. 7, Act. 8A, Act. 9, Act. 10A, Act. 13, Act. 20A, Act. 21A, Act. 21B, Act. 23, Act. 24A, Act. 28A.

Show the chapter video episode at any point in the chapter that you see fit and do all or selected activities in class. Note: Content of the video supplements the cultural material in the chapter and activities reenter chapter grammar and vocabulary.

¡Que vivan los novios!

un/a amigo/a íntimo/a	a very close friend
¿No te/le/les parece?	Don't you think so?
mientras más vengan, mejor	the more, the merrier

 *La boda*

Practice expressions: Write them on the board. Tell students that you have some friends that are planning a wedding and that they are planning to invite a lot of people because **mientras más vengan, mejor.** Ask them **¿No les parece una buena idea?** Ask them whether they think it's better to invite only **a sus amigos íntimos.**

◂ Chicas argentinas tiran las cintitas de un pastel de boda.

Actividad 1 Las bodas Marca qué costumbres asocias generalmente con bodas de tu país (MP), de varios países hispanos (PH) o de ambos (A).

1. __MP__ ceremonia civil o religiosa
2. __PH__ ceremonia civil y religiosa
3. __MP__ damas de honor como madrinas
4. __PH__ padres y madres como padrinos
5. __A__ pajes con anillos
6. __A__ tirarles arroz a los novios al salir de la iglesia
7. __A__ fiesta con baile
8. __A__ pastel de boda

Act. 1: Have students share their answers. #2. In many Hispanic countries, a civil wedding is mandatory; a growing number of couples only celebrate this type of wedding. #3. Sometimes in Venezuela (believed to be an import from the U.S.). #4. In many countries it is typical for the parents to be the **padrinos.** In Mexico, the best man and maid of honor are a married couple who are friends of the bride and groom. Other traditions will be discussed in the listening passage.

Actividad 2 Otras costumbres **Parte A:** Escucha el programa de radio "Charlando con Dolores" para enterarte de, por lo menos, dos costumbres hispanas relacionadas con las bodas.

Parte B: Escucha el programa de radio otra vez y apunta todas las costumbres hispanas que se mencionan. Debes estar preparado/a para contárselas con detalle al resto de la clase.

Parte C: En parejas, describan costumbre de su país relacionadas con las bodas, que no se hayan mencionado en la actividad anterior.

Act. 2A: Tell students not to concentrate on the details of the traditions since they will do that in Part B.

Act. 2B: Discuss how to take notes. Tell students to write phrases or words, not sentences. You may want to pause after each tradition is discussed in the call-in show, and have students retell it.

Act 2C: Pair students and have them discuss other customs from their country. Then have them share with the rest of the class.

Act. 3: Set up the activity, form groups, and begin. Make sure students justify their opinion. Option: Assign a sentence for each group to discuss.

Actividad 3 ¿Qué opinas? En grupos de tres, discutan las siguientes ideas relacionadas con las bodas en su país.

1. Los padres de la novia deben pagar todos los gastos de la fiesta.
2. Los invitados sólo deben comprar regalos de la lista de regalos.
3. Las madrinas de la novia deben comprar el vestido que la novia elija por más feo que sea.
4. El novio y la novia pueden celebrar su despedida de soltero/a como quieran.

¿LO SABÍAN?

Entre las muchas tradiciones en torno a las bodas de los países hispanos se encuentran las serenatas en Colombia. Aunque esta costumbre parezca anticuada, todavía a veces se dan serenatas. En el pasado, el novio generalmente le mandaba a su futura esposa uno o varios músicos que le tocaban canciones frente a la ventana muy tarde por la noche. Hoy día, es más común que el novio le lleve el conjunto de "serenateros" uno o dos días antes de la boda, generalmente la noche que reciben los regalos, y juntos con la familia pasan un rato escuchando música. Poco a poco las costumbres cambian y a veces los cambios son buenos y otras veces no tan buenos. Comenta qué opinas de esta tradición y si te gustaría recibir o mandarle una serenata a alguien. ¿Es una tradición cursi o romántica? ¿Hay algunas tradiciones que se están perdiendo en tu país?

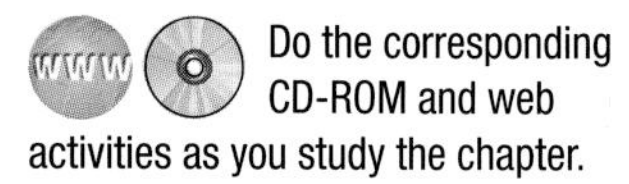

Do the corresponding CD-ROM and web activities as you study the chapter.

I. Stating Future Actions

The Future Tense

Drill future tense:

1. Have students mention what they plan to do after they finish college: **Me iré de esta ciudad. Me casaré. Estudiaré medicina.**

2. Have students predict their own and their classmates' future for the year 2015: **Bob y yo trabajaremos en computación. Lynn y Ted tendrán tres hijos. Viviré en España.** (etc.)

In the radio program, you heard a caller say, **"Y la que se saque el anillo es la que se casará el año que viene"**, in reference to an action that will take place in the future. To do this, she used the future tense. You are already familiar with the two most common ways to refer to future actions: a construction with **ir a** + *infinitive* and the present tense.

1. The present tense is frequently used to refer to the near future, and a sense of certainty about the future is implied. **Ir a** + *infinitive* can be used to talk about both the near and distant future.

Esta noche **se casan** Wilson y Marta.	*Tonight Wilson and Marta are getting married.* (near future and sense of certainty)
En una semana **van a volver** de su luna de miel.	*In a week they are going to return from their honeymoon.* (near future)
El año que viene mi novia y yo **vamos a casarnos.**	*My girlfriend and I are going to get married next year.* (distant future)

2. Another way to refer to actions both in the near and distant future is by using the future tense (**el futuro**). In everyday speech, this tense is not as common as the present or **ir a** + *infinitive*. The future tense is formed by adding the following endings to the infinitive form of the verb.

us**ar**		vend**er**		viv**ir**	
usar**é**	usar**emos**	vender**é**	vender**emos**	vivir**é**	vivir**emos**
usar**ás**	usar**éis**	vender**ás**	vender**éis**	vivir**ás**	vivir**éis**
usar**á**	usar**án**	vender**á**	vender**án**	vivir**á**	vivir**án**

For additional information on the formation of the future tense, see Appendix A, page 344.

Los recién casados **saldrán** para Cozumel esta noche.	*The newlyweds will leave for Cozumel tonight.*
Con el tiempo, **tendrán** dos o tres hijos.	*In time, they will have two or three children.*
Ellos **querrán** que sus hijos estudien otro idioma desde niños.*	*They will want their children to study another language starting from a very young age.*

*Note: In sentences requiring the subjunctive, if the independent clause contains the future, use the present subjunctive in the dependent clause.

3. You can use the future tense to make promises and predictions.

—Necesitamos llegar a la boda a tiempo.	*We need to arrive at the wedding on time.*
—**Estaré** en tu casa a las ocho.	*I'll be at your place at eight.* (promise)
—¿Sabes si ya compraron apartamento? —No, pero me imagino que **vivirán** cerca de los padres de él.	*Do you know if they bought an apartment yet?* *No, but I imagine that they will live near his parents.* (prediction)

Actividad 4 ¿Cómo serán? En parejas, describan cómo creen que será físicamente la otra persona cuando tenga setenta y cinco años. A continuación hay algunas ideas que pueden ayudarlos. Justifiquen su descripción.

Act. 4: Begin by predicting what you will look like at 75. Encourage creativity in responses. Check by asking some students to share their responses.

Follow-up: Ask students to predict other aspects of their partners' lives (type of house, wealth, memberships in clubs, etc.).

tener pelo blanco, canoso o teñido (*dyed*)
ser calvo/a
llevar peluca (*wig, toupee*)
ser activo/a o sedentario/a
tener buena o mala salud
ser gordo/a o delgado/a
llevar anteojos bifocales o trifocales
tener arrugas (*wrinkles*)
tener cuerpo de gimnasio o ser fofo/a
estar senil o tener la mente lúcida
oír bien o mal
? ? ?

Act. 5: When finished, check by asking who will do a few of the activities mentioned.

Actividad 5 ¿Lo harán? En parejas, túrnense para preguntarse cuáles de las siguientes actividades no harán nunca y cuáles harán si pueden. Expliquen sus respuestas.

▶ —¿Tendrás gatos?

—Sí, tendré gatos porque me encantan los animales.

—No, jamás tendré gatos porque les tengo alergia.

1. ganar un dineral
2. hacer un viaje al Oriente
3. vivir en la misma ciudad que sus padres
4. dedicarse a ayudar a los necesitados
5. adoptar a un niño
6. hacer el doctorado
7. aspirar a ser famoso/a
8. presentarse como candidato/a para un puesto del gobierno
9. matricularse en otro curso de español
10. aprender a hacer alas delta

Act. 6A: As a review, point out the use of the imperfect for describing habitual actions in the past. Do in class (whole class activity or pairs) or assign as HW. Collect HW and/or have students compare answers and share in class.

Actividad 6 El pasado y el futuro **Parte A:** Lee cómo era la vida en el año 1900 y luego di cómo será el mundo en el año 2075.

1. En el año 1900 las personas no viajaban mucho porque usaban caballos, barcos o trenes y cada viaje llevaba muchos días. En el año 2075...
2. En el año 1900 se pagaba en las tiendas con monedas o billetes. En el año 2075...
3. En el año 1900 la gente cerraba las puertas con llave y para entrar tenía que tener la llave. En el año 2075...
4. En el año 1900 casi ninguna mujer ocupaba un puesto en el gobierno. En el año 2075...
5. En el año 1900 existían tiendas donde se compraba comida, ropa, etc. En el año 2075...

Act. 6B: Follow same procedure as in Part A. You may need to brainstorm some vocabulary so that students can express their ideas.

Parte B: Ahora usa la imaginación e imita el estilo de la Parte A para describir otros aspectos de la vida del año 1900 y después di qué pasará en el futuro.

1. las bodas
2. hacer las labores domésticas
3. el cáncer
4. trabajar 40 horas o más por semana
5. las guerras
6. las escuelas públicas

Act. 7: Could be assigned as HW. List answers given on the board. When finished, ask students which changes will occur sooner than others.

Actividad 7 La estructura familiar En grupos de tres, lean las siguientes descripciones sobre la estructura familiar actual de los Estados Unidos y digan cómo creen que será esta estructura dentro de veinte años.

1. La mujer trabaja en la casa más que el hombre.
2. Hay desigualdad entre el sueldo que ganan los hombres y las mujeres.
3. Las parejas generalmente se casan entre los 25 y los 30 años.
4. Las familias tienen generalmente dos hijos.
5. Hay bastante gente soltera con hijos.
6. Muchos jóvenes no pueden seguir sus estudios por falta de dinero.
7. Los adolescentes salen por la noche con permiso de los padres.
8. El porcentaje de divorcios es alto.
9. Existen familias no tradicionales, pero no son la mayoría.

Actividad 8 Promesas **Parte A:** Te vas a casar y quieres preparar una lista de cinco promesas para leerle a tu novio/a el día de la boda. Selecciona cinco de la siguiente lista y luego añade una promesa original al final.

Act. 8A: Assign as HW or do in class. Encourage students to create an original vow.

_____ decirle la verdad siempre
_____ serle fiel
_____ ayudarlo/la en todo
_____ quererlo/la para toda la vida
_____ apoyarlo/la
_____ respetarlo/la
_____ hacerlo/la feliz
_____ escucharlo/la siempre
_____ no gritarle
_____ tener presentes sus deseos
_____ estar con él/ella en las buenas y en las malas
_____ ____________________________________

Parte B: En parejas, mírense a los ojos y díganse las promesas.

Act. 8B: Pair students and have them role play the situation. Follow-up: Have students create vows for famous couples who want to reaffirm their vows. (Bill and Hillary Clinton, Sarah Jessica Parker and Matthew Broderick).

II. Expressing Conditions, Giving Advice, and Making Requests

The Conditional Tense

 **FLR** link: **Lectura 1**

Drill conditional:

Ask students for advice on different topics: **Voy a alquilar un apartamento nuevo. / Voy a comprar un coche usado. / No sé adónde ir para mis vacaciones de verano.** Ss: **Yo que tú/Ud., miraría los anuncios del periódico.**

1. To express what someone would do in a given situation, use the conditional tense (**el condicional**).

Sería interesante hacer un estudio sobre los hombres que ganan menos dinero que su esposa. ¿Cómo **describirían** ellos su papel en la familia?	*It would be interesting to do a study about men who earn less money than their wives. How would they describe their role in the family?*

2. The conditional is formed by adding the following endings to the infinitive form of the verb.

us**ar**		vend**er**		viv**ir**	
usar**ía**	usar**íamos**	vender**ía**	vender**íamos**	vivir**ía**	vivir**íamos**
usar**ías**	usar**íais**	vender**ías**	vender**íais**	vivir**ías**	vivir**íais**
usar**ía**	usar**ían**	vender**ía**	vender**ían**	vivir**ía**	vivir**ían**

For additional information about the formation of the conditional, see Appendix A, page 344.

3. The conditional is frequently used to give advice when prefaced by the phrases **yo que tú/él/ella/ellos...** and **(yo) en tu/su lugar.**

Yo que tú, me casaría con ella.	*If I were you, I would marry her.*
(Yo) en tu lugar, les **diría** la verdad.	*If I were in your place, I would tell them the truth.*

You may want to explain that **quisiera** is frequently used instead of **querría** to create a softer request: **¿Querría/Quisiera hacerme un favor?**

4. You can also use the conditional to make very polite requests. The following requests are listed from the most direct (commands), to the most polite (conditional).

Dime dónde es la ceremonia.	Haz esto.
¿Me dices dónde es la ceremonia?	Quiero que hagas esto.
¿Quieres decirme dónde es la ceremonia?	**Me gustaría** que hicieras esto.*
¿**Podrías** decirme dónde es la ceremonia?	**Querría** que hicieras esto.*

In everyday language it's common to hear **Me gustaría que hagas eso.**

*Note: When expressing influence, if the independent clause contains the conditional, use the imperfect subjunctive in the dependent clause.

Act. 9: Assign as HW or do in class.

Actividad 9 Una emergencia Estás en el trabajo y acabas de enterarte que tu padre tuvo un accidente grave. Fuiste a pedirle algunos favores a una compañera, pero no la encontraste. Por eso, le pediste los mismos favores a tu jefa. Cambia lo que ibas a pedirle a tu compañera a la forma de Ud. y usa frases como: **¿Me podría...?, Querría que..., Me gustaría que...**

1. ¿Me puedes ayudar?
2. ¿Me dejas usar tu carro?
3. ¿Puedes cancelar mis citas con los clientes?
4. ¿Me puedes prestar cien dólares?
5. Quiero que llames a mi madre para decirle que iré enseguida al hospital.
6. No quiero que le digas nada a nadie en la oficina.

Act. 10A: Assign as HW or do quickly in class.

Actividad 10 Situaciones de la vida diaria **Parte A:** Lee individualmente las siguientes situaciones de la vida diaria y marca qué harías en cada una.

1. Estás en el banco y la mujer que está delante de ti sólo habla español y tiene problemas porque el cajero sólo habla inglés. ¿Qué harías?
   a. ayudarla y traducirle b. no hacer nada c. buscar un cajero que hablara español
2. Llegas a tu casa solo/a de noche y encuentras la puerta abierta. ¿Qué harías?
   a. entrar para investigar b. buscar a un vecino c. llamar a la policía
3. Un vendedor te devuelve diez dólares de más en una tienda. ¿Qué harías?
   a. devolverle el dinero b. darle las gracias e irte c. comprar algo más en esa tienda
4. Un amigo que tiene novia te cuenta que está saliendo con otra chica. ¿Qué harías?
   a. decirle la verdad a la novia b. no hablarle más a tu amigo c. sugerirle a él que se lo dijera a su novia
5. Viste a una señora poner un disco compacto en su bolso, pero no la vio nadie de la tienda. ¿Qué harías?
   a. avisarle a un vendedor b. decirle algo a ella c. no decirle nada a nadie

(continúa en la página siguiente)

6. Hay un incendio (*fire*) en una casa y hay niños gritando adentro, pero parece muy peligroso entrar. ¿Qué harías?
   a. llamar a los bomberos con tu móvil
   b. entrar en la casa y sacar a los niños de allí
   c. buscar a un vecino para que te ayudara
7. Un amigo que bebió seis cervezas mientras miraba un partido de basquetbol en tu casa quiere manejar a su casa. ¿Qué harías?
   a. llevarlo a casa
   b. dejarlo ir solo
   c. ofrecerle un lugar para dormir en tu casa

Parte B: En parejas, miren las situaciones de la Parte A otra vez y marquen individualmente lo que creen que respondió su compañero/a. No pueden consultar con él/ella.

Act. 10B: Form pairs and have students mark predictions of their partner's responses. You may want to have students sit back-to-back so as not to peek at responses.

Parte C: Ahora hablen sobre las respuestas y las predicciones que hicieron.

► A: ¿Qué haría yo en la primera situación?
B: Yo creo que no la ayudarías porque eres muy tímido/a.
A: Soy tímido/a, pero también soy amable y hablo bien español.

Act. 10C: Encourage students to support their opinions. Check by asking about one or two specific items.

Actividad 11 ¿Qué harías? En parejas, digan qué harían en las siguientes situaciones y por qué. Reaccionen a lo que dice su compañero/a usando las siguientes expresiones.

Act. 11: Share responses in pairs. Option 1: Encourage or assign some students to be **sinvergüenzas.** Check by asking for different possible courses of action in each circumstance. Encourage connected discourse. Option 2: Check and ask what a person who is **responsable/ irresponsable** would say.

Ángel is always masculine.

Positivas	Negativas	
¡Qué decente!	¡Qué caradura!	*Of all the nerve!*
¡Qué responsable!	¡Qué sinvergüenza!	*What a dog/rat!*
Eres un ángel.	¡Qué desconsiderado/a!	*How inconsiderate!*
Eres un/a santo/a.	Francamente creo que tú...	*Frankly I think that you . . .*
Eres más bueno/a que el pan.	Ésa es una mentira más grande que una casa.	*That's a big fat lie.*

Situaciones para el/la estudiante A

1. Has gastado más de $4.000 con la tarjeta de crédito y no tienes más crédito. En la cuenta bancaria tienes sólo $1.600 y quieres hacer un viaje a México con tus amigos durante las vacaciones.
2. Has chocado contra un auto estacionado y a tu auto no le ha pasado nada, pero el otro está un poco dañado. Calculas que el arreglo no costará más de $200. Nadie ha visto el choque y estás solo/a.

Situaciones para el/la estudiante B

1. Acabas de comprar un móvil sin seguro. Al salir de la tienda se te cayó al suelo y se te rompió.
2. Estás en un examen sentado al lado del mejor estudiante de la clase y puedes ver bien su examen porque escribe con letra muy grande. Estudiaste mucho para el examen pero te resulta muy difícil y no te parece justo.

Act. 12: Form pairs assigning A and B roles. Model the activity and begin. Check by asking for advice about a few of the situations.

Actividad 12 Yo que tú... En parejas, un/a estudiante mira las situaciones A y la otra persona mira las situaciones B. Cuéntense sus problemas usando sus propias palabras y dense consejos usando las expresiones **yo que tú/él/ella/ellos** y **yo en tu/su lugar.**

A

1. Mi madre no quiere que yo acepte un trabajo en Bolivia, quiere que me quede aquí.
2. Mis padres van a ir a Europa y no saben si alquilar un carro o comprar un "Eurail pass".
3. Un amigo quiere que yo salga en el programa de Jerry Springer.

B

1. Un amigo me acusó de robarle el radio.
2. Mi padre no quiere que mi madre trabaje, pero ella quiere trabajar.
3. A mi hermano que está casado y tiene hijos le ofrecieron un buen trabajo en una fábrica, pero es por la noche y no sabe qué hacer.

Drill probability about the present:

Have students wonder about a classmate who is absent. T: **No veo a** (absent student). **¿Dónde estará?** S: **Estará en su cuarto.**

You may want to teach it's also possible to say **Probablemente están/estén haciendo algo malo.**

III. Expressing Probability

The Future and Conditional Tenses

The conditional to express probability about the past will not be emphasized in this text due to its low frequency, except in instances expressing states (time, age, etc.).

Drill probability about the past:

1. Tell students that someone broke into your office this morning. Then give them clues. For example: T: **Encontré esto** (take out a basketball). **¿Quién sería?** Ss: **Sería Jennifer porque juega al basquetbol.** T: **Pero también encontré...** Continue to implicate different students with the clues given. Then ask: **¿Qué querría?** Students give possible responses: **Querría su libro de notas/el examen final/una prueba/**etc.

2. Ask students questions about famous people and events: **¿Cuántos años tenía Joe Montana cuando dejó de jugar al fútbol americano? ¿En qué año se jugó la Copa Mundial de Fútbol en los Estados Unidos?**

When you are not sure about something, you may express probability. For example, you may wonder about how old someone is, or if a person is late, you may wonder where he/she might be.

1. To wonder or to express probability about the present, use the future tense.

—¿Qué **estarán haciendo** los niños?	*I wonder what the kids are doing.*
—**Harán** alguna travesura porque están tan callados.	*They must be doing something bad because they are so quiet.*
—¿Cuántos años **tendrá** Ramón?	*I wonder how old Ramón is.*
—**Tendrá** unos cincuenta.	*He's probably about fifty.*

2. To wonder or to express probability about the past, use the conditional tense.

—¿Por qué se divorciaron?	*Why did they get divorced?*
—No tengo idea. **Tendrían** muchos problemas y tal vez ella **estaría** muy descontenta.	*I have no clue. They probably had a lot of problems and maybe she was very unhappy.*

Actividad 13 ¿Qué pasará? En parejas, miren las situaciones y usen la imaginación para hacer tres conjeturas sobre qué pasará en este momento en cada situación.

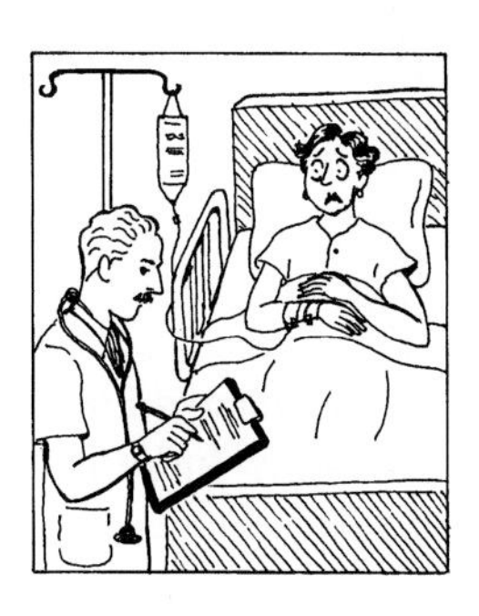

Act 13: You may want to do this activity in pairs or as a whole class. Set a time limit for pairs to come up with their conjectures (or assign as HW and have students share ideas) and then ask **¿Quién llamará? ¿Qué ocurrirá? ¿Qué tendrá la paciente?**

Actividad 14 Solos en casa Ha habido muchos robos últimamente y te has puesto un poco paranoico/a. En parejas, Uds. están solos en una casa por la noche y hacen conjeturas acerca de lo que pasa. Sigan el modelo y miren la siguiente lista.

▶ Oyen un ruido en otra habitación.

A: ¿Oíste ese ruido?
B: Sí. ¿Qué será?
A: Será el viento.

1. Un perro empieza a ladrar.
2. Suena el teléfono y al contestar, no habla nadie.
3. Oyen un grito que viene de afuera de la casa.
4. Escuchan la sirena de la policía.
5. Alguien llama a la puerta.

Act. 14: Introduce the activity by acting paranoid about a sound you hear in the hall. Inform students that they are somewhat paranoid. Form pairs and do the activity. Check by asking how they responded to the different items or by role playing different situations.

Actividad 15 ¿En qué año sería? Intenta decir el año o la edad exacta que tenían ciertos famosos cuando ocurrieron los siguientes acontecimientos. Si no estás seguro/a, mira las opciones que se presentan y usa expresiones como: **sería a principios de los.../a fines de los.../en el año.../de... a...** o **tendría... años.**

▶ llegar / Armstrong a la luna

a. a principios de los 60 b. a fines de los 60 c. a principios de los 70

Armstrong llegó a la luna en 1969. Sería a fines de los sesenta cuando Armstrong llegó a la luna.

1. ser / las Olimpiadas en Barcelona
   a. en el año 1988 b. en el año 2000 c. en el año 1992
2. Penélope Cruz / ser / protagonista de una película norteamericana por primera vez
   a. 18 años b. 25 años c. 28 años
3. norteamericanas / ganar / la última Copa Mundial de Fútbol
   a. a mediados de los 70 b. a finales de los 80 c. a finales de los 90

(continúa en la página siguiente)

Act. 15: Do as a whole class activity or in groups of three. Answers: 1. **c** (The Olympics were hosted in Barcelona in 1992 because it was the 500th anniversary of Columbus' arrival in this city from the Americas. Barcelona was his first port of call because Ferdinand and Isabella were there.) 2. **b** (Her first American movie was *Woman on Top*) 3. **c** (1999 – Note they also won in 1991 at the first World Cup for women in soccer.) 4. **b** 5. **b** (Ask students who recently won the Tour de France *six* consecutive times. Answer: Lance Armstrong, United States from 1999 to 2004.) 6. **b** (Her first album in English was *Laundry Service*.)

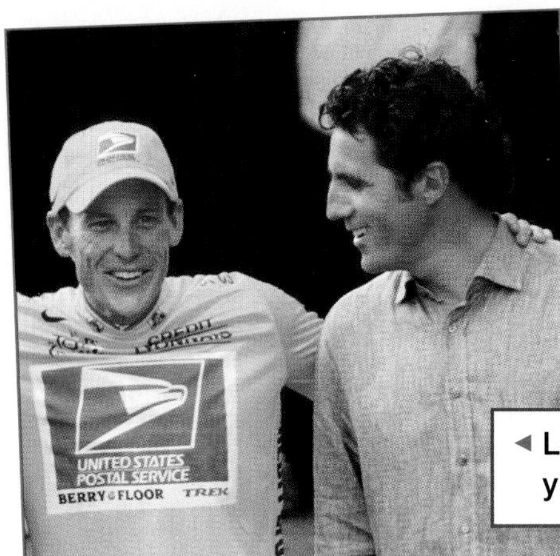

◄ Los ciclistas Lance Amstrong y Miguel Indurain.

4. JFK / morir / asesinado en Dallas, Texas
   a. 36 años b. 46 años c. 56 años
5. Miguel Indurain / español / ganar el Tour de Francia cinco veces consecutivas
   a. de 1974 a 1978 b. de 1991 a 1995 c. de 1998 a 2002
6. Shakira / producir / su primer álbum en inglés
   a. 20 años b. 24 años c. 27 años

IV. Discussing Societal Issues

FLR link: **Lectura 2** discusses traditional ideas about men and women in the Hispanic world.

La sociedad

The title *Cuernos* is taken from the expression **ponerle los cuernos a alguien** = *to cheat on someone* (literally, to put horns on your partner).

Cuernos

La relevancia que le damos a la **fidelidad** sexual, independientemente de la edad, es altísima; sólo un 2,7% la considera "poco importante". Pero además **confiamos en** nuestros compañeros sentimentales: más del 68% de los españoles no cree que sus **parejas** les **hayan sido infieles,** mientras que el 30,5% de los varones y el 10,7% de las mujeres reconocen haberlo sido alguna vez. Estos son algunos datos de la muestra que Sigma Dos ha realizado en la última semana de julio en exclusiva para *Magazine*. El escritor, político y demógrafo Joaquín Leguina analiza los resultados de la encuesta y señala que "estas proporciones de infieles subestiman la realidad". Pero si algo ha llamado la atención del autor del libro *Cuernos* es el porcentaje de menores de 30 años que sostienen como motivo inevitable de ruptura **una cana al aire**: "La permisividad de los jóvenes españoles **queda muy en entredicho".**

fidelity

we trust

partners

have been unfaithful, have cheated

(echarse) una cana al aire = (to have) a one-night stand

is very questionable

La pareja y la familia

el asilo/la casa/la residencia de ancianos	nursing home
la crianza, criar	raising, rearing; to raise, rear
ejercer autoridad	to exert authority
entrometerse (en la vida de alguien)	to intrude, meddle (in someone's life)
la falta de comunicación	lack of communication
la generación anterior	previous generation
la igualdad de los sexos	equality of the sexes
inculcar	to instill, inculcate
independizarse (de la familia)	to become independent (from one's family)
infidelidad	
el machismo	
malcriar	to spoil, pamper (a child)
matriarcal, patriarcal	
moral, inmoral	
la niñera	nanny
rebelde, rebelarse	rebellious; to rebel
sumiso/a	submissive
tener una aventura (amorosa)	to have an affair
el vínculo	bond
vivir juntos/convivir	to live together

Practice vocabulary:

1. Give definitions and have students say the corresponding word. T: **Es la acción de no comunicarse con su pareja.**

2. Give a verb and have students give a related noun or vice versa: **crianza, ser fiel, independencia, comunicarse.**

3. Ask students **¿Qué problemas tienen las parejas? ¿Qué problemas existen entre padres e hijos?**

You may want to tell students that the term "baby sitter" does not exist in Spanish and instead, people may say, **cuido a los hijos de unos amigos de mis padres.** Some people use the English term with Spanish pronunciation: **¿Por qué no llamas a la baby sitter** *(pronounced beibi síter)***?**

Actividad 16 Es la misma palabra En parejas, una persona mira solamente la columna A y la otra mira la columna B. A debe definir las palabras pares y B debe definir las palabras impares sin usar la palabra en la definición. Al escuchar a su compañero/a, digan si la palabra que tienen bajo ese número es la palabra que su compañero/a define. Recuerden que no pueden utilizar la palabra en la definición. Usen frases como: **Es la acción de..., Es el lugar donde..., Es una cosa que...**

A	B
1. criar	1. inculcar
2. serle fiel a alguien	2. serle fiel a alguien
3. sumiso/a	3. sumiso/a
4. malcriar	4. criar
5. independizarse	5. vivir juntos
6. inmoral	6. inmoral
7. entrometerse	7. ejercer autoridad
8. matriarcal	8. patriarcal

Act. 16: This activity practices circumlocution. Form pairs and have one student in the pair cover column B while the other covers column A or copy lists A and B on separate pages and distribute. Model activity by describing the first word in column A without using the word in your definition, and have B students tell you whether their word under #1 is the word you are describing. If they are not sure, they can ask you questions until they are sure enough to tell you (**no**) **es la misma palabra.** Set a time limit and begin. Check by giving definitions and have the class shout out responses.

Act. 17: Encourage students to be inventive when answering question #3. Follow-up: Ask for what other reasons people marry (money, status, to have children, to get out of their home, etc.).

The word **pareja** can mean *partner* or *couple*.

Actividad 17 El matrimonio en el futuro En una época, el matrimonio por amor y no por conveniencia se consideraba una idea muy radical. En parejas, discutan las siguientes preguntas sobre el matrimonio.

1. Cuando en generaciones anteriores el matrimonio era un arreglo, ¿qué tipo de conflictos tendrían los hombres y las mujeres?
2. ¿Qué tipo de problemas tendrán ahora las parejas que generalmente se casan por amor?
3. ¿Qué tipo de vínculo creen que se establecerá entre dos personas en el futuro?

Act. 18A: Allow students a moment to skim this portion of the article. When finished, ask comprehension questions about content.

Actividad 18 La mujer mexicana **Parte A:** El siguiente párrafo es parte de un artículo que apareció en una revista mexicana. Léelo para enterarte de cómo predice que será la mujer del año 2025.

ASÍ SERÁ LA MUJER

La mujer del año 2025 será realista, optimista y se sentirá cómoda con su incorporación a todos los ámbitos de la vida social. Formará una familia distinta a la tradicional, basada en las nuevas relaciones de pareja: el hogar dejará de ser el "reposo del guerrero", y el hombre compartirá las labores domésticas. Las cualidades que más valorará en su compañero serán la ternura, la inteligencia y el sentido del humor. Rechazará el papel de *superwoman* y no deseará ser perfecta. En el trabajo accederá a puestos de mayor responsabilidad, pero no cambiará su calidad de vida por conseguir el éxito a cualquier precio.

Act. 18B: Instruct students that to determine what the Mexican woman is like today, they must read between the lines. Remind them to use the future of probability because they are talking about the present. Example: **El artículo dice que en el futuro será** (future) **realista y entonces ahora será** (future of probability) **idealista o no muy realista, soñará demasiado.** Form pairs and begin the activity. Check by asking students' opinions of each response. Have students justify responses based on the reading. Follow-up: Ask if they believe whether the article's predictions will be possible or not and why.

Parte B: Ahora en parejas, deduzcan las respuestas a estas preguntas sobre la vida de la mujer mexicana de hoy basándose en lo que acaban de leer.

1. ¿Cómo será la mujer mexicana actual?
2. Por lo general, ¿qué tipo de familia tendrá ahora?
3. El hogar se ve en la actualidad como el "reposo del guerrero". ¿Qué significará esta frase?
4. ¿Qué tareas hará el hombre mexicano en el hogar hoy día?
5. ¿Cuáles serán las cualidades que más valora la mujer en un hombre?
6. ¿Qué papel creen que le asigne ahora la sociedad a la mujer?
7. Generalmente, ¿qué tipo de trabajo tendrá ahora la mujer fuera del hogar?

Actividad 19 La tele y la familia **Parte A:** En grupos de tres, miren el siguiente chiste de Quino, caricaturista argentino, y comenten las ideas que lo acompañan.

Act. 19A and B: When finished doing the activity, discuss answers to each question. Follow-up questions may include: **Imagina que tu televisor está descompuesto y no te lo van a arreglar hasta el mes próximo. ¿Qué harías durante ese tiempo? ¿Crees que la computadora también afecte la comunicación entre miembros de una familia?**

1. la televisión y la falta de comunicación en la familia
2. la televisión como un miembro más de la familia
3. la televisión como niñera
4. la televisión para inculcar valores tanto positivos como negativos

Parte B: Ahora comenten las siguientes preguntas relacionadas con la televisión y su infancia.

1. horas de televisión que veían
2. tipos de programas que veían
3. si la televisión era su niñera y por qué sí o no
4. de qué modo creen que les haya afectado la televisión

Parte C: Estudios recientes afirman que los niños que miran mucha televisión cuando son muy pequeños tienen luego problemas de concentración y son más hiperactivos. Teniendo en cuenta ese dato, ¿qué reglas para mirar televisión usarán con sus hijos?

Actividad 20 Los más jóvenes y los ancianos **Parte A:** En grupos de tres, discutan estas preguntas sobre la educación infantil y el cuidado de los ancianos.

Act. 20A: Could be assigned as HW and discussed in class.

1. Imaginen que tienen un niño menor de dos años. ¿Lo dejarían en una guardería todo el día? ¿Cuáles serían tres ventajas y tres desventajas?
2. Si vivieran cerca de la casa de sus padres, ¿dejarían al niño todos los días con ellos? ¿A ellos les gustaría?
3. ¿Quién debe ser responsable de la crianza de los niños y por qué?
4. ¿De qué forma creen que los padres malcríen a los niños? ¿Por qué creen que lo hagan?
5. ¿Qué papel desempeñan/desempeñaron sus abuelos en su familia?
6. Imagínense que sus padres son ancianos y necesitan cuidados especiales. ¿Cuáles serían tres ventajas y tres desventajas de que ellos vivieran con Uds.?
7. ¿Pondrían a sus padres en una casa de ancianos? ¿Cuáles serían las ventajas y desventajas de hacerlo?

Act. 20B: After doing Part B, have a class sharing. Then ask students where their parents live and where their married brothers and sisters live. Ask students how far their parents live from their grandparents. Ask if their aunts and uncles live in the city where their parents live. Ask students where they think the people in the Venezuelan's family live in relation to each other.

Fuente hispana

Parte B: Ahora lean lo que dice una venezolana acerca del cuidado de los niños y de los ancianos en su país. Luego en su grupo, comparen lo que dice ella con lo que contestaron Uds.

"En Latinoamérica, una familia con hijos pequeños nunca los llevaría a una guardería antes de los dos años para que allí se los cuidaran. Preferiría en todo caso contratar a una niñera que les ayudaría con la parte pesada de ese trabajo, como es el bañarlos, darles de comer, cambiarles los pañales, supervisar sus juegos. Ahora bien, en caso de no tener recursos económicos para contratar ayuda, acudirían a la madre o a la suegra. Ellas, sin duda, lo harían con mucho amor, sin esperar ningún tipo de compensación económica.

Por otro lado, si los padres de la pareja son muy ancianos y no pueden valerse por sí mismos, ellos esperarán que sus hijos los cuiden. Vivirán en la casa de uno de sus hijos y, si es necesario y si tienen los recursos, les contratarán a una enfermera particular para que se encargue de ellos. Por nada en el mundo se les ocurrirá buscarles lugar en un asilo para personas mayores, pues, si lo hacen, sus padres sentirán que los hijos los han abandonado."

venezolana

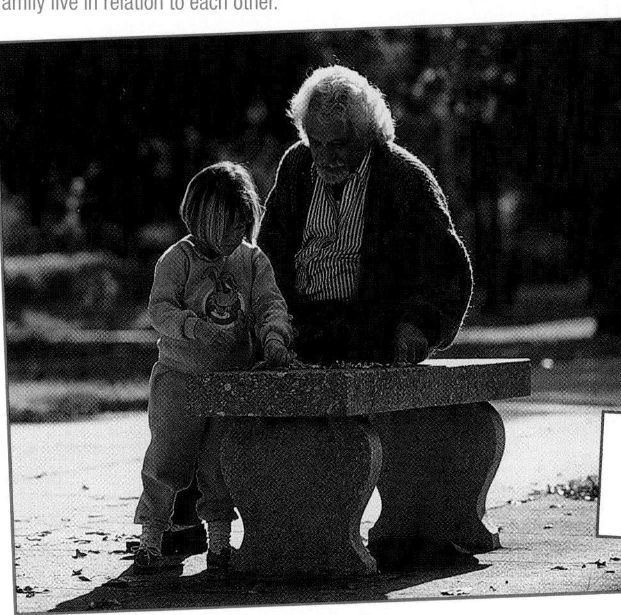

◄ Un abuelo y su nieta se divierten en un parque de La Habana, Cuba.

www *El rol de la mujer*

Act. 21A and B: This activity and Act. 22 all revolve around the topic of attitudes and customs. Option 1: As HW have students answer questions in Part A as an American would respond and then in Part B as they think a Hispanic would. Option 2: As HW have half the pairs answer questions as an American would and the other half as they think a Hispanic would. If you have foreign students, have them respond according to their culture.

Actividad 21 ¿Costumbres semejantes? **Parte A:** En parejas, lean las siguientes preguntas y discutan sus respuestas basándose en sus ideas sobre la sociedad norteamericana.

1. ¿Es común que un hombre soltero o una mujer soltera de treinta años viva con sus padres?
2. ¿Con quién viven los ancianos? ¿Tienen Uds. algún pariente en una casa de ancianos?
3. ¿Hay presión para que los recién casados tengan hijos?
4. ¿Comparten por igual el padre y la madre la crianza de los niños?
5. ¿Quién cuida a los niños durante el día?
6. ¿Cómo dividen las responsabilidades de la casa las parejas casadas?
7. ¿Tiene la mujer de hoy más independencia que antes? Expliquen.

Parte B: En parejas, lean las preguntas nuevamente y traten de imaginar lo que contestaría un hispano.

▶ Un hispano diría que (no) es común que un hombre de treinta años viva con sus padres.

Parte C: A continuación hay una lista de respuestas que dieron una mexicana y una española a las preguntas de la Parte A. Algunas respuestas fueron similares y otras no. Comparen estas respuestas con lo que respondieron Uds. en las Partes A y B de esta actividad. Los números corresponden a las preguntas de la Parte A.

Act. 21C: Give students a few moments to compare their answers to the answers given by a Mexican and a Spaniard. Note: the Spaniard said that the cost of living today, especially the cost of housing, has provided an impetus for change in Spain.

Fuentes hispanas

Las respuestas similares

- "Es común y aceptable que un hombre o una mujer de treinta años viva con sus padres si todavía no se ha casado." (1)
- "En general, la madre es la que más se ocupa de la crianza de los niños." (4)
- "Los abuelos y otros familiares suelen vivir en la misma ciudad y ayudan a cuidar a los niños cuando los padres lo necesitan." (5)
- "Dentro de la casa, generalmente la mujer sigue ocupándose de la mayoría de las labores domésticas." (6)
- "La mujer de clase media tiene cada vez más independencia y trabaja más fuera del hogar." (7)

mexicana	española
• "Relativamente pocas personas tienen parientes en casas de ancianos." (2)	• "Las cosas han cambiado ya que la mujer trabaja fuera de casa, y por eso ahora hay más personas en residencias de ancianos. También existen las residencias de día, son como guarderías pero para mayores." (2)
• "La familia espera que los recién casados tengan hijos pronto, pero últimamente esto está cambiando en las grandes ciudades." (3)	• "Normalmente tienen hijos dos o tres años después de casarse, si los tienen. Las mujeres tienen el primer hijo más o menos a los 30 años." (3)

Actividad 22 Una pareja hispano-norteamericana **Parte A:** Después de discutir las preguntas de las Actividades 20 y 21, en grupos de tres, hagan conjeturas sobre qué conflictos habría si se casaran una mujer de este país y un hombre de un país hispano. Luego hagan lo mismo para un hombre de este país y una mujer de un país hispano.

Act. 22A: Have students close books, form groups of three, allow a few minutes to generate ideas, and share answers when finished. Follow-up: Ask which combination they think would have fewer cultural conflicts and why.

Parte B: A veces las diferencias culturales en una pareja pueden ser grandes como, por ejemplo, si se debe tener a un pariente mayor y enfermo en casa o en una casa de ancianos. Pero también existen pequeñas diferencias culturales que pueden causar conflictos. Lean los comentarios de personas de diferentes países hispanos que viven en los Estados Unidos y que están casadas con norteamericanos. Luego digan si sus comentarios son parecidos a los que mencionaron Uds. en la Parte A o si les sorprenden algunos de los comentarios.

Act. 22B: After reading these comments, ask students what they reveal about the cultures in question.

"A mí me sorprendió ver a mi esposa caminando por la casa sin zapatos o zapatillas. En mi país jamás se hace eso y se dice que si uno anda descalzo se puede enfermar. Otra cosa que nunca voy a entender es

cómo se puede comer sólo un sándwich para la comida. ¿Dónde está el arroz? ¿Cómo se puede comer tan poco?"

colombiano

"Mi marido no entendía por qué yo siempre le planchaba la ropa. Su primera mujer, que era norteamericana, no lo hacía. Yo le expliqué que hacerlo era para mí un acto de amor."

peruana

"Me sorprendió que en la cocina de una típica familia norteamericana no suele haber una olla de presión. Aquí parece que muchas personas compran la sopa en latas o en sobres y no la preparan con carne, chorizo, huesos, garbanzos, vegetales, etc. El puré como primer plato no lo conocen. Echo de menos un buen puré de **puerros** y patatas. También echo de menos el pan español."

leeks

español

"La primera vez que fui a una cena formal, al final de la comida mi suegro se levantó para ver un partido de fútbol americano y muy poco después todos se levantaron. Me pareció muy extraño. Me sorprendió que ninguno estuviera interesado en conversar; comer era lo único importante. Eché de menos la sobremesa cuando en mi país, después de comer, todos se quedan y platican sobre cualquier tema."

puertorriqueña

V. Hypothesizing About the Future and the Present

Si Clauses (Part One)

FLR link: **Lectura 3**

Drill hypothetical future situations:

Do a chain drill: Have students say what they will do if they get a good job when they graduate. S1: **Si consigo un buen trabajo, no estudiaré más.** S2: **Si consigue un buen trabajo, ella no estudiará más, pero yo comenzaré a hacer la maestría.** (etc.)

In this section, you will learn to discuss hypothetical situations about the future and the present.

1. When making a hypothetical statement about possible future situations, use the following formula.

Referring to the future

si + *present indicative,*	present indicative **ir a** + *infinitive* future command

Si Paco tiene tiempo,
If Paco has time (which he may or may not),

le hablo del problema.
I am going to speak to him about the problem.
le voy a hablar del problema.
I am going to speak to him about the problem.
le hablaré del problema.
I will speak to him about the problem.
háblale del problema.
talk to him about the problem.

2. When you want to express hypothetical situations about the present, use the following formula. Notice that the **si** clause contains a contrary-to-fact statement (if I were a rich man—which I am not).

Drill contrary-to-fact situations:

Do a chain drill: S1: **Si fuera más rico, iría a Europa este verano.** S2: **Si él fuera más rico, él iría a Europa y si yo fuera más rica, compraría un carro nuevo.** S3: **Si ellos fueran más ricos, él... y ella..., y si yo fuera más rico, yo...**

Referring to the present

si + *imperfect subjunctive*, *conditional*

Si tuviera el dinero, *If I had the money* (which I do not),	**viajaría** por todo el mundo. *I would travel all over the world.*
Si estuvieras de visita en Santo Domingo, *If you were visiting Santo Domingo* (which you are not),	**irías** a la playa todos los días. *you would go to the beach every day.*
Si mi hermana **fuera** piloto, *If my sister were a pilot* (which she is not),	**conocería** muchos lugares. *she would know many places.*

3. In all sentences with **si** clauses, the **si** clause can start or end the sentence.

If needed, state that the present subjunctive is not used in a **si** clause.

Si Uds. me ayudan, terminaremos pronto.	=	Terminaremos pronto si Uds. me ayudan.
Si nos escucháramos más, nos pelearíamos menos.	=	Nos pelearíamos menos si nos escucháramos más.

Actividad 23 Situaciones para niños Imagina que eres un/a niño/a y acabas de participar en un taller (*workshop*) sobre seguridad personal. Di qué harías en las siguientes situaciones.

Act. 23: This could be assigned as HW and checked in class.

1. Si alguien te preguntara en la calle cómo llegar a un lugar, ...
2. Si un amigo o una amiga te ofrecieran un cigarrillo, ...
3. Si un amigo o una amiga te sugirieran que Uds. robaran algo en una tienda, ...
4. Si tú estuvieras solo/a en casa y una persona llamara por teléfono y preguntara por uno de tus padres, ...
5. Si en la calle alguien te ofreciera un dulce, ...

Act. 24A: Assign as HW or allow a short period of time in class to complete.

Actividad 24 ¿Alondra o búho? **Parte A:** Los cronobiólogos aseguran que existen personas orgánicamente más dispuestas al trabajo físico y mental diurno y otras al trabajo nocturno. Contesta este cuestionario para averiguar a qué grupo perteneces. En el cuestionario usan el reloj de 24 horas.

1. De poder elegir[1] con toda libertad y sin ninguna restricción laboral o de otro tipo, ¿a qué hora se levantaría?
   A- entre las 5 y las 6
   B- entre las 6 y las 7
   C- entre las 7.30 y las 10
   D- entre las 10 y las 11
   E- entre las 11 y las 12
2. Supongamos que Ud. se ha presentado a un nuevo trabajo y que tiene que realizar una prueba psicofísica que dura algunas horas y es mentalmente cansadora, ¿a qué hora le gustaría que le tomaran la prueba?
   A- entre las 8 y las 10
   B- entre las 11 y las 13
   C- entre las 15 y las 17
   D- entre las 19 y las 21
3. Si pudiera planear su noche con toda libertad y sin ninguna restricción laboral o de otro tipo, ¿a qué hora se acostaría?
   A- entre las 20 y las 21
   B- entre las 21 y las 22.15
   C- entre las 22.15 y las 0.30
   D- entre las 0.30 y la 1.45
   E- entre la 1.45 y las 3
4. Supongamos que se ha decidido a hacer ejercicio físico (un deporte, como el tenis, por ejemplo) y un amigo le sugiere hacerlo entre las 7 y las 8 de la mañana. En base a su predisposición natural, ¿cómo se encontraría Ud. si aceptara la invitación?
   A- estaría en muy buena forma
   B- estaría bastante en forma
   C- me sería difícil
   D- me sería muy difícil
5. Si tuviera que realizar dos horas de ejercicio físico pesado, ¿cuáles de estos horarios elegiría?
   A- de 8 a 10
   B- de 11 a 13
   C- de 15 a 17
   D- de 19 a 21
6. Si Ud. se fuera a dormir a las 23, ¿en qué nivel de cansancio se sentiría?
   A- nada cansado
   B- algo cansado
   C- bastante cansado
   D- muy cansado
7. ¿Se siente cansado durante la primera media hora luego de levantarse?
   A- muy cansado
   B- medianamente cansado
   C- sin cansancio pero no en forma plena
   D- en plena forma
8. ¿A qué hora del día se siente mejor?
   A- de 8 a 10
   B- de 11 a 13
   C- de 15 a 17
   D- de 19 a 21
9. Supongamos que otro amigo le sugiere hacer jogging entre las 22 y las 23, tres veces por semana. Si no tuviera otro compromiso y en base a su predisposición natural, ¿cómo se encontraría Ud. si aceptara la invitación?
   A- estaría en muy buena forma
   B- estaría bastante en forma
   C- me sería difícil
   D- me sería muy difícil

RESULTADO

Sume los puntos obtenidos de acuerdo con el siguiente puntaje:

Puntaje

Pregunta 1: A=1, B=2, C=3, D=4, E=5
Pregunta 2: A=1, B=2, C=3, D=4
Pregunta 3: A=1, B=2, C=3, D=4, E=5
Pregunta 4: A=1, B=2, C=3, D=4
Pregunta 5: A=1, B=2, C=3, D=4
Pregunta 6: A=4, B=3, C=2, D=1
Pregunta 7: A=4, B=3, C=2, D=1
Pregunta 8: A=1, B=2, C=3, D=4
Pregunta 9: A=4, B=3, C=2, D=1

Interpretación del resultado

9-15: Definidamente matutino
16-20: Moderadamente matutino
21-26: Ni búho[2] ni alondra[3], intermedio
27-31: Moderadamente vespertino
32-38: Definitivamente vespertino

[1] si pudiera elegir [2] owl [3] lark (known for its early morning song)

Act. 24B: Before sharing answers, have students predict if certain people are night owls or early birds. Do a poll by a show of hands to see how many are early birds or night owls. Discuss characteristics of each.

Parte B: En grupos de tres, hablen de las siguientes preguntas.

1. ¿Eres búho o alondra?
2. Si eres una persona matutina, ¿te casarías con una persona vespertina? ¿Cuáles serían los pros y los contras de ese tipo de unión?
3. ¿Cómo clasificas a diferentes parejas de tu familia o de amigos tuyos? ¿Son dos búhos o dos alondras? ¿Es una persona vespertina y la otra matutina? ¿Qué parejas funcionan mejor y por qué?

Actividad 25 Acciones poco comunes **Parte A:** Entrevista a personas de la clase para averiguar si han hecho o harían, si pudieran, las actividades de la siguiente lista. Debes hacerle sólo una pregunta a cada persona que entrevistes y escribir sólo un nombre para cada acción. Sigue el modelo.

Act. 25A: Instruct students to ask a question and write the name of the respondent in the appropriate space. Only one question to one person and then they must move on. Note: **El/La maratón** are both accepted.

▶ A: ¿Alguna vez has comido ancas de rana?

B: Sí, lo he hecho.
↓
A: ¿Cuándo las comiste?
↓
B: El verano pasado y me gustaron mucho.

B: No, nunca lo he hecho.
↓
A: ¿ Las comerías si pudieras?
↓
B: No, nunca lo haría. / Creo que sí lo haría.

	Lo ha hecho	Nunca lo haría	Lo haría si pudiera
1. correr en un maratón	________	________	________
2. escalar una montaña muy alta	________	________	________
3. ser participante de un "reality show"	________	________	________
4. hacer un viaje por la selva amazónica	________	________	________
5. vivir por lo menos un año en un país de habla española	________	________	________
6. actuar en una película de Hollywood	________	________	________
7. nadar sin traje de baño	________	________	________
8. ser reportero/a para un periódico de chismes	________	________	________

Parte B: Ahora en parejas, díganle a la otra persona los datos que obtuvieron.

Act. 25B: Do in pairs or have a full class sharing.

▶ Beth dice que si pudiera, comería ancas de rana.

Actividad 26 ¿Cómo serías? En parejas, túrnense para decir cómo sería su vida si Uds. fueran diferentes en ciertos aspectos.

Act. 26: Use the example in the text and expand to model talking about yourself if you were taller/shorter. Encourage students to be creative in their responses.

▶ ser más alto
Si yo fuera más alto, podría ser un buen jugador de basquetbol. Practicaría todos los días y también viajaría mucho para jugar partidos.

1. ser más bajo/a o alto/a
2. estudiar más/menos
3. tener más/menos dinero
4. hacer más/menos ejercicio
5. ser más/menos atractivo/a
6. ser famoso/a
7. (no) estar casado/a
8. (no) tener hermanos
9. (no) cambiarse el color del pelo
10. vivir en un país de habla española

Act. 27: Form groups of three and have students discuss the first two questions; then have a group sharing of ideas. Follow this procedure with the second two and last two questions. This will help to move the discussion along quickly.

Actividad 27 La clonación Mientras hacían las últimas actividades, Uds. tuvieron la oportunidad de explorar un poco la variedad de personas de la clase y sus opiniones: decidieron si eran matutinos o vespertinos; hablaron de las acciones que a cada uno le gustaría hacer o no; especularon qué diferencias habría en su vida con ciertos cambios. Durante siglos se decía que no había dos personas iguales en el mundo. Ahora, en grupos de tres, van a discutir las siguientes preguntas sobre la clonación (*cloning*).

1. ¿Qué significa el término "planificación familiar"?
2. Si la clonación y los mapas genéticos de embriones estuvieran al alcance de todos, ¿cómo cambiaría la definición de "planificación familiar"?
3. ¿Creen que la clonación sea moral o inmoral? Justifiquen su respuesta.
4. ¿Creen que muchas personas se harían un clon de sí mismas si pudieran?
5. ¿Cómo se sentiría un niño si supiera que es producto de una clonación?
6. ¿Qué consecuencias tendría la clonación para la estructura familiar? ¿Cómo cambiaría el concepto de "hermanos" o el de "padres"?

www.gaturro.com

Si pudieras pedir un hijo como pides una hamburguesa, ¿cómo te gustaría que fuera?

Act. 29 (on p. 267): ▶ Discuss the tradition of **piropos** with students. You may also want to mention that in Hispanic cultures it is not uncommon for people to stare at others. Then discuss the ramifications of acknowledging both a **piropo** and a stare. If you have received (or given) any **piropos**, share them with the class. Ask the women in the class how they would feel if someone **le echara un piropo en un país hispano.**

Pair women with women and men with men if possible to create **piropos**. When checking you might have people act like they are walking down the street while others give them **piropos;** of course, the person receiving the **piropos** should not acknowledge them.

Act. 28A: Do the activity as a whole class or in pairs. If done in pairs, check by seeing how students responded to questions 4 and 5. Could be assigned as HW and answers shared in class.

Act. 28B: Form groups and begin. Finish by having students share their ideas with the class and give examples of commercials or ads to illustrate their point.

Actividad 28 Un anuncio publicitario **Parte A:** Mira el anuncio de la página 267 y contesta estas preguntas.

1. ¿Qué ofrece el anuncio?
2. ¿A quién está dirigido?
3. ¿Qué supone el anuncio que la persona esté haciendo?
4. Si una empresa quisiera ofrecerle algo a ese consumidor en los Estados Unidos, ¿aceptaría el consumidor ese tipo de anuncio o lo interpretaría como ofensivo?
5. Si tuvieras que hacer un anuncio para ofrecerle ese tipo de servicio a un hombre, ¿qué dirías en el anuncio?

Parte B: En grupos de tres, lean las siguientes ideas sobre los anuncios comerciales y digan qué opinan.

1. En los anuncios, el hombre vende productos caros y la mujer vende productos baratos.
2. Los anuncios para adelgazar son para las mujeres.
3. Los anuncios de juguetes para niños están dirigidos a los niños y a sus madres.
4. Muchos anuncios presentan a la mujer como un "premio".

Actividad 29 El piropo Existe una costumbre en países de habla española llamada el piropo. El piropo suele ser una frase agradable que le dice normalmente un hombre a una mujer en la calle. Por lo general, la mujer no le hace caso a su admirador. Aunque hoy día no se oyen tantos piropos como antes y aunque se dice que la calidad también ha bajado, todavía es posible oír algunos muy bien expresados. Aquí hay algunos ejemplos.

"Le voy a preguntar a tu mamá dónde queda la juguetería donde compró esta muñeca."
"¿Quién se murió en el cielo para que los ángeles estén de luto (*in mourning*)?" (dicho a una mujer vestida de negro)
"Si fuera un caramelo, me gustaría derretirme (*melt*) en tu boca."
"Si pudiera hacerlo, volvería a ser niño para ser tu primer amor."
"Desearía ser tu perfume para besar tu cuello constantemente."

En parejas, escriban un piropo para hombres o mujeres para cada una de las siguientes categorías.

1. Un piropo que haga referencia al padre/a la madre de la persona porque su bello aspecto físico y su manera de ser tan agradable debe tener algo que ver con su padre/madre.
2. Un piropo que haga referencia a un ángel. Puesto que los ángeles son símbolos de lo ideal y de la pureza, muchos piropos se refieren a la persona como a un ángel.
3. Un piropo con esta fórmula: **Si yo fuera un/a** + *sustantivo*, + ...
4. Un piropo con esta fórmula: **Si yo pudiera...,** + ...
5. Un piropo con esta fórmula: **Desearía ser tu** + *sustantivo* + **para** + ...

Actividad 30 Lectura entre líneas **Parte A:** En grupos de cuatro, Uds. son empleados de una fábrica. Uno de Uds. tocó una tecla equivocada en la computadora y aparecieron en su pantalla los mensajes electrónicos entre Pura Morales, que es la nueva presidenta del sindicato, y el dueño de la fábrica. Lean los mensajes de las páginas 268–269 (en orden cronológico, es decir, de abajo hacia arriba) y hagan conjeturas sobre lo que ocurrió. Usen frases como: **Aquí dice que..., pero antes decía que...; Sería que ellos...; Esto implicaría que...; Será posible que...**

Señora, haga ya sus compras sin quitarse su máscara verde de belleza.

Nuestros vendedores la atenderán como si no la vieran, pero con una cordialidad especial para lectores de La Nación.

4343-8930 al 35

USTED ES DE LOS NUESTROS.

En vez de decir **Desearía ser tu...**, se puede decir **Me gustaría ser tu...** o **Quisiera ser tu...**

Para leer más piropos, haz una búsqueda en Internet con la palabra "piropo". ¡Ojo! Existen diferentes tipos de piropos, unos son chistosos, otros simpáticos y algunos poéticos, pero también existen piropos de muy mal gusto y en Internet vas a encontrar un poco de todo.

Act. 30A: Form groups of four and set up the activity. Tell students to be office gossips while doing the activity. Tell them they must read a few emails before being able to discern what they think happened. Allow sufficient time for groups to form opinions. As they work, ask how much more time they need to help move them along. When finished, share possible scenarios.

De: Felipe Bello [fbello@sistema.com]
Fecha: 18/4
A: Pura Morales [puramo@sistema.com]
Tema: Una rosa roja

Pura, ¡qué día! Hace mucho tiempo que no me divertía tanto. Desde luego, entre nosotros no hay falta de comunicación. Cuando te vea el viernes, tendré una rosa roja para que la lleves entre los dientes. Hasta el viernes próximo en Le Rendezvous a las ocho.
>
>----Mensaje original----
>**De:** Pura Morales [puramo@sistema.com]
>**Fecha:** 7/4
>**A:** Felipe Bello [fbello@sistema.com]
>**Tema:** A las ocho
>
>Felipe, obviamente no quiero entrometerme en tu vida familiar.
>El sábado que viene está perfecto. Estaré allí a las ocho.
>
>----Mensaje original----
>**De:** Felipe Bello [fbello@sistema.com]
>**Fecha:** 6/4
>**A:** Pura Morales [puramo@sistema.com]
>**Tema:** Le Rendezvous
>Pura, me es imposible. Este sábado me toca cuidar a los niños ya que
>no me gusta dejarlos con la niñera. Lo siento mucho, pero ¿qué tal el
>sábado que viene? Seguro que puedo decirle a mi mujer que voy a un
>partido de fútbol y así no podrá comunicarse conmigo.
>
>----Mensaje original----
>**De:** Pura Morales [puramo@sistema.com]
>**Fecha:** 5/4
>**A:** Felipe Bello [fbello@sistema.com]
>**Tema:** El secreto
>Felipe, ¿qué te parece si vamos al restaurante Le Rendezvous este
>sábado? El dueño es un íntimo amigo mío y es de confianza. Él no
>le dirá nada a nadie. Seguro que el dueño nos puede dar una sala
>especial sólo para nosotros donde podamos escuchar tangos.
>

(continúa en la página siguiente)

>----Mensaje original----
>**De:** Felipe Bello [fbello@sistema.com]
>**Fecha:** 4/4
>**A:** Pura Morales [puramo@sistema.com]
>**Tema:** Nuestro secreto
>Pura, no sabes cuánto me gustó conocerte. Eres una persona muy
>especial. ¡Hay pocas mujeres tan valientes! Confía en mí, no voy a
>decir nada a nadie de lo nuestro. Dime cuándo puedes reunirte
>conmigo.
>
>----Mensaje original----
>**De:** Felipe Bello [fbello@sistema.com]
>**Fecha:** 31/3
>**A:** Pura Morales [puramo@sistema.com]
>**Tema:** Reunión
>Srta. Morales: No tengo ningún inconveniente. Ya es hora de que nos
>conozcamos personalmente.
>
>----Mensaje original----
>**De:** Pura Morales [puramo@sistema.com]
>**Fecha:** 30/3
>**A:** Felipe Bello [fbello@sistema.com]
>**Tema:** Reunión
>
>Sr. Bello: Me gustaría hablar con Ud. el lunes, 3 de abril, a las 15:00.
>¿Estaría bien y le convendría esa hora? La cita no es para hablar de
>trabajo.

Parte B: Para ver qué pasó de verdad, lean el artículo que salió en el boletín (*newsletter*) de la fábrica a principios de mayo y comparen sus deducciones con la información del boletín. (Ver página 315.)

Act. 30B: Have students read the article to confirm or reject their theories.

Parte C: Antes de discutir el tema de la fidelidad, lean en la página 256 la información que se publicó en España sobre el tema. Luego compárenla con lo que creen que ocurre en este país.

Act. 30C: Ask students if they think there is a double standard for men and women that have affairs. You may want to discuss other double standards in relationships—for example, age differences between the man and the woman. If students say there is a double standard, ask if they think the society is **machista.**

1. ¿Creen que sea común la infidelidad entre personas que tienen un vínculo amoroso? Si supieran que la pareja de un amigo íntimo le pone los cuernos a un amigo, ¿bajo cuáles de estas circunstancias le dirían algo?
   - si fueran novios
   - si vivieran juntos, pero no estuvieran casados
   - si pensaran casarse
   - si estuvieran casados sin hijos
   - si estuvieran casados con hijos

2. ¿Cambiaría su respuesta si fuera una amiga íntima?
3. Si estuvieran Uds. en cualquiera de esas situaciones, ¿les gustaría que alguien les dijera la verdad? ¿Preferirían enterarse de otra forma? ¿Preferirían no saber nada?
4. Si un político casado tuviera una aventura amorosa, ¿cómo reaccionarían los ciudadanos? Si una mujer política casada tuviera una aventura amorosa, ¿cómo reaccionarían los ciudadanos?

Do the corresponding CD-ROM and web activities to review the chapter topics.

Vocabulario activo

La pareja y la familia

el asilo/la casa/la residencia de ancianos	*nursing home*
confiar en	*to trust*
la crianza	*raising, rearing* (of children)
criar	*to raise, rear*
(echarse) una cana al aire	(*to have*) *a one-night stand*
ejercer autoridad	*to exert authority*
entrometerse (en la vida de alguien)	*to intrude, meddle* (*in someone's life*)
la falta de comunicación	*lack of communication*
la fidelidad	*fidelity*
la generación anterior	*previous generation*
la igualdad de los sexos	*equality of the sexes*
inculcar	*to instill, inculcate*
independizarse (de la familia)	*to become independent* (*from one's family*)
la infidelidad	*infidelity*
inmoral	*immoral*
el machismo	*male chauvinism*
malcriar	*to spoil, pamper* (a child)
matriarcal	*matriarchal*
moral	*moral*
la niñera	*nanny*
la pareja	*partner; couple*
patriarcal	*patriarchal*
ponerle los cuernos a alguien	*to cheat on someone* (literally, to put horns on your partner)
rebelarse	*to rebel*
rebelde	*rebellious*
ser fiel/infiel	*to be faithful/unfaithful*
sumiso/a	*submissive*
tener una aventura (amorosa)	*to have an affair*
el vínculo	*bond*
vivir juntos/convivir	*to live together*

Expresiones útiles

un/a amigo/a íntimo/a	*a very close friend*
mientras más vengan, mejor	*the more, the merrier*
¿No te/le/les parece?	*Don't you think so?*
Eres un ángel.	*You're an angel.*
Eres un/a santo/a.	*You're a saint.*
Eres más bueno/a que el pan.	*You are better than gold.* (literally, You are better than bread.)
Ésa es una mentira más grande que una casa.	*That's a big fat lie.*
Francamente creo que tú...	*Frankly I think that you . . .*
¡Qué decente!	*How decent.*
¡Qué responsable!	*How responsible.*
¡Qué caradura!	*Of all the nerve!*
¡Qué sinvergüenza!	*What a dog/rat!*
¡Qué desconsiderado/a!	*How inconsiderate!*

Vocabulario personal

Capítulo 11

Drogas y violencia

Metas comunicativas

- hacer hipótesis sobre el futuro y el pasado
- expresar influencia, emociones y otros sentimientos y reacciones pasadas
- hablar sobre delitos y violencia

Meta adicional

- usar palabras de transición

May be assigned: Grammar, vocabulary, **¿Lo sabían?,** Act. 5, Act. 6, Act. 7A, Act. 11A, Act. 21A, Act. 23, Act. 25, Act. 27, Act. 28, Act. 29, Act. 30A.

Show the chapter video episode at any point in the chapter that you see fit and do all or selected activities in class. Note: Content of the video supplements the cultural material in the chapter and activities reenter chapter grammar and vocabulary.

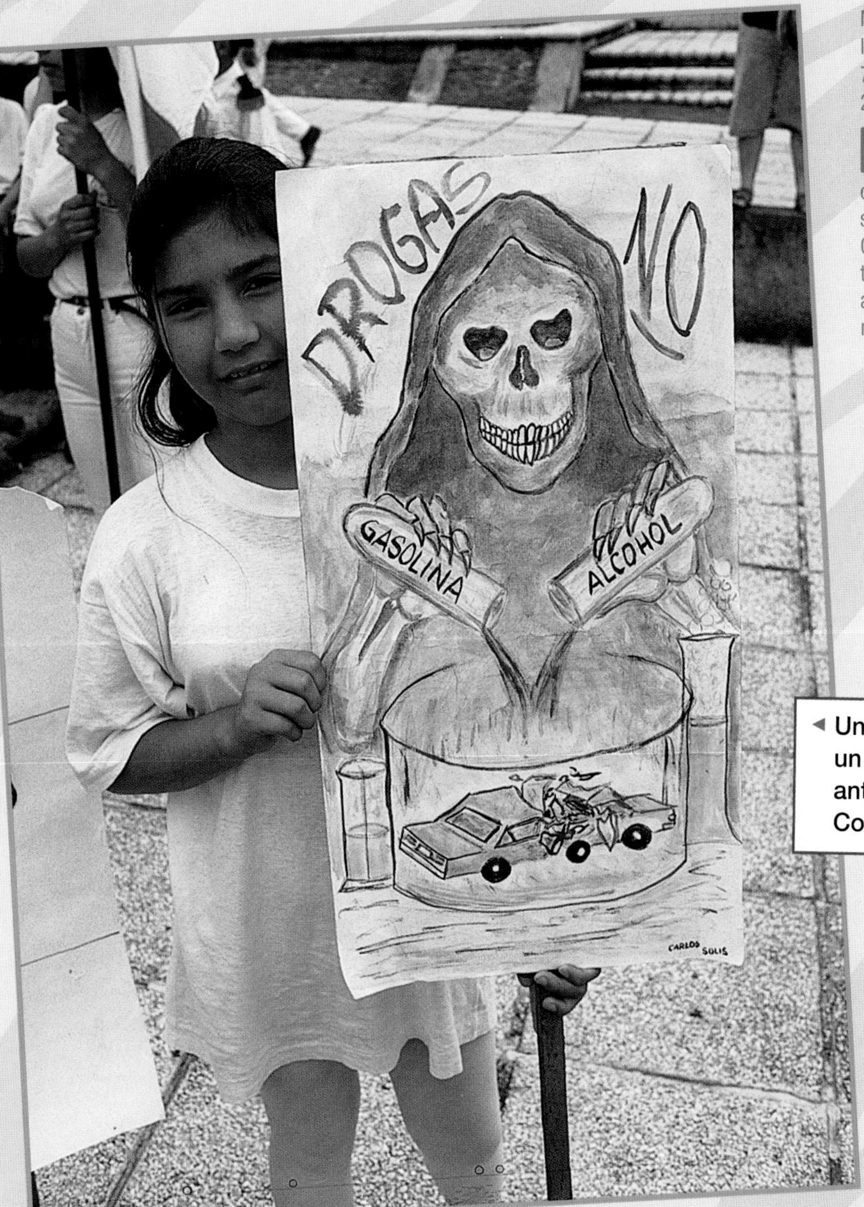

Una estudiante muestra un cartel en una campaña antidrogas en San José, Costa Rica.

¿Coca o cocaína?

La coca

Pretende aprobar el examen aun cuando no ha estudiado. = He attempts (and hopes) to pass the exam even when he hasn't studied.

Practice expressions: Create a context around a news item or something pertinent to the class. Write the expressions on the board and say: **El gobierno pretende convencer a los jóvenes que no consuman drogas con campañas que son malas. Se espera que para dentro de diez años no tengamos problemas de drogas. A veces la juventud les lleva la contraria a las autoridades a propósito.**

a propósito	on purpose
(para) dentro de (diez) horas/días/años/etc.	in (ten) hours/days/years/etc.
pretender + *infinitive*	to attempt (and to hope) + *infinitive*

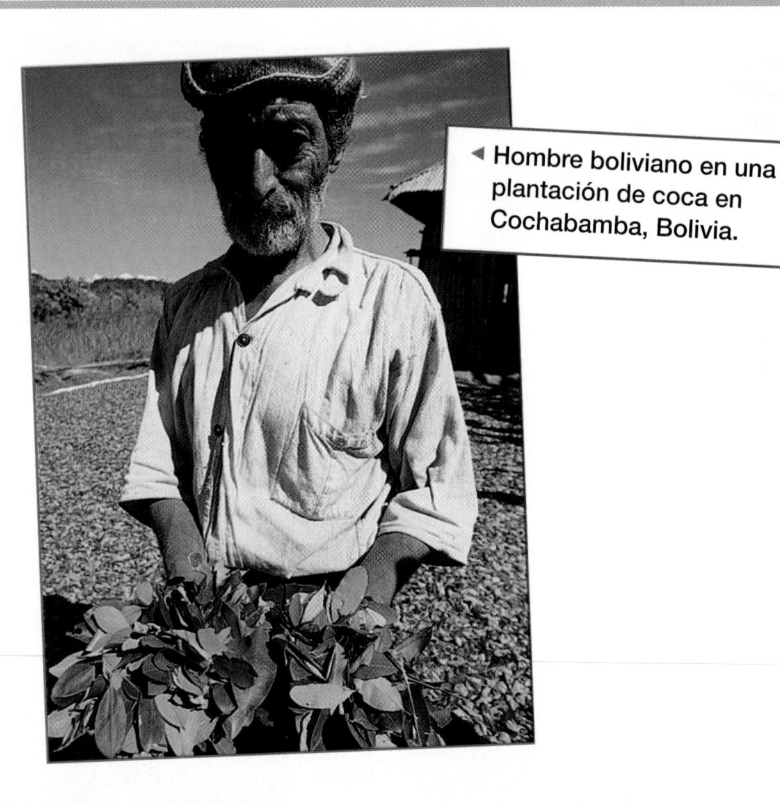

◂ Hombre boliviano en una plantación de coca en Cochabamba, Bolivia.

Act. 1: Do in pairs or as a whole group. Have students account for their answers. Explain that **droga** can have a positive or negative connotation.

Actividad 1 ¿Es droga o no? Lee la siguiente definición sobre la droga. Después, decide cuáles de las siguientes sustancias son drogas.

Droga: "Se dice de cualquier sustancia de origen vegetal, mineral o animal que tiene un efecto depresivo, estimulante o narcótico."

el café	las pastillas para adelgazar
el alcohol	la Coca-Cola
los somníferos	el cigarrillo
el té	la heroína
la hoja de coca	la mariguana
el éxtasis	

Actividad 2 ¿Cuál es su opinión? Mientras escuchas a un boliviano hablar sobre la diferencia entre la coca y la cocaína, determina cuál de las siguientes ideas representa su opinión.

1. _____ La cocaína es una droga, pero no debe ser ilegal.
2. __✓__ La coca no es una droga y no debe ser ilegal.
3. _____ La coca y la cocaína son drogas que deben ser ilegales.

Act. 2: Play the interview, then check response.

Actividad 3 ¿Qué es la coca? Ahora, lee las siguientes preguntas y después, para contestarlas, escucha la entrevista otra vez.

1. ¿Cuál es la diferencia entre la coca y la cocaína?
2. ¿En qué países se consume la coca?
3. ¿Con qué bebida compara el narrador el mate de coca?
4. Según el narrador, ¿cuáles son algunos de los grupos que consumen coca y por qué la consumen?
5. ¿Qué ha hecho el gobierno boliviano con respecto a la coca?
6. ¿Qué hizo la reina Sofía de España cuando llegó a La Paz?

Act. 3: Have students read the questions prior to listening. Option 1: Play the interview and then check responses. Option 2: Play the interview pausing it whenever an answer is given and checking responses.

Answers: 1. **La coca es una planta; la cocaína es una droga.** 2. **en los países andinos** (**Perú, Ecuador, Bolivia**) 3. **con un café fuerte** 4. **las clases trabajadoras para aguantar jornadas de trabajo largas; estudiantes de clase media cuando tienen que trasnochar; turistas para combatir el soroche** 5. **campañas para erradicar las plantaciones de coca** 6. **Tomó mate de coca.**

La hoja de coca es utilizada de diferentes maneras por indígenas en Perú, Bolivia, el norte de Argentina, Ecuador, Colombia, Venezuela, Brasil y Chile:

- como unidad monetaria para intercambiar alimentos
- en ceremonias religiosas (nacimientos, bautizos, casamientos, actos relacionados con la naturaleza, etc.) porque se considera una planta sagrada
- como medicamento para enfermedades de la piel, el aparato digestivo y el sistema circulatorio, se considera un remedio popular y de bajo costo

En los Estados Unidos esta hoja se utilizó por primera vez en 1884 en una bebida llamada Vino Francés de Coca inventada por el Dr. Pemberton en Atlanta. Años después él creó la Coca-Cola (con la hoja de coca y la nuez kola) que era una gaseosa y a la vez un medicamento para el dolor de cabeza.

Actividad 4 ¿Qué harían? En grupos de tres, discutan qué harían Uds. en las siguientes situaciones.

1. ¿Tomarían mate de coca si estuvieran en La Paz como turistas?
2. Si Uds. fueran el/la presidente de los Estados Unidos y estuvieran de visita en Bolivia, ¿tomarían mate de coca si se lo ofreciera el alcalde de una ciudad? Si aceptaran, ¿cómo lo interpretaría el pueblo norteamericano? ¿Y el pueblo boliviano?

Act. 4: While checking, discuss ramifications of the actions of people in power. Relate this to the drinking of **mate de coca** by Queen Sofía upon arrival in La Paz. Discuss the political implications of this.

I. Discussing Crime and Violence

Delitos y consecuencias

FLR link: **Lectura 3**

El siguiente es parte de un artículo que apareció en la publicación digital *Honduras*.

watchman
assault, attack, robbery
armed

fight / crime, criminal activity

a criminal offense, a crime
Students will discuss this article in Act. 8.

"Aló, habla el vecino **vigilante** al volante y llamo para reportarles en este momento el **asalto** a la agencia bancaria ubicada en la entrada de la colonia El Roble. Son cinco individuos **armados** que..." Así podría ser una llamada de uno de los cinco mil quinientos teléfonos celulares que este 4 de octubre serán entregados a igual número de taxistas, buseros y dirigentes patronales con el fin de fortalecer la **lucha** contra la **delincuencia** mediante el programa "Vecino vigilante al volante". El programa municipal consiste en que los poseedores de los celulares, sin riesgo alguno, reporten de inmediato a las autoridades policiales cualquier **delito** que ocurra en la ciudad o sus alrededores.

Asesinar refers to all homicides and not just to those of important people. **Crimen** means serious crime as well as homicide. .

Delincuente is someone of any age who breaks the law

Delincuencia does not refer only to criminal activity committed by youth, but by people of any age.

Practice vocabulary:

Give definitions and have students guess the words. Then pair up students, and have them take turns giving definitions and guessing the words.

Personas	Hechos y cosas	Acciones
el/la asesino/a	el asesinato	asesinar
el asaltante	el asalto	asaltar
	el atraco (*holdup; mugging*)	atracar
	el castigo (*punishment*)	castigar
el/la carcelero/a (*jailer, warden*)	la cárcel (*jail, prison*)	encarcelar
el/la condenado/a (*convict*)	la condena (*the sentence*)	condenar (a alguien) a (10) meses/años de prisión
el/la delincuente (*criminal*)	la delincuencia (*criminal activity*)	
el/la drogadicto/a	la droga	drogarse
	la legalización	legalizar
el/la narcotraficante	el narcotráfico	traficar en drogas
el/la pandillero/a (*gang member*)	la pandilla (*gang*)	
	la prohibición	prohibir
	el rescate (*ransom*)	rescatar (*to rescue*)
	el robo (*robbery*)	robar
el/la secuestrador/a (*kidnapper; hijacker*)	el secuestro	secuestrar

el/la sentenciado/a	la sentencia	sentenciar
	el soborno (*bribe*)	sobornar
el/la suicida	el suicidio	suicidarse
el/la terrorista	el terrorismo	
el/la violador/a (*rapist*)	la violación	violar (a alguien)

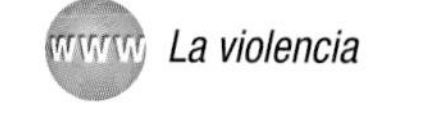

La violencia

Otras palabras relacionadas con el delito

la adicción	addiction
la cadena perpetua	life sentence
el cartel (de drogas)	
consumir drogas	to use drugs
detener	to arrest
el homicidio	
el ladrón/la ladrona	thief
la libertad condicional	parole
la pena de muerte/pena capital	death penalty
el/la preso/a	prisoner
el/la ratero/a	pickpocket
la sobredosis	drug overdose
el toque de queda	curfew
la víctima	
la violencia	

Víctima is always feminine even when referring to men: Él fue **la única víctima.**

Actividad 5 ¿Cuánto sabes? Habla sobre las siguientes personas, instituciones o cosas usando palabras de la lista de vocabulario. Sigue el modelo.

Act. 5: Assign as HW and check in class.

▶ Jesse James fue un **ladrón** que participó en muchos **robos** durante el siglo XIX. **Robaba** bancos y trenes y finalmente fue **asesinado**, pero nunca estuvo en la **cárcel**.

1. Bonnie y Clyde
2. Alcatraz
3. la silla eléctrica
4. Charles Manson
5. la escuela Columbine de Colorado
6. John Wilkes Booth
7. John Lennon
8. ? ? ?

Act. 6: Assign as HW or do in class. Point to the possible use of historical present in headlines. Have students expand on the headlines by describing what they think happened or will happen.

Actividad 6 Los titulares Lee los siguientes titulares (*headlines*) y complétalos con palabras de la lista de vocabulario.

Se discute en el Senado la ___legalización___ de la mariguana

Se ___suicidó___ la jueza Roviralta
Saltó del balcón de un 10° piso

Comienza el ___toque de queda___
Calles sin menores de 18 después de las 22 hrs.

___Detuvieron___ a 8 jugadores de fútbol
No pasaron el control antidrogas

A 3 años de la muerte del Presidente Ramírez, condenan al ___asesino___ a ___cadena perpetua / (10 años)___

Act. 7A: Assign as HW or quickly do individually in class. Then form groups of three and have them decide on the two most and least important. When finished, have groups report back to the class.

Actividad 7 El país **Parte A:** Piensa en este país y numera del 1 al 12 los asuntos (*matters*) que te preocupan, del que más te preocupa al que menos te preocupa. Luego en grupos de tres, comparen el orden que escogió cada uno y expliquen por qué ciertos asuntos les preocupan más/menos que a sus compañeros. Intenten decidir cuáles son los dos más importantes y los dos menos importantes.

▶ A mí me preocupa más/menos... porque...

_______ Acceso a la educación
_______ Alto costo de la vida
_______ Bajos salarios
_______ Corrupción
_______ Delincuencia, inseguridad
_______ Desempleo
_______ Drogadicción
_______ Mal estado o ausencia de servicios públicos
_______ Malos servicios de salud
_______ Pobreza
_______ Violencia, incumplimiento de leyes
_______ Otro(s)
¿Cuál(es)? _________________

Act. 7B: Form groups of three, compare responses, and discuss reasons behind choices. See if answers are different for men and women. Have the class vote on the most and least important.

Parte B: En grupos de tres, miren los resultados de una encuesta realizada a un grupo de guatemaltecos sobre los asuntos que les preocupan de su país. Comparen sus respuestas con las de Uds.

Principales problemas a resolver en Guatemala

	N	%
Delincuencia, inseguridad	736	32,0%
Desempleo	421	18,3%
Alto costo de la vida	351	15,2%
Pobreza	189	8,2%
Acceso a la educación	163	7,1%
Violencia, incumplimiento de leyes	122	5,3%
Corrupción	114	4,9%
Malos servicios de salud	85	3,7%
Mal estado o ausencia de servicios públicos	42	1,8%
Drogadicción	24	1,1%
Bajos salarios	23	1,0%
Otros	9	,4%
Ninguno	6	,3%
Ns-Nr	15	,7%
Total	**2301**	**100,0%**

Multirespuesta
Demoscopía S.A.

Ns - Nr = No sabe. / No responde.

¿LO SABÍAN?

Hoy día la gente no sólo se preocupa por la delincuencia sino también por el terrorismo. ETA es una organización terrorista en España que busca la secesión del llamado País Vasco—región que se encuentra en la parte norte del país—del resto de España, argumentando que tienen su propio idioma y su propia cultura diferente del resto del país. En septiembre de 1998, ETA y el gobierno español acordaron una tregua (*truce*) como un principio para resolver este conflicto, pero desde el año 2000 ha habido un promedio de 20 muertos por año. Desde principios de los años 60, han sido asesinadas más de 800 personas, en su gran mayoría representantes del gobierno como políticos y policías.

In 2004, there was a terrorist attack in Madrid and ETA was a suspect. It was soon determined that they were not at fault and that the attackers were possibly tied to Al Qaeda.

04 de Agosto de 2002. **Los nacionalistas vascos ponen una bomba al lado de la Casa-Cuartel de la Guardia Civil de Santa Pola (Alicante) y muere Cecilio Gallego Alarias que estaba en una parada de autobús próxima, y la hija de un guardia civil, Silvia Martínez Santiago, de 6 años de edad, que se encontraba jugando en su habitación.**

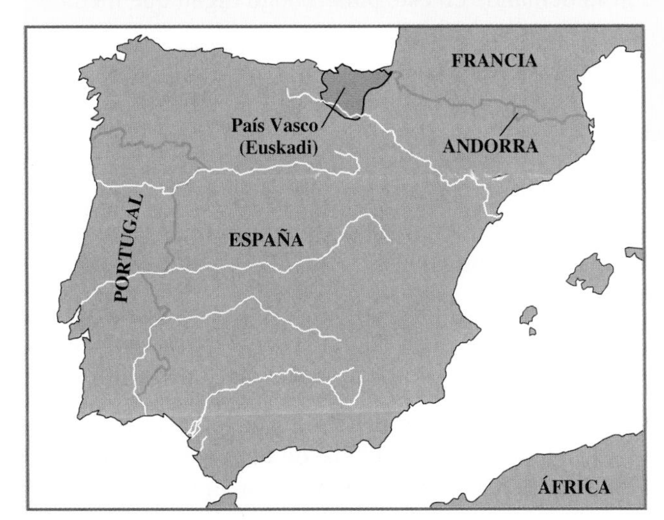

▼ Manifestación en San Sebastián en contra de los actos terroristas de ETA en España.

Actividad 8 Combatir la delincuencia En la sección de vocabulario de la página 274 aparece parte de un artículo hondureño que explica una forma de combatir la delincuencia. Léelo y luego en grupos de tres discutan las siguientes preguntas.

1. ¿Qué forma de combatir la delincuencia describe el artículo?
2. ¿Qué consecuencias positivas y negativas puede tener?
3. ¿Alguna vez han usado un móvil para informar sobre un accidente, un robo o un delito? Si contestan que sí, ¿qué ocurrió? Si contestan que no, si vieran algo y tuvieran móvil, ¿notificarían a las autoridades?
4. ¿Creen que se podría implementar un plan similar al del artículo en su ciudad? Justifiquen su respuesta.
5. ¿De qué otra forma se podría reducir la delincuencia en su ciudad?

Act. 9A: You may want to have the class summarize the Peruvian's statement before students express their opinions or you may want to elicit opinions by asking questions such as **¿Creen que la gente aceptaría ganar menos dinero?**

Fuente hispana

Act. 9B: Encourage students to be creative. When finished, list ways to reduce the demand for drugs on the board. Then ask them which of these measures they were exposed to when they were younger.

As a follow-up, ask students who is more guilty, the person that uses drugs, the person that sells it, the person that produces it, or are they all equally guilty. Note: this chapter ends with a debate on the legalization of drugs. This activity will help to get students thinking about the subject.

Act. 10: Option 1: Form groups of three and allow a period of time for discussion. When finished, have groups report back to the class. Option 2: Form groups of three and assign each group a question. When finished, have each group report back.

Actividad 9 La oferta y la demanda **Parte A:** El problema que genera la cocaína y su erradicación es un tema que preocupa a todos. Lee la opinión de una peruana sobre cómo eliminar las plantaciones de coca en Perú y luego, en grupos de tres, digan qué piensan de esa idea.

> "En Perú hay muchos campesinos que trabajan en las plantaciones de coca y es muy fácil decir que uno de los pasos para eliminar el problema de la droga es quemar esas plantaciones. Algunos dicen que en vez de plantar coca podrían plantar café, pero una planta de café tarda cuatro años en dar frutos. ¿Y qué haría la gente mientras tanto? Creo que la solución es que el gobierno peruano implemente un plan integral en el que se diera subsidios a los trabajadores durante esos cuatro años para que cambien de cultivos. Pero el plan también debe incluir el construir escuelas y postas médicas. Con plantaciones que no fueran coca, la gente ganaría menos dinero, pero creo que no le importaría si tuviera ciertos servicios básicos cerca del lugar donde viven. Trabajé en esa zona y viví con los campesinos. En mi opinión lo único que quieren es vivir en paz y con dignidad."
>
> ***peruana***

Parte B: Ahora, hagan una lista de lo que hace y de lo que podría hacer el gobierno actual para reducir la demanda en este país. Luego digan qué medidas (*measures*) les parecen más eficaces y por qué.

Actividad 10 La violencia En grupos de tres, discutan las siguientes preguntas relacionadas con la violencia.

1. ¿Cuáles son las cinco causas más importantes de la violencia en este país? ¿Cómo se podría solucionar este problema?
2. Algunos dicen que la televisión fomenta la violencia en la sociedad, pero para otros la programación es sólo un reflejo de una sociedad enfermiza. Den dos argumentos a favor de la primera idea y dos a favor de la segunda.
3. ¿Qué tipo de programas televisivos prefieren los niños de hoy? ¿En qué se diferencian estos programas de los que veían Uds. de niños? ¿Son más o menos violentos? ¿Más o menos educativos? Mencionen algunos ejemplos.
4. ¿Creen que los programas de noticias que muestran la reconstrucción de un asesinato sean beneficiosos para la sociedad? ¿Es buena idea dejar que los niños vean ese tipo de programa? Si contestan que no, ¿cómo se podría lograr que no lo vieran?

¿LO SABÍAN?

En varios países hispanos como Colombia, España y Argentina el gobierno les prohíbe a los canales de televisión presentar programas de contenido pornográfico o con mucha violencia antes de las diez de la noche y exige que se le recuerde al televidente la finalización de este horario con anuncios como "Aquí termina el horario de protección al menor. La presencia de los niños frente al televisor queda bajo la exclusiva responsabilidad de los padres". Di si crees que sería bueno utilizar este sistema de control en tu país.

Sexo y violencia en televisión

El Congreso de los Diputados aprobó el jueves 30 con carácter definitivo, la ley por la cual se incorpora al derecho español la directiva comunitaria de "televisión sin fronteras". En ella se atribuye al Ministerio de Obras Públicas el control e inspección de todas sus disposiciones, incluidas las emisiones pornográficas o de "violencia gratuita", que los espectadores no podrán recibir entre las seis de la mañana y las diez de la noche.

—El País

Actividad 11 Decidan ustedes **Parte A:** En parejas, comenten las siguientes situaciones y usen las expresiones de la lista.

Act. 11A: Assign as HW and compare answers and justifications in pairs in class. When finished, have groups share answers and try to reach group consensus in each case.

1. Un criminal violó y mató a una niña de ocho años y fue condenado a cadena perpetua. Después de ocho años, salió en libertad condicional.
2. Un muchacho de 15 años que mató a una anciana de 75 años y le robó su dinero fue encarcelado, pero a los 21 años lo soltaron por haber cometido el crimen cuando era menor de edad.
3. Un hombre de 58 años que siempre mantenía su inocencia fue declarado inocente después de que le hicieron un análisis de ADN. Estuvo en la cárcel 27 años.

ADN = DNA

¿Y a ti qué te parece?	What do you make of it?
¿Qué opinas sobre esta situación?	What do you think about this situation?
Desde mi punto de vista...	From my point of view . . .
A mi modo de ver...	The way I see it . . .
Es un acto despreciable.	It's a despicable act.
¡Qué barbaridad!	Wow!/How terrible!
¡Qué injusticia!	How unfair!/What an injustice!

Parte B: En grupos de tres, cuéntenles a sus compañeros, con detalle, un crimen o un delito reciente.

Actividad 12 Los jóvenes y el alcohol **Parte A:** Lee lo que dice una española sobre el consumo del alcohol entre los jóvenes de su país y luego compara la situación con la de este país.

"Soy española y estudiante de posgrado en una universidad norteamericana donde doy clases de español. Al llegar aquí me sorprendió muchísimo el lugar que ocupa el alcohol en la vida estudiantil norteamericana. No quiero decir que en España la gente no beba,

El consumo del alcohol por persona es más alto en España que en los EE.UU., pero el índice de alcoholismo y de abuso es más bajo.

El número de muertos por enfermedades del hígado (*liver*) es tres veces más alto en España que en los EE.UU.

Act. 12A: You may want to tell students that young people in Spain generally do not go out with the express purpose of getting drunk, and although some people do get drunk, they don't usually brag about it the following day.

simplemente que hay diferencias y esas diferencias se reflejan en el idioma. Por ejemplo, en español no existen palabras para *binge drinking* o *keg party* y la idea de tomar una cerveza rápidamente, o sea, lo que llaman *chugging* o *funneling*, es un concepto totalmente desconocido para los españoles.

Normalmente los españoles empiezan a beber en casa a una edad temprana ya sea vino con gaseosa a la hora de comer o una copa de champán en un día especial. Luego, los jóvenes entre 14 y 16 años experimentan un poco con el alcohol y cuando los universitarios salen a los bares, pubs o a una discoteca suelen tomar, pero lo importante es que el propósito de la salida es hablar con los amigos, bailar, ligar, o sea, pasarlo bien."

española

Act. 12B: Form groups of four and set a time limit. Have a group sharing when finished.

Parte B: La edad mínima para beber alcohol en este país es de 21 años. En grupos de cuatro, discutan si la edad mínima para beber debe ser de 18 años o no y por qué.

II. Hypothesizing About the Future and the Past

A. The Future Perfect and the Conditional Perfect

Drill future perfect:

1. Write clues on the board and have students say things you will have done by next year or the following one: **comprar un apartamento, viajar por Centroamérica, casarse,** etc. Ss: **Para dentro de un año Ud. ya habrá comprado un apartamento.**

2. Ask students what life will be like in 20 years. If needed, give clues like **Marte, transporte público, clima.**

In Chapter 10, you studied how to express probability about the present and the past using the future and the conditional. In this chapter you will learn how to hypothesize about the future and the past. In the interview you heard at the beginning of this chapter, the Bolivian used the future perfect when he said **"para dentro de diez años, el mundo ya habrá entendido la diferencia entre uno y otro"** to express what *will have happened* in ten years.

1. When talking about what will have happened by a certain time in the future, use the future perfect (**futuro perfecto**), which is formed as follows.

haber (future)		
habré	habremos	
habrás	habréis	+ *past participle*
habrá	habrán	

Note: To review formation of past participles, see Appendix A, pages 348–349.

—Dentro de un mes ya **habré dejado** de fumar.	*In a month I will have already quit smoking.*
—Y **¿habrás comenzado** a sentirte mejor dentro de tres meses?	*And will you have started to feel better in three months?*

2. When talking about what *would have happened* in the past, use the conditional perfect (**condicional perfecto**), which is formed as follows.

Drill conditional perfect:

Tell students that last week you found a wallet in the street and that you went and got a massage at a spa. Have them say what they would have done in your place.

haber (conditional)		
habría	habríamos	+ *past participle*
habrías	habríais	
habría	habrían	

—La muchacha les contó a sus padres que su hermano era drogadicto. ¿Qué **habrías hecho** en su lugar?

The young woman told her parents that her brother was a drug addict. What would you have done in her place?

—Yo le **habría hablado** a mi hermano primero.

I would have talked to my brother first.

Act. 13: Practice question formation, form pairs, and do the activity. Check by calling on individuals for responses. Encourage connected discourse by asking students to support their answers with anecdotes from the news.

Actividad 13 El cigarrillo Hoy en día se habla mucho del cigarrillo y sus efectos. En parejas, hablen de cuál será la actitud hacia el cigarrillo dentro de cinco años. Sigan el modelo.

▶ el gobierno / prohibir / fumar en presencia de los niños

—¿Crees que dentro de cinco años el gobierno ya habrá prohibido fumar en presencia de los niños?

—Sí, el gobierno ya lo habrá prohibido.

—No, el gobierno no lo habrá prohibido todavía.

1. el gobierno / prohibir / fumar en todos los bares y restaurantes de todo el país
2. los médicos / inventar / un método para dejar de fumar en un día
3. algún niño / demandar (*to sue*) / a sus padres por fumar en casa
4. las máquinas que venden cigarrillos / desaparecer
5. las compañías tabacaleras / hacer / un cigarrillo que no produzca humo (*smoke*)
6. el número de fumadores menores de 18 años / reducirse / drásticamente
7. el gobierno / limitar / la cantidad de nicotina en los cigarrillos

Act. 14: Practice question formation, form pairs, and do the activity. Check by calling on individuals to say what their partners will be doing.

Actividad 14 Tu futuro En parejas, entrevisten a su compañero/a para averiguar cómo habrán cambiado ciertos aspectos de su vida dentro de tres y diez años, y escriban la información de forma breve.

▶ —¿Cómo habrá cambiado tu vida sentimental dentro de tres años?
—Me habré casado/a...

Vida	3 años	10 años
sentimental	______________	______________
familiar	______________	______________
profesional	______________	______________
turística	______________	______________

Act. 15: Model by reading the example and giving and eliciting other excuses such as: **Se lo habría prestado, pero yo tenía que usarlo.** Form pairs and begin. Check by having a few pairs report back to the class.

Actividad 15 La mejor excusa En parejas, inventen el contexto en que se hicieron estas preguntas y las excusas que se dieron en cada caso. Sigan el modelo.

▶ —¿Por qué no le prestaste el coche a tu hermano?
—Estábamos en el centro y él quería irse a casa (*contexto*). Se lo habría prestado, pero él estaba borracho (*excusa*).

1. ¿Por qué no lo invitaste a salir?
2. ¿Por qué no te pusiste los pantalones negros que te regalé?
3. ¿Por qué no devolviste el DVD?
4. ¿Por qué no le abriste la puerta?

Act. 16: Option 1: Form groups of three, set a time limit, and call time for students to go to the next situation. When finished, have some groups report back. Option 2: Assign a different scenario to each group, have them discuss and, when finished, have groups report back. Follow-up: For HW, assign students to write statements on each situation.

Actividad 16 Situaciones difíciles En grupos de tres, lean cada situación y luego discutan qué habrían hecho Uds. en cada caso y por qué.

1. Teresa estaba en una tienda de regalos y sin querer rompió un animalito de cristal muy caro, pero nadie vio lo que ocurrió. En la tienda había un cartel que decía: "Si lo rompe, es suyo". ¿Qué habrían hecho Uds. en el lugar de Teresa y por qué?
2. John estaba en una discoteca en un país extranjero con leyes muy estrictas y conoció a unos muchachos que lo invitaron a ir a un bar. En el carro uno de los muchachos encendió un porro (*lit a joint*) y se lo ofreció a John. ¿Qué habrían hecho Uds. en el lugar de John y por qué?
3. Mariano y Silvia siempre se pelean a causa de los amigos del otro. El sábado organizaron una cena y un amigo de Silvia encendió un cigarrillo inmediatamente después de terminar de comer. Mariano odia el humo y no sabía qué hacer porque no quería causar tensión entre él y su esposa. ¿Qué habrían hecho Uds. en el lugar de Mariano y por qué?
4. Era un día lindísimo y la playa estaba llena de gente. Patricio se metió en el mar para refrescarse y una ola gigantesca lo revolcó en el agua. Cuando se recuperó, se dio cuenta de que había perdido el traje de baño. ¿Qué habrían hecho Uds. en el lugar de Patricio y por qué?

B. *Si* Clauses (Part Two)

In Chapter 10 you studied how to make hypothetical statements about the future and the present: **Si tengo tiempo, iré. Si tuviera tiempo, iría.** In this chapter you will learn how to hypothesize about the past.

FLR link: **Lectura 2**

Drill hypothetical situations about the past:

1. Tell students they missed a great party yesterday for the reunion of the *Friends* cast. Have them say what they would have done if they had gone to the party. List cues on the board: **bailar, comer, cantar, pedir un autógrafo, darle un beso, darle un abrazo.** S: **Si hubiera ido a la fiesta, le habría pedido un autógrafo a Jennifer Aniston.**

1. When you want to make hypothetical statements about the past, use the following formula. Notice that the **si** clause contains a contrary-to-fact statement.

Referring to the past	
si + *pluperfect subjunctive,*	*conditional perfect*

Remember that the **si** clause can start or end the sentence.

Si hubiera ido a la fiesta, / *If I had gone to the party* (which I didn't), — **habría visto** a Christina Aguilera. / *I would have seen Christina Aguilera.*

Si **hubiéramos tenido** más dinero, / *If we had had more money* (which we didn't), — **habríamos ido** a más países. / *we would have gone to more countries.*

2. Do a chain drill: Have students say what their life would have been like if they had been born in a big/small family, in a big/small town. S1: **Si hubiera nacido en una familia numerosa, habría tenido muchos hermanos.** S2: **Si ella hubiera nacido en una familia numerosa, habría tenido muchos hermanos; si yo hubiera nacido en una familia numerosa, mis padres no habrían podido pagarme los estudios.**

2. The pluperfect subjunctive (**pluscuamperfecto del subjuntivo**) is formed as follows.

haber (imperfect subjunctive)		
hubiera	hubiéramos	
hubieras	hubierais	+ *past participle*
hubiera	hubieran	

There is an optional form, frequently used in Spain and in some areas of Hispanic America, in which you may substitute **-se** for **-ra**; for example: **hubiera** = **hubiese.**

To review the formation of past participles, see Appendix A, pages 348–349.

3. The following summarizes hypothetical situations with **si.**

Referring to the future	
si + *present,*	+ *future*

Si **tengo** tiempo, / *If I have time* (which I might), — **iré** a la fiesta mañana. / *I will go to the party tomorrow.*

To review other **si** clauses that *can* refer to the future, see pages 262–263.

Referring to the present	
si + *imperfect subjunctive,*	+ *conditional*

Si **tuviera** tiempo, / *If I had time* (which I don't), — **iría** a la fiesta. / *I would go to the party.*

Referring to the past	
si + *pluperfect subjunctive*,	+ *conditional perfect*

Si **hubiera tenido** tiempo,	**habría ido** a la fiesta.
If I had had time (which I didn't),	*I would have gone to the party.*

Drill **como si:**

Use knowledge of students to have them make contrary-to-fact statements: **Jason juega al tenis como si..., Mary habla español como si...**, etc.

4. The phrase **como si** (*as if*) is ALWAYS followed by the imperfect or pluperfect subjunctive to make contrary-to-fact statements.

Habla **como si fuera** el rey de España.	*He talks as if he were the king of Spain* (which he is not).
Me mira **como si** yo **hubiera cometido** un crimen.	*She's looking at me as if I had committed a murder* (which I didn't).

Act. 17: Be sure that students realize that they are pretending to be finished with their studies. Therefore, set the scene by saying that it is the year X and that they are at an alumni gathering (**reunión de ex alumnos**) and are discussing campus safety. Follow-up: When finished, ask them to rank the items from most to least important.

Actividad 17 La seguridad en la universidad Imagina que ya terminaste la universidad. Di qué habrías hecho para mejorar la seguridad en tu universidad si hubieras podido.

▶ Si hubiera podido, yo...

1. aumentar el número de policías
2. crear un servicio de guardias que acompañara a la gente de noche
3. mejorar el sistema de alumbrado (*lighting*) de los estacionamientos
4. instalar más teléfonos de emergencia
5. expulsar a los estudiantes problemáticos
6. financiar un sistema de transporte nocturno gratis
7. poner cámaras de video en las bibliotecas
8. ofrecerles a los estudiantes un curso sobre seguridad personal

Act. 18 and Act. 19: Encourage students to be creative with their responses. Check by calling on individuals for responses. Get multiple responses for each situation.

Actividad 18 Un mundo diferente En grupos de tres, terminen estas frases con una cláusula que explique de qué manera habría sido diferente el mundo en las siguientes situaciones.

1. Si en 1491 los aztecas hubieran descubierto Europa, ...
2. Si Portugal, en vez de España, hubiera financiado los viajes de Colón, ...
3. Si México hubiera ganado la guerra con los Estados Unidos en 1848, ...
4. Si no hubieran construido el Canal de Panamá, ...
5. Si Oswald no hubiera asesinado a JFK, ...
6. Si no hubieran atacado las torres gemelas de Nueva York, ...

Act. 19A: Elicit a quick summary of the historical facts before moving on to the hypotheses.

Actividad 19 La tecnología en la historia **Parte A:** En parejas, miren estos chistes de la versión mexicana de la revista *MAD* de la página 285 y contesten las preguntas para hablar sobre lo que habría pasado si la tecnología hubiera invadido la historia.

¿Y si Moisés hubiera tenido un fax?

¿Y si Vincent Van Gogh hubiera tenido un walkman?

Due to advances in technology, it is common to borrow words from other languages for newly created items. Use may vary from country to country and it takes time for a lexical item to become accepted as standard. Such is the case with *fax*, *walkman*, and *beeper*.

¿Y si Alexander Graham Bell hubiera tenido espera de llamadas?

¿Y si los caballeros medievales hubieran tenido imanes para refrigerador?

¿Y si Nerón hubiera tenido una máquina de Cantaré?

¿Y si Paul Revere hubiera tenido un beeper?

Parte B: Ahora, inventen dos preguntas semejantes sobre la tecnología y la historia. Luego háganle sus preguntas al resto de la clase.

Actividad 20 La escuela y los mediadores Lee parte del siguiente artículo publicado en Internet por el Ministerio de Educación de Chile sobre una escuela que logró reducir la violencia escolar. Luego, en grupos de tres discutan las preguntas de la página 286.

PALABRAS EN VEZ DE GOLPES

En la escuela Valle de Lluta de San Bernardo, los alumnos resuelven sus diferencias conversando. Con la acción de niños mediadores desterraron los golpes del aula. Los protagonistas quisieron contar sus vivencias para que otras comunidades escolares puedan mejorar su convivencia.

"Antes de que fuéramos mediadores había muchas peleas en la sala y en el patio", dice Kathia (15 años). Su compañero Luis (16 años) agrega, "Y no sólo golpes, también había **alegatos** que no se terminaban nunca. Ahora, los mediadores les decimos a los que pelean, que la gente se entiende conversando". Entre los ochocientos alumnos de la escuela, 24 son quienes tienen la función de mediar los conflictos. Ellos son niños y jóvenes que tienen condiciones de líderes —en su versión positiva o negativa— y fueron escogidos por el profesor jefe para capacitarse en la técnica de la mediación.

alegatos: arguments

1. ¿En qué consiste el programa de la escuela Valle de Lluta para reducir la violencia escolar?
2. ¿Había mediadores cuando Uds. estaban en la escuela secundaria?
   - Si contestan que sí: ¿En qué consistía el trabajo del mediador? ¿Alguna vez estuvieron en un conflicto que se resolvió con la ayuda de un mediador? ¿Fueron Uds. mediadores? ¿Creen que el uso de esta técnica de resolución de conflictos haya sido eficaz en su escuela? Si Uds. hubieran sido el/la director/a de su escuela, ¿qué otras técnicas habrían usado?
   - Si contestan que no: Si Uds. hubieran sido el/la director/a de su escuela, ¿habrían usado esta técnica para resolver conflictos? ¿Por qué sí o no? ¿Les hubiera gustado ser mediadores/as? ¿Qué otra técnica habrían usado?
3. ¿Había en su escuela estudiantes que llevaran armas?
   - Si contestan que sí: ¿Qué hacía el/la director/a de la escuela para prevenir ese problema?
   - Si contestan que no: ¿Había detector de metales en la puerta para ver si los estudiantes llevaban armas? ¿Revisaba la escuela el contenido de los armarios (*lockers*) de los estudiantes con/sin su permiso?

Act. 21A: May be assigned as HW. Make sure that when students do Part A they do not mention the person's name in the sentence since it will be used in Part B. While students are formulating sentences, circulate to correct errors.

Act. 21B: Model by reading a sentence and having the class guess who it refers to: **Si no hubiera comido la manzana, no habría tenido que salir del paraíso.** Have students read their sentences and have the class guess who it is.

Act. 22: Set up the activity by listing or eliciting some of the differences between being an only child vs. having brothers and sisters, living in a small vs. a big city, going to a private vs. a public school. Form pairs, do the activity, and follow with a group sharing.

Actividad 21 Los remordimientos **Parte A:** Mucha gente se arrepiente de (*regret*) no haber hecho ciertas cosas en su vida o de haber hecho otras. Escribe los remordimientos (*regrets*) de conciencia que podrían haber tenido tres personas famosas. No menciones el nombre de las personas.

▶ Si yo no hubiera mentido, no habría tenido que renunciar a la presidencia. (Richard Nixon)

Parte B: Ahora, léele tu mejor oración a la clase para que tus compañeros adivinen quién podría haber tenido ese remordimiento.

Actividad 22 ¿Cómo habría sido tu vida? En parejas, cuéntense con detalle cómo habría sido su vida si hubieran ocurrido las siguientes cosas. Sigan el modelo.

▶ (no) ser hijo único
Si yo no hubiera sido hijo único, habría tenido pocos juguetes. También me habría peleado mucho con mis hermanos y habría tenido que compartir la habitación con ellos.

1. (no) ser hijo único
2. (no) crecer en una ciudad pequeña
3. (no) ir a una escuela secundaria privada

Actividad 23 Como si... Anoche estuviste en una fiesta y oíste sólo partes de algunas conversaciones. Escribe posibles finales para estas frases que oíste.

Act. 23: Assign as HW and check in class.

1. Odio a la gente que habla como si...
2. Hay gente que va muy elegante a la universidad como si...
3. Mi profesor de literatura nos manda leer un montón de libros como si...
4. Ayer mi mejor amigo tenía una cara larga como si...
5. En el último partido, nuestro equipo jugó como si...

Actividad 24 Un anuncio comercial En parejas, inventen un anuncio comercial o informativo de treinta segundos para las siguiente cosas. Incluyan un lema (*motto*) y la expresión **como si** en su anuncio. Sigan el modelo.

Act. 24: Set up the activity, then form pairs, set a time limit, and begin. Check by having groups read their ads.

Zara es una tienda española de ropa.

▶ Zara, la tienda que lo soluciona todo. Ropa para cada ocasión. Con la ropa de Zara, lucirán como si fueran modelos.

un carro híbrido
el café de Colombia
clases de tango
las donas de Krispy Kreme
un viaje por el Caribe en un crucero Princesa
el chicle de nicotina

III. Expressing Past Influence, Emotions, and Other Feelings and Reactions

The Pluperfect Subjunctive

1. You have already seen in this chapter how to use the pluperfect subjunctive to hypothesize about the past. Like other tenses of the subjunctive, the pluperfect can be used after expressions of emotion, doubt, influence, or desire, and in descriptions of the unknown. In all these cases, the pluperfect subjunctive usually refers to an action that preceded another past action. Look at the following sentences.

Remind students that the present perfect subjunctive is used when expressing present emotions, doubt, etc., about the past. **Me alegra que ella haya dejado el alcohol.**

La policía **buscaba** a alguien que **hubiera visto** a la narcotraficante. — *The police were looking for someone who had seen the drug dealer.*

Unknown: Chapter 7

Me alegré de que ella **hubiera dejado** el alcohol. — *I was happy that she had quit drinking.*

Emotions: Chapter 6

Habría querido que la policía **hubiera sido** más dura con los ladrones.* — *I would have liked the police to have been tougher with the thieves.*

Influencing: Chapter 5

*Note: This combination of **habría** + *past participle* + **que** + **hubiera** + *past participle,* is frequently used to express hindsight: **Habríamos preferido que él no hubiera venido el domingo.**

Drill pluperfect subjunctive:

1. Do a transformation drill. T: **Me alegra que tú hayas venido a clase hoy.** S: **Ayer le alegró que yo hubiera venido a clase.** Other cues: **Busco un estudiante que haya estado en México. Dudo que Uds. hayan ido al laboratorio hoy.** (etc.)

2. Put phrases on the board and have students express hindsight, hopes, and desires about their childhood. For example: **Habría querido que mi escuela..., Habría querido que mis profesores/consejeros..., Me habría gustado que mis padres...**, etc.

3. Have students express what others felt about them: **Mis padres habrían querido que yo..., A mis profesores les habría gustado que yo...**

2. Compare the following sentences containing either the imperfect subjunctive or the pluperfect subjunctive and note the difference in meaning conveyed by each.

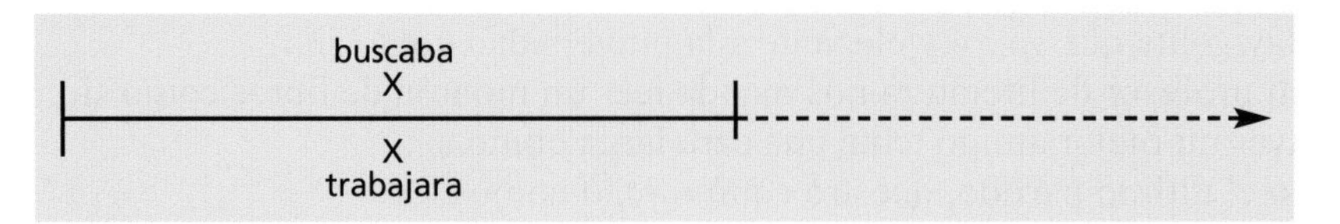

La policía **buscaba** a alguien que **trabajara** con drogadictos.	*The police were looking for someone who worked with drug addicts.*

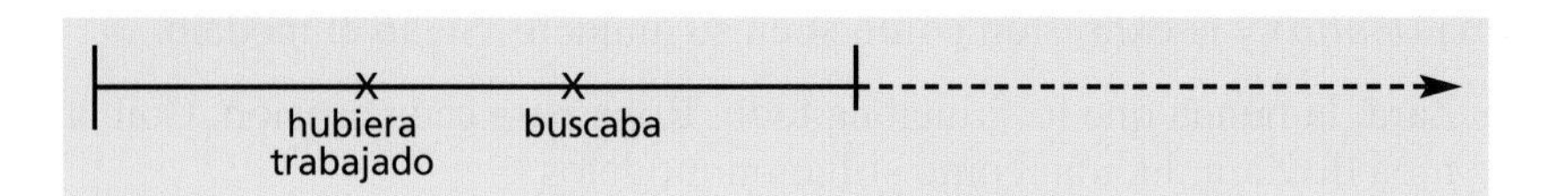

La policía **buscaba** a alguien que **hubiera trabajado** con drogadictos.	*The police were looking for someone who had worked with drug addicts.*

Act. 25: Assign as HW and check in class.

Actividad 25 No estaba de acuerdo Completa con detalle estas situaciones para indicar cómo se sintieron las personas en cada caso. Usa el pluscuamperfecto del subjuntivo.

1. Marta me dijo que ella había visto un robo en la calle y que unos policías habían atrapado al delincuente y le habían pegado mucho, pero como Marta siempre cuenta historias, yo no creía que... porque...
2. José, de catorce años de edad, llegó a casa después de una fiesta con un olor a alcohol muy fuerte, pero les juró a sus padres que él no había bebido. Ellos dudaban que... porque...
3. La hija del Sr. Salinas era contadora, tenía cuarenta años y estaba en la cárcel por haber cometido fraude en el trabajo. Su padre habría querido que... porque...
4. Hace unos años quedé embarazada y fumé durante todo el embarazo. Mi médico habría preferido que... porque...

Act. 26: Encourage connected discourse by having students justify their choices. Poll members of the class to see how many wish their parents had been stricter or more lenient, etc.

Actividad 26 Mirar al pasado En grupos de tres, digan cómo habrían querido que hubieran sido ciertos aspectos de su infancia y adolescencia. Sigan el modelo.

▶ mis profesores / darme / materia más (menos) difícil
Habría querido que mis profesores me hubieran dado materia más difícil porque así (yo) habría estudiado más y...

1. mi escuela / ofrecer / más (menos) actividades extracurriculares
2. mis padres / ser / más (menos) estrictos
3. mis padres / tener / más (menos) hijos
4. mi escuela / dar / explicaciones más (menos) explícitas sobre la sexualidad
5. mi familia / residir / en una zona más urbana (rural)
6. mis amigos / participar / más (menos) en las actividades de la escuela

IV. Linking Ideas

A. *Pero, sino,* and *sino que*

Pero, sino, and **sino que** are conjunctions (**conjunciones**), that is, they join different parts of a sentence.

Drill **pero, sino,** and **sino que:**

Have students finish these ideas about last weekend: **Iba a estudiar, pero..., No fui al cine sino..., No fui a una discoteca sino que...,** etc.

1. Pero means *but* (when *but* means *however*) and can be used after affirmative or negative clauses.

Iba a ir a clase, **pero** estaba muy cansado.	*I was going to go to class, but/however I was very tired.*
No iba a ir a clase, **pero** tenía un examen.	*I wasn't going to go to class, but/however I had an exam.*

Note the use of a comma before **pero.**

2. Sino and **sino que** also mean *but* (when *but* means *but rather* or *but instead*). These words can only be preceded by a negative clause. **Sino** is followed by a word or a phrase that does not contain a conjugated verb, and **sino que** introduces a clause that contains a conjugated verb.

No fui a clase **sino** a la cafetería.	*I didn't go to class but rather to the cafeteria.*
No quería estudiar **sino dormir.**	*He didn't want to study but rather to sleep.*
No estaba estudiando **sino durmiendo.**	*He wasn't studying but rather sleeping.*
No fui a clase **sino que me quedé** en la cafetería.	*I didn't go to class but instead I stayed in the cafeteria.*
No manejaban al trabajo **sino que caminaban.**	*They didn't use to drive to work but instead they walked.*

Actividad 27 Consejos para un amigo **Parte A:** Tienes que darle consejos a un/a amigo/a que está por irse de viaje al extranjero. Termina las ideas usando **pero, sino** o **sino que.**

Act. 27A: Assign as HW and check in class.

1. No debes llevar joyas de oro ____sino____ de fantasía.
2. No debes llevar bolsa ____sino que____ debes llevar una riñonera (*fanny pack*).
3. Puedes llevar dinero en efectivo, ____pero____ es mejor usar el cajero automático.
4. Nunca debes dejar la cámara fotográfica en un auto estacionado ____sino____ tenerla contigo en todo momento.

(continúa en la página siguiente)

5. Puedes llevar el pasaporte contigo, ____pero____ también es buena idea tener una fotocopia del pasaporte en el hotel.
6. No debes obtener dinero local en el aeropuerto ____sino____ en un cajero automático porque te da más dinero por cada dólar.
7. En el aeropuerto no debes dejar las maletas solas ____sino que____ debes llevarlas contigo a todos lados.

Act. 27B: When finished, call on individuals to tell their stories.

Parte B: En grupos de tres, discutan si Uds. o personas que conocen han estado en algunas de las situaciones que se mencionan en la Parte A, en el extranjero o en este país. Digan si les han robado algo alguna vez. Describan qué ocurrió.

B. *Aunque, como,* and *donde*

You may want to explain the difference between **siempre estudian aunque están cansadas** (factual) and **siempre estudian aunque estén cansadas** (whether or not the situation exists). The distinction is often subtle and mastery is not expected at this level.

Drill **aunque, como,** and **donde:**

1. Write cues on the board and have students talk about their habits: **estudiar / aunque / costar mucho; comer mucho / aunque / no tener hambre; vestirse / como / querer; estacionar / donde / poder.**

The conjunction **aunque** and the adverbs **como** and **donde** are used as follows.

1. Aunque (*even if, even though, although*) is used to disregard information. It is usually followed by the subjunctive.

Siempre estudian por la noche **aunque estén** cansadas.	*They always study at night although they may be tired.* (It doesn't matter if they are tired.)
Aunque te vayas temprano mañana, quiero ir contigo al aeropuerto.	*Even though you may be leaving early tomorrow, I want to go to the airport with you.*
Paco nunca probaría drogas **aunque** se las **ofrecieran.**	*Paco would never try drugs even if they were offered to him.*

Don't confuse **cómo** and **dónde,** which are question words, with **como** and **donde,** which are adverbs.

2. Como (*as, how, any way*) and **donde** (*where, wherever*) use the indicative when referring to a specific manner or place, and the subjunctive when referring to an unknown manner or place.

2. Drill **aunque** + *imperfect subjunctive* by writing cues on the board and having students say what they would do: **ir a una fiesta / tener un examen.** S: **Iría a una fiesta aunque tuviera un examen al día siguiente.** Other clues: **dar la vuelta al mundo / quedarse sin dinero; comprar un coche / tener que pedirle dinero al banco.**

Specific: Indicative	Unknown: Subjunctive
La sentenciaron **como** yo **quería.** *They sentenced her as I wanted.*	Bueno, senténciala **como quieras.** *OK, sentence her any way you want.*
Se vistió **como quería.** *She dressed as she wanted.*	Dile que se vista **como quiera.** *Tell her to dress any way she wants.*
Cuelga el cuadro **donde** yo **quiero:** allí. *Hang the painting where I want it: over there.*	Cuelga el cuadro **donde quieras.** *Hang the painting wherever you want.*
Busqué la ciudad **donde había** poca delincuencia. *I looked for the city where there was little crime.*	Busqué una ciudad **donde hubiera** poco delincuencia. *I looked for a city where there was little crime.*

Actividad 28 Combinaciones Combina ideas de las dos columnas para formar oraciones lógicas.

A	B
Seguiremos viajando aunque...	enseñarte / la semana pasada
Nunca te dejaría aunque...	estar / muy cansados
Generalmente trasnochamos aunque...	pasar / su adolescencia
Ella volvió al lugar donde...	dejarme / de querer
Busco un apartamento donde...	querer
Puedes ir vestido a mi fiesta como...	poder vivir / cómodamente
Prepara el mate de coca como yo...	quedarse / sin dinero

Act. 28: Assign as HW and correct in class. Answers will vary and may include: **Seguiremos viajando aunque nos quedemos sin dinero. Nunca te dejaría aunque me dejaras de querer. Generalmente trasnochamos aunque estemos muy cansados. Ella volvió al lugar donde pasó su adolescencia. Busco un apartamento donde podamos vivir cómodamente. Puedes ir vestido a mi fiesta como quieras. Prepara el mate de coca como yo te enseñé la semana pasada.**

Actividad 29 Delitos mayores Termina las siguientes ideas sobre delitos mayores.

1. Un hombre que viola a una mujer a veces sale en libertad condicional aunque...
2. Queremos vivir en un lugar donde...
3. Muchos criminales cometen crímenes horribles aunque...
4. Es necesario implementar el toque de queda donde...
5. Muchos asesinos parecen personas normales aunque...
6. El acusado del secuestro fue sentenciado como...

Act. 29: Assign as HW and check in class. Ask for multiple responses to each situation.

Actividad 30 ¿Legalización o no? **Parte A:** La legalización de las drogas en varios países del mundo, inclusive en este país, es un tema muy controvertido. Lee las siguientes ideas sobre su legalización e indica si crees que muestran una posición a favor (AF) o en contra (EC). Luego comparte tus ideas con el resto de la clase.

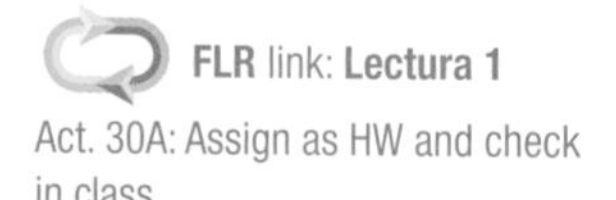

Act. 30A: Assign as HW and check in class.

1. __AF__ Una de las formas de combatir el narcotráfico es la legalización, pero esto no significa legalizar a los capos del narcotráfico.
2. __AF__ Los narcotraficantes obtienen ganancias increíbles debido a la prohibición de la droga. Hay que acabar con esta situación.
3. __EC__ Sería muy peligroso legalizar la mariguana en un país democrático. Esto podría crear la imagen de una narcodemocracia.
4. __EC__ Es factible (*feasible*) que la legalización de la droga traiga como resultado un aumento del consumo.
5. __EC__ La legalización no es una buena solución pues la droga siempre va a estar prohibida para alguien, como por ejemplo, los menores de edad.
6. __EC__ Para terminar con la droga hay que acabar con los narcotraficantes.
7. __AF__ La muerte de poderosos narcotraficantes no ha afectado el mercado.
8. __EC__ Legalizar las drogas sería como perdonar y olvidar todos los crímenes cometidos por el narcoterrorismo.
9. __EC__ Los países productores no producirían tanta droga si no hubiera una demanda tan intensa de parte de los países consumidores. Hay que reducir la demanda.

Do the corresponding CD-ROM and web activities to review the chapter topics.

Parte B: Ahora, formen dos grupos: uno a favor de la legalización de la droga en este país y el otro en contra. Tomen unos minutos para preparar sus argumentos usando ideas de la Parte A como punto de partida. Luego, hagan un debate sobre la legalización de la droga.

Act. 30B: Separate the class into two groups: pro and con. Have them get together on different sides of the room. Assign a leader for each group. You may have students select the side they would like to debate or simply assign members to a group. Allow five minutes for students to compile information to support their argument. Then seat the two groups facing each other and conduct the debate.

Vocabulario activo

Delitos y consecuencias

armado/a — *armed*
asesinar — *to murder*
el asesinato — *murder*
el/la asesino/a — *murderer*
el asaltante — *assailant*
asaltar — *to assault*
el asalto — *assault, attack, robbery*
atracar — *to hold up; to mug*
el atraco — *holdup; mugging*
la cárcel — *jail, prison*
el/la carcelero/a — *jailer, warden*
castigar — *to punish*
el castigo — *punishment*
la condena — *sentence*
el/la condenado/a — *convict*
condenar (a alguien) a (diez) meses/años de prisión — *to convict (someone) to (ten) months/years in prison*
el crimen — *serious crime; homicide*
la delincuencia — *crime, criminal activity*
el/la delincuente — *criminal*
el delito — *criminal offense, crime*
la droga — *drug*
el/la drogadicto/a — *drug addict*
drogarse — *to get high, take drugs*
encarcelar — *to jail, imprison*
la legalización — *legalization*
legalizar — *to legalize*
la lucha — *fight*
el/la narcotraficante — *drug dealer*
el narcotráfico — *drug traffic*
la pandilla — *gang*
el/la pandillero/a — *gang member*
la prohibición — *prohibition*
prohibir — *to prohibit*
rescatar — *to rescue*
el rescate — *ransom*
robar — *to steal; to rob*
el robo — *robbery*
el/la secuestrador/a — *kidnapper; hijacker*
secuestrar — *to kidnap*
el secuestro — *kidnapping*
la sentencia — *sentence*
el/la sentenciado/a — *person sentenced*
sentenciar — *to sentence*
sobornar — *to bribe*
el soborno — *bribe, bribery*
el/la suicida — *person who commits suicide*
suicidarse — *to commit suicide*
el suicidio — *suicide*
el terrorismo — *terrorism*
el/la terrorista — *terrorist*
traficar en drogas — *to deal drugs*
el/la vigilante — *watchman/woman*
la violación — *rape*
el/la violador/a — *rapist*
violar (a alguien) — *to rape (someone)*

Otras palabras relacionadas con el delito

la adicción	*addiction*
la cadena perpetua	*life sentence*
el cartel (de drogas)	*drug cartel*
consumir drogas	*to use drugs*
detener	*to arrest*
el homicidio	*homicide*
el ladrón/la ladrona	*thief*
la libertad condicional	*parole*
la pena de muerte/pena capital	*death penalty*
el/la preso/a	*prisoner*
el/la ratero/a	*pickpocket*
la sobredosis	*drug overdose*
el toque de queda	*curfew*
la víctima	*victim*
la violencia	*violence*

Expresiones útiles

a propósito	*on purpose*
(para) dentro de (diez) horas/días/años/etc.	*in* (*ten*) *hours/days/ years/etc.*
pretender + *infinitive*	*to attempt* (*and to hope*) + infinitive
¡Qué barbaridad!	*Wow!/How terrible!*
¡Qué injusticia!	*How unfair!/What an injustice!*
¿Qué opinas sobre esta situación?	*What do you think about this situation?*
¿Y a ti qué te parece?	*What do you make of it?*
A mi modo de ver...	*The way I see it . . .*
Desde mi punto de vista...	*From my point of view . . .*
Es un acto despreciable.	*It's a despicable act.*

Vocabulario personal

Capítulo 12

Meta comunicativa

- narrar y describir en el presente, pasado y futuro (repaso)

La comunidad latina en los Estados Unidos

May be assigned: Grammar, **¿Lo sabían?,** Act. 5, Act. 7A and B, Act. 10A and B, Act. 11A, Act. 15 (also could assign research on discrimination against immigrants in Argentina and Spain), Act. 16.

▲ Niños danzan en el Festival Boliviano de Arlington, Virginia.

Show the chapter video episode prior to or after doing Act. 20 and do all or selected activities in class.

Un poema

A través de este programa de español has aprendido sobre diversos aspectos del mundo hispano incluyendo el mundo hispano de los Estados Unidos. En este capítulo se presentará información sobre la historia y las vivencias no sólo de los inmigrantes que han llegado a este país sino también de los descendientes de estos inmigrantes.

FLR link: **Lectura 3**

Actividad 1 **Proyecciones** Mira la siguiente tabla sobre la población de los Estados Unidos y discute las preguntas que la acompañan.

Distribución de edad por sexo y origen hispano: 2002

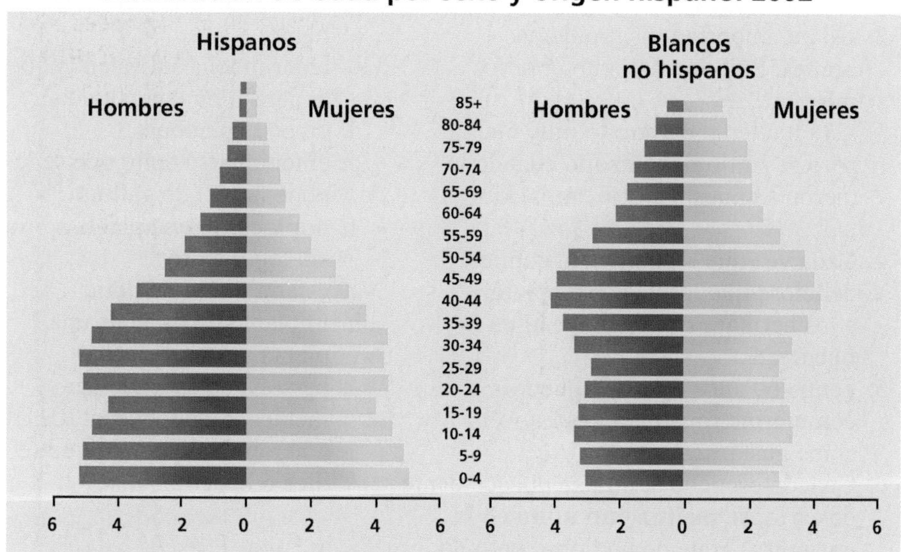

Cada barra representa el porcentaje de la población hispana o no hispana blanca que cae dentro de cada grupo por su edad y sexo.

(Fuente: Censo de EE.UU.)

1. Según este gráfico del censo estadounidense, ¿cuál de los dos grupos tiene un porcentaje mayor de gente joven?
2. Más o menos, ¿qué porcentaje de la población hispana tiene menos de 18 años? ¿Y de la población blanca que no es hispana?
3. Teniendo en cuenta que las mujeres dejan de tener hijos normalmente antes de cumplir los 40 años, ¿qué significa esto en cuanto al crecimiento de la población hispana y la no hispana en este país?

Act. 1: 1. **hispanos** 2. Actual answers are: **34,4% hispanos y 22,8% no hispanos blancos** 3. **La población hispana va a crecer más rápidamente que la población no hispana blanca porque proporcionalmente hay más mujeres hispanas jóvenes que pueden tener hijos.**

Interesting data to give and later discuss ramifications: It is estimated that by the year 2050, Hispanics may comprise 25% of the U.S. population. From 1990 to 2000, some states experienced a large growth in Hispanic population: North Carolina 394%, Arkansas 337%, Georgia 300%. Even a northern state such as Minnesota rose 166%.

Act. 2A: After checking response to question # 1, tell students that according to U.S. Census Bureau Statistics over 94% of the population of Laredo, Texas is Hispanic. Only East Los Angeles is higher with 97%.

Actividad 2 Un poema **Parte A:** La locutora de un programa de radio de Laredo, Texas va a leer un poema escrito por una estadounidense de ascendencia mexicana. Antes de escucharlo, busca la ciudad de Laredo en el mapa que está al principio del libro y contesta las siguientes preguntas.

1. ¿Cómo crees que sea la población de Laredo?
2. ¿Crees que sea una ciudad típica de los Estados Unidos? ¿Por qué?
3. ¿Qué idiomas crees que se hablen allí?
4. ¿Crees que la poeta se identifique con la cultura estadounidense, con la cultura mexicana o con las dos? ¿Por qué?

Parte B: Ahora vas a trabajar con algunas palabras que aparecen en el poema. Lee las siguientes oraciones y luego asocia las palabras en negrita con su significado.

1. A ella le molesta **andarse con tiento** y no poder decir lo que piensa. __j__
2. No me importan los problemas **ajenos.** Sólo me preocupo por los míos. __d__
3. Antonio tenía un puesto muy bueno, pero se sintió **desplazado** cuando le dieron su puesto a otro empleado. __b__
4. Cada vez que recuerdan la comida deliciosa que les hacía su madre, a los hermanos **se les hace agua la boca.** __c__
5. Tengo 60 años **¿y qué?** Puedo comprarme ropa para gente joven, si me gusta. __a__
6. Cuando escuché la noticia del accidente de carro, **se me hizo un nudo en la garganta.** Traté de no llorar, pero no pude contener las lágrimas. __g__
7. Para hacerle un **injerto** a esa planta, le hice un corte y le puse otra… __h__
8. … Pero mi experimento no resultó pues la planta **no pegó** y se murió. __f__
9. Odio que me llamen **pocho.** Yo soy mexicano, vivo en EE.UU. y punto. __i__
10. Cuando el nadador olímpico escuchó el himno nacional al recibir el premio en los Juegos Olímpicos, **se le enchinó el cuero.** __e__

a. y no importa lo que piensen los demás
b. que lo han quitado de su lugar
c. tener mucha saliva en la boca al pensar en una comida
d. de otras personas
e. emocionarse tanto que se le pone la piel de gallina
f. implantarle una planta a otra sin tener éxito
g. estar a punto de llorar
h. implante de parte de una planta a otra
i. persona de ascendencia mexicana que vive en EE.UU.
j. tener cuidado con lo que se dice o hace

Parte C: Ahora usa la información de la Parte A y el vocabulario de la Parte B para predecir el tema del poema llamado "Soy Como Soy Y Qué" de Raquel Valle Sentíes. Luego escucha el poema para confirmar tu predicción.

Act. 2C: You may choose to have students read along as they hear the poem or simply listen to it with books closed. You might want to tell students that titles in Spanish do not usually take caps except for the first word. The use of caps in the name of this poem is the author's choice. Although this may not have been a conscious choice, it also shows the mixing of cultures by imposing English rules for capitalization on a title in Spanish.

Raquel Valle Sentíes was born in Laredo, Texas, and she has lived both in Veracruz, Mexico, and in Laredo, Texas. In 1997 she received an award for Chicano literature from la Universidad Autónoma de Ciudad Juárez. She has been writing since 1988. Her play *Alcanzando un Sueño* received an award at the Chicano Literary Contest at UC Irvine in 1990. Her play *La Mala Onda de Johnny Rivera* was performed at the Teatro de la Esperanza in San Francisco in 1996.

Soy flor injertada que no pegó.
Soy mexicana sin serlo.
Soy americana sin sentirlo.
La música de mi pueblo,
la que me llena,
los huapangos, las rancheras,
el himno nacional mexicano,
hace que se me enchine el cuero,
que se me haga un nudo en la garganta,
que bailen mis pies al compás,
pero siento como quien se pone
sombrero ajeno.
Los mexicanos me miran como diciendo
¡Tú, no eres mexicana!

El himno nacional de Estados Unidos
también hace
que se me enchine el cuero,
que se me haga un nudo
en la garganta.
Los gringos me miran
como diciendo,
¡Tú no eres americana!
Se me arruga el alma.
En mí no caben dos patrias
como no cabrían dos amores.
Desgraciadamente,
no me siento ni de aquí,
ni de allá.

Ni suficientemente mexicana.
Ni suficientemente americana.
Tendré que decir
Soy de la frontera.
De Laredo.
De un mundo extraño
ni mexicano,
ni americano.
Donde al caer la tarde
el olor a fajitas asadas con mesquite,
hace que se le haga a uno agua la boca.
Donde en el cumpleaños
lo mismo cantamos
el *Happy Birthday* que las mañanitas.
Donde festejamos en grande
el nacimiento de Jorge Washington
¿quién sabe por qué?
Donde a los foráneos
les entra *culture shock*
cuando pisan Laredo
y podrán vivir cincuenta años
aquí y seguirán siendo
foráneos.
Donde en muchos lugares
la bandera verde, blanca y colorada
vuela orgullosamente
al lado de la *red, white and blue.*

Soy como el Río Grande,
una vez parte de México,
desplazada.
Soy como un títere
jalado por los hilos de dos culturas
que chocan entre sí.
Soy la mestiza,
la pocha,
la Tex-Mex, la Mexican-American,
la hyphenated,
la que sufre
por no tener identidad propia
y lucha por encontrarla,
la que ya no quiere cerrar los ojos
a una realidad que golpea,
que hiere
la que no quiere andarse con tiento,
la que en Veracruz
defendía a Estados Unidos
con uñas y dientes.
La que en Laredo
defiende a México
con uñas y dientes.
Soy la contradicción andando.

En fin, como Laredo,
soy como soy y qué.

Act. 3: Answers: 1. **de la autora misma, vive en Laredo** 2. **de EE.UU., se siente que no es de allí ni de México** 3. **los mexicanos creen que ella no es de México, los americanos creen que ella no es de EE.UU.** 4. **Sienten un choque cultural y nunca llegan a pertenecer a Laredo.** 5. **que ella es una contradicción** (**como Laredo**) **y lo acepta, no le importa ser como es**

Actividad 3 La "hyphenated" Antes de escuchar el poema otra vez, lee las siguientes ideas. Luego escucha el poema para buscar la información correspondiente.

1. ¿De quién habla y dónde vive?
2. ¿De qué país es y de dónde se siente que es?
3. ¿Qué conflicto tiene con los mexicanos y con los americanos?
4. ¿Qué problema tienen los foráneos (las personas de otro lugar u otro país) en Laredo?
5. ¿A qué conclusión llega la persona que habla?

Act. 4: Follow-up: In groups of three, have students write a poem about how they feel about living where they do and whether they feel they belong to that place.

Actividad 4 Tu opinión **Parte A:** Después de escuchar el poema, expresa tu reacción al conflicto que tiene la poeta.

Parte B: En parejas, una persona es el/la locutor/a del programa de radio y la otra persona llama para decir si le gustó o no el poema. Justifiquen su opinión.

¿LO SABÍAN?

La autora de "Soy Como Soy Y Qué" escribe en español, pero usa el inglés para describirse a sí misma como *"la Mexican-American, la hyphenated"*. Ella representa una fusión de culturas: la mexicana, que es una combinación de la cultura española mezclada con las culturas indígenas que estaban en México cuando llegaron los españoles, y también de la cultura más prevaleciente de los EE.UU. Cuando la autora se describe a sí misma como *"la Mexican-American, la hyphenated"* probablemente lo hace en inglés o porque la terminología para describir lo que quiere decir es más precisa en ese idioma o porque tanto el concepto como el término no existen en la cultura hispana o porque quiere expresar con la mezcla de idiomas su cultura mezclada.

En los EE.UU. una manifestación de la fusión de culturas se ve en el idioma; muchos hispanos alternan entre el español y el inglés dentro de una misma conversación y, con frecuencia, lo hacen inconscientemente. Mientras que los hispanos de primera generación se sienten más cómodos hablando español en casa y en situaciones sociales y de trabajo, la preferencia por el uso del español disminuye con la segunda y tercera generación. Según *Voy,* el 65 % de los hispanos de segunda generación se sienten más cómodos hablando inglés, mientras que el porcentaje aumenta al 70 con los de tercera generación. ¿Tienes parientes o amigos que alternen entre el inglés y otro idioma o que se sientan más cómodos hablando otro idioma que no sea el inglés? ¿Cómo le explicarías a una persona que no habla inglés el término *hyphenated* que usa la autora?

Voy es una compañía que se dedica a entretener a la gente a través de diferentes medios de comunicación como el cine, la televisión, la música e Internet.

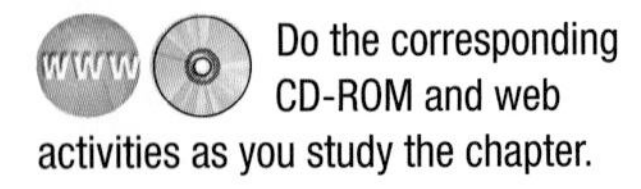

Do the corresponding CD-ROM and web activities as you study the chapter.

I. Narrating and Describing in the Past, Present, and Future (A Review)

In this chapter you will review how to narrate and describe in the past, present, and future. Before reviewing each, read the following chart, which is a synopsis of the life of a man and his family. First, read the columns vertically. Then go back and compare the horizontal columns to each other.

Have students analyze uses vertically and horizontally. This will help focus them for the rest of the chapter.

Past	Present	Future
Cuando era joven, Juan vivía en Puerto Rico.	Ahora Juan vive en Nueva York con su familia.	Juan va a comprar una casa en Puerto Rico y vivirá allí durante los veranos.
Tenía 17 años cuando terminó la secundaria.	Tiene 40 años y trabaja en el Hospital Monte Sinaí.	Tendrá 65 años cuando se jubile.
Sus padres querían que él fuera a los Estados Unidos a estudiar medicina.	Tiene una hija y quiere que ella pase los veranos con sus abuelos en Puerto Rico para que aprenda bien el español.	Él y su esposa querrán que su hija también estudie en Harvard.
Como había sacado buenas notas en la escuela, lo aceptaron en Harvard.	Como ella saca buenas notas en la escuela, no tiene que estudiar durante el verano.	Seguramente ella sacará buenas notas y será médica como sus padres.
Mientras estaba estudiando en Harvard, conoció a su esposa Marta.	Mientras su esposo está en el hospital, Marta que también es médica, trabaja con niños que padecen de SIDA.	Mientras ella esté estudiando la carrera universitaria, trabajará como voluntaria en un hospital.
Siempre decía que si se hubiera quedado en Puerto Rico, nunca la habría conocido.	Si Marta tuviera más tiempo, iría a las escuelas para hablar sobre la prevención del SIDA.	En caso de que pueda, tratará de trabajar, igual que su madre, con niños que padezcan de SIDA.

Now you will review how to discuss past, present, and future actions and states. If you feel you need more in-depth explanations, consult the pages given in the annotations in the margin.

A. Discussing the Past

To review narration and description in the past, see pages 41–51, 65–69, and 97–98. Note that throughout the chapter, topic titles and page references are given in the margin to tell you where you can review the topic.

FLR link: Lectura 1

1. Look at how the preterit and imperfect are used to talk about the past as you read this brief summary of Cuban immigration to the United States.

Preterit	Imperfect
	• **Setting the scene** Durante la década de los 50, **había** en Cuba mucha corrupción en la dictadura de Batista.
• **Completed action** **Hubo** una revolución en 1959 y después Fidel Castro **subió** al poder.	• **Age** Castro **tenía** sólo 32 años.
• **End of action** La revolución le **puso fin** a la dictadura de Batista.	• **Action or state in progress** Pero muchas personas le **tenían** miedo al nuevo régimen comunista.
• **Beginning of action** En 1959 **empezó** el gran éxodo de cubanos hacia los Estados Unidos y en 1966 **comenzó** la salida de Cuba de otra ola de refugiados.	• **Habitual or repeated action** Cada día **llegaba** a los Estados Unidos, más y más gente que **buscaba** asilo político.
• **Action in progress interrupted** Cuando **intentaban/estaban intentando** salir de Cuba en embarcaciones pequeñas, muchos **murieron.**	
• **Action over specific period of time** Entre 1965 y 1971 los Estados Unidos **permitieron** la entrada de 250 mil cubanos.	• **Simultaneous ongoing actions** Mientras **llegaba** un grupo de cubanos en 1980, mucha gente **protestaba** contra su entrada a los Estados Unidos porque muchos eran delincuentes.
	• **Ongoing emotion or mental state** En los Estados Unidos, muchos cubanos **sentían** y sienten nostalgia por su isla y por su vida anterior al gobierno de Castro.

Past action preceded by other past actions, see page 51.

Buena Vista Social Club was a group of retired Cuban musicians that got together after a long hiatus from performing. They were a new sensation and performed all over the world including venues as prestigious as Carnegie Hall.

Narrating in the past, see page 105.

2. To denote a past action that preceded another past action, use the pluperfect.

En 1999, **se estrenó** la película *Buena Vista Social Club* sobre un grupo de músicos cubanos, pero dos años antes ya **había salido** el CD del mismo nombre.

3. To ask the question *Have you ever?* and to refer to past events with relevance to the present, use the present perfect.

—¿**Has leído** algún artículo sobre la situación cubana actual?
—Últimamente no **he visto** nada sobre Cuba en el periódico.

4. To describe something that may or may not have existed, use the imperfect subjunctive in dependent adjective clauses.

Imperfect subjunctive, see pages 231–233.

Los cubanos que salieron de Cuba querían ir a **un lugar donde pudieran** empezar una vida nueva.

5. To refer to a pending or not yet completed action in the past, or to express possibility, purpose, and time in the past, use the imperfect subjunctive in dependent adverbial clauses.

Pending actions, see pages 188–189 and 231–233.

Possibility, purpose, time, see pages 206–207.

Muchos refugiados políticos pensaban quedarse en los Estados Unidos sólo **hasta que cambiara** el gobierno de Cuba. (Pending action in the past)
Trabajaban **para que** sus hijos **tuvieran** un futuro mejor. (Purpose in the past)

6. To talk about past actions or states after expressions of influence, emotion, and other feelings and reactions, use the present perfect subjunctive, the imperfect subjunctive, or the pluperfect subjunctive in the dependent clause.

Present perfect subjunctive, imperfect subjunctive, and pluperfect subjunctive, see pages 152–153, 231–233, and 287–288.

Es una pena que tantas familias **se hayan separado** por razones políticas.	*Present emotion* (**Es una pena**) *about a past action: present perfect subjunctive* (**se hayan separado**)
Mucha gente **quería que** Kennedy **interviniera** militarmente contra Castro.	*Past influence* (**quería**) *about a past action: imperfect subjunctive* (**interviniera**)
Cuando era pequeño, **me sorprendía que** mis padres **hubieran dejado** a mis abuelos en Cuba y **hubieran venido** a Miami, pero ahora lo entiendo.	*Past emotion* (**me sorprendía**) *about an action that happened before that emotion: pluperfect subjunctive* (**hubieran dejado... hubieran venido**)

7. To hypothesize about a past occurrence that is contrary to fact, use **si** + *pluperfect subjunctive,* + *conditional perfect.*

Hypothesizing about the past, see pages 280–281.

Si yo **hubiera sido** un exiliado político, no **habría podido** volver a mi país.

Actividad 5 Los inmigrantes hispanos Habla de la llegada de los tres grupos principales de hispanos (mexicanos, cubanos, puertorriqueños) a los Estados Unidos usando los datos que están a continuación. Incorpora el nombre del grupo apropiado en tus oraciones.

Puerto Rico y Cuba

Act. 5: Could be assigned as HW or done in class (whole class or paired activity) followed by a check phase. Encourage students to use their imagination if they don't know an answer.

Answers: 1. **mexicanos** 2. **cubanos** 3. **puertorriqueños** 4. **mexicanos** 5. **cubanos** 6. **cubanos** 7. **puertorriqueños** 8. **cubanos** 9. **cubanos**

► en 1959 / empezar a salir de la isla / cuando subir / al poder Fidel Castro
En 1959 los cubanos empezaron a salir de la isla cuando subió al poder Fidel Castro.

1. vivir / en la zona que se extiende de Texas a California antes que los primeros inmigrantes anglosajones
2. llegar / como refugiados políticos
3. en 1917 / recibir / el estatus de ciudadanos estadounidenses
4. en 1848 / firmar / el Tratado de Guadalupe Hidalgo con los Estados Unidos

(continúa en la página siguiente)

5. para 1980 / ya / vivir / en Chicago, Los Ángeles, Miami, Filadelfia y el norte de Nueva Jersey
6. establecerse / principalmente en Miami
7. después de la Segunda Guerra Mundial / comenzar / la movilización a Nueva York
8. llevar / a EE.UU. / la industria del puro (*cigar*)
9. no querer / que sus hijos / vivir / bajo un régimen comunista

Act. 6A: You may want to discuss other groups as well. Answers: 1. 1881 to 1914 Jews from Eastern Europe—homelessness, pogroms, economic problems. 1930's Jews from Germany and Austria escaping the Nazi movement. 2. From 1846 to 1855 over 2 million Irish people emigrated due to starvation from a potato blight. 3. Africans came due to slavery, began in 1619—importation of slaves banned in 1808. 4. Vietnamese, Cambodians, and Laotians came post 1975 due to the economic and political hardships of the aftermath of the Vietnam war. 5. Japanese came after the Gold Rush in 1848 because workers were needed in the mining, railroad, and construction industries.

Act. 6B: Encourage students to make a variety of statements about each person using past and present tenses. Answers: 1. **checoslovaca, tenista** 2. **alemán, físico, Premio Nobel** 3. **francés, violoncelista** 4. **inglesa, actriz** 5. **canadiense, periodista** 6. **escocés, hombre de negocios y filántropo** 7. **chino, arquitecto**

Actividad 6 Otros inmigrantes **Parte A:** Di por qué llegaron los siguientes grupos a los Estados Unidos y más o menos cuándo lo hicieron.

1. los judíos
2. los irlandeses
3. los africanos
4. los vietnamitas, camboyanos y laosianos
5. los japoneses

Parte B: Los siguientes inmigrantes han aportado mucho a la cultura y la historia norteamericana. En grupos de tres, digan de dónde son y qué han hecho las siguientes personas.

1. Martina Navratilova
2. Alberto Einstein
3. Yo Yo Ma
4. Ángela Lansbury
5. Peter Jennings
6. Andrew Carnegie
7. I. M. Pei

Crecimiento por grupo racial/étnico en los Estados Unidos
Porcentaje de crecimiento de abril, 2000 a julio, 2002

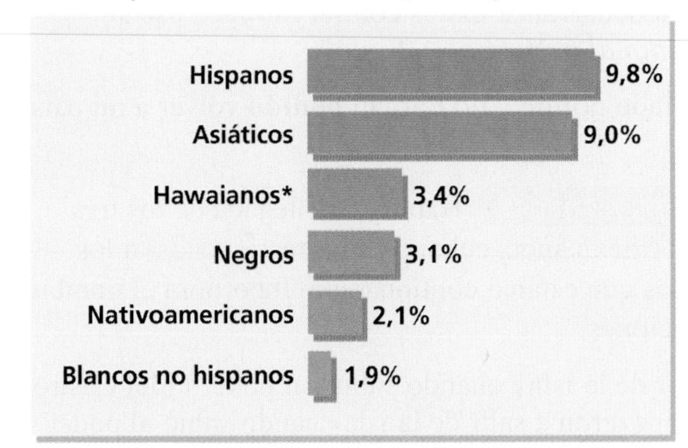

*Hawaianos: Incluye a gente de islas del Pacífico.
(Fuente: Censo de EE.UU.)

¿LO SABÍAN?

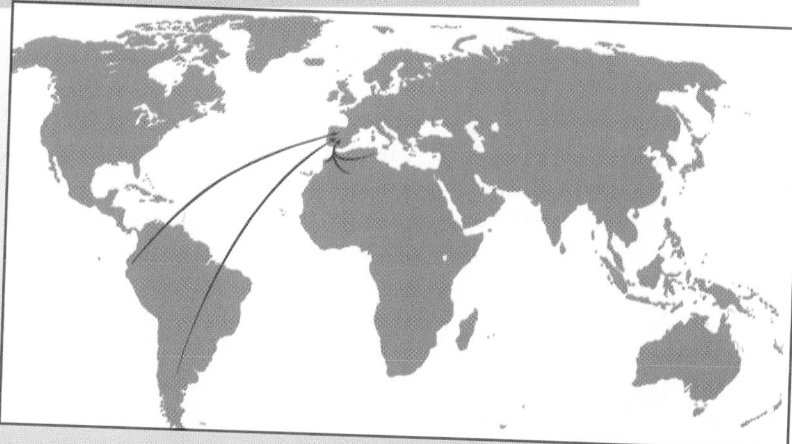

Aunque a lo largo de su historia los Estados Unidos han recibido inmigrantes de diversos países, no es el único en esta situación. Por muchos años los españoles, al igual que otros europeos, emigraron a países de América en busca de un mejor futuro. Hoy día España goza de un gobierno democrático y una economía estable que la hace atractiva a inmigrantes de otros países que tienen problemas politicos y económicos. Entre los inmigrantes a España más recientes se encuentran los ecuatorianos, los argentinos y los magrebíes (gente de Marruecos, Argelia y Túnez) que han contribuido al crecimiento de la población del país. Debido a esta inmigración reciente, el país se enfrenta a cuestiones de discriminación que antes no existían. ¿Quiénes son los últimos inmigrantes que han llegado a tu país? ¿Sufren algún tipo de discriminación?

Actividad 7 Hispanos famosos: Parte A: Lee la siguiente biografía que está escrita en el presente histórico y cámbiala al pasado.

www *Hispanos famosos*

Sandra Cisneros nace en Chicago en 1954. Su padre es mexicano y su madre chicana. Tiene seis hermanos y ella es la única hija mujer. Su abuela por parte del padre vive en México y su familia se muda a ese país con frecuencia por diferentes períodos de tiempo. Debido a esta situación y al hecho de que, con frecuencia, cambia de escuela, Sandra es una niña tímida e introvertida. En la escuela secundaria empieza a escribir poesía y en 1976 recibe una especialización en Literatura de la Universidad de Loyola en Chicago. Luego, mientras realiza estudios de maestría en la Universidad de Iowa, descubre su voz para escribir. Esto la lleva a escribir *The House on Mango Street.* A través de los años, recibe diferentes premios por sus libros y trabaja como maestra de estudiantes que dejan la escuela secundaria.

Sandra Cisneros, escritora de ascendencia mexicana.

Act. 7A: Assign as HW or do in class. Discuss the use of the **presente histórico** briefly.

Parte B: En parejas, lea cada uno la información sobre uno de los siguientes hispanos famosos para luego contársela a la otra persona, usando verbos en el pasado donde sea apropiado.

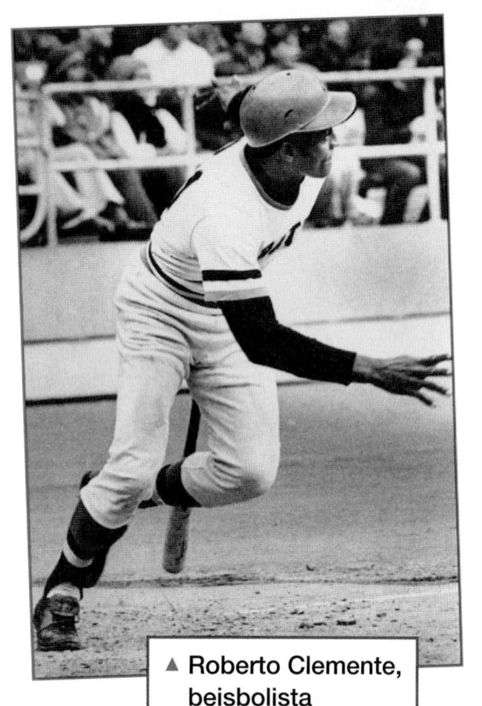

▲ Roberto Clemente, beisbolista puertorriqueño.

Act. 7B: Option 1: Assign half the class to do Clemente and the other half Garzón as HW and read in class to a partner the next day. Option 2: Form pairs, assign roles, and give a few moments to prepare; then have students tell about their person's life.

Roberto Clemente (1934–1972)

- nacer / en Puerto Rico
- mientras / jugar / con los Piratas de Pittsburg / dar / 3.000 batazos (*hits*)
- ayudar / a su equipo a ganar dos Series Mundiales
- llegar a ser / cuatro veces bateador campeón de la Liga Nacional
- los puertorriqueños / considerarlo / héroe nacional
- ser / muy generoso
- mientras / viajar / a Managua, Nicaragua para ayudar a víctimas de un terremoto / morir / en un accidente de avión en 1972
- ser / elegido al Salón de la Fama de Béisbol en 1973

Baltasar Garzón (1955–)

- nacer / en España
- estudiar / en monasterios católicos
- su familia / creer que / ir / a ser cura
- ser / expulsado el último día de clase por darle una serenata a una chica
- mientras estudiar / abogacía / trabajar / en una gasolinera para pagar sus estudios
- cuando tener / 32 años / ser / nombrado juez para la corte de casos criminales más importante de España
- en 1998 hacerse / famoso por luchar para detener al ex dictador chileno Augusto Pinochet en Londres
- querer / extraditarlo a España y tortura pero / no poder
- hoy día ser / conocido como el "superjuez" por detener a políticos corruptos, a narcotraficantes y a terroristas tanto nacionales como internacionales

▲ Baltasar Garzón le firma un autógrafo a una de las Madres de Plaza de Mayo.

Act. 8: Form pairs, encourage students to be creative. Set a time limit and begin. Check by calling on a few individuals.

Actividad 8 ¿Qué pasó? En parejas, escojan a una de las siguientes personas e inventen cómo era su vida en su país, cómo fue su emigración y adaptación a los Estados Unidos y cómo se hizo famosos.

Arnold Schwarzenegger (austríaco)	Michael J. Fox (canadiense)
Isabel Allende (chilena)	Mario Andretti (italiano)

Actividad 9 La nostalgia Una inmigrante mexicana a los Estados Unidos habla de su nostalgia. Lee lo que dice y luego, en parejas, discutan si alguna vez han sentido nostalgia de algo, y digan de qué y por qué.

"Después de un tiempo de estar en los Estados Unidos, comencé a **extrañar** todo lo relacionado con el folclor. La música de mariachi, ciertas comidas como los dulces típicos mexicanos que son de calabaza o **camote** (pues en el norte de California adonde yo llegué no había tanta concentración de latinos y era difícil conseguir casi todo). También extrañaba muchísimo la celebración del 12 de diciembre. Este es un día nacional en México donde celebramos la aparición de la virgen de Guadalupe. Extrañaba la misa, la comida y el festejo de ese día tan especial. Otra cosa que extrañaba mucho eran las posadas, la celebración de la Navidad, pues en México es una celebración larga y de mucha tradición. Es irónico porque en México odiaba poner el nacimiento para el niño Dios, pero al estar lejos y ya no verlo más, mandé pedir uno. Ahora lo conservo como una reliquia. Finalmente, antes de venir a los Estados Unidos no apreciaba todo lo rústico referente al arte mexicano. Ahora todo lo que tengo en cada rincón de mi casa es de arte rústico mexicano: muebles tallados en México, cerámica, pinturas de Rivera, Siqueiros, Kahlo y todo lo que uno pueda imaginarse... Hasta el canasto donde pongo las tortillas."

mexicana

to miss
sweet potato

Act. 9: Transition to Act. 9 by asking if the class thinks the people in Act. 8 felt nostalgic for their country. Have students read the comment by the Mexican and ask comprehension questions. Discuss when you have been nostalgic. Then form pairs and set a time limit for their discussion. When finished, ask general questions like: **¿Quién asistió a un campamento de verano cuando era pequeño?** Some students raise their hands. **¿Sentiste nostalgia?**

Act. 10A: Could be assigned as HW and checked in class.

Note: The use of **hubiéramos** in the result clause in the ad is common throughout the Spanish-speaking world although it is not grammatically correct.

Actividad 10 Un anuncio comercial **Parte A:** Mira el siguiente anuncio comercial y busca pistas (*clues*) que indiquen que está dirigido específicamente a hispanos inmigrantes en los Estados Unidos.

Parte B: Contesta las preguntas que siguen.

1. ¿Por qué crees que McDonald's haya hecho un anuncio comercial dirigido a inmigrantes? Justifica tu respuesta.
2. Si este anuncio hubiera aparecido en inglés en una revista como *Time* o *Sports Illustrated,* ¿habría tenido éxito? Justifica tu respuesta.
3. En el anuncio Ernesto dice: "¡Qué chiquito es el mundo!" ¿Estás de acuerdo con esa frase?
4. Mientras estabas en otra ciudad u otro país ¿alguna vez te has encontrado con (*have you run into*) alguien a quien conocías? ¿Qué pasó?
5. Estando de vacaciones, ¿has conocido a alguien que era de tu estado o tu ciudad? ¿Sentiste alguna afinidad con esa persona?
6. Si cuando eras niño/a, se hubieran tenido que trasladar (*transfer*) tus padres a otro país, ¿dónde te habría gustado vivir? ¿Por qué?

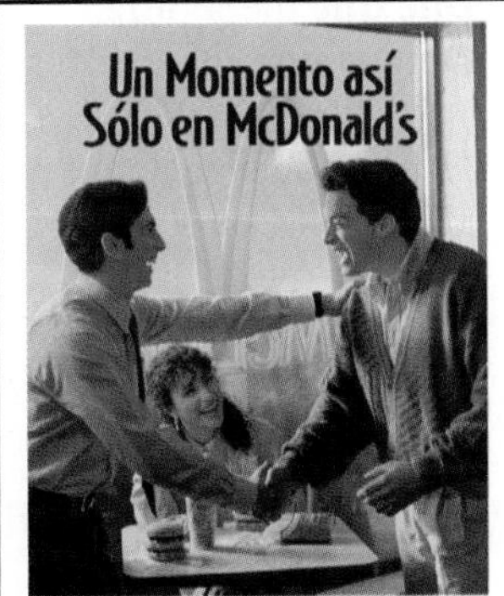

McDonald's Corporation

¡Qué chiquito es el mundo! Mira que encontrarme a Rubén aquí en Estados Unidos después de tanto tiempo.

Yo estaba almorzando con una compañera del trabajo en el McDonald's de aquí a la vuelta y lo vi entrar.

"*Rubén*", le grité.

"*¡Ernesto!*", y nos dimos tremendo abrazo.

"*¿Qué haces aquí?*", pregunté.

"*Lo mismo que tú, a punto de comerme un Big Mac*", me contestó vacilándome como la hacía antes.

Me contó que se casó con Lupe, su novia de todo la vida, qu tienen dos niñas preciosas y que lo acaban de transferir aquí a Estados Unidos.

Y así se nos pasó el tiempo.

Si no hubiera sido porque teníamos que regresar a trabajar, nos hubiéramos quedado el resto de la tarde platicando en McDonald's.

¡Qué agradable reecontrarnos!

Lo que quieres, aquí está.

vacilar = to kid (around)

Act. 10B: Could be assigned as HW and checked in class or done as a whole in-class activity or in pairs followed by a group sharing.

B. Discussing the Present

FLR link: Lectura 2

Narrating in the present, see pages 17–18 and 22–23.

1. To talk about present habitual actions or present events or states, use the present indicative.

Nunca **tengo** tiempo para hacer todo lo que **quiero.**
Hoy en día muchos hispanos **ocupan** puestos importantes en el gobierno.
Hace calor y **estoy** cansada.

2. To discuss actions in progress at the moment of speaking, you may use either the present indicative or the present progressive.

Ellos **estudian/están estudiando** en la biblioteca ahora.

Describing the unknown, see pages 183–184.

3. To describe something that may or may not exist, use the present subjunctive in the dependent clause.

Quiero ir a **un lugar donde no existan** los prejuicios.

Present subjunctive, see pages 118–120 and 147–149.

4. To talk about present actions or states after expressions of influence, emotion, and other feelings and reactions, use the present subjunctive in a dependent clause.

Es sorprendente que el 90 por ciento de los trabajadores agrícolas de California **sean** hispanos.

Present subjunctive, see pages 118–120 and 124–125.

Commands, see pages 126 and 129.

5. To influence someone's actions, use a command or the present subjunctive after an expression of influence.

Ayúdame.
Dile que me **ayude.**
Quiero que me **ayudes.**

Hypothesizing about the present, see pages 262–263.

6. To hypothesize about present contrary-to-fact situations, use **si** + *imperfect subjunctive,* + *conditional.*

Si fuera político (*which I am not*), **haría** todo lo posible para obtener el voto hispano.

Act. 11A: Assign as HW or do in class. Do not give correct answers until doing Part B.

Actividad 11 ¿Cuánto sabes? **Parte A:** Usa la imaginación y lo que sabes sobre la población hispana de los Estados Unidos para completar este cuestionario.

1. En el año 2015, se calcula que la población negra va a representar el 13,6% de la población estadounidense y que la hispana va a representar el __________.
   a. 12,5% b. 13,9% c. 15,8%
2. En la población norteamericana hay 2,4 personas por familia. En la familia hispana hay __________.
   a. 2,8 b. 3,5 c. 4,5

3. El hispano mira un promedio de 58,6 horas de televisión por semana, 4,4 horas más que el que no es hispano. Entre el primer grupo, el ________ prefiere ver televisión en inglés, el ________ prefiere programas en español y el ________ no tiene preferencia.
   a. 40%, 33%, 27% b. 26%, 51%, 23% c. 18%, 48%, 33%
4. El sueldo promedio en los Estados Unidos es de $46.133; el del hispano es ________.
   a. $30.775 b. $34.515 c. $39.210
5. El 24% de la población estadounidense es católica. El porcentaje de hispanos católicos es del ________.
   a. 57% b. 70% c. 80%
6. En los Estados Unidos la edad promedio es de 35,3 años; entre los hispanos es de ________.
   a. 25,8 b. 30,1 c. 38,0
7. Según el censo del año 2000, en los Estados Unidos hay ________ personas que hablan español en casa. Esto representa 1 de cada 10 habitantes de los EE.UU.
   a. 17.000.000 b. 22.000.000 c. 28.000.000
8. De las personas que indicaron que hablan español en casa, ________ dice que habla inglés con fluidez.
   a. más de la mitad b. el 40% c. el 25%

Parte B: Ahora en grupos de cuatro compartan y justifiquen sus opiniones con el resto de la clase usando expresiones como: **Creo que..., Dudo que...**

Act. IIB: Have students share and support answers in groups of four. Then supply correct answers and have students react to the statistics saying **(No) Me sorprende que los hispanos...** Correct answers: 1. **c** 2. **b** 3. **a** 4. **b** 5. **b** 6. **a** 7. **c** 8. **a**

Note: One Hispanic contribution to the U.S. included the utmost sacrifice: **Los hispanos sufrieron el 20% de las bajas en Vietnam aunque solo constituían el 5% de las tropas.** To find out more about Hispanic participation in the armed forces, read *Hispanics in America's Defense*, Gordon Press Publisher.

¿LO SABÍAN?

Hay muchas personas de países latinoamericanos que emigran a los Estados Unidos, pero cada día son más los norteamericanos que se van a vivir a países como México y Costa Rica cuando se jubilan. Esto se debe en parte a que las casas son más económicas y el costo de vida es más bajo que en los Estados Unidos. Costa Rica cuenta con 20 mil jubilados norteamericanos mientras que México tiene 600 mil. Hoy día hay grupos que están presionando al gobierno de los Estados Unidos para considerar extender el sistema de Medicare fuera del territorio estadounidense y así cubrir las necesidades de sus ciudadanos residentes en México. ¿Qué cosas tomarías en cuenta a la hora de elegir un lugar para jubilarte? ¿Te gustaría vivir en otro país como jubilado/a?

Note: It is not typical for people from Spanish-speaking countries to move when they retire. Therefore, one will not find retirement communities for the 55 and over population complete with golf courses and swimming pools. This is not part of the culture and may be because their families and friends are most likely in the same city.

Actividad 12 Emigración e inmigración **Parte A:** En parejas, hagan una lista de cinco motivos por los cuales hay más inmigración a los Estados Unidos y menos emigración de los Estados Unidos a otros países. Estén preparados para explicar los motivos.

Act. 12A: Form pairs, set a time limit, and begin. Check by asking pairs to give some reasons. Write these on the board in two columns: **Hay mucha inmigración porque... / Hay poca emigración porque...**

Act. 12B: Call on different pairs when checking each item to get a variety of responses.

Parte B: Si este país pasara por una situación económica desastrosa y fuera muy difícil continuar viviendo aquí, ...

1. ¿Adónde irían a vivir?
2. ¿Con quién(es) irían?
3. ¿Qué llevarían?
4. ¿Cómo se sentirían?
5. ¿Cómo sería la adaptación?
6. ¿Qué cosas extrañarían?
7. ¿Los aceptaría la población local?
8. ¿Qué harían para integrarse?

Act.13: Allow time for students to create a few pieces of advice and then have a group sharing. If anyone is planning to go abroad or has recently returned from studying abroad, ask them which piece of advice they think is the best.

Actividad 13 En el extranjero En parejas, imaginen que un amigo va a ir a estudiar por seis meses a un país de habla española. Denle recomendaciones para que aproveche (*take advantage of*) bien el viaje. Usen expresiones como: **Te recomendamos que..., Es importante que..., No te olvides...**

Act. 14: It is important that students realize that they'll be doing this anonymously so they'll be more apt to say what they really think. You may want to create a handout to fill out. Once anonymity is assured, follow this procedure, which will help students explore different opinions and attitudes, and possible reasons for them while never having to express their own opinion publicly: 1. Have students rate each item. 2. Collect the papers. 3. Shuffle them. 4. Hand them out to the students in a random fashion. 5. Poll the class for each item (students report what is on the paper they have). 6. After each item, ask why they think that some people may have said what they did.

Actividad 14 Un cuestionario Vas a dar una opinión **anónima** sobre puntos importantes concernientes a los hispanos en este país. Escribe en una hoja los números del 1 al 12 y, mientras lees cada oración del cuestionario, asígnale una letra (a, b, c). Luego entrégale la hoja a tu profesor/a y sigue sus instrucciones.

a. estoy de acuerdo
b. no estoy completamente de acuerdo
c. no estoy para nada de acuerdo

1. Muchos inmigrantes intentan pasar por refugiados políticos cuando en realidad vienen por cuestiones económicas.
2. Los inmigrantes son muy trabajadores.
3. Debemos mandar a todos los inmigrantes ilegales a su país de origen.
4. Los inmigrantes ilegales sólo deben recibir servicio médico en caso de emergencia.
5. La pobreza de México es la causa del alto índice de personas que emigran de ese país a los Estados Unidos.
6. La gente que emplea a los trabajadores indocumentados tiene la culpa de que haya tantos inmigrantes ilegales.
7. Solamente los hijos de ciudadanos de este país deben poder asistir a las escuelas públicas.
8. La inmigración ilegal existe porque hay una relación de oferta y demanda: los Estados Unidos necesitan la mano de obra barata y los inmigrantes ilegales necesitan trabajo.
9. Los inmigrantes indocumentados contribuyen al progreso de la economía del país.
10. Si pudieran, muchos inmigrantes no saldrían de su país de origen; sólo lo hacen por necesidad económica o política.
11. El gobierno debe vigilar más las fronteras del país.

Act. 15: Assign as HW and discuss answers in class. Have students research discrimination in other countries. For example: Bolivians in Argentina; Argentineans, Ecuadorians, and people from Northern Africa in Spain; Spaniards in Germany. Once finished they could do short presentations in groups or to the class on the topic.

Remember: **discriminar a alguien.**

Actividad 15 La discriminación Contesta las siguientes preguntas sobre la discriminación.

1. ¿Qué significa discriminar? ¿Por qué discrimina la gente?
2. ¿Alguna vez has sido (o ha sido alguien que conoces) víctima de discriminación?
3. ¿Quiénes discriminan a quiénes?

(continúa en la página siguiente)

4. ¿A quién se discrimina en este país?
5. ¿A qué grupos discriminaba la gente en el pasado?
6. ¿Existe discriminación en tu universidad?
7. En los Estados Unidos, se habla de *reverse discrimination*. ¿Qué significa? ¿Crees que exista?

Actividad 16 ¿Qué falta aquí? En parejas, lean este anuncio y discutan las preguntas siguientes.

1. ¿De quiénes habla el anuncio y cómo los describe?
2. ¿A quién está dirigido?
3. ¿Cuál es el propósito del anuncio y quién lo patrocina (*sponsors*)?
4. Durante el régimen de Castro, muchos cubanos han venido a los Estados Unidos como refugiados políticos. ¿Conocen Uds. a hispanos de otros países que también hayan sido aceptados en este u otro país como refugiados políticos? ¿Cuál era la causa?

Act. 16: Assign as HW and discuss answers in class. At the end of 2003, Ecuador was receiving between 900 and 1000 Colombian refugees monthly who were fleeing the country due to the violence of a 40-year civil war and the effects of narcotrafficking.

¿QUÉ FALTA AQUÍ?

Observa detenidamente este grupo de personas. Todas ellas tienen algo. Algunas tienen herramientas, otras portan una maleta, conducen un vehículo o llevan cualquier utensilio. Todas ellas podrían considerarse normales, gente corriente.

Sin embargo, hay una excepción. Ese buen hombre, el segundo por la derecha, en la tercera fila, parece no tener nada.

En efecto, no tiene nada. Es un refugiado. Y, como en principio habrás podido notar, es una persona como todas las demás. Porque los refugiados son gente corriente. Como tú y como yo. Gente normal con una pequeña diferencia: todo lo que tenían ha sido destruido o confiscado, arrebatado tal vez a cambio de sus vidas.

No tienen nada.

Y nunca más lo tendrán si no les ayudamos.

Por supuesto, no podemos devolverles aquello que les fue arrebatado. Pero sí podemos ofrecerles nuestra solidaridad. Por eso no te pedimos dinero, aunque la más mínima contribución siempre es una gran ayuda. Ahora lo que más necesitan es sentirse recibidos con cordialidad.

Tal vez una sonrisa no parezca gran cosa. Pero para un refugiado puede significarlo todo.

El ACNUR es una organización con fines exclusivamente humanitarios, financiada únicamente por contribuciones voluntarias. En la actualidad se ocupa de más de 19 millones de refugiados en todo el mundo.

Naciones Unidas
Alto Comisionado para los refugiados

ACNUR
Alto Comisionado para los Refugiados
Apartado 69045
Caracas 1062a
Venezuela

Cambio 16

You may want to tell students that Archbishop Oscar Romero's death in El Salvador in 1980 raised people's consciousness and sparked more to participate in the Sanctuary Movement.

¿LO SABÍAN?

Durante los años 70 y 80 muchos de los habitantes de El Salvador y Guatemala huyeron de su patria porque su vida corría peligro, cruzaron México e intentaron entrar en los Estados Unidos. Se prohibió la entrada a los inmigrantes de los dos países y el gobierno norteamericano decidió no aceptarlos como refugiados políticos. Fue así como muchas iglesias se organizaron y fundaron el movimiento "Santuario" para ayudarles a cruzar la frontera y darles casa, comida y apoyo tanto económico como espiritual. Algunos de los líderes norteamericanos del movimiento fueron encarcelados por su participación. Di si crees que un grupo religioso que quebranta la ley debe ser procesado (*prosecuted*) por participar en lo que considera actividades humanitarias.

▲ Una familia de refugiados salvadoreños se cubren la cara para no ser identificados por las autoridades de Inmigración (Cincinnati, Estados Unidos, 1982).

C. Discussing the Future

Future actions, see pages 8 and 248–249.

1. To refer to a future action, you can use the following.

a. the present indicative	Esta noche **hay** una reunión de inmigrantes guatemaltecos.
b. **ir a** + *infinitive*	Para el año 2050, los hispanos **van a formar** el 25% de la población estadounidense.
c. the future tense	En el futuro los hispanos **ocuparán** más puestos en el gobierno.

Present subjunctive, see pages 118–120 and 147–149.

2. To talk about future actions or states after expressions of influence, emotion, and other feelings and reactions, use the present subjunctive in dependent clauses.

Las grandes compañías **quieren que** los hispanos **compren** sus productos.
Para educar a la gente, **es importante que hagan** más anuncios sobre los efectos del cigarrillo.

Pending actions, see pages 188–189.

3. To describe actions that are pending or have not yet taken place, use the present subjunctive in dependent adverbial clauses.

Pienso ir a México a hacerle una visita a mi familia **cuando tenga** vacaciones.

4. To say something will have happened by a certain time in the future, use the future perfect.

Hypothesizing about the future, see page 281.

Para el año 2015, la población hispana de los Estados Unidos **habrá alcanzado** el 15,8 por ciento.

5. To hypothesize about the future use **si** + *present indicative,* + *future* / **ir a** + *infinitive*.

Hypothesizing about the future, see pages 262–263.

Si los Estados Unidos **incrementan** sus exportaciones a Hispanoamérica, **crearán/van a crear** más empleos.

Actividad 17 El poder adquisitivo El poder adquisitivo de los hispanos en los Estados Unidos llegará en unos tres años a 926 mil millones de dólares y, por supuesto, las grandes empresas no pueden darle la espalda a ese mercado. En grupos de tres, Uds. trabajan en una empresa de mercadeo y deben hacerles recomendaciones a compañías de *Fortune 100* teniendo en cuenta lo que han aprendido en este capítulo y usando el mapa que aquí se presenta. Piensen en los siguientes factores.

mil millones = one billion

- a qué sector de la población hispana le ofrecerán productos
- qué tipos de productos ofrecerán
- qué medios de comunicación usarán
- a qué lugares de la comunidad irán para regalarle muestras (*samples*) gratis a la gente

El poder adquisitivo hispano y sus diez principales estados.

Act. 17: Prior to doing this activity, ask students questions about the Hispanic population in the USA. Questions may include: average age of the population, language preferences, largest number of people from which countries, geographic concentrations of people from different countries of origin, etc.

Actividad 18 Un anuncio de Coca-Cola Lee el siguiente guion de un anuncio comercial que ha hecho la empresa Coca-Cola para la televisión. Después, contesta las preguntas de la siguiente página.

padre (*México*) = **chévere** (*Caribe*)
camión (*México*) = **guagua** (*Caribe*)

A: ¡Oye! ¡Qué padre! Un jueguito de fútbol ¿no?
B: Muchacho, ¿cómo que "padre"? Se dice "chévere".
C: Ya comenzaron de nuevo.
B: ¿Qué pasa?... Mira, "gaseosa".
A: Que ya se dice "soda".
C: No, "refresco".
B: No, no, no, no, no, ya... una Coca-Cola.
A: Ándale, ya nos entendemos.
B: Salud.
C: Salud.
B: ¡Oye! Mira, flaco, nos va a dejar la guagua.
C: ¿La "guagua"?
A: Es el "camión".
C: No, es el "bus".
A: No, el "camión".
C: No, es el "bus".
B: "Guagua".

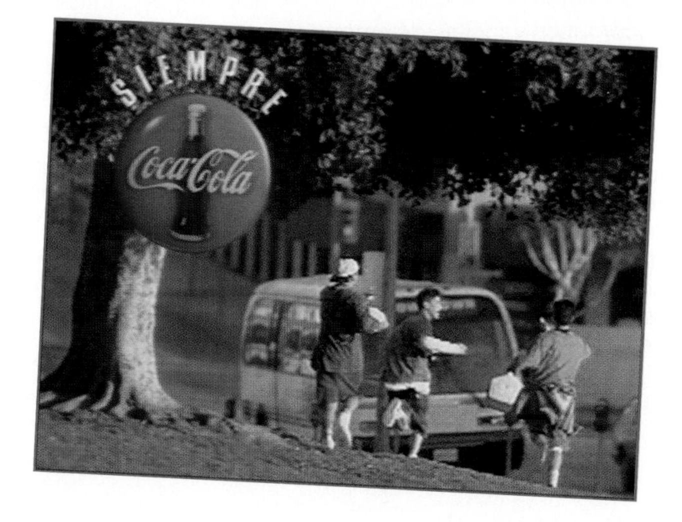

Act. 18: Begin by discussing differences in English between the U.S. and England (lift/elevator), or between different parts of the U.S. (pop/soda, water fountain/bubbler, milkshake/frappé). Then have students read the text of the TV ad, which features people of Latin America, including a Mexican and a Caribbean person, and answer the questions, justifying all responses. Note: This ad would be shown in the U.S. where there is a large Spanish-speaking population from different parts of the Hispanic world. The words used in this ad reflect the diversity of the population.

1. ¿Qué hicieron los muchachos antes de tomar el autobús? ¿Qué harán cuando bajen del autobús?
2. ¿Cuáles son las dos expresiones sinónimas de **¡qué bien!**? Hay tres expresiones diferentes que usan los muchachos para referirse al tipo de bebida que es la Coca-Cola, ¿cuáles son? ¿Qué palabras usan para decir **autobús**?
3. ¿A qué grupos de inmigrantes hispanos creen que se mostrará este anuncio comercial?
4. En tu opinión, ¿Coca-Cola usará este anuncio comercial en España? ¿En Chile? ¿En Venezuela? ¿Por qué sí o no?

¿LO SABÍAN?

En los Estados Unidos la población consumidora hispana consta de unos veinte subgrupos que incluyen a más de 40.000.000 personas. De ellos casi el 70% son de origen mexicano, casi 9% de origen puertorriqueño y un poco menos del 4% son de origen cubano. Pero también hay personas de todos los otros países latinoamericanos y también hay gente de España. Cada subgrupo se caracteriza por tener su propia cultura y diferencias lingüísticas, lo cual presenta un dilema al promocionar un producto. Algunos anuncios presentados en el oeste son dirigidos a la comunidad mexicana, mientras que los anuncios presentados en la Florida se dirigen principalmente a los cubanos. Por supuesto, muchas veces resulta más eficaz crear anuncios comerciales más generales para toda la comunidad hispana y usar un acento y vocabulario relativamente comunes y fáciles de entender para todos.

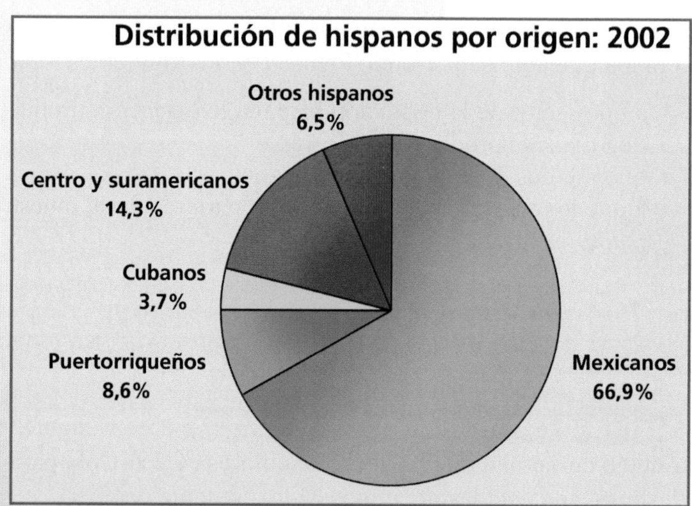

Act. 19: Read through all information in the instructions, divide the class in two groups: pro and con. Assign one person to be a secretary in both groups, allow time to prepare arguments, and conduct the debate.

Twenty years later in 2003, a bill was introduced in the House of Representatives of the United States to declare English the official language of the United States. This issue continues to be debated at the highest levels.

Actividad 19 English Only Como consecuencia de la gran cantidad de inmigrantes que viven hoy en los Estados Unidos, en 1983, el entonces senador Hayakawa de California creó el movimiento de *U.S. English* para lograr, entre otros, los siguientes objetivos:

- adoptar una enmienda (*amendment*) constitucional para que el inglés fuera el idioma oficial de este país
- limitar los fondos gubernamentales para la educación bilingüe

Dividan la clase en dos grupos para debatir si el inglés debe convertirse en el idioma oficial de este país. Cada grupo tiene que preparar un argumento a favor o en contra. Lean las siguientes citas para apoyar sus ideas. Su profesor/a va a moderar el debate.

"Si se hablan muchos idiomas, ¿cómo es posible conducir los asuntos oficiales?"

"Para la defensa del país, es necesario que tengamos personas que hablen otros idiomas."

"El inglés sigue siendo el idioma predominante aunque se hablen otros idiomas."

"Quiero que mis empleados hablen sólo inglés para saber de qué hablan."

"Mis bisabuelos hablaban italiano y no aprendieron inglés al llegar a este país, sus hijos sí lo hablaban y les traducían cuando lo necesitaban."

"Es obvio que los inmigrantes quieren aprender inglés, pero a veces, es difícil hacerlo."

"La educación bilingüe es necesaria para que nuestros niños sean competitivos en un mercado global. Privarlos de esa ventaja afectaría el futuro económico de este país."

"Cuando las agencias del gobierno ofrecen servicios en otros idiomas, desaparece el incentivo de estudiar inglés."

"El 94 por ciento de la población de los Estados Unidos habla inglés. Estamos gastando millones de dólares en clases bilingües."

"Los inmigrantes pueden tener una vida mejor si aprenden inglés."

"Hablar una variedad de idiomas contribuye a la riqueza cultural de un país."

"Los estudiantes americanos que hablan inglés van a 'English class' durante doce años. Los niños hispanos deberían estudiar tanto inglés como español durante doce años también."

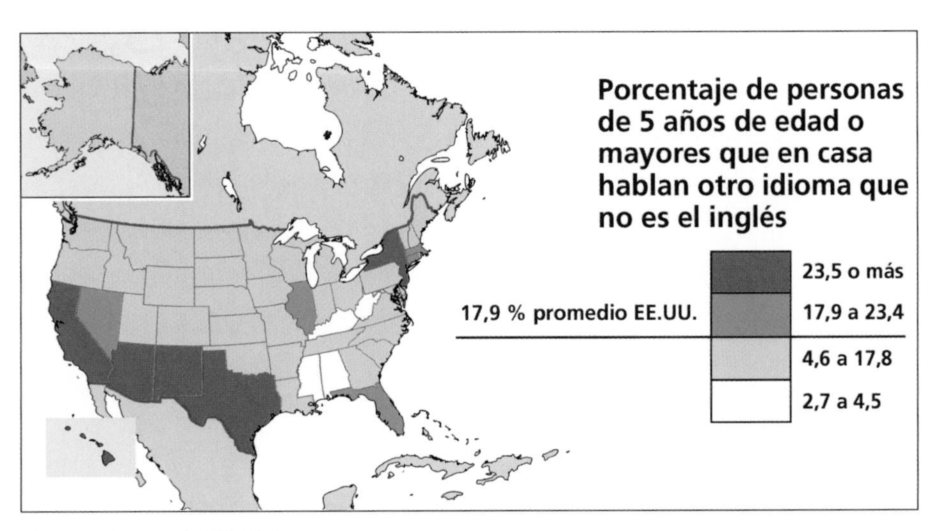

(Fuente: Censo de EE.UU.)

La página del idioma español

Act. 20: Encourage students to be very creative in their responses. When they finish giving their responses, tell them about past students you may have had and how they have used their knowledge of Spanish. If you are a beginning instructor, discuss how knowledge of Spanish is helping your peers.

Actividad 20 El futuro ¡Felicitaciones por haber terminado este curso de español de nivel intermedio! Algunos de Uds. van a dejar el estudio del idioma después de este curso, otros irán a un país de habla española en un futuro próximo para poner en práctica lo que han aprendido y otros van a continuar sus estudios del idioma en la universidad. En el futuro, todos Uds. van a usar el español de una forma u otra, sea en un viaje a un país de habla española, al mirar una película en español o posiblemente al hablarlo en el trabajo. En grupos de tres, discutan cómo creen que usarán el español en el futuro.

International Tax Manager

You are a CPA with 3-5 years' experience in planning the International Tax Function of a multinational corporation. In addition to in-depth knowledge of Subchapter C, 482 and Subchapter N of the IRC, your knowledge of Foreign Tax Laws will benefit you in this fast-paced environment. Specifically, you will be responsible for planning and compliance for EMC's foreign operations. You will assist in tax evaluations of international acquisitions and reorganization, taxation of foreign currency transactions and FSC maintenance and planning, as well as foreign tax credit planning to ensure utilization. BA/BS in Accounting, MST or LLM required. Some travel required. **Job Code: GS**

SR. WIC NUTRITIONIST

F/T to oversee nutrition services, assess, counsel & certify WIC participants. Bachelors Degree in nutrition w/min. 2 yrs. exper. in community setting, Masters pref'd., WIC exper. pref'd. Excel counseling skills req'd. Spanish language a plus. Resume & cover letter by 8/26/94 to Personnel Dir. Community Action, Inc., 25 Locust St., Haverhill, MA 01832. Affirmative Action, Equal Oppty. Employer.

EDITOR

Music Magazine Editor. We're looking for a talented editor with strong organizational skills who can manage a start-up. Experience in the music/entertainment field required; expertise in Latin music and Spanish language proficiency highly desirable. Competitive salary and excellent benefits pkg. Send resume, cover letter and clips.

RECEPTIONIST/SECRETARY

BI-LINGUAL (SPAN/ENG.) Two (2) positions available in small law office. Must have H.S. Diploma, type 60 wpm, & have word processing skills. Good benefits. Salary dependent on experience. Send resume to Ross, Martel & Silverman, 59 Temple Place, Suite 605, Boston, MA. 02111

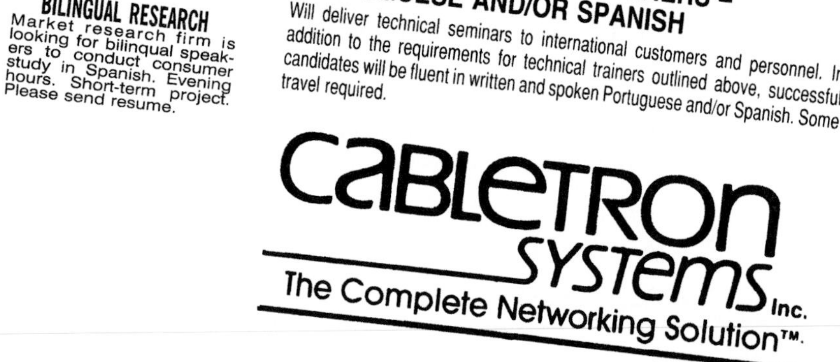

Do the corresponding CD-ROM and web activities to review the chapter topics.

This is also a good time to encourage students to continue their language studies at your university or to participate in programs abroad. (Upon successful completion of this course, students will meet the linguistic requirements for most of these programs.)

Do the video either before or after Act. 20. The content of the video is the benefits of studying abroad from four participants who studied in five different countries.

Vocabulario personal

Buena comida y ¿un tango sensual?

Como todos los años, los trabajadores de la fábrica tuvieron una fiesta en el restaurante Le Rendezvous después de Semana Santa. Esta reunión fue algo extraordinario. La nueva presidenta del sindicato ha sido fiel a su palabra: dijo que mejoraría las relaciones entre la dirección y los empleados y prometió que no lo haría de una manera convencional. Este viernes cumplió con su palabra cuando bailó un tango sensacional con Felipe Bello.

El tango fue una representación cómica e irónica de las relaciones entre la gerencia y el sindicato. Él

llevaba un saco con sus iniciales y ella una camiseta blanca con el símbolo del sindicato. Él ejercía el control mientras ella bailaba con una rosa entre los dientes. Los dos se burlaban del control que tiene un jefe y de cómo puede abusar de los empleados. Pero poco a poco cambió el baile y al final, él tenía la rosa entre los dientes y era ella quien ejercía el control.

Un reportero le preguntó al Sr. Bello qué significaba el final cuando él estaba tendido en el suelo con la rosa en una mano y el pie de la mujer sobre su estómago. Él le explicó que la presidenta había negociado un aumento de sueldo a partir del primero de mayo. El anuncio inesperado fue recibido con grandes aplausos del público eufórico.

VIDEOFUENTES

Capítulo 1 ¿Cómo te identificas?

Antes de ver

Act. 1: When checking, point out that **latinoamericano** also includes people that may speak Portuguese (Brazil). Also note that not all **chicanos** nor **mexicoamericanos** speak Spanish.

Actividad 1 Términos hispanos Explica la diferencia entre los términos **chicano, latinoamericano** y **mexicoamericano** que ya discutiste en clase.

Mientras ves

Actividad 2 ¿Cómo se identifican?

Parte A: Mientras escuchas a varios hispanohablantes que explican cómo se definen, completa la siguiente tabla.

► Jessica Carrillo Fernández

Even though he says he is American, he was born in Colombia.

Nombre	País	Se identifica como...
Rodrigo	Argentina	argentino, latinoamericano
Cecilia	Argentina	argentina, latina, latinoamericana
Gregorio*	España	español, hispano
Jessica*	Perú	peruana
Mirta*	México	latina, mexicana
John*	See annotation	latinoamericano, latino, americano de ascendencia latina
Carmen*	República Dominicana	hispana
Alberto	EE.UU.	latino, hispano, cubanoamericano

*Personas que no fueron entrevistadas en su país.

Parte B: Ahora escucha las entrevistas otra vez y marca las definiciones que los entrevistados asocian con los siguientes términos.

1. d, e latinoamericano
2. a, b hispano
3. c latino

a. hablar español, compartir tradiciones
b. poder hablar español
c. ser gente cálida y tener cosas en común
d. la unión de muchos pueblos
e. la unión del continente

Many Hispanics in the U.S. tend to refer to the heritage of their parents and grandparents when discussing their own nationality. This is especially true for first or second generation Americans. People even often refer to themselves as African-Americans, Italo-Americans, etc. On the other hand, although Irish, Italians, Spaniards, Germans, Koreans, Africans, etc., went to Latin America, it is not common to be a **chileno alemán**, if born in Chile, but a **chileno.**

¿LO SABÍAN?

En el video que acabas de ver, John Leguizamo y Alberto Vasallo III son las únicas dos personas que, al definirse a sí mismos, hablan del origen de sus padres. El primero llegó a los Estados Unidos cuando era muy pequeño y el otro nació en ese país. Por lo general, la gente de habla española que no vive en los Estados Unidos se identifica con su país natal cuando se le pregunta de dónde es y no hace referencia al país natal de sus padres. ¿Por qué muchas personas de habla española que nacieron en los Estados Unidos suelen hablar del país de origen de sus padres?

Después de ver

Actividad 3 **¿Cómo te identificas tú?** En el video algunos hispanohablantes dicen que se identifican como parte de Latinoamérica. En grupos de tres, discutan las siguientes preguntas sobre Uds.

1. ¿Se identifican como parte del continente americano o con un país específico?
2. ¿Con qué países del continente se identifican más o menos? Miren las ideas de la lista para justificar su respuesta.

- tener costumbres similares
- hablar el mismo idioma
- pensar de forma similar
- escuchar la misma música
- ver los mismos programas de televisión
- leer a los mismos escritores

Act. 3: When discussing answers to this activity, have students note the power that language has to unite people. In the video, the woman from the Dominican Republic states that to be **hispano** one needs to speak Spanish. Ask students if they think that when one loses one's ancestral language, one loses the culture as well.

Capítulo 2 España: ayer y hoy

Antes de ver

Actividad 1 **¿Qué recuerdas?** Antes de ver un video sobre la historia de España, di cuáles son algunos de los grupos que habitaron la península Ibérica. Luego menciona personas famosas que están relacionadas con la historia de España.

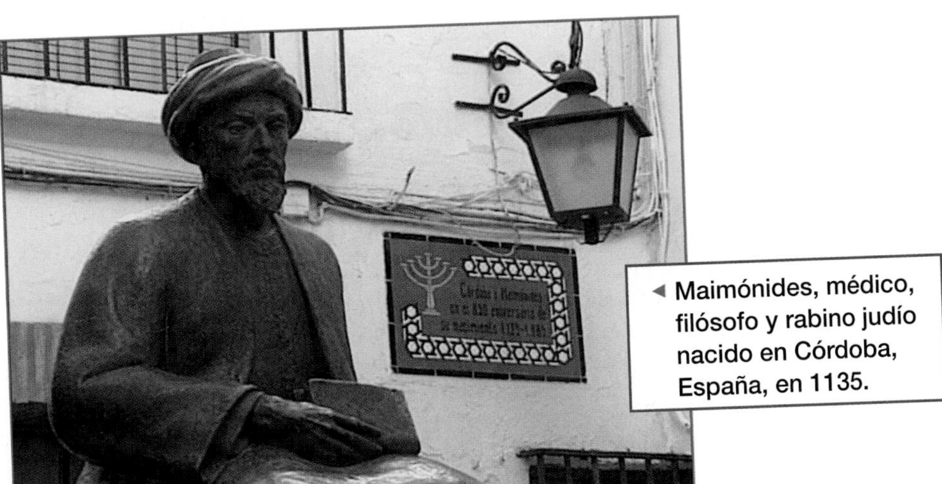

◄ Maimónides, médico, filósofo y rabino judío nacido en Córdoba, España, en 1135.

Act. 2: Answers 1. a. **los romanos**; b. **un par de siglos antes de Cristo** c. **costumbres, leyes, ingeniería (el acueducto de Segovia), arte** 2. a. **los moros** b. **711**; c. **casi 800 años** d. **arquitectura, la cultura del agua y de las huertas, arte ornamental**; e. **Córdoba y Granada** 3. **La Reconquista fue una serie de batallas que duró siete siglos para retomar la península de los moros. Covadonga es donde empezó la Reconquista.** In the video you see the Basilica at Covadonga, the statue of Pelayo, and La Santa Cueva which houses a statue called la Santina, the patron saint of Asturias. People make pilgrimages to the cave by walking up 100 steps or by going through a tunnel that connects with the basilica. The tomb of Pelayo is in the tunnel.

Act. 3: Answers: 1. **Empieza a las ocho de la tarde y dura doce horas.** 2. **Va a los bares o a discotecas, al cine, sale con los amigos a conversar, escucha música, toma una copa con los amigos.**

Act. 4: After students have discussed the history of their own country, you may want to assign individuals to research what historical sites to see in specific Spanish cities. This could be done as extra credit. Possible places to research include Mérida (Museo Nacional de Arte Romano and Roman ruins including the amphitheater and the theater), Segovia (the Roman aqueduct and the Alcázar), Granada (the Alhambra, the Generalife, and the cathedral with the tombs of Ferdinand and Isabel). Other possibilities include El Camino de Santiago and Romanesque architecture, the mixing of cultures as present in Mudejar architecture, and the mixing of cultures under Alfonso el Sabio.

Mientras ves

Actividad 2 Los invasores Ahora lee las siguientes ideas y luego, para buscar la información, mira el video hasta donde se empieza a hablar de Madrid.

1. a. nombre de un grupo que invadió la península Ibérica
   b. cuándo llegaron
   c. en qué se vio su influencia
2. a. nombre de otro grupo que invadió la península Ibérica
   b. cuándo llegaron
   c. cuánto tiempo estuvieron
   d. en qué se vio su influencia
   e. dos lugares importantes que ocuparon en la península Ibérica
3. la importancia de la Reconquista y de Covadonga

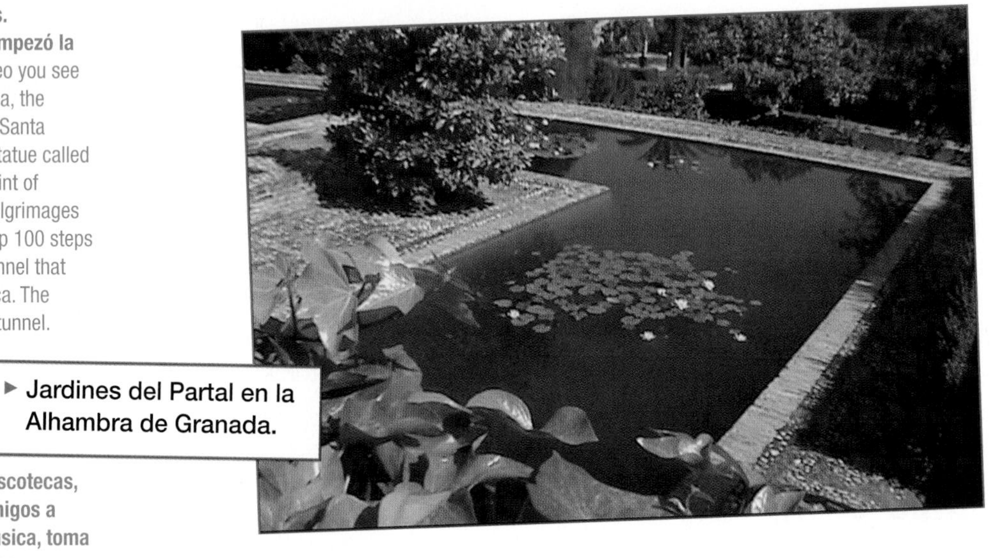

▶ Jardines del Partal en la Alhambra de Granada.

Actividad 3 Madrid Ahora mira el segmento sobre Madrid para contestar las siguientes preguntas sobre su vida nocturna.

1. ¿A qué hora empieza la vida nocturna y cuánto tiempo dura?
2. ¿Qué hace la gente para divertirse?

Después de ver

Actividad 4 La historia de tu país En grupos de tres, hablen sobre los siguientes datos de su país.

1. a. quiénes fueron sus primeros habitantes
   b. influencias que se ven hoy día
2. a. qué grupos llegaron al país
   b. cuándo llegaron
   c. influencias que se ven hoy día
3. dos momentos importantes en la historia de su país

Capítulo 3 Los mayas

Antes de ver

Actividad 1 Indígenas de América Latina Antes de mirar un video sobre un grupo indígena de América Latina, habla sobre la siguiente información.

- grupos indígenas que habitan América Latina
- la zona con que los asocias
- algo sobre sus tradiciones o conocimientos

Mientras ves

Actividad 2 La cultura maya **Parte A:** Mira la primera parte del video sobre la cultura maya, hasta donde empieza a hablar el guía turístico, y busca información sobre los siguientes lugares.

Act. 2A: Possible answers: Mérida: fundada en 1542, arquitectura colonial, gran presencia maya; **Tulum: sitio arqueológico de gran interés, en la costa, centro comercial maya; Chichén Itzá: el sitio arqueológico más visitado del Yucatán, habitado durante casi ocho siglos, hasta 1204.**

- Mérida
- Tulum
- Chichén Itzá

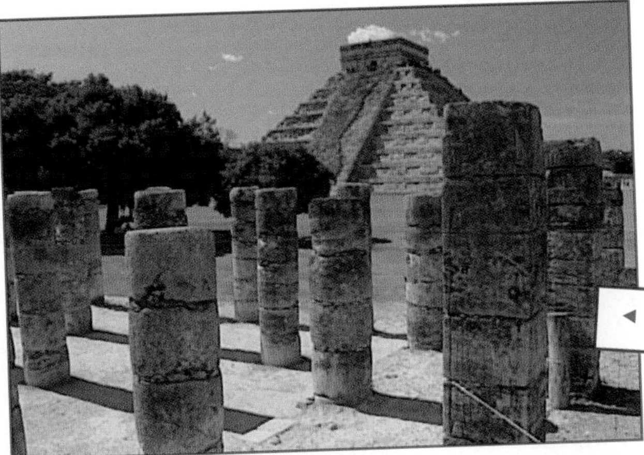

◄ Chichén Itzá.

Parte B: Lee las siguientes preguntas y luego mira el resto del video para contestarlas.

1. ¿Quién era Kukulkán?
2. ¿Qué ocurre dos veces al año en su templo de Chichén Itzá?
3. Según el guía, ¿cómo desaparecieron los mayas?
4. ¿Cómo son físicamente los mayas?
5. ¿Por qué los jóvenes mayas se sienten avergonzados de ser mayas?

Act. 2B: Answers: 1. **el dios más importante de la cultura maya** 2. **Con el reflejo de la luz en la estructura se ve la forma de una serpiente descendiendo las escaleras del templo.** 3. **enfermedades, guerras internas, la llegada de los españoles** 4. **bajos, fuertes, tienen piel oscura** 5. **por no saber hablar español al entrar en la escuela**

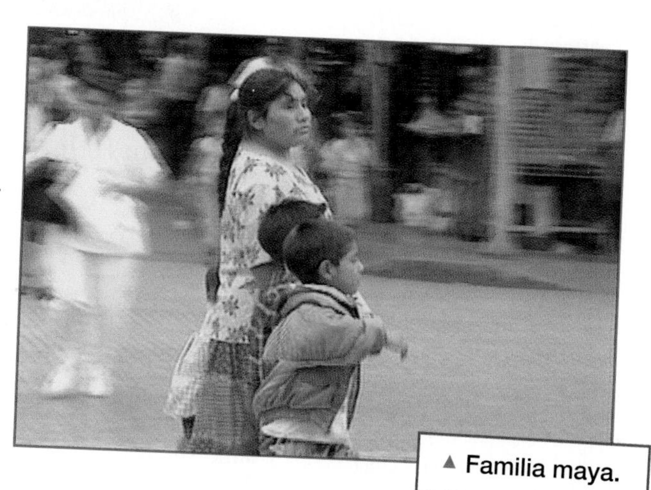

▲ Familia maya.

Act. 3: 1. Answers will vary, but for the U.S. will most likely include Hopi, Navajo, Apache 2. Answers will vary, but may include certain Indian reservations and places like Canyon de Chelly, Acoma, Taos Pueblo. 3. Answers will vary. 4 Answers will vary, but will most likely include the Navajo (they were used in WWII to send secret messages that the enemy was unable to comprehend). Note: Many indigenous languages in North America have become extinct (some due to imposed assimilation) or are in danger of extinction today since few young people speak them fluently. There are people trying to revive some of these languages today. In Latin America, many native languages have not survived, but others are thriving such as Quechua, Nahuatl, and Guaraní (one of the official languages of Paraguay). In Guatemala 23 indigenous languages are spoken by 40% of the population.

Después de ver

Actividad 3 La revalorización En las últimas décadas se han empezado a apreciar más las culturas de los pueblos originales de América Latina. En grupos de tres, discutan las siguientes preguntas sobre las culturas indígenas de su país.

1. ¿Qué grupos indígenas existen hoy día en su país?
2. ¿Qué lugares indígenas se pueden visitar? ¿Han estado en alguno de ellos?
3. ¿Conocen a alguien de origen indígena? Si contestan que sí, ¿saben si habla o no el idioma de sus antepasados? Si eres de origen indígena, ¿hablas el idioma de tus antepasados?
4. ¿Qué grupos indígenas conservan su idioma?

Capítulo 4 La legendaria Celia Cruz

Antes de ver

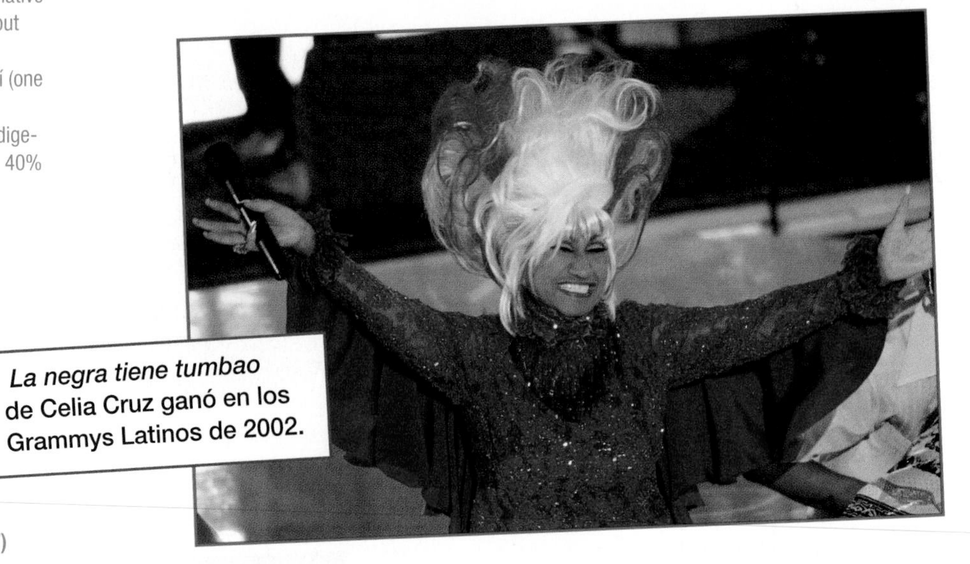

► *La negra tiene tumbao* de Celia Cruz ganó en los Grammys Latinos de 2002.

La negra tiene tumbao = The black woman's got style

Act. 1: **E. Presley (1935–1977) cantante de rock; B. Holiday (1915–1959) cantante de jazz; J. García (1942–1995) guitarrista y cantante del grupo Grateful Dead; J. Morrison (1943–1971) cantante del grupo The Doors; E. Fitzgerald (1917–1996) cantante de jazz; J. Garland (1922–1969) actriz y cantante; B. Haley (1925–1981) cantante de rock con el grupo The Comets; B. White (1944–2003) cantante de blues; F. Sinatra (1915–1998) cantante de jazz y de otros estilos; J. Lennon (1940–1980) guitarrista y cantante con el grupo The Beatles.**

Actividad 1 Los famosos Antes de ver un video sobre Celia Cruz, di cuántas personas de la primera lista conoces y si tienes CDs de algunas de ellas. Luego en grupos de tres, discutan la lista de ideas de la segunda columna.

Elvis Presley
Billie Holiday
Jerry García
Jim Morrison
Ella Fitzgerald
Judy Garland
Bill Haley
Barry White
Frank Sinatra
John Lennon

- qué hicieron estas personas
- por qué fueron una leyenda en vida o después de su muerte
- qué talento tenían
- cómo se vestían para el escenario
- cuáles eran sus innovaciones
- edad de la gente que los escuchaba
- qué aspectos tenían en común con otras personas famosas

Mientras ves

◄ Funeral de Celia Cruz en Nueva York.

Actividad 2 **Su vida** **Parte A:** Ahora mira el primer segmento del video hasta donde la reportera pregunta quién es Celia Cruz. Mientras miras el video, piensa en la siguiente información para después comentarla.

1. ritmos que influyeron en la salsa
2. año en que nació Celia Cruz
3. edad que tenía cuando llegó a los Estados Unidos
4. premios que recibió
5. año en que murió
6. lugar del funeral
7. bandera que llevaba el ataúd (*casket*)
8. lugares donde era famosa

Act. 2A: 1. **ritmos caribeños con influencia del jazz de Nueva York** 2. **1925** 3. **35 años en 1960** 4. **ganó cinco Grammys** 5. (el 16 de julio de) **2003** 6. **en la catedral de San Patricio en Manhattan** 7. **la bandera cubana** 8. **en todo el mundo**

Parte B: Primero, lee las siguientes preguntas y después mira el resto del video para buscar las respuestas.

1. ¿Sabía hablar inglés?
   a. sí
   b. no
2. ¿Qué edad tenía el público que escuchaba a la cantante?
   a. 18-30 años
   b. 30-50 años
   c. mayores de 50 años
   d. gentes de todas las edades
3. ¿Qué crees que hacía ella para mantener la atención de este público? (Es posible marcar más de una respuesta.)
   a. Cantaba diferentes tipos de música.
   b. Se cambiaba el color del pelo con frecuencia.
   c. Sonreía mucho.
   d. Se vestía de maneras divertidas.
   e. Era optimista siempre.
   f. Bailaba mientras cantaba.
4. ¿Cómo se sentía respecto a su país natal?
   a. Nunca quería volver.
   b. Estaba enojada.
   c. Sentía nostalgia.
5. ¿Qué gritan al final los cantantes que le rinden homenaje (*pay homage*)?
   a. ¡Viva Celia!
   b. ¡Azúcar!
   c. ¡Rumba!

Act. 2B: 1. **b** 2. **d** 3. **a, b, c, d, e, f** 4. **c** 5. **b**

Después de ver

Act. 3A: Ask comprehension questions about the contents of the paragraph. Additional information: The wake in Miami took place at the Freedom Tower, which served as a type of Ellis Island processing center for half a million Cubans who fled Cuba after Castro took control. Fifth Avenue in NYC was closed to traffic for the funeral. The director of the funeral home said that it was the largest wake he had ever seen—even larger than Judy Garland's.

Actividad 3 El funeral **Parte A:** Lee la descripción del funeral de Celia Cruz y contesta las preguntas de tu profesor/a.

Celia Cruz murió el 16 de julio de 2003 en su casa de Fort Lee, Nueva Jersey. Después de su muerte, el cuerpo de la cantante fue trasladado a Miami para un velorio al que asistieron más de cien mil admiradores incluyendo a Cristina Saralegui, la Oprah latina. Después hubo otro velorio en Nueva York donde fueron miles de admiradores, entre ellos la senadora Hillary Clinton y el diputado Charles Rangel.

El funeral de Celia Cruz se realizó en la catedral de Nueva York. Asistieron actores y cantantes como Antonio Banderas, Melanie Griffith, Jon Secada, y Gloria y Emilio Estefan. El alcalde de Nueva York, Michael Bloomberg, acompañaba al marido de Celia al entrar en la catedral y Patti LaBelle cantó el Ave María durante la ceremonia. Se enterró a la cantante en el cementerio del Bronx, como era su deseo, ya que quería estar en ese barrio entre los latinos y los negros. Allí se encuentran personalidades famosas como Miles Davis, Irving Berlin y Duke Ellington.

In 2004, Celia Cruz won a Latin Grammy posthumously. In 2005, the Smithsonian had an exhibition paying tribute to her, and her biography was published with a foreword written by Maya Angelou.

Act. 3B: Option 1: Do in class and encourage students to be creative. Set a time limit for students to create answers. When finished have a group sharing. Option 2: Assign this as individual HW and have students write a newspaper article covering the funeral. (Note: There are many articles in Spanish on the Internet about Celia's funeral that could be copied and used as an example.) If time is limited, simply elicit from students impressions/reactions of Celia's life.

Parte B: En grupos de tres o cuatro, imaginen que la semana pasada murió un/a artista muy famoso/a. Decidan quién era e incluyan la siguiente información para describir el funeral.

- de qué o cómo se murió
- quiénes asistieron
- dónde fue
- quiénes hablaron y cantaron
- qué hacían sus admiradores mientras el ataúd pasaba por la calle
- dónde se enterró a la persona

Capítulo 5 Entrevista a John Leguizamo

Antes de ver

Actividad 1 Hispanos famosos

Antes de ver la entrevista a un hispano famoso, di el nombre de hispanos famosos que viven en los Estados Unidos, explica de dónde son o de qué origen es su familia y qué hacen.

Mientras ves

Actividad 2 Leguizamo y su vida Mira la primera parte de la entrevista con el actor y cómico John Leguizamo hasta donde explica en qué idioma siente. Contesta las siguientes preguntas.

1. ¿De dónde es? ¿De dónde son sus padres?
2. ¿Cuántos años tenía cuando llegó a los Estados Unidos?
3. Según el cómico, ¿en qué idioma piensa y en qué idioma siente? ¿Por qué crees que dice que piensa en un idioma y siente en otro?

Act. 2: Show the first part of the video. Answers: 1. **Nació en Colombia. Sus padres son de Colombia y Puerto Rico.** 2. **Tenía cuatro años.** 3. **Piensa en inglés, pero siente en español.** Answers to second part will vary.

Actividad 3 Los inmigrantes Mira ahora el resto de la entrevista y piensa en las siguientes preguntas.

1. ¿Qué mensaje quiere el cómico que entendamos?
2. Según el cómico, ¿cuál es la dura realidad del hispano que emigra a los Estados Unidos?
3. ¿Qué les recomienda a las personas que estudian español?

Act. 3: Answers to these questions will vary. Note that his advice on learning Spanish reflects the process that he has had to go through while learning it. Students may find pronouncing Spanish harder than reading it.

Después de ver

Actividad 4 Los estereotipos **Parte A:** En el video, vemos cómo John Leguizamo se ríe de los estereotipos de los latinos que viven en los Estados Unidos. En grupos de tres, discutan en qué consiste el estereotipo de la gente norteamericana que existe en otros países.

Parte B: Ahora en su grupo, digan cómo quieren Uds. que el resto del mundo vea a la gente de los Estados Unidos.

Act. 4A and B: Form groups of three and have students discuss the stereotype. Then have them discuss how they want to be seen. Note: You may want to change the content depending on your circumstances to people from Canada, from a certain state/city/region, or from your university instead of people from the U.S.

Capítulo 6 En busca de la verdad

Antes de ver

Actividad 1 ¿Qué recuerdas? En grupos de tres, antes de ver un video sobre algo que ocurrió durante la dictadura militar en Argentina entre 1976 y 1983, hablen sobre lo que saben de las siguientes ideas.

- los desaparecidos de Chile y el general Pinochet
- Sting y los derechos humanos
- los desaparecidos de Argentina y las Madres de Plaza de Mayo

Act. 1: Form groups, set a time limit, and check. Accept all correct answers, but do not elaborate since they will learn a great deal of information in the video.

Mientras ves

Act. 2: 1. **más de 30.000** 2. **Fueron secuestrados, torturados y asesinados; fueron adoptados ilegalmente.** 3. **Madres de Plaza de Mayo y una organización de abuelas (Abuelas de Plaza de Mayo); las madres protestaron contra el gobierno; las abuelas buscan a sus nietos.**

Actividad 2 Los desaparecidos Lee las siguientes preguntas y luego, para contestarlas, mira el video sobre los desaparecidos, hasta donde Horacio empieza a hablar de sus padres.

1. ¿Cuántas personas desaparecieron en Argentina?
2. ¿Qué les ocurrió a los desaparecidos? ¿Y a sus hijos?
3. ¿Cuáles fueron los grupos de protesta que se formaron y cuáles eran sus objetivos?

▶ Mercedes Meroño, vicepresidenta de la Asociacíon Madres de Plaza de Mayo.

Act. 3: Answers: 1. **Trabaja en Abuelas de Plaza de Mayo.** 2. **Sus padres eran estudiantes de sociología y psicología. Detuvieron al padre y no se supo más; a la madre la mataron.** 3. **Unos militares lo llevaron de una clínica.** 4. **No era como los demás en su familia y tenía sus dudas; miró la página de las abuelas en Internet donde vio una foto y se hizo una prueba de ADN.** 5. **No se puede olvidar porque, si se olvida, puede pasar otra vez.**

Actividad 3 La historia de Horacio Ahora lee las siguientes ideas y luego mira el resto del video para escuchar la historia de Horacio.

1. qué hace Horacio
2. quiénes eran sus padres y qué les ocurrió
3. cómo llegó Horacio a su nueva familia
4. cómo descubrió su verdadera identidad
5. por qué es importante no olvidar lo que ocurrió

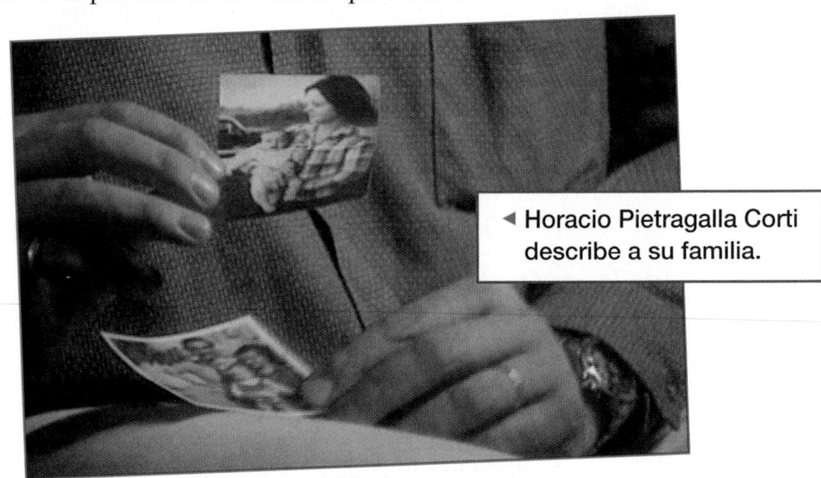

◀ Horacio Pietragalla Corti describe a su familia.

Después de ver

Act. 4: Answers will vary. Possible answers for question # 2 for the U.S.: **Detenidos afganos en Guantánamo, prisioneros de guerra iraquíes. El gobierno detuvo a japoneses en los EE.UU. durante la Segunda Guerra Mundial.**

Actividad 4 Nunca más En grupos de tres, discutan las siguientes preguntas sobre los derechos humanos. Al hablar, usen expresiones como: **Dudo que... haya..., Creo que..., Es terrible que...**

1. ¿Conocen otros países donde hubo o hay hoy día violaciones de derechos humanos? ¿El mundo hizo o hace algo para detenerlas? ¿Alguien hizo o hace algo para juzgar a los culpables?

(continúa en la página siguiente)

2. ¿Alguna vez ha violado el gobierno de este país los derechos humanos de sus ciudadanos? ¿Y de los ciudadanos de otros países? Si contestan que sí, ¿el mundo hizo algo para detenerlo? ¿Alguien hizo algo para juzgar a los culpables? ¿Cómo reaccionaron los ciudadanos del país?
3. ¿Qué creen que se pueda hacer para que los gobiernos del mundo respeten esos derechos? Mencionen por lo menos cuatro ideas.

Capítulo 7 El turismo rural

Antes de ver

Actividad 1 La provincia de Asturias Antes de ver un video sobre Asturias, España, mira las siguientes fotos y usa la imaginación para decir qué deportes se pueden practicar allí y qué clima tiene la región.

◄ Montañas asturianas.

► Costa asturiana.

Act. 2: Answers: 1. **la costa, los valles y las montañas** 2. **turismo deportivo (o activo) y turismo rural; La gente se aloja en una casa y aprende y participa en tradiciones asturianas.** 3. **el pony asturcón y la gallina (pita pinta)** 4. **Estas construcciones tienen su origen en la cultura celta; son almacenes de comida que están elevados del suelo.** 5. **Se recogen las manzanas entre septiembre y diciembre, entran en la bodega, se pican/cortan, se prensan y se van fermentando.** 6. **La sidra se echa desde alto y debe chocar contra el borde del vaso porque así se genera una especie de oxigenación.** NOTE: Only a small amount is poured into the glass—enough for a good gulp or two. When the first person is finished, another person pours a small amount into the same glass. One glass is shared by a group of people.

Mientras ves

Actividad 2 Un turismo diferente Lee las siguientes ideas y luego mira el video y apunta esta información.

1. las tres zonas principales de Asturias
2. tipo de turismo que se puede hacer en la zona y en qué consiste
3. dos tipos de animales que están en peligro de extinción
4. descripción de los hórreos
5. proceso para hacer sidra
6. cómo se sirve la sidra y por qué

¿LO SABÍAN?

Las zonas rurales de España, y de otras partes de Europa, pierden habitantes cada año porque mucha gente prefiere la vida urbana. Debido a ese éxodo, especialmente de gente joven, es difícil mantener vivas las costumbres de las diferentes regiones. Por eso, en los últimos veinte años han surgido casas rurales que cumplen un papel importante por las siguientes razones.

- Ofrecen una oportunidad para conectarse o reconectarse con la vida del campo.
- Ayudan a crear una conciencia en cuanto a la importancia de proteger el medio ambiente.
- Mantienen vivas las costumbres y transmiten esas costumbres a través de talleres donde la gente participa activamente.
- Luchan contra la extinción de especies animales.
- Promueven el turismo que es otra fuente de ingresos para la gente de la zona y la alienta a no abandonar el campo.

Act. 3A and B: Option 1: Form groups of three, go over the instructions, set a time limit, and begin. At the end, poll the groups about their **casas rurales.** Part B can be done individually, in groups, or omitted. Option 2: Assign Part A as a brainstorming activity and assign Part B as written HW to be done individually. The day the descriptions are due students could be put in groups to try to convince each other to go to their **casa rural.**

Después de ver

Actividad 3 Turismo rural en tu país **Parte A:** En grupos de tres, Uds. van a crear una casa rural similar a la Quintana de la Foncalada, pero en su país. Miren las siguientes ideas y la información sobre la Quintana para pensar en las cosas que necesitan. Al hablar, usen expresiones como: **Buscamos un lugar que..., Tenemos una persona que..., Vamos a enseñarles... para que...**

- tipo de lugar que necesitan
- región del país donde puede estar la casa rural
- proceso que pueden enseñarles a los turistas
- animales que Uds. van a proteger que pueden estar en peligro de extinción

Parte B: Individualmente, lee la siguiente descripción que aparece en Internet de la Quintana de la Foncalada. Después, crea una descripción de tu casa rural, parecida a la siguiente, que incluya toda la información necesaria.

Casería tradicional asturiana totalmente rehabilitada en una finca de una hectárea. Alojamiento rural con apartamento para 2, para 4 personas y 4 habitaciones con baño. En la finca tenemos un parque infantil, mesas para merendar. Finca ganadera con razas autóctonas en peligro de extinción: ponis asturcones, ovejas xaldas, pitas pintas. Producción ecológica de cordero, sidra. Planta de energía solar térmica y fotovoltaica. Ecomuseo del Asturcón con exposiciones y actividades relacionadas con las especies ganaderas asturianas. Taller de alfarería, con producción y cursos de cerámica tradicional asturiana.

CASA:	La Quintana de la Foncalada
PROPIETARIO:	Severino García & Daniela Schmid
DIRECCION:	Foncalada 26, 33314 Argüero. Villaviciosa. Asturias
TELEFONO:	985 876365 / 655 69 79 56
FAX:	985 876365
E-MAIL:	foncalada@asturcon-museo.com
WWW:	http://www.asturcon-museo.com
ABIERTO:	Todo el año
IDIOMA:	Español, francés, inglés
PRECIO/NOCHE:	Temporada alta: 2 personas 45,00 € apartamento (4 p.) 85,00 € Temporada baja: 2 personas 35,00 € apartamento (4 p.) 60,00 € Cama supletoria: 12,00 € Desayuno 4,00 € cena 12,00 €

Capítulo 8 Almodóvar y los estereotipos

Antes de ver

Actividad 1 ¿Con quién asocias este trabajo?

Antes de ver algunas escenas de una película de Pedro Almodóvar, mira la siguiente lista de ocupaciones y di si generalmente las asocias con un hombre o con una mujer. Justifica tus respuestas.

1. doctor/doctora
2. enfermero/enfermera
3. general/mujer general
4. maestro/maestra de jardín infantil
5. piloto/mujer piloto
6. portero/portera
7. presidente/presidenta de este país
8. profesor/profesora de química
9. torero/torera

The term **la presidente** is also accepted.

Act. 1: As a class have students shout out responses. While doing this activity, ask questions like **¿La última vez que volaste el avión tenía piloto o mujer piloto? ¿Te ha atendido alguna vez un enfermero?** (etc.) Ask or explain to students who Almodóvar is. You may want to show a picture of him that is on p. 52.

The actress in the photo is the daughter of the late Lola Flores, a famous Spanish entertainer.

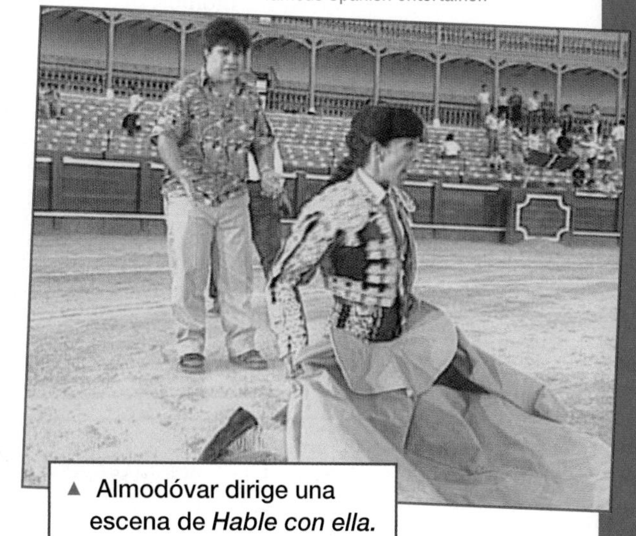

▲ Almodóvar dirige una escena de *Hable con ella.*

Mientras ves

Act. 2A: Answers: **enfermero (ser enfermero requiere atributos femeninos, los hombres gay tienen estos atributos), portera (le gusta chismear, saber todo sobre la vida de otros), torera (su vida amorosa es más importante que su vida profesional)**

Actividad 2 Hable con ella **Parte A:** Vas a mirar tres clips de la película *Hable con ella* donde se ven hombres y mujeres que tienen diferentes trabajos. Mira el video hasta donde terminan los clips y piensa en las siguientes ideas.

- las ocupaciones que se presentan
- si un hombre o una mujer tiene el trabajo
- estereotipo(s) que se presenta(n) en cada clip

Act. 2B: Answers: *Clip 1:* 1. **¿Cuál es su orientación? A la cultura americana.** 2. **indignado** *Clip 2:* 1. **Porque no ha ido ningún paparazzi a entrevistarla.** 2. **Está en la cárcel, pero es inocente.** 3. **Probablemente le va a hacer preguntas al amigo de Benigno todo el tiempo.** *Clip 3:* 1. **En un programa de entrevistas.** 2. **Porque la usó para hacerse famoso.**

Act. 2B: In the movie, Almodóvar gives the male nurse the name of **Benigno,** who may or may not be so *benign*, and **Lydia** is the name given to the bullfighter because she is a person **que lidia toros.**

Parte B: Ahora lee las siguientes preguntas y luego, para contestarlas, mira los clips otra vez.

Clip 1

1. ¿Qué pregunta dice Benigno que le ha hecho el padre de la chica? ¿A qué cultura le atribuye la pregunta?
2. ¿Cómo se siente Benigno con la pregunta que le hizo el padre?

Clip 2

Marcos, un amigo de Benigno, va a alquilar la casa de Benigno y habla con la portera.

1. ¿Por qué está sorprendida e indignada la portera?
2. ¿Qué información recibe ella sobre Benigno?
3. ¿Cómo crees que ella va a obtener más información sobre Benigno?

Clip 3

1. ¿En qué tipo de programa de televisión aparece la torera?
2. ¿Por qué dice la entrevistadora que el torero llamado el Niño de Valencia se ha burlado de ella?

Act. 2C: Answers will vary. Encourage students to support opinions using connected discourse.

Parte C: En el siguiente segmento, Pedro Almodóvar habla sobre el personaje de Lydia, la torera, que trabaja en una profesión de hombres donde hay mucho machismo. Mira la entrevista a Almodóvar y luego di si existen otras profesiones donde haya machismo y no se acepte a las mujeres como iguales.

► Escena de *Hable con ella.*

Después de ver

Actividad 3 Tus estereotipos **Parte A:** En grupos de tres, contesten estas preguntas y justifiquen sus respuestas.

1. Cuando tengan hijos pequeños, ¿van a emplear a un hombre o a una mujer como babysiter? Imaginen que hay dos maestros (un hombre y una mujer) para la clase de primer grado y Uds. pueden elegir: ¿van a elegir al hombre, a la mujer o van a dejar que la escuela decida?
2. En el trabajo, ¿prefieren trabajar para un jefe, una jefa o les da igual?
3. En el gobierno, ¿prefieren un presidente, una presidenta o les da igual? ¿Cambia su respuesta si la persona tiene hijos adolescentes?
4. En cuanto a la salud, ¿prefieren ir a un doctor, a una doctora o les da igual? ¿Depende del problema que tengan?
5. En el ejército, ¿las mujeres deben servir igual que los hombres? Imaginen que Uds. tienen un hijo que es soldado y está en la guerra: ¿prefieren que la persona que combata junto a su hijo sea hombre, mujer o les da igual?

Parte B: Discutan las siguientes preguntas teniendo en cuenta sus respuestas de la Parte A.

1. ¿Existen prejuicios contra la mujer en el campo laboral? ¿Y contra el hombre?
2. ¿Uds. mismos tienen prejuicios?
3. Los idiomas evolucionan con los cambios en la sociedad. Hoy día hay ocupaciones que se asociaban o se asocian típicamente con un solo sexo. En inglés, la palabra *president* puede referirse a un hombre o a una mujer, pero en algunos casos se usa una palabra diferente si la ocupación la ejerce un hombre o una mujer. ¿Pueden pensar en ejemplos de palabras como éstas?

Act. 3B: Here are a few examples for item 3: male nurse (*male* is added), chairman/woman/person, congressman/woman/person, mail carrier (*mailwoman* sounds incorrect), flight attendant (preferred term vs. *steward/stewardess*), actor (preferred term vs, *actor/actress*). Compare the changes in the English language to some that have occurred in Spanish: **el piloto/la pilota/la mujer piloto** all accepted, **el cartero/la cartero** (since **la cartera** = *pocketbook*), **el fontanero / la mujer fontanero** (same with **plomero**); **el político/la mujer político, el/la chofer, el/la soldado/la mujer soldado, el policía/la mujer policía, el mecánico/la mujer mecánico,** etc.

Capítulo 9 El arte de Elena Climent

Antes de ver

Act. 1: Do this as a full class activity calling on a variety of individuals for each question.

Actividad 1 Tu carrera y tu futuro laboral Antes de ver el primer segmento sobre cómo y por qué empezó a pintar la artista mexicana Elena Climent, habla sobre las siguientes preguntas.

1. ¿Ya sabes qué trabajo te gustaría tener cuando termines la universidad? ¿Cuándo lo supiste y cuántos años tenías? Si no sabes, ¿qué crees que te pueda ayudar a tomar esa decisión?
2. Cuando terminaste la escuela secundaria, ¿qué querían tu padre o tu madre que estudiaras? ¿Hiciste lo que querían?
3. ¿Están de acuerdo tus padres con la carrera que estudias? ¿Por qué? Si no has elegido una especialización todavía, ¿les preocupa eso a tus padres?
4. ¿Estudias la misma carrera que estudió alguien de tu familia? Si contestas que sí, ¿qué influencia tuvo esa persona en la elección de tu carrera?

▼ Elena Climent pintando en su casa.

Mientras ves

Act. 2: Play the first part of the video. Stop and correct answers. 1. **Tenía dos años. Vio a su hermana pintando y se le antojó muchísimo.** 2. **Era pintor.** 3. **Le preocupaba que al tener hijos, ella no iba a tener tiempo para pintar.**

Actividad 2 La pintora y su infancia Ahora mira el primer segmento sobre Elena Climent hasta donde explica por qué su padre no quería que ella pintara. Mientras miras, piensa en las siguientes preguntas. Luego comparte las respuestas con el resto de la clase.

1. ¿Cuántos años tenía la artista cuando empezó a dibujar y por qué empezó?
2. ¿Qué ocupación tenía el padre?
3. ¿Por qué no quería el padre que ella pintara?

Act. 3: Play the rest of the video and check answers. You may want to rewind and stop at different points when checking. Possible answers include: 1. **Definición: Los objetos tienen alma; ella tiene una relación con los objetos. Ejemplo:** Students will discuss objects in her paintings, why she may have included them. 2. **Definición: Los mexicanos reciclan las cosas; las usan para otro próposito que el original. Ejemplo: Una lata que se usa como una maceta para plantas.** 3. **Definición: Todo lo que entra en México se va integrando a lo que es México — los mexicanos lo hacen mexicano. Ejemplo: Cómo colocan cosas como las botellas de Coca-Cola en el cuadro.**

Actividad 3 La influencia mexicana Aunque esta artista mexicana vive en Chicago, se ve en su obra mucha influencia de su país natal. Observa el resto del video para escuchar la definición de los siguientes términos. Después busca ejemplos de cada uno en sus pinturas.

1. animismo
   definición: ______________________________
   ejemplo: ______________________________
2. reciclaje
   definición: ______________________________
   ejemplo: ______________________________
3. sincretismo
   definición: ______________________________
   ejemplo: ______________________________

Después de ver

Act. 4A: Form groups of three and set a short time period for students to discuss. When finished discuss their comments. If time permits, you may want to show the video again and have students discuss some of her other paintings.

Actividad 4 Mirar un cuadro **Parte A:** En grupos de tres, observen el siguiente cuadro y describan todos los elementos que ven. Luego den, por lo menos, dos ejemplos de elementos que muestren la influencia mexicana.

► *Mesa de mosaicos con espejo.*

Parte B: Climent pone en los cuadros partes de su vida que representan momentos de su pasado. En su grupo de tres, imaginen que cada uno de Uds. tiene una mesa enfrente de una ventana y tiene que ponerle cosas que reflejan algún aspecto de su vida: su juventud, su familia, su escuela, su ciudad o pueblo, etc. Las cosas pueden ser una foto especial, un libro, una llave, lo que quieran. Expliquen qué van a poner en la mesa y cómo van a colocarlo todo. Digan también qué se puede ver por la ventana que está detrás de la mesa.

Act. 4B: Option 1: Assign as HW and have students draw or create a collage to represent their table. Have them include a narrative to describe their choices of objects. Hand in or use as a paired activity the next day in class. Option 2: In groups of three or pairs, have students discuss what they would paint and have them justify their responses.

Capítulo 10 *En la esquina* (cortometraje)

Antes de ver

Actividad 1 ¿De qué se trata? En el siguiente cortometraje chileno llamado *En la esquina*, aparecen un chico, su novia y una segunda chica. En grupos de tres, miren el título del corto, la foto y usen la imaginación para inventar lo que creen que va a ocurrir.

El cortometraje *En la esquina* ganó premios en Chile, Italia, Cuba y los EE.UU.

Act. 1: Form groups of three, set a time limit, and begin. When finished, have a group sharing, accepting all answers as possible.

Mientras ves

Actividad 2 El cortometraje **Parte A:** Mira el cortometraje y prepárate para hablar de las siguientes ideas. ¡OJO! El cortometraje termina después de que aparecen los títulos de crédito (*final credits*).

- quiénes son los personajes
- qué ocurre en la esquina
- cuál es el final de la historia
- qué creen que ocurrirá después del final que se presenta

Act. 2A: Play the tape all the way through; make sure not to stop the tape until after the credits are completed since there is additional footage with the credits. Discuss answers to the questions.

Parte B: El cortometraje muestra realidad y fantasía. En grupos de tres, discutan qué partes creen Uds. que son reales y cuáles no.

Act. 2B: Form groups and have students report back to the class.

Después de ver

Act. 3A: Form pairs and have students alternate asking each other questions 1–6. Stop and share answers.

Actividad 3 Las relaciones amorosas **Parte A:** Ahora en parejas, discutan las siguientes preguntas sobre las relaciones amorosas.

1. ¿Qué harían si estuvieran en el lugar del chico de la película y por qué?
2. Si fueran la chica de la esquina y el chico les hablara, ¿qué le dirían?
3. ¿Alguna vez han visto a alguien muy atractivo mientras tenían novio o novia? ¿Qué hicieron? ¿Imaginaron algo?
4. ¿Alguna vez han visto en la calle a un ex novio o ex novia? ¿Qué hicieron y por qué?
5. En su opinión, ¿creen que algunas parejas estén juntas por costumbre y no porque realmente se quieran?
6. ¿De qué modo cambia la gente su comportamiento cuando está delante de alguien que le gusta mucho?

Act. 3B: Explain the meaning of the second **refrán** and have students discuss the sayings in pairs. Discuss their responses.

Parte B: Ahora miren los siguientes refranes y expliquen cómo se reflejan en la película que acaban de ver.

- Más vale malo conocido que bueno por conocer.
- Del dicho al hecho hay largo trecho.

Act. 4: Option 1: Do in class and have a few groups perform. Option 2: Assign as a skit to perform in class or to film. Have students write scripts, which should be handed in and checked prior to performing in class or filming.

Actividad 4 En la esquina (Segunda parte) En grupos de tres, escriban el argumento de un segundo cortometraje con los mismos personajes. Luego prepárense para actuar la situación delante de la clase.

Capítulo 11 Día latino en Fenway Park

Antes de ver

You may want to supply words like **pegatina** ("My son is an honor student at XXX school"), and **promedio** (*GPA*).

Actividad 1 Premios y honores En la escuela primaria y secundaria de este país los estudiantes reciben premios (*awards*) y honores por ser buenos estudiantes. En grupos de tres, den ejemplos de algunos de esos premios y honores. Digan también si alguna vez recibieron algún premio en la escuela.

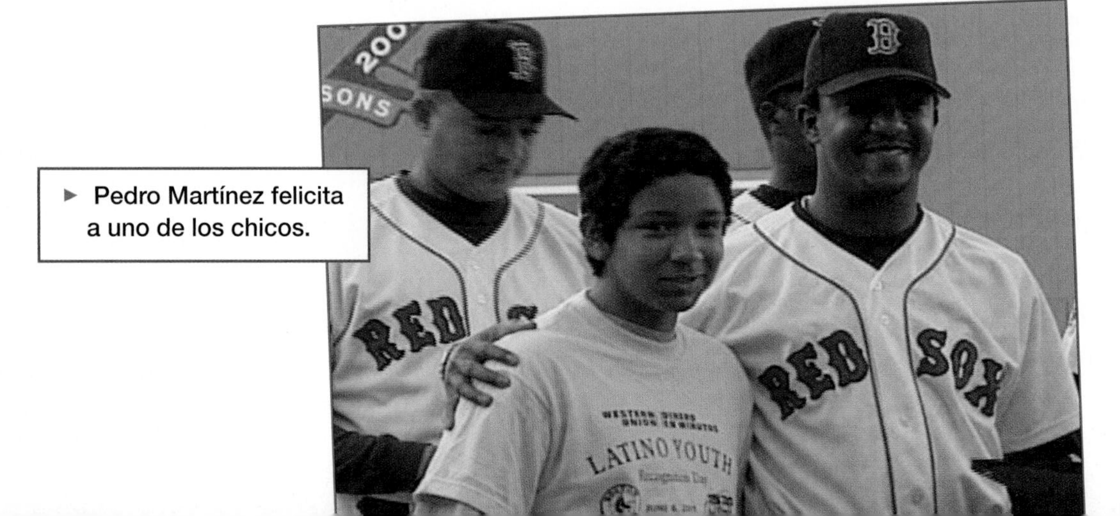

▸ Pedro Martínez felicita a uno de los chicos.

Mientras ves

Actividad 2 Un día de reconocimiento Lee las siguientes preguntas y mientras ves el video sobre el *Día de reconocimiento de los jóvenes latinos*, contéstalas. Mira el video hasta que los estudiantes empiezan a dar consejos.

1. ¿Dónde tiene lugar este evento?
2. ¿Por qué se premia a los estudiantes?
3. ¿Quién organiza el evento?
4. ¿Quiénes les dan los premios a los estudiantes?
5. ¿Adónde se transmite el evento?

Act. 2. Have students read the questions and then play the tape. Answers: 1. **Fenway Park en Boston.** 2. **Para motivarlos a tener éxito académico.** 3. **El periódico *El Mundo* y Los Red Sox (las Medias Rojas).** 4. **Los jugadores (muchos de origen latino como Pedro Martínez).** 5. **Por todo Nueva Inglaterra a través de siete cadenas de radio en español.**

Actividad 3 Los consejos **Parte A:** Ahora lee esta lista de consejos y mira el resto del video para marcar los consejos que ofrecen los estudiantes.

✓ estar en contacto con sus padres
✓ estudiar mucho
___ hablar con los profesores
✓ portarse bien
✓ tener un horario para hacer la tarea
___ no andar con malas compañías
✓ no descuidar los estudios
___ no estar en una pandilla
✓ no faltar a clase
___ no hablar en clase
✓ no meterse en problemas

Parte B: En parejas, digan otros consejos para que un estudiante no tenga problemas en la escuela. Sigan el modelo.

▶ Es importante que duerman ocho horas cada noche.

Act. 3B: Form pairs, set a short time limit, and begin. Check by having a group sharing.

Después de ver

Actividad 4 Voluntarios y los niños **Parte A:** Lee qué hizo una estudiante americana que pasó un semestre en Ecuador y contesta las preguntas de tu profesor.

Soy estudiante de Boston College y pasé el segundo semestre de mi tercer año estudiando en Quito. Allí asistí a clases, pero también trabajé como voluntaria en la cárcel de mujeres. Hay una ley en Ecuador que dice que en caso de que no haya parientes para cuidar al hijo de una mujer acusada de un delito, el niño debe ir a la cárcel para vivir con la madre. La mayoría de los niños tienen menos de cinco años, pero hay unos de ocho o hasta 12 años, también. Mi trabajo consistía en ayudar a las mujeres que trabajan allí con los niños. Les daba comida, les enseñaba a contar, los ayudaba con proyectos de arte, los cuidaba cuando estaban jugando afuera. Pero sobre todo, creo que mi trabajo era prestarles atención en forma individual, abrazarlos, ayudarlos a calmarse cuando lloraban y decirles que los quería mucho. Esa fue una experiencia inolvidable para mí y espero que también para ellos.

Parte B: Averigua qué oportunidades ofrece tu universidad para trabajar como voluntario/a y ayudar a niños. Para informarte, puedes preguntar en diferentes oficinas de tu universidad, hablar con amigos que son voluntarios o buscar en Internet. Para la siguiente clase debes estar preparado/a para hablar de una posibilidad, por lo menos.

Act. 4B: Option 1: Have students discuss any programs they know in class as a group activity. Option 2: Have students find out about at least two programs and come to class the next day to inform each other. The next day place them in groups of four to discuss opportunities. Option 3: Have students write a composition containing a description of a program and an interview with a volunteer. Option 4: Give each student different programs to find out about and to be ready to explain in the next class period.

Capítulo 12 Estudiar en el extranjero

Antes de ver

Actividad 1 Tus amigos en el extranjero Antes de ver un video sobre estudiantes que vivieron en el extranjero, di si conoces a gente que haya estudiado en el extranjero y explica lo que sabes.

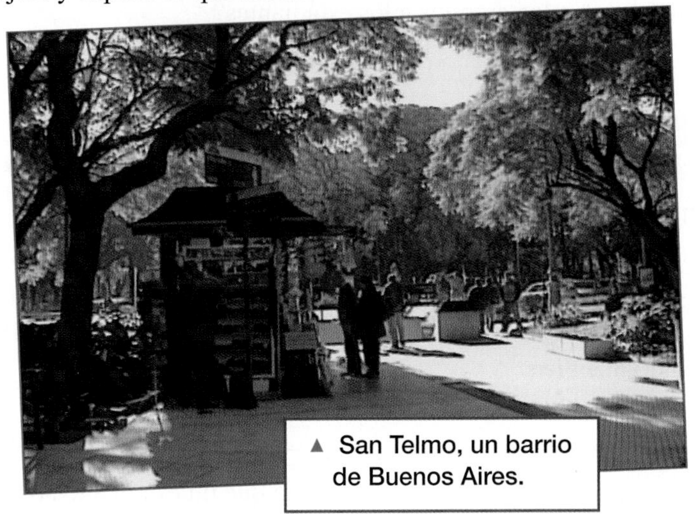

▲ San Telmo, un barrio de Buenos Aires.

Mientras ves

Actividad 2 En el exterior Ahora mira el video sobre cuatro jóvenes que vivieron en el extranjero y completa la tabla de la página 335.

► Nicole

	Andrés	Sarah	Stephanie	Nicole
dónde estuvo	Buenos Aires	Salamanca, España	El Salvador y México, D.F.	Quito
cuánto tiempo	no dice	10 meses	1 año	1 año
qué le gustó	• vivió con una familia increíble • le gustó la ciudad	• oportunidades para viajar y conocer España • la comida y la vida nocturna	• la hospitalidad de la gente, la comida y la cultura latinoamericana	• su familia y amigos ecuatorianos

Después de ver

Actividad 3 Vivencia en el extranjero **Parte A:** Mira las siguientes oraciones y escoge la respuesta que crees que sea correcta.

1. Cada año, más de __c__ estudiantes universitarios de los Estados Unidos reciben crédito por haber tomado clases en otros países.
   a. 100.000 b. 125.000 c. 150.000
2. Al principio del siglo XXI, el número de estudiantes estadounidenses que realizaron estudios en otros países subió cada año por más del __c__.
   a. 3% b. 4% c. 5%

Parte B: Como se puede ver con las respuestas de la Parte A, mucha gente opina que estudiar en otro país es una experiencia que vale la pena. En grupos de tres, discutan las siguientes preguntas.

1. ¿Han estudiado en el extranjero? Si contestan que sí, ¿adónde fueron? ¿Les gustó la experiencia? Si no han estudiado en el extranjero, ¿han considerado ir? ¿Adónde les gustaría ir y por qué?
2. En los últimos años, se ha hecho más y más énfasis en la importancia de estudiar en otro país. Según el periódico *U.S. News* hay 42 universidades en los Estados Unidos donde más del 50% de los estudiantes han estudiado en el extranjero. En su opinión, ¿cuáles son las cinco razones más importantes de estudiar en el extranjero?

Act. 3A and B: Every year articles are written about the importance of knowing a foreign language and many times there is information about the importance of studying abroad. You may want to do a quick search online for a few of those articles and email them to your class or copy them for your students to look over. Possible answers for #2: **aprender sobre otra cultura y, como consecuencia, tener menos prejuicios; aprender a respetar otras formas de pensar y de ser; mejorar su habilidad de comunicarse con otros al entender su manera de vivir y sus costumbres; saber adaptarse a otra cultura; poder llegar a ser bilingüe; ver monumentos, obras de arte y arquitectura; tener algo más para agregar a su curriculum; ser la mejor época de la vida para hacerlo; hacer amigos; poder aprender y divertirse simultáneamente; aprender a ser más aventurero/a; ser una persona más culta.**

Reference Section

Appendix A: Formation of Tenses

Appendix A contains rules for verb conjugations in all tenses and moods. Since you may already be familiar with much of the information in this appendix, you should read through the explanations and focus on what is new to you or what you feel you may need to review in more detail. Highlighting portions of the explanations might help you study more efficiently. Inexpensive reference books that may help you find specific verb conjugations are *201 Spanish Verbs* and *501 Spanish Verbs*, published by Barron's Educational Series. There are also verb conjugation sites on the Internet.

- While studying these rules, remember that most compound verbs are conjugated like the base verb they contain: con***seguir***, ob***tener***, re***volver***, etc.
- Reflexive verbs can be used in all tenses and moods. To review placement of reflexive pronouns and other object pronouns, see pages 354–355.
- To review accentuation rules, see page 358.

The Present Indicative Tense–*El presente del indicativo*

A. Regular Forms

1. To form the present indicative of regular verbs, drop the **-ar, -er,** or **-ir** ending of the infinitive and add the appropriate endings to the stem.

dibuj**ar**		corr**er**		viv**ir**	
dibuj**o**	dibuj**amos**	corr**o**	corr**emos**	viv**o**	viv**imos**
dibuj**as**	dibuj**áis**	corr**es**	corr**éis**	viv**es**	viv**ís**
dibuj**a**	dibuj**an**	corr**e**	corr**en**	viv**e**	viv**en**

2. Certain verbs are regular but need spelling changes in the **yo** form to preserve the pronunciation. Remember these spelling conventions to help you.

Hard "g" sound: **ga gue gui go gu**
exting**ui**r: exting**o,** extingues, extingue, etc.

Soft "g" sound: **ja ge gi jo ju**
diri**gi**r: diri**jo,** diriges, dirige, etc.
esco**ge**r: esco**jo,** escoges, escoge, etc.

Other common verbs of this type are: ele**gi**r, exi**gi**r, reco**ge**r.

B. Irregular Forms

1. The following verbs have irregular **yo** forms. All other forms are regular.

caber → quepo	hacer → hago	salir → salgo	valer → valgo
caer → caigo	poner → pongo	traer → traigo	ver → veo
dar → doy	saber → sé		

Most verbs that end in **-cer** and **-ucir** have irregular **yo** forms.

cono**cer**: cono**z**co, conoces, conoce, etc.
tra**ducir**: tradu**z**co, traduces, traduce, etc.

Other common verbs of this type are: establе**cer,** prod**ucir.**

2. Verbs that end in **-uir** have the following irregular conjugation.

constr**uir**:	constru**y**o	constru**y**es	constru**y**e	construimos	construís	constru**y**en

Other common verbs of this type are: distrib**uir,** contrib**uir,** reconstr**uir.**

3. Verbs ending in **-uar** (but not **-guar**) and some verbs ending in **-iar** require an accent to break the diphthong.

conf**iar:**	confío	confías	confía	confiamos	confiáis	confían
contin**uar:**	contin**ú**o	contin**ú**as	contin**ú**a	continuamos	continuáis	contin**ú**an
But:						
averi**guar:**	averiguo	averiguas	etc.			

Other common verbs of this type are: cr**iar,** env**iar.**

4. The following verbs require an accent on certain verb forms to break the diphthong.

reunir:	**reú**no	**reú**nes	**reú**ne	reunimos	reunís	**reú**nen
pro**hi**bir:	pro**hí**bo	pro**hí**bes	pro**hí**be	prohibimos	prohibís	pro**hí**ben

5. The following verbs are irregular and should be memorized.

estar:	estoy	estás	está	estamos	estáis	están
haber:	he	has	ha	hemos	hais	han
ir:	voy	vas	va	vamos	vais	van
oír:	oigo	oyes	oye	oímos	oís	oyen
oler:	huelo	hueles	huele	olemos	oléis	huelen
ser:	soy	eres	es	somos	sois	son

Note: *There is/are* = **hay.**

C. Stem-Changing Verbs

Stem-changing verbs have a change in spelling and pronunciation in the stem in all forms except the **nosotros** and **vosotros** forms, which retain the vowel of the infinitive. The change occurs in the *stressed* syllable of the conjugated verb, which is also the last syllable of the stem. There are four categories: **e → ie, o → ue, e → i,** and **u → ue.** All stem-changing verbs are noted in vocabulary lists and in dictionaries by indicating the change in parentheses: **volver** (**ue**).

perder (**e → ie**)		probar (**o → ue**)	
pi**e**rdo	perdemos	pru**e**bo	probamos
pi**e**rdes	perdéis	pru**e**bas	probáis
pi**e**rde	pi**e**rden	pru**e**ba	pru**e**ban

pedir (**e → i**)		jugar (**u → ue**)	
p**i**do	pedimos	ju**e**go	jugamos
p**i**des	pedís	ju**e**gas	jugáis
p**i**de	p**i**den	ju**e**ga	ju**e**gan

Stem-changing verbs that also have irregular **yo** forms include the following.

decir (**e** → **i**) → **digo** tener (**e** → **ie**) → **tengo** venir (**e** → **ie**) → **vengo**

Note that **reírse** has an accent on the **i** of all forms to break the diphthong: **me río, te ríes, se ríe, nos reímos, os reís, se ríen.**

Some common stem-changing verbs are:

e → ie	o → ue	e → i
cerrar	almorzar	decir*
comenzar (**a** + *infinitive*)	costar	elegir* (**a** + *person*)
empezar (**a** + *infinitive*)	devolver	pedir
entender	dormir	repetir
mentir	encontrar (**a** + *person*)	seguir* (**a** + *person*)
pensar **en**	morir(se)	servir
pensar + *infinitive*	poder	
perder (**a** + *person*)	probar	
preferir	soler + *infinitive*	
querer (+ *infinitive*); (**a** + *person*)	volver	**u → ue**
tener*	volver a + *infinitive*	jugar (**al** + ...)
venir*		

*These verbs have an irregular **yo** form or spelling change.

The Present Participle–*El gerundio*

1. The present participle is formed by dropping the **-ar** of regular and stem-changing verbs and adding **-ando** and by dropping the **-er** and **-ir** of regular verbs and the **-er** of stem changers and adding **-iendo.** (For **-ir** stem changers, see point 2 below.)

cerr**ar** → cerr + ando → cerr**ando**
corr**er** → corr + iendo → corr**iendo**
viv**ir** → viv + iendo → viv**iendo**

2. The **-ir** stem changers have a change in the stem of the present participle. In dictionary listings, stem changers are followed by vowels in parentheses. The first vowel or vowels in parentheses indicate the change that occurs in the present indicative tense: **dormir** (**ue,** u), **vestirse** (**i,** i), **sentirse** (**ie,** i). The second vowel indicates the change that occurs in the present participle: **dormir** (ue, **u**), **vestirse** (i, **i**), **sentirse** (ie, **i**). (Also see the discussions of the preterit and present subjunctive.)

dormir → d**u**rmiendo vestirse → v**i**stiéndose* sentirse → s**i**ntiendo

3. Verbs with stems ending in a vowel + **-er** or **-ir** (except a silent **u**, as in **seguir**) take a **y** instead of the **i** in the ending.

construir → constru**y**endo

Common verbs that fit this pattern include the following.

leer → le**y**endo
destruir → destru**y**endo
creer → cre**y**endo
caer → ca**y**endo
oír → o**y**endo

The Preterit–*El pretérito*

A. Regular Forms

1. To form the preterit of regular **-ar, -er,** and **-ir** verbs and **-ar** and **-er** stem changers (but not **-ir** stem changers), drop the **-ar, -er,** or **-ir** ending of the infinitive and add the appropriate endings to the stem.

cerr**ar**		vend**er**		viv**ir**	
cerr**é**	cerr**amos**	vend**í**	vend**imos**	viv**í**	viv**imos**
cerr**aste**	cerr**asteis**	vend**iste**	vend**isteis**	viv**iste**	viv**isteis**
cerr**ó**	cerr**aron**	vend**ió**	vend**ieron**	viv**ió**	viv**ieron**

Notice that the **-ar** and **-ir** endings for **nosotros** are identical in the present and the preterit.

---

* To review placement of object pronouns with present participles, see page 355. To review accents, see page 358.

2. Certain verbs are regular but need spelling changes in the **yo** form to preserve the pronunciation. Remember these spelling conventions to help you.

> Hard "g" sound: **ga gue gui go gu**
> pag**ar**: pa**gué,** pagaste, pagó, etc.

Other common verbs of this type are: ju**gar**, ne**gar**, re**gar**, lle**gar**, ro**gar**.

> Hard "c" sound: **ca que qui co cu**
> bus**car**: bus**qué,** buscaste, buscó, etc.

Other common verbs of this type are: to**car**, practi**car**, criti**car**, expli**car**.

> "z": **za ce ci zo zu**
> empe**zar**: empe**cé,** empezaste, empezó, etc.

Other common verbs of this type are: almor**zar**, comen**zar**, ca**zar**, re**zar**, apla**zar**, organi**zar**.

B. Irregular Forms

1. The following verbs have irregular forms in the preterit.

dar:	di	diste	dio	dimos	disteis	dieron
ir:	fui	fuiste	fue	fuimos	fuisteis	fueron
ser:	fui	fuiste	fue	fuimos	fuisteis	fueron
estar:	estuve	estuviste	estuvo	estuvimos	estuvisteis	estuvieron
tener:	tuve	tuviste	tuvo	tuvimos	tuvisteis	tuvieron
poder:	pude	pudiste	pudo	pudimos	pudisteis	pudieron
poner:	puse	pusiste	puso	pusimos	pusisteis	pusieron
saber:	supe	supiste	supo	supimos	supisteis	supieron
hacer:	hice	hiciste	hi**z**o	hicimos	hicisteis	hicieron
venir:	vine	viniste	vino	vinimos	vinisteis	vinieron

2. The verbs **decir, traer,** and verbs ending in **-ducir** take a **j** in the preterit. Notice that they drop the **i** in the third person plural and are followed by **-eron.**

decir:	dije	dijiste	dijo	dijimos	dijisteis	di**jeron**
traer:	traje	trajiste	trajo	trajimos	trajisteis	tra**jeron**
producir:	produje	produjiste	produjo	produjimos	produjisteis	produ**jeron**

3. Verbs with stems ending in a vowel + **-er** or **-ir** (except the silent **u**, as in **seguir**) take a **y** instead of the **i** in the third person singular and plural.

construir:	construí	construiste	constru**y**ó	construimos	construisteis	constru**y**eron
leer:	leí	leíste	le**y**ó	leímos	leísteis	le**y**eron
oír:	oí	oíste	o**y**ó	oímos	oísteis	o**y**eron

Note: *There was/were* = **hubo.**

C. *-Ir* Stem-Changing Verbs

Stem-changing verbs ending in **-ir** only have a stem change in the third person singular and plural. In dictionary listings, these changes are the second change listed: **morir** (ue, **u**).

d**o**rmir (ue, **u**):	dormí	dormiste	d**u**rmió	dormimos	dormisteis	d**u**rmieron
m**e**ntir (ie, **i**):	mentí	mentiste	m**i**ntió	mentimos	mentisteis	m**i**ntieron
v**e**stirse (i, **i**):	me vestí	te vestiste	se v**i**stió	nos vestimos	os vestisteis	se v**i**stieron

The Imperfect–*El imperfecto*

A. Regular Verbs

To form the imperfect of regular verbs, drop the **-ar, -er,** or **-ir** ending of the infinitive and add the appropriate endings to the stem. Notice that all **-ar** verbs end in **-aba** and **-er** and **-ir** verbs end in **-ía.**

cerr**ar***		conoc**er**		serv**ir***	
cerr**aba**	cerr**ábamos**	conoc**ía**	conoc**íamos**	serv**ía**	serv**íamos**
cerr**abas**	cerr**abais**	conoc**ías**	conoc**íais**	serv**ías**	serv**íais**
cerr**aba**	cerr**aban**	conoc**ía**	conoc**ían**	serv**ía**	serv**ían**

*Note: Stem-changing verbs do not change in the imperfect.

B. Irregular Verbs

Common irregular verbs are:

ir:	iba	ibas	iba	íbamos	ibais	iban
ser:	era	eras	era	éramos	erais	eran
ver:	veía	veías	veía	veíamos	veíais	veían

Note: *There was/were* = **había.**

The Future—*El futuro*

A. Regular Verbs

To form the future of regular verbs, add **-é, -ás, -á, -emos, -éis, -án** to the entire infinitive.

habl**ar**		com**er**		**ir**	
hablar**é**	hablar**emos**	comer**é**	comer**emos**	ir**é**	ir**emos**
hablar**ás**	hablar**éis**	comer**ás**	comer**éis**	ir**ás**	ir**éis**
hablar**á**	hablar**án**	comer**á**	comer**án**	ir**á**	ir**án**

Note: There is no accent in the **nosotros** form.

B. Irregular Verbs

Some verbs have irregular stems in the future, but all add to the stem the same endings used above.

Infinitive	Future stem	Infinitive	Future stem
caber	cabr-	querer	querr-
decir	dir-	saber	sabr-
haber	habr-	salir	saldr-
hacer	har-	tener	tendr-
poder	podr-	valer	valdr-
poner	pondr-	venir	vendr-

Note: *There will be* = **habrá.**

The Conditional—*El condicional*

A. Regular Verbs

To form the conditional of regular verbs, add **-ía, -ías, -ía, -íamos, -íais, -ían** to the entire infinitive.

habl**ar**		com**er**		**ir**	
hablar**ía**	hablar**íamos**	comer**ía**	comer**íamos**	ir**ía**	ir**íamos**
hablar**ías**	hablar**íais**	comer**ías**	comer**íais**	ir**ías**	ir**íais**
hablar**ía**	hablar**ían**	comer**ía**	comer**ían**	ir**ía**	ir**ían**

B. Irregular Verbs

Irregular conditional forms use the same irregular stems as for the future (see the explanation for the future tense) and add the same endings used above.

Note: *There would be* = **habría.**

The Present Subjunctive–*El presente del subjuntivo*

A. Regular Forms

1. The present subjunctive of most verbs is formed by following these steps.

- Take the present indicative **yo** form: **hablo, leo, salgo.**
- Drop the **-o: habl-, le-, salg-.**
- Add endings starting with **e** for **-ar** verbs and with **a** for **-er** and **-ir** verbs.

habl**ar**		le**er**		sal**ir**	
que habl**e**	habl**emos**	que le**a**	le**amos**	que salg**a**	salg**amos**
habl**es**	habl**éis**	le**as**	le**áis**	salg**as**	salg**áis**
habl**e**	habl**en**	le**a**	le**an**	salg**a**	salg**an**

2. Certain verbs are regular but need spelling changes to preserve the pronunciation. Remember these spelling conventions to help you.

Hard "g" sound: **ga gue gui go gu**
pa**gar**: que pa**gue,** que pa**gues,** que pa**gue,** etc.

Other common verbs of this type are: lle**gar**, ju**gar**, ne**gar**, re**gar**, ro**gar**.

Soft "g" sound: **ja ge gi jo ju**
ele**gir**: que eli**ja,** que eli**jas**, que eli**ja,** etc.

Other common verbs of this type are: esco**ger**, exi**gir**, reco**ger**, diri**gir**.

Hard "c" sound: **ca que qui co cu**
sa**car**: que sa**que,** que sa**ques,** que sa**que,** etc.

Other common verbs of this type are: bus**car**, to**car**, criti**car**, expli**car**, practi**car**.

"z": **za ce ci zo zu**
empe**zar**: que empie**ce,** que empie**ces**, que empie**ce,** etc.

Other common verbs of this type are: almor**zar**, comen**zar**, organi**zar**, ca**zar**, re**zar**.

B. Irregular Forms

Common irregular forms include the following.

dar:	que dé	des	dé	demos	deis	den
estar:	que esté	estés	esté	estemos	estéis	estén
haber:	que haya	hayas	haya	hayamos	hayáis	hayan
ir:	que vaya	vayas	vaya	vayamos	vayáis	vayan
saber:	que sepa	sepas	sepa	sepamos	sepáis	sepan
ser:	que sea	seas	sea	seamos	seáis	sean

Note: *There is/are* = **que haya.** *There will be* = **que haya.**

C. Stem-Changing Verbs

1. Stem-changing verbs in the present subjunctive ending in **-ar** or **-er** have the same stem changes as in the present indicative tense.

almorz**ar:**	que alm**ue**rce	alm**ue**rces	alm**ue**rce	almorcemos	almorcéis	alm**ue**rcen
quer**er:**	que qu**ie**ra	qu**ie**ras	qu**ie**ra	queramos	queráis	qu**ie**ran

2. Stem-changing verbs ending in **-ir** have the same stem changes in the present subjunctive as in the present indicative except for the **nosotros** and **vosotros** forms, which require a separate stem change. In dictionary listings, this is the second change indicated and is the same change as in the preterit and the present participle: **dormir (ue, u)**.

m**e**ntir (ie, **i**):	que mienta	mientas	mienta	m**i**ntamos	m**i**ntáis	mientan
m**o**rir (ue, **u**):	que muera	mueras	muera	m**u**ramos	m**u**ráis	mueran
p**e**dir (i, **i**):	que pida	pidas	pida	p**i**damos	p**i**dáis	pidan

Commands—*El imperativo*

A. Negative Commands

All negative commands use the corresponding present subjunctive forms.

———	¡No comamos eso!
¡No comas eso!	¡No comáis eso!
¡No coma (Ud.) eso!	¡No coman (Uds.) eso!

B. Affirmative Commands

1. Use the third person forms of the present subjunctive to construct affirmative **Ud.** and **Uds.** commands.

hable (Ud.)	salga (Ud.)	vaya (Ud.)
hablen (Uds.)	salgan (Uds.)	vayan (Uds.)

Note: Subject pronouns are rarely used with commands, but if they are, they follow the verb.

2. To form regular affirmative **tú** commands, use the third person singular of the verb in the present tense.

habla (tú)	come (tú)	duerme (tú)

Note: Subject pronouns are rarely used with commands, but if they are, they follow the verb.

Irregular affirmative **tú** commands include the following.

Infinitive	*Tú* Command	Infinitive	*Tú* Command
decir	di	salir	sal
hacer	haz	ser	sé
ir	ve	tener	ten
poner	pon	venir	ven

3. Affirmative **nosotros** commands (*let's + verb*) use the corresponding present subjunctive forms.

hablemos	comamos	salgamos

Exception: The affirmative **nosotros** command for **ir** is **vamos** (not **vayamos**).

4. The affirmative **vosotros** commands are formed by replacing the final **r** of the infinitive with a **d.** If a reflexive pronoun is added, the **d** is deleted.

habla**d**	come**d**	sali**d**	levantaos*

The only exception is **irse: idos.**

Note: It is common simply to use the infinitive form as an affirmative **vosotros** command in colloquial speech.

*To review placement of object pronouns with commands, see page 355.

The Imperfect Subjunctive–*El imperfecto del subjuntivo*

1. The imperfect subjunctive is formed by following these steps.

- Take the third person plural of the preterit: **decir** = **dijeron.**
- Drop **-ron** to create an imperfect subjunctive stem: **dije-.**
- Add either of the following sets of endings.

-ra endings		**-se** endings	
-ra	-ramos	-se	-semos
-ras	-rais	-ses	-seis
-ra	-ran	-se	-sen

Note: The **-ra** endings are used by more speakers of Spanish. The **-se** endings are common in Spain and in some areas of Hispanic America.

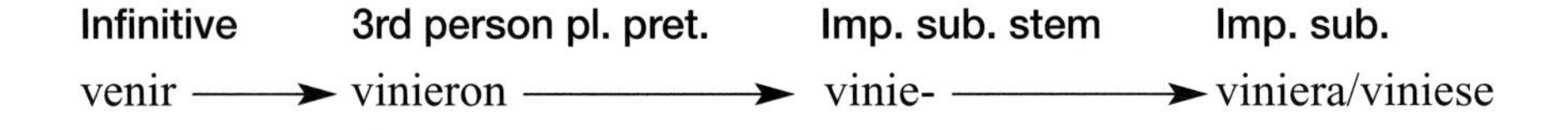

-ra forms		**-se** forms	
que vinier**a**	vinié**ramos**	que vinie**se**	vinié**semos**
vinie**ras**	vinie**rais**	vinie**ses**	vinie**seis**
vinie**ra**	vinie**ran**	vinie**se**	vinie**sen**

Note: The **nosotros** form always takes an accent.

2. All imperfect subjunctive verbs follow this pattern. There are no irregular verbs in the imperfect subjunctive; they are all are based on the third person plural of the preterit. Review the preterit tense, especially the third person plural, to ensure proper formation of the imperfect subjunctive.

Note: *There was/were* = **hubiera/hubiese.**

The Past Participle–*El participio pasivo*

The past participle is a verbal form that can be used either as part of a verb phrase or as an adjective modifying a noun. When used as part of a verb phrase, the past participle has only one form, which ends in **-o.** When used as an adjective modifying a noun, the past participle agrees with the noun in gender and number.

A. Regular Forms

The past participle of **-ar** verbs is formed by adding **-ado** to the stem. The past participle of **-er** and **-ir** verbs is formed by adding **-ido** to the stem.

compr**ar** → compr**ado**   vend**er** → vend**ido**   decid**ir** → decid**ido**

The past participle of **ser** is **sido** and of **ir** is **ido.**

B. Irregular Forms

1. Common irregular past participles include the following.

Infinitive	Past Participle	Infinitive	Past Participle
abrir	abierto	morir	muerto
cubrir	cubierto	poner	puesto
decir	dicho	resolver	resuelto
describir	descrito	romper	roto
escribir	escrito	ver	visto
hacer	hecho	volver	vuelto

Note: Compound verbs are usually conjugated like the verb they contain.

de*volver* → **de*vuelto***   des*hacer* → **des*hecho***   re*poner* → **re*puesto***

2. Some past participle forms differ if used as part of a verb phrase (e.g., **he bendecido**) or as an adjective (**está bendito**). The following is a list of common verbs that have two different forms.

Infinitive	Past Participle in a Verb Phrase	Past Participle as an Adjective
bendecir	bendecido	bendito/a
confundir	confundido	confuso/a
despertar	despertado	despierto/a
freír	freído	frito/a
imprimir	imprimido	impreso/a
soltar	soltado	suelto/a

The Perfect Tenses—*Los tiempos perfectos*

The perfect tenses are formed by using a form of the verb **haber** + *past participle.* See the explanation of the formation of past participles if needed.

The Present Perfect—*El pretérito perfecto*		
he	hemos	+ *past participle*
has	habéis	
ha	han	

The Present Perfect Subjunctive—*El pretérito perfecto del subjuntivo*		
haya	hayamos	+ *past participle*
hayas	hayáis	
haya	hayan	

The Pluperfect—*El pluscuamperfecto*		
había	habíamos	+ *past participle*
habías	habíais	
había	habían	

The Pluperfect Subjunctive—*El pluscuamperfecto del subjuntivo*		
hubiera	hubiéramos	+ *past participle*
hubieras	hubierais	
hubiera	hubieran	

Note: There is an optional form, frequently used in Spain and in some areas of Hispanic America, in which you may substitute **-se** endings for **-ra** endings: **hubiera = hubiese.**

The Future Perfect—*El futuro perfecto*		
habré	habremos	+ *past participle*
habrás	habréis	
habrá	habrán	

The Conditional Perfect—*El condicional perfecto*		
habría	habríamos	+ *past participle*
habrías	habríais	
habría	habrían	

Appendix B: Uses of *ser*, *estar*, and *haber*

1. Use **ser:**

 a. to describe the being or essence of a person, place, or thing. This includes personality traits, physical characteristics, and place of origin.

 Mi amigo Walter **es** muy divertido. (*personality*)
 Es bajo y un poco gordo. (*physical characteristics*)
 Es de Guatemala. (*origin*)

 b. to state an occupation.

 Es estudiante universitario.

 c. to tell time and dates.

 Ahora **son** las cuatro de la tarde.
 Los exámenes finales **son** entre el 2 y el 10 de mayo.

 d. to indicate possession.

 Los libros que usa para estudiar **son** de su primo Carlos.

 e. to state when and where an event takes place.

 El examen de química **es** a las once de la mañana y **es** en el Appleby Center.

2. Use **estar:**

 a. to describe condition or state of being of a person, place, or thing.

 Hoy **está** cansado porque no durmió mucho anoche.
 Su habitación **está** sucia y tiene que limpiarla.

 b. to describe the location of a person, place, or thing.

 Ahora Walter **está** en la clase con sus amigos.
 Su universidad **está** en el centro de la ciudad.
 El examen de química **está** en el escritorio del profesor.

 c. as a helping verb with the present progressive to describe actions in progress.

 Él y sus amigos **están** haciendo planes para el fin de semana.

3. Use a form of **haber** to state the following.

 there is/are (not) = (**no**) **hay**
 there was/were (not) = (**no**) **hubo** (*preterit*)/**había** (*imperfect*)
 there will (not) be = (**no**) **habrá**
 there would (not) be = (**no**) **habría**

 Hay 50.000 estudiantes en esa universidad.

Appendix C: Gender of Nouns and Formation of Adjectives

A. Gender of Nouns

1. Most nouns that end in **-l, -o, -n,** and **-r** are masculine.

un carte**l** **el** partid**o** **el** exame**n** **el** televiso**r**

Common exceptions: **la imagen, la mano, la mujer.** Remember that **la foto** (**fotografía**) and **la moto** (**motocicleta**) are feminine.

2. Most nouns that end in **-a, -ad, -ión, -umbre,** and **-z** are feminine.

la lámpar**a** **la** liber**tad** **una** canc**ión** **la** cost**umbre** **una** lu**z**

Common exceptions: **el camión, el avión, el día, el lápiz, el pez.**

3. Feminine nouns that begin with a stressed **a-** sound (**agua, área, arpa, hambre**), use the articles **el/un** in the singular, but still use the articles **las/unas** in the plural. If adjectives are used with these nouns, they must be in the feminine form.

el alma pur**a** **el a**gua fresc**a**

las alm**as** pur**as** **las** agu**as** fresc**as**

Note: There is one exception; the word **arte** begins with a stressed **a-** and is normally masculine in the singular and feminine in the plural: **el a**rte modern**o**, **las** bell**as** **a**rtes.

4. Memorize the gender of nouns that end in **-e.** Common words include:

Masculine: **el accidente, el cine, el coche, el diamante, el hombre, el pasaje, el viaje**
Feminine: **la clase, la fuente, la gente, la noche, la tarde**

5. Many nouns that are borrowed from languages other than Latin are usually masculine in Spanish. Here are a few nouns that are borrowed from English: **los blue jeans, el hall, el kleenex.**

6. Many nouns that end in **-ma** and **-ta** are masculine and are of Greek origin: **el drama, el idioma, el planeta, el poema, el problema, el programa, el sistema, el tema.**

B. Use and Formation of Adjectives

1. With few exceptions, adjectives agree in number (singular, plural) with the nouns they modify. The plural is formed by adding **-s** to adjectives that end in an unaccented vowel (usually **-e, -o,** or **-a**) and **-es** to those that end in a consonant or an accented vowel (usually **-í** or **-ú**). Adjectives ending in **-o** and **-or** agree not only in number but also in gender (masculine, feminine) with the noun they modify. Adjectives ending in **-ista** agree in number only. See the following charts.

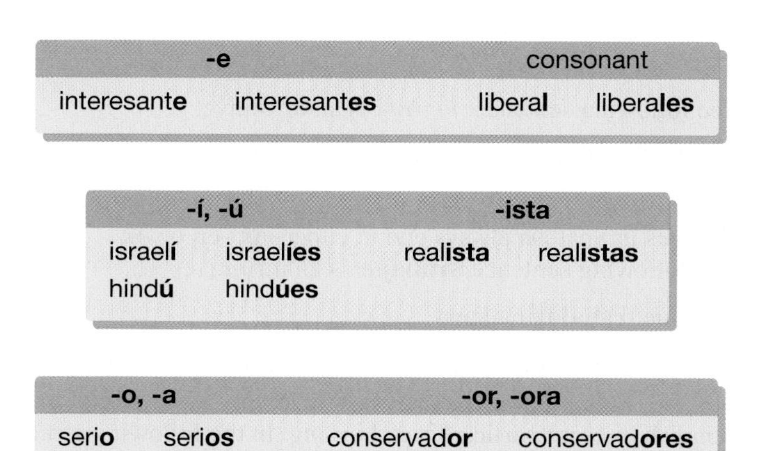

-e		consonant	
interesant**e**	interesant**es**	libera**l**	libera**les**

-í, -ú		-ista	
israel**í**	israel**íes**	real**ista**	real**istas**
hind**ú**	hind**úes**		

-o, -a		-or, -ora	
seri**o**	seri**os**	conservad**or**	conservad**ores**
seri**a**	seri**as**	conservad**ora**	conservad**oras**

una clase interesante	unas clases interesantes
una profesora seria	unas profesoras serias
un artículo liberal	unos artículos liberales
el estudiante conservador	los estudiantes conservadores
un profesor realista	unos profesores realistas

2. Adjectives of nationality that end in **-és** or **-án** drop the accent from the masculine singular and add the appropriate endings to agree in gender and number with the nouns they modify.

ingl**és**	ingl**eses**	ingl**esa**	ingl**esas**
alem**án**	alem**anes**	alem**ana**	alem**anas**

3. Adjectives that end in **-z** change **z** to **c** in the plural.

feli**z** → feli**ces**   capa**z** → capa**ces**

Appendix D: Position of Object Pronouns

Prior to studying the position of object pronouns (direct, indirect, and reflexive), you may want to familiarize yourself with the following terms.

1. Infinitives—**Infinitivos**

   a. In the following sentence, *to work* is an infinitive.

   I have *to work* tomorrow.

   b. The infinitive is the verb form listed in Spanish dictionaries.
   c. Infinitives in Spanish always end in either **-ar, -er,** or **-ir.**
   d. In the following sentence, **trabajar** is an infinitive.

   Tengo que **trabajar** mañana.

2. Present Participles—**Gerundios**

   a. In English, present participles end in *-ing.* In the following sentence, *studying* is a present participle.

   I am *studying.*

   b. In Spanish, present participles end in **-ando, -iendo,** or **-yendo.** In the following sentence, **estudiando** is a present participle.

   Estoy **estudiando.**

3. Commands—**Órdenes**

   a. Commands are direct orders given to people to do something. In the following sentence, *help* is a command.

   Help me!

   b. In the following sentence, **ven** is a command.

   Niño, ¡**ven** aquí en seguida!

4. Conjugated Verbs—**Verbos conjugados**

   a. In the following sentence, *am* and *is* are conjugated verbs. Their infinitive is the verb *to be.*

   I *am* smart and this *is* easy.

   b. Conjugated verbs are any verbs that are not infinitives, commands, or present or past participles.

c. Conjugated verbs can be in the present, past, future, or conditional tense, as well as part of the perfect tenses, and they can be in both the indicative and subjunctive moods. In the following sentences, the conjugated verbs are in bold.

Ella **trabaja** para IBM.
¿Dónde **comieron** Uds. anoche?
Quería que ellos **vinieran** a mi casa.

A. Pronoun forms

1. Object pronouns include direct objects (**me, te, lo, la, nos, os, los, las**), indirect objects (**me, te, le, nos, os, les**), and reflexive pronouns (**me, te, se, nos, os, se**).

2. When an indirect- and a direct-object pronoun are used in succession, **le** and **les** become **se** when followed by **lo, la, los,** or **las.** When two object pronouns are used in the same phrase, they are not separated and must be used in succession.

B. Placement

The placement of object pronouns is as follows.

1. before a conjugated verb

Lo habré hecho para el lunes.

Si **lo hiciera** ahora, no podría terminar.

Lo haré el lunes.

Lo hice el lunes pasado.

Te lo voy a hacer el lunes.*

Lo hacía los lunes.

Quiero que **lo hagas** el lunes.

Lo había hecho el lunes antes de trabajar.

Lo hago los lunes.

Si él **lo hubiera hecho,** yo no **lo habría sabido.**

Te lo estoy haciendo.**

2. before the verb in a negative command

¡No **lo hagas**!

¡No **se lo compre**!

---

* See point 4, page 356.
** See point 5, page 356.

3. after and attached to an affirmative command

¡Hazlo! **¡Cómpreselo!*** **¡Dáselo!***

a. When the reflexive pronoun **os** is attached to the **vosotros** command, the **-d** is dropped.

Bes**aos.** Quer**eos.**

The only exception is the verb **irse: idos.**

b. When the reflexive pronoun **nos** or the indirect-object pronoun **se** is attached to the **nosotros** command, the **-s** is dropped.

Comprémonos* un coche. **Comprémosela.***

4. after and attached to an infinitive

Voy a **hacerlo** el lunes. Voy a **hacértelo** el lunes.

5. after and attached to a present participle

Estoy **haciéndolo*.** Estoy **haciéndotelo*.**

---

* When another syllable is added to a present participle, a command consisting of two or more syllables, or when two pronouns are added to monosyllables, place an accent over the stressed syllable.

Appendix E: Uses of *a*

Use the word **a**:

1. to indicate destination: **ir a** + *article* + *place*.

Van **a la** playa.
Vamos **al** cine. (remember: **a** + **el** = **al**)

2. to discuss the future: **ir a** + *infinitive*.

Ellos **van a estudiar** esta tarde.

3. after certain verbs when followed by infinitives. These verbs include **aprender, comenzar, empezar,** and **enseñar.**

En esa escuela **enseñan a pintar.**

4. in prepositional phrases to clarify or emphasize the indirect-object pronoun.

¿**Le** diste el dinero **a Carlos?**

Note: A prepositional phrase can also be used to clarify the indirect object with verbs like **gustar, encantar,** and **fascinar.**

A mí me encanta la música de Celia Cruz.

5. when the direct object is a person.

Vas a ver **a Felipe Pérez** y **al hermano de Alicia** si vas a la fiesta.
¿Conociste **a la profesora Vargas?**

Appendix F: Accentuation and Syllabication

A. Stress—*Acentuación*

1. If a word ends in **-n, -s,** or a **vowel,** the stress falls on the *next-to-last syllable.*

lava**pla**tos | **exa**men | **ho**la | aparta**men**to

2. If a word ends in any **consonant** other than **-n** or **-s,** the stress falls on the *last syllable.*

espa**ñol** | us**ted** | regu**lar** | prohi**bir**

3. Any exception to rules number 1 and 2 has a written accent mark on the stressed vowel.

televisi**ó**n | tel**é**fono | **á**lbum | cent**í**metro

Note: Words ending in **-ión** lose their written accent in the plural because of rule 1: **naci*ó*n**, *but* **naci*o*nes.**

4. Question and exclamation words, e.g., **cómo, dónde, cuál, qué,** always have accents.

5. Certain words change their meaning when written with an accent although the pronunciation remains the same.

cómo	how	**como**	like, I eat
dé	give (*command*)	**de**	of, from
él	he/him	**el**	the
más	more	**mas**	but
mí	me	**mi**	my
sé	I know	**se**	*3rd person pronoun*
sí	yes	**si**	if
sólo	only (*adv.*)	**solo**	alone
té	tea	**te**	you (*object pronoun*)
tú	you	**tu**	your

6. You may see demonstrative pronouns with a written accent to distinguish them from demonstrative adjectives (except for **esto, eso,** and **aquello,** which are neuter pronouns and never have an accent).

este niño éste estas blusas éstas

Nos vendieron **aquellos** caramelos. — *They sold us those candies over there.* (**Aquellos** modifies candies and is a demonstrative *adjective* and therefore has no accent.)

Aquéllos nos vendieron caramelos. — *They sold us candies.* (**Aquéllos** is a demonstrative *pronoun* and refers to those people way over there and can take an accent.)

7. One-syllable words (other than those listed in #5 on page 358) are not accented. Some examples include: **guion, rio** *(he/she laughed)*, **vio, fe**, etc. NOTE: This is a recent change to the Spanish rules of orthography, so some texts printed before the change was made official may show these words with accents: **guión, rió, vió, fé.**

B. Diphthongs—*Diptongos*

1. A diphthong is the combination of a weak vowel (**i, u**) and a strong vowel (**a, e, o**) or the combination of two weak vowels in the same syllable. When two vowels are combined, the strong vowel or the second of the weak vowels takes a slightly greater stress in the syllable.

v**ue**lvo ***au***tomático t**ie**ne conc**ie**nc***ia*** c***iu***dad

2. When the stress of the word falls on the weak vowel of a strong–weak combination, the weak vowel takes a written accent mark to break the diphthong. No diphthong occurs because the vowels belong to different syllables.

pa-**ís** **dí-a** **tí-o** en-v**í-o** Ra-**ú**l

Note: **Ma-rio,** *but* **Ma-*rí*-a.**

C. Syllabication—*Silabeo*

1. A single consonant between vowels always goes with the second vowel. Remember that **ch, ll,** and **rr** are considered a single consonant in Spanish.

A-**mé**-ri-**ca** to-**ma**-**te** ca-**je**-**ro** *But:* pe-**rr**o

2. When there are two or more consonants between vowels, the second vowel takes as many consonants as can be found at the beginning of a Spanish word (English and Spanish allow the same consonant groups at the beginning of a word, except for **s** + *consonant* which does not exist in Spanish). The other consonants remain with the first vowel.

Pa-**blo** (*bl* starts words, as in **blanco**)
es-**pe**-ran-za (**s** + *consonant* does not start words in Spanish)
ex-**plo**-rar (**xpl** does not begin words, **pl** does)
tra**ns**-**p**or-tar (**nsp** does not begin words, **sp** does not start words in Spanish)

3. A diphthong is never separated. If the stress falls on the weak vowel of a strong–weak vowel combination, an accent is used to break the dipthong and two separate syllables are created.

a-m**ue**-blar c**iu**-dad ju-l**io** *But:* **dí-a**

Note: Two strong vowels never form a diphthong: **po-e-ta, le-er.**

Appendix G: Thematic Vocabulary

The following lists contain basic vocabulary. For more advanced vocabulary on some of these topics, see the vocabulary entries in the glossary.

La ropa

la blusa	blouse
la camisa	shirt
la chaqueta	jacket
la corbata	tie
la falda	skirt
las medias	socks
los pantalones	pants
el saco	sports coat
el sombrero	hat
el traje de baño	bathing suit
el vestido	dress
los zapatos	shoes

Los colores

amarillo/a	yellow
anaranjado/a	orange
azul	blue
blanco/a	white
gris	gray
marrón	brown
morado/a	purple
negro/a	black
rojo/a	red
rosa, rosado/a	pink
verde	green

Los días de la semana

lunes	Monday
martes	Tuesday
miércoles	Wednesday
jueves	Thursday
viernes	Friday
sábado	Saturday
domingo	Sunday

Los meses del año

enero	January
febrero	February
marzo	March
abril	April
mayo	May
junio	June
julio	July
agosto	August
septiembre	September
octubre	October
noviembre	November
diciembre	December

Las estaciones

el invierno	winter
la primavera	spring
el verano	summer
el otoño	fall

La comida

el ajo	garlic
la carne de res	beef
la cebolla	onion
el cerdo	pork
la coliflor	cauliflower
el cordero	lamb
los espárragos	asparagus
la fruta	fruit
las habichuelas	green beans
los huevos	eggs
el jamón	ham
el jugo	juice
la lechuga	lettuce
la mantequilla	butter
la mermelada	marmalade
el pan	bread
la pimienta	pepper
el pollo	chicken
el queso	cheese
la sal	salt
el tomate	tomato
la tostada	toast
el vinagre	vinegar
el yogur	yogurt

Los deportes

el basquetbol	basketball
el béisbol	baseball
el fútbol	soccer
el fútbol americano	football
el golf	golf
la natación	swimming
el squash	squash
el tenis	tennis
el voleibol	volleyball

El arte

el/la artista	artist
la copia	copy
el cuadro/la pintura	painting
dibujar	to draw
el dibujo	drawing
la escena	scene
el/la escultor/a	sculptor
la escultura	sculpture
la estatua	statue
la exhibición	exhibition
el mural	mural
el original	original
el pincel	brush
pintar	to paint
el/la pintor/a	painter

El medio ambiente

la basura	trash
la ecología	ecology
en peligro	in danger
la energía nuclear	nuclear energy
la energía solar	solar energy
la fábrica	factory
la lluvia ácida	acid rain
el reciclaje	recycling
reciclar	to recycle

Los números ordinales

primer(o)/a	first
segundo/a	second
tercer(o)/a	third
cuarto/a	fourth
quinto/a	fifth
sexto/a	sixth
séptimo/a	seventh
octavo/a	eighth
noveno/a	ninth
décimo/a	tenth

Los números cardinales

0 cero
1 uno, un/a*
2 dos
3 tres
4 cuatro
5 cinco
6 seis
7 siete
8 ocho
9 nueve
10 diez
11 once
12 doce
13 trece
14 catorce
15 quince
16 dieciséis (diez y seis)
17 diecisiete (diez y siete)
18 dieciocho (diez y ocho)
19 diecinueve (diez y nueve)
20 veinte
21 veintiún, veintiuno/a*
22 veintidós (veinte y dos)
30 treinta
31 treinta y un, uno/a*
32 treinta y dos
40 cuarenta
50 cincuenta
60 sesenta
70 setenta
80 ochenta
90 noventa
100 cien
101 ciento un, uno/a*
110 ciento diez
200 doscientos*
300 trescientos*
400 cuatrocientos*
500 quinientos*
600 seiscientos*
700 setecientos*
800 ochocientos*
900 novecientos*
1.000 mil
2.000 dos mil
100.000 cien mil
200.000 doscientos mil*
500.000 quinientos mil*
1.000.000 un millón (de)**
2.000.000 dos millones (de)**
1.000.000.000 mil millones (de)**

---

* These numbers agree in gender with the nouns they modify. **Había *trescientas personas* en la conferencia.**

** **De** is used before a noun: **Había un millón de personas**.

Notes:
a. Numbers ending in **uno** drop the **-o** before a masculine noun: **veintiún libros, cuarenta y un libros.** *But:* **veintiuna chicas.**
b. The numbers 16 through 29 are more commonly written as one word: **veintitrés** instead of **veinte y tres.**
c. The numbers **dieciséis, veintidós, veintitrés,** and **veintiséis** have an accent.
d. The word **y** is only used with numbers 16 through 99: **treinta y dos,** *but* **tres mil doscientos cuatro.**
e. *1,000,000,000 = one billion*, but **1.000.000.000** = **mil millones.**

Spanish-English Vocabulary

This vocabulary includes both active and passive vocabulary found throughout the chapters. The definitions are limited to the context in which the words are used in the book. Exact or reasonably close cognates of English are not included, nor are certain common words that are considered to be within the mastery of a second-year student, such as numbers, articles, pronouns, and possessive adjectives. Adverbs ending in **-mente** and regular past participles are not included if the root word is found in the vocabulary or is a cognate.

The gender of nouns is given except for masculine nouns ending in **-l, -o, -n, -r,** and **-s** and feminine nouns ending in **-a, -d, -ión,** and **-z.** Nouns with masculine and feminine variants are listed when the English correspondents are different words (e.g., *son, daughter*); in most cases, however, only the masculine form is given (**carpintero, operador**). Adjectives are given only in the masculine singular form. Irregular verbs are indicated, as are stem changes.

The following abbreviations are used in this vocabulary.

adj.	adjective	*irreg.*	irregular verb	*p.p.*	past participle
adv.	adverb	*m.*	masculine	*prep.*	preposition
conj.	conjunction	*n.*	noun	*pro.*	pronoun
f.	feminine	*pl.*	plural	*sing.*	singular
inf.	infinitive				

a: a fines de at the end of; **a la vuelta de** around the corner from; **a las...** at . . . o'clock; **a menos que** unless; **a menudo** often, frequently; **a pesar de que** even though; **a principio(s) de** at the beginning of (*time*); **a propósito** on purpose; **A que no saben...** Bet you don't know. . . ; **a través de** through; **a veces** sometimes
abarrotar to become packed (*with people*)
abierto (*p.p. of* **abrir**) open
absoluto: no, en absoluto no, not at all
abuela grandmother
abuelo grandfather; *pl.* grandparents
aburrido bored; boring
aburrirse (de) to become bored (with)
abusar to abuse
abuso *n.* abuse
acabar to finish; to run out (of); **acabar de** (+ *inf.*) to have just (done something)
acallar to stifle, silence
acampar to go camping
acaso: ¿Acaso no sabías? But, didn't you know?; **por si acaso** just in case
acceder to assent, consent
aceite *m.* oil
aceituna olive
acogedor welcoming, warm
aconsejable advisable
aconsejar to advise
acontecimiento event
acordarse (ue) de to remember
acoso harassment
acostarse (ue) to go to bed
acostumbrarse (a) to become accustomed (to)
actitud attitude
activismo activisim
actriz actress
actual present-day, current
actualidad: en la actualidad at the present time
actualmente at present, nowadays
actuar to act
actuación *n.* acting
acuerdo *n.* agreement; pact; **de acuerdo a** according to; **estar de acuerdo** to be in agreement
acusado accused
adelgazar to lose weight
además *adv.* besides; **además de** *prep.* besides
adivinar to guess
adoptivo: hijo adoptivo adopted son; **hija adoptiva** adopted daughter
afeitarse to shave
agobiante exhausting
agradecerle to thank someone
agrandarse to grow larger
agregar to add
agridulce sweet and sour
agrio sour
agua *f.* (*but* **el agua**): **agua con gas** sparkling water; **agua mineral** mineral water
aguacate *m.* avocado
agua fuerte *m.*: **grabado al agua fuerte** etching
aguantar to tolerate, stand
águila *f.* (*but* **el águila**) eagle
aguinaldo end-of-the-year bonus
aguja needle
agujero hole
ahorrar to save
aire *m.* air; **al aire libre** outdoors

aislado isolated
aislarse to isolate onself
ajo garlic
ajustado tight
al tanto up-to-date
alas: hacer alas delta to hang-glide
alcalde *m./f.* mayor
alcanzar to be sufficient; to reach, attain
alegrarse (de) to become happy (about)
alemán *n., adj.* German
alfabetización literacy
álgebra *f.* (*but* **el álgebra**) algebra
algo something; **algo así** something like that
alguien someone
algún/alguna/os/as + *n.* a, some, any; **sin duda alguna** without a doubt
alianza alliance
alimenticio *adj.* nutritious
alimento food
almendra almond
almorzar (ue) to have lunch
alondra lark
alquilar to rent
alquiler *n.* rent
alto stop; **alto en calorías** high in calories
altura height
alumbrado *n.* lighting
ama de casa *f.* (*but* **el ama**) housewife
amante *m./f.* lover
amargo bitter
ambiente *m.*: **medio ambiente** environment
ámbito atmosphere; field
ambos both
amenaza threat
amenazar to threaten
amigo friend; **amigo íntimo** a very close friend
analfabeto *n., adj.* illiterate
ancas de rana *pl.* frogs' legs
anchoas *pl.* anchovies
anciano: asilo de ancianos nursing home; **residencia de ancianos** nursing home
andar *irreg.* to work, function
ángel angel
anidamiento nesting
anillo ring
anoche last night
anorak *m.* parka
anteanoche the night before last
anteayer the day before yesterday
antepasado ancestor, forefather
anterior previous
antes *adv.* before; **antes de** *prep.* before; **antes (de) que** *conj.* before
anticuado old-fashioned, antiquated, obsolete
antropología anthropology
añadir to add
año: año clave key year; **año escolar** school year
apagar to turn off
apariencia appearance
apenas hardly
aperitivo appetizer
aplazar to postpone
apoyar to support
apoyo *n.* support
apreciar to appreciate
aprieto: sacar a alguien de un aprieto to get someone out of a jam
aprobar (ue) to pass (*a course*); to approve
aprovecharse de to take advantage of
apuntar to write down; to make note of
apuntes *m. pl.* class notes
argumento plot (*of a book, movie*)
armado armed
armario closet
arqueología archeology
arquitecto architect
arrancar to start (*a motor*); to tear out (*weeds*)
arrebatar to snatch, seize
arrecife *m.* reef
arreglar to fix; **arreglarse** to make oneself presentable
arreglo repair; agreement
arrepentirse (ie, i) to regret
arrestar to arrest
arroz *m.* rice
arruga *n.* wrinkle
arte *m. sing.* art; **artes** *f. pl.* arts
artesanía crafts
artista *m./f.* artist
arvejas *f. pl.* (*Latinoamérica*) peas
arzobispo archbishop
asado barbecue
asaltante *m./f.* assailant
asaltar to assault
asalto assault, attack, robbery
ascendencia ancestry
asegurar to assure
asemejarse a to resemble, be like
asesinar to murder
asesinato *n.* murder
asesino murderer
así: algo así something like that
asignatura subject, course
asilo: asilo político political asylum; **asilo de ancianos** nursing home
asimilarse to assimilate
asimismo in the same way, likewise
asistir a (una clase/una reunión) to attend (a class/a meeting)
asombro amazement
asombroso astonishing
aspiradora vacuum cleaner
aspirar a ser to aspire to be
astuto clever
asunto político/económico political/economic issue
atender (ie) to attend to; to pay attention to
atentado *n.* attemped crime
atento polite, courteous
atracar to hold up; to mug
atraco holdup; mugging
atrevido *adj.* daring; *n.* daredevil, bold person (*negative connotation*)
atribuir (y) to attibute
atroz huge
atún tuna
audaz daring (*positive connotation*)
aumentar to raise, increase; **aumentar el sueldo** to raise the salary
aumento *n.* raise, increase
auto de fe public punishment by the Inquisition tribunal
autoridad: ejercer autoridad to exercise authority
autorretrato self-portrait
ave *f.* (*but* **el ave**) bird
aventura: tener una aventura (amorosa) to have an affair
averiguar to find out (about)
avisar to inform, notify; to warn
avisos clasificados *m. pl.* classified ads
ayer yesterday
ayudante de cátedra *m./f.* teaching assistant
ayunas: en ayunas before breakfast
azafata airline stewardess
azúcar sugar

bajar: bajar el fuego to lower the heat; **bajar el sueldo** to lower the salary
ballena whale
bandeja tray
bañarse to bathe
banda sonora sound track
bar bar, café
barajar to shuffle
barba beard
barbaridad: ¡Qué barbaridad! Wow! (literally, What a barbarity!), How terrible!
barbilla chin
barra (de chocolate) (chocolate) bar
bastante quite, very
basura garbage
batalla battle
batazo hit (*in baseball*)
batido shake (*drink*)
bautismo baptism

bautizar to baptize
beber to drink
bebida drink
beca scholarship
belleza beauty
beneficio laboral work benefit
berenjena eggplant
bienestar común the common good
bigotes *m. pl.* mustache
bilingüe bilingual
bisabuela great-grandmother
bisabuelo great-grandfather
blanco *adj.* white; **voto en blanco** blank vote
blando soft
boda wedding
bodegón still life
boletín newsletter
bolsa bag
bombero firefighter
bono bonus (pay)
boquiabierto open-mouthed, shocked
borrador first draft
bosque *m.* woods
botella bottle
botón button
breve brief (*in length*)
brindar to offer
brocha paintbrush
bruscamente abruptly
bucear to scuba dive
buceo scuba diving
bueno: ¡Qué bueno...! How good . . . !
bufón buffoon
búho owl
bullicio noise, din
burla mockery
burlarse de to mock, make fun of
buscar: buscar nuevos horizontes to look for new horizons**; pasar a buscar a alguien (por/en un lugar)** to pick someone up (at a place)
búsqueda *n.* search

caballero gentleman; knight
caber to fit; **no cabe duda** there is no doubt
cabeza: No tiene ni pies ni cabeza. It doesn't make (any) sense to me./I can't make heads or tails of it.
cabina telefónica telephone booth
cadena chain; **cadena perpetua** life sentence
caer to fall; **caerle bien/mal (a alguien)** to like/dislike (someone); **caerse** to fall down
café: color café *adj.* brown; *m.* coffee; an espresso; **café con leche** coffee with lots of hot milk
cafeína: con cafeína with caffeine
caja box; cash register
cajero cashier
calabaza pumpkin
calamares *m. pl.* calamari, squid
cálculo calculus
calentar (ie) to heat
calidad quality
callarse to shut up
calorías: alto/bajo en calorías high/low in calories
calvo bald
calzoncillos *m. pl.* boxer shorts; briefs
camarera waitress
camarero waiter
camarón shrimp
cambio: en cambio instead
camino a on the way to
camiseta T-shirt
camote *m.* (*México*) sweet potato
campaña electoral political campaign
campesino peasant; farmer
camping *m.* campsite
campo field (*business, farm, sports*)
Canal de la Mancha English Channel
canasto basket
canela: piel canela *f.* cinnamon-colored skin
canoso white-haired, gray-haired
cansancio tiredness
caña (*España*) glass of beer
capa de ozono ozone layer
capacitación *n.* training; **cursos de capacitación** training courses
capaz capable
caprichoso capricious, fussy
cara larga long face
caradura: ¡Qué caradura! Of all the nerve!
¡Caray! Geeze!
cárcel *f.* jail, prison
carcelero jailer, warden
cariño affection; **con cariño** fondly
cariñoso loving, affectionate
carne *f.* meat
carnet *m.* ID card
carpintero carpenter
carrera professional studies
carrito cart
carta de recomendación letter of recommendation
cartel (de drogas) drug cartel
cartelera: seguir en cartelera to still be showing (*movie*)
cartero mail carrier
casa de ancianos nursing home
casado married
casamiento marriage, wedding
casarse (con) to get married (to)
casero homemade
caso: en caso (de) que in the event that, if
castaño: pelo castaño brown hair
castigar to punish
castigo punishment
casualidad: por casualidad by chance
catarata waterfall
cátedra: ayudante de cátedra *m./f.* teaching assistant; **dar cátedra** to lecture someone (on some topic)
cautiverio: en cautiverio in captivity
cazar to hunt
cebolla onion
celoso jealous
cenar to have dinner/supper
censura censorship; censure
censurado censored; censured
censurar to censor; to censure
cepillarse (el pelo/los dientes) to brush (one's hair/teeth)
cercano *adj.* near, nearby
cerdo pork
cerrado closed; narrow-minded
cerrar (ie) to close
cesante *adj.* unemployed
césped *m.* lawn
chaleco vest
chaqueta jacket
charlar to chat
chévere: ¡Qué chévere! (*Caribe*) That's cool.
chisme *m.* piece of gossip
chismear to gossip
chismoso gossipy
chiste *m.* joke; **chiste verde** dirty joke
chocar to crash
choque cultural *m.* culture shock
chofer *m./f.* chauffeur, driver
cicatriz scar
ciego blind
cielo heaven; sky
ciencia: ciencia ficción science fiction; **ciencias políticas** *f. pl.* political science
científico scientist
cierre *m.* zipper
cierto certain; **(no) es cierto** it's (not) true; **por cierto** by the way
cine *m.* movie theater; **ir al cine** to go to the movies
cinturón belt
cirugía surgery
cita appointment; quote
ciudadanía citizenship
ciudadano citizen; **hacerse ciudadano** to become a citizen
claro clear; **tener en claro** to have it clear in your mind
clase particular *f.* private class
clave *sing. adj.* **años/palabras clave** key year/words
clavo: dar en el clavo to hit the nail on the head

clérigo clergy
clonización cloning
cochinillo roast suckling pig
cocinero *n.* cook
cóctel cocktail
código code
codo elbow
coger el sueño to fall asleep
cola: cola de caballo pony tail; **colas (de películas)** previews
colar (ue) to drain
colgar (ue) to hang
colocar to place
color: color café brown; **color miel** light brown
colorín, colorado esta leyenda ha terminado and so the legend ends
combinar to match
comenzar (ie) a to begin, start to
comer to eat; **comérselo todo** to eat it all up; **ser de buen comer** to have a good appetite
comestible *m.* food
cometer to commit (*a crime*)
cómico *adj.* funny
comienzo beginning
como si as if
compartir to share
complacer to please
completar una solicitud to fill out an application
comportamiento behavior
comprobar (ue) to prove
comprometerse (con) to get engaged (to)
compromiso commitment, engagement
computación computer science
con: con cafeína with caffeine; **con frecuencia** frequently; **con gran esmero** with great care; **con tal (de) que** provided that
concienzudo conscientious
concierto concert
concurso contest
condena sentence (*jail*)
condenado *n.* convict
condenar: condenar (a alguien) a (10) meses/años de prisión to convict someone to (10) months/years in prison
condicional: libertad condicional parole
conejo rabbit
confianza trust
confiar to trust
congelado frozen
conjetura conjecture, guess
conmover (ue) to move, touch (*emotionally*); **me conmueve** it moves me
conquista conquest
conquistador conqueror
conquistar to conquer
consciente aware
conseguir (i, i) to obtain
consejero advisor
consejo (piece of) advice
conservador *adj.* conservative
consiguiente: por consiguiente therefore
constar de to consist of
consumir to consume; to use; **consumir drogas** to take/use drugs
contabilidad accounting
contador accountant
contaminación pollution
contaminante *adj.* contaminating
contaminar to contaminate, pollute
contar (ue) to tell
contenido *n.* content; **de alto/bajo contenido graso** high/low fat content
contraer *irreg.* to contract, catch (*a cold*)
contratar a alguien to hire someone
contratiempo: tener un contratiempo to have a mishap that causes one to be late
contribuir (y) to contribute
convenir *irreg.*: **te conviene** it's better for you
convivencia living together, cohabitation
convivir to live together
cónyuge *m./f.* spouse
coquetear to flirt
cordero lamb
cordillera mountain range
cordón shoelace
Corea Korea
coreano *n., adj.* Korean
corona crown
correo electrónico email
correr to run
corriente *adj.* ordinary
cortado *n.* coffee (small cup) with a touch of milk
corto short (*in length, duration*)
cortometraje *m.* (movie) short
cosechar to harvest
cosquillas: hacer cosquillas to tickle
costar (ue) to cost
costumbre *f.* custom, habit
cotilleo *m.* gossip
creador creator
crear to create
creencia belief
creído vain
crema cream
cremallera zipper
crianza upbringing, raising (*of children*)
criar to bring up, raise (*a child*)
crimen serious crime; homicide
cristal glass (*material*)
cristiano Christian
crítica *n.* critique
criticar to criticize; to critique
crítico *n.* critic
cuadrado square
cuadro painting
cuando when; **de vez en cuando** every now and then; **siempre y cuando** provided that
cuanto: en cuanto as soon as; **en cuanto a** with reference to
cuchara spoon
cuello collar; neck
cuenta bill, check (*in a restaurant*)
cuerda *n.* rope; string
cuerdo *adj.* sane
cuerno horn; **ponerle los cuernos a alguien** to cheat on someone
cuerpo body; **tener cuerpo de gimnasio** to be buff
cuesta hill
cuidar (a) niños to baby-sit
culpa guilt, blame
culpabilidad guilt
culpar to blame
cultivo crop
cumplir to fulfill
cuñada sister-in-law
cuñado brother-in-law
cura *m.* priest
curriculum (vitae) *m.* résumé
cursar (una clase) to take, study (a class)
cursi tacky
curso course
cuyo whose, of which

dañado damaged
dar *irreg.*: **dar a luz** to give birth; **dar cátedra** to lecture someone (on some topic); **dar en el clavo** to hit the nail on the head; **dar una película** to show a movie; **dar una vuelta** to go for a ride/walk; **darle igual (a alguien)** to be all the same (to someone); **darle la espalda (a alguien)** to turn one's back on; **darle pena (a alguien)** to feel sorry; **darse cuenta (de)** to realize
de: de acuerdo a according to; **de alto/bajo contenido graso** high/low fat content; **de hecho** in fact; **de pocos recursos** low income; **de por vida** for life; **de repente** suddenly; **de todos modos** anyway; **de una vez por todas** once and for all; **¿De veras?** Really?/You're kidding./Don't tell

me!/You don't say!/Wow!; **de vez en cuando** every now and then
deber *n.* duty; *v.* should, ought to
debido a due to
década decade
decano dean
decidir to decide
decir *irreg.* to say, tell; **Es decir...** That is to say . . . ; **el qué dirán** what others may say; **¡No me digas!** Don't tell me!/You don't say!/Wow!; **Te lo digo en serio.** I'm not kidding.
dedicarse a to devote oneself to
deducir to deduce
degenerarse to degenerate
dejar to quit, stop; **dejar a medias** to leave unfinished; **dejar plantado (a alguien)** to stand someone up
delantal apron
delincuencia crime, criminal activity
delincuente *m./f.* criminal
delito offense, crime
demanda: oferta y demanda supply and demand
demandar to sue
demás: los demás others
dentro *adv.* inside; **dentro de (diez) horas/días/años** in (ten) hours/days/years
deportista *m./f.* athlete
derecho law; **derechos humanos** human rights; **violar los derechos humanos** to violate human rights
derrotar a to defeat
desafiar to challenge
desaparecer to disappear
desaparecidos *m. pl.* missing people
desaparición disappearance
desarrollo development
desbordar to overflow
descafeinado decaffeinated
descalzo barefoot
descansar to rest
descendiente *m./f.* descendant
descomponerse *irreg.* to break down
descompuesto (*p.p. of* **descomponerse**) broken
desconsiderado inconsiderate
desconocido *n.* stranger; *adj.* unknown, unidentified
descortés impolite
descubridor discoverer
descubrimiento discovery
descubrir to discover
descuidar to neglect
desde: desde... hasta... from . . . to . . .; **desde luego** of course; **desde mi punto de vista** from my point of view
desechable *adj.* throwaway, disposable
desechar to throw away
desecho rubbish, waste
desempeñar to fill; to occupy; to play (*a role*)
desempleado: estar desempleado to be unemployed
desequilibrar to throw off balance
desequilibrio imbalance
desesperado desperate
desfile *m.* parade
desgracia: por desgracia unfortunately
deshacer *irreg.* to undo; **deshacerse de** to get rid of
deshecho (*p.p. of* **deshacer**) undone
desigualdad inequality
desnudo naked
desovar to lay eggs (*turtles*)
desove *m.* egg laying (*turtles*)
despacho office
despedida de soltero/a bachelor/bachelorette party
despedir (i, i): despedir a alguien to fire, dismiss someone; **despedirse de** to say good-bye to
desperdiciar to waste
desperdicio *n.* waste
despertarse (ie) to wake up
despistado absent minded
desproporcionado disproportionate, out of proportion
después *adv.* later, then, afterwards; **después de** *prep.* after; **después (de) que** *conj.* after
destierro exile, banishment
destruir (y) to destroy
desventaja disadvantage
desvestirse (i, i) to undress
detener *irreg.* to arrest; to stop
detenidamente thoroughly, closely
detrás: ir detrás del escenario to go backstage
devolver (ue) to return, give (something) back
día *m.*: **día feriado** holiday
dibujar to draw
dictadura dictatorship
dibujo drawing
dieta: hacer dieta to be on a diet
difícil difficult
difundir to spread (*news*)
digas: ¡No me digas! Really?/You're kidding./Don't tell me!/You don't say!/Wow!
dignidad dignity
dineral great deal of money
dirán: el qué dirán what others might say
dirección address; management
director de cine movie director
dirigir to direct
discriminación discrimination
discriminar (a alguien) to discriminate (against someone)
disculpar to forgive
disculparse to apologize
discurso speech
discutir to discuss; to argue
disentir (ie, i) (de) to dissent (from)
diseñador designer
diseño *n.* design
disfrazar to disguise
disfrutar to enjoy
disgustarle to dislike, displease
disminuir (y) to decrease, diminish
disponerse *irreg.* **a** to get ready to
dispuesto willing, ready
diurno *adj.* day, daytime
divertido fun
divertirse (ie, i) to have fun, have a good time; **divertirse un montón** to have a ball, a lot of fun
divorciado divorced
divorciarse (de) to get divorced (from)
dolor ache, pain
domicilio domicile, residence
dominador dominator
dominar to dominate
dominio mastery, command
dorar to brown
dormir (ue, u) to sleep; **dormirse** to fall sleep
dormitorio bedroom
drama *m.* drama
droga drug
drogadicto drug addict
drogarse to take drugs; to get high
ducharse to take a shower
duda: no cabe duda there is no doubt; **por si las dudas** just in case; **sin duda alguna** without a doubt; **sin lugar a dudas** without a doubt
dudar to doubt
dudoso doubtful
dulce *adj.* sweet
duque *m.* duke
durante during
durar to last
durazno peach

echar to pour, put in; **echar a perder** to waste, to spoil, ruin; **echar de menos** to miss; **echar un vistazo** to glance at
ecologista *m./f.* ecologist
economía economics; **economía sumergida** underground economy
edulcorante *m.* sweetener
efectivo: en efectivo cash
efecto: efecto invernadero greenhouse effect; **efectos especiales** *m. pl.* special effects

eficaz effective
eficiencia efficiency
egoísta *m./f., adj.* selfish
ejemplo: por ejemplo for example
ejercer: ejercer autoridad to exercise authority
ejército army
electricista *m./f.* electrician
elegir (i, i) to choose, select, elect
embarazada pregnant
embargo: sin embargo nevertheless
emborracharse to get drunk
embrión *m.* embryo
embutidos *m. pl.* types of sausages
emigrar to emigrate
emisora broadcasting station
empezar (ie) a to begin to, start to; **empezar de cero** to start from scratch
empleado employee
empleo job; **solicitar un empleo** to apply for a job
empresa company, business
empujar to push
en: en absoluto not at all; **en ayunas** before breakfast; **en cambio** instead; **en caso (de) que** in the event that, if; **en cuanto** as soon as; **en cuanto a** with reference to; **en el extranjero** abroad; **en la actualidad** at the present time; **en plena forma** fully awake, alert; **en seguida** at once; **en torno** around
enamorarse (de) to fall in love (with)
encantador *adj.* charming
encantarle to really like
encarcelar to incarcerate, imprison
encargar to commission (*a painting*); **encargarse de** to take charge of; to look after
encender (ie) to light
encontrar (ue) to find; to meet; **encontrarse a/con** to run into
encuentro finding; meeting
encuesta *n.* survey
enfadarse to get angry
enfermarse to get sick
enfermero nurse
enfermizo sickly
enfocar to focus
enlatado canned
enmienda amendment
enojarse (con) to become angry (with)
enorme enormous
enseguida at once
enseñanza teaching
entender (ie) to understand
enterarse de to find out about
entrada ticket (*to an event*)
entregar to hand in
entrenamiento training
entrevista *n.* interview
entrevistarse (con alguien) to be interviewed (by someone)
entrometerse (en la vida de alguien) to intrude, meddle, interfere (in someone's life)
entusiasmarse to become excited
envase *m.* container
enviar to send
envolver (ue) to wrap
envuelto (*p.p. of* **envolver**) wrapped
época era, period of time
equivocado wrong
equivocarse to err, make a mistake
escasez shortage
escalar (montañas) to climb (mountains)
escaleras *f. pl.* staircase; stairs
escenario stage; **ir detrás del escenario** to go backstage
esclavo slave
escoger to choose
escolar: año escolar school year
esconder to hide
escrito (*p.p. of* **escribir**) written
escritor writer
escuchar música to listen to music
esforzarse (ue) to make an effort
esmero: con gran esmero with great care
espalda: darle la espalda a to turn one's back on
espárragos *m. pl.* asparagus
especia spice (*food*)
especializarse (en) to specialize (in); to major (in)
especie *f.* species
espejo mirror
esperanza *n.* hope; **esperanza de vida** life expectancy
esperar to hope
espesar to thicken
espiar to spy
espionaje: película de espionaje spy movie
espontáneo spontaneous
esposa wife
esposo husband
esquí: hacer esquí acuático to water-ski; **hacer esquí alpino** to downhill ski; **hacer esquí nórdico** to cross-country ski
esquina corner
estabilidad stability
estacionamiento parking lot
estampilla stamp
estrenarse to premiere
estreno premiere, openning
estar *irreg.*: **estar de acuerdo** to be in agreement; **estar de moda** to be in style; **estar pasado de moda** to be out of style; **estar rebajado** to be on sale; **no estar de acuerdo del todo** to not completely agree
estricto strict
estupefaciente *n. m., adj.* narcotic
etapa period of time; state, phase
ético ethical
evitar to avoid
exigencia *n.* demand
exigente demanding
exigir to demand
éxito success; **tener éxito** to be successful
expectativa expectation; hope; prospect
experiencia laboral work experience
experimentado experienced
explotador exploiter
expresar to express
expulsar to expel
extinguirse to become extinct
extranjero *n.* foreigner; *adj.* foreign, alien; **en el extranjero** abroad
extrañar to miss
extraño *n.* stranger; *adj.* strange
extremo *n.* end

fa: ni fu ni fa it doesn't do anything for me
fábrica factory
fácil easy
factible feasible, possible
facultad school, college
falta de comunicación lack of communication
faltar: faltar (a) to be absent (from); **faltarle** to be lacking, missing (*something*)
fama fame
fascinarle to really like
fastidio: ¡Qué fastidio! What a nuisance/bother!
faz face (*metaphorical*)
felicidad happiness
feliz happy
feriado: días feriados holidays
ferrocarril railroad
ficha index card
fidelidad fidelity
fiebre *f.* fever
fiel faithful; **serle fiel (a alguien)** to be faithful (to someone)
fijarse (en) to notice
fila row; **sentarse (ie) en la primera/última fila** to sit in the first/last row
filosofía philosophy
final: al final de at the end of
finalmente finally
finca farm

fines: a fines de at the end of (*time*); **sin fines de lucro** nonprofit
flan custard
flauta flute
flequillo bangs
flirtear to flirt
flujo flow
folleto pamphlet
fomentar to foment, stir up
fondo background (*of a painting*)
foráneo foreign
forma: en plena forma fully awake, alert
fornido strong, strapping
frac *m.* tuxedo
fracasar to fail
francamente frankly
francés *n., adj.* French
frasco jar
frecuencia: con (gran) frecuencia frequently
frecuentemente frequently
freír (i, i) to fry
frenillos *m. pl.* braces
frente: hacer frente a to stand up to
fresco fresh
frijol bean
frontera *n.* border
fronterizo *adj.* on or near the border
fruta fruit
fu: ni fu ni fa it doesn't do anything for me
fuego heat; fire; **bajar/subir el fuego** to lower/raise the heat
fuente *f.* fountain; **fuente de inspiración** source of inspiration
fuera *adv.* outside
fuerza: por la fuerza by force, forcibly
fumar to smoke
fundación founding
fundador founder
fundar to found

gambas *f. pl.* (*España*) shrimp
ganancia earning, profit
ganas: se me fueron las ganas de (+ *inf.*) I didn't feel like (doing something) anymore; **tener ganas de** (+ *inf.*) to feel like (doing something)
gandules *m. pl.* (*Caribe*) pigeon peas
ganga good buy, bargain
gas: agua con gas (*f. but* **el agua**) sparkling water
gaseosa soda pop
gastar (dinero) to spend (money)
gasto expenditure, expense
generación anterior previous generation
general: por lo general in general
género genre; gender (*grammar*)
genial brilliant, great (*idea*)
gerencia management
gerente *m./f.* manager
gimnasio gymnasium; **tener cuerpo de gimnasio** to be buff
glorificar to glorify
golpe de estado *m.* coup d'état
gorra cap (*hat*)
gozar to enjoy
grabado: grabado al aguafuerte etching
gracioso funny, amusing
grande big
graso: de alto/bajo contenido graso high/low fat content
gratis free of charge
grato pleasing, agreeable
grave serious
gritar to shout
guapo good-looking
guardería (infantil) daycare center
guerra war
guerrero warrior
grueso thick
guion *m.* script
guisada: carne guisada *f.* stew
guisantes *m. pl.* (*Spain*) peas
gustar: me gustaría... I would like to . . .

había there was/were; **había una vez...** once upon a time, there was/were . . .
habichuelas beans
habilidad innata innate ability
hacer *irreg.* to make; to do; **hacer alas delta** to hang-glide; **hacer algo contra su voluntad** to do something against one's will; **hacer dieta** to be on a diet; **hacer ecoturismo** to do ecotourism; **hacer esquí acuático** to water-ski; **hacer esquí alpino** to downhill ski; **hacer esquí nórdico** to cross-country ski; **hacer frente a** to stand up to; **hacer investigación** to do research; **hacer preguntas** to ask questions; **hacer senderismo** to go hiking; **hacer una locura** to do something crazy; **hacer una pasantía** to do an internship; **hacer vela** to sail; **hacerle cosquillas** to tickle someone; **hacerse ciudadano** to become a citizen; **hacerse la América** to seek success in America
hacia toward
hambre (*f. but* **el hambre**) hunger; **tener un hambre atroz** to be really hungry
hasta: hasta que until; **desde... hasta...** from . . . to . . .
hecho (*p.p. of* **hacer**) made, done; *n.* fact; **de hecho** in fact
heredar to inherit
herida wound
hermana sister; **media hermana** half sister
hermanastra stepsister
hermanastro stepbrother
hermano brother; **medio hermano** half brother
hervir (ie, i) to boil
hija daughter; **hija adoptiva** adopted daughter; **hija única** only daughter
hijastra stepdaughter
hijastro stepson
hijo son; **hijo adoptivo** adopted son; **hijo único** only son
histérico hysterical
hogar home
holgado loose
holgazán/holgazana lazy
hollywoodense: ser muy hollywoodense to be like a Hollywood movie
homicidio homicide
honradez honesty
honrado honest
hora: ¿A qué hora es...? What time is . . . at?; **a la hora de** (+ *inf.*) when the time comes to (+ *verb*)
horario schedule, timetable
horizonte *m.* horizon
hormiga ant
hormiguero anthill
hoy: hoy en día these days
hoyuelo dimple
huelga strike
huérfano orphan
hueso bone
huésped *m./f.* guest
humo smoke
humor: sentido de humor sense of humor

idealista *m./f.* idealist
idioma *m.* language
iglesia church
igual: darle igual (a alguien) to be all the same (to someone)
igualdad equality; **igualdad de los sexos** equality of the sexes
imagen *f.* image, picture
impar *adj.* odd (*number*)
impermeable *m.* raincoat
importarle to matter
imprescindible essential
impuesto *n.* tax
incendio *n.* fire
incentivo incentive
incertidumbre *f.* uncertainty

incierto uncertain
inclusive even, including
incómodo uncomfortable
inculcar to instill, inculcate
independizarse (de) to become independent (from)
índice *m.* rate
indígena *m./f.* native person; *adj.* indigenous, native
ineficiencia inefficiency
inesperado unexpected
inestabilidad instability
infantil: guardería infantil child care center; **película infantil** children's movie
infiel: serle infiel (a alguien) to be unfaithful (to someone)
infidelidad infidelity
influencia influence
influir (y) en to have an influence on
informe *m.* report
ingeniería engineering
ingeniero engineer
ingenioso resourceful
inglés *n., adj.* English
ingresos *m. pl.* income
iniciativa initiative, drive
injusticia injustice; **¡Qué injusticia!** How unfair!
inmaduro immature
inmediatamente immediately
inmigrar immigrate
insistir en to insist on
insoportable unbearable
insulso bland (*food*)
intentar to try, attempt
intercambiar to exchange
interesar: interesarle to interest; **interesarse (por)** to take an interest (in)
íntimo: amigo íntimo very close friend
inundación flood
invasor invader
inversión investment
invertir (ie, i) to invest
investigación *n.* research; **hacer investigación** to do research
irritarse to become irritated
irse *irreg.* **(de)** to go away (from), leave
isla island

jamás never
jarabe *m.* syrup
jarrón vase
jaula cage
jefa boss (*female*)
jefe *m.* boss (*male*)
jerga slang
jeringa syringe
jeroglífico *n.* hieroglyph
jornada working day
joya de fantasía costume jewelry
jubilado: estar jubilado to be retired
judío *n.* Jew; *adj.* Jewish
jugar (ue) to play; **jugar al (nombre de un deporte)** to play (a sport)
juguete *m.* toy
juguetón/juguetona *adj.* playful
junta militar military junta
juntarse con amigos to get together with friends
junto *adv.* together; *adj.* **vivir juntos** to live together
jurado jury
jurar to swear
justo fair, just
juventud youth

laboral: experiencia laboral work experience
lacio: pelo lacio straight hair
lácteo: producto lácteo dairy product
lado: por otro lado on the other hand; **por un lado** on the one hand
ladrón/la ladrona thief
lamentable: es lamentable it's a shame
lamentar to lament, be sorry
langostino prawn
lanza lance
lápiz de labios *m.* lipstick
largo long
largometraje *m.* feature-length film
lástima: es una lástima it's a shame; **¡Qué lástima!** What a shame!
lata *n.* can
lavaplatos *sing./pl.* dishwasher
lavarse (el pelo/las manos/la cara/etc.) to wash (one's hair/hands/face/etc.)
lazo *n.* tie, bond
lealtad loyalty
lechería dairy store
lechón suckling pig
lechuga lettuce
lector reader
leer *irreg.* to read
legumbres *f. pl.* legumes
lejano: pariente lejano distant relative
lengua tongue; language; **lengua materna** mother tongue
lenguado sole (*fish*)
lenteja lentil
lento *adj., adv.* slow
leve *adj.* light (slight)
leyenda legend
libertador liberator
libertad: freedom; **libertad condicional** parole; **libertad de palabra/de prensa** freedom of speech/of the press
licencia leave, leave of absence; **licencia por enfermedad/maternidad/matrimonio/paternidad** sick/maternity/wedding/paternity leave; **licencia de manejar** driver's license
licenciatura BA or BS degree
lienzo artist's canvas
ligar (*España*) to pick someone up (*at a club, bar*)
ligero *adj.* light
lingüística linguistics
linterna flashlight
liquidación sale
liviano *adj.* light (weight)
llamarle la atención to catch someone's eye
llanta *n.* tire
llanura plain (*flat land*)
llegar a un acuerdo to reach an agreement
llevar: llevar a cabo to carry out (*a task*); **llevarle a alguien...** to take someone (*a period of time to do something*)
locura: hacer una locura to do something crazy
locutor announcer, commentator, speaker
logotipo logo
lograr to achieve
logro achievement
loncha slice (of ham)
lucha *n.* fight
luchar to fight
lucro: sin fines de lucro nonprofit
luego later; **desde luego** of course
lugar: tener lugar to take place
luna de miel honeymoon
lunar beauty mark
lunes: el lunes on Monday; **el lunes pasado** last Monday; **los lunes** on Mondays
luz: dar a luz to give birth

machacar to crush, mangle
machismo male chauvinism
madera wood
madrastra stepmother
madre *f.* mother
madrina maid-of-honor
madrugada daybreak, early morning
maestra: obra maestra masterpiece
maestría master's degree
mago magician
maíz *m.* corn; **palomitas de maíz** *f. pl.* popcorn
mal evil
malcriar to spoil, pamper, raise badly
maletín briefcase
malhumorado moody, ill-humored

mancha stain
mandamiento commandment
mandíbula jaw
maní *m.* (*pl.* **maníes**) peanut
manifestación demonstration, protest
mano de obra *f.* labor, manpower
manta blanket
manzana apple
mapa *m.* map
maquillarse to put on makeup
maravilloso: es maravilloso it's marvelous
marca brand name
marcha: ponerse en marcha to start off (*on a trip*); to start up
marginar to marginalize (someone)
mariposa butterfly
mariscos *m. pl.* seafood, shellfish
más: más de lo debido more than required; **más seguido** more often; **más tarde** later
masticar to chew
matar to kill
materia subject, course; material
materno *adj.* on your mother's side
matrícula tuition
matricularse to register
matutino *adj.* morning (*person*)
mayorista *m./f.* wholesaler
mecánico *n.* mechanic; *adj.* mechanical
medalla medal
media: media hermana half sister; **medias: dejar a medias** to leave unfinished
medicamento medicine
médico doctor
medida measurement
medio: medio ambiente *m.* environment; **medio hermano** half brother
mejilla cheek
mejillones *m. pl.* mussels
mejor: es mejor it's better
mejorar to improve
melocotón peach
melodrama *m.* melodrama
membrete *m.* letterhead
menor de edad minor (age)
menos less, lesser, least; **a menos que** unless; **echar de menos** to miss; **por lo menos** at least
mensaje *m.* message
mensual *adj.* monthly
mentir (ie, i) to lie
mentira *n.* lie; **una mentira más grande que una casa** a big, fat lie
menudo: a menudo often, frequently
mercadeo marketing
merluza hake (*fish*)
mermelada jelly
mestizo *person of mixed European and American indigenous blood*
meter to put; to insert; **meterse** to meddle, interfere; **meterse en** to get/go into
mezcla *n.* mix
mezclar to mix
miedo: tener miedo (de) to be afraid (of)
miel *f.* honey; **color miel** light brown; **luna de miel** honeymoon
mientras: mientras (que) while, as long as; **mientras más vengan, mejor** the more, the merrier
militar military person
mínimo minimal**; salario mínimo** minimum wage
minusválido handicapped
mío: el mío también/tampoco mine too/neither
mirar (la) televisión to watch TV
mitología mythology
mochila backpack
moda: estar de moda to be in style; **estar pasado de moda** to be out of style
modales de la mesa *m. pl.* table manners
modo: a mi modo de ver... the way I see it . . .; **de todos modos** anyway
mojado wet
mojado *n.* wetback (*derogatory slang*)
molestar to bother; **molestarle** to be bothered by, find annoying
molesto *adj.* bothersome, annoying
moneda currency; coin
monja nun
monje *m.* monk
montar: montar a caballo to ride a horse; **montar en bicicleta de montaña** to ride on a mountain bike
montón: un montón a lot; **divertirse (ie, i) un montón** to have a ball, a lot of fun
moreno dark-skinned
morir(se) (ue, u) to die
moro *n.* Moor, Moslem; *adj.* Moorish
mosaico mosaic
mosca *n.* fly; **por si las moscas** just in case
mostrador counter (*store, airline*)
mostrar (ue) to show
mucama (*partes de Suramérica*) maid
muchas: muchas personas many people; **muchas veces** many times
mudarse to move (*to a new residence*)
mudas: películas mudas silent films
muerto (*p.p. of* **morir**) dead; **estar muerto** to be dead
muestra *n.* sample
mujer policía *f.* policewoman
mujer política *f.* politician (*female*)
mujeriego *adj.* womanizer
mulato mulatto (*person of mixed European and black blood*)
multa *n.* fine, citation
mundial *adj.* world, worldwide

nacimiento birth
nada nothing, not anything
nadie no one
naranja orange (*fruit*)
narcotraficante *m./f.* drug dealer
narcotráfico drug traffic
naturaleza muerta still life
navaja suiza Swiss army knife
navegante *m./f.* navigator
necesitado needy, poor
negar (ie) to deny; to negate; **negarse a** to refuse
negocio business; **hombre de negocios** *m.* businessman; **mujer de negocios** *f.* businesswoman
nevar (ie) to snow
nexo connection
ni: ni... ni neither . . . nor; **ni (siquiera)** not even; **ni fu ni fa** it doesn't do anything for me; **ni me va ni me viene** it doesn't do anything for me; **No tiene ni pies ni cabeza.** It doesn't make (any) sense to me./I can't make heads or tails of it.
nieta granddaughter
nieto grandson
ningún/ninguna (+ *singular noun*) *adj.* not any; **de ningún modo** no way
ninguno/a *pro.* not any, none, no one
niñera nanny
niñez childhood
nivel del mar sea level
no: No, en absoluto. No, not at all.; **no obstante** nevertheless
noche *f.*: **noche de bodas** wedding night; **la noche está en pañales** the night is young
nostalgia: sentir (ie, i) nostalgia to be homesick; to feel nostalgic (about)
nota: sacar buena/mala nota to get a good/bad grade
noticias *f. pl.* news
novato novice, beginner
novedoso novel, new
noviazgo courtship
nuera daughter-in-law
nuez nut (*food*)
número par/impar even/odd number
nunca never

o... o either . . . or; **o sea** that is to say
obra: obra abstracta abstract work (of art); **obra maestra** masterpiece; **ser mano de obra barata/gratis** to be cheap/free labor
obstante: no obstante nevertheless
obvio obvious
occidente *m.* west
ocio leisure time; relaxation
ocuparse (de) to take care (of)
odiar to hate
oferta y demanda supply and demand
oficina de reclamos complaint department
ola *n.* wave
óleo oil painting
oler *irreg.* to smell
olla *n.* pot; **olla de presión** pressure cooker
olor smell, odor
olvidarse (de) to forget (about)
olvido *n.* forgetfulness
ondulado: **pelo ondulado** wavy hair
opinar: Opino como tú. I'm of the same opinion.
opinión: en mi opinión in my opinion
optimista *m./f.* optimist
oratoria speech
ordenador (*España*) computer
orgullo *n.* pride (*emotion*)
orgulloso proud (*negative connotation*)
oriundo *adj.* to come from, be native to; **ser oriundo de** to be originally from
osado daring (*negative connotation*)
osito de peluche teddy bear
ostra oyster
otro other; **por otro lado** on the other hand
ovalado oval
oveja sheep

paciente *adj.* patient
padecer to suffer from
padrastro stepfather
padre *m.* father; priest; **padres** *m. pl.* parents; fathers; priests
padrino best man
pago mensual/semanal monthly/weekly pay
paisaje *m.* landscape
paja straw
palabra word; **Pido la palabra.** Can I speak?
paladar palate
paloma *n.* dove
palomitas de maíz *f. pl.* popcorn
pandilla gang
pandillero gang member
pantalla screen
pañales *pl.*: **la democracia/la noche/la fiesta está en pañales** the democracy/night/party is young
pañuelo scarf, handkerchief
papa (*Latinoamérica*) potato
papel: hacer el papel to play the role
paquete *m.* package
par even (*number*)
para que in order to, so that
pardo *adj.* hazel (*eye color*)
parecer: ¿No te/le/les parece? Don't you think so?
pared wall
pareja pair; partner; significant other; couple
parentela relatives
pariente *m./f.* relative; **pariente lejano** distant relative: **pariente político** in-law
paro work stoppage
parte *f.*: **por otra parte** on the other hand; **por parte de mi madre/padre** on my mother's/father's side; **por una parte** on the one hand
particular *adj.* private, personal
partido *n.* game; (political) party; **partido demócrata** Democratic party; **partido republicano** Republican party
pasa *n.* raisin
pasado: el lunes/fin de semana/mes/año/siglo pasado last Monday/weekend/month/year/century; **pasado de moda** out of style
pasaje de ida *m.* one-way ticket
pasantía internship
pasar: pasar a buscar/recoger a alguien (por/en un lugar) to pick someone up (at a place); **pasar tiempo con alguien** to hang out with someone; **pasar la noche en vela** to pull an all-nighter, to stay awake all night; **pasarlo bien/mal** to have a good/bad time
pasatiempo hobby
pasear: pasear al perro to walk the dog; **pasear con el auto** to go cruising
pastel cake; pie
pastelería pastry shop
pastelito cake, pastry
pastilla pill
paterno *adj.* on your father's side
patillas *f. pl.* sideburns
patinar to skate
patrocinar to sponsor
pavo turkey
pecar to sin
pecas *f. pl.* freckles
pechuga: pechuga de pollo chicken breast
pedazo piece, slice
pedir (i, i) to ask (for); **pedir algo de tomar** to order something to drink; **Pido la palabra.** Can I speak?
peinarse to comb one's hair
película: película de espionaje spy movie; **película infantil** children's movie; **películas mudas** silent films; **dar una película** to show a movie; **ser una película taquillera** to be a blockbuster
peligroso dangerous
pelirrojo redhead
pellizcar to pinch
peluca wig, toupee
peludo hairy
pena: darle pena (a alguien) to feel sorry; **es una pena** it's a shame; **pena capital/pena de muerte** death penalty; **¡Qué pena!** What a shame!
pensar (ie) (+ *inf.*) to plan to (do something); **pensar en** to think about
pepino cucumber
pera pear
perder (ie) to lose (*someone/something*); **echar a perder** to waste, to spoil, ruin
pérdida loss
perdón excuse me
perdonar to forgive
perezoso lazy
perfeccionamiento: tomar cursos de perfeccionamiento to take continuing education courses
perfil *n.* profile
periódico newspaper
perjudicial harmful
permanente *n. f., adj.* permanent; **tener permanente** to have a permanent/perm
perpetua: cadena perpetua life sentence
personaje *m.* character
pertenecer to belong
pertenencias *f. pl.* belongings
pesa weight, dumbell
pesado heavy; **ser un pesado** to be a bore
pesar to weigh; **a pesar de que** even though
pescado fish (*that is eaten*)
pescar to fish
pesimista *m./f.* pessimist
pez *m.* fish (*the animal*); **pez vela** sailfish
picar to chop; to nosh, nibble on something

piel *f.* skin
piedra rock
pies: No tiene ni pies ni cabeza. It doesn't make (any) sense to me./I can't make heads or tails of it.
pila battery
pimiento (verde, rojo) (green, red) pepper
pincel paintbrush (*art*)
pincho: pincho de tortilla (*España*) slice of a potato omelet
piña pineapple
pisar to step on
piscina swimming pool
pista *n.* clue
placa license plate; plaque
planchar to iron (*clothes*)
plantado: dejar plantado (a alguien) to stand someone up
plátano plantain
platicar to chat (*México*)
plato: primer/segundo plato first/second course; **platos** *m. pl.* dishes
plena: en plena forma fully awake, alert
plomero (*Latinoamérica*) plumber
pluma feather
pobreza poverty
pocas: pocas personas few people
poder *irreg.* to be able to, can; **no poder más** to be full, to not be able to take it any more; **(no) puede ser** it can(not) be
poderoso powerful
policía *m./f.* police officer; *f.* police (force); **mujer policía** policewoman
política *n.* politics; policy; **la mujer política** politician (*female*)
político *n.* politician (*male*); *adj.* political
pómulo cheekbone
poner *irreg.*: **poner la mesa** to set the table; **ponerse** to put on (*clothing*); **ponerse de acuerdo** to agree, reach an agreement
por: por casualidad by chance; **por cierto** by the way; **por consiguiente** therefore; **por desgracia** unfortunately; **por ejemplo** for example; **por esa razón** that's why, for that reason; **por eso** that's why, for that reason; **por lo general** in general; **por lo menos** at least; **por lo tanto** therefore; **por otra parte** on the other hand; **por otro lado** on the other hand; **por parte de mi madre/padre** on my mother's/father's side; **por si acaso** just in case; **por si las dudas** just in case; **por si las moscas** just in case; **por supuesto** of course; **por un lado/por el otro** on the one hand/on the other; **por una parte/por la otra** on the one hand/on the other
porción serving
porquería junk (*food*)
porro joint (*marijuana*)
portar to carry
posadas: las posadas *Mexican Christmas custom re-enacting Mary and Joseph's search for shelter*
poseer to have, own, possess
posgrado *adj.* postgraduate
postal: tarjeta postal post card
postre *m.* dessert
postura stand, point of view
precioso lovely, adorable
preciso: es preciso it's necessary
predecir *irreg.* to predict
preferir (ie, i) to prefer
preguntas: hacer preguntas to ask questions
prejuicios: **tener prejuicios contra alguien** to be prejudiced against someone
premio prize
prendedor pin, brooch
prender to start (*a motor*)
prensa press; **libertad de prensa** freedom of the press
preocuparse to become worried; **preocuparse (de, por)** to worry (about), to take care (of)
preparado: ser una persona preparada to be an educated person
prepararse (para) to prepare oneself (for)
presencia: la buena presencia good appearance
presión pressure
preso prisoner
préstamo *n.* loan
prestar atención to pay attention
presupuesto estimate, budget
pretender (+ *inf.*) to attempt (and to hope) (+ *inf.*)
prever *irreg.* to foresee
previsto (*p.p. of* **prever**) foreseen
primer plato first course
primero *adj.* first
primo cousin
primordial primary, fundamental
principio *n.* beginning; **a principios de** at the beginning of
prisa: tener prisa to be in a hurry
prismáticos *m. pl.* binoculars
privar to deprive
probador dressing room
probar (ue) to taste; to try; **probarse** to try on (*clothing*)
producir *irreg.* to produce
producto product; **producto lácteo** dairy product
productor producer
profecía prophesy
profesorado faculty
prohibir to prohibit
promedio *n.* average
prometer to promise
promoción advertising
pronto soon; **tan pronto como** as soon as
propietario owner
propina gratuity, tip
propio *adj.* own
proponer *irreg.* to propose
propósito purpose; **a propósito** on purpose
protector solar sunblock
proteger to protect
provecho: ¡Buen provecho! Enjoy your meal!; **sacar provecho** to take advantage of
proveedor supplier
provenir *irreg.* to come from
psicología psychology
psicólogo psychologist
pudrir to rot
pueblo people, nation; town
puesto *n.* position (job); **solicitar un puesto** to apply for a job; (*p.p. of* **poner**) put, placed, set (*table*)
pulir to polish
pulpo octopus
puntaje *m.* score (*sports*)
punto: punto de partida point of departure; **y punto** and that's that
puro *n.* cigar; *adj.* pure

que: A que no saben... Bet you don't know . . .
qué: ¿Qué? What?; **¡Qué +** ***adj.*****!** How + *adj.*!
quebrantar to break
queda: toque de queda *m.* curfew
quedar to stay behind; **quedar a una hora con alguien** to meet at an agreed upon time; **quedarle bien/mal** to (not) fit well (*clothing*)
quehaceres *m. pl.* household chores
quejarse (de) to complain (about); **No sirve para nada quejarse...** It's not worth it to complain . . .
quemar to burn
querer *irreg.* to want; to wish; to love; **querer repetir** to want a second helping
quién: ¿Quién diría...? Who would say . . . ?
química chemistry
químico *n.* chemist; *adj.* chemical
quiosco kiosk

quisiera... I would like to . . .
quitarse to take off (*clothes*)

raíz (*pl.* **raíces**) root
raptar to kidnap
raro strange, unusual
rasgo feature
ratero pickpocket
razón *f.*: **por esa razón** that's why, for that reason; **tener razón** to be right
realista *adj.* realistic
realizar to carry out (*a plan*)
rebaja sale
rebajado: estar rebajado to be on sale
rebanada (de pan) slice (of bread)
rebelarse to rebel
rebelde rebellious
recargable rechargeable
recargar to recharge
receta recipe
rechazar to reject
rechazo rejection
recién casados *m. pl.* newlyweds
reclamo claim; complaint
reclutar to recruit
recoger: recoger información to gather information; **pasar a recoger a alguien (por/en un lugar)** to pick someone up (at home, etc.)
recomendar (ie) to recommend
reconocimiento gratitude, recognition
recto *adj.* straight (*as in a line*)
recuerdo memory; souvenir
recursos: recursos humanos *m. pl.* human resources, personnel; **recursos naturales** *m. pl.* natural resources; **ser de pocos recursos** to be a low income person
redactar to compose (*prose*), write
redondo round
reducir *irreg.* to reduce
reemplazar to replace, substitute
reemplazo replacement
referencias *f. pl.* references (*job*)
reflejo reflection
refrán proverb
refugiado político political refugee
regalo gift
regar to water
reina queen
reírse (i, i) (de) to laugh (at)
relaciones: relaciones exteriores *f. pl.* foreign affairs; **relaciones públicas** *f. pl.* public relations
reliquia relic, heirloom
remojar to soak
remordimiento remorse, regret
renta income
repelente *m.*: **repelente contra insectos** insect repellent
repente: de repente suddenly
repetir (i, i) to repeat; **querer repetir** to want a second helping
reponer to replenish
reposo resting place, repose
rescatar to rescue
rescate *m.* ransom; rescue
residencia de ancianos nursing home
resolver (ue) to solve
respetar to respect; **respetar los derechos humanos** to respect human rights
respirar to breathe
restringir to restrict
resuelto (*p.p. of* **resolver**) resolved
resumir to summarize
retratar to paint a portrait of; to photograph
retrato portrait
reunión meeting; gathering
reunir to join
reunirse (con) to meet (with)
revalorizar to revalue
revendedor (ticket) scalper
revivir to revive
revolcar (ue) to knock over
revolver (ue) to mix
revuelto (*p.p. of* **revolver**) overturned; scrambled (*eggs*)
rey *m.* king
rezar to pray
rígido rigid, stiff
rincón corner
riñonera fanny pack
riqueza riches
rizado: pelo rizado curly hair
róbalo bass (*type of fish*)
robar to rob, steal
robo robbery, theft
rogar (ue) to beg
romper to break
roto (*p.p. of* **romper**) broken
rubio blond
ruido noise

sábalo shad (*type of fish*)
saber *irreg.* to know; **¿A que no saben... ?** Bet you don't know . . . ?; **¿Acaso no sabías?** But didn't you know?; **No saben la sorpresa que se llevó cuando...** You wouldn't believe how surprised he/she was when . . . ; **¡Ya sé!** I've got it!
sabio wise
sacar to get, obtain; **sacar a alguien de un aprieto** to get someone out of a jam; **sacar a bailar a alguien** to ask someone to dance; **sacar buena/mala nota** to get a good/bad grade; **sacar entradas** to get tickets; **sacar provecho** to take advantage of
sacarina saccharine
saco de dormir sleeping bag
sagrado sacred
salado salty
salario mínimo minimum wage
salchicha sausage
salir *irreg.* to leave, go out; **salir a dar una vuelta** to cruise, go cruising, go for a ride/walk; **salir bien/mal (en un examen)** to do well/poorly (on an exam); **salirse con la suya** to get his/her way
saltar to jump
salvar to save
salvavidas *m./f. sing./pl.* lifeguard
sangre *f.* blood
sandía watermelon
sano healthy
santo saint
sardina sardine
sátira satire
satisfecho: estar satisfecho to be full
sea: o sea that is to say
secador de pelo hair dryer
secadora (de ropa) clothes dryer
secarse (el pelo, la cara, etc.) to dry (one's hair, face, etc.)
secuestrador kidnapper; hijacker
secuestrar to kidnap; to hijack
secuestro *n.* kidnapping; hijacking
seda silk
seguida: en seguida at once
seguir (i, i) to follow
según according to
segundo *adj.* second; **segundo plato** second course
seguro *adj.* sure; **es seguro** it's certain; **(no) estar seguro** to (not) be sure; **seguro médico/dental/de vida** *n.* health/dental/life insurance
selva forest
semana pasada last week
semanal *adj.* weekly
semilla seed
sencillo simple
senderismo hiking; **hacer senderismo** to go hiking
Sendero Luminoso Shining Path (*Peruvian guerrilla group*)
sensato sensible
sensible sensitive
sentarse (ie) to sit down
sentencia (*prison*) sentence
sentenciado the person sentenced
sentenciar to sentence
sentido: (no) tener sentido (not) to make sense; **sentido de humor** sense of humor

sentir (ie, i) to be sorry**; sentir nostalgia** to be homesick, to feel nostalgic (about); **sentirse** to feel; **sentirse rechazado** to feel rejected
señal *f.* signal
ser *irreg.*: **ser un pesado** to be a bore; **(no) puede ser** it can(not) be; **serle fiel/infiel (a alguien)** to be faithful/unfaithful (to someone); *n. m.* being; **ser humano** human being
serenata serenade
serio serious; **¿En serio?** Really?; **Te lo digo en serio.** I'm not kidding.
servir (i, i) to serve; **No sirve para nada quejarse...** It's not worth it to complain . . .
siempre always; **siempre y cuando** provided (that)
silvestre wild
símbolo symbol
sin: sin duda alguna without a doubt; **sin embargo** nevertheless; **sin lugar a dudas** without a doubt; **sin que** *conj.* without
sindicato labor or trade union
sinvergüenza: ¡Qué sinvergüenza! What a dog/rat!
siquiera: ni siquiera not even
smoking *m.* tuxedo
sobornar to bribe
soborno *n.* bribe
sobredosis *f.* drug overdose
sobremesa after dinner chat at the table
sobrina niece
sobrino nephew
sofreír (i, i) to fry lightly
sofrito lightly fried dish
soga rope
solapa lapel
soler (ue) (+ *inf.*) to do . . . habitually; to usually (do something)
solicitar un puesto/empleo to apply for a job
solicitud application; **completar una solicitud** to fill out an application
solomillo filet mignon
soltar (ue) to free
soltero single (*marital status*)
sombra shadow
someterse to submit
somnífero sleeping pill
sonora: banda sonora sound track
sonreír (i, i) to smile
sonrisa smile
sordo deaf
soroche *m.* altitude sickness
sorprenderle (a alguien) to be surprised
sorpresa: ¡Qué sorpresa! What a surprise!
soso bland
sostén bra
sostener *irreg.* to support; to hold up
subir to raise; **subir el fuego** to raise the heat
subrayar to underline
suceder to happen
suceso event; **sucesos del momento** current events
sucio dirty
sudadera sweatsuit, sweatshirt
suegra mother-in-law
suegro father-in-law
suela sole (*of a shoe*)
sueldo salary; **bajar/aumentar el sueldo** to lower/raise the salary
sueño: coger el sueño to fall asleep
sugerencia suggestion
sugerir (ie, i) to suggest
suicida *m./f.* person who commits suicide
suicidarse to commit suicide
suicidio suicide
sumar to add
sumergido underground
sumiso submissive
sumo enormous, great
superar to overcome; to surpass
supervivencia survival
suplicar to implore, beg
supuesto: por supuesto of course
suya: salirse con la suya to get his/her way

tacaño stingy, cheap
tachar to cross out
tal: con tal (de) que provided that
taller workshop
tamaño size
también: Yo también. I do too./Me too.
tambor drum
tampoco: Yo tampoco. I don't either./Me neither.
tan pronto como as soon as
tanto so much; as much; **al tanto** up-to-date; **por lo tanto** therefore; **¡Tanto tiempo!** Such a long time!
tapar to cover
taquillera: ser una película taquillera to be a blockbuster
tarde *adv.* late**; más tarde** later
tarjeta card; **tarjeta verde** green card (*residency card given to immigrants in the United States*)
tarta (*España*) cake; tart
tatarabuela great, great grandmother
tatarabuelo great, great grandfather
tatuaje *m.* tattoo
taxista *m./f.* taxi driver
teatro theater
tecla key (*typewriter, piano*)
tejer to weave; to knit
tela material, fabric, cloth
telenovela soap opera
tema *m.* theme, topic
temer to fear
temprano early
tendido stretched, spread out
tener *irreg.* to have; **tener en claro** to have it clear in your mind; **tener ganas de** (+ *inf.*) to feel like (doing something); **tener lugar** to take place; **tener prejuicios** to be prejudiced; **tener prisa** to be in a hurry; **tener que** (+ *inf.*) to have to ...; **(no) tener sentido** (not) to make sense; **tener título** to have an education/a degree; **tener una aventura (amorosa)** to have an affair; **tener un contratiempo** to have a mishap (that causes one to be late); **tener un hambre atroz** to be really hungry
teñido dyed
tercero *adj.* third
terminar to finish; to run out (of); **al terminar** after finishing
ternera veal
ternura tenderness
terremoto earthquake
terrorista *m./f.* terrorist
tesoro treasure
tía aunt; **tía política** aunt-in-law
tibio lukewarm
tiempo: ¿Cuánto tiempo hace que...? How long have you . . . ?; **¡Tanto tiempo!** Such a long time!; **trabajar medio tiempo** to work part-time; **trabajar tiempo completo** to work full-time
tienda de campaña tent
tiernamente tenderly
tijeras *f. pl.* scissors
tío uncle; **tío político** uncle-in-law
tira cómica comic strip
tirar to throw away
título title (*book, person*); degree; **tener título** to have an education/a degree
todavía still, yet; **todavía no** not yet
todo everything; **todo el mundo** everyone; **todos** everyone; **todos los días/domingos/meses** every day/Sunday/month
tomar cursos de perfeccionamiento/capacitación to take continuing education/training courses
tomate *m.* tomato
torno: en torno around
torpe clumsy
torta cake
toque de queda *m.* curfew

tostar (ue) to toast
trabajar: trabajar de sol a sol to work from sunrise to sunset; **trabajar medio tiempo/tiempo completo** to work part-time/full-time
trabajo escrito written paper
traducir *irreg.* to translate
traficar en drogas to deal drugs
traición betrayal
traidor traitor
trailers *m. pl.* previews (*movies*)
trampa trick, trap
tranquilo calm
transpiración perspiration
trasladar to transfer
trasnochar to stay up all night
trastorno *n.* inconvenience, upheaval
tratado treaty
través: a través de through
travieso mischievous
trenza braid
trigo wheat
trigueño olive-skinned
trilingüe trilingual
trillizos *pl.* triplets
tristeza sadness
tronco trunk (*of a tree*)
trozo piece
turnarse to take turns
turquesa turquoise

ubicarse to be located
una vez once
unirse to unite
uno: uno a(l) otro each other; **(los) unos a (los) otros** one another (more than two)
útil useful

vacilar to kid around
vacuna vaccine
vaina pod (*bean*)
valer: vale la pena to be worthwhile; **(No) vale la pena** (+ *inf.*) It's (not) worth it to (+ *verb*); **valerse por sí mismo** to manage on one's own
valioso valuable
vanidoso vain
valor value; valor, courage
variedad variety
vasco *n., adj.* Basque
veces: a veces sometimes; **muchas veces** many times
vecino neighbor
vela: hacer vela to sail; **pasar la noche en vela** to pull an all-nighter, to stay awake all night
vencedor conqueror
vencer to defeat
vencimiento conquest
vendedor salesperson
vender to sell
veneno poison
venir *irreg.* to come
venta sale
ventaja advantage
veras: ¿De veras? Really?/You're kidding./Don't tell me!/You don't say!/Wow!
verdad: no es verdad it's not true
verde green; **chiste verde** *m.* dirty joke; **tarjeta verde** green card (*residency card given to immigrants in the United States*)
verdura vegetable
vergüenza: ¡Qué vergüenza! What a shame!
verter (ie) to shed (*tears*)
vespertino *adj* evening
vestido de fiesta evening dress
vestimenta clothes, garment
vestirse (i, i) to get dressed
vestuario costumes
vez: de una vez por todas once and for all; **de vez en cuando** every now and then; **una vez** once
víctima (*f. but refers to both males and females*) victim
vida: de por vida for life
videojuegos: ir a los videojuegos to go to the video arcade
vientre *m.* belly: **la danza del vientre** belly dancing
vigilante *m./f.* watchperson, sentry, lookout
vínculo bond
vino wine
violación rape
violador rapist
violar to rape; **violar los derechos humanos** to violate human rights
viruela smallpox
vistazo: echar un vistazo to glance at
vitrina store window
viuda widow
viudo widower
vivienda housing
vivir to live; **vivir juntos** to live together
vivo *adj.* smart; alive
voluntad will; **contra su voluntad** against one's will
volver (ue) to return, come back; **volver a** (+ *inf.*) to do something again; **volver a empezar de cero** to start over again from scratch
voto en blanco blank vote
vuelta: a la vuelta de around the corner from; **dar una vuelta** go for a ride/walk

xenofobia xenophobia (*fear of strangers or foreigners*)

ya already; yet; **ya no** no longer, not anymore; **¡Ya sé!** I've got it!; **¡Ya voy!** I'm coming!
yerno son-in-law
y punto and that's that

zanahoria carrot
zapatería shoe store
zapatillas *f. pl.* slippers

Index

Permissions and Credits

Text Permissions and Sources

The authors and editors thank the following persons and publishers for permission to use copyrighted material.

Chapter 3: page 63, Legend based on Otilia Meza, "La leyenda del maíz," *Leyendas del antiguo México: Mitología prehispánica* (México, D.F.: Edamex, 1985). **Chapter 5:** page 117, Data taken from Raymond Sokolov, *Why We Eat What We Eat* (New York: Summit Books, 1991); 136 (Ponce), From Luis Martínez, "Los buenos modales en el olvido," *El Universal*, (http://noticias.eluniversal.com); 136 (Calderero), From José Fernando Calderero, "En la mesa," *Los buenos modales de tus hijos mayores*, ed. Palabra, Madrid, 1.997 (www.edufam.com); 138, Adapted from *Más*, Univisión, New York, N.Y. **Chapter 7:** page 185, Data for items 1 and 2 taken from 1993 *Earth Journal Environmental Almanac and Resource Directory* (Boulder: Buzzworm Books, 1993); 185, Data for items 3, 4, and 6 found on Aug. 16, 2003 from World Resources Institute (http://pubs.wri.org); 185, Data for item 5 from Revista Integral #283, p. 28, Julio 2003, España; 195–196, Reprinted with permission from the Instituto Costarricense de Turismo, San José, Costa Rica. **Chapter 8:** page 210, Adapted and translated from www.executiveplanet.com, Jan. 15, 2004. **Chapter 10:** page 256, Excerpted from Joaquín Leguina, "Cuernos," *El Mundo*, Aug. 17, 2003, Feb. 17, 2004 (www.el-mundo.es/magazine/2003). **Chapter 11:** page 273, Data taken from Instituto Indigenista Interamericano (III), *La coca: Tradición, rito, identidad* (México, D.F.: Instituto Indigenista Interamericano, 1989); 274, Excerpted from "Celulares, nueva arma contra la delincuencia," *Honduras Revista Internacional*, Feb. 17, 2004 (www.hondurasri.com); 277, Excerpted from "Resumen de atentados mortales," Feb. 17, 2004 (www.interbook.net/personal/angelberto); 279 (first student annotation), Data from Elizabeth M. Whelan, Sc.D. "Perils of Prohibition: Why We Should Lower the Drinking Age to 18," *Newsweek*, May 25, 1995, Feb. 17, 2004 (www2.potsdam.edu/alcohol-info/YouthIssues); 279 (second student annotation), Data from NIAAA Task Force on College Drinking, "Clinical Protocols to Reduce High Risk Drinking in College Students: The College Drinking Prevention Curriculum for Health Care Providers," Feb. 17, 2004 (www.collegedrinking prevention.gov/Reports); 285, Excerpted from Ministerio de Educación de Chile, "Convivencia en la Escuela Valle de Lluta: Palabras en vez de golpes," Feb. 21, 2004 (www.mineduc.cl/revista/anteriores). **Chapter 12:** page 297, "Soy Como Soy Y Qué" by Raquel Valle Sentíes, reprinted by permission of the author; 298, Data from "The Opportunity," *Voy*, Feb. 21, 2004 (www.voy.tv/the_opportunity/index.html); 304 (Clemente), Some data taken from Nicolas Kanellos, ed., *The Hispanic American Calendar*, (Detroit: Gale Research, 1992); 304 (Garzón), www.gill.stanford.edu/depts/hasrg/latinam/ garzon/AboutHim.html and www.lanacion.com.ar/Archivo/Nota.asp?nota_id=212184& aplicacion_id=4; 306, Data from "The Emergence of Latinos in America," *Milwaukee Journal Sentinel*, Aug. 24, 2003. Crossroads, p. 01J, and the following sites on 21 Feb. 2004: www.ameristat.org, www.hispaniconline.com, *San Antonio Express-News* (www.religionwriters.com), U.S. Census Bureau (www.census.gov); 307, Data taken from "Background Note: Costa Rica," Feb. 21, 2004 (www.state.gov/r/pa/ei/bgn/2019.htm), and from *NewsMax.comWires*, "U.S. Retirees Flock to Mexico," Feb. 6, 2001, Feb. 21, 2004 (www.newsmax.com/archives/articles/2001). **Videofuentes:** page 327, www.comarcasidra.com/plantillaalojamientos.php?id=33.

Realia

Preliminary Chapter: page 9, Courtesy of Khandle Hedrick. **Chapter 1:** page 20, Reprinted with permission from Moto Paella, Madrid, Spain; 34, Reprinted by permission of the League of Women Voters from Getting Out the Vote. **Chapter 2:** page 42, La Feria del Libro de Buenos Aires. **Chapter 4:** page 104, www.gaturro.com. **Chapter 5:** page 115,

Restaurante Tocororo; 117 *bottom*, Green Giant and Mexicorn are registered trademarks of General Mills. Used with permission of General Mills; 117 *top*, SOS Cuetara, S.A.; 129, Reprinted with permission from Univisión, New York, N.Y. **Chapter 6:** page 157, Copyright © Quino/Quipos. **Chapter 7:** page 185, Reprinted with permission of the City of Los Angeles, Department of Public Works, Bureau of Sanitation. **Chapter 8:** page 203, AIESEC; 206, www.gaturro.com. **Chapter 9:** page 229 *top*, Reprinted with permission from Estancia el Carmen S.R.L.; 229 *left*, © Café de Colombia; 229 *right*, Reprinted with permission from Aeroméxico, New York, N.Y. **Chapter 10:** page 256 *bottom*, Photo by Alvaro Villarrubia/elmundo.es; 258, *Revista Mía de México*, Editorial Televisa/Publicaciones Continentales de México; 259, Copyright © Quino/Quipos; 266, www.gaturro.com; 267, Reprinted with permission from *La Nación*, Buenos Aires, Argentina. **Chapter 11:** page 275, Center for Disease Control, Atlanta, G.A.; 276, encuestadelsiglo@sigloxxi.com; 279, Copyright © 1994 *El País*; 281, California Department of Health Services; 285, Reprinted with permission from *MAD en México*. **Chapter 12:** page 305, Reprinted with permission of McDonald's Corporation; 309, Reprinted with permission from The United Nations High Commission for Refugees; 311, Reprinted with permission from Hispanic Trends; 314 *top middle*, Reprinted with permission from Community Action, Inc., Haverhill, M.A.; 314 *bottom left*, Reprinted with permission from Ross, Martel & Silverman, Boston, M.A.; 314 *bottom right*, Cabletron Systems. **Videofuentes:** page 334 *bottom left*, Courtesy of Stephanie Valencia.

Illustrations

Anna Veltfort

Photographs

Preliminary Chapter: pages 1 and 2, Ulrike Welsch; 3, Frerck/Odyssey/Chicago; 10, Bob Daemmrich/The Image Works. **Chapter 1:** page 14, Pablo Corral Vega/Corbis; 15, Richard Nowitz/Photo Researchers; 22, Owen Franken/Corbis; 27 *left*, Ron Dahlquist/Tony Stone Images; 27 *right*, Image 100/Royalty-Free/Corbis; 28, Margot Granitsas/The Image Works; 35, Robert Fried Photography. **Chapter 2:** page 38, John and Lisa Merrill/Corbis; 39, Frerck/Odyssey/Chicago; 44, Figaro Films; 50, Nik Wheeler; 52, Reuters Newmedia Inc./Corbis; 54, culturalianet.com; 58, Corbis/Bettmann. **Chapter 3:** page 62, Corbis/Bettman; 64, Nik Wheeler; 70, Comstock; 75, The Image Works Archives; 78 *left*, © Classmates.com; 78 *right*, © Classmates.com; 79 *left*, © Classmates.com; 79 *right*, Corbis; 87, Guillermo Aldana E. **Chapter 4:** page 90, Miguel Cabrera, *Escena de mestizaje*, 1763. Museo de América, Madrid; 91, Courtesy Alexandre Arrechea; 92, Digital File © The Museum of Modern Art/Licensed by SCALA/ Art Resource, N.Y. Lam, Wifredo (1902–1982), *The Jungle*, 1943. Gouache on paper mounted on canvas, 7′10″ × 7′6 1/2″. Inter-American Fund (140.1945) The Museum of Modern Art, New York, N.Y.; 93, Courtesy of Marcela Domínguez; 96, Reuters Newmedia Inc./Corbis; 108, Patrik Giardini/Corbis. **Chapter 5:** page 114, Sandy Felsenthal/Corbis; 122, Tom Bean/Corbis; 128, Pablo Muñoz; 132, Danny Lehman/Corbis; 133, Stuart Cohen/The Image Works; 135, Bob Daemmrich/The Image Works; 139, Pablo Muñoz. **Chapter 6:** page 144, Martin Thomas/Liaison Agency; 145, Rafael Wollman/Liaison Agency; 154, Corbis; 156, Reuters/Corbis; 158, Alyx Kellington/Liaison Agency; 168, Juan Barreto/AFP/Getty Images. **Chapter 7:** page 172, Copyright © 2003 Tom Dempsey/Photoseek.com; 173, James D. Nations/DDB Stock Photo; 174, Galen Rowell/Corbis; 176, Michael J. Doolittle/The Image Works; 187 *top*, DDB Stock Photo; 187 *right*, Frerck/Odyssey/Chicago; 187 *bottom*, Frances S./Explorer/Photo Researchers, Inc.; 190, Beryl Goldberg; 195, Buddy Mays/Travel Stock; 196, Alan & Sandy Carey/Sygma. **Chapter 8:** page 199, Danny Lehman/Corbis; 205, Reuters/Corbis; 208, Oscar Bonilla/Impact Visuals; 209, Gary I. Rothstein/Reuters Newmedia Inc./Corbis; 217 *top, left, and bottom right*, Courtesy Debbie Rusch. **Chapter 9:** page 222, Owen Franken/Corbis; 223, B. Brent Black; 224 *top*, Jeff Greenberg/The Image Works; 224 *bottom*, Kahlo, Frida (1907–1954). © Banco de México Trust. *The Two Fridas*, 1939. Museo Nacional de Arte Moderno, Instituto Nacional de Bellas Artes, Mexico City, D.F., Mexico. Schalkwijk/Art Resource, N.Y.; 227 *top*, Commissioned by the Trustees of Dartmouth College, Hanover, New Hampshire; 227 *bottom*, Barbar Alper/Stock Boston; 229 *bottom*, Rufino Tamayo, *Women of Tehuantepec*, 1939, oil on canvas, overall: 33 7/8′ × 57 1/8″ (86.04 × 145.09 cm.), Albright-Knox Art Gallery, Buffalo, New York, Room of Contemporary Art Fund,

1941; 230, Courtesy of Ma. Estela E. de Santos; 234, Velásquez, Diego Rodríguez de Silva y (1599–1660). *Las meninas*, 1656. Prado, Madrid. Bridgeman Art Library, N.Y.; 237, Ayuntamiento de Córdoba. Area de Servicios Socioculturales. Dirección de Museos Municipales; 238 *top*, Botero, Fernando (b. 1932). © The Marlborough Gallery. *The Presidential Family*, 1967. Oil on canvas, 6′8 1/8″ × 6′5 1/4″. Gift of Warren D. Benedek (2667.1967). Digital Image © The Museum of Modern Art/Licensed by SCALA/Art Resource, N.Y. 238 *bottom*, *La tamalada*, © Carmen Lomas Garza; 244 *left*, Ulrike Welsch; 244 *middle*, Jack Picone/Liaison Agency; 244 *right*, Bettmann/Corbis. **Chapter 10:** page 246, Pablo Corral V/Corbis; 247, Marcelo A. Geiler; 256 *top*, Peter Dejong/AP/Wide World Photos; 260, © José Azel/Aurora. **Chapter 11:** page 271, David J. Sams/Stock Boston; 272, Carrion/Sygma; 277 *right*, Juan Herrero/AFP/Getty Images. **Chapter 12:** page 294, Rob Crandall/The Image Works; 303 *bottom*, Eric Gay/AP/Wide World Photos; 304 *left*, Bettmann/Corbis; 304 *right* Reuters/Corbis; 310, AP/Wide World Photos; 311, Courtesy the Coca-Cola Company. "Coca-Cola Classic" and "The Genuine Coca-Cola Bottle" are registered trademarks of the Coca-Cola Company. **Videofuentes:** page 320, AP/Wide World Photos; 321, Telemundo News, Miami, F.L.; 327 and 328, el deseo s.a., Madrid, Spain; 329, Big Camera, Chicago; 330, Elena Climent, *Mesa de mosaicos con espejo*, 1997. Courtesy of Mary-Anne Martin/Fine Art, New York; 331, Rodrigo Silva Rivas and Aldo Aste Sambuceti AAS. Creación Audivisual Viña del Mar, Chile; All other photos in Videofuentes section, Frank Konesky, TVMAN/Riverview Productions, Dover, M.A.